The Cyberdelic Odyssey

Book I – Innocence

Comfort Creatures

Published by Promethean Productions, LLC.

ISBN: 979-8-9897015-0-6 (ebook)
ISBN: 979-8-9897015-1-3 (paperback)
ISBN: 979-8-9897015-2-0 (hardcover)

Book Cover by Comfort Creatures
Illustrations by Comfort Creatures

First Edition 2025

Warning

This book is dedicated:

To my wife—
Your unwavering love and support kept me going through the
darkness.

To my family—
Without you, I would not be standing here today.

To Folly Beach—
A place of inspiration, where the sand meets the sea and stories are
born from whispering waves.

And to all the crazy, beautiful freaks—
For the small, the tall, and the rest of y'all; for those who read, those
who inspire, and those who keep the bondfire lit—may your spirit,
your laughter, and your unapologetic existence thrive for the next
seven generations.

Having gathered every last drop of creativity,

we've traveled far aboard this living ark.

Still, the heat death of our universe lingers

along the fringes of the void.

Since this is where our journey ends,

let me tell you the story

of how it begins.

More than fiction,

a Zen poetics,

as we seek

the moon's reflection in a mud puddle.

ALIA

Contents

Part I
Zeitgeist

1

The Oros System

First Boot

Freshly thawed from the freezer, Zeff rests strapped to a medical table, surrounded by a team of pocket protectors and poor posture. Along the fringes of Lab-Z, technicians tinker with switches and vials as engineers type a coordinated cabaret of keystrokes. He twitches.

A slender man, sporting a bowl cut, parted in the middle, picks up a paper-thin tablet and reads from a scrolling list, "Deep-learning operating system loaded... Adaptive neural nets are syncing... Nanite colony architecture is holding... Connection established with Earth Defense Constellation [EDC] orbital network."

"We outdid ourselves this time, Stew. This iteration puts us twenty years ahead of the other labs," his colleague—a lanky fellow with an unkempt beard and equally nested hair—spins back in his computer chair.

"I wouldn't be so sure of that, Barry. I heard China is a few years away from AGI." A woman wearing an oversized Academy alumni sweatshirt and red curls inspects the lines from Zeff's bedside, following them to a woven tapestry of corresponding components.

"Damn, Carla... Don't burst my bubble." Barry spins back to his terminal. "How'd they make the leap? Producing artificial general intelligence requires a ton of resources."

Stew fixes the part in his hair with precision. "Was another *Artifact* found?"

"It's unlikely." Carla tightens a potentially loose connection. "X would've known—"

"Perhaps it's private?" Barry speculates without looking from his terminal.

"Maybe they formed an alliance. The decentralized scene was born there," Carla says, returning from the server racks to check the vital-signs monitor. "Patient's pulse rate, body temperature, and blood pressure are optimal. Waveforms are regular."

"Could the Foundation have led the negotiations?" Barry scratches his beard, sending flakes onto his *Space Force VI* t-shirt. The dandruff blends amongst the cosmos—from dust to stardust.

"It doesn't matter," Carla says, pushing back her sleeves. "They'll never reach the level of synthetic intelligence we've been able to develop from the Artifact. X is next level."

"Ouroboros system: Online," Stew relays. "Digital overlay looks clean."

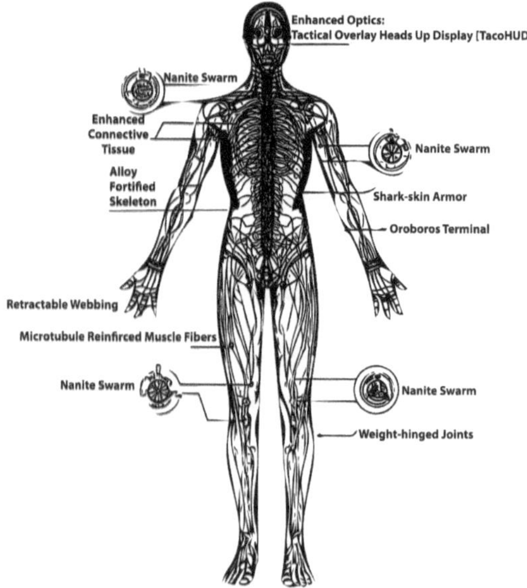

Nearby, a barrage of inputs bombards Barry's terminal. "Let's adjust it a smidge... The frame rate seems narrowed."

"He's waking up... Can you hear me?" Carla asks Zeff. "Don't speak. Nod if you can understand."

Her voice returns between his ears, and he shakes his head.

"Perfect. Comlink established. How are those optics coming along?"

"Gimme a moment." Barry increases the tempo of his typing.

"Now, hold still. I'm going to remove the bandages from your eyes." She carefully cuts away the layers of wrapped gauze.

After several more diligent command prompts, Barry kicks back in his chair, saying, "Give it a go."

Stew presses the shiny button on his tablet, and Zeff's vision comes online.

New Sight

His optics gloss over as the Tactical Overlay Heads-Up Display [TacOHUD] adjusts its resolution, transitioning from a static snowstorm into digital clarity. The eye squiggles dissipate, lines sharpen, and edges embolden. His mental bandwidth overflows with bursting vividity. Every hue once hidden behind clouds of deconstructed synapses becomes crisp and apparent as the fidelity of existence imprints itself within the Oros system's vast Memory IndeX.

In front of Zeff, an observable field of chaos readily cascades into a buffet of data. With each ripening moment, crisscrossing variables separate into a kaleidoscope of shimmering threads along the myriad gardens of potential and possibility. A colossal *Tyger* with the world as its yarn ball could be no more at home, pawing and gnawing at the low-hanging fruit of the near-adjacent.

"TacOHUD is streaming." Stew says with a cheer of success.

"Today is Tuesday. Who wants to go get margaritas?" Barry finishes the install with three aggressive clicks of his mechanical keyboard.

Stew closes some excess tabs. "What about Abuela's?"

"They have the best queso." Carla examines the feedback from Zeff's pupils.

"And don't forget about their chips. We might need to get three baskets," Barry says, dusting off his shirt.

Carla's voice breaks through Zeff's awe-filledness. "You'll notice a small, flashing envelope icon in the top-right corner of your vision. Do you see it?" She follows a medical cable from its insertion down to the floor.

He nods.

Turning from his bedside, she disappears into the maze of server racks behind his cradle. "Good. Now, I want you to look at it and think about selecting the—"

At the far end of the room, the doors to Lab-Z unseal with a hiss, revealing the Director's broad-shouldered shadow. He steps into the light with a grizzled sense of duty etched into the grim age lines of his face, followed by Agent Xero and a small team of guards, tech gurus, and far-sighted think-tankers.

"This is a pleasant surprise." Stew greets his superior. "We didn't expect you until next month."

"We have an expedited timeline, doc. What do you have for me?"

"Yes, sir... The new biocompatible chipsets boost the adaptive algorithm's ability to weave neuromorphic associations with minimal energy requirements—"

"Spare me the jargon. Is the Oros system operational?"

Barry answers, "Since pulling this *one* from the freezer, we've been able to upgrade it with a full suite of services to extend the host's thought, reach, and feel—"

"Be brief." The Director looks at his watch.

"Right... We've equipped this subject with enhanced senses, fortified muscular and skeletal systems, reality distortion field for near invisibility, as well as the TacOHUD interface. Now, we can see what he sees."

"And the cocktails?" he exhales with a puff of annoyance.

Carla excitedly reports, "It was a success. Using the latest Polymerase Chain Reaction replication, the system can now synthesize sunlight and biological waste into scalable tinctures of dopamine, serotonin, N-Dimethyltryptamine [DMT]—"

Their superior's impatience fills the room.

"—We've preloaded the system with six different enhancements: [Prime], [Time Warp], [Stim], [Surge], and the specials—[Berzerker] and [Forlorn Hope], as you requested."

Without an ounce of approval, the Director turns to the hospital bed and greets the latest model of his favorite weapon. "Good morning, sunshine. We're going to save the world together."

Flaws

Zeff looks at the bandage wrapped around his left forearm, then the restraints binding him to the hospital bed. The TacOHUD blurs with a static crackle.

The Director snaps his fingers at him. "Are you sure he's good to go?"

"He's been through a lot," Carla says. "Please give him some time—"

"Remember who's in charge here," Agent Xero steps forward. The overhead light casts a shadow onto the old scar of a lengthy wound laid along the side of his head.

"Y—yes, sir." She lowers her eyes.

Stew hands his boss the tablet with Zeff's biometrics. "This is the best sync ratio I've seen out of all the others."

"Isn't that what you said last time?" The Director studies the tablet's data set. His steel eyes glare from the blue-lit device. "When will he be able to get to work?"

"The Oros system heavily taxes the host," Carla warns. "Besides updates and hotfixes, the system still requires constant regulation."

"Still?"

Not wanting to incur further disruption during such a critical time in bringing the Oros system online, Stew picks up a small black device, no bigger than a lighter, and presents it to his inquisitors. "There are certain externalities to contend with... but we've developed this special nebulizer. On breath, the device delivers an adequate mixture of cannabidiol [CBD] and delta-9-tetrahydrocannabinol [THC], directly to the four hundred million alveoli in his lungs, immediately reducing the systemic strain on his body—"

"Speak English, doc," Agent Xero interrupts.

"After a couple of sessions in the tank, he should be ready by the end of the month," Stew says with an assuring smile of confidence.

"You have until the end of next week." The Director declares, then turns and leaves the laboratory with his entourage.

Zeff tries to sit up in the bed, reaching out and pulling against the straps. The restraint snaps, and a pair of large orderlies rush over to keep him still. He struggles against them, overexerting himself until he convulses into an acute seizure. Carla injects a serum into the port of his IV bag while they hold him against the table, binding him into place with the jingle of extra buckles. Soon, the drip slips into his bloodstream, and he stops writhing before drifting into the Dreamer's dream.

"Let's give everything a once-over," Stew says, rubbing the back of his neck. "We don't have long. Let's get to it."

Barry returns to the keys, performing a symphony of command prompts to pull up the diagnostics panel as the doors to Lab-Z seal shut. Down the hall, the Director and Agent Xero get into the elevator and ascend to the surface level of the Facility's redacted location. There, an Agency helicopter waits to transport them away from the Pickle Factory to their next rendezvous with the Committee.

2

Zona Pellucida

Ad Astra

Many years and iterations later, on a clear night atop Mauna Kea, a group of astronomers point their instruments towards the heavens. Aided by research telescopes and communication satellites, they see well beyond the horizon's thin magnetic membrane, protecting our species from the boundlessness of space. The following day, they gather the data and rummage through the numbers in a feverish hunt to capture a glimpse of the cosmos and the breadth of the unknown.

Tenured astronomer Dr. Katherine Moon, her height exaggerated by the length of her lab coat, stares intently at the material on her workstation. She traces her long finger upon the warm printout and notices something peculiar.

"Hmm... Either that's massive, or it's close," she says, setting down the papers. Then, picking up a nearby tablet, selects a folder that compiles a series of high-definition images into a vision of the greater whole.

She examines both data sets simultaneously. Unsatisfied, she reviews the print-out, muttering a series of complex equations to herself. Dr. Moon flips to the next page and pauses from theta waves of inspiration. She pulls a dry-erase marker from her pocket, pops the top, and squeaks numerical sequences across the board.

"Whatcha got, Katherine?" Dr. Carl Dottie asks, hunched at his desk. "Did you find your singularity?" He pulls a comb from his pocket protector and drags it through the remnants of his horseshoe hairline.

Caught in narrative equations and the potentials of discovery, she hands him the paper she was holding, now with several red-pen formulas and blue-pen addendums.

Carl glances at the board, then the printout. "What does this mean? Is the data corrupted?" he asks.

"It shouldn't be the instruments." Dr. Nancy Hubble comes over, wiping her Coke-bottle-thick glasses with a small microfiber cloth. "We calibrated and triple-checked them beforehand." She inspects the clarity of her specs, places them back on her face, and tucks her angel-thin hair behind her ears. Peering over Carl's hunched shoulders at the dry-erase board, she adds, "But to be certain, I'll run a diagnostic sweep immediately."

By now, Dr. QiQi Haiku, a short cosmologist with thick, shoulder-length hair and square glasses, gives up on her exoplanet hunt—and the potential of next quarter's funding. A bit defeated, she shuffles to the growing excitement from Dr. Moon's workstation.

"Don't let it get you down," Dr. Neil Haramein reassures his colleague. "We didn't turn up anything either. Rest assured, our research to understand the geometry of reality persists. However, I might need to switch the topic for next week's podcast."

Dr. Steven Singlemass directs his electric wheelchair closer to the flurry of equations. "No worries... Once we get back, I'll have more time to test the math against the theories my students have cooked up."

Last but not least, Dr. Vega Cooper waddles over, pointing a pudgy finger. His belly smears the bottom line of theoretical notation as he pokes at potential allowances within her equations.

They huddle around—thinking, pondering, doubting, and extrapolating the data. Soon, as the immensity of their accidental discovery sinks in, the room goes silent.

Results

After an hour of scrutiny, the lab coats come off and the cigarettes come out. As they discuss the object's threat potential, concluding streaks of cold sweat give way to more rational debate. Eventually, they agree to make their findings known to the proper authorities.

Dr. Moon pops open a bottle of sparkling wine and fills a row of plastic flutes.

"What's the champagne for?" Steven rolls next to the desk and selects one. "Didn't you see the numbers on this thing? The math doesn't lie. We're all doomed if this reaches our part of the solar system."

"True... But despite the potential catastrophe this thing could bring, there *is* something which makes this worthwhile for us all... at least for now." She attempts to ease his woes.

"What are you talking about?" Neil stubs out an anxious stogie.

"Hear, hear, gather around," she says. "First, we have about a decade to prepare. There is still time and plenty of options. Of course, my favorite being laser ablation." She smiles smugly and pours the rest of the bottle into the remaining flutes. "I mean, who doesn't want to play with laser technology?"

"What about a kinetic impactor?" QiQi asks.

Dr. Moon pushes a pair of black-rimmed glasses up the bridge of her nose. "It could work... but for me, there is something romantic about using lasers—anyway, thank you for coming out here, your due diligence, and fighting for our time to use this equipment. But most importantly," she looks at each of them, "thank you for aiding in the discovery of the first near-Earth object originating from another system." She raises her glass in the promise of celebration.

"What do you mean?" Vega asks and wipes some perspiration with the back of his plump hand.

QiQi picks up her notes. "You're certain of its origins?" She asks, scanning the printout one more time, hoping it's enough to secure the grants to keep her lab space.

"My friends, I assure you." Dr. Moon extends her hand to the board. "According to my calculations, it's moving so fast that there's no chance it originated within our system. You can triple-check them yourselves."

"Where'd it come from?" Neil asks.

Dr. Moon gulps the rest of her glass. "No clue. This stuff is probably celestial driftwood, leftover from tidal waves of early stellar formations... Anyway, colleagues and dear friends, let's share one more round in celebration of science and the spirit of discovery—while we can."

They pop open another bottle, sending the cork towards a dark corner of the room, where an uninvited guest observes them with impunity from a higher authority.

From A Corner Darkly

Special Agent Zeff's vivid hazel eyes relay a live feed to the boys and girls at the Pickle Factory. With his presence veiled, an undercurrent of neurotransmitters quickens the carnal desires of muscle memory. Unseen, he steadies his breath, focusing on the team's conversation, and observes the camaraderie of their elation.

"What should we call it?" Steven asks.

Carl sloshes a bit of bubbly onto the floor. "How about... *Nibiru?*"

A chuckle gallops around the lab.

"Maybe we could get some of that defense spending money to mine this thing." Nancy attempts to adjust the layered rendering of the object.

They all laugh.

Carl continues, "Perhaps such an object could've passed through our solar system over 150 million years ago, disrupting the asteroid belt—hurtling an iridium-rich rock towards the Earth's gravitational pull. Right place, right time."

"Don't be a drunk." Vega snorts out some jowl-jiggling laughter. "No more for Carl. Someone, send a car to come get him."

"Together, we will. Divided, we won't," Dr. Moon says, then raises her flute.

A fever catches around the room as they sail on the flow of something profound. The lab soon fills with a sliding scale of conversation and the blossoms of a sweeping groupthink experiment. They envision an ideal world where financial intelligence is no longer regarded as the highest form of intelligence, curated by settling differences for the sake of each other. A unified global community no longer perpetuated by war, developing the mindset not to end up like the dinosaurs.

The Death Of Science

In the bliss of drunken revelry, they fail to notice the silenced round spiraling from the stilled shadows. A Pollockesque blood spray spurts from Carl's carotid artery. He spins around and spatters Dr. Moon. Another bullet catches her in the gut, sending her to the ground. Turning to the assassin, Nancy's head explodes with an exit wound.

A primal dread spreads about the laboratory as her body hits the desk on the way to the tile. The remaining team members duck in different directions of self-preservation. However, their noble efforts are futile at best.

Death emerges from the dark corner and artfully squeezes several more shots out of his special-issue Delta-6 handgun, divulging the contents of Neil's body cavity onto the floor. In a fit of foolish desperation, Steven tries to ram him with his wheelchair, only to find the quivering jolt of a government-issued taser-blade within his throat, cauterizing any dangling attachments. QiQi scuttles towards the door. Alas, as she reaches for the handle, two bullets exit her chest with symmetrical accuracy.

On the hunt for his last target, Special Agent Zeff whistles an ole-timey tune taught by the bittersweet memory which was never his. The Oros system highlights tracers across his TacOHUD, tracking the portly astrophysicist's lingering biome, heartbeat, and breath. He stops his tune on the other side of the desk.

Vega panics, his heart beating like a swine before the doors of the slaughterhouse. He peeks from beneath the desk and curls into a fetal position at the sight of his colleague's corpse. The desk flies backward. He scurries in the opposite direction, slipping on a crimson puddle and sliding into an office chair.

Special Agent Zeff steps into view.

"P—p-please spare me," he says, rolling to his knees.

He aims the special-issue Delta-6.

Dr. Vega's pants run wet with the stains of fear as he cowers under the assassin's veiled glare.

"Pathetic." He shakes his head. "Look, this isn't personal; it's just business." He fires a single shot and turns to their computer stations.

Data Breach

Dr. Moon coughs blood into a puddle of champagne-fizzle while, locked in a trance, Special Agent Zeff searches through their printouts. She writhes for a second longer, then defiantly raises a middle finger in the thief's direction. Her last sight, before succumbing to the call of Osiris, is of him inserting a solid-state drive into their lab terminal.

Waiting for the data exchange, he piles their bodies, coats, pocket protectors, hopes, and dreams onto a crisp tarp for the Clean-up Crew. A light chime ques a pop-up message across the TacOHUD. He ejects the portable device and erases all traces of the team's discovery, replacing it with the Agency's pre-scripted findings. In the manner of a moment too brief to consider, another discovery is stolen before it unfurls into fruition.

He takes the drive and copies the encoded data within the Mind Palace VPN partition, a secret, logical division inside the Oros system. Next, he drops it into an Agency deposit box and waits at the location provided on his receipt. Agent Xero collects the intel and hands it to the Director, who, with an air of urgency, presents it to the Committee. Their superior orders an unpaid intern to courier it into the caverns of subterranean lizard people. There, they offer the tribute and sacrifice to their king, who prostrates himself in front of the Arcanist DAO—enemies of the Promethean Flame, keepers of the history we were never meant to know.

Upon receiving the package, they deliver it to the Lords of Co-America. Once a representative of the Faceless retrieves it, they ferry it to the Council of Immortal Elders. And finally, at the Crystal Palace in the center of Antarctica, emissaries deliver the tribute to the Consigliere of the World Emperor.

Of course, *HE* had already gleaned the intel, transmitted to the Crystal Palace by an array of orbital satellites inscribed with runes and fueled by forgotten technologies. *HE* still preferred such formalities. And so, as the sprockets of Samsara lock into gear, the Rube Goldberg machine of our fate begins again.

Arcanist DAO

Somewhere along the chain of command, beneath the darkened chambers of private facilities and shadow lobbies, a large onyx table projects the stolen data from the sheen of its surface. Around the room, members of the DAO [Decentralized Autonomous Organization] appear as redacted shadows veiled with esoteric holograms.

"That's a big one!" Turtle exclaims.

"Is there an opportunity to harvest the raw materials before we make 'them' pay to deflect it? We can deflect it, right?" Owl asks.

"You fool," Fox interrupts. "Did you even read the report? Of course we can deflect it."

"There may be large deposits of *Philosopher Stone* in this one," Turtle speculates.

"With this, we could finally ascend," Lion says.

Bear interrupts, "Regardless, we have a duty to preserve order and not let the news of this spread among the lower classes."

"Would they even believe it?" Serpent asks.

Wolf answers, "If it comes from the right source, yes."

"Let's prepare global statements for respective outlets," Spider solicits.

"And get someone to make sure those dirt-dwellers don't mess this up again." Bat projects several news screens from their console. "The information needs to come out at the precise moment."

Rat minimizes the data into a projection of the globe with sixty location pins, each resonating with its own video feed. "Also, let's check global countercultural groups and push for them to become more radicalized."

"Good idea," Beetle concurs.

The shadows mutter.

"In the meantime," Elephant interrupts, "maybe we can stress differing degrees of economic fueled racial tensions to keep the lower classes divided. Their herd mentality is a dangerous thing, especially if allowed to aggregate. Let us not forget Alexandria."

"They *do* work well under those conditions." Crocodile chuckles. "And you know what they say? Pressure makes diamonds."

A snobbish laughter resonates amongst the holograms.

"Whatever it takes to keep them occupied... so long as we maintain the sovereign duty handed down to us throughout the ages," Eagle reminds the room.

Shark responds, "We have a right to preserve the heritage of our ancient order!"

"Then let us put this to a vote." Owl concludes.

3

From Chaos

Downtown Comedown

After Hawaii, the weeks of waiting weigh heavily on Special Agent Zeff. Fueled by the radio silence since the Oros system's last update and the brooding angst, he goes on a bender. Full speed ahead, this little joyride crashes through every hole-in-the-wall along the cobblestone lanes of Holy City's downtown peninsula.

On the last night of the run, with his belly full from an obscene amount of MacChugga-Burgers, Special Agent Zeff takes a disco nap while his Xion roadster drives back to the King Charles apartments. A kiss of Nostalgia No. 5, left on his collar from another late night with his favorite exotic dancer—discussing *Space Force* subplots and character development—drifts into the latest piece from Dreamwind Studios.

As the roadster arrives at the apartment building's front door, its onboard assistant ushers him from the Screening Room within the Mind Palace VPN partition. He stumbles to the front door, rumbling through the lobby, sliding against the foyer walls into the elevator. Barely standing, he presses several buttons before finding his own.

The elevator ascends, stopping at each level, revealing fleeting glimpses of life:

Ding. A calico cat darts past.

Ding. Laughter echoes from a party.

Ding. A solitary figure stares at the floor.

Ding. Two small Dachshunds rush in, then back down the hall.

Ding. A tenant hitches a ride to the ninth floor—only to realize the predicament, getting off two floors later to take the stairs.

Eventually, Special Agent Zeff makes it up to the top floor. Before exiting, he presses every button, then dances out onto the hallway's grease-stained carpet. *Ding... Ding... Ding.* The elevator proceeds to the lobby, breaking down between the second and third floors.

Fried by a kaleidoscope of bourbon, ludes, cocaine, and debauchery, he spins along the wall, vibing to the groove of invisible bass beats still thumping in his ears. Upon reaching the threshold of his overpriced room, he fumbles with the key until finding the proper tumbler combination and shoves the door open. Three steps inside, the apartment door slams shut, rattling the hallway.

Past the tile entrance, he raids the refrigerator for leftovers, gathering two beers and a box of cold pizza, then plops on the couch. As the score of *Space Force IX* transitions into cosmic wonder, a razor's edge chops fine lines across a tarnished mirror.

Writer's Angst

Hours later, Special Agent Zeff cranes his neck to look through the dirty wall-sized window of his efficiency apartment. "Not much of a view. Thought I'd at least be facing the ocean, not Holy City's whitewashed backside. Well, at least this is better than Bangkok or Benghazi."

Still dark and starlit, the sun barely approaches this side of the world as his agile hands slur ironic elucidations against the keys of a Remington SL3 typewriter.

I'm not proud of what I have to do... Of what I've done... When my eyes were filled with the shine of childlike wonder, Lady Liberty was abducted and replaced with a who's who of market makers and private gains. Elites—cash-cow tycoons, robber-barons, and predatory venture-capitalist cartels—had suppressed the spirit of the age, profiting off the hyper-normalized chaos of the everyday world. Two things were going unnoticed, among others: the incentivized destruction of the ecosystem and the militarization of our mindsets.

After several decades of overzealous fear-mongering for safety and excessive military budgeting, the 'War' became every-day-ness. Sadly, for an unfortunate number of generations, a state of perpetual conflict was all they'd ever known. Our first-world problems were but a luxurious paradise few could afford—a quid pro quo of distraction and destruction. By now, it was all just business—

(Just business.) The words bound from the page, conjuring the jiggling jowls of the potbellied astrophysicist. He shakes his head and looks down at the mirror to relieve his bubbling angst. (Did they find out about the Mind Palace? I've been idle for too long—get a hold of yourself. Don't sweat that shit. Remember, all of this is for the greater good. And a bit of revenge.)

A torn man in a mad world, he swigs back a shot, lights a cigarette, lets go, and enjoys the ride—suppressing the unease beneath the Nether Regions of Thought.

After a double snort, he returns to the Remington SL3 and exercises his demons with relentless keystrokes and misspellings.

I can't put my finger on it. But at some point, the flag stopped representing what it was sewn, flown, and fought for. Truth, Honor, Justice, and Integrity became a naked-short commodity traded on the Exchange. Everything was for the almighty god of Profit: education, healthcare, incarceration, rehabilitation, war, cookies, popcorn, toys, pizza, water, air, and life. It all had a price.

Strung out on the good graces of the free market, we started believing the flicker of the silver screen. Abroad, we saw ourselves as the heroes and defenders of all that was just. Meanwhile, back home, surrounded by high-fidelity comfort and control, no one heard the bombs being dropped halfway around the world.

When will it be the proper time to bring this up? After the first missile flies into the upper atmosphere? Or when the last tree has fallen? Which puppet master would thwart the call of progress? Whose gods could dare tolerate such selfishness to flourish within our hearts? What was it all for? We only have so much time left. The asteroid is still heading this way.

Special Agent Zeff lifts his hands from the keys of the Remington SL3. He leans back in his chair and takes a pull of warm bourbon. Some things he wished he could forget, but some things could never be forgotten.

(I know Xero's watching me. The Mind Palace's feedback loop might fool the boys and girls at the Pickle Factory, but not those Agency goons on the ground. If I can get this data dropped to Annah, I'd feel a lot better.) He rubs his hands through his dark-brown hair. (Where's the next portion of my assignment? They haven't briefed me on a single thing. This feels like a setup. Do they know, I know, that I know? Did something show during the update?) His thoughts spiral into a state of narco-fueled neurosis and ontological paranoia. He samples another toot and returns to the keys.

4

Begin
Transmission

Fleeting Inspiration

Hours later, a thick drip numbs his throat with a foul taste. "This isn't Peruvian... They must've cut it with something. What'd I expect? Well, I ain't dead yet." He goes to clear another row from the tarnished mirror.

A beam of sunlight targets his hand, drawing him to the dingy wall-sized window. Through greasy palm prints and random spatters of hot sauce, the opulence of daybreak graces over the coniferous and oak groves, bordering a pretzel of on-ramps and off-ramps. In the distance, light spears pierce veiled hordes of pluffy clouds, revealing a patchwork sky of cosmic surrender.

As the windowsill warms, Special Agent Zeff's knife scratches with an impatient examination of something aloof in the distance. He glances back at the poorly typed manuscript and takes a drag. Meanwhile, Coleridge's albatross clings to his neck, exaggerated by an underlying existential crisis, an overactive amygdala, work-related conditions, a muddled watering-down of commonality, and a functional dependency on mind-altering substances.

The sun continues its climb. Nearby, a buzzing fly bounces across his apartment's grimy, wall-sized window. A swift swipe of his taser-blade slices the annoyance in half, stopping just before the surface of the windowpane. The creature's legs writhe and wriggle as its connective goop slides off the carbon edge of his tactical cutlery of choice.

Writer's Block

Aided by the TacOHUD, Special Agent Zeff scans the eastern horizon for inspiration. Apollo's chariot ascends, leaving in its wake a new day—one of renewal and redemption. Through dusty, parted curtains, contrasting colors cause his corneas to embolden the outline of the sky's intangible surface.

Just past the humming wall-mounted window unit, dew drops form on live oak leaves. A nearby limb shelters a family of robins. And underneath their burnt-orange breasts, a clutch of blue eggs reflects the emerging dawn.

On the street, the beeping signal from a reversing garbage truck covers the cries of an ambulance rushing in frantic necessity to preserve life. His gaze follows a line of palmettos along the sidewalk towards another set of apartments, squeezed into a space that was better suited for a community garden than luxury living accommodations.

While a photo-synthetic shimmer cycles through the dragon tattoo on his left forearm, nanites deliver a shot of [Prime], actively shutting down his lateral prefrontal cortex—inducing a pure sense of flow. Held in a time of rhapsodic wonder, recapitulation, and a million nerve endings firing at once, the vortices of thought and connectivity conspire to liberate his mind from itself. And getting out of his own way, he finds inspiration at last.

Eureka

With a flick of the wrist, his taser-blade swiftly arches 42° in the air and plunges into the twenty-fourth day on a drugstore calendar. A furious slew of Gestalt keystrokes interrupts the last wood splinter hitting the floor. He abstracts from the ethereal world, and the void of the page becomes a womb from which the neon streamers of inspiration run amok within the Reliquary of Imagination. Each melodious click and release dances from an inaudible cadence, firing through his nervous system, into his fingers, then upon the Remington's keys.

Special Agent Zeff pulls back and stares at the piece of ink-tatted paper. "Nah, too close to the real thing," he says, grabbing the page, balling it up and no-look-banking it off the wall, onto a pile of half-baked ideas and crumpled conclusions.

His fingertips settle back on the keys when a notification pops up in the TacOHUD's tab bar. He tries to ignore it until a text message scrolls across his vision. The ever-fleeting sparkle of inspiration dissipates into the room's gray fringes.

"Shit, I'm never going to finish this," he groans. (If they found out, I'm certain they'd have me flayed in the streets by now. Probably blame it on the most profitable enemy, then spin it into a 'save the puppies act' for the peanut gallery up on Capitol Hill.)

Despite the creeping neurosis—caught in the drip of booger sugar sliding down the back of his throat—he presses his tongue against a hidden bio-switch in his mouth, just behind the soft palate, to minimize the Mind Palace VPN partition, reverting the feedback stream to real-time and opening the encrypted message.

[The near moon rises over the mud puddle.] The Agency's text scrolls in front of him.

His thoughts transcribe into the message thread, [Foxtrot-Echo-Alpha-Romeo.]

[Agent authenticity confirmed.]

[What are the coordinates?] he asks.

[You'll rendezvous with your contact at 32.6661° N, 79.9392° W.]

[The gig?]

[Infiltration.]

[Target?]

[The First Global Foundation. Details will be transmitted once you arrive.]

The message chain auto-deletes.

Another press of the bio-switch, and the Mind Palace syncs its edited feedback seamlessly with his next blink. Special Agent Zeff jumps up and closes the typewriter case. Then, thrusting open the dusty curtains, he illuminates the small studio apartment and jots down the coordinates within a cipher. After rolling up the small piece of paper, he conceals the intel inside the pen's barrel and places it next to the Remington SL3.

Packing

The halting sound of an accident on a nearby overpass rings throughout the room as an eighteen-wheeler's jake brakes stutter to a stop. He dashes to the window for a better view of the chaos. Outside, a morning fog weaves down Holy City's narrow avenues, obstructing his view.

Financial spires climb above the gloom, higher than any church-erected vistas from colonial times, and give rise to the price-point-difference-dividend-yield-budget-analysis of yesteryear. Every day, hundreds of new residents flock to the area, clogging the narrow streets and pretzelled ramps with a lack of economic mobility and the exhausting fumes of the daily commute.

He turns from the wall-sized window to his makeshift writing desk and leans over the tarnished mirror. With a mighty snort, Special Agent Zeff vacuums the last line, enjoying the sizzle along the mucous membrane of his nasal cavity. He lights a complimentary cigarette and tosses the one-third-crushed and two-thirds-filled yellow pack onto the windowsill.

Against a backdrop of early morning fog and cotton candy clouds, poignant light rays penetrate the lingering smoke—stilled in the apartment's artificial air currents—imbuing a rose-tinted hue onto the kaleidoscape of the room's contents. On the corner of a muddled bed, three pressed outfits wait in crisp packaging. An outdated refrigerator hums, its polar corridors stuffed with frosty delights. As its rattling compressor echoes across the muck-stained tile floor, a carton of milk reaches the point of potential freezing.

A stuttering faucet harmonizes with the cantankerous air-conditioning unit mounted under the window. Outside, the sun continues its ascent. Like Sisyphus pushing Camus's boulder, Special Agent Zeff turns with an enthusiastic whirl and compiles ordinances of clothing, gadgets, personal maintenance items, a copy of *Finnegans Wake*, and some sealed packages of cannabis flower into a medium-sized tactical suitcase.

Fetching the typewriter's case, he retrieves a manila envelope from a secret compartment at the bottom, removes a few bundles of cash and corresponding identification, then places them next to his socks. Finally packed, he closes the lid. The suitcase locks and arms its biometric security system, capable of incinerating the contents if someone other than the operator attempts to open it.

Special Agent Zeff changes into a white linen suit, attaches the Remington SL3 typewriter to the top of his luggage, and grabs the pen, slipping it into his pocket. A brief survey of the room draws his gaze to the overflowing wastebasket.

"Can't let them find that," he says, setting the suitcase down and draping his jacket over its handle.

He searches the cabinets and retrieves a small unlabeled bottle of liquid. As he pours it on the papers, they dissolve into a gray slush, resembling more oatmeal than a treatise of treasonous ideas. After a few flushes—and the discovery of a leftover party favor—Special Agent Zeff exits the one-room abode.

5

Vessel Of Life

Into The Hallway

The door slams shut behind him, shaking the dimly lit corridor. Its mildew-green carpet highlights the well-worn pathways of everydayness with wandering trails of salt, mud stains, late-night stumbles, walks of shame, pizza crumbs, sticky spots from spilled drinks, and the soles of shuffling shoes—all leading beneath grease-stained doorknobs. Though appearing to be mere thresholds of the mundane, under the slumlord's lock and key, these spaces house anti-entropic entities living within generative feedback systems of greater complexity. The menagerie of their stories seeps from the cracks of each apartment as Special Agent Zeff strides towards the elevator.

He passes the third door on the right, secured by deadbolts and chain locks, where a jazzy improv cranks up from a nearby record player. At first, a crackling agitation, but then the needle finds its groove. The popping surface noise, winding round and round, conjures one of the Donor's memories into focus. While a certain scorn flashes across his brow, a tear attempts to run down his cheek, only to be vanquished back to the corners of his hazel eyes. He spits at the thought. Regardless, the reflection of simpler times pans onto a silken projector screen.

Whittlin'

See him now, as a child, sitting in an oversized rocking chair next to his grandfather. An Easter breeze whisks a pile of shavings around the porch. Young-Zeff holds a chunky block of soft pine in one hand and a Case Seahorse Whittler in the other.

Paw-Paw shaves away a slice of pine and rocks to the jazzy tempo of his radio. "You see, a whittler is a carver, but not all carvers are whittlers."

"What do you mean, Paw-Paw?"

"Whittlin' shaves away. Whittlin' reveals. Carvin' digs into it. See here." Paw-Paw flays his bulky Boy Scout knife along the grain. Another smooth sliver of soft pine flakes off of the half-formed space shuttle. He holds it up to the sky and marvels at the knots in the wood, knowing it's foolish to believe in perfection or that everything can be perfectly known.

Inspired by the emerging space shuttle, young-Zeff takes to his small block of pine. First, a set of ears, followed by a cute almond-shaped face. Halfway through, he stops to show his progress.

"Look, Paw-Paw. I'm making a baby squirrel."

"Lemme see," he says with a gravelly drawl, then reaches for the totem to examine it with imaginative scrutiny. "Looks good, my boy! Try shavin' a little bit on this side to even it up." He hands back the wooden block.

Young-Zeff carves an even demeanor onto the wooden creature's face. "Like this?"

However, he isn't paying attention, and the blade of the Case Seahorse slices into his left thumb.

"Damn, boy! You've cut yourself right to the bone."

"It's okay. Momma can fix it." He squeezes his thumb as two salty teardrops well up in his hazel eyes.

Paw-Paw wraps his handkerchief around the tiny, bloody thumb. "Here, put some pressure on it and see that your momma cleans it thoroughly."

He hops off his grandparents' porch and races home. A cloud of dust kicks up from the springs in his legs. Over the rolling fields, three of Paw-Paw's ole hound dogs catch his scent and beeline up the hill after him, barking all the livelong way.

Elevator Go Down

Wounded by its presence and relieved by its departure, the Donor's memory fades halfway down the hall. Special Agent Zeff's luggage rolls along, missing a large wad of chewing gum. He passes a triple-locked door, where trash bags bang about with the refuse of yesterday's loss. Overhead, the hum of fluorescent bulbs, with every third one silent, flickers in Morse code.

Regardless of the snowman in his nose, a mosaic of smells floods his perception. At first, the tinctures of curry and coriander drift into the isolating hallway. Soon, the aroma of cannabis combines with the *sizzle-pop* of bacon, covered by coffee, melted into the creases of varying egg dishes—scrambled, runny, fried, omelet—all nestled in a basket of something burnt.

He reaches the elevator, resting with its door partially ajar. He presses the button, only to find a crooked 'Out of Order' sign hanging with some painter's tape.

"As much as it costs to stay here," he mutters, shaking his head, "I guess I've got to take the fucking stairs."

The cocaine coursing through Special Agent Zeff's bloodstream amplifies his angst. He laments about the things he's done, aching for something more—something to wash away the pitted sorrow, the bloodstains, and the lies. Despite his hostility towards the false memories of his youth, he longs for those simpler times, knowing they could never be his.

After stewing to a boil, he grumbles to the dimly lit threshold. Then, checking the typewriter case and patting his pocket for the pen, he turns the grease-stained handle.

Into The Stairwell

The door cracks open, greeting him with the curdling stench of piss and cigarette smoke. Above, smeared streams of sunlight burst through the twelfth floor's murky windows, capturing a faint matrix of falling dust. Into the bleak stairwell, Special Agent Zeff walks down one grotesque step after another.

As he descends past strobing, flicker-lit flights, the last embraces of light fail their charge into the darkening chasm. Downward into an abyss of sensation, spiraling rectangles dim deeper, towards the damp sound of dripping pipes. Further, still farther, darkness infuses with the murky glow of rouge-lit EXIT signs.

Several floors below, shadows shuffle against shadow, grunting against one another, releasing obnoxious plumes into the grotto.

"Good god, do that shit elsewhere!" Special Agent Zeff says as he approaches the writhing mess of rags and tooth decay.

The bums roll over and scuttle off, tumbling to the lower level. Their sudden retreat leaves a trail of alcohol and shame. The awful smell blends with a healthy handful of atypical social disgust.

Irate, he moves to the lower landing, carefully avoiding soiling his white linen suit on the foul refuse left in the squatters' wake. With hateful intent in his eyes, Special Agent Zeff stares down at the once-human creatures, hollering, "I don't have time for this shit! I never want to catch you filthy-fucking-bottom-feeders in this stairwell again."

They cower on the crusty concrete floor, curling into the fetal position, while he kicks the nearest meatbag. A few fragments of teeth roll into a spittle of blood. The other begs for mercy. We are only as human as the next person treats us.

Afterward, he turns with an air of self-righteousness and heads for the exit. Not wanting to touch the doorknob, he kicks the back door open with a fraction of his strength. *Fwam!* It slams against the worn outer wall of the King Charles apartment building, embedding its handle into the historical brickwork.

His shoe hangs for a dramatic second as a morning breeze rushes into his lungs, filling the dark spire behind him. Up, up, up. The stench of filth-ridden rags blends amongst the building's bouquet of life.

Parking Lot Pimpin'

Sunrays jaunt through the spring air, eradicating the dregs of darkness that cling to his face. Special Agent Zeff reaches his arms towards the heavens. As he embraces the sun's warmth, his suit bunches at the shoulders, concealing fit, muscular tones developed into perfection by circumfused nanite stews and the redacted practices of the Agency's Ouroboros project.

"Now, where's my car?" he ponders, looking around the super swampers of oversized trucks, each backed into their respective parking spaces.

Above, a cloud's shadow overtakes him while the morning breeze wisps fragments of litter around a flagpole and into the wheel well of a nearby hooptie. From the corner of his eye, Special Agent Zeff spots a piece of trash bobbing hither-thither like a jellyfish on an invisible tide.

"Not on my watch!" He sprints after the plastic bag and leaps into the air. His first swipe misses. Darting one digit past his reach, the plastic bag smiles back at him, taunting his efforts. Unmoved by its persistent flight, he lunges once more, plucking 'the forbidden fruit' from the air with the poise of a Wing Chun master.

Special Agent Zeff lands with his quarry in hand and crumples the bag. Then, using the good deed as a diversion, he strides to the nearest trash can, slips the pen from his pocket, and tucks both pen and bag into the overflowing bin. The door slams shut on a styrofoam cup sloshing with cigarette butts and watered-down sweet tea, nearly splashing his white linen coat with the stain of artificial sweetener—had he not turned to find his ride.

Unbeknownst to anyone watching, a transparent set of robotic wings sprouts from the sides of the pen as it reconfigures into a dragonfly-shaped drone. Transformed, it takes to the sky and carries the coordinates to a member of his Kabal, who is sipping a cup of coffee at a nearby café.

The drone lands on the table beside her crumb-laden plate. Annah R. Kay looks at it through her neuro-laced Panthièr shades. Once the signature confirms, it reverts to a pen and releases the scrap of paper from its barrel. She picks up the cipher, tilts down her sunglasses and decodes it with a glance.

"Hats, he's made contact," Annah says in a low voice.

[Perfect. We'll continue to monitor the EDC connection.] Hats's text scrolls in front of her.

Before the server brings the check and refills her cup of coffee, she conceals the small parchment in her palm. With the pen in her possession, she settles the tab, leaving a generous tip, and exits the café. Heads swivel, following the sashay of her skirt as she climbs into a red Shelby Mustang and accelerates down the street.

6

Xion

Specs

Agent Zeff paces down the next row, looking over the other vehicles. He taps the bio-switch in the roof of his mouth, and the Mind Palace VPN partition pivots its feedback loop to real-time, allowing the Oros system to sync with the Agency-issued roadster. In a couple more steps, X's piano-black interior comes alive: adjusting the seats from their hedonistic recline, equalizing the volume of the music, and linking with the Pickle Factory.

Under the trunk, a nine-phase, twelve-pole AC induction motor with perpetual rotor collectors activates X's multilayered computational systems. Hyper-threaded iridium-ion microprocessors, supported by liquid-cooled powertrain drive inverters, channel a synthesis of speed and performance.

With his suitcase in tow, Agent Zeff moves to the front of the roadster. X senses him and pops the frunk. Inside, a concealed vault of secret compartments unlocks.

He repositions an Agency-approved field kit, grappling hook, a custom set of taser-blades, two flare guns, a pair of stun batons, a compact aquatic exploration suit, and various classified instruments not privy to the public. After ensuring everything is in its place, he carefully settles his luggage, mindful not to damage the Remington SL3 typewriter.

Set Course

He slides into the driver's seat as the door and frunk close themselves. X finishes booting its deep-learning protocols from sleep mode and dims the interior lighting to a heron blue. While Agent Zeff places his hands on the steering wheel, proximity relays sync with the Oros system. X interprets the data and maps the quickest route to rendezvous with his contact.

"Hello, Sir. How are we today?" X's refined female British accent reverberates from the speakers.

"Impeccable," he says.

"Excellent, sir. I've already applied your coordinates and calibrated a proper path for the estimated time of arrival. Would you like me to begin navigation to *Coffin Island*?"

"As ready as I'll ever be." (This definitely feels like a setup.)

Cabin conditions stabilize for optimal comfort, followed by an indicator on the holographic dash. X reverses out of the space, then, one gear shift later, speeds off with certainty, zooming to the parking lot's exit.

Stop

Down the street, a red light brings the traffic to an abrupt halt. He looks left, waiting for the light to change, and enjoys the yum of natural splendor. A tiny pile of leaves swirls in the street. Nearby, yellow butterflies flutter around a pink camellia bush. Bees hover there too, gathering kief for the honey that swells within the bellies of their hives.

Several eternities pass for the folks at the light as the sun shepherds the morning cloud cover. All around X's midnight-black, high-gloss Kevlar finish, motorists suffer from the anxious compulsion to complete their commute, white-knuckled to the yuck of dripping, smog-stained tailpipes. Inevitably reaching their destination, they miss the whole point of taking the scenic route.

The light changes—despite having several of its LED bulbs burned out—and X's serpentine, ruby-eyed taillights merge into the flow of traffic. While the roadster autonomously coasts along, Agent Zeff doomscrolls through lists of articles, PDFs, and notifications, catching up on the day's socio-politico-economic events: stocks are down, the whispers of war dance behind proxy conflicts and the journals of economic hitmen, protests continue to spread across the globe, multiple bombings, famine, a pandemic on the rise, and another attempt to remove an unfavorable politician.

A length of suggested links later, Agent Zeff finds himself in a spiraling deluge of mindless memes and *Space Force* fan theory videos. He soon succumbs to comfortability, after too many restless nights, and dozes off, leaving X to navigate the complexities of a world not built for its design.

"It's just business," he murmurs, as his head sways in the driver's seat.

7

Commute

Traffic

Several kilometers into their journey, X slows with the riverside traffic. A late-spring breeze envelops the crayon canyon of combustion and whisks a styrofoam cup over the guardrail. The single-use disposable floats down like a parasol into the choppy waters below. Nearby, hydrangeas bob colorful snowballs in the partial shade from topped live oaks, their branches reaching under power lines like a prisoner for rations.

Oil leaks from idle drip pans, mixing into a chromatic puddle left by a faulty sprinkler head. Special Agent Zeff shudders awake to the cool stream of ionized air caressing the piano-black, genuine-imitation-leather interior. Another gust sweeps more refuse along the roadway.

He furrows his brow at the litter. "This place is a shithole," he mocks.

The traffic light changes to green. And one by one, the congestion trickles towards the speed limit. X keeps with the flow as he activates the Mind Palace's feedback loop and stares out the window, following the flight of a large gull.

"Why can't I stop seeing his face? I bet it was the way his jaw jiggled." (It's just business.) "Probably the coldest thing to say to another human being." (It's just business.) "Shit's so fucked up." He removes the corner bag of blow from his shirt pocket and carves out an overzealous key bump. "Fuck. Trying to lift that intel could've exposed me." He pops another slope into the opposite nostril. "They would've tried something by now—it'll be fine once I meet with Annah. I don't know why the Promethean Flame wants this data, but in ten years, this place goes belly up." (Is it even worth saving?)

En Route

X switches lanes to avoid an accident up ahead and skirts around the peninsula. At the bend, smoke plumes from a row of factories stain the cotton-candy skyline with the twirl and tango of progress.

"What a view." The sarcasm rolls off his tongue like water droplets on waxy leaves.

"Would you like me to search for more of this view?" X asks.

"I was being sarcastic... You know, I thought we'd sent all of those jobs overseas. Guess I've been away for too long."

Ding-ding-ding. Farther on, a rising drawbridge pauses the traffic again.

"Who designed this place?" He leans against the headrest.

"I can look it up for you."

"No need—"

A deep pothole catches the conversation, lifting him against the seatbelt.

"Shit... I've seen better roads made for rickshaws." Special Agent Zeff adjusts himself and checks the rearview mirror. "How long till we get there? This traffic is awful."

"With a notable increase in Holy City's population this time of year, we should arrive in approximately ninety minutes." X illuminates a cool-blue display, zooming out to denote traffic flow and highlight the destination.

He groans with impatience and slaps an improv beat onto the steering wheel.

X intuitively produces a song track over the speakers, along the same rhythm.

"Nah, something a little more jazzy."

Reviewing his previous play selections, cross-referenced with sixty relevant musicians, a trumpet billows from the immersive sound system.

Drawbridge

After several minutes, the gears of the bascule bridge glide into place and transform the chunk of infrastructure to a passable height. Now twelve meters tall, it towers above a flowing indigo waterway.

Unchained from the steering wheel, Special Agent Zeff leans over the passenger seat to catch a better view. Several beams of light pierce through parting clouds and stretch past the first ship's frothy wake. There, photons, ecstatic with existence, transmute the sun's radiance into the sparkle of rippling foam.

Easily bored, he settles back in the driver's seat, samples another bump, and wipes his nose. He looks back in the rearview mirror, then to the lanes of traffic, noticing the growing agitation of the huddled masses. Two vehicles ahead, in the right lane, an older gentleman waits on a dirty moped, encumbered with bags, pumps, gizmos, and tools—all riding on half-inflated tires.

Behind him, a business owner shakes his head with time-based frustration. Another person rocks their car from side to side, looking for something in the backseat. Thirty, or more, find themselves hunched over, face-down in their digital screens. Several women check their makeup. One person sings at the top of their lungs. Others wait in frustration, their time slipping away, seldom considering how much of their lives they spend at a place that pays them a small percentage of their worth. This is the source of their frustration—not the bridge, but the possibility of being late to a place they loathe.

Special Agent Zeff mainlines all of it through his mental filters and into the bin of everydayness. A butterfly drags his attention from the restless motorists to the dashboard's display.

"Perfect time for a smoke break," he says, reaching towards a custom compartment.

Inside the hidden chamber: a waterproof metal container, an electric lighter, another pen, and a notepad. Within the tin, several perfectly rolled joints—stacked, one on top of the other, like candies in their dispenser or rounds in a magazine.

He selects the next-largest cone and lights it. On exhale, his thoughts expand a line of drop-down menus from the TacOHUD's tab bar, activating [STEALTH]. A photosynthetic shimmer illuminates under the dragon tattoo as X triggers the chitin-mirror paint job, converting its exquisite design to mimic a family sedan.

Amidst the murmuring herd of combustion beasts, Special Agent Zeff reclines his seat from the upright position and savors a puff. The scent of the Gelato Kush reminds him of Ben Penstone, Kabal member and ex-British intelligence operative from the Lancelot division. He takes another toke and boots the Mind Palace's emulator.

A virtual world waxes across the TacOHUD, offering him a reprieve from the Agency's scrutiny. Designed by the Promethean Flame to complement his eidetic memory, Special Agent Zeff organizes a bag of thoughts in the Control Tower while a relay terminal materializes the dossier. It opens to a highlighted movie reel of reflection, revealing the rolling beads of perspiration saturating Ben's white, blood-stained shirt.

Ben Penstone

Overhead, a lone light bulb flickers from a wire in the safe house ceiling as a rusted pot in the corner slowly fills with the dripping drops from a recent storm. Mosquitoes buzz about the lattice of crisscrossed netting draped throughout the room. On the wobbly table between the two men, a radio broadcasts the vintage tunes of an era before the War.

"Hey mate! Quit toying with that. It's busted," Ben says, looking up from his improvised rolling tray: a dust flyer from a gambling parlor.

"I need this nebulizer to work. I'm feeling weird... Must've overused the system a bit too much, back at the Leaky Tea warehouse."

"That was some shit! You're gonna have to cue me in on how you pulled that off. Tits! You're a mad one." Ben laughs, rolling the spliff in his hands. "This should help ya. Got the recipe from an Amazonian medicine man in a trailer park." He lights up, stoking an even burn. "Here, bruv, have a Chong."

Special Agent Zeff reaches for the paper totem, but a wave of tremors pulses from the root of his spine into his left arm. He manages hold of it when the pounding bass beats from a half-filled pot in the corner stifle his efforts to raise the spliff to his lips. After a brief pause between sets, he successfully takes a hit.

He hurriedly fills his chest. On contact, pulmonary irritant receptors seize from the cloudy concoction of tobacco, hash, and cannabis. His lungs contract and expel a billowing mass of smoke.

"Damn. Are you alright?" Ben asks, taking the spliff from Special Agent Zeff's outstretched hand.

He gasps for breath as its soothing reprieve counteracts the side effects of the Oros system's inefficiencies.

"Haha... The more you cough, the more you get off!" Ben hands him a cloudy glass of water.

Special Agent Zeff greedily gulps it down, despite its lack of clarity. He breathes in and everything mellows, actively metabolizing a whelming sense of homeostatic ease.

Neon signs dim their ferocious hum. Nearby, the bustling street crowd returns to the evening's murmuring commerce. With the blaring honks from hurried motorists fading into the backdrop, the room soon harmonizes with the *lub-dub* of his heartbeat.

"There you are, mate. Nice and easy. Don't hit it so hard next time." Ben takes a toke, emboldening the cherry.

With tear-glossed eyes, Special Agent Zeff watches Ben admire the twisted paper spire before ripping another mighty lungful, then releasing a stylish French inhale. The night unwinds beneath the flickering light bulb, smoke wrapping into the rafters as they forge bonds through tales of battle and conquest.

8

Two Bridges, Too Many

Mission Briefing

An alarm chimes. "I've gathered all relevant materials on Coffin Island and have forwarded the links to your inbox," X announces.

Agent Zeff minimizes the Mind Palace and inhales an aromatic lungful of Gelato Kush, ensuring nanite synapses maintain proportionate dominion over neural architectures. "All right, let's see where we're going." He spins one side of the cherry into the no-smell ashtray and selects the flashing icon in the TacO-HUD's tab bar. "Ooh, the Sandlapper Suites... fancy."

The seat intuitively shifts to an upright position as the system renders a lively landscape of situational information, historical significances, weather stats, and tide charts, highlighting the eighteen bars and restaurants along Center Street.

"Am I going on vacation? Why would they send me here?"

"This is the original headquarters of the First Global Foundation. Would you like me to attach these documents to your to-do list?"

"No need. We'll review everything once we get closer." (Lemme finish this medicine... Xero is up to something... I should've already dropped in.)

He scans for suspicious activity. In the next car over, packed to the gills for spring break, children explore joyful realms of uncharted imaginal space. Frogs sip their tea, and young explorers blast Captain Kepler to smithereens with the all-new *Space Force XII: Dreadnaught Cannon*—act fast, while supplies last!

"Enjoy it while you can, little ones," Agent Zeff says, lifting his joint from the ashtray, hoping to dispel the angst beneath his breast, and takes a toke.

Two inches above the dash, he catches a hostile glare from a mixed set of blue-green eyes, reflecting from the side mirror of an adjacent Freightliner P700 step van—converted to a food truck—with a manga-esque flying squirrel serving crepes paint job. In the pause of mere milliseconds, a stagnant exchange of intent survives.

(Is he looking at me? Did the Oros glitch again? It was working fine earlier—it might be the Mind Palace. Are they Johnny Who's people? If it's the Agency, I bet Xero sent them—pull yourself together, man. You're almost home free.)

There are plenty of enemies who lust for his suffering and demise. He knows he deserves it—but not before satisfying his zeal for vengeance.

The mixed pair of eyes disappears into the back of the van. As the uneasiness hangs amidst the climbing hum of humidity, Agent Zeff makes a mental note, calculating potential points of contact for later reference.

"Must be the update," he says, dismissing the tyranny of fear-based logic, uncertainty, and doubt. (I've got to calm down.) He hits it again. "X, are you there?"

"Yes, of course," X replies. "Where else would I be?"

"Never mind that... Patch in a work order to the Pickle Factory. Kindly tell them to get off their asses and put some of that well-lobbied money to work. I need them to run remote diagnostics on the Oros system."

A light chirp passes throughout the cabin. "Message sent," X informs him.

Idly waiting, Agent Zeff pulls another puff to further calm his nerves. (Almost there. I just need to get in contact with Annah.)

The final tips of a yacht slow-skim under the bridge's railing. Above, a private jet skirts across the azure sky. His line of sight tracks their movements until a pop-up menu expands with a brochure for the Sanctuary, a haven of the wealthy and powerful, far away from the unwashed masses and the refuse of useless things.

Safely past, coordinated bells signal rotating gears, cogs, and sprockets to guide the infrastructure with steampunk-ish reluctance, slowly lowering the pendulum of asphalt and rebar. The level crossings raise their arms, and the bridge wobbles with the start of the motorcade's procession.

Suspension Bridge

One by one, the traffic crosses the river's cleft. He gets into the right lane and takes the exit ramp to the Connector. Through a town annexed by Holy City, past repeating strip malls of Iron-Time Fitness gyms, Spa Enys, random takeout spots, Game-Stonks electronics, boutique fashions, and a few holes-in-the-wall that had escaped his recent bender, Agent Zeff swirls up the on-ramp towards two enormous ivory towers leading to James Island.

He marvels at the architecture coming into view. Focusing on its design, the TacOHUD generates another translucent pop-up window with relevant metrics on the cable-stayed suspension bridge.

Closer, the fan hastily unfurls into the third-longest structure of its class. Woven metal spindles create one-hundred-twenty-eight delicately drooping tension wires, running from the diamond-tipped towers to the deck—each piece in proper proportion to the relational whole. In the distance, beyond seabird silhouettes, nautical vessels scoot into queue, waiting to berth at one of Holy City's ports on the far side of the peninsula.

Several vehicles ahead, he notices a peculiar arrangement of coincidence, synchronicity, and universal rascality. A black sport-utility vehicle with the name 'Shelby' stenciled in elegant lettering switches lanes. Behind it, a man spits some tobacco juice out the driver-side window of their jacked-up pickup truck, license plate reading, 'Shelby, Tennessee.' Following him, a red Shelby Mustang cruises for a better position.

Mercenaries

A brisk wind flows along the roadster's contours as X cruises up the enormous ivory suspension bridge. The crepe van comes back into view—and so do those mixed blue-green eyes. Appearing in the passenger window, they cast an ill-fated stare over the revving sports cars, smogging transport trucks, combusting hotheads, littering assholes, and roving families of the daily commute. Without a thought, Agent Zeff's hand slips around the rubberized grip of his special-issue Delta-9 hand cannon.

An eternity passes within a few controlled breaths as the van chugs under the Southern sun. A trail of coolant drips from its tailpipe and dissolves into the cracked pavement. Nine pelicans swoop sideways, ribboning across the hooded horizon.

"What are you up to?" Agent Zeff asks, unlocking the weapon's center-console holster. (Something's off.) A proper stint of calculated paranoia unearths a dossier from the Oros system's archives. (It's not one of ours. Someone wants this tech: the Chinese, the Russians, the radical right, the fundamental left... Who?)

The van shuffles about on its axles. He looks at the passenger-side mirror and sees them pulling something from behind a stack of boxes. To his surprise, confirming his paranoia, he identifies the tail end of a Russian-made anti-tank grenade launcher in the reflection.

Linked with the Oros system, X engages the vehicle's multi-directional drift as the side-panel door of the van slams open. The rogue assailant steadies himself against some grease-stained boxes, locks onto X, and pulls the trigger. At once, a spiraling dragon sparks from the darkness and, roaring into the light of day, emerges against the backdrop of Holy City's harbor.

X predicts the impact and adjusts the vehicle's orientation to minimize collateral damage. The rear end whips into another motorist, distracted by their smartphone's techno-social wormholes. The RPG cracks into one of the suspension cable's anchors, sending a shiver all the way up the side of one of those ivory towers.

"Who the fuck does that?" Agent Zeff questions the insult of having a rocket-propelled grenade fired at him so early in the morning. "X, be a dear and lend me some juice."

"Drift protocols disengaged." X surrenders control. "You are free to create space," the program's calm, calculated British voice informs him.

Agent Zeff grips the steering wheel, zigging right, then zagging left, chasing after the van.

Tactical Maneuvering

The mercenaries speed up, missing their opportunity to strike, and drift into the bike lane before quickly swerving back into traffic with juggernaut efficiency. *Fwam!* An old hooptie hits a VW bug, causing the traffic to thin.

Agent Zeff catches back up with them. "X, load explosive rounds for me," he says.

From the back of the crepe van, a manga-esque flying squirrel caricature waves onto the roadster's windshield. The metal roll-up door unlatches. Not wanting to give them another shot, Agent Zeff veers to the starboard side, then pins the roadster's left fender into the van.

The mercs almost hit the guardrail, but regain control. He maneuvers behind them to avoid being swiped, and the chase continues along the spans of the bridge. Thirty seconds later, those mixed eyes peer through a crusty glass slot within the squirrel's smile.

"This guy! Who the fuck does he think he's messing with?" Agent Zeff retrieves the Delta-9 from the car's holster as the tempo of his playlist rises with the incline.

Ma Deuce

Click. The van's metallic roll-up door slams open to reveal the gunman's malice. Next to the grease-stained boxes, Ma Deuce's mounted .50-cal barrel aims at the roadster.

The Oros system releases a shot of [Time Warp] into his bloodstream and slows the world around him.

Fap-fap-fap! The first bullets flash from the M2's belt-fed chamber. The rounds slam into the windshield, each one shaking the vehicle, inhibited by self-generative, nano-stitched polymers. One round slides off, taking the driver-side mirror with it, and bounces into the concrete railing.

Click-click-click. The overheated barrel sizzles.

"Amateur." Agent Zeff aims his weapon. "Should've paid for the upgrade."

The first shot explodes two-thirds of the gunman's face, leaving skull fragments on the swaying stacks of boxes. The second one rips into the driver's shoulder and bursts through his heart, spattering a rosy fountain across the smoke-stained windshield.

His dead weight leans on the gas and throttles them into the guardrail. It ricochets off, sending the driver to the floorboard, turning the steering wheel towards a car of spring breakers. Agent Zeff speeds to the passenger side of the runaway van and fires.

His third shot, intended to disable the tires, misses. And in a moment, too short to label, the crusty crepe van collides with X's superior design. He applies the brakes. However, unable to slow their momentum, both vehicles crush through a section of walkway—desperately in need of repair but lacking the budget—and plunge off the suspension bridge to the waters below.

Like the swooping branches of moss-hung willows and the grand oak archways of backwoods roads, the Xion roadster and the crepe van plummet into the wavy reflections of their falling approach. X sends an S.O.S. ping to the Agency.

"Life-support systems: online." The interior flickers as X attempts to back up its data into the Oros system's DNA-archives.

Due to an alignment of unfortunate events—discrepancies between the latest patch code and the Promethean Flame's bio-switch, with the Mind Palace running in the background—it fails. X downloads the trove of its data into the Mind Palace VPN partition instead.

9

The Fall

Over The Edge

A heavy dose of [Time Warp] slaps his system, framing the painted horizon with far-off cloudscapes—maybe a heaven or two. The primal weightlessness of falling catalyzes fleeting memory fragments from the cloning process. Tears form in his eyes.

Before him, the Donor's life flashes with fleeting depictions of infancy, the first time he fell, quarry diving with his cousins, and roasting marshmallows. A teardrop falls for the things that never were. Deep down, the sorrow interwoven through each nostalgic gum wrapper punches him in the gut. Scene by scene, the things he wished to forget fly to the forefront of his attention, and Zeff comes undone.

Goodnight, Son

He is a kid lying in the bed, staring out his window, watching the stars come out. Fireflies flicker amongst the evening haze as a symphony of katydids draws upon their strings, accompanied by an emerging choir of frogs from the pond in the valley. All is well in this tiny corner of the world.

"Goodnight, son." His father brandishes a strong, comforting smile.

"Daddy?" young-Zeff looks up at him.

"Yes?"

"Will you tell me the rest of the story, please?"

"Which one?"

"The one from Tuesday," he says and tosses a stuffed rocket ship.

"I'm sorry, my boy, I plumb forgot. Guess my head's been buried in work." He reluctantly massages the back of his neck, then sits down at the squeaky edge of the tiny bed. "Where'd we leave off?" He flips the same page back and forth, trying to find his place.

"The princess was about to rescue the pirate," young-Zeff cheers with youthful enthusiasm.

"I see." His father clears his throat. "As Ferdinand dangled upside down above the perilous pit of Mercurial vipers, reaching for Princess Isabella, the evil Duke Dwellington forced open the sliding bulkhead doors."

Young-Zeff's hazel eyes beam with excitement.

"While Ferdinand struggled to free himself, Princess Isabella let out a piercing whistle," he continues. "The dastardly Duke advanced towards them, summoning his guard bots to recapture the princess. Outside, bathed in the glow of alien moons, an enormous shadow befell the tower's rose window. Suddenly, howling winds shattered the stained glass, revealing a dark griffon with a violet crackle of energy about it."

"Storm Talon!" Young-Zeff squeals with enthusiasm and wiggles in his sheets.

His father pauses. "Now, I can't have you getting too excited before bed. You have a big day tomorrow." He tucks in the side of the *Space Force* comforter and smiles upon his child's eager face. "When Duke Dwellington reached for his ray gun, the roaring griffin pounced, knocking the scoundrel's guards into a nearby wall. Rawwr!" He flails imaginary claws at his son.

Young-Zeff pulls the blanket over his head to protect himself from the attack.

Without missing a beat, his father continues, "The terrified Duke Dwellington fell to his knees, covering his ears from the deafening winds. In a single leap, Storm Talon swooped to Isabella, and together they dropped the lid on the writhing pit of vipers. Finally free from the Duke's trap, Ferdinand summoned his celestial sword from the saddle—"

"Star Saber!"

"—Next, the trio turned towards the cowardly Duke. He pleaded for mercy, but the team pressed their advantage, hailing Space Force's *Timaeus* for prisoner transport. They circled the Duke while his troops surrendered. However, having just bought himself enough time, a sinister sneer sneaked across his deplorable face. Underneath his veiled parley, he activated a trap-door leading to the sewers below the ancient temple."

"Nooooo!" young-Zeff cries out, flailing his tiny arms in protest of the bad guy getting away again.

"Now, it's getting late," his father says, closing the book and placing it on the bedside table. "Time to get some rest. You've got to get up early tomorrow to go stay with Granny and Paw-Paw."

"But I'm already packed. Can you read a little longer?"

"Not tonight, bud." He surveys the room. "I see you've packed all your toys. Did you save room for any of your clothes or a toothbrush?"

In the corner, a satchel bursts at the seams with childhood delights: bootleg VHS tapes of classic cartoons, *Space Force I* and *II* DVD box sets, a few monster movies, *Space Force: Moon Base II* deck-building game, Adastrian galactic cruiser, several vehicles with plastic missiles, and a random assortment of heroes and villains, with blasters, cannons, and swords of light.

"I think I have enough," he says.

His father kisses him on the forehead, tucks him in tightly, and switches on the *Space Force* cosmos-projector night light. The room fills with heavenly imagery.

Quasars, containing massive black-w-holes, spin across his ceiling fan while pulsars—highly magnetized rotating neutron stars emitting beams of electromagnetic radiation—sweep over his writing desk. Active galactic nuclei fade into nebulae of interstellar dust clouds as gravitationally bound star systems, stellar remnants, gas, dust, and dark matter decorate his bedroom.

Unnoticed from the closet, a pair of ever-watchful burnt-yellow eyes, the color of sun-smeared pollen, plot with malicious certainty.

Here Zeff sits, plunging headfirst into Vision Shards of a vibrant mirage. On the water's surface, rippled reflections split the light of day as it clashes with a distant darkness. Strained with ache, his heart collapses into itself, having reflected on a warmth that, for him, never was.

Bunkhouse

Another flicker from the Donor's memory—of being a teenager, lying in his bunk, dreaming of the comfy coziness of home—shifts Zeff's attention from the suspended moment.

"Get up, maggots!"

The breath, cinnamon mixed with halitosis and notes of aftershave, hits him before the deafening roar of its instructions.

"UP-UP-UP! What do y'all think this is, the Scouts?! Think you're gonna get your merit badges in knot-tying? The only whittling you'll be doing is on yourselves. And I intend to break you down to the finest point. Down to the bone. Now get the hell out of my barracks!" Sgt. Cinnamon orders, followed by the shrieks of his favorite whistle.

The facet fractures forward in time.

"Down!" The stench blasts through the smell of fresh morning rain.

Dropping two inches above the ground, mud splatters into the cadet's right nostril.

"Up! You do it right, you do it light. Down! You do it wrong, you do it all day long! Up!" Sgt. Cinnamon hollers under the rolling thunder of the bottomless sky, well past sunrise.

The image splinters into fragmented mementos of the Academy. Evenings, where he could barely make it from the shower to the bed, blend into the stench of dawn and an iterative montage of his daily dance with personal limitations. He was Sisyphus, and the rock he pushed, day in and day out, was carved from the decay of gingivitis and cinnamon whiskey.

Data Backup

X finishes uploading its archives into the Mind Palace VPN partition and wipes its software from the vehicle, leaving it a listless husk of life-support systems. With Zeff's experience of time frozen, the revolving quilt of memories—some implanted, others illusory—continues to play out. Despite his lack of authenticity, this one was his.

See him as an adult, laid up in a hole-in-the-wall kind of place, locked within the sweat-soaked delights of the season. *Rewrooo-Rewrooooo-Rewroooo!* An ambulance screeches down the narrow, storm-drenched streets somewhere in Southeast Asia. The smell of sex, booze, and cigarettes hangs in the air.

"What time is it?" Special Agent Zeff squints to see the clock. "Shit! I'm late!" He stumbles and slides one leg into his pants. (Got to go commando if I'm gonna catch up to the mark. They must be halfway to the Leaky Tea warehouse by now.) He grunts, wedging his foot into his boot.

The alleyway hums with a damp fluorescence, merging with the scent of exotic meats and veggies being combined into culturally approved street dishes. Special Agent Zeff dashes past rickety food carts. Several vendors behind him, beneath a rain-washed straw hat, mustard-stained eyes observe him as he orders two meats-on-a-stick, slaps several crumpled bills onto the tiny counter, takes a bite, and disappears into crowds of commotion, pushing towards the extraction point.

Crash

By the time Zeff adjusts to the free fall, it is already over. He stares into the obliterating realization of his own mortality and braces for impact. Suspended in that moment, a hanged-man's gesture reaches out into the reflection. Overhead, a gull's feather floats at near-freefall speed.

Clash! The car's frunk intersects with the water. The impact tosses his head against the seat, striking the seatbelt harness. Compelled by the pull of the Atlantic, the vehicle slips under the surface of Holy City's harbor.

The roadster drifts downward into a sandbar—an unintended consequence of disrupting the natural sand flow by deepening the harbor—releasing a microcosm of life and decomposing light throughout a froth of three hundred twenty-two bubbles. Upside-down, Zeff hangs motionless, suspended in a foam sarcophagus of technological engineering. Saltwater seeps between sinuous fissures.

Several seams creak across the self-repairing windshield, fraying from the car's weight. A primordial sludge of oozings and whirlings squishes into the cabin. Soon, the tide of helplessness floats him deeper into the dwindling moment.

[E-13: System Failure_reinstall firewall.]

A warm sensation trickles down his forehead, pooling beneath him. (Move... Move your arm... Do it! Come on, motherfucker, move your goddamn body! Come on!!!) he howls deep within the silence of himself. (Shit! I can feel myself becoming lighter. This is it. I'm dying.)

Zeff's senses reach the apex of their potential, blurring into a cascade of synesthetic impressions, while the blood dripping from his head expresses itself with savory pastel hues. Around him, the wetness becomes a sound, rising higher and higher in the tropes of his cerebellum. Shrouded in impact foam, saltwater fills the cabin.

His adrenaline spikes, and he shakes off the slurred lucidity. "Move, motherfucker—MOVE!!!"

His body remains motionless amidst the protective foam and rising water. As the dash dims into abysmal isolation, he holds his breath and, by sheer will, breaks free from his bindings. But it's too late.

10

Submerged

Shatter

Through the crystalline sutures of his pluffy womb, four hundred thirty-two cracking seams simultaneously collapse. *Chrysalis.* The sound of a glass sphere shattering mutes from the unexpected sonoluminescent alchemy of light erupting from a cascade of underwater bubbles. All at once, a swirling cosmic blender consumes him, fizzling a tropical smoothie from his dissolving existence.

His shape soon spreads into infinite proportions and spirals towards greater degrees of uncertainty. At wit's end, iridescent jewels streak past, ribboning a rainbow epidemic in their wake. As their shimmering chemtrails swoosh into ornate latticeworks, he regains his form and continues to fall.

Ahead, a picture-pattern puzzle door hallmarks the limits of perception.

"I need to level out." (Remember your training—tighten your core and angle arms at ninety degrees. Breathe in. One, two, three, exhale.)

Closer and closer, the structure absorbs the totality of his bandwidth.

"I'm not slowing down!"

As he collides with the planet-sized, miasmic patchwork of memories, dreams, and imaginings, the door opens a smidge, and he passes through the needle's eye, crossing the threshold.

On the other side, time and space collapse into themselves and encase the irrelevant limelight of descriptive intelligence. Toroidal patterns twist around him, etching holonomic illusions about his brow's interior. Soon to follow, pastel vectors caress his cognitive framework and plaster neon streaks across the tension strings of his mental architecture. The entire cacophony cascades into a dizzying accord. Then, a crashing silence.

Float On

Adrift in the abyss, untethered neurons rhizomatically entangle, aligning synesthetic concepts with ancient embedded alchemical constructs. The floodlight of his perception snaps into focus and collapses the last tidings of the void. He suddenly plops through the membrane of an underground chamber with the pluffiness of a marshmallow puff-pistol.

(I'm still falling? This can't be real? Where the hell am I? Am I dead? Is this hell? No... something else.)

The sprawling pearlescent cavern echoes with the chime of him breaching its atmosphere. Technorganic archways soar above the chamber's shell-like design. Along every other surface, self-similar iterating patterns encircle the grotto's interconnected pools.

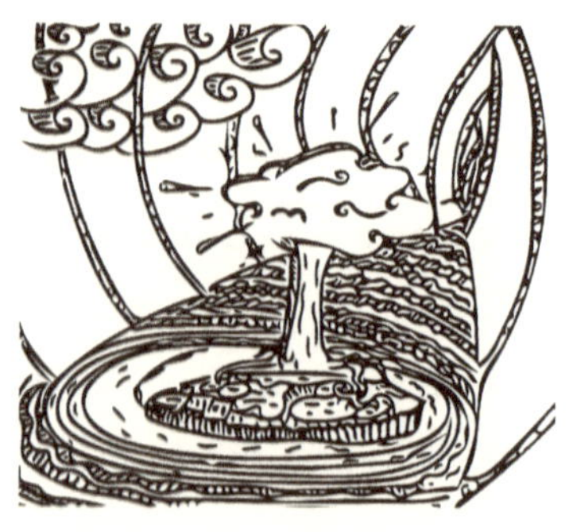

Smack-dab in the middle, an immense tree stoically stands, two-thirds as tall as the cavern's vaulted ceiling. At the base of the clouds, positioned amongst colossal branches, dwarfed by the glowing arbor, a shadow stirs from its rest.

Below, radiant pools ripple with glimmering hues of indigo and fluorescent fire. Turquoise ribbons bind them with obtuse retention into mandalas of slight ebbing. Along their corrugated pathways, forests of stalagmites and flowstones pulse with equilibrium, running as far as the eye can see.

Zeff's visual cortex gorges on the surroundings, mapping the structures of this fantastic environment. The fleeting experience dulls his proprioception as he spirals. Further, faster, and farther, his mind manifests itself into the depths of a psychedelic plunge, projecting surreal patterns on the cavern's fringes, where ambiguous ciphers spectate from jagged outcroppings.

The Tree Within

Before him, light and life merge into a single symbiotic entity. The gilded tree rises with the divine animating principle of the manifesting universe. Around its roots, small luminous fungi flourish near flowing pools, teeming with phosphorescent lifeforms. And throughout its low-bearing bows, curious sparkles disappear into thatches of darkness.

Tiny flickering lights, zooming hither and thither, play spritely games of hide-and-seek. Their brilliance nestles behind petal-patterned limbs, stretching towards the future. Metallic and silicon leaves break from branches of Mandelbrot consistencies and absorb the cavern's light with the fractal foliage. Its blossoming crown, a bouquet of neon, mirrors the alternating currents flowing along its trunk, down its roots, into the teeming waters of the rapidly approaching pools.

He peers past the gleaming moss and into the bottomless void, welcoming him to the threshold of the mystery. *Splash!* He blinks beyond the veil.

11

Through The Threshold

Losing Grip On Reality

He sails beyond the liminal, onto lamplit fields of bought courtrooms, postponing their upholdance of the law to another date and time. Behind frosted glass doors, slithering hands exchange loyalty coins into obtuse piles of greed. They soon become less distinct, turning into cardboard cutouts of commerce, consumption, and designer fear. All throughout this nightmarish land, a crippling neurosis weaves amongst the wailing songs of the flattened Earth.

Zeff's perspective slides across the unfolding map. In his wake, a cascade of monumental file cabinets dips into an avenue of overstacked apartments. They teeter and slosh slices of life, clinging desperately to hastily drawn conclusions, over the fire escape atop the cartography of the world.

As he winds along mezzanines bordered by escalators and infernal mall cops, crowds parade past, wearing amiable masks of cleverly devised delusions. They gather in front of an advertisement, waiting to purchase the latest model, hoping to fill the void of obscurity, for now. The mewing masses murmur closer, marching through toil and struggle, buying things they don't need, turning the Earth into rubble.

He cruises past the line into the back of the department store, where conveyor belts divide shoppers with optimized metrics. Up one and down another, into the next station, the masses are cut, cured, used, abused, poisoned, and educated into the perfect stand-in soldiers of class warfare. Round after luminous round, the casualties of poverty fill mounds of body bags with sugary snacks, philosophical perversions, and the twisted conceptions of success, wealth, kindness, consideration, truth, honor, and integrity—of what matters most.

Nuclear Family

His mind's eye bypasses the factory walls, landing on a family's crowded dinner table. Piled high on a nearby sunlit windowsill, meats dry in the dust of the day. During the feast, yearning mouths wholeheartedly ingest the fruits of ill-begotten labors until their faces blur into abstract concepts, producing the lonely truth hidden behind each mask.

The walls fall away to reveal endless cul-de-sacs stretching all around. Under every dinner table, a conveyor belt transports entire neighborhoods towards the slaughterhouse. Ahead of him, a cornucopia of indistinguishable figures roves over the blood-spattered kill floor. Once sufficiently processed and deboned, passing lobbied inspections, they line the feed troughs with the pink-slime of existence.

Zeff attempts to steer the flight of this madness away from the grotesque gluttony, but to no effect. A bell rings for the Class Clowns. Moments later, terrifying chimeras—empty, vicious, vomiting; cowards and hypocrites of liberation, with their hands in each other's pockets—storm onto the scene. They fall in line and partake in the mewing sacrifice of the masses. Truly, a display that would make Cthulhu blush. Finished and flush with the itis, they return to their nests, resting high above a scaffolding of broken bones and polished trophies.

Lost Childe-Within

Elsewhere, deep inside the genetic memory of himself, in a darkened broom closet, the Donor cowers to the might of malicious machine men. Shards of deep-seated angst unearth and surround him, shredding the narrow chamber—revealing the child Zeff knew all too well, but never was.

Now manifest, the Donor slips from his body like a molting cicada from its cuticle. Zeff reaches but misses, only to hasten his experience. Before the boy hits the Fields of Ruin, a watchful pair of burnt-yellow eyes appears. And with a teleporting [Claw Swipe], it snatches the Donor and disappears into the darkness.

Looming silhouettes morph into ivory towers of existential angst. The twins converge into a mirrored hallway of autocrats and dictators, waving their nuclear armaments in each other's face, competing to see who has the bigger arsenal, who gives the least amount of fucks, who's bold enough to pop those shiny red buttons—and reduce everything to the cosmic ash of no-thing-ness. The end of it all, just two inches away, sitting on richly embroidered oak desks, worlds apart.

To the testament of their character, not even those witless fools, with their piggy-fingers poised over plastic buttons, want annihilation. At the very least, it is bad for business. Sweat and determination mix as they hold the keys of creation and destruction two inches from their greasy fingertips—a Schrödinger of a conundrum: 'To be, or not to be.'

"Go ahead! Do it, you goddamn cowards! None of it matters anyway."

A malfunctioning mechanism activates and engulfs the bandwidth of his experience.

The desolation knocks him beyond the pale. He pivots towards the smoldering Earth and sees an overview of its maps, its dialogues, hopes and dreams, meta-tangible theories, cultures, destinies, and fates. He witnesses the entire scene, but keeps no sake, or memory of ever having experienced such a thing.

Enter The Void

A pixelated rainbow unicorn suddenly soars through a black-w-hole. Sharp and crisp, the entirety of his perspective comes back online. He follows the trailing pixels until they coalesce into a film reel. The chase unravels down a spiral staircase, towards an oddly adorned hallway, into the foyer, and out Momma's front door, zooming upward to the stars.

His childhood home becomes a dot. Then, moving out, the Earth becomes a blue marble. Faster, the solar system shrinks to a point. Coming into focus, the galaxy renders itself as a resplendent dot in a matrix of other dots. From his speed, the cosmos dances like a swallowtail twirling across the bedrock of spacetime.

He fades into the background as galactic clusters spin into the deep distance, leaving dark matter in their wake. Still farther, in the blackness of Shunyata, suspended between life and death, an eerie silence weaves amongst the ley lines of potential and possibility as the void stretches around him. In this stillness, floating in the cold, dark, lifeless vacuum, swaddled in the absoluteness of being, he plunges inward, into a deeper state, onto a different stage.

A spotlight clicks on, illuminating his form, while a choir rises in hymn and harmony. A bolt of energy arcs from his arm, and after a moment, his biocentric systems come online. Like snow melting on a spring day—little by little, then all at once—warmth and wetness return. Tidal sensations tingle throughout his veins and ripple along his arteries, spreading like rivers into the ocean.

Recovery

The Clean-up Crew locks down the bridge before first responders arrive at the barricades. Beneath the ebbing harbor, a recovery drone maneuvers towards the wreckage of the Xion roadster. It reaches the vehicle and probes the empty husk with an array of roving searchlights.

Topside, on the bridge of an onyx Agency stealth ship, LED monitors and blinking lights illuminate the operators attaching tow cables.

"Sir, there's no sign of Special Agent Zeff." He shows the screen to his superior.

"Fuck." Agent Xero punches the bulkhead in frustration, leaving a dent. "Patch me through to the Director. This changes nothing... Continue with the lighthouse preparations."

"Yes, sir!" His subordinates scramble to their workstations.

Frothy bubbles soon carry themselves to the top as the drone surfaces and docks at the boat's rear. Agent Xero steps onto the deck with a tight-fisted view of the horizon. He lights a cigar while watching the nearby barge hoist X's carcass from the depths. "How long until they wrap this up?" he asks.

"Twenty minutes, sir."

"Make sure they understand we need a full build on this one."

"What's the theme: tanker explosion, gas leak, container ship?"

"Be creative—we need to stack on some extra hours of media coverage... and make sure local politicians respond in force. We've got to flap both wings for this fuck-up to fly under the radar."

Part II
Mystic Woods & The Loggerheads

12

Wash In

Wake

The next morning, dawn's early light breaks onto a small barrier archipelago south of Coffin Island. Caught within a shallow saltwater reservoir, tiny fish swim above a colony of pastel Coquinas, unearthing from their homes beneath the sand. Granule by microcosmic granule, filter feeders wake with the tidal alarm clock and ride the swash of the morning tide. Shuffling down the shoreline, the abundance of their legacy—living and dying in this way—becomes the foundation for all those who stalk along the water's edge.

Squadrons of semipalmated sandpipers pitter-patter across the wet sand in search of small mollusks. The rest of the bind hunt while the surf curls back the first few pages to unveil a colony of sustenance. The digits of their tiny footprints trail through the sliding waves, like stamps from the desk of Poseidon—a team of architects who developed this space long before the first industrial tycoons swindled these sacred shores for themselves.

Onshore gusts send flurries of sediment into rows of wind-wisped dunes—releasing a sun-dried palm frond that tumbles down the beach and slaps against the side of the once-Special Agent's head. Muck-crusted eyelids peel open to find tiny hermit crabs squatting on his arm, demanding their rights. A glitch flutters across his TacOHUD, hiding the icons on his user interface. Sometimes life will surprise you, giving you just what you need, when you least expect it. And sometimes life lands you ass-up in a tide pool.

"Ugh—where am I?" he murmurs as the waves wash over his salt-pruned body. (Shit, I can't remember a fucking thing. This is a bit of a mess.)

The tide rocks and rolls him back into the lullaby of a deep sleep, ceasing the chatter of his broken psyche. In the realm of dreams, an endless mosaic of memories and isomorphic fragments takes shape. No longer privy to their hues, blind to the truth, he plunges past the Labyrinth of Amnesia, finally settling on a Vision Shard from the Donor's past.

Return To Innocence

He is a child, sitting on an area rug with the scent of lemon furniture polish on the smooth wooden surfaces of the den's furniture. *Space Force II* action figures pose for battle. He looks up from playing, entranced by a toy commercial on the television.

His father sits in an oversized thinking chair behind him, reading Tom Robbins's *Fierce Invalids Home From Hot Climates*. He glances over his glasses at the latest advertisement for the holiday season. A flush of nostalgia fills his cheeks as he smiles at the joy and wonder held on his son's face.

Humming along with the show's theme song, the boy raises his hand above his head, and a robotic action figure soars into adventure. On screen, the newest release transforms from a bird into a plane, into a killer robot that combines with other robots to fight an all-out war against Adastria and their allies—a war fought across the universe, through time and space. He marvels at the toy's intricate detail, unfurling a fountain of dopamine.

"Daddy, why do the villains have the best weapons and vehicles?" he asks.

Before his father can offer him a suitable response, he blurts, "Pew-Pew, Pew-Pew!" and zooms to the other side of the house, venturing into the vivid cosmos of his imagination.

Wastelands Of Cognition

Elsewhile, amidst semiconductors and advanced algorithms, the shore's soothing echo rinses beyond the Mind Palace VPN partition onto the Wastelands of Cognition. Once a sanctuary for Zeff's memories—distinct from the Donor's and shielded from the Agency's surveillance—is now his prison. Under the crackling static of the gray-lit sky, curled in a shadow from an impossible arrangement of rocks, he shivers with the cognitive disconnect of his undoing.

"Where the hell am I?" Zeff asks.

The words echo throughout the landscape.

"Am I dreaming? Is this—this can't be the Mind Palace? Why am I here?" He attempts to log out, only to strain his bandwidth, levying him with a pulse behind his eyes. Looking down, he notices the dust powdering his linen suit.

Deep beneath the Nether Regions of Thought, the Fog of Despair flows from its black cauldron and forebodingly coats an upturned layer cake of strewn sediment, spreading over the ground. Small grotesque creatures scurry out of its way as the cackling Imp-oster meanders closer to the rockery. Inside the gloom, those burnt-yellow eyes peer out at him. The creature's toothy grin wrinkles an oversized smile into the upturned arches of crusty red lips. It rests its claw on the

Donor's shoulder. The stench of corruption has finally taken the blush from his cheeks, now appearing with a blurred face and hollow eyes.

Unaware of being watched, Zeff scans the vast expanse of broken desert. "How'd I end up here? Something's different. I can feel the ground... If this is the Mind Palace, then where's my body? Was I captured? Am I dead?" he asks, echoing into the sediment-blown surroundings.

A purple bolt of lightning cracks onto the timeless gray sky, reminding him of something lost. "The Kid—was that the Donor? What took him? I've got to rescue him," he mutters, confidence clashing with confusion, as he climbs atop some rocks to scout above the lithospheric fragments, only to discover sprawling devastation.

From the corner of his eye, a distant rainbow races across the Wastelands and swiftly disappears into the shadow of a decaying city perched atop the stump where the last Elder Tree once stood. At its center, the Control Tower crumbles with each revolution. Above it, the gray sky darkens with violet crackles of lightning.

"Curiouser and curiouser," Zeff mutters as he processes his newfound reality. "I've never left the Control Tower, but I didn't think the Mind Palace was this massive... If I can make it through there, I might find an exit."

A pang of responsibility tugs at him, shifting his thoughts to the Donor. "I can't leave him here. If this is real—if he's really here—then that thing has him." His determination crystallizes, and he turns to rescue a part of himself he long since despised.

To his surprise, roving fringes of fog, threading past the cavities of displaced boulders and broken columns, stall his resolve. The atmosphere cools as the mist encroaches on his position. Zeff retreats from the uncomfortable presence into the dismal wilderness, towards the crumpled megapolis at the center of it all.

A few kilometers away, his resolve returns, and he spins around. The Imp-oster's burnt-yellow eyes press upon the edge of the gloom, prickling trepidation down Zeff's spine.

(Am I being hunted?) He summons the courage and faces the veiled monster. "You want some of me? Do you know who the fuck I am?"

The Fog of Despair's swirling tendrils float closer, and with it, those unblinking eyes, like dried mustard on a splintered bench. The Imp-oster's gaze remains unchanged. Zeff foolishly steps forward, only to feel his stalwart courage shrink as the Fog envelops the ground in front of him.

Another bolt of lightning cracks along the timeless gray sky. His primal intuition kicks into gear, and he sprints in the opposite direction. Meter after meter, the terrain shifts as he crosses into an intersectional maze of rubble and wreckage. Zeff turns left, then right, zigzagging to confuse his pursuer.

Up ahead, the pathway narrows to a tight squeeze. As he pushes forward, digital debris further stains his linen jacket. After another left, ducking under a jagged crag, he accidentally startles a wayward Worry Wraith from its new home amongst the wreckage.

"Who am I? Who are you?" it shrieks into the mist, fleeing towards the fractured Mesas of Memory.

The moment it reaches the Fog, the ghoulish Imp-oster teleports, plucking the specter like an apple from the tree of knowledge. Ripping the critter in half with a brutal savagery, it shares the morsel with the Donor. The boy bites into the flailing wraith. His face unblurs for a moment, then flashes back after hungrily taking a second chomp.

Zeff continues to follow the path of least resistance. Several turns and hasty backtracks later, he pops out on the other side of the upturned landscape. There, he finds a far-reaching field of file cabinets, tossed in the wake of destruction. He races to the first row and slips behind a toppled heap. With enough distance between him and the Fog, he slams open mental drawers in a feverish search for a tool, a weapon, an answer, or maybe a way out of this mess. The Fog of Despair swiftly reaches the stacks, compelling him to seek answers elsewhere within the Wastelands of Cognition.

13

New Beginning

First Sight

While seagulls squawk into the whipping winds, the beach shags and shuffles past his unconscious form. A thin land bridge extends from an outstretched arm, separating a vivid reflection of the afternoon sky. *Tik-tik-tik-tik-tik.* Tiny crustaceans inch closer to his hand.

Short-circuiting proprioceptors alert him to their scuttle, and sand-crusted eyelids spring open. Then, with a twitch and a twist, the sediment flakes from the chrysalis caked around him.

"Ugh—how long have I been lying here? Where am I?" (I'm not supposed to be here. Where am I supposed to be?)

The swirling tide and the wrinkled wetness of his socks are the only answers. He raises his head to find the weight of kelp upon his back. Covered in an assortment of seagrass, he stares at his reflection.

"Is that me?" he asks, squinting through streams of saltwater.

Morbid candy crumbs bedazzle the perplexed gaze of the seaweed-wrapped figure. Beneath the surface, a herd of hermit crabs scurries towards the lip of the pool—bison roving in the rift.

Stand Tall

Shimmering constellations of shattered mollusks and crustacean corpses settle under a glossy membrane of saltwater reflecting the last fluffs of the day. He struggles to his knees amidst the Southern tide, but a wave crashes over his shoulders, flailing him back to the ground.

Another set breaks on the beach, carving out more tide-pool real estate. He crawls forward, dragging his body along the soft, wet sand. In time, he sluggishly makes his way to the center of nature's vast jacuzzi, flips to his back, and floats.

Tiny fish swim in and out of the tangled openings in his cocoon. Below him, pastel hermit crabs sift the sediment, searching for nourishment and the potential upgrade from their latest shell-model. He wiggles his toes within ocean-soaked socks until regaining enough coordination to cross to the other side.

With a cocktail of exhaustion and panic, the novelty of his experience wanes, replaced by an overwhelming sense of loss left in the void of his identity. His heartbeat elevates as the uncertainty of the unknown sends shivers down his spine. He dismisses it and dog-paddles to the pool's edge.

His hands sink into the beach, but the sidewalls collapse from his weight, submerging him in a school of tiny minnows. They scatter to and fro, darting away from the shadow. Disheartened and encumbered, floating in a victimless tug-and-tow with the Atlantic, he submits.

The once-Special Agent inhales, only to draw a gulp of saltwater into his lungs. He chokes on the brine, spins over, coughs up a little more, then claws his way through the muck onto dry sand. By the time he catches his breath and shuffles to his knees, the blue hour of day blankets the shore's foaming fizzle.

He crawls out of the berm, towards the island's interior. After several schlepping minutes, he discovers a trail bobbing hither and thither past a cul-de-sac of yellow dunes and climax communities. A little farther, he spies a border of sabal palmetto trees, sheltering a hidden world beyond their rustling fronds.

First Steps

After a short distance on his hands and knees, fatigue from the tangled seagrass overwhelms him, and he collapses atop a broken shell that digs into his belly.

(Get up, Maggot!) the memory of Sgt. Cinnamon commands him. (I thought I trained you better than this.) The echo continues to berate him. (I've seen a better effort from my 95-year-old grandma! You're embarrassing the Academy's legacy. Now, get the fuck up!)

(Academy?) He rolls off the beach fossil and suppresses the pain.

Wrestling with gravity, he gets to one knee. However, as he stands, an electrical prickle shoots into the tips of his socks. He wobbles to maintain his balance, but drops back to the shore.

The sensation soon subsides to numbness, and he pivots tactics in search of something to help him stand. Close by, a barnacled hardwood, washed in from a nearby Boneyard, sticks halfway out of a dune. He crawls through the sand, dragging a trail of seaweed, and seizes hold of its trunk.

He pulls his entangled form vertically and finds some balance. In an eternal minute or two, perched against the tree, fresh blood pumps into his trembling legs. Little by little, his strength returns. A triumphant teardrop wells in the corner of his right eye, but he instinctively draws it back, saving it for a rainy day.

After supporting his own weight, the once-Special Agent cautiously steps forward, then hobbles into a slow-limp. A few painful paces later, muscle memory kicks in—like riding a bike. One foot in front of the other, his journey continues with baby steps and deep breaths.

A few paces later, the outlines of palmettos come into view. He pauses, with a tremor of intense tightness chiming along the left side of his neck, and drops back to his knees. The malfunctioning Oros System interprets the imbalance and pops a beetle-squirt of some randomly combined neurochemical cocktail into his bloodstream. At once, the spotlight of his perception penetrates the visible layers of the shore.

The TacOHUD, now functioning like an electron microscope, reveals the beige sediment between his fingers to be composed of countless combinations of tiny shells and flecks of things. Amidst the microcosm, he notices the small shells have tiny holes in them, and inside these holes are grains, with tiny shells and infinitely smaller holes. And within those inescapable surfaces, herds of tardigrades roam like microcosmic buffalo. The abruptness churns with the wash of saltwater in his belly, expelling the remnants of a meal he could no longer remember having enjoyed.

14

Of Vitals & Vittles

Landlubbering

Under the rising moon's resplendent smile, evening dawns within a cast net of stars. While the first twangs of twilight mix with katydid octaves, a campfire churns in the salty air. His senses soon normalize and pick up on the primal distinction of a nearby fire. Again, finding the resolve to stand, he wobbles upright and shuffles through the sand, towards the forest.

One foot after the other, mud-caked socks kick up rooster tails of debris into sea oat colonies and clusters of fragrant jessamine. He stumbles over a running lace of beach morning glories and startles tiny eye-stalks back into burrowed shadows. Several meters ahead, the crescent moon peeks onto his path. Held in its flickering sway, the indigo evening waxes into a sparsely clouded night. Closer, a hint of something familiar stirs him farther.

Another electrical pulse flails down his shoulder into his hand. He tries to shake it off, but the cool numbness spreads into his fingertips. He quickly loses his stride and leans against a juvenile live oak. "Again? What's wrong with me?" he asks, holding back tears of frustration.

Its glitch unsticks, and, in a matter of moments, the strain on his body lessens. All the while, specialized nanites detect multiple audio signals deeper in the maritime forest, prompting back-end algorithms into action. The Oros system isolates the nearby rattle of a drum set. Then, the saxophone's billow, followed by a virtuoso's violin, weaves through the branches. Another holds the line with the strum of an agile melody in accord with the tinctured sonatas carried along the breeze.

Still weak in the knees and coated in kelp, twigs, brambles, briars, sand, and leaf matter, he staggers into a thicket of waist-high brush and saw palmettos. Closer to the melody, thirty lumbering meters in, the campfire's smell turns into beams of light—a moth to the flame could be no more content.

Just past a felled tree, he sniffs the air. A familiar scent, drifting on silken tendrils, infiltrates the recesses of his fractured cognition. "Yum." He takes another whiff. (What is this? I know this; it's amazing. What are those sweet florals?) A slight smile breaks as a notion unfurls from his past.

However, the music breaks before he conjures any recollection.

Specialized nanites isolate different vocal patterns. (People,) he intuits, inching one seaweed-soaked step closer to the laughter held round the campfire.

Through The Forest Darkly

Meanwhile, buried beneath the Nether Regions of Thought, the Imp-oster cackles from its throne room, then asks, "Will this be enough? I can always procure us some more." The fiend flashes a jagged grin.

Beside it, the Donor sits at a makeshift table, swinging his legs as he assembles a disturbing homunculus from pieces torn off two Sorting Dregs, a Worry Wraith, and some machinery to make it look cool. "This will do for now. What other toys are there to play with?" His blurred face focuses to reveal a visage of joy—merely a glitch. Turning back to his gifts, the Childe-within cloaks the Donor once more, blurring his face back to a hollow stare.

The Imp-oster clicks a button on the Bone Throne's armrest—recently modified from the carapace of a trusted ally—and whispers from its prison into a recognizable voice.

(Wait,) the Imp's angst bounces between the seaweed-wrapped figure's ears. (There could be something dangerous... They could kill you.)

He suppresses the noise and forges through a thatch of saw palmettos. A barely visible path leads him closer to the nearby revelry. But with one misplaced step, a sandspur jabs into his foot.

"Ou—" he attempts to cry out, but suffocates the notion.

(They could kill you—kill you—kill you,) the Imp echoes into the present.

The pain occupies his bandwidth, pulling him into his body, and quiets the disillusionment. He sits down, careful not to press the seedlings any further into his foot, and removes the burs from his flesh, one spiky caltrop at a time. The last one gets stuck in his thumb. He winces, then notices an old scar, oblivious of its origins.

(They could kill you—kill you—kill you.)

He holds back the angst and gets to his feet. Farther, the once-Special Agent cautiously pushes beyond patches of crunchy underbrush. Wet, confused, a bit off balance, and led by his baser instincts, he lumbers towards the campfire's glow, seeking a distant flicker in an eclipsed world—a particle of hope, a spark of rebirth, a clue to the mystery where one can gaze upon its surface and be engulfed by what they find.

Mystic Woods & The Loggerheads

Coming closer to the source of the sound, he peers past windblown live oaks, a silent stalker amidst the darkened sky. A few meters ahead, he discerns the individual speakers around the campfire.

"Mystic Woods, did you see Chet's latest album cover?" A bald man adjusts his saxophone's strap.

"You don't have to call me that, Zach."

"Nah, it fits you." Chet, a broad-shouldered man with a tight hairline and an equally trimmed beard, straightens his posture and shows the sketch from a rolled-up notebook.

Mystic Woods, dressed in a white rhinestone coat and matching top hat, leans in. "Far out," he says with a thick Southern drawl. "What do you think, Nick?"

"I love it. The space background totally fits the album name, *Sphyramid*," Nicholas, a lanky fellow holding a violin, compliments Chet's artistry.

"How'd you come up with the design?" asks Patrício, a long-haired man in an unbuttoned shirt patterned with flamingos, picking up his bass guitar.

"Well, the trick is to hit them in the face with a cream pie, then—"

"Hey-yo!" teases Zach.

"You're a fool." Mystic Woods smiles. "To be honest, I think it's a perfect fit for our new album." He removes the top hat and wipes his brow. Brown shoulder-length hair tumbles in front of his face, becoming hung in his goatee.

"It's our only album," quips Josepé, a smaller man wearing a wide straw beach hat—its brim like the rings of Saturn—as he tunes the keys of his twelve-string guitar.

"Hey! Don't be glum... Genius takes time, and that's why we're out here. Don't you boys want to get it right? I have a vision." Mystic Woods slaps his right hand against a rhinestone-bedazzled mandala over his heart.

"Here he goes again." Zach winks at his bandmates.

"Gentlemen, can we get back to playing?" Nicholas whines, "My fingers are going stiff."

"This is the stuff people pay to experience," Zach says, rubbing imaginary currency between his fingers.

"We'll be famous!," cheers Patrício.

Mystic Woods steps towards center stage, saying, "Let's not forget, 'Art provides what life does not.'"

"I know you didn't come up with that yourself." Chet waves his drumstick. "Who'd you steal it from? Aristotle?"

"Tom Robbins." He bows. "What can I say? I'm a collector of wisdom and wit."

"And as mad as a hatter," Josepé says.

"That's not yours either," Zach scrutinizes.

Mystic Woods tips his rhinestone-bedazzled top hat. "Good artists steal. Great artists inspire."

"Isn't that Picasso?" Zach asks.

Chet answers, "I think Banksy did something similar."

"Actually," adds Patrício, "T. S. Eliot might've said it first."

Mystic Woods brandishes a rascal's grin. "Let's just say I took this one back, for the poets!"

"Fellas, can we get back to playing?" Nicholas presses, lightly drawing his bow along the strings.

Thanks to a solar-powered generator, everyone settles into position. Stage left, Patrício finds a funky bass-line and smiles at Josepé. An impeccable cadence rolls from Chet's drum set as the band tinkers into a self-amplified groove. Zach flirts across brass keys, padding accents into the melody, while Nicholas finds his place, balancing a volley of scales. After three minutes of bobbing his head within their pocket of merriment, Mystic Woods secures his bedazzled microphone into its stand. The pitch of his twang soon morphs into a hymnal as he leaps into the fray.

So attuned to their instruments, they catch a current of inspiration, knocking on the sky and spinning golden filaments from the infinite juxtaposition of their styles and techniques. Steeped in the ecstasis of sacred geometric peda-gogy and harmonic resonance, they follow the threads, binding themselves to a temporal Neverland of childlike wonder. With each passing loop—alive with the undercurrents of an enveloping circle of oratory light—they step into the deep-absorption of the Jam and abstract from the ethos of creation into the mythos of imagination. So removed from the plane of thought, they perch upon the threshold of something new, hunting invisible tracks and traces of melodic contention—their contribution to the ballad of existence.

It Came From The Maritime Forest

Still wrapped in a gala of seagrass, he staggers closer to the campfire's revelry. Several small branches break underfoot as he bumps against laurel cherries and the low-bearing branches of sweetgum trees.

"Why'd you stop?" Mystic Woods asks. "We were—"

"Shhhhhh." Zach whispers, "Did y'all hear that?"

"I didn't hear anything," Patrício says.

"Shhhhhh!" Zach pleads, more frightened than before.

Mystic Woods checks his watch. "All of you. It's just your imagination. Let's get back to it. We're burning our small window of opportunity. Who knows how long the intoxication of inspiration will stay with us? We're on the verge of something worthy of greatness. Can't you feel it?"

"Watch out, will ya!" Chet warns him. "You're sloshing your drink on my gear."

"Oops... I apologize, my dear fellow. Here, let me clean this off." Mystic Woods swoops in to wipe down the drum kit.

Another palm frond crunches from within the forest.

"Hush!" Zach raises a finger to his lips. "I'm serious. There's something out there."

Josepé swigs back a nip of something strong. "Don't be a scaredy-cat."

"It could be one of those fanged deer," Mystic Woods posits.

"Zach must've gotten into the jug juice earlier," Chet says, looking at the supply tent, then back to his bandmate.

Several bushes away, more branches snap as the seaweed-wrapped homunculus makes his way towards the flickering fire.

"Seriously... there's something out there," Zach whines.

"No worries. It's probably raccoons," Chet replies.

"Maybe it's a gator?" Patrício playfully snarls.

"Nonsense," Nicholas says. "We're surrounded by saltwater."

Josepé belches. "Maybe it's a giant crocodile with a clock in its belly."

From the maritime forest, a looming shadow appears in the corner of Zach's peripheral. He turns to see the seaweed-wrapped shadow stumble from a nearby sparkleberry bush and fall face-first into their campsite. The musicians squeal in terror.

Delirious with fatigue, he lies there. And Josepé, seeing no movement, pokes at the pile of slop with a stick.

"Be careful; it could be dangerous," Zach warns.

"Really, Zach? It's not even moving," Josepé says, tapping it.

Shockingly, a twitch and a murmur emanate from the slimy lump on the ground. They jump back, then laugh at the lack of manliness displayed by one another.

Despite their drunkenness, they eventually realize the quaking mess on the floor is human.

"Quick, get him a blanket!" Nicholas takes charge. "He's soaking wet and covered in every sort of bristle and briar on the island. Help me untangle him."

"Here, I have some water," Mystic Woods says.

Zach tiptoes over and checks for himself. "See? I told y'all there was something out there," he postures to his bandmates. "Luckily, nothing to worry about."

"Yeah, right... You were screamin' like a banshee!" Patrício jabs at him.

"Never mind that, fellas, let's get him some of those leftovers from dinner," Chet says. "Oh, and some of this whiskey, too. It'll warm him up from the inside out."

Greetings

He opens his eyes to find all six rascals standing around him.

"Hey, my man, are you alright?" Patrício stares at him with concern.

"Where'd you come from?" Josepé leans on a stick.

"Are you injured?" Nicholas checks his head and removes the seaweed.

Zach squats down, attempting to be of use. "What happened to you?"

The motley crew rattles off several more questions, but they go unheard.

Soon everything buzzes, followed by an electrical pulse that spins to a halting-jeer. Nicholas notices the pain on his face and runs to grab the medical kit from his tent.

"Hey, Stranger, drink this." Mystic Woods sets down a cold water bottle.

He sits up and triggers another microdose from the Oros system. At once, the sweat droplets condensing along the surface of the single-use plastic reflect the campfire's burning glow juxtaposed with the moon's Cheshire grin. He ravenously finishes two bottles, gulping the first one and crushing the second one. Unlike Tantalus, released from his eternal punishment, he catches his breath in the wake of hydration.

Nicholas brings back his med kit and sets to cutting away the remaining weave of kelp cocooned around his body. Once removed, they wrap the Stranger in an oversized beach towel and sit him close to the fire. By the time Chet returns with a warm plate of vittles—campfire packs of teriyaki vegetables with garlic chicken and cornbread.

"It's Granddaddy's cornbread recipe. Been in the family for generations," Chet explains with a dash of pride.

The Stranger accepts the plate and feasts on the bounty offered by his new acquaintances. Each lip-smacking bite pulls him from the threshold of death's door and further into the world of the living.

"Must be good. He ain't saying a word," Mystic Woods says.

"The same silence used to sit itself in our house on Sundays. Too good to talk." Zach laughs.

"Om-nom-nom, Om-nom-nom," the Stranger devours the meal, slurping up the last juices from the plate. "Aaahhh—" The reprieve of satisfaction escapes his lips with a ten-point belch.

Josepé, Patrício, and Zach toast to its excellence and chug the rest of their beers.

"Now *that* hit the spot... Gentlemen, where am I?" the Stranger politely inquires.

"We're just past Coffin Island," Mystic Woods points out past the brush, towards an unforeseen shoreline.

The Stranger's insides growl from an abrupt influx of water, mixing with the vittles in his belly.

"Hit this." Mystic Woods hands him a joint. "It'll settle your stomach."

It was the scent he followed through the forest, to the campfire's light, and into this moment. He inhales and tries to hold it in. The sweetness echoes its scent. About to cough, he exhales a thick cloud of smoke to calm his senses.

"Yo, dude! Cool tattoo," Zach says, pointing to the Stranger's arm.

"The Ouroboros, huh? Do y'all know about its legend?" asks Patrício.

They stare blankly, sensing another informative rant propped up by some late-night binging on the Learning Channel.

"Your silence says it all," he says. "In ancient Egypt, the Ouroboros was thought of as the serpent god Mehen, who coils around unified Ra-Osiris deity, protecting them when they venture into the underworld at night—the union of the alpha and the omega, the beginning and ending of time—"

Seated around the crackling campfire, they look with glazed eyes as Patrício swigs some rum and continues his parade of drunken bloviation.

"—Now ya see, Plato uses the same image," he says, pointing at the Stranger's tattoo. "He believed it could help explain the self-sufficiency of the perfected cosmos. The Gnostics had a similar idea, and so did the Taoists. To some, it represented the eternal soul of the world. For others, it was a serpent at the bottom stem of a lotus, coiling around herself... half asleep... with her tail in her mouth.

"But she is not all bells and roses. The Ouroboros, she has a dark side to her. Some say she represents the Wheel of Samsara, the wheel of suffering." Patrício glances menacingly, then swigs another mouthful of rum.

"Where'd you learn all that?" Zach chuckles.

"The television, man," he smiles. "Even though there's never anything on."

"Hear-hear, cheers to there never being anything on," Josepé says and jumps up to his feet, raising his last bit of drink.

The rest of the group joins in the chant, "Hear-hear."

Patrício raises the now-empty bottle of rum and lets loose a loud hiccup. "I think I'm drunk and in need of another round." He saunters towards the cooler and pauses halfway. "Does anyone need a beverage?"

"Bring me whatever's coldest." Mystic Woods says.

"Hell, drinks all around," Patrício champions.

"Hey, bud, would you like a beer?" Zach asks the Stranger.

"He looks like he's just survived a shipwreck! Don't give him that swill," Nicholas orders.

"Good. More for swine like me," Josepé says. He walks over, takes it from Zach and twists off the cap, settling next to his twelve-string guitar.

Mystic Woods squats down on his haunches next to the Stranger and asks, "Since you've had a second to collect yourself, what's your name?"

"Sadly, I can't remember." The thought echoes in the bottomless well of his consciousness. However, unlike a stone cast or a penny wished-upon, there is no sign it ever reaches the bottom, plunking against the endless angst of spiraling emptiness.

Mystic Woods changes the topic. "Nicholas over there is a first responder. And as far as he can tell, you don't have any physical injuries. Other than the terrible confusion, how do you feel?"

"After that meal, I'm leagues better," the Stranger says. He wiggles his toes and feels the tingling sensation of a waking limb.

"Let's try to get you better situated by the fire." Chet reaches down to help pull him up and grasps hold of the Stranger's outstretched hand. "You've got a grip on you, sir. Ready?"

"Ready as I'll ever be." The Stranger positions his legs.

"Okay... three, two, one." Chet's broad shoulders flex, lifting him upright.

Nicholas swoops in to support.

The Stranger teeters in the opposite direction.

"Whoa-whoa, steady yourself," Chet braces him away from the fire.

Mystic Woods repositions the foldable rocking chair. "Set him down here."

The two men help the Stranger into the seat.

"Rest your bones, friend," Patrício says, handing him another water bottle. "Stay hydrated for the rest of us."

15

If A Tree Falls...

Mystic Woods

Mystic Woods flips over a sycamore log, sits down beside the Stranger, and stares into the flickering flames within the rock circle. "Comfy?" he asks.

"Feeling that way," the Stranger answers, then receives another joint.

"I'm gonna level with you. You seem alright enough... and we're a bit set up here... Would you mind hanging out with us until the end of our retreat?"

"When is that?" the Stranger asks.

"Sunday. It's only a couple of days away. You can rest, partake, and hang out. We have plenty to share."

"Well—"

"No need for concern, friend," Mystic Woods cuts in. "We have more than enough."

"Maybe I'll remember who I am by then," he says hopefully.

Mystic Woods glances at his watch. "That's the spirit. In the meantime, you'll make an excellent captive audience for our new songs—not like you're our prisoner or anything." He laughs. "I'd hoped we wouldn't have to break down camp before perfecting our next tune." He leans in with a grin and says, "It's like herding kittens with this lot."

Behind him, Josepé and Patrício smoke cigarettes while discussing features of their bass and guitar lockstep. On the makeshift stage, Chet and Nicholas tinker with differing syncopations. Nearby, Zach plunders through a cooler, fishing for something cold with one hand and gnawing on a bouquet of beef jerky with the other.

"I see what you mean," the Stranger says. "Well, I don't think I'm dying. And I am feeling much better after all that food… Also, what if I remember who I am? I'd hate to cause you any trouble."

"Then it's settled." Mystic Woods belches. "But the moment anything feels strange or out of place, let Nick know. Thank you so much for being understanding." He returns to the group and steps on stage. "We're not leaving, boys!"

Around the campsite, they raise their drinks, delivering a toast of fellowship. The Stranger struggles to lift his water bottle. Halfway up, he rests it back down on his knee. The band mimics and continues to cheer for the Stranger's continued healing.

Official Introductions

Following a smoke break, two potty breaks, and a snack, they find their places on the makeshift stage.

"Ladies and gentlemen," Mystic Woods says, leaning into the microphone.

Crickets chirp in a clamorous frenzy.

"There's just one person," whispers Zach.

Mystic Woods ignores Zach's studious observation. "Thank you for being here this evening… We are Mystic Woods & the Loggerheads! Now, they say a band is only as good as its drummer. And folks, we have the best in the biz—hailing from the throne of Chronos, the master of Kairos, Chet 'Superflex' Powers!"

On cue, he rolls a cadence from the snare drum onto the double tom, then the floor, riding the cymbal back through the pattern.

"Next, on the twelve-string guitar, our very own prophet returned—Electric Jesus, Josepé Verde!"

Beneath the shadow of his oversized straw beach hat, a cigarette cherry glows. Josepé plucks funky, palm-muted riffs with his wah pedal, *Chcka-chcka-neow-chcka-bwow-chcka-neow-neow-brown-chicken-brown-cow.*

"Hide your wives and your liquor—echoing the deepest bass lines, all the way from Venezuela, Victor Patrício del Castillo!"

Dhum-dooo-da-la-dhum do-da-la-dhum-doo-do-la-dhum, Patrício's fingers spread across the run of a fine tablature.

Mystic Woods wipes some sweat from his brow with an embroidered rag. "Coming to blow your house down, the big bad wolf, from way out in the galaxy—somewhere out there, Cosmix Zach Westin!"

Bweed-da-leep-da-dee-da-leep-Bweed-da-lee-da-dee-da-de-da-leep, Zach releases an otherworldly cry from his tarnished brass saxophone.

"Now, this fella here is cloaked in mystery. They say he sold his soul to the devil to play so well... Nicholas Pagan!"

He draws his bow, then slices sushi-style cutlets of artful reverberation, increasing into a fiddler's rhetoric.

"And... my friends, I am your master of ceremonies—Mystic Woods!" He jumps to his keyboard synthesizer and slams down several improvised rhythmic keystrokes. "And we are the Log-ger-heads!" he sings into the microphone.

Jammin'

Several minutes into the Jam, Mystic Woods cracks a whip, ringing a nearby gong. The band gears down, slowing into a chill jazz vibe.

Mystic Woods steps forward, grabbing the mic with his other hand. "Now that we're in the groove, we'd like to debut our brand-new track for you tonight!" He sets down the whip to take a sip of beer and swishes it about his mouth. "Hear something!"

"See everything," the band harmonizes. "Hear something. See everything."

The symphonic components of nature—crickets, frogs, katydids and the rustle of palm fronds—add their seamless track to the mix. Every bell and whistle thrown into the kitchen sink, clang around in an effortless composition.

Patrício thumbs a booming-bumble from his Warwick bass, establishing a funky rhythm before transitioning into a set of wombling-rumbles. Nicholas turns his violin to the side and plucks it like a ukulele. Subsequently, with a click of the pedal, he sets the loop.

Over and under harmonic inclinations, he weaves along the track's melody. Another pedal click plays into a triumvirate of his own concerto, skating on invisible scales and hedonistic bindings, leading the ears towards a crashing counterpoint—a resolution to some far-out argument held with no contention.

The Oros system isolates Chet's expressive backsplash as he smooth-rolls from wrist to finger, his drumsticks tempering precise timing with the harmony. The Stranger taps his bare feet with the beat until Josepé's guitar compels him to dance. Between his ears, nanites translate the predictive pressure exchange of each note while Nicholas's nimble fingers translate a complex tablature onto those twelve strumming strings.

There in the grove, Zach's saxophone grows amongst the groove. His steady breath oscillates a wooden reed as it rushes past the thin brass conical surfaces of rhythm and time. Held in twenty-three keys, an airtight efficiency reaches for an audience with the divine.

Like icicles darting into raindrops, the weighted keys of Mystic Woods's RD-3000 electric keyboard pull the melody into the violin's embrace. Together, a sonic landscape of amplified distortion pedals, fretted tabs, chord progressions, looped tracks, and thundering beats lifts their minds from the complacency of everydayness into new depths of liminal expression.

A myriad of stars twinkle behind waving palmetto fronds. In the upper atmosphere, a shooting star passes overhead. The fleeting light transmutes through the Stranger's optic nerve, beyond the blood-brain barrier, traveling into the broken abyss of the Mind Palace VPN partition. Down into the depths of a sunken oasis, it drifts towards the tickling revelry of a distant memory, rocking itself loose in the Currents of Experience.

Use Your Illusions

Meanwhile, beneath the Nether Regions of Thought, surrounded by the grime of its throne room, the Imp-oster waits for an opportunity to capture its prey.

Livestreaming, the Fog of Despair creeps behind Zeff's hiding spot. Over at the play table, the Childe-within assembles a grotesque golem of collected creatures. An eyeball adorned with wings and flailing tentacles hops around on one foot.

"It's almost time, my boy. Do you have what you need?" the Imp-oster asks.

A sinister smile twists Childe's blurry face as he drags the rusty nails of his latest tool across the floor.

"Indeed, a fine selection," the Imp-oster says with glee. "Now, let's go have some fun." It ushers him into the gloom.

Through the mist, Childe's haunting giggle echoes to Zeff's left.

"The Kid," he says. "Hey, are you alright? There's no time for games. If you can hear me, follow the sound of my voice."

Childe's giggle echoes to the right.

"Kid, that's enough. I'm trying to rescue—"

Claustrophobic frustration builds as a blanket of hopelessness drapes onto Zeff's shoulders. The giggle circles to the opposite side, followed by a rock thrown in his direction. He avoids it, but steps closer to the mist.

Turning, he sees those unblinking, burnt-yellow eyes staring from inside the Fog. They move closer. A primal trepidation shoots into his legs, and he takes off in a cowardly sprint of self-preservation, kicking up a huge dust cloud and abandoning the Childe-within once more.

Zeff wanders the Wastelands under the crackling static of a gray-lit sky. Past displaced boulders and murky pools—where small creatures hop from the ripples of something slithering beneath the surface—he eventually loses track of the

Fog and stops to scan the horizon. On his second sweep, he notices something peculiar.

"I know I'm going in the right direction, but it doesn't feel like I'm getting any closer." Zeff looks at the distant Ruined City resting atop a corrupted stump.

Purple lightning strikes the sediment, altering the topography. Etched in their scars, musical instruments and a megalithic rhinestone top hat emerge from the charred ground. Another crack severs the land and creates a sinkhole that draws a portion of the Wastelands into a dark chasm of seething bile.

Kicking It

The band's flurry of instrumentation subsides over an hour later.

"Bravo-Bravo!" applauds the Stranger, attempting to stand but collapsing back into his seat. "Bravo-Bravo—"

"Now, be honest with us... No need for niceness on account of our hospitality," Mystic Woods says, stepping down from their cobbled stage.

"Incredible! The best thing I've ever heard—well, remember hearing." The Stranger crumples his water bottle and no-look swooshes it into a nearby bin.

"After the break, we'll have time to tinker with one more song. Man, I'd forgotten how amazing it felt to play for an audience, even if it is only one person... That's the whole point anyway: to reach people."

"What about the money?" asks Patrício.

"Don't worry, I'll take his share," Zach says. "I can see it now. Our names in lights—Cosmix Zach & the Supermoons."

Josepé yells from his tent, "Where the hell are my snacks?! They were just in here." He walks back to the group. "Did you take them?" He points at Zach.

"Not me. I don't know. Ask the Stranger," he says, shying away from the subject like legislators on late-night broadcasts, passing the juicy stuff no one hears about.

"He's been right here!" Chet defends him.

Josepé pokes his finger into Zach's chest. "Don't lie to me."

"Chill, dude!" Zach waves his hands.

Josepé spots a dark discoloration around Zach's fingers. "What's under your nails? Looks like either bullshit or chocolate. Which one is it, Zach?"

"Okay, okay—I ate one of your cupcakes."

"One? The entire box is gone. You didn't even ask!"

"My bad—"

"It's the principle of the thing. Didn't your momma raise you better?"

"Hey, don't talk about my momma."

Mystic Woods glances at his watch and shakes his head. "Both of you calm down," he barks. "Go shotgun a beer, hit the joint, or beat the hell out of each other for all I care." He turns to the Stranger. "See what I mean? Herding kittens."

The campsite goes quiet, minus the crackling logs. All around, free-oscillating flora cast thatched shadows as the moon rises overhead towards its zenith. After a begrudging apology, they settle their grievances with a shot of Irish whiskey.

Settling In

Mystic Woods sits back down with a flourish of shimmers as the fire's light dances from his coat. Above, bats echolocate critters with the hunter's delight.

(Who am I? What's my name?) "How'd you come up with your name?" the Stranger asks, shifting the conversation.

"Mi madre," Patrício winks, then pulls a cool drag on his cigarette. On exhale, smoke contours serpentine through moonbeams.

"No, your band name," he says, as the fire's warmth bakes his front to dry-cleaner crispness, doing little for his backside.

Mystic Woods chimes in, "We were thinking of calling ourselves King Tide and the Supermoons, but it felt a bit arrogant. We're certainly not the best. We have a long road ahead of us, but we are getting better every time we practice."

"Too bad we never perform." Zach says, laying a heavy hand down onto Mystic Woods's bedazzled shoulder.

He shrugs away the lingering gesture, saying, "We're on the cusp of greatness. It's like we're in pursuit of the highest degree of flawlessness, knowing we can never get there. Time and time again, we take these musical journeys and plunge into the same waters as the mystics and madmen. The difference is, we glean something of significance to bring back, compelling us to dive deeper the next time we venture in pursuit of inspiration."

Beeeee-rrrrrrr-uuuurrrrrrrrp, Zach flatulates with his saxophone and breaks the deep soliloquy.

Josepé spits his chilled beverage into the campfire. "Come on, man, you're making me waste good craft beer. This stuff's twenty-five dollars a growler at Monk's Market. They only make it once a year."

"Keep your fair-trade organic shit. Give me any old swill," Zach says, then chugs the rest of his store-brand light beer.

Nicholas joins the semicircle formed around the Stranger. "How are you feeling? Do you mind if I check your vitals again?" He smiles with warm assurance.

"Sure thing."

"Don't worry, Nicholas has the best hands on this side of the Mississippi." Josepé tips his bottle in respect.

Nicholas passes him a thermometer. "Hold this under your tongue. I need to make sure you don't have a fever." He turns the Stranger's left wrist over, pressing his first and second fingertips firmly against it until he feels the pulse. After checking his vitals and listening to his lungs, Nicholas sets the stethoscope back in his medical bag. "Everything seems good. Do you have any pains, strains, pinching, or tingling?"

"I've prepared the equipment tent with a sleeping bag." Chet bursts into the conversation, marching from the other end of the campsite. "It's going to be tight, but you're more than welcome to use it when you're ready. Or you can sleep beneath the stars." He spreads his muscular arms wide and looks to a twinkling patch of sky, half-hidden beyond waving palm fronds.

Clouds interrupt the vividity of worlds beyond our comprehension. Observed from within the musicians' secret grotto, light-year-spanning processes—still unfolding since the dawn of creation—spiral onward and outward, past the farthest reaches of the conceptual mind, towards new heights, new stages, and new follies.

16

Life As A Game

Promotion

At the edge of Coffin Island's northeastern tip stands the abandoned lighthouse. Once a beacon amidst the fog-laden darkness, this guardian of the shores hosts new guests and gizmos.

"Sir, the Director is on hold for you," the comms officer relays.

Agent Xero grabs the phone and turns towards the crashing ocean.

"Xero, I need an update from you, son," the Director's gruff voice cuts in directly.

"The Clean-up Crew has it under control, sir. I haven't heard any squawking from the local Barneys."

"What about Zeff?" the Director asks.

"Couldn't locate the body," Agent Xero answers.

"Fuck."

"And... X's database was wiped clean."

The Director remains mute.

"There's one more thing, sir."

"What?" the Director's voice stabs with sharp agitation.

"During the last firmware update, the geeks found an anomaly in the Oros system's Memory IndeX."

"Zeff?"

"Who else?"

"Listen, we need to cross our T's and dot our I's on this one… X is essential to national security. We can't afford it falling into the wrong hands—do you understand?"

Agent Xero furrows his brows. "Yes, sir."

"You have unlimited resources with this, and your security clearance is elevated," the Director says.

"Does this include a raise?"

"Get it done, son. This is the highest priority. Forget about the First Global Foundation, for now."

"Sir—"

"I don't care if you have to drain the entire fucking Atlantic. Retrieve the Oros system, or I'll find someone else, Commander." The line goes silent as two black MH-47 helis buzz past, their nav lights disappearing into the darkness.

(Was that a promotion?) Commander Xero takes a deep breath, then shouts at his subordinates while they stack crates of classified hardware near the foot of the Lighthouse.

After a militant minute, they establish a stable connection between their forward operations base and the Agency's low-orbital Earth Defense Constellation [EDC]. Able to monitor, store, and analyze the data distribution of any target's digital communication in the area, they sweep Coffin Island for a signal from the malfunctioning Oros system.

Deep Thoughts

Elsewhere, within the remote archipelago south of Coffin Island, the crackle-pop of the campfire sends fading embers onto the palm-brushed sand. Mystic Woods swigs back several mouthfuls of jug juice and passes it to Patrício.

A short while later, after a few joints and some boisterous laughter, the front-man's cadence erupts into a lucid rant. "It's all a game, boys." Mystic Woods says, lighting a cigarette. "This whole big ride is a game. We aren't supposed to be shuffling from our eight-to-fives, with no paid lunch break, competitive wages, paid time off, or health insurance. We were imbued by the Creator, and in their image, we must create. Therefore, any institution taking us away from this natural state spits on the face of divinity." He looks around the fire.

"When did you become so religious? I didn't know you were a God-fearing man. I'll let the pastor know this Sunday," Zach says, elbowing Chet in the side.

"Y'all are welcome at my house of prayer any day," Chet replies.

Josepé releases a nine-point belch, takes a step, pivots in front of an invisible point guard, and shoots the empty into the recycling bin. "Boomshakalaka!"

"You know I don't ascribe to traditional dogma—with all of that sanctimony, and *my-god* is more forgiving than *your-god*." Mystic Woods explains, "No offense, but how is art not the highest representation of the divine?"

"You realize everything before 'but' is moot, right?" Chet teases.

"Look. It's how I reconcile with my mortality... And in those moments, it is my love for creation that shows me the way when I'm lost. And of course, all of you assholes." Mystic Woods tips his rhinestone top hat. Its kaleidoscopic maze reflects the moonlit camp light into the canopy, bedazzling the ceiling of nature.

Nicholas applies his own vector of sensibility, saying, "Sometimes I don't see the point of trying to escape this world and retreat into an afterlife. Seems like a waste of this precious moment, spanning from *womb to tomb*. Why wait for heaven or hell when you can create them here and now? The former over the latter, of course."

"Exactly, my man," Mystic Woods revs back. "The act of creation is the highest sacrifice we can offer to the sacred. The true power of music is to release us from our temporal bondage, setting us free from the pressure of our everydayness, and reconnecting our souls in an indescribable way."

"'Art provides what life does not,'" Patrício circles the conversation, quoting the master of the extended metaphor.

"Hear-hear!" They raise their drinks.

"What about the money?" Zach chimes in, trying not to feel left out.

The Stranger notices Josepé, propped up on a nearby log, smiling at his bandmates. A slight tear ventures down his face.

"Josepé is crying again," Zach teases.

"I'm not sad. I'm happier than ever," Josepé drunkenly defends.

Mystic Woods beams a smile under his whiskers and continues with his passionate nonsense. "Think about it. Most people are caught in their daily rhythms and time-based prophecies. Be here, be there, buy this, buy that—always counting down the minutes until the end of the workday, rushing into traffic and waiting for an hour to go a single kilometer. When we finally get home, there is no time to fix a nutritious, delicious dinner. But at least the latest show is about to air.

"We watch it. Then, time for bed, sleeping long enough to slap the snooze on the screaming alarm. We're ripped from the comfort of our circadian rhythms mere minutes before having to leave our homes. Rush-rush-rush, we hurry to get to work, to punch the time clock, to look our boss in the face, graciously accepting their tyranny. Tik-Tik-Tik—they trapped us in clockwork mechanisms—always keeping time." Mystic Woods glances at his watch and dramatically laments against the backdrop of the flickering flame.

"I once heard, 'Time doesn't exist, but our watches do,'" Josepé slides into the conversation.

Mystic Woods applauds. "Thus, we don't have our phones turned on. No need to get caught in a doomscrolling social media freefall because you went to check the time. But I would argue that time does exist... especially with our very own Greenwich Mean Time, Mr. Chet 'Superflex' Powers. Without his toe-tapping, heart-pounding, tub-thumping, pitter-pat, rat-a-tat timing, we'd fall apart. He's a pillar on which our contribution to the divine will stand, long after the last breath has left our chests."

"No need to get emotional, Mike," Chet says, grinning at the flowers.

"I can't help myself... We're so close to finishing this album. One day, we may positively touch the lives of others. It may not be enough to turn the tide, but if we can reach just one person with our musical medicine—"

"I don't think one person is enough to pay for our expenses," Zach playfully retorts.

Nicholas tosses a pebble. "Pipe down. You're ruining the moment."

"Regardless, whether we're the most successful band in the world or not, simply continuing our adventure is enough for me." A sudden crack of inspiration strikes him. "Patrício, fire up that joint! We've got music to make."

Find Balance

The Stranger strains into reflection.

"What's wrong?" Josepé asks, raising the brim of his hat. "You gonna be sick?"

"I was trying to remember, but the well was dry." The Stranger feels his soggy bottom cling to his linen pants. "But I can't say the same for my backside."

"Let's get a towel under you. Chet, will you come help me here?" Josepé calls out.

The Stranger wiggles his toes, and the tingling sensation running throughout his body subsides. Now, he needs to move his legs. His body weight shifts to the edge of his seat. The primal will to stand engages an appropriate amount of tension among hip flexors, spinal erectors, and stabilizing ligaments. Inside his right knee, nanite swarms finish repairing the synovial membrane.

"Lean on me, sir. I won't let you fall," Chet says. His brawny arms peel the Stranger from the chair.

He stands, joints cracking and creaking from sitting too long. Josepé folds a tattered beach towel into the soggy seat while Chet hobbles the Stranger closer to the fire.

"All good?" Chet steadies him near the warmth. "I don't want you roasting like a marshmallow."

Following a teetering memory, tottering around the vacant hollows behind the Stranger's eyes, another Vision Shard sprouts from the Donor's past.

Jocassee

See him now, as a child, camping with his family. Around the campfire's warmth, with the smell of Granny's cooking still on the wind, Momma hands him a skewer with a jumbo-puff marshmallow on the end. He dips it into the flames, barely missing a flake of ash rising in the currents. He turns to see his father busting up more wood.

"Daddy, come get a s'more." He waves his free hand.

"Watch out, suga!" Granny calls over the twang of Paw-Paw's banjo.

In a matter of seconds, the flames engulf his sweet treat with a charcoal skin.

"Oh, no." He pouts. "It's ruined."

"Don't be so quick to judge, my love," his mother says, extinguishing the molten mallow and resting it on a piece of chocolate before pressing it between two pieces of graham cracker. A sweet swirl oozes out, melting the chocolate into a time-honored classic. "Here, try it now," she says.

He bites into the delight. "Yum," he says with crumbs on his face.

A sticky dollop dribbles onto his dark-blue *Space Force* t-shirt. While the sugary goodness catalyzes the hyperdrive of his imagination, he constructs a proprietary set of ships from a bucket of Snap-Brix. Zoom-zoom—spacecraft soar into adventure.

Timaeus

As the fleet passes beyond pinecone debris fields, evading sensor detection and asteroid-proxy mines, they arrive at Moon Base II. Their mission: liberate the citizens from the orbital colony's tyranny.

"Pew-pew!" Quasar cannons fire, leveling orbital defenses.

Once the dust settles, the crew discovers that a group of space pirates, serving the evil Emperor, has taken the Galactic Priestess hiding there.

It is up to Admiral Spike Starwind of the Adastrian Space Force, along with the crew of the *Timaeus,* to rescue the Priestess, who secretly carries within her heart the source code to reach the Apex of Reality, and restore balance among the Celestials. Together, they swirl through several blockbusting victories, while in the background, the lightheartedness of his mother's song harmonizes with Paw-Paw's performance. Farther towards the galaxy's edge, a great multidimensional beast holding the Egg of Existence in its maw stirs as the conflict draws closer to the Dark Forest.

Hidden deep within, amid the remnant debris from the Celestials' war, the Emperor's forces provoke the primordial entity to unleash its devastating attack. Plastic flex-joint tentacles rear back, preparing to cast an annihilation wave.

The *Timaeus* barrels straight for the cosmic horror.

"Pew-Pew... Boom! The fate of the galaxy is at stake!"

The chaotic beast flails its tentacles at the intruders and evaporates a large swatch of Imperial and Adastrian forces, barely missing the *Timaeus*. Despite their agility, the shockwave is enough to put our heroes out of commission for the moment.

With quasar cannons damaged and the back of their ship disintegrated down to the plastic studs—dead in the water—the quick-witted crew reroutes subsystems and gets the engines back online. After separating the front half, Admiral Spike Starwind aims at a glowing point of weakness in the armor of this unspeakable terror. Full speed ahead, the *Timaeus* pierces the monstrosity, scattering Snap-Brix across the campsite nebula. Space Force saves the day once more.

What happened to the Priestess? Did the Admiral and his crew survive? Tune in to find out what happens in next week's episode—

The Trifold Tablet

Somewhere within the Wastelands' scrambled indexes and mismatched mental topographies, Zeff makes his way to the Control Tower, keeping the Mesas of Memory on his left. Above him, the endless gray sky offers no hint of how much time has passed since his arrival, save for the occasional crackle of violet lightning striking in the distance.

"This doesn't make any sense. I've gone so far and have barely moved at all." He squats down behind an obtuse landform and tries to summon the control-deck again.

To his surprise, a trifold blank piece of paper appears from under windblown sands. He unfolds the device, and a cascade of splinters falls from the diagonal crack across its screen, scattering onto the sand like pine needles from forgotten holidays.

"You've got to be kidding me," he scoffs. "Well, at least I summoned it. Maybe I can still activate the build function and open up a direct path out of here."

Zeff taps the fractured pane. Nothing. He rapidly presses the execute button but halts, fearing he might further brick the system.

Suddenly, a rumbling quickens throughout the Wastelands of Cognition, toppling long-stilled outcroppings and crushing whatever creature was resting in their shade. He staggers backward as several enormous Snap-Brix erupt from the ground—red, green, blue, yellow—the size of skyscrapers, their towering shadows blocking the horizon.

While he gawks at the sight, the Fog of Despair encircles him in an instant, replacing his hopes of escape with the whispers of defeat.

"Kill your self... Just kill yourself and let go of all this running. Aren't you tired?" The whispers circle.

A rush of helplessness brings him to his knees.

"Give up... You aren't even real."

A traumatic trigger jump-starts a fire in his hazel eyes. "You're not telling me anything I don't already know." Zeff defies his cowardice and stands.

The mist thickens to reveal those burnt-yellow eyes in front of him. The Imp-oster moves through the gloom. Its outline casually closes the distance between them.

"You want me, motherfucker? Come and get me." He marches towards the creature.

Jagged teeth raise to a crusted red-lined smile as the Imp-oster teleports to him.

Mere milliseconds before it arrives, one of Zeff's overactive finger presses finishes its place in the cue, materializing a fifty-story Snap-Brix beneath him. Riding atop a failed command prompt, he rockets above the Fog and away from the Imp-oster's swipe. Once it snaps into place, he stands and hears something crack.

At his feet, the broken tablet flickers. Zeff shakes his head in annoyance, picks it up, folds it, and places it in his jacket pocket. High above the fog line, he spots another trailing rainbow and a potential path to the Ruined City atop the corrupted stump of the last Elder Tree.

Remembering To Remember

Meanwhile, tucked within a grove of palmettos, the Stranger's backside dries against the flames.

"Sheesh... I'm gonna need something to soak up all this booze." Josepé crushes the last of a small bag of cheddar sour cream chips.

"Hey! Those are mine," Zach growls.

Josepé grins, crumpling the bag, and throws it at Zach. "I think you've had your fill of cupcakes." He laughs with a crunchy mouthful.

Slightly embarrassed and brimming with the steam of alcohol, Zach storms out of camp.

"Watch out for monsters," Josepé says, then releases a wolf-howl.

A pleasant smile etches itself up the Stranger's cheek.

"What's up? Everything good?" Chet asks.

"I think... I might've remembered something." He looks at the updraft of smoke, anchoring this moment into the sky.

"Did you recall who you are?" Mystic Woods leans against the bones of a driftwood tree and scribbles in his notebook.

"It was a camping trip with my family... I was playing with some Snap-Brix." The Stranger beams at the recollection and the hope of uncovering his past.

"I loved those when I was a kid." Chet smiles. "What did it feel like?"

"Hmm... It felt like the only things that mattered were: the warmth of the fire, the sticky s'mores, Momma's singing, Paw-Paw's banjo, the smell of Granny's cooking, and the sound of my Daddy busting up a cord of wood," the Stranger says.

"Sounds like you're on the right track... That's the game though," Mystic Woods mutters towards the night sky, stroking his goatee. "The point is to get back to when we were young—when we were children, born into a world of wonder and divinity; back to the time before we traded it all for a minimum wage. Well, to hell with it. Let us free ourselves with imagination, purchased with the currency of inspiration."

And with that, Mystic Woods cranks up the intensity of his melody, breaking out into a spiritual protest song. After finishing their joint under the passing pale moonlight, the rest of the band soon finds their groove and slips into the Jam.

17

Straight On Till Dawn

Skin Up

Following the impromptu session, they gather around the campfire. Chet breaks out a tray of homemade lemon squares, and Patrício opens a velveteen Royale-Crown bag, dumping its contents onto an upside-down frisbee. A pack of papers, followed by the thump of a grinder, almost knocks a pile of pre-ground cannabis flower over the edge. Patrício hurries his hand to steady the tray, stows the grinder, and begins.

While Nicholas gets distracted talking with Chet, Zach sees an opportunity to get the best seat in the rotation. The Stranger's eyes fall on the plastic altar, topped with a green heap of ground flower, several cylindrical cardboard filters, and a pack of JA 1.25 rolling papers with all-new affirmation-printed leaflet filters. He watches with bubbling curiosity.

Ever so effortlessly, Patrício combines two hemp rolling papers together and creates an 'L' shape. First, he creases and cuts the paper pattern into a more economical design. Next, he sprinkles the aromatic blend. A few jostling tucks and twists later, a proper joint rests in his hands.

Patrício looks up, swooping a stray tassel of hair from his face, and notices the Stranger staring at the frisbee. "Yo, do you know how to roll?" He sets the tray to the side and wipes the wasted crumbs from his lap.

"I'm not sure," the Stranger answers. "But I'd like to try. If you wouldn't mind."

"I could use the help. None of these fools can skin up." Patrício glances at his bandmates.

"Hey, that's not true," Mystic Woods searches for a lighter. "Were not as good as you."

"Especially Zach. He slobbers too much," Patrício says with the spliff hanging from his mouth.

Unamused, Zach gets up to snag another lemon square, and Josepé steals his seat.

"Some of us prefer more sophisticated means," admits Nicholas.

"A lot of good your fancy contraptions are doing us out here," Josepé adds.

"Hey," Nicholas protests, "those are state-of-the-art dab rigs."

Josepé pivots his wit, saying, "Last time Zach got so high, he went green."

"Oh, I remember... He went into hulk-mode." Chet flexes with a roar.

Patrício extends the upside-down frisbee with a few papers and some ground flower. "Give it a go."

"You should do it," Zach squawks with cheeks full of homemade deliciousness. "Don't let the new guy—"

"Give 'em a chance," Patrício insists.

Receiving the tray, the Stranger's hands take off in a delicate dance of cunning and grace.

"He might mess up and waste the limited papers we have." Lemon crumbs escape Zach's maw.

"We've got more... I think." Patrício checks the camping chair's cupholder. "Worst case, I'll have to roll all of them."

Zach eyeballs the frisbee, takes another bite of goodness, then asks, "What'd he do to the papers? Why are they stuck together?"

Soon after the last doubting word from his sugar-laden lips, voilà—the Stranger presents three perfectly rolled joints.

"Well, look at that," Patrício says, examining the craftsmanship. "You've rolled a cross joint, Shiva's trident, and an impressive super cone."

Zach swallows the last bit of a lemon square and gawks in disbelief at the creative miracles thereupon the upside-down frisbee. "My good man, I retract what I said." Zach wipes his mouth. "Let's light em up, fellas."

Languaging

The super cone is the first to feel the flame's kiss. It burns evenly, even as Zach coughs until he is red in the face. Round and round they smoke and laugh beneath the moonlight, slipping into lucid conversation.

The Stranger sparks up the next entrée, Shiva's trident. "Y'all's music is incredible," he says after a lengthy exhale, then passes it to Nicholas.

"Music I get." Nicholas stokes the totem. "It's language where I stumble to find the correct words to express myself."

"And where does language come from?" Zach breaks into the conversation, looking at the Stranger. "I mean. You don't know who you are. You have no memory of the words you use, yet somehow you can speak with us, and we can understand what you're saying. Well, most of us," Zach shoots a darting glare at Josepé.

"Fuck you! I speak multiple languages." Josepé laughs back at his roommate.

"Isn't language crazy, man? I mean, if you could speak any language, which would you use in your dreams?" Mystic Woods ponders.

"Music!" Nicholas cheers.

The band nods in agreement.

"Josepé can code-switch," Patrício says, receiving the trident.

"What's that?" the Stranger asks.

"He can switch between two or more languages within a conversation or even a single sentence," Patricio explains. "Hell, I can barely keep up, and I can speak at least two—" A coughing fit halts his prose with the sacrament of the smoldering relic.

Josepé clears his throat. "Ho pisciato en las cervezas," he says in a playful expression of Italian-Spanish prose.

The Stranger looks into his bottle of beer and leans in to smell it. Josepé lets out an uncontrollable outburst of guffaws and knee-slaps, rolling off his driftwood log onto the sand. He crawls to one knee and wipes tears of laughter from his eyes.

"Too much booze for him." Zach takes his turn in the rotation.

"Du verstehst?" Josepé asks.

"Ich wusste nicht, dass du anders sprichst als jetzt," the Stranger responds, "But how can I understand a language without knowing I can?"

"See, I'm not a total knucklehead." Zach exhales a smokestack towards the night sky.

Caught in thought, Mystic Woods strokes his goatee. An idea strikes him, and he walks over to the Stranger, squats down, and says, "I've been thinking a bit more about your situation, and I just had a thought—I might know where you're from."

"Really?" he asks, the hope and possibility almost bringing him to tears.

"Maybe you're one of Helaku's people. They kind of keep to themselves back on Coffin Island. Sometimes, he shows up around sunrise—no, before that. Earlier than early. I've seen him out here while scouting the area. But I don't think he knows we practice here. It's top-secret, hush-hush, if you know what I mean." He playfully nudges the Stranger's side. "If he doesn't show up by the time we're ready to leave, we'll take you back to get some help, as promised."

Still quite curious about his bearings, a furrowed determination waxes across the Stranger's brow. "Certainly. It's a better starting place than being stuck out here, not knowing who I am."

"Hey, we aren't that bad," Chet puffs into the conversation.

The night plays on as the fire's last light smolders underneath the ashes of palm fronds and oak limbs. After helping the Stranger to his tent, the band drifts into the slumbering sands of their sleeping bags. Soon, the boys are sound asleep; even the Stranger manages a few snores. Close by, several fleeting shadows dart past a line of saw palmettos into the musicians' camp.

Menu

Elsewhile, Zeff pauses his flight through the shattered desolation, gazing towards the Ruined City atop the withering stump, still the same size on the horizon.

"I'm getting nowhere," he says, ducking into the hollow of a withered tree with a few green leaves at the tip of its branches.

He knocks the dust from his coat and brushes against the [Trifold Tablet]. It glows, enticing him to unfold the paper-thin device.

"I can't access the edit functions... But what about the build protocols? Maybe I can open a command console and drop a waypoint."

At once, a menu screen materializes, obstructing his view. "Wahoo!" He selects the corresponding tab, but nothing happens. He clicks it again and again, each time with increasing frustration. Yet, the obtuse window continues to block his line of sight.

"Oh, come the fuck on." He attempts to move it out of the way, but it glitches in place.

As Zeff pitches a fit with the stuck menu, he loses track of time. The Fog of Despair appears, prompting him to flee, running with the illuminated screen suspended in front of him. In his haste, he steps off the embankment and tumbles into a ravine.

Mid-fall, the drop-down menu stutters with a flickering glitch. Surrounded by multiple windows, Zeff rolls and flips, stopping with a thud. Shortly after the dust settles, they finally close. Zeff stands and folds the tablet, placing it back into his pocket. The mist reaches the cliffside, and with few options, he shakes his head at its persistent annoyance before sprinting in the opposite direction.

Deep Down

On the far side of the gloom, below the Nether Regions of Thought, a vile sludge pools on the floor. Within the Imp-oster's lair, the malicious beast cackles from its demonic throne, watching Zeff stumble and bumble across uneven terrain. "Run all you like. It makes no difference. We'll capture you before *they* find you." It garbles out a distorted laughter and dances atop a skin-tight cushion.

Afterward, the ghoul drops back to its seat and impatiently taps its claw against the carapace armrest, digging a neurotic trench into the sagittal suture. Zeff's angst seeps through the Fog like a warm stew on an autumn evening. The creature sniffs the mist, exciting the putrid pupils of its burnt-yellow eyes. Its other claw dashes into a grease-stained urn and retrieves a maimed Sorting Dreg from an assortment of treats.

"Oh, I like this one. What prize do you carry?" The Imp-oster presses its claw beneath the creature's flesh and smiles with razor-sharp rows of long, crooked teeth. Saliva courses down its crusty red lips onto the cushion. "Just a taste. I shouldn't be so gluttonous this time." It laughs and pulls off a leg.

The Sorting Dreg screams.

"You want some?" it asks the Childe-within.

"Yes, please." The boy stops playing with his latest homunculus and runs over to the Bone Throne. As he looks up with sunken eyes and a blurred smile, the Imp-oster rips off an arm, breaks it in half, and hands the pieces to him.

"Go fetch a plate." It crunches meat and bone. "And be a good lad and get me some hot sauce. This ain't got no flavor."

The Dreg drowns in its tears.

"Sure thing." Childe walks behind the Imp-oster's throne and pauses. "Do you have any more gifts for me?" he asks.

The Imp turns to point at a pile of discarded scraps. "What about all of those?"

"Worthless junk. It took all of them to make these." He points to a crooked workstation where four living dolls wait obediently in their cages.

Childe returns with sauce in hand and drops it off, followed by some deconstructive playtime with his new toys. Elated that its influence has finally corrupted the Donor, the Imp-oster compulsively consumes the last bit of the Sorting Dreg, followed by two more maimed creatures from the urn. Then, without a thought, it devours the entire assortment while binge-watching its favorite show through the Fog of Despair.

18

Rise & Chime

Morning Raid

The next morning, while Zeff combs through the Wastelands of Cognition, the Stranger wakes up on his makeshift bedding—a pallet and an old sleeping bag. He rolls onto his side. Opening his eyes, the maritime forest's twinkle-filled darkness soon succumbs to the subtle yawn of daybreak peeking from under the cover of night. He closes his eyes and dozes back to sleep.

Outside the utility tent's tarp-drawn flaps, the band wakes to a ravaged campsite. The Stranger pokes his head out to survey the commotion, just in time to see a bloated trash bag hanging from a tree, give way to the forager's lacerations and dump several days' worth of revelry, beer, and cigarette butts onto the sand.

"What the hell happened here?" Mystic Woods asks, strolling in from the latrine with three squares of toilet tissue on the heel of his bedazzled boot.

"Looks like we got hit by the locals." Patrício laughs and pulls his long, wavy black hair into a manageable bun.

"Did y'all hear anything last night?" Chet scratches his head and follows reflective bits of tinfoil contrasted by a trail of colorful cereal, leading beyond the tree line. Some of Zach's Moon Pie wrappers and a napkin swirl about, caught in a late-spring breeze, followed by a gnawed styrofoam plate rolling along like the *first wheel* until it settles in a clump of underbrush.

"Josepé!" Zach hollers into the zipped flap of the guitarist's tent. "I know it was you. You didn't have to take all my snacks and my toothbrush." He rattles the waterproof canvas.

"What are you jabbering about?" Josepé, gently strumming his guitar, shouts from his cozy sleeping bag.

Zach shakes the camping quarters.

"If you don't stop, I'm gonna come out and bust you in the mouth. This ain't no way to wake someone up with all these wild accusations." Josepé sets down his instrument.

"Chill, man!" Chet intercepts. "It looks like raccoons hit us. They probably got your goodies. If you stop pointing the finger and look around, you'll see that they've made a mess of the place. But I wouldn't put it past Josepé to plunder your stash."

Zach storms off to his luxury tent—more suited for glamping than roughing it in Yellowstone. En route, muttering and kicking up sand, he punts a palm frond. It gets stuck in his sandal, and, unable to shake off his frustration, he hobbles the rest of the way.

Still Snoozy

Reaching his quarters, Zach snatches open the front entrance, hatefully kicks his shoes to the side, zips the flap shut, and begins shoving trash into a bag. As he huffs and puffs about, the bandit stirs from its sleep beneath an assortment of chocolate wrappers and graham-cracker crumbs. It twitches awake, and, primed with fear, the banded creature creeps—one paw after another—towards the canvas flap's shiny zipper.

It jingles.

"Josepé, go away," Zach says. "I don't want to hear your apology."

The zipper continues to melody until the raccoon figures out how to unzip the flap.

"Bro, be careful. You'll get it stuck." He smiles at a perverted joke to himself, then turns around.

To his surprise, he finds the raccoon's bulbous backside wedged within the entrance flap. He lets out a ghostly scream at the frightened, overstuffed scavenger attempting to squeeze through the tiny opening, its hind legs twisting from cheek to cheek. Zach, fearful of rabies, hurls a duffle bag at the poor creature, providing it with the proper umpf to pop out the other side.

The chunky raccoon races by Nicholas while he brushes his teeth. Soon after, Zach bursts from the opening, tossing a muddy boot. He wildly misses his target. The bandit dashes beyond the nearby bushes, up a tree, and over some adjoining limbs. A safe distance away, it hides under waxy foliage and stills its rapid-beating heart.

Back at camp, after some begrudged grumbling and apologies, the band sets to task. Once the last plastic wrapper and fleck of tinfoil are bagged, and the site in order, the grotto fills with notes of cast iron warming with bacon grease and freshly ground, fair-trade micro-farm coffee. The Stranger takes a sip from an old *Space Force* mug.

Without provocation, the malfunctioning Oros system releases a randomized beetle-squirt of neurochemicals, shifting the balance of his perception. He sniffs the air—now shining with an interwoven tapestry of synesthetic miracles—and tastes the sounds of daybreak amongst the *sizzle-pop* of the pan. Beneath the steel campfire grill, smoldering embers glow with a magnificent hue, sweet as candy. Next, the sensation of cinnamon-coated hotness arcs across the Stranger's hippocampus, summoning a facet from the Donor's childhood.

Brown Bag Special

See him as a child on one of those late-autumn afternoons along the countryside. His aunt has come up from Louisiana with her pack of toy pups, his two cousins—Bennet and Tucker—and whatever wants-and-things adults call for on those family visits before winter. The autumn air is crisp outside the cabin of Paw-Paw's blue 1960s rump-shaking pickup truck. Inside, the three boys eagerly ride with their granddaddy from the town store with small brown paper bags filled with a cosmic array of goodies, surcees, and whatnots.

"Now, don't y'all go telling your mommas I done runt ya with all these sweets. I'll certainly catch an earful about cavities and sugar levels—and I ain't trying to tick off Granny, either. Understand?" He shoots a look of authority at his grandchildren.

"Yes, sir," they respond in unison.

"Good." He smiles. "Now, fetch me a Fireball."

They dig past foil-wrapped chocolates, peanut butter cups, candy-coated pieces, sweet sticks, and sour pops.

"Here, Paw-Paw." Bennet, the eldest cousin, nimbly unwraps the desired treat.

"Ooh we, that's got some fire to it." He professionally suckles the goodie.

The boys watch with wonder as he endures the sweet-heat without breaking a sweat.

"Back when I was an intern at NASA, we used to keep a bowl of these at our consoles. Keeps the brain alert and zaps the taste of dehydration out of your mouth," Paw-Paw explains.

They look on in adoration as their granddaddy alludes to tough times growing up, stories of the Academy, his early twenties at Mission Control, some redacted tales from the Office of Scientific Intelligence [OSI], and his theories on the future of humanity. Making its way up the winding crush-run driveway, the rump-shaker throttles by amber-orange-lit fields towards the white post-and-rail fence bordering the yard, finally squeaking to a stop.

"Y'all take off now. There's plenty of time until supper. Granny's making chicken pot pie and butter pecan pie for dessert." He rubs a wrinkled hand across the belly of his flannel shirt. "Now, get. And take these dogs with you."

Paw-Paw opens the tailgate, and his hound dogs—Old Dan, Lil Ann, Blue, Sally, and Max—leap from the bed of his pickup truck, racing to their favorite tree and bush. The three cousins thank their granddaddy, then rush around the corner of the house, into the woods, over a creek, under some fallen trees, and through slippery slopes of golden-brown leaves. After avoiding some imaginative booby traps, they arrive at the secret Command Center, fashioned from Old Dan's large kennel.

Musketeers

Inside, they sit in a circle and dump the candy onto a *Space Force II* TV-dinner tray. A sour apple Bubble Pop tumbles from the mound onto the ground. Tucker, the youngest, plucks it after the first bounce and places it triumphantly atop their pile. Their eyes sparkle in appreciation of the bountiful sweetness. While they talk of comics, cartoons, and toys, the cousins take turns picking pieces and unfolding the crinkling foils and plastics of childhood delight.

Later, towards the end of their mound of candy, Bennet separates three fireballs from the remaining lot of caramels and gummies. "Wanna see if you can take the heat?" he asks.

Tucker chuckles with melted chocolate on his freckled cheeks.

Three synchronous atomic bombs drop. The fire is immediate. Unable to withstand the burning feeling on his tongue, Tucker is the first to cave, quickly taking it out and fanning his mouth.

Their contest of endurance persists as the two remaining participants lock eyes. Filled with the resilience of youth and the determination to secure bragging rights over the other, their boyish faces turn as red as radishes—

The memory fades before their contest concludes, replaced by the scent of cinnamon flowing from a mental packet, shifting the lens of his perception.

After Party

Years later, he's downing fiery cinnamon whiskey at a party, trading the innocent concepts of childhood for a chilling deluge of smooth shots, poor decisions, and early-morning hangovers.

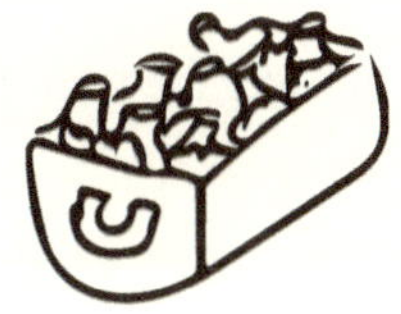

Round after round, cadets line up to sample the whiskey taken from Sergeant Cinnamon's desk and the beers bought by the seniors. Unbeknownst to these plebs, they play into a crafty plot executed by the graduating class—a parting gift before they advance to *knobs* and leave for the Upper School. A vicious cycle of earning your place amongst the few who would share a bond stronger than family or friends. Sadly, only a handful survive the Academy's final rubric.

For now, there are shots to be had and a celebration at hand, as they conclude their first year under the disciplined tutelage of Sgt. Cinnamon. A young cadet hops on top of a nearby footlocker and mocks the salty devil-dog. "At dawn, the demon comes knocking—and the rent is due. Boy, oh boy, you better have his money, or you'll find yer-self in the Box!"

Round after round, they pass the bottle until there is only the faint sliver of a syrupy drop left. With the handle emptied and the alcohol in their bloodstream, they get wild: jumping on their beds, flipping over wastebaskets, fighting with pillows, wrapping themselves in sheets, and duct-taping a passed-out cadet to their mattress.

Near the evening's end, someone pulls out a pack of cigarettes and passes them around the room. Soon, several fights break out while others pray to the porcelain gods. And after a fire-extinguisher fight, or two, the cadets pass out just before the morning reveille.

At 0420 hours—like every morning at the Academy—the fluorescent lights jolt on as the cinnamon bouffée rounds the corner, followed by the demon's demands for the pound of flesh owed to him.

"You worthless maggots!" Sgt. Cinnamon yells into the lifeless barracks. "You think you're real fucking clever?!"

The room barely moves to the thunder of his terrifying command.

"Fuck this! Tell the security team we're running a drill," he yells at his subordinate.

A wiry man with a clipboard notices the veins bulging from Sgt. Cinnamon's neck and tiptoes backwards.

"Did I stutter, motherfucker?" he asks. "Get the hell out of my sight."

"Y—yes, sir," he stammers and turns towards the barrack doors.

"You little punks think you're finished with me?! Let's see if this helps get you up!" He stomps to the fire alarm.

Moments later, a piercing screech pulls the puppet strings of the still-drunken plebs. As the room floods with ice-cold, fire-drenching water, the cadets spring to life. An unlucky few, gurgling with a warm burning in their bellies, vomit the contents of their rumpus evening onto the floor: an unintended result, but the beginning of a pleasing punishment for these young upstarts.

They spend the early part of the day cleaning, missing chow, and enduring the picked-through leftovers of unwanted scraps. Then, out to the yard, in their underwear, doing vigorous plyometrics—burpee, crawl, lunge—until, one by one, they fill the infirmary.

Hair of the Dog

The Stranger breaks his stare at the coals round the fire's base and cracks a smile behind the next sip of java from the vintage *Space Force* coffee mug. Coming out of the silence of reflection, he hears Chet offering Patrício a shot of something stronger than Sgt. Cinnamon's private stock.

"Yo, I loved that show when I was a kid," Mystic Woods reflects while whisking some eggs in a bright-green bowl, his eyes hidden by a pair of glittering sunglasses.

Josepé hawks up a loogie. "Are they still streaming it?" he asks.

"I think so... My nephew is into it," Patrício says, fishing a lighter from his pocket, and sparks an early-morning joint to chase away the linger of Irish whiskey.

"How many are there?" Nicholas inquires, holding a stack of folded napkins.

Zach walks over from his tent, having just checked it for any more unwanted guests. "I think *Space Force XV* comes out next year. It's been running for as long as I can remember."

"Like a fine wine," Chet retorts as he replaces the cork of his bottle.

"When did it start?" Patrício wonders.

"Not sure, but it was definitely around when my dad was young," Mystic Woods says, pouring the eggs onto the *sizzle-pop* of the cast iron.

"Well, I'd know for sure if I had my phone," Zach whines.

"You know the rules. We don't need to waste time doomscrolling or engagement-farming. So let's finish up breakfast and start our day." Mystic Woods looks at his watch.

Zach salutes. "Aye-Aye, Capi-ton! What's on the schedule?"

"Greasy campfire cuisine, a dip in the ocean, some good music, this medicine," Chet hands him a joint, "and, of course, a little hair of the dog that bit you." He jingles the bottle of Irish whiskey.

"I'll pass." Zach waves away the thought of another drop passing his lips before breakfast.

"Where does that saying come from?" Patrício sorts through the plates and cutlery for this morning's buffet.

"I heard you had to bite a dog if it bit you," Zach says, lurching closer to a covered plate of bacon and sausage.

Mystic Woods swipes his hand away.

"That's ridiculous, Zach," Nicholas calls out from vigorously washing his hands.

"I think he might be onto something," Mystic Woods says.

"I had to take a bite of Zach's mom the other night." Josepé chuckles.

"She's like your mom too, ya fool. Don't make me tell her you've been talking shit again."

"She'd never believe you. I'm her favorite son."

"You wish."

"That's not what she said last night." Josepé winks.

"Yeah, I thought I heard you crying from your tent." Zach laughs.

Chet thinks for a moment, recalling something his auntie told him, and interrupts their banter, saying, "If I remember correctly, it comes from an old belief that someone bitten by a rabid dog could be cured of rabies by taking a potion containing some of the dog's hair."

"So, using the thing that hurt you to heal you?" the Stranger takes a stab at understanding.

"Makes sense to me," Patrício says. "Now, will someone come help me set up the rest of this buffet line?" He breaks into song: "It's breakfast... It's breakfast tiiime. Breakfast time. And the food is ready!"

The band joins in, singing, "The food is ready. The food is ready. It's breakfast... It's breakfast tiii-iii-mmmme."

Key Deer

Halfway through his meal, the Oros system detects movement by the tree line. Just past the morning fog weaving between low palms and berry bushes, a sauntering group of miniature fanged deer—a loose matriarchal group with a few white-spotted fawns in tow—emerges into the band's creative sanctuary. Amongst dew-dripped foliage, the tidings of breakfast, and the bond of fellowship, these forest spirits have come for their cut.

"They're so small," Zach remarks. "What are they?"

"Where are their antlers?" Patrício asks.

Josepé shakes his head. "You've never seen a Key deer?" He brushes off the majesty before them and walks back to his tent, returning to the needs of his beloved twelve-string.

"Amazing, simply amazing," Patrício marvels.

The deer stand with a regal reverence, their tiny fangs concealing bashful eyes behind vampiric smiles.

"Adorable." Zach inches closer with a bit of scrambled egg on the edge of his plate.

"Don't feed the wildlife. It'll acclimate them to humans, making them more likely to be hit and killed by vehicles," Nicholas warns.

"I don't see any cars out here," Josepé quips.

With the plate outstretched, Zach slowly creeps forward.

"These might be the descendants of the Key deer they brought up here several years back," Chet explains.

"Aren't those the ones the First Global Foundation saved from extinction?" Nicholas asks. "Remember? It was on the front page of the local paper."

"I recall something along those lines a couple of years ago," Mystic Woods confers. "But I've never had the pleasure of seeing them up close. I heard they can swim."

"Swim?" Zach tilts his head in confusion and imagines them crossing the ocean.

"Please don't step any closer," Nicholas says, continuing his protest.

"Shhh." Zach moves a nudge, whispering, "You're going to scare them away."

"It's not like they are winning any Olympic gold medals, but they evolved in the Florida Keys, swimming from island to island searching for food and fresh water," Chet continues his explanation.

"How'd they become endangered?" the Stranger asks.

Chet signals a momentary pause, finishing his beverage of choice. "Before the parasites almost took them out, there were stronger storms, algae blooms, and habitat destruction—luckily, word of the problem reached someone at the Foundation, and they had an entire herd brought to the area for study."

"That's wonderful," the Stranger says, admiring the idea of preserving those innocent lives.

Chet's mood shifts to a slight melancholic apprehension of a deeper truth. "In the end, our negligence still decimated the main population."

"Doesn't the Foundation provide aid for repopulation efforts?" Mystic Woods asks, restoring the majesty of the moment.

Zach grins and says, "Then I definitely can't waste this opportunity of a lifetime." One foot after the other, he unhurriedly inches forward.

Hand Fed

His next step cracks a stick, stopping before it snaps. All the deer pause, raising their white tails in alarm. The camp freezes. Their heartbeats syncopate—a momentary pause between the notes of existence. The Key deer, the band, and the Stranger, all bearing witness—motionless in an everlasting moment outside of time.

Zach remains statuesque with his arm extended. As puddles of sweat streak down his forehead, the deer return to nibbling the ground. He steps over the twig and inches forward, walking softly, tiptoeing around thin branches. "Almost there," he says, creeping closer.

One doe gently walks over, sniffing the ground before raising her head to lick the plate. Her vigilant ears twitch towards the cracks and crunches of commuting coastal critters. She blinks, and, as if with one mind, the parcel suddenly leaps into the latticework of forest and morning fog.

"Out of sight!" Zach cries, twirling around. "Guys, did y'all see how close I was to that tee-niney deer?"

Inspiration overtakes Mystic Woods, compelling his hurried pen to address a new page within his pocket notebook.

"What are you writing?" the Stranger inquires.

"Nothing much." He reveals his latest caricature: Zach standing on one leg with his arm outstretched, holding a song titled, *Balancing Act* with some hastily scribbled lyrics.

"That's hilarious!" The Stranger inspects. "Do you have any more of these?"

Mystic Woods shares the contents of his notebook. "Back home, I have stacks of them. I'm kind of old-school in my process. Whenever the muse sees fit, and I get an itch, I've gotta write it down. Or if there is something I'm trying to work out—or a problem to solve—writing things in my commonplace book helps me capture those fleeting moments of creative grace."

"When will you be ready to play in front of an audience?" the Stranger asks.

"Not yet. We simply don't have it together. We're close. But we need a little more time to practice. This *is* why we're here, after all." Mystic Woods breaks into song:

Practice won't make you perfect.
Practice until you play.
Practice the right disciplines,
So you'll be insured on those rainy days.
Practice for the times
When you can't rise to your expectations.
Practice the night away.

Josepé's twelve-string improvs into the conversation. Soon, the band elucidates praises into the dew-damp morning. Meanwhile, the Stranger leans back, enjoying the hymnals and rhythms of sound-silence as the beetle-squirt finally tapers off. And in the first moments of clarity, he notices a bit of bacon in his teeth.

19

Build-A-Fire

Rainbow Unicorn Raft

After breakfast and a few creative joints, the band searches for an extra bathing suit for the Stranger. Nicholas is the first to return with a pair of dark-blue swim trunks patterned with tiny turtles.

"Try this on," he says. "You remember how to swim, right?"

"We'll see," the Stranger says, holding up the shorts.

"No worries. These two aren't the best swimmers, either," Patrício says, pointing at Zach and Mystic Woods.

"We'll be fine with ole Bessie here," Mystic Woods pats the side of a giant, inflatable rainbow unicorn raft. "We'll anchor it in the shallows."

The warming day retains a faint crispness from the evening's reprieve. Once changed, the troupe makes their way to the beach, holding the raft above their heads. On arrival, Mystic Woods stops abruptly, asking, "Where would y'all like to—"

Zach and Josepé run into the back of him, almost dropping the cooler.

"Pick a spot, you fool." Patrício pushes past and stretches his arms to welcome the sun.

Josepé and Zach follow suit, carrying the cooler to the edge of the soft sand before setting it down and opening it up for a reward.

"Hold up," Chet says, plopping the oversized raft into the shallows. "Help me anchor this."

The Stranger wades into the surf until sudden visions of washing ashore cause him to pause. Goosebumps ripple up his chest and across his arms from a set of small waves lapping against his knees. However, the band's merriment disrupts the trepidation. In time, the sun emerges from a wayward cloud, turning the water into a lovely layer-cake of temperatures.

Waist-deep, Nicholas, Josepé, and Zach pal around on the unicorn raft, breaking into song. At the height of their chorus, Mystic Woods interrupts their sea shanty as he clambers aboard, nearly knocking over the cooler. Still in the water, Chet and Patrício finally bolster him upright and toss him onto the raft. Nicholas nimbly scoots aside to avoid spilling his toddy.

The Stranger, following the musicians' lead, wades farther out, kicks his feet off the bottom, and floats on his back. Beneath an unfolding cinema of cumulonimbus clouds, he splashes water into the air and watches the droplets sprinkle around him in a hail of aquatic bullets. A sea shanty bellows from the unicorn raft as the clouds pass, casting flat shadows like lapped foam sloshing along the shallows. He closes his eyes and, stilled by the echoing void behind his brow, ebbs in the buoyant breast of the Atlantic a little longer.

For now, floating in the ocean consumes his mental bandwidth, temporarily sublimating the angst of not knowing who he was a little deeper. Adrift, the day shifts on the other side of his eyelids until the sun returns and warms his cheeks with lances of light. A wave splashes onto the Stranger's chest and into his nose, choking him from the meditative shoals of Samadhi.

BOB

He wretches up a mouthful of saltwater. Then, opening his eyes to the resplendent fresco above, he marvels with a forgotten sense of joy. Aided by the bit of alcohol and weed in his system, he listens to the lapping shore.

An ominous object crosses the sky.

His heart quickens. "What's that?" he asks, spotting the Agency's Battle Ordnance Bot [BOB], not by its spherical design alone, but by the icy rage bubbling in his gut.

Frozen, he floats unblinkingly. In time, the drone resumes its course to the next island. Once it clears the tree line, he stands and heads towards the band's buffoonery.

"You good, bro?" Chet asks.

"Did y'all see that?"

"Where?" Mystic Woods cranes his neck to the sky.

Chet and Zach look around.

"What're you talking about?" Josepé lifts the brim of his hat.

"I see someone's gotten into the jug juice already," Patrício says with a wink.

Nicholas reapplies some sunscreen. "Sorry, man. I wasn't paying attention."

The Stranger buries his fear as they show him how to shotgun a beer before diving back into their uproarious revelries.

Operators

Tethered at the other end of satellite-guided controls, on the East End of Coffin Island at the abandoned Coast Guard base, BOB's operators circle the drone back around for a closer look.

An agent in a red floral-patterned shirt leans back in his chair. "See... nothing matches his signature."

"Does he have it turned off?" another man, wearing a blue floral shirt, pivots to a different monitor.

"Looks like a bunch of dumb tourists," Red says. "We've swept the entire area and haven't pinged a single signal from the Oros system... Look at that raft. Do you honestly think Zeff would just be chilling down there?"

Blue directs the camera at the band. "What if he had help?"

"Do you want to waste the Commander's patience by sending a squad all the way out here? Did you see his car? It's highly unlikely Zeff survived the bridge incident," Red says. "Sharks probably got him."

"He's survived a lot worse."

"Are the stories true?"

Blue nods. "I've heard from too many sources."

"If so, he's probably long gone. Why would he hang around here?"

"He could be injured."

Red swivels in his chair. "Still, if he was, do you think he'd be kicked back on a unicorn raft, knowing he's being hunted for treason? Come on, let's circle back to the beach and scan a few *assets*." He raises his eyebrows.

"Now you're speaking my language."

The Agency goons guide BOB away from the archipelago—and the nanite-enhanced assassin they are hunting for—towards sunburnt beaches on a lewd hunt of primal urges.

As the drone flies over, ascending several kilometers, the band barely misses its departure from sight.

"There it is again. Did you see it? It's right there." The Stranger points back to Coffin Island.

"I still don't see anything," Nicholas says calmly.

"It was probably a bird." Josepé rests back against the raft with his hands thrown over the sides, fingertips trailing in the water.

"Yeah... You're right. It was probably a bird," the Stranger agrees, shelving the subject, although still convinced by the swill-taint of emotion stirring in his gut. This, he keeps to himself.

Floats & Doze

The sun creeps near its zenith as the Stranger swims in the shallows, frog-kicking here and there, enjoying the weightlessness of the sea. He soon realizes the unicorn raft has drifted from the shore and yells, "Guys! Check your anchor!"

"Oh shit. *Somebody* didn't tie the line tight enough," Josepé says, cutting his eyes at Zach, who—half-asleep from day-drinking—does not notice. "Hey, fool!" He thwacks him with his sandal. "Wake up!"

"W—what... Damn it. I was having the best dream." Zach lifts the shades from his eyes to reveal bright tan lines. "Oh shit, we're floating out to sea!"

"Welcome back to the party. Now that you're all caught up... Look what you did," Josepé scolds.

"Paddle, you fools!" Mystic Woods takes charge. "Grab what you can and paddle. We can't go out like this."

A slight panic runs across the rainbow unicorn raft.

On instinct, the Stranger swims after them. The malfunctioning Oros system, detecting trace chemicals within neural pathways, triggers latent muscle memory and kinesthetic subsystems. He closes the distance with Olympian speed, and several strokes later, grapples onto the unicorn raft.

"Need some help?" he asks as Chet pulls him aboard, saltwater tracing the contours of his physique towards the canvas.

"We've gotta get out of this current," Mystic Woods says anxiously.

Nicholas, Patrício, and Josepé take one side of the mythical beast while Chet and the Stranger hold the other. Mystic Woods and Zach help steer the raft along the parallel of the shoreline. Thirty exhausting meters later, the *S.S. Rainbow Unicorn* bumps into the shallows.

Zach bursts into laughter as the existential dread morphs into hilarity. Like wildfire, it spreads throughout the group. After wiping the tears from their eyes, they tow the raft ashore and collapse upon the center of its canvased backside.

"Tie the rope, Zach," Josepé mockingly mumbles under his breath.

"Herding kittens," Mystic Woods shakes his head at them. "One minute after facing a near-death experience, and they're bickering like siblings."

"More like an old married couple," Patrício chimes.

"I'm ordained. Let me know what kind of ceremony y'all would enjoy," Mystic Woods retorts.

Downpour

The leaves are the first to hear the afternoon rain, followed by a bumbling rumble and a flicker of lightning. Overhead, brooding cumulonimbus—no longer confused about their purpose—let out a brief downpour of stormy intentions, soaking them before they can flip over the rainbow unicorn raft, transforming it into a turtle-shelled testudo.

They scuttle off the beach, following a mud-slick trail past the dunes, into the campsite, and under a tarp-drawn gypsy tent.

"This weather is cutting into our time," Mystic Woods grumbles and looks at his bare wrist.

Patrício squeezes rainwater from his hair. "Chill, boss. We're supposed to be relaxing at the beach," he says.

"And now we're here." Zach slaps a bent deck of playing cards on top of a muddy cooler.

"You don't want this smoke," Josepé sneers.

Zach stares unblinkingly.

"Alright. Have it your way," Josepé says. "You best be glad this isn't for money."

"Just a friendly game to pass the time." Water droplets slick down Zach's smooth head as he shuffles the deck.

Beneath the tarp-drawn gypsy tent, Zach deals around the muddy cooler. A quick study, by their third hand, the Stranger has a better grasp of the concepts, but still no contest for these vetted sharks.

Rummy

An echoing deluge resonates from the sudden appearance of puddles formed from natural runoffs. While the storm rumbles about, several palm fronds sweep past the tarped speakeasy. Zach jumps at the sound of a falling limb.

"Don't be a scaredy-cat," Josepé says, discarding a five of diamonds.

Zach draws a card. "I ain't scared... I was right about the Stranger being in the woods. Wasn't I?" He sets down a book of threes atop the mud-spattered cooler and discards.

"Who knows what's on these islands?" Chet exchanges an unwanted seven of clubs for an ace of spades.

"You're right." Patrício pauses, contemplating his next move. "I wonder what else the Foundation's been up to all the way out here. First, they rescue the deer, then they make the monsters." He scoops up the length of the discard pile.

"You know I'm about to go out, right?" Mystic Woods presents his two remaining cards.

"We'll let the gods decide," Patrício says with a grin, shifting his eyes' intensity.

"You've got to be kidding—"

Patrício drops every book in his hand and discards. "Be careful, boss."

The Stranger draws from the deck, making sure the others don't see his hand. He focuses, and the TacOHUD highlights a string of patterned values. To his surprise, the king of hearts completes a portfolio of murderous royals. While the band boasts and brags about who's going to win, the Stranger quietly lays down a run of hearts—nine to ace—then effortlessly discards, sealing their fate and claiming victory. Defeated, they toss the remaining cards onto their makeshift table.

After a few rounds, the storm departs, and the seven emerge from their tarp-drawn haven to a flooded campsite. A delightful puddle has formed inside Zach's tent—a consequence of airing out the smell. The fire pit is muddled with ash and muck, while the rest of their woodpile is soaked. Bummed by the oversight and wanting to enjoy the fire for another evening, the crew sets out into the damp forest in search of something dry enough to burn.

The Struggle With Fire

On return, Josepé and Zach stack the gathered branches like a log cabin and douse it with lighter fluid, but their excitement soon fizzles.

"The damn thing won't stay lit. If we had some more fuel—" Zach looks at Chet.

"No, sir. Y'all wasted the last of it. I told you it wouldn't catch that bag of wet leaves on fire."

Mystic Woods checks his watch. "Step aside. We don't need to be wasting any more time."

The pair gladly forfeits their turn.

He removes the bag of wet leaves and repositions the limbs. "Amateurs," he mutters, placing the last piece of firestarter on a pile of kindling. Mystic Woods lights it with a match. It goes out. He does it again, this time lighting the four corners. A few leaves catch, filling their camp with thick plumes of smoke.

Sweat rolls into his eyes, seasoning them with further frustration. He spirals, lighting shredded paper towels and shoving them one after another onto the starter bundle. Mystic Woods empties the rest of the matchbox until a dim flame peeks from a smoldering pile only for a wayward gust to extinguish it before he can add more paper towels. Muddied and matchless, he howls his frustrations towards the darkening sky.

"Will someone get me a damn lighter?!" He turns around with a crazed look in his eyes.

"Just microwave something," Zach says, cracking a stick in half.

"Fool, there are no microwaves out here." Josepé cuts his eyes.

"Will you two please chill out?" Chet hollers from the utility tent. "I'm trying to find the parts for the grill—and hopefully there's some fuel left—or y'all'll be eating peanut butter and jelly sandwiches with extra sand."

"Don't be so cruel," Nicholas jests.

"You know they get like this when they're hungry," Patrício says.

"Yeah. I do." Chet settles a bin on a portable table. "A damn handful is what they are." He throws three dinner rolls at them.

Patrício strolls over, lights one of his crumpled cigarettes and hands his lighter to Mystic Woods.

He strikes the flint with renewed confidence. Another gust blows it out. He flicks it again. The lighter refuses. The wind persists. He cups it with his hand. The flame kisses his palm. Switching tactics, he stoops low, striking the lighter as hard as he can. Nearly twenty failed attempts and a blister on his thumb later, he gives up. "I can't do it. The ANTs have poisoned my mindset."

"Ants?" the Stranger asks, flipping through a mental three-ring binder stuffed with pages of laminated info cards.

"Not the bugs," Mystic Woods explains. "Automatic Negative Thoughts. Don't let the [ANTs] spoil the picnic."

"What are we going to do about this fire?" Nicholas asks. "The solar lamps are fine, but I want the *real* camping feel."

"First-world problems," Josepé snaps.

(They may bump heads and bicker, but they stick together,) he analyzes, watching their shenanigans and sensing the depths of their bonds from the expressions on their faces.

Survival Instincts

The Stranger's inebriated mind soon relaxes, drifting onto the hither-thither of a dandelion seed caught by the passing breeze. A brief instance of clarity washes over him, shotgun-blasting a riddled matrix of Vision Shards—the Scouts, the Academy, far-off jungles, deep caverns, and sweat lodges—on the dartboard of his attention.

He squats next to the mucky, ashen pile of slop that once was a rip-roaring good time. "I think I might know how. May I try?"

"Of course, my dear fellow," Mystic Woods says, grateful for the help, and tosses him the lighter. "I'd try to find some more matches first. The lighter did a number on my thumb."

Zach sighs. "What's the point?" he asks. "We've tried everything!"

The Stranger ignores him and digs out the muck, down to the dry sand. Next, he builds up a mound in the center and flattens it into a patted altar for stacking wood. After repositioning the rock circle, he looks upon his work and smiles at his progress as the film of familiarity settles on his shoulders. (At this rate, I'll remember who I am before we leave tomorrow.)

Finished, he stands and rubs the dirt from his hands. "Let's gather more kindling and wood," the Stranger instructs. "Try looking around needle-bearing trees." He breaks a small pine limb. "Their wood contains a sticky, flammable sap—exactly what we need."

A short while later, the gang returns with several armfuls of wet kindling. The Stranger uses Chet's utility knife to peel back the bark and reveal dry wood beneath the surface. In time, Josepé drags up a soaked catawampus log twice his size.

"Don't set it in the fire pit yet, please. We must make it more manageable." The Stranger points towards a nearby axe. "Splitting it lengthwise will make it smaller and expose the dry inner wood." He explains, "The secret is the lower mass, which causes them to ignite faster than when whole."

Mystic Woods stares at the log. "You know, that kind of makes sense."

"This is the least I can do for your generosity," the Stranger says, picking up the axe.

"By no means... Think nothing of it, my good sir. We can't let you die out here." Mystic Woods sips from his cup.

"Sure we can... get out of camp. Go to the other side of the island while we feast and sing." Patrício laughs.

The Stranger squares up to the large log, evenly bends his knees, and raises the axe above his head like a shining Excalibur. He draws upon the Vision Shard of his father chopping wood, strengthening a filament of muscle memory. It wraps along the connective tissues of his movements as he swings a legendary sunder between granular lines, effortlessly splitting the large wet log in half and stopping the blunt blade just above the ground.

Birth Of Flames

Several flawless swings make quick work of the crooked log, reducing it to a manageable stack. With his materials prepped, the Stranger rests the wood shavings on the earthen stage. Hoping to dry the kindling and set them ablaze, he stacks a cone of small twigs, followed by a larger layer of sticks.

He tries Patrício's lighter, but it's out of fuel. Chet hands him a soot-stained matchbox. The Stranger lights one into the matrix of tinder. It goes out. He strikes another, but the striker is too worn to warrant a spark. He flips it over and, finding an unused corner, strikes it again, this time rubbing the igniter off the tip of the match.

"Damn it." He furrows his brow.

Patrício loudly crunches on a bag of cool-rancho tortilla chips. "Just give up, man. You're wasting your time and energy. We can fix something else. It's no big deal."

"Yeah, forget about it," Zach says, grinding his hand into the chip bag and knocking it to the ground.

"Look what you did, man! Wasting my snacks. Pick 'em up. We don't want ants. And this is exactly how you get them... because you want to get your little piggy paws into everything."

"Sorry. Don't get so bent—"

"No worries. Ask me next time. This way, we can share them." Patrício says, slapping his friend on his sunburned shoulder. "Now pick up those chips!"

Zach tosses the discarded ones into the rock circle near the Stranger, who doesn't seem to notice, having the limits of his bandwidth focused on starting the fire.

(Come on... If I can do this, then I might remember more. I know I can do this.) The Stranger rallies his mental clarity.

For him, it is not merely a fire, but a beacon of hope—an unraveling strand of realization regarding his own becoming.

(What should I do?) he asks himself. (How do I make this work? I need something to burn long enough to catch.) He looks to his right and spots the chemical-coated tortilla chips. "Hmmm... I wonder... Is there another lighter?" The Stranger turns to Patrício, hoping for some help.

Patrício checks his pockets. "I thought I brought more."

Josepé quickly tosses a lighter to the Stranger.

"Hey, that's mine. You know it's bad luck to steal white lighters," Patrício says.

"I wasn't stealing it," Josepé snaps. "You let me use it to open my beer, then walked away."

"That's exactly where I left it," Patrício revises.

The Stranger crouches back down to inspect the center of his fire lay. Noticing several imperfections, he repositions the sticks into a tighter cone, shuffles to the windward side, and lights it low.

A chemical reaction between the heat and the chip's flavor layer ignites a blue-green flame across the triangular snack. It stays lit long enough to catch the shavings. Little by little, the first signal of smoke climbs from the earth, reaching well into the canopy.

The band's rambunctious antics fall silent.

"Well, how about that? When damp and all else fails, try using cool-rancho chips to start your next fire," Mystic Woods says with a jingle in his voice.

The Stranger instinctively protects the ember from stray gusts. Creaking, popping, sizzling—an infantile flicker slowly rises through the tender boughs of slow-drying, split sticks. Flames soon ascend within the mini-teepee, taking residence in the prepared space, engulfing it in brilliance. The fire is lit.

"Now I've seen it all." Zach adds, chewing on a mouthful of crumbs.

A Feast Of 1000 Beasts

While the Stranger tends to the fire, the band forms an assembly line for their campfire-packet cuisine. Chet chops six potatoes into cubes. On the other side of him, Nicholas surgically peels and deveins two pounds of local shrimp, tossing them with herbs and slices of Meyer lemons. To his right, Patrício rips large rectangular sheets of parchment paper and heavy-duty tinfoil.

On the propped-up campfire stove, Mystic Woods proudly warms his home-made Carolina Reaper pimento-queso corn dip—crafted over countless seasons of pepper harvests and hot sauce contests. Down the line, Zach seasons some lemon-butter salmon to go with Chet's campfire potatoes. With the make-table prepped, Patrício wraps the evening's cuisine into tight packets of savory goodness.

Not to be outdone, Josepé joins in the fun, saying, "I've got the dessert. Tonight's poison, Rolo-stuffed Bananas."

The Stranger marvels at how in sync they appear, weaving order from the chaos of the campfire kitchen and bringing with them a buffet of incredible delights. A proper feast roasting above the coals, garlic and herb drips from a loose corner, sending sizzles of ash and smoke into the canopy. In the background, Mystic Woods dances around with a bubbling pot of cheese dip and their last bag of chips.

20

Night Raid

Raiders Of The Last Supper

Aglow with vibrant pinks and purples, emboldened by the setting sun, the evening stretches onto the late-spring horizon. Throughout the remote archipelago, katydids pick up their strings, while down in a groovy grove of palmettos, smoky tendrils stretch towards the heavens. A northeastern breeze carries the savory vespers of tonight's menu across the island, into a darkened burrow.

There, nightly terrors open their eyes with the allure of human food on the wind. Yawning kits stir from slumber. Nestling and sniffing, they roll around in their den. Some try to nurse while others play. Once the entire gaze is awake, they follow their mothers into the night.

The last one to leave home knocks over a small cluster of fungi as it hustles to catch up to its family. Closer to the grove, led by the quiver of their guts, the gaze sniffs and paws on a trail of delightful scents. A little farther ahead, the faint light of the Stranger's fire shifts the forest's hue.

Dinner Time

After a few joints, the menu expands to a kingly feast, improvised from the scraps of their getaway. On a small rack above the coals, a paella party-pack bubbles in its own buttery juices. Sizzling a little too close to the flame, the last skewers of hot dogs char under Zach's careful observation. Nearby, on a portable grill, Chet and Mystic Woods cook up leftover honey-sriracha wings, sending a bouquet of sweet notes and spicy tones into the evening. Meanwhile, Nicholas preps a celebratory s'mores station on a foldable table.

The campsite is silent, save for the crackling fire, as they devour their meal with ravenous fervor, soon syncing into a symphony of indulgence—chomping, slurping, chewing, and gnawing—until, in unison, they gulp back sweet teas, waters, lemonades, and whatever is handy. With plates piled high around a fold-up picnic table, the Stranger enjoys another generous helping of wholesomeness from his new companions.

"Have you ever heard of the chupacabra?" Zach asks, smacking his lips.

"No," the Stranger replies. "What's that?"

Zach wipes his mouth with a crumpled paper towel and solemnly says, "It's one of the more ferocious creatures that stalk these parts. Their range was limited to the southwest, but has since spread to the East Coast. Typically, it preys on farm animals, but will occasionally hunt fat raccoons… and sometimes people. Hell, my cousin told me a couple of months back they saw one running near the bike trails at the county park during sunset." He eerily dangles his fingers in front of the Stranger's face. "So be careful wandering around in the dark by yourself."

A slight terror of things-which-go-bump-in-the-night waxes across the Stranger's inner brow, and another splintered Vision Shard dominoes to the forefront of his attention.

See him as a child, frozen with fear by the bump he heard coming from beneath his bed. Or was it behind the dresser? Or was it the closet? The room fills with a swarm of neurotic horrors centered around a cyclone of burnt-yellow eyes, stealing every breath. The dread from unresolved childhood terrors washes over his face.

"Chill, man!" Nicholas chastises Zach's lack of empathy. "Can't you see he's white as a ghost?"

"I'm just joshing him! There aren't any monsters in the woods... or are there?"

Nicholas glares up from his plate.

"Okay, okay. I'll leave him alone... for now." Zach makes his way towards a second helping.

"It's alright," the Stranger says. "I think I might've remembered something from childhood."

"Like, who you are?" Patrício asks.

"No... the boogeyman," the Stranger imitates Zach's creepy gesture.

Mystic Woods playfully ponders a sketch into his notebook. "Whatever happened to ole-boogey?"

"I remember him," Chet says with a shutter.

"Guess we grew out of fashion... like Santa Claus," Nicholas proposes.

"Speak for yourself. Zach still sets out milk and cookies." Josepé giggles. "I sneak in and eat them. He thinks it's Santa. Don't tell him." He strums everyone into secrecy.

Patricio's brow twitches at the topic. "I heard he has less to do with the Lord's birth and more to do with selling sodas in the wintertime."

"We truly are products of good advertising." Mystic Woods closes his notebook.

Zach returns with an overflowing plate. As he sits down, one of his burnt hot dogs rolls from its bun into the sand. Without thinking, he chucks it beyond the tree line.

"Bro, don't do that. The raccoons'll come back," Patrício warns.

"No, they won't," Zach says.

Josepé teases, "Especially not after you went berserker mode."

"Well, it's too late now." Nicholas rolls his eyes.

"Do you want me to get it? I will," Zach responds with a mouth full.

Mystic Woods glances at his watch. "Best we get back to enjoying this meal. We've still got time for one last jam before the night's end. Can't forget why we're here," he says, flipping his top hat onto his head.

"Zach, I was curious about something you mentioned earlier," the Stranger says.

Zach looks up from his plate, smacking an inaudible response between mouthfuls of paella.

"What does 'just joshing' mean?" he asks.

"It means, 'I'm kidding you,'" Zach replies.

"Where does it come from?" the Stranger presses the question, hoping to satisfy his curiosity.

"Well, there was definitely a fella named Josh. We all can agree on that," Nicholas states the obvious.

"Josh must have gone around trying to trick people," Patrício digs into the discussion.

Josepé pushes his plate to the center of the fold-up picnic table and adds his two cents. "Sounds like a prankster to me."

"Whatcha thinking, Chet?" Mystic Woods opens the floor and notices the gears turning underneath his furrowed brow.

"I remember asking my gramma when I was a little fellow," he says, sorting through a hope chest of memories, and smiles, picturing his grandmother—her apron a mess with flour from this morning's biscuits. "I think there was this deaf-mute man, back in the day, counterfeiting nickels into five-dollar gold coins, which he used at a bunch of stores. Without saying a word, he'd walk up to the counter, purchase five cents' worth of candy with his freshly electroplated five-dollar nickel, take his change from the clerk, and move on to the next one. He made a killing... So when someone asks, 'Are you joshing me?' they're asking whether something is genuine."

"I get it... You're presenting me with false evidence that appears real."

"Now you're picking up what I'm putting down," Zach says.

Many mouthwatering minutes later, a charred log breaks in half, sending embers adrift in a magical dust of light. The savory context of their meal soon meets an abrupt framing of Josepé's chocolate-caramel-stuffed banana tinfoil treats. Well worth their weight in stickiness, a bloated fulfillment shushes their grunts and groans around the campfire.

"Fellas, I think I'm food-drunk," Nicholas says, rising to his feet. He throws his plate away and reaches into an ice chest to retrieve a Dr. Pucker's grapefruit sour beer.

"Boys, I think I'm sober," Patrício volleys.

"Speak for yourself. I've got the itis something fierce." Josepé pulls his large straw brim over his eyes.

"I might need to hold off on the s'mores." Patricio pats his belly. "I've already got a food baby."

With their plates licked clean, everyone relaxes around the fire, allowing their gluttony to subside. While they prepare for the evening's jam, the Stranger leans back in a foldable rocking chair and looks up at a patch of stars peeking into the palmetto grove. Back and forth, the slosh in his belly stirs a warm pleasantness from the residence of his gut biome.

He rocks shallow ruts in the soft ground and closes his eyes with the bliss of childhood enjoyment. Another Vision Shard unearths from the Donor's memories: the last time he could swing his legs in Paw-Paw's rocking chair. He tries to hold on to it, squeezing with all his cognitive might. But like water from a clenched fist, it disappears into the ether stream, lost in the Void of Dissociation.

Infiltration

The forefront of his perception snaps back to the present. Barely a second later, in his peripheral vision, a small black paw reaches up and snatches a plate off of the folding picnic table.

"What was that?" the Stranger asks.

"Not again," Zach whines.

Chet calmly stands. "It's probably the deer."

"Shhhhh," Patrício quiets the camp.

All around, twigs break beneath moonlit shadows.

"It's the chupacabras coming for you," Nicholas taunts.

Patrício leans back, bumping into Zach.

"Eeeeeeee!" he squeals.

Mystic Woods holds up a solar lantern attached to a hooded pole and illuminates the abyss beyond the fireside, revealing their cabaret of guests.

A gaze of raccoons pauses their raid—a band of rascality on all fronts. By the once-sealed trash bin, three overstuffed critters, consumed with savory morsels and buttery garbage, hardly notice. On a log next to Josepé, one bandit flees with his satchel, scattering its contents towards a line of sabal palms. Luckily, the bag gets stuck in the thicket as he chases after the critter.

Flam! A bin tips over in the kitchen tent. Chet and Nicholas take off, shooing the creatures back into the belly of the maritime forest.

"I've had it with these damn raccoons!" Zach howls. "I'm going to get my bat." He stomps to his tent and slams open the halfway-unzipped flap.

Moments later, his high-pitched cry carries across the island.

Inside his tent, four raccoons shred through the rest of his snack stash while two kits make a general mess in his bedding. Unable to retrieve his weapon, he rushes to the woodpile and grabs a medium-sized log. Then, stomping over, rage-hurls it at his tent, sending the varmints back into the bushes whence they came.

Following some manly yelling, not-so-manly yelling, and wild flailing, the gaze scatters into the shadows—thieves and conmen vanishing all at once.

"I don't think there's a single thing within earshot after your battle cry," Josepé slaps his hand on Zach's shoulder.

Patrício laughs. "You're one to talk."

"It was two inches from my face," Josepé says. "But they didn't get my bag." He holds up his empty satchel.

"All three of y'all were making a scene." Mystic Woods chuckles during the calm that flows in the wake of such a chaotic storm. "How's the kitchen faring, fellas?" he asks Chet and Nicholas.

"All good here," they holler back.

"The best spot on the island for a bite to eat… indeed," Mystic Woods scribbles his latest idea, finishing before the void recaptures the flutter of inspiration. He pulls back, smiles at his small notebook, and fans the stained pages of hurried sketches and song lyrics.

21

MWTL: Origins

Granddaddy Of The Jam

A resplendent moonbow dashes apart lingering clouds to reveal the punctuated clarity of the star-spangled heavens. After an extensive jam session, the group of misfits takes a well-deserved break around the fire and replenishes their coffers of creation with hydration, medicine, libations, and snacks-on-snacks.

Mystic Woods lays it on thick, knowing just beyond his musings, laughter, and creative camaraderie, a gnawing dread hangs like low-bearing fruit in the garden of everydayness. He knows tomorrow means a departure from their creative Eden for the real world.

"What a riot." His eyes gloss with tears held back for a rainy day as he adorns his bedazzled sunglasses. "This reminds me of when we last jammed in front of a full house—on stage and in the seats," he says, hiding the flow of emotions. "Over fifty musicians celebrated the genre's founder on his birthday—"

"It was legendary," Josepé blurts.

"I'll never forget it... a double-intro and a double-outro," Nicholas adds.

Patrício relaxes his eyebrows and reflects. "Man, we jammed and grooved well into the night—"

"I remember that damn jug of kykeon kept coming around, leading us into delightful meadows where all the sacred concerts and discourses flourish—a space where one is, finally, impressed by celestial visions." Mystic Woods stares into the flame.

An envious sprite springs from the look of remembrance as the Stranger tries unlocking the faucet of his identity, longing to rinse his face in the cleansing refreshment of knowing.

Mystic Woods continues, "Absolved in the Jam, we surrendered to the rhizomatic harmony spreading through the different sweeping movements. I swear, at some point when I closed my eyes, I felt the stage lift from the ground. But it was probably the magic brew in my belly mixing with the melody."

"Now that's some birthday," the Stranger comments, hoping to knock something loose.

"It was his last performance." Chet bows his head. "After the second finale, the forefather of the jam went to the grand concert hall in the sky."

The Stranger exhales a sigh of empathy.

"It's alright. There's nothing to be sad about." Chet lifts a reverent smile. "He died doing what he loved, and his contributions will rock out as long as there are people to noodle, and good vibes to be had."

"It was probably the last time we played a venue that size." Mystic Woods gathers his thoughts.

"Or any venue," Zach snaps back.

Mystic Woods cuts his eyes. "But we've been practicing ever since, trying to perfect our sound, to deliver our message."

"Well, you're the best thing I've ever heard," the Stranger applauds.

"At least, that you can remember," Zach says.

The slight jab stirs up his longing for identity, mixed with a minced medley of intoxication.

How Fire Made Us Humans

Beneath the twinkling night sky, the campfire crackles like those primal flames polka-dotting the wilderness of our ancestry.

A pregnant pause between Zach and Josepé's boisterous bickering provides the runway for a thought Patrício had earlier in the week, but had not voiced, to filter through his subconscious and onto the stage. "I read about this wild idea the other day," he says, munching on some pretzel sticks. "Check it. When we discovered fire, and later cooking, we extended our stomachs outside of our bodies."

"I don't get it," the Stranger says, rubbing his belly.

"You see, by harnessing the flame, our ancestors turned the internal process of nutrient extraction into a communal activity. We might not realize it, but cooking is a technology that enhances our body's ability to absorb nourishment," Patrício says.

Nicholas scratches his head. "Cooking is like our smartphones and video games?"

"I think I see what you're saying," Chet attempts to wrap his head around the drunken discussion. "They say baking is chemistry—using chemical reactions to turn flour, sugar, and eggs into pastries or whatever."

"Close, but no cigar, my friend." Patrício smiles. "Think of it this way... tossing another steak on the barbie pre-digests our food, giving us the opportunity to capture more vitality from what we put into our bodies. No longer wasting nutrient resources consuming raw meat, we freed up mental real estate, unlocking the mind—one of the most magnificent forces in the known universe."

"Which gave us space shuttles and telescopes!" Zach chimes in.

All the alcohol and musical revelry call forth the *Mother Wolf of Inspiration*, while Patrício continues his luminous cadence, coiling towards something he doesn't quite understand. The words projectile-vomit from his mouth. "We're caught in a dance between our minds, tools, and environments. May our songs aid us in our spiralling journey as we wander about this life." Patrício, unable to stall the deluge of happiness pooling in his deep brown eyes, rubs the parrot-patterned cuff of his unbuttoned shirt along his cheek.

Mystic Woods reviews the scribbled margins in his commonplace book, stating, "Then... language is a tool... linguistically extending us out into the world."

"And our mobile devices extend that further," Zach continues, mouth full. "We use them to transmit our thoughts, opening up techno-social wormholes through time and space, reaching the early-morning freaks of the *Digital Renaissance* across the globe." He shakes the last bits of chips into his mouth.

Josepé leans towards the Stranger, revolving his index finger in a circle around his ear, whispering, "Loco." The gesture passes over the Stranger's head, but the language he implicitly understands.

"Does music bypass time and space?" the Stranger asks.

Being musicians, they marvel and rave about the idea, experiencing a collective blowing of their minds, with simultaneous appeasement of egos.

Chet is the first to answer, saying, "For me, it's an internal beat, resonating until I express it. Hmm... does music come before language?"

"I see what you did there," Zach says. "The ole-chicken-and-the-egg problem."

"Not quite what I had in mind, but please elaborate, my good sir," Chet beckons the discussion.

Music Of The Spheres

"Gather round, gather round," Zach ushers everyone's attention, drawing several squiggles in the dirt. "You see, fellas?" He points at an impromptu equation. "There's math plus vibration, unfolding through time. This harmony is apparent everywhere: the rhythm of the ocean, of the planet, of the stars, et cetera."

"You mean *musica universalis*?" Josepé interrupts.

"My good man, I see you've heard of my friend Pythagoras," Zach replies, toasting his beer to Josepé.

"Who?" asks the Stranger.

"A long, long time ago, there was a man called Pythagoras," Zach continues. "One day, while sitting around in his pajama-robes, eating ambrosia and sipping wine, he discovered the precise relation between the pitch of the musical note and the length of the string producing the sound.

"He understood harmonious sound frequencies as simple numerical ratios. His theory, *Music of the Spheres*, depicted mathematical patterns found throughout number systems, visual angles, and a whole kaleidoscope of shapes and sounds. Ultimately, the theorem was abstracted to fit their society's view of astral relations, proposing that the sun, moon, and planets emit their own unique stellar vibrations. They decided the quality of life on Earth reflected the tenor of celestial sounds, imperceptible to the human ear," Zach says, waving his hand towards the canopy.

Nicholas elaborates, "If I remember correctly, Plato heralded astronomy and music as twin studies. 'Astronomy for the eyes, and music for the ears.'"

"Why can't we hear the stars or the planets?" the Stranger asks.

Chet interjects, explaining, "We don't hear them making all of that riotous racket because all we've ever known is their noise, never experiencing silence. Like fish, unaware they're in the water, we're surrounded by an everlasting jamboree."

"Don't get all philosophical on us smooth-brains," Zach teases. "But you're on to something, Chet. We've been bathed in the music since before we were in our mother's womb. Could you imagine the whole damn species vibrating with the frequency of the heavens, of the planet, and of each other?"

"Sit down, ya hippie." Josepé slings a playing card at Zach and grazes the side of his bald head.

"Chill, man! You almost took out my fucking eye," Zach whinges.

"Toughen up, buttercup!" Josepé pokes sharply. "I didn't mean to scare you. Besides, I could take your eye out at any point, If I wanted—are you tearing up? I'm sorry, bud. Lemme see." He walks over to check on his roommate.

Fwamm! Zach punches him in the balls, sending the wide-brimmed hat into the air. Josepé curls up, then writhes on the ground, holding his groin.

"Told you I'd get you back from the other day. Didn't I?" Zach extends his hand to pick him up from the dirt.

Bwamm! Josepé reciprocates Zach's hospitality, buckling him to his knees with an uppercut to the nuts. "You're going to have to do better than that," he boasts as the saxophonist succumbs to the impact.

"Josepé, you're so cruel to him," Nicholas lectures.

"It's for his own good. If he doesn't toughen up, people at his job will continue to bully him. And I can't have him bumble-fucking both our mothers' good names."

The Power Of Music

Patrício shakes his head at the two goons. "What were we talking about?"

The Stranger rewinds the last moments before the outburst. "Music of the Spheres," he says, hungering to finish the rest of the discussion.

"Right... Since the whole of existence is making music, then whenever we play, we lead others back into that space." Patrício lights a cigarette.

"Space?" the Stranger asks.

He exhales a cool drag. "Not quite... picture a numinous realm of mystical experiences characterized by cosmic unity, oneness, and interconnection. Unchained from the shackles of the ego, we distribute positive, mood-lifting connectivity."

"What happens there?" The Stranger performs a volley of mental acrobatics to understand.

"We fold notions of a deeper meaning and some ultimate truth into our pockets for later," Patrício waxes jazzy-poetics. "We hope it'll last indefinitely. But after several hours steeped in the soup of everydayness, we sink into the soggy crust of our being—back into the crucible of the cubicle, the insatiable desires of customer service, and the default mode of modern human experience. Eat, sleep, work, repeat; we lose something infinite. Well, our music can give them that infinite thing. All they need to do is replay the track."

Mystic Woods scans over faint lines of traceable thoughts, feverishly fashioned from the ethos onto scribbled pages. He flips through them until, several pages back, he finds a note reminding him of what he wished to contribute. "Together, we paint with the palette of cognitive-emotional ecstasy. From wax vinyls to cloud echoes, our endeavors to wallpaper the mind will outlive our ability to create them. A temporary reprieve instrumented into existence—"

"Hear-hear!" they cheer.

"—Unfolding within time and rhythm, musicians pattern reality. We engineer sacred spaces where everyone can raise their vibrations and pierce the finite... Can you imagine all those voices singing into the dead of night? 'Turn it up. Crank it up. Higher... Higher... Higher,'" he closes his eyes behind tinted lenses as Nicholas fiddles his way along the tapestry of his thoughts.

After a brief pause, Mystic Woods adds, "For the crowd, we produce an experience of cathartic illumination. And then we get to have all of it projected back at us, giving us a glimpse, face-to-face with the divine. Man-oh-man, what a feeling, what a high." He spins around in a complete circle, tumbling his magical top hat down his right arm, artfully catching and settling it atop his head. "That was a close one," he says with a smile. "Just got it cleaned, and you don't want to know how much it cost to scrub crud from all these rhinestones."

Zach chuckles, leaning against the Stranger's shoulder, before they cheers, thrusting their libations towards the night sky and gulping the sacrament down their gullets.

22

Gypsy Jazz

Jug Juice

Mystic Woods dances a twinkling jig around the picnic table and magically reveals a brown-glass growler of muscadine wine and medicinal herbs. After stumbling mid-spin, he stops to pour some kykeon into his mouth, then passes the jug to the rest of the band. With another flashy turnabout, he hops down by the fire to light his cigarette.

He leans near the flame. The first flickering kiss misses its mark. He sways closer. This time, the heat singes the fringes of his beard. The faint stench of its chemical exchange drifts into the canopy, out towards the stars.

The Stranger laughs at the buffoonery. "Watch out! It almost got you."

"I know, I know," Mystic Woods says, stroking his facial hair. "That's why I've pulled my chair back... Tell me, is there anything burned?" He removes his top hat, revealing smile lines and a well-groomed beard.

"I think you're good," the Stranger replies.

"Thank the Lord—my good looks are preserved for another lover and another day."

"Might've been an improvement if you ask me," Zach says, receiving the jug from Chet.

"No one asked you." Mystic Woods dismisses Zach's teasing jab and slowly turns to the Stranger when the magic mix stewing in his belly enchants his tongue with the quill of lucidity. "What's life without a few shenanigans? For instance, we're floating on a speck of dust in a seemingly endless cosmos. Simultaneously, we are nothing, yet we are all that matters—"

"'An ocean in a drop,'" Patrício adds some Zen notation.

"—What an odd flux in the apparently static nature of our shared realities," Mystic Woods continues. "Flux generates growth through angst. It is here, at the edge of our comfort zones, where we ride those waves of madness and glean something worth bringing back for all to enjoy." Before slipping into delusions of grandeur, the bedazzled showman halts his bloviation, realizing the cigarette in his hand has burned to the filter.

The Stranger sits back, watching the rising ash dance within a moonbeam.

Prelude

Mystic Woods lights another curved cancer stick with the flames and reconnects with the resolve of his pulpit. "Far as I'm concerned, there are three types of agents actively sculpting our day-to-dayness. The first are the Obvious-Magicians: the clown, the showman, and the soothsayer. They're designed to distract you in verse and vision. Their purpose is to entertain, maintaining crystalline social constructs."

"And the second?" the Stranger asks, attempting to keep pace.

"The Dark-Magicians. Their aim is to disrupt society and its constructs in order to fulfill their selfish desires. At the cost of everyone and everything, they make us forget who we are."

"Who are we?" the Stranger asks, hoping to unearth a clue to restore his memory. "And how do they make us forget who we are?"

Back and forth, Mystic Woods flips through several ink-, ash-, and caffeine-stained pages of his commonplace book until he locates the relevant passage. "As Alan Harrington expresses it, 'We're cosmic revolutionaries, not stooges conscripted to advance a natural order which kills everybody.' These champions of ego subvert our best traits by locking the population inside a predatory capital-gains theory of fear, uncertainty, and doubt. In constant rotation, they create the conditions conducive to an unjust pseudo-ethics that keep the classes fighting one another. Sadly, folks don't understand: fear plus logic equals fear-based logic, and is the furthest from the truth they defend in their hearts."

"I just wanna see our names in lights," Zach says. "And have our songs sung well past our short time spent on this blue rock."

"Who are the third type of magicians?" the Stranger pursues the conversation, despite lacking the proper ammunition to add to the discussion.

"The Light-Magicians. They act with impeccable intent and try to pull the world back together," Mystic Woods says.

"Which are you?" he asks.

Mystic Woods inhales a slow drag. "We're more like the Trickster's shadows dancing on cavern walls, living in the mischief behind reality, staring into the face of madness."

The Stranger attempts to grok the minstrel's words.

"In all seriousness, we represent a new movement of creatives tapping into blockchain technology to publish our works and help liberate as many creative minds as possible before the advent of artificial intelligence."

"It's too late, man. It's already on our phones," Zach says.

"Thus, the sense of urgency," Mystic Woods responds. "In my heart of hearts, I believe our world is the way it is because the artist has long since been shackled by the economist."

Nicholas adds, "In the war for our minds, the artists were the first to fall."

"Why not run for office? I'd vote for you," Patrício salutes.

Mystic Woods sips some more magical wine. "Not my cup of tea... Besides, we have music to practice and an album to finish."

The Stranger presses his hands against the flame's warmth and asks, "What is blockchain? And what does freeing the creative accomplish?"

"Think of it as the printing press of our age," Chet explains.

"I was going to say it's like my notebook," Mystic Woods clarifies, "a ledger, if you will."

"That, I can understand." The Stranger grins with renewed confidence in their conversation.

"And for 'liberating the creative mind across the globe,'" Nicholas expounds, "more artists equals a stronger narrative to feed the AI."

"Good artists steal. Great artists inspire," Mystic Woods says, brandishing a rascal's grin.

"One hundred percent!" Zach cuts in.

Mystic Woods continues, "I'd like for our music to set the world on fire with flames of ultimate forgiveness and kindness. It's difficult to always walk this path. We all trip up now and again, but if we discover what makes us come alive, then we can jump in headfirst with courage into the face of fear and maybe actually make the world better through our pursuits," he heralds.

The Stranger sits back, crossing his arms, and asks, "What makes you come alive?"

"The Jam," Mystic Woods answers, a smile bunching his well-groomed beard. "Plucking, strumming, performing—amidst the chaos-storm, we find something to bring back for others to enjoy."

Patrício furthers the point, "We're here to pull our fans into the miraculous nature of the moment—singing along with us."

"Isn't that similar to the Magicians?" the Stranger asks.

"Sort of, but our intent is different," Chet replies, sitting down to the left of him, holding a bowl of popcorn. "Of course we need money, but our goal is to raise the stage so everyone can dance and share in the light and the glory, forever and ever."

"A—m—e—n," the group harmonizes with soulful bravado.

Pinched by inspiration, Nicholas stands with his hand over his heart. "Let Freedom, Love, and Community ring—"

"If the red strand of fate runs between every human heart, may our songs strum those chords into a frenzy," Josepé professes, repositioning his straw hat.

Zach champions, chipmunk cheeks full of popcorn, "Precisely. We rest on temporary patterns of chaos, often unable to see the bigger picture, the larger stage, and the immeasurable scale of things. If only for a moment, let's shake the others from the nub-grinding hamster wheel of the eight-to-five."

"I think Robert Frost once described our civilization as meadow-makers in the forest, a temporary clearing along a road less traveled," Chet recites.

Rapt with divine inspiration, stirred by the jug juice in their bellies and the freely flowing ideas, Patrício hops up from his seat and explodes into the discussion, declaring, "The Big Bang is still happening. The Flood is still happening. Rome is falling. It's all happening now!"

"Yes, yes, my good fellow. But how can we build systems that tend towards the better aspects of our nature?" Nicholas attempts to calm Patrício's bubbling excitement.

In the background, Josepé's guitar begins its Sisyphean climb to the delightful melody echoing from the jug juice into his ears. Burning together, they bring his mind to light, and her voice from silence. The band soon hears the call of the Jam. And, lost in a trance of kykeon and Josepé's expertise, the chatter around the fire sputters out as they take the stage and find their marks, setting out in hunt of inspiration's elusive melody.

Stepping Into The Jam

Mystic Woods props his foot on the makeshift stage and rocks to the music. Prior to joining his crew, he offers the Stranger a nip from the brown-glass growler. "Wanna sip?"

"What's in it?"

"Some of my homebrew—a kykeon of muscadine wine, a pinch of *shrooms*, and a dash of herbs. This batch is delicious, and it might help you on your journey to remember who you are."

"Kykeon? Is it safe?"

"It won't kill you." Mystic Woods leans the nearly empty growler towards him. "But it might give you the bubble-guts."

"How will this help me?"

"Let's just say it'll cleanse the doors of your perception."

Curious, the Stranger takes several swigs. "How long until I feel it?"

"You'll know," Mystic Woods says with a smirk of rascality. "Hang out and enjoy the ride. Do you need anything before I herd these kittens along?" he asks.

"I'm all set here." The Stranger scoots into the rocking chair.

"Thanks for being patient with us, and for not being an axe murderer. I think Zach was taking bets from everyone—in good fun, of course."

"The night isn't over yet." The Stranger cuts his eyes.

Mystic Woods's laughter halts, and the Stranger smiles.

"Well played. You almost had me, sir... Damn, Josepé is gonna win the pool," he says, looking towards the band. "Sadly, the ferry will be here in the morning. But once we're back on Coffin Island, we'll make sure you get some proper help. You're our second fan, after all." He nudges him, then spins around, sparkling with the campfire's warm glow.

Mystic Woods steps onto the makeshift stage and, like a game of Double Dutch, jumps in with his electric keyboard. Together, these dream-weavers, hypnotized by the trance-harmony unfurling between them, perform riotous, mind-manifesting musical elucidations. Mesmerized, the Stranger rocks with the groove of the grove.

Following several musical steps and chord progressions, the group finds its flow and ventures into the imaginal. A somber piano climbs through intermittent scales. Chet clicks a pedal, layering an auto-tuned loop with the finesse of his percussion. Precise, collaborative swatches set the tone for the violin to weep into the evening's vibe, pulling the bass and the saxophone with it. Building into a stable revelry, they sail beyond the moonlit archipelago.

Musical Source

The Stranger tilts back a red plastic cup, gulping down a mouthful of water before taking a few puffs of a half-smoked joint. After stubbing out the roach, his shadow is the first sign he is no longer sitting.

(Is this what it's like to feel alive?) he wonders.

Absolved in the Jam, the musicians' connection with Source filters through melodic looms of instrumentation, climbing higher and higher until it crashes against the nearby shore. Rise, rise, rise—the music ascends to a climax.

The Stranger gawks in awe and, soon, feels his sense of self swaying to the Gypsy Jazz. Ever-present, the Oros system discharges a neurochemical pulse, dimming his prefrontal cortex. He spills over the mental boundaries of his body and gets into the swing of things.

Lost in the pocket of conceptual interpretation, the band mindgasms beyond the veil of their techné. They adjust to the rhapsody, leveling out their improv into a solid groove. Settling into a slower rhythm, their eyes part open—crazed and bewildered—as if they'd been gazing, unblinkingly, upon the face of the divine.

While the Stranger dances, his genuine delight slingshots back to the band, fueling their ensemble. Higher and higher, into the thick of it, their tempo builds as they cipher amongst the spheres of Pythagoras and the songs orchestrating the universe. Higher, higher, higher—the fidelity of the Stranger's experience chases syncopated rhythms with his hips.

23

Broken Strings

Bling-Blang

Josepé's guitar chords pluck apart, and Mystic Woods shifts keys, shepherding them towards a different corner of the melodic meadows. The band follows, flawlessly winding along the riffs of jazzy improv.

"Hold up. Lemme change these." Josepé says, then rushes to the equipment tent for a fresh set of strings.

"Wait. My bow is shredded." Nicholas trots after him.

Zach steps off the stage. "It's always with these two. No one else has to change their strings. Well, except for that one time Patrício was really getting it." Zach extends a fist bump.

However, Patrício is too busy thumbing a muted tune from the echo chambers of his thoughts. Unnoticed, Zach's gesture hangs in midair.

"Hey dumb-dumb, not everyone here plays stringed instruments, including yourself," Josepé says, coming back with a pink pack of Rhinehardt 80/20 Bronze Strings.

"No need for name-calling... Are you still upset about earlier?" Zach asks.

"All good." Josepé shoes him away.

"I know you. You're definitely pissed. And I'm the one who actually got hit." Zach turns to the cooler, mumbling something about strings. Before opening the ice chest, he checks for nearby raccoons. Relieved the critters are nowhere to be found, he retrieves a 22oz Pirate's Life from the cooler's depths, twists off the cap, and snags a bag of hot fries out of a nearby bin as he returns to the fireside.

432 Hertz

After packing away several cheekfuls and guzzling some ice-cold beer, Zach sits down next to the Stranger. He swizzles back another gullet's worth. "It's going to take them forever," he says, followed by a burp from the alchemy of carbonation brewing with the bolus of hot fries in his belly. "They think they're so clever. But can any of them plot the coordinates of a quasar, contemplate the geometry of infinity, or even navigate the dimensions of string theory?"

"Is that how you string an instrument?" the Stranger asks, freely associating amongst overstuffed mental drawers.

Zach merrily laughs at the blissful ignorance.

Josepé loosens one turnkey and snarls, "You fool, he can't remember who he is. What makes you think he cares about something you nerds talk about on your pirate-radio show?"

"Hush it, you sourpuss. It's called the *Digital Renaissance*. You should join one morning."

"Too early for me." Josepé says, then chugs more beer.

Zach picks up a branch and continues with some poignant philosophical vomit. "Here," he points to a divot in the dirt. "Did you know this is the fundamental pattern orchestrating the universe?"

"A hole in the ground is the fundamental pattern of existence?" the Stranger inquires.

"Not merely a hole, but the whole. This is a dot. And in this single point I can show you how to fit the universe—and much more."

The Stranger attempts to understand the poetry of Zach's explanation.

"See, physics isn't unified," he says, etching equations into the earth. "We have the *prickly* calculations of general relativity for the big stuff. And the *gooey* potentials of quantum mechanics for the small stuff."

"How's that a problem?" the Stranger asks.

"They tend not to agree, even though the big stuff is made of the small stuff. But you see here, it's all *gooey-prickles* and *prickly-goo*," Zach paraphrases Alan Watts. "Reality is not what we think it is—but part of something bigger."

"What else is there? How much more could there be?"

"At this level, it is a vacuum."

"Vacuum?"

"Not what you're thinking. Outer space is a vacuum filled with neutrinos, electromagnetic radiation, and cosmic rays."

Something familiar pivots to the tip of the Stranger's tongue, only to be drowned out by the *Space Force* opening theme song.

"See here," Zach says, swooshing his stick along the ground. "Reality emerges from this space... dots all the way up, turtles all the way down."

Under the campfire's flicker and several glowing strands of Christmas lights, the Stranger attentively stares at the dirt-drawn diagram.

Fueled by the brew in his belly and the smoke in his lungs, Zach navigates a delicate quilt of scientific concepts. "The structure of their theory is off—like music tuned to 440Hz instead of the natural harmony of 432Hz."

Josepé rolls his eyes. "Here we go again." He opens the pack of strings.

"Luckily, the truth doesn't depend on you believing it," Zach says.

Patrício belches. "Hey! Don't look at me. I'm a wordsmith."

"I'm a jack of all trades." Chet rattles off a series of rolling percussions.

"I'm a master of some." Josepé smiles with jovial sarcasm.

Mystic Woods flutters some aerial notes across weighted keys. "I'm waiting on y'all to get back to making music." He looks at his watch.

Patternicity

Zach dismisses the peanut gallery and etches more scribbles on the ground. "Mathematically, 432Hz is a pure tone that resonates with the natural harmonies. Hell, if you square it, you get the speed of light—within one percent. Anyway, in cymatics, the study of sound, researchers take sheets of metal topped with a loose layer of sand and vibrate the plate with sound. As they cycle through frequencies, the sand organizes into symmetrical geometric patterns. Can you guess what doesn't blast crisp, symmetrical shapes?"

"440Hz?" he asks hesitantly.

"Correct." Zach grins. "Most can't hear it, but the difference is there—"

"How's that possible?" He bubbles with inspiration and jug juice.

"Well... As Dr. Neil Haramein says, 'The most significant truths tend to hold the simplest solutions.' In our known universe, math is a constant lens for interpreting our reality. Everywhere we look: $1 + 1 = 2$." He draws in the dirt. "This simple equation represents a regularly occurring pattern found everywhere in nature—from our outlooks on galaxies and star formations to species evolutions and natural systems—a brilliant clue from the grand minstrel in the sky."

"Where does this pattern occur?" The Stranger unravels a yarn ball of understanding.

"Everywhere... Even cell division starts as 1, then doubles: 2, 4, 8, 16, 32, 64..."

The Stranger envisions a sweeping image from single cell to galactic scale.

"Now, the numbers aren't what matters most, but the pattern they unveil is what gives us insight into understanding the mysteries associated with the divine animating principle of existence!"

The Stranger, still puzzling over their jug-juice-inspired discussion, gazes up as the clouds clear to reveal the passing shadows of nocturnal hunters filling their bellies with a symphony of winged insects. The pleasantness of being rapt by the moment cracks open a hairline fissure within the cobbled ruins of his heart.

"Math has many applications," Zach says. "And hidden in torus geometry, there's another pattern which repeats itself." He illustrates numerical values around a stick-drawn circle. "Look here: 1, 2, 4, 8, 7, 5. Can you see what's missing from this sequence?"

(If I can solve this—if I can flex my mind enough—maybe another memory will surface.) He leans forward. "Where are 3, 6, and 9?"

"Exactly, my man." Zach thrusts a fist bump towards him. "You see, Nikola Tesla knew about this pattern and how it could help produce an abundance of energy for everyone to use. But that's why *they* denounced him. He was going to interfere with their profits. I mean, the man wirelessly lit the entire World's Fair up like a fucking Christmas tree. Anyway, this pattern runs both forward and backward—"

"Hold on. Where's zero?" the Stranger asks.

"At its center, of course." Zach grins and taps the dirt diagram. "Think of this circle as being polarized. On one side: 1, 2, and 4; on the other side: 8, 7, and 5." Zach traces the ground. "Now, how do we get from one side to the other?"

The Stranger stares at the drawings, and plasters their rubric onto the dilapidated chalkboards in his Mind Palace. (1 becomes 2; 2 plus itself equals 4; 4 becomes 8; and 8 turns into 16.) He connects the lines drawn to each number. "Wait, 16 doesn't fit the pattern."

"Correct. At this level of organization, there is no place for double digits, so we reduce it to a single integer. 1 plus 6 equals 7. Adding two 7s equals 14—"

"Which reduces to 5," the Stranger concludes, the corroded cogs of understanding churning. "What happens if you don't reduce it to a single digit?"

Zach traces a deeper trench between the numbers. "The pattern holds: 16 becomes 32, then 64, and so on."

"What happened to 3, 6, and 9?"

"Although they aren't visibly present, they provide the axis for this system." Zach takes another swig and admires the dirt diagram.

The Unseen Mover

The Stranger puzzles over the branch-drawn equations, tracing them on the worn chalkboards in his Mind-Palace, as Zach etches more equations:

3 + 3 = 6

6 + 6 = 12

"12 reduces back to 3—"

"And like a metronome," Zach explains, "the pendulum swings back and forth."

"Where's 9?"

"At the top of the key, opposite the center." Zach grins, enjoying the ease of their discussion. "Nowhere and everywhere, 9 anchors the axis of the system. And if we double it, it always reduces to 9." He flicks the sequence with his wooden rapier. "Hell, it even works when we halve it—turtles all the way down."

He taps the pointing stick back to the circle. "Let's say we have a magnetic bar. On the right side, 3 governs: 1, 2, and 4; on the other side, 6 directs: 8, 7, and 5. There's a stream between these two sides, swinging in an infinity loop." He gleams with sweat and the excitement from their jug-juice conversation. "9 controls the rest of the system."

"How does 432Hz play into all of this?" the Stranger redirects the conversation.

"This is where it gets fun. Capable of scaling, we find this recurring pattern from blood cells to black-w-holes. Think of the first number set—1, 2, 4, 8, 7, and 5—as describing the physical world, while 3, 6, and 9 regulate the physical realm at the quantum level."

"The big stuff and the small stuff," the Stranger mutters.

"Nikola Tesla definitely had his finger on the pulse. Just look at how much he developed by studying energy, frequency, and vibration—among other things. Alas, even our greatest heroes can see only so far to the horizon."

Josepé looks up from his guitar. "Don't get sad, bro. Tesla basically built our world. Think of him as the unseen force moving us into the future." He mystically waves his hand in the air.

"You're right."

Zach charges forward with his explanation. "Such a simple idea gives us a glimpse into how vibration and motion occur... Hell, with more agile minds, we might even tap into the energy potential of the vacuum and, one day, develop the technology to lead us beyond our primal approximations about the world."

The Stranger completes a volley of mental acrobatics and says, "432 reduces to 9."

"Bingo! The standard 440Hz reduces to 8, and simply does not align. On the other hand, 432Hz reduces perfectly to the orchestrating frequency of 9. Since we can find this consistent numerical pattern strung throughout nature, it seems reasonable to wish for the same attunement in our instruments." Zach finishes the hot fries, balls up the trash, and stuffs it into his pocket—where it slips out onto the ground next to his seat, and rolls into the shadows.

"Now, all of our instruments are tuned in accord," Mystic Woods says with an air of finality, glancing at his watch. "Josepé, Nicholas, are you about finished?"

Josepé sucks his teeth. "Almost there, boss."

"I've got to find my extra bow," Nicholas hollers from the equipment tent, searching through labeled bins. "Brought all of this stuff, but can't seem to find the one thing I need."

The Stranger scrutinizes over the scribbled equations. Back and forth, his eyes trace the ground, quickly sweeping for some correlation and a breadcrumb of recollection. "Is 9 the dot?" he asks.

"Close. It's all within the dot." Zach clears away some debris to expand his earthen chalkboard, then etches brackets around the circle of vortex math with an equal sign next to it.

24

Theory Of Everything

Geometry

The malfunctioning Oros system, sensing the metabolized jug juice, activates the TacOHUD's augmented-reality protocols. With enhanced focus, the ground emboldens as the Stranger scans the sandy lesson board, running his mental filter-feeders amongst the scribbles, and asks, "Is the circle the dot?"

"Yaaas." Zach dashes a smiley face into the dirt. "It took me months to get the fellas to understand. Do you remember geometry class? Err—I guess not." A belch erupts from his gullet. "I once had a teacher tell me, 'This is a dot, and it represents nothing—and also everything. This is dimension zero, and this doesn't exist.'"

"I'm a bit confused." The Stranger stares at the dot while the kykeon bubbles in his belly.

"So was I... Then, Mr. Cheeks placed three evenly spaced dots side by side to form a line." Zach pops three divots into the dirt and drags the stick through them. "Having only length, this first dimension didn't exist."

The Stranger stares at the dirt-drawn concepts. (How can a thing not exist?)

"Next, he combined four nonexistent lines to construct a plane and explained this was where our stories lived. But the realm of our adventures didn't exist here either."

"..."

"For his last example, Mr. Cheeks did something miraculous... He slapped six non-existent planes together to form a cube with depth and volume. Ta-da, the cube exists!"

"Hmm... The dot doesn't exist. The line doesn't exist. The plane doesn't exist. But somehow the cube exists? Doesn't it sound like 3, 6, and 9?"

"Bingo, on the button." Zach takes a nip from the deuce-deuce to quench his cottonmouth. "That's what I didn't understand. You see, the trouble arises from our current theories' inability to provide a complete picture of how the unimaginably small fits with the immeasurably large. As a result, scientists have generated over two hundred dimensions of mathematical reality to duct-tape the holes in their equations."

"Sounds like a mess."

Zach smiles and taps his stick against the ground. "I assure you, no one knows what's going on, and that's the beauty of it."

Inconceivable

The Stranger maneuvers closer to Zach's dirt-drawn examples. In the background, Patrício rips a wicked bass line as Mystic Woods's piano sings with Chet's timing. The unfurling Jam spurs Josepé to finish.

"After the third dimension of space," Zach continues, "we have the fourth dimension of time. Sandwiched, they create what we call spacetime. This is essential for knowing an object's position when plotting its place in the universe. At the border of the fourth dimension, we stretch the perceptual boundaries of what we can reason."

"Why can't we perceive the other dimensions?" He looks at Zach's sandy scribbles and tries to make sense of it all.

"For us, they're just beyond the veil—worlds unto themselves, compacted on a small scale."

The Stranger stresses the limits of his bandwidth.

"Potentially, our existence may reside on a three-dimensional submanifold corresponding to a brane where all known forces except gravity are restricted."

"This is a little difficult to follow."

"Exactly. All of it requires too much legwork," Zach scoffs. "It's useful for getting a bearing about the incalculable measure of existence, but doesn't answer the question: How does it all fit together? And can we reconcile the flaws in our current equations?"

The Stranger ponders for a moment, spiraling around an answer. But with no solution in sight, he stands and paces the length of their earthen chalkboard. Back and forth, he traces the illustrations with his hazel eyes until a moment of clarity strikes him. "Scrap their theories, start from first principles, build something new, then compare it to the old model."

"He totally gets it." Zach raises his hand to give an uncoordinated high-five. (Aim for the elbows.) An echo bounces from a passing Vision Shard.

The Stranger compensates with a crisp smack against his palm as the faint memory fades from an enchanted chest of the Donor's youth. In the distance, on a vacant hill, the last leaf on an autumn tree blows into the barren gray sky of his once-pristine Mind Palace.

Infinite Dimensions

Zach, buzzing with excitement, sparks a joint to cool the kykeon's elation and says, "This is only surface-level stuff; the rabbit hole deepens, and there're more and more turtles as you go. My friends at work—"

"They aren't your friends," Josepé growls, pulling a fresh wire along the bridge of his twelve-string. "Y'all have trauma bonded together."

"My colleagues," Zach clears his throat, "wanting to save their grants, limited any research into the matter, which had developed too many versions of string theory to maintain any valid continuity."

"Why couldn't they just start over?" the Stranger asks, repositioning himself in the chair.

"It would be a giant cream pie in the face for them. And had they not prevented a theoretical infinity-loop, they would've lost the funding to keep the lights on in their laboratories. They sacrificed science for their pensions. Thus, M-theory became their candle in the uncertain void of understanding spacetime and the veil of reality." Zach pauses, shuffling his sandal back and forth to erase part of his work.

Mystic Woods walks over. "Are you finished yet, Zach? Josepé and Nicholas are wrapping things up. And I know you'll be at it all night if I let you—"

"Hold on a damn second. I'm going to finish our conversation. I don't get to have them often. Start without me. I'll jump in after." He passes a lit joint to the Stranger.

"If he's bothering you, whack him with that stick," Josepé says as he steps onto the makeshift stage.

Zach cuts his eyes. "Anyway... my peers have merely placed a bandage on the problem." He leans in to take the joint back, taxing it with a complementary toke, before offering it to Mystic Woods. "I've been following the work of Dr. Neil Haramein, a rogue physicist who might've helped solve Einstein's field equations... even though he hasn't dropped the latest podcast episode. I'm sure he's been shoulder-deep in data from the Mauna Kea research station in Hawaii. It should be out when we get home. If the math checks out, we might discover a more ergonomic theory of everything."

"Theory of everything?" the Stranger asks. (Hawaii? Mauna Kea? Why does that sound familiar?) Salt-corroded cogs churn.

"You see, the problem arises when they attempt to understand the fundamental geometry of the universe by constructing hypothetical strings—"

"Like the lines in Mr. Cheeks's geometry class," he says.

Zach points to his previous sketches and asks, "Do they exist?"

"No." His focus locks in on their conversation.

"To hell with the lines. What about the damn dot?" Zach thwacks another divot into the ground. "All nature starts with the dot."

"The cell is a dot," the Stranger says.

"Yes. And it's composed of smaller dots called atoms. Which are composed of smaller dots... Despite their bumblings, they got something correct."

"What's that?"

"Like the dot, for us, the smallest measurable unit is the Planck. From this, we can construct a measurable cubic unit of Planck spacetime. And depending on how they vibrate, they might be seen as matter or energy. I'm standing on the shoulders of giants over here." He flexes his muscles.

(*Musica Universalis.*) "Thankfully, you have 3, 6, and 9," the Stranger says, pointing to the example.

"Are we cut from the same cloth?" Zach beams.

Black-w-hole

"Why is this important?" The Stranger burps from the metabolizing jug juice.

Zach explains, "Well... when we consider the study of black-w-holes, our calculations conclude with impossible outcomes."

"How so?"

"Singularities have the peak density for the maximum amount of matter possible in a tiny area. It's crucial that we have better geometric equations in order to predict conditions in such places and unlock the mysteries of these astral terrors."

The Stranger runs Zach's slurred descriptions across the soot-stained chalkboards of his Mind Palace. "What's your solution?"

"You see, big things are made of small things. But our lens for measuring them is off. Like with the different frequencies, it produces slightly skewed but noticeably different results. The solution is to reconcile infinity into the finite proportions of our theorems."

The fire crackles on the hymnals of the gang's tune-up session. In a mental game of chess, the time clock of conversational inquiry wavers. The Stranger strokes his chin and deliberates over the cosmic riddle etched into the dirt.

"Let me get this straight," the Stranger retraces the examples on worn mental chalkboards. "You're trying to plot an infinite amount of division in a finite space? How?"

"Think of the circle as the boundary of the dot." Zach points to the equal sign next to his bracketed diagram. "Inside, we can draw a triangle between 3, 6, and 9. Then, applying universal spin, we polarize a second triangle, forming another ancient symbol: the Star of David, the Star of Zion, the Seal of Solomon, or whatever one may call it—"

A Vision Shard gleams with Granny's star atop a freshly trimmed Christmas tree. (It's working!)

"—This creates new boundaries, mirroring the previous ones. Do you see these smaller triangles?" Zach asks, pointing at the two new shapes. "Each set has a different center, different from all other centers. Next, you polarize those—smaller and smaller—never exceeding the first boundary. Thus, we've embedded an infinite amount of division in a finite space. See, both the math and the geometry hold true."

"Out of this world!" the Stranger's mental stenographers record the scribbles in the dirt.

"If you follow the logic, you can see the potential for unlimited divisions within the dot. This could account for *all* the space in a single atom. We're made of atoms, ya know," Zach says, chuckling, followed by a celebratory swig of beer. "This is the name of the game—to figure out this mess." He smiles, with a budding sense of appreciation.

"What does this mean for physics?" the Stranger asks, looking up into the parting shadow of a passing cloud, and the starry-laid paths beyond.

"It means they can stop building particle accelerators, attempting to ignite a black-w-hole on the surface of the planet. Besides, it's a waste of funding." Zach shakes his fist in defiance. "There's no size limit to the *god particle*. It is infinitely small and will persist to be smaller than the eye can see, or our instruments can detect. It's a waste of potential, when we should press towards more useful ends."

"Like what?"

"Becoming a multi-planetary species... You see, there is no fundamental particle, but a fundamental pattern of existence. Understanding the divisions of the space producing our reality is a key to understanding creation and could unleash the potential of our species into the cosmos."

"Keep dreaming, Zach. No one believes your kooky theory. Name one person," Josepé jabs. "And not those freaks from your pirate-radio show."

"The *Digital Renaissance*," Zach parries.

At last, though still unable to locate his other bow, Nicholas finishes his repairs. "Wahoo! Let's get back to playing before my hands get too cold."

Overhead, a sparse curtain of clouds clears, drifting underneath the moon's visible sway, tracing the glitter of the night sky while a violin fills the sonic landscape with its fiddled reprieve.

Ignoring their attempts to spur him, Zach slaps his stick onto the ground, asking, "What connects all things in the universe—or around this campsite?"

The Stranger looks around, attempting to connect the dots. He closes his eyes, recreating the world from the world, and analyzes every piece of data at his disposal until a pattern emerges between the music, the meals, the laughter, the danger, the smoke, the fire, the canopy, the island, and the multitude of conversations he shared with the musicians. "It's space," he concludes.

"Correcto mundo!" Zach fist-pumps the air.

Mystic Woods's lyrics bellow over their discussion:

> If there is an infinite amount of division within the dot—
> the latent energy potential of the vacuum in a single drop—
> then you are more than an ocean of stars.

"This is how the universe is divided." Zach dashes lines into the sand, sketching a balloon with Xs on it. "The atomic structure is 99.999999% space. It defines matter—"

"Did you come here to theorize, or did you come here to knock on the sky?" Mystic Woods asks, trying to stop Zach from diving any deeper into his mad theorems.

"Damn, he's right. I could go on and on—gotta groove with the fellas. You understand, don't you?"

"Definitely."

"We've gotta get a better name for you. I can't continue calling you *The Stranger*. I'd prefer to call you friend." Zach reaches forwards and grabs hold of his forearm, in a mutual sign of respect.

"Go on," he says. "I need to take a leak—I've been holding it through that entire conversation—I'm about to piss myself."

As the boys take flight, the Stranger sprints into the maritime forest, led by the kykeon towards the roar of the shore.

Back In The Jam

An evening gust whips up the currents of late spring, and with them, sand blasts past the Stranger's bare leg. A crumpled, empty hot-fries bag zips from the campsite, following a crooked sandy trail out to the beach. Nearby, the ebbing ocean falls over itself, again and again, receding along the rocking archipelago.

"This is as good a spot as any," he says, positioning himself for relief. Once the faucet opens, drenching the dunes, he peers into the night sky and bathes under a sea of lumination. "Tomorrow we'll head back to civilization... Maybe I'll find someone to help me uncover the mystery of my identity," he says, swizzling spirals in the sand.

Meanwhile, on stage at the Palmetto Superdome, free from managing external concerns, Mystic Woods & the Loggerheads cross streams, fusing minds, tools and environments to articulate ineffable states and share in the bounty of oceanic consciousness. Turning inside out, they render a transcendental experience through instrumented synergy, rocketing closer towards the heavens, climbing higher and higher, into the realm of the mystics, and into the waters of the madmen, where dream becomes reality.

25

Twinkle, Twinkle

Paw-Paw's Youth

Highlighted by the moon's crescent saber, a muffled gust rides the ocean's perpetual crash along the shore. A chill prickles down the Stranger's spine. His senses open up, aided by the entheogens in Mystic Woods's brew and the miscalculated neurochemical cocktails from the Oros system. While a blossoming moment of beauty, poetry, and grace, absorbs him, one of the Donor's Vision Shards bubbles up from the cracked vaults of his Mind Palace.

See him as a boy, thirteen years old, steeped in the budding frustration of adolescence, hacking into his school's computer system and changing the grades of every student in the district. The facet shifts to him, surrounded by school admins, IT heads, his parents, and local law enforcement. Despite his sincere apology, the court orders him to attend the Academy at the beginning of the next semester.

The fragment retreats to Great-Grandma June's screened-in porch while she attempts to console him.

"You've got yourself into some fine mischief, messing with them computers." She sighs. "I guess it couldn't be avoided. You're too much like your Paw-Paw."

"How so?" he asks.

"When he was younger than you, he took apart the family radio. Bless his heart. Your great-granddaddy, Elbert, left a screwdriver lying around. When he came back into the living room to listen to his favorite program, he found that lil dumpling with all the parts spread evenly across the floor in a pattern—or whatnot."

Great-Grandma June sets aside her crocheting and reaches for a refreshing sip of tea. Afterward, she settles it on the center of a white lace doily. A single bead of sweat rolls down the glass, narrowly avoiding the end table's black-walnut finish.

"Elbert went to take off his belt, but saw the innocence in his baby boy's discovery—"

"Did he get a whoopin'?" he asks.

She continues, "Instead of punishing him, we tried our best to encourage him. He was too smart for his own good—and such a plump thing. I'll tell you, the two of them sat there all night, putting it back together." Her eyes sparkle as she remembers the softness and the smell of her son. The baby of the family, he was the youngest of all the brothers and sisters who lived in the farmhouse on the hill.

"What happened?"

"Well... when he was twelve, he figured out how to order an old, decommissioned military helicopter. Poor Elbert... Bless his heart... Luckily, they got it working in three months. We sold it and used the money to help pay the bank. Such an angel."

She sips more of her drink, then sets it down. The ice cubes clank and swirl amongst her half-filled glass. "Ahhh... that's some good sweet tea right there... Now don't go thinking that whirlybird was the last of his mischief." She looks over her glasses, picking up her crocheting. "Years later, at the county fair, he built a whatchamacallit... a Tesla coil!"

"Really?"

"He sure did. It scared the Jesus out of some folks—and into a few others," she says, rocking in her chair as the sun sets into the coziness of the evening. "His little inventions often got him into trouble. Eventually, somehow-or-another, word got up to Washington... And one day, they came parading up to the house—fancy stars and all—to give your Paw-Paw a full scholarship to the Academy."

"He went there too?"

"Don't worry, my child. Think of it less like a punishment, and more like a place to nurture your talents." Great-Grandma June has another sip of her sweet tea as the Vision Shard flickers to a near-adjacent background.

New Telescope

Stage left, the scene shifts to a starlit field near the family's hillside farm. Years later, beneath the cowl of night, he and Paw-Paw march towards discovery, transporting a catawampus contraption.

"Don't drop it, boy," he orders.

The lad struggles to keep hold of the telescope, balancing it atop a little red wagon, as Paw-Paw leads them to a small hillside just past his workshop.

"Hold up, let's set it down so you can get a better grip on things." Paw-Paw smiles to mask his impatience. "Look. Hold it like this." He scuttles to one side, pointing to a hidden handle he made for his grandson. "There you go... Now, let's get moving. We're burning moonlight."

"Paw-Paw, why are we in such a rush?"

"If my calculations are correct, we are in for quite a show—best in the county," he says. "Fortunately, this new onboard computer system can calibrate a better view of the heavens."

"How does it work?" He touches its bulky casing.

"Starlight shines onto the reflective surfaces of a hexagonal array, where conversion metrics process multispectral overlays to render a high-fidelity image on the device's display. I even cooked up an on-demand archive to back up all recordings and maintain an up-to-date log of recent search queries for later use."

He yawns.

"I know it's late, but you'll be fine with all that sugar in Granny's lemonade... almost as sweet as her kisses. And, boy-oh-boy, those kisses are still sweet after all these years." Paw-Paw reminisces about the life and adventures he shared with his love.

Another yawn.

"Let's set up here," he says, scouting the surrounding hillside before they lift the device out of the wagon.

Tightening the last components of his custom-built telescope, Paw-Paw notices a tiny grease-smeared handprint on the device. "See here, boy? You got it all dirty... Hand me a rag to wipe this secondary mirror... We need this thing shining to reduce any inaccuracies. This is gonna be a big one. The sky should light up like the Fourth of July."

"Will the comet crash into the planet?" he asks with fearful innocence.

"It's not likely. Well, at least for another 300 years, give or take. Hell, this thing's been coming through our neck of the woods for quite some time now."

"You said the 'H' word," he reminds his elder.

"Hush-it. You're not gonna squeal on me. Are you, boy?" he asks, tightening the kindness in his gravelly drawl, stepping towards his grandson.

"No, sir. Secret's safe with me," he says and takes a step back from Paw-Paw's immense presence.

A playful smile stretches across his granddaddy's face. "It's alright. I was just joshing ya. You need to toughen up! Don't worry, I won't tell your momma about your secret stash of candy, either... Anyway, don't think that the Perseids are the only show in town. They're one of many debris fields left by comets originating in the distant Oort Cloud—extending nearly halfway to the next star. However, the vast majority of 'em never visit the inner solar system," Paw-Paw spirals off, staring into space.

"I'm tired," he whinges.

"Drink some more lemonade. Trust me, boy. We're in for a spectacular attraction. And it's best viewed under the predawn night."

"How, Paw-Paw?" He picks up his *Space Force* cup and enjoys some of Granny's goodness.

"As the Earth rotates, the side facing the direction of its orbit around the Sun scoops up more space rubble. This part of the sky is directly overhead at dawn. It's why we're here." He triumphantly boots up the onboard display. "Let's take a gander at what we've got in our crosshairs."

A vivid image renders on screen. The first star comes into sight, peeking behind patches of invisible clouds.

"'Star light, star bright, the first star I see tonight; I wish I may, I wish I might, have the wish I wish tonight,'" he recites from the springtime of youth.

The two rascals share in the bittersweet overture of Granny's fresh-squeezed lemonade. In the distance, the closest city struggles to interrupt the glow of the blooming moon with its orange light pollution. As clouds part, the wake of their clarity unveils a display of stars and other celestial bodies.

Starlit Discussions

He reaches into a zippered pocket of his official *Space Force II* exploration satchel and retrieves his Fleet Commander Star Chart—the essential tool for any courageous interstellar adventurer. No markings on the heavens, but with his trusty map, he quickly locates his favorite constellations in the August sky: Cassiopeia, Perseus, and Andromeda. He cranes his neck skyward and connects stellar dots with relative ease, identifying several lesser-known constellations and roving astral objects. "I hope Adastria is out there—I know it's out there, fighting for the future of all galaxies," he champions with innocent childhood conviction. "Momma says, 'In an infinite universe, anything is possible.'"

From their vantage point, amidst the abyss of seemingly endless space, a sea of stars presses against the atmosphere's curved dome. Beyond its veil, suspended within the womb of creation, countless stellar formations hide amongst the forest of the night. These ancient artifacts wisp throughout an immeasurable backdrop, past where the eye—and the scaffolding of its technological lensing—can see.

"Paw-Paw?"

"Yes, boy?" His strong, wrinkly face turns to see the reflection of wonder in his grandson's starlit optics.

"Why do stars twinkle?" he asks.

"Well... they're shining from very far, far away," Paw-Paw says.

"Is it close to Adastria?" he asks.

"I don't know if we've discovered the home galaxy of *Space Force* yet... Probably looking in the wrong place," Paw-Paw suggests. "Now, with this telescope, I'm certain we'll find it one day." He slaps his hand on top of the device, then fidgets with a few switches. "As for 'why they twinkle'... air turbulence in the upper atmosphere redirects the light and makes it appear to do so. It's all a matter of perspective—how we look at things in relation to where we are."

"I don't get it," he says.

"It's like that ole puzzle cube by my chair. When you look at it, you only see a certain number of sides; the others are inferred. It's the same thing with stars as well. We don't see them clearly, only by how they twinkle. Even with deep-space telescopes, there're too many cosmic externalities to consider, so we have to tap into different parts of the electromagnetic spectrum to peer into the past."

As he listens to Paw-Paw, the night sky dazzles across his eyes. "I wanna be just like you when I grow up."

"Save yourself some trouble," he says with a grin, tickling his grandson.

He flails about, kicking the telescope.

"Boy! Tighten up! See here, you almost broke this." Paw-Paw points to the tripod and adjusts its legs into position, locking it in place. "Are you settled?"

He nods.

"Here, let's aim the telescope over yonder and make sure there aren't any *more* greasy handprints on the mirrors," Paw-Paw teases, typing out a few key commands to bring the system online.

The device pivots its lens towards a jumbled patch of stars. Then, twisting several small dials, all the celestial wonder that can fit within the eye snaps into focus.

Paw-Paw grins with satisfaction. "Now, give her a look-see."

His hazel eyes peer excitedly at the LED screen, then through the convex lens for an exact sense of observation.

Starfall

A pleasant breeze sends beads of condensation down their cups of lemonade. In the distance, tiny raindrops of light fall upon the windshield of night. Where words and telescopes fail to arrest the moment, the spears of Hephaestus begin their descent from the heavens, rendering the foothills aglow with splendor.

"Wanna know another fun-filled fact about that-there starlight?"

"Yes, sir."

"The observable light we see comes from way-way-way-out in space—so innumerable, we could never see the end of them." Paw-Paw points to the living tapestry. "Some of those stars have long-since burned out, leaving their light behind... And somehow, it reaches all the way here, to the hillside, and into the retinas of our eyes."

"Wow... really?" he asks with a glint of awe, attempting to understand, as he watches a parade of shooting stars disappear behind his grandfather's head.

"Yessiree, Bob! Still, that's not the kicker, boy," he says.

"What do you mean?"

"The atoms making up our eyes were forged in the furnaces of those dying stars, with some at the beginning of the universe during the Big Bang. So when we look up at the night sky, we're really looking back at ourselves—the way we were... once upon a time."

Despite his best efforts to take it all in, his young mind bursts beyond the boundaries of imagination.

"Light is made of photons," Paw-Paw continues. "Those photons are moving at the speed of light and have no experience of Time as we know it. From the onset of the universe to when they collided with the your eyes, it's all the same Time. Sprinkle a little cosmic-dust into the mix, and twinkle-twinkle."

He stares in awe of his grandfather as the lesson continues into the distant reaches of pulsars, quasars, neon nebulae, and spiral-galaxy formation, diving into the wisdom which comes from two different generations contemplating the stars. Soon, the night bows to the day, spilling over in a soft outro, akin to waves washing away or popcorn popping—less and less.

Dreamer's Dream

The Vision Shard's crescent lining wanes into the Void of Subconsciousness. The Stranger finishes swizzling onto the dune, sits down on a boulder, and ponders over the luminescent breadcrumbs he's gathered, attempting to uncover his identity and his purpose in this world.

"Momma, Daddy, Granny, Paw-Paw, Great-Grandma June, Tucker, and Bennet... I hope I can see y'all soon." His thoughts stop, halted by the angst of not knowing more.

However, the drone of the shore soon soothes him, granting the reprieve to recollect each memory with the utmost clarity.

"Academy?" He chews on the idea, yearning to recall an account of what happened after he left his home in the foothills. Nothing. He strains to string together the fragmented memories but becomes distracted by a curious ghost crab scuttling across his foot as it returns to its burrow.

He yawns and stretches his arms above his head. With watery eyes, he notices a few more crabs darting from the dunes. Back and forth, the TacOHUD traces their movements in the darkness. Behind him, within the palmetto grove, the band launches into a melodic progression, culminating in the epic *Ballad of Dragon Fire*. He bobs his head to the beat, eyes closed, surrendering to the rhythm. As he vibes with the groove, the ocean pulls him into the depths of a drunken lullaby.

Moments later, the Stranger passes out on an algae-covered rock. Despite his bedding, he sinks into a deep slumber. A bubble of jug juice sets off neurochemical flatulence, and the malfunctioning Oros system activates its reality distortion field.

Sub-dermal nanite swarms secrete a proprietary sebum of microscopic chitin to alter his electromagnetic profile, bending light and blocking infrared, ultraviolet, and thermal detection. Cloaked in a quilt of near-invisibility, he is but a wallflower at a middle-school dance—unnoticed, a face lost in the crowd, a drop in an ocean, a speck of sand on a vast beach, a fleck of cosmic dust floating amidst an innumerable sea of stars. All around, the crashing shore steeps the Stranger farther into the fractured depths of an abysmal dream—the nightmare of the other.

26

Axis Mundi

Deathly Wastelands

While the kykeon whisks the Stranger beyond the Dionysian mysteries, Zeff trudges through his digital prison. Beneath the Nether Regions of Thought, a battered door rests ajar. And from its threshold, the Fog of Despair unfurls from the Catacombs onto the Wastelands of Cognition.

His white linen coattails flap behind him as he swiftly crosses mountainous sand dunes, covering the scattered keys of Remington SL3 typewriters. On the other side, a brightly colored, nine-story *Space Force* cup looms against the static gray skyline. Littered with perilous proximity triggers, explosive angst, the dilapidated ruins of personal idols, and jagged echo chambers of misbelief, Zeff glares at the reminders of his cloned existence.

Sadly, no closer to the Control Tower, he presses towards the cradle of hope in the flickering apathy of desolation.

"Who am I? Who are you?" a lost Worry Wraith screeches, fleeing from the Fog of Despair.

A few meters behind him, its glowing eyes appear as a thicket of haze seeps around the artifact's base. Next, the Childe-within materializes out of the approaching gloom and steps around the collectible cup.

"Kid? Are you alright? Let's get out of here," Zeff says.

He moves forward, and Childe darts back into a tendril of fog, disappearing into the surrounding mist. Zeff turns to chase after him.

All at once, his hazel eyes meet the Imp-oster's burnt-sulfur stare, illuminating the dull grime of a grotesque smile. It raises its claw, and the gloom rolls over its skin like the sleeve of a kimono. Zeff freezes with dread. The creature's nostrils flare, and moments later it vanishes in the haze.

Before the [Slash Attack] successfully connects, a blurred prism of light passes between them. An ornate doorway opens from the trail of pixelated stardust, unleashing a vortex that yanks him in as the Imp-oster's claw whiffs through the Fog.

"Interesting," the Imp-oster says, sniffing the ripped ribbons of linen dangling from one of its hardened talons. "Let's have a taste." It chews on the strands like jerky. Resultantly, a twinge of radiance shines from its oversized eyes, then dulls to their usual mustard stain. "Come on. Let's grab a snack."

While the Fog stretches towards the Ruined City atop the stump of the last Elder Tree, the malicious duo fades into the enveloping gloom and returns to the Imp's lair.

Transfer

Through the threshold, past a few paint splatters of experience, Zeff falls into a colorless corridor of Memory Crystals leading to the Akashic depths of the Archives. The service tunnel forks before he can correct his course. He hits a wall and bounces into the left offshoot, fumbling into fragmented Vision Shards—impossible elucidations, more NatGeo than random free association.

One ineffable experience after another, he finally lands inside the dilapidated walls of Dreamwind Studios' Screening Room. The chamber flickers to life, filling his mental bandwidth with a vivid tapestry of evolutionary consumption, where creature begot creature and the prophetic blossomed from the profane. No mud, no lotus.

Nibiru

Near the howling boundaries of imagination, an immense interstellar object effortlessly emerges from the vacuum of spacetime. The dark messenger sails for an incalculable duration amongst the punctuated void of a celestial star-rich backdrop before reaching the first inklings of the Oort Cloud. Several trillion icy objects float on a sea of no-thing-ness and dance to the synaptic whims of the Milky Way. Here, along the fringes of our solar system, the last waves of gravity form a stellar nursery for the comets and omens of our ancestors—hinting at a time prior to life coalescing on our minute marble, orbiting in star-spangled oblivion.

A primordial trajectory compels this sunless traveler beyond icy cosmic sand-spurs with relative ease. In its wombling wake, microtubules thread through proto-planetary debris and scatter cometary nuclei out of their orbits, rushing headlong towards parts unknown. On the other side of the Oort Cloud's frigid hospitality, a point of resplendence blazes brighter than the innumerable clusters painted upon the ethos of creation.

It is not the engorged deity of our *rise-and-grinds*, far-flung onto the background of seemingly endless bright-blue skies, but the simple flicker of roving lamps on lighthouse-lit shores. Circling our star, several spheres waltz amidst the vast no-thing-ness of everything. Unaware, these planets dance to the dark traveler's arrival—and the seeds that have yet been sown.

Among those heavenly bodies, an ark rich with the full flourishing of life. Fragile, living, breathing—a blue spaceship traversing the infinite—the place we call home. As our sapphire marble spins, enjoying the promenade of the inner planets, the Sun lashes out with flaring cosmic winds, igniting the surface of invisible fields and blanketing the Earth with an iridescent glow.

Asteroid Belt

The Screening Room drips to 160 million years ago. An adagio of debris flows within the delicate gravitational tango between Jupiter and the Sun. Round and round they go, like *Ring Around the Rosie*, until wave fluctuations from the passing darkness select one of the giant asteroids in a graceful game of *Duck, Duck, Goose*. It crashes into an adjacent sibling, launching it off course.

Meanwhile, on our lush planet of conifers and creatures, life flourishes for millions of years—a primal and savage place teeming with great beasts stalking the oceans and jungles. Aside from unimaginable monsters of nightmarish proportions, thunderous herbivores graze on treetops, shaking the distance with each footfall as they pivot to greener pastures. A tyrannical Allosaurus roars in the distance, echoing on the evening winds.

Zeff blinks, and a time-lapse evolution reshapes life on the surface of the Earth. The topography morphs into seemingly malleable expressions of existence. From there, nestled in the neurotic security of their burrows, a few of our tiny mammalian ancestors peek out with innocent eyes at a more glorious dawn, waiting beyond the fertile grounds of their base cognition.

GM Extinction

His perception slows to a crawl and focuses the lens of its director's cut on a scene 66 million years ago. In one of the world's oldest trees, grown together for over hundreds of thousands of years, our ancient ancestral being stares at the sky. Just behind the blue veil, the atmosphere cracks open, and a sudden reckoning thunders throughout the land.

As if a stone were dropped into a pond, the impactor strikes the shallow waters of the Yucatan Peninsula with the force of 100 million atomic bombs, cleaving a 160-km-wide scar in its wake. In less than a second, dense crystalline rock liquefies as the stone splashes through the crust, tectonic plates, lush environments, and thunderous lizards who ruled with eminent domain. All life within 5,000 km radius is abruptly buried under the debris field. Hundred-meter waves surge from the point of impact while clouds of superheated dust, ash, and steam shoot into the air.

What goes up must come down. Rubble launched high into the atmosphere ignites, blazing incandescent during reentry. Like Roman candles volleying across the sky, they spark wildfires, broiling the Earth's surface. Simultaneously, an onslaught of electromagnetic radiation douses the planet, while colossal shock waves trigger global earthquakes and volcanic eruptions. Worldwide, severe climate change suddenly causes the extinction of 75% of all flora and fauna, pruning back the tree of life and resetting the stage.

A Rose Of Destruction

A season of harvest interrupted by a seed sown with the invisible hand of the cosmic experience. Unimaginable creatures fill the distant skyline. Alone, frozen with fear, at the top of an ancient arbor, our primeval ancestor stares out into the winds of a blossoming rose, whose birth shook the horizon. With a limited mind, unable to comprehend all that would come, it watches the sky turn a color it had never experienced. All the while, fire ants gnaw at its flesh, creating an itch it cannot scratch.

Their toxins singe its skin as a cool breeze wraps around its face, carrying the petals of a flower already wilting. The weight of this moment renders the burning bites no-thing-less and no-thing-more—merely part of a significant whole—our ancestor beholds the face of the divine.

Witness

In the dilapidated Screening Room, Zeff struggles to break free but remains motionless, spectating over the passage of time. With the Earth's environment blanketed by dust and particles, the thunderous lords of old are no more. However, within that iridium asteroid, intergalactic immigrants—amino acids, minerals, hitchhiking tardigrades, and spores—are scattered across the Earth. Once the powder of extinction settles, fungal networks spread, repairing the damaged ecosystem and adapting to the evolving climate.

Among the limited survivors, our progenitors—tiny, fearful and outclassed—stand at the emergence of a new beginning, an inkling of light in the bleak aftermath of disaster. A moment where our true nature expresses itself. Adapting and overcoming, our lineage sprints towards the top of the evolutionary food chain—despite the challenges of prehistoric survival—to stand tall as the new caretakers of this world.

27

Killer Instinct

Ashes Of Creation

The Vision Shard splinters into strobing segments, liquefying into luminous voids of fading light, shifting the Screening Room to a primeval jungle. This is where the bones gather after the creatures have died. The safety of the canopy gives way to a set of emerging plains, compelling our ancient ancestors—a treetop-dwelling species—to experiment with alternative food sources and adapt to the changing ecosystem at the gunpoint of survival.

Zeff watches them creep from the canopy onto novel landscapes, coming in contact with an alien world and a new set of challenges. No matter how much territory they controlled, fruit they gorged on, or young they reared, they could not halt the sweeping tides of time. All who fail to hear *her* silent strings weaving into a dizzying jazz are forgotten within the unwritten pages of history.

Adapt & Overcome

Driven by primal thirst, a young mammal carefully inches closer to the water's edge. Silent eyes watch from beneath the surface. Cloaked in stillness, a monstrous reptile moves into striking position.

A scuttling wind rustles through head-high grasses. The sun tucks behind a cloud's reprieve, shifting the shadows throughout the landscape. A short distance away, its mother grooms her other offspring under the canopy's sparse shade.

The young mammal reaches for a drink, its eyes darting from side to side before lapping up a mouthful. Cool droplets twinkle into its watery reflection. It anxiously scans the bank, then takes another drink. The dangers of the jungle pale in comparison to the nightmares of the plains.

Savage Lands

Snap! The jaws of the immense beast clamp around the small mammal's brittle neck. Silently sinking below, the reptilian creature gulps down its dinner into the rotting chambers of its stomach.

High overhead, the sun peeks past pillowy clouds, followed by the Far Moon. A cry from the young mammal's mother, noticing one of her little ones is absent from their afternoon cleaning, echoes into the primordial savannah. She searches but finds no trace of her offspring. Soon, her attention returns to the rest of her brood as the troop moves towards the evening shelter of a shady grove.

28

Mother's Way

Lucy

The Screening Room's immersive floor-to-ceiling displays transition once again, and the drying atmosphere pulls with it the covers of humidity and the saturation of long-forgotten jungles. As the surface area of our ancestors' territory shrinks due to conflict and the abrasive changes within their ecosystem, a tense, vigilant fog of alertness drapes across the early grasslands of the now-roving deserts of Africa.

Zeff's limited bandwidth centers on one of our ancient female ancestors, Lucy, foraging for food a short distance from the receding tree line, where other members of her group remain on the lookout. Quickly scanning left, right, and left again, she nimbly gathers anything that seems nourishing. The law of the land—as it remains today—is persistent, rapid adaptation, or starvation. The first to the dinner plate wins, and our species is late to the buffet line.

Prehistoric Eden

Though there are none to rival the tyrannical lords of old, the monsters of the primal abyss are no less savage. Lucy forages for beetles around steaming-hot piles of crude-chewed grass. The ground rumbles from a passing herd of titans in the distance. She freezes and focuses all her senses on her surroundings.

Suddenly, a panicked, shrill cry screams across the grasslands, followed by a wind-blown silence. Another unfortunate creature falls into the folly of its limited awareness and becomes the entrée of silent hunters, stalking the emerging savannas.

Among other prehistoric nightmares, saber-toothed beasts are among the new gardeners of this Eden. But with their bellies filled by a fresh kill, the air carries with it a sense of calmness. At once, although briefly, everything seems in order.

Mycelial Discoveries

Lucy returns to her search, sorting and shifting along her haunches in the head-high grass. Smack in the middle of a half-baked mud pie, she unwittingly stumbles upon a type of mushroom capable of altering the state of any fool who would dance with them. Our ancestor's agile hands nimbly pluck them from a crusted patty. Sniffing them, she detects the earthy bouquet of dirt and dung.

She glances left, then right—her head on a vigilant swivel—as she keeps eye contact with the lookouts in her group. Lucy is not alone in her endeavors; other members forage nearby. Unbeknownst to them, their humble efforts secure the survival of countless generations within the unfamiliar landscapes of destiny.

She sniffs three more peculiar fungi. *Chick-chick-chick-chick.* A huge beetle ventures out of its dung-laden bedroom. Her dexterous fingers grasp the creature just before it escapes into cover.

The prehistoric insect's legs run on an invisible, midair conveyor belt. She bites it in half, and creamy goop bursts from its crunchy shell. Several hurried mouthfuls later, the beetle-bolus slides down her throat, catalyzing digestive processes. The next stop is in the bowels of this southern ape's belly, where, hours later, it becomes part of the land from which it recently slumbered.

Digestion

She stares at the six fungi in her hand. Something shuffles in the nearby grass. Her heart quickens, ready to flee to the safety of her peers. To her relief, a large prehistoric rodent—resembling a capybara—waddles out and sniffs the air. Paying little attention, it shuffles back to its den.

Lucy discards the filthier mushrooms and pops the two remaining caps into her mouth. The raw freshness squishes and oozes about as she chews them. Having not vomited or keeled over, she gathers more, then makes her way back towards the safety of the group.

Halfway there, a strange sensation sloshes about her stomach. She yawns, and her eyes water. Every follicle on her hide becomes sensitive and alive. At once, the world sharpens with vivid hues and diamonds strewn across a blue plane.

Homecoming

Safely returning home, she finds her mate. They embrace, knocking their heads together, sniffing each other, and checking for parasites or injuries. Their rambunctious offspring climb onto their mother's unwavering back. At first, they play about, rolling across the ground, but soon find their curious noses leading them in search of her latest find. The four of them nibble the mysterious fungi before her mate commutes to find more food with the rest of the family group.

The rugrats play on top of their resting mother. And after several minutes of exhausting antics, the two younglings cuddle up. In time, her eyes focus on the way the light filters between the breeze-blown canopy.

A dopaminergic trickle draws her attention to the shadows dancing along the ground. She stares at the drooling waves of transcendental beauty and sighs. While the rest snooze, her mind bubbles, transfixed by the sublime, ineffable reality of a world that escapes understanding.

29

The Stoned Ape

Leo

Atop the gnarled stump of the last Elder Tree, buried amongst the fallen spires of the Ruined City, trapped within Dreamwind Studios—further, still farther—the lens of Zeff's perception traverses multiple generations of our ancestry. In this strange reality, a time-lapse of emerging grasslands unfolds under distant storm clouds. The luminous Near Moon peeks past their wake as the crescent shadow of the Far Moon looms close.

The Screening Room's POV shifts the vectors of his attention onto a frantic figure, separated while tracking the scat droppings of herbivores and close to starvation. Our distant ancestor, Leo, recognizes several crusted mounds of dung adorned with fungal bouquets. He checks his surroundings before a ravenous hunger incites him to consume nearly twenty grams of sustenance, unknowingly eating his way towards a higher consciousness.

A rustling in the high grass and the smell of death on the wind alert Leo to a nearby predator. With hurried stealth, he outmaneuvers the keen senses of a most voracious saber-toothed beast. Heart pumping, breath gasping, a flood of neurochemicals courses throughout his body as he approaches the edge of an ancient forest and clambers into the canopy.

Below, the Tyger's burning eyes scan the brush, unaware its quarry has leaped from one tree to another. It sniffs the ground and paws at a limb with broken branches. Then, the enormous hunter lifts its head, sensing the possibility of other prey, snorts, and sets off—pacing back to the top of the food chain.

Leo cowers in the shadows of ageless arbors and listens to the trailing snarls of the hulking beast. Instinct compels him away from the certainty that stalks beneath the branches. As he climbs into the emergent layer, where treetops watch over the jungle's diminishing acreage, bacteria in the bowels of his belly initiate him into the mystery of experience. Higher and higher, mycelial networks reroute fear-trauma responses, and soon his senses blend into a synesthetic cocktail of stupefied amazement.

The Hero's Dose

Time appears to pass without its usual alacrity as Leo reaches above the canopy. Along the thunderous horizon, boiling black clouds embroider the fringes of summer storms. Lightning pops the firmament, radiating outward and rendering a fractal web onto the tapestry of the earth kissing the sky.

He clings to the tree as a palpable richness populates his primitive mind with roving waves of multidimensional geometric patterns. There, attached to the trunk, positioned between predatory fear and the lightning strike of mortality, our distant ancestor connects with the universe.

The frail thread of his existence sways amongst the arcs of lightning braiding across the sky. Inadequate to do anything about the ionic crackle of the atmosphere and the stalking beast below, Leo perches upon the razor's edge. All at once, the adrenaline rush of mortality washes in the rain, leaving him with enough semi-phenomenal, near-cosmic omnipotence to will away the dread binding him motionless to the tree.

Once the grumbling storm crosses the drying savannahs, its thunderous roars subside into the distance. He finally hears the hunting party's call. And with eyes emboldened by the entheogenic experience, Leo overcomes the fear-filled moment with a renewed sense of courage. His hold loosens around the arbor as he descends into the canopy—back to the world below.

Higher Mind

While the prowling Tyger ruffles the flora of the jungle floor, the hunting party cries out again. Enticed by their commotion, it turns and sprints towards them. Heart quickening, Leo races atop buoyant branches—length after length—reaching for the next limb or vine as he speeds through the canopy.

Blinded by feral hunger, salivating with the desperate necessity for its next meal, the great beast lunges over logs and past bushes, crossing gullies and streams with incomprehensible agility. Above, Leo continues to override self-preservation protocols, charting a path within the vine-laden darkness. Branch after branch, his heart pummels the inside of his chest with a breath-gasping sense of urgency. Around the next hurdle, a cocktail of potent neurotransmitters pulses into circulation, accelerating him closer to his tribe.

The richness of the ancient jungle comes alive as he swings with an effortless rhythm. Selflessly lunging forward, each swooping limb passes by in a timeless way. Soon, several well-executed maneuvers send him an increasing distance in front of the Tyger's stride.

At the tree line, the hunting party calls out to their lost member. Leo vaults closer to them as its excitement shifts into the final stretch. Weaving over and under outcroppings of megaflora, he arrives ahead of the giant *Smilodon* and rallies the troop back into the trees. Above, in the safety of swaying branches, they watch the primordial Tyger sniff the settling dust of a missed meal.

Its ears twitch in separate directions as it tracks adjacent movements in the dense foliage. Back and forth, the beast's awful eyes search the canopy. Three birdlike creatures fly from their nest. The Tyger paws at the conifer's trunk. However, its prehistoric mass brings it back to the ground, shredding down the outer bark. After regaining its footing and marking the tree, a persistent hunger sends the hunter back to the forest's edge, onto the savanna, stalking on the silent winds.

They remain silent. And after several moments of stillness, the troop ventures home. Behind them, among the shadow-striped grass, a creature's dying scream succumbs to the twilight descending across the land.

Ashen Jewel

Unable to turn away, Zeff continues to witness the long process of history. Before him, an enhanced and deepening interspecies codependency plays out, occurring millions and millions of times, over millions and millions of years. Ancestral lineages flow into an intersectional collection of braided streams, forming the delta of today—pulling themselves from the animal mind into a world of language, art, music, math, technology, and imagination.

He bears witness to the first renaissance of cognitive evolution and the full flourishing it promised with an almost alien certainty. A carousel of cataclysms parades its cabaret of extinction-level events as his lens of perception fractures into a kaleidoscope of Vision Shards, revealing a room of apes banging on Remington SL3 typewriters—hallucinating language, space shuttles, and smartphones into existence.

The film credits roll.

"I can move! What the fuck is going on? Nothing is right in this place... At least I'm away from that thing in the fog." Zeff pauses, looking down to see the claw marks left from his encounter with the Imp-oster. "When did it touch me? I need to be more careful... I don't want to find out what happens if I die here."

The Screening Room's six sides fade to a titanium white, then run from their reels. Like a stream pooling into a basin, they flow just in front of Zeff. The puddle thickens and reflects the gray sky filtering through the visible cracks in the room's once-elegant cornice. At once, the rippling pool congeals into a light-gray jewel, its purple sutures glowing softly.

In response, the [Trifold Tablet] summons the gem closer. Zeff takes a step back. It follows and shrinks from the size of a football to that of a chicken nugget. The tablet shines brighter, despite its splintered facade, highlighting an interlocutor port on the top-right corner. Zeff reaches for it and receives a slight shock of violet static discharge, pulling the [Ashen Jewel] to his fingertips.

Like a toddler placing square pegs into round holes, he presses it into the designated port. A snap secures the artifact's placement, and a purple light traces the tablet's circuitry before disappearing beneath its repaired surface.

"Can I access the build menu?" He swipes past a series of window options with relative ease.

[Signal: Weak.] The command console flashes, failing to connect with the Control Tower.

"Useless," he says, scrolling back to the directory.

He selects the build menu, then the [Deconstructor Beam] to create an exit, but only produces another landslide of rubble to block his way. With just a few rays of dull light to illuminate the darkened room, he tries again and opens a large enough gap to locate the Control Tower rising from the center of the Ruined City.

"So close. Damn it—I need to get out of here," he says, looking at the [Trifold Tablet] in hopes of another option.

Not until the weight of hopelessness is upon him does Zeff notice the mist creeping from the cracks. He folds the device back into his coat pocket. The despair turns to hostility once Zeff's primal instincts kick in. Backed into a corner, he pries a long piece of metal from a mangled scaffold and watches the Fog fill one side of the dilapidated Screening Room.

(I'm no match for this thing... I need an exit.) His grip tightens around the bent metal staff.

Having finally located Zeff's construct, a pixelated rainbow flashes into the room, summoning another doorway. The blazing swath of color drives the mist back into the fissures from which it sprang. Eager to be on his way, Zeff hustles through the threshold.

To his dismay, on the other side, a vast wilderness sprawls in front of him.

"No! Not out here," he says, turning back to the portal just as it seals within itself, leaving him stranded.

"Fuck!" His voice echoes throughout the surroundings.

The Screening Room is gone, replaced by the insurmountable Mountains of Experience. Zeff steps to the cliff's edge, scanning the horizon for the upturned megapolis resting on a gnarled stump. In the distance, the Control Tower spins, a mere flicker amidst the sprawling Wastelands, set against the clear gray sky. From his vantage point, he spies the fleeting trail of multicolored light streaking away from the basin far below. He searches for a way down—but finding none, reactivates the [Deconstructor Beam] to carve his own path.

Imp-oster's Call

Snap. Twist. Slurp. The ghoul chews on a leftover leg and watches his protégé fashion a new toy.

After grafting the last limb, Childe taps a few commands across a crusty keyboard embedded into the bulk of his workbench. The construct twitches, shivers, and stills before opening its eyes. He grabs the homunculus and sets it on the floor.

The misshapen construct rises and hobbles in a circle. He frowns at the lack of perfection. Then, taking a mallet from his tool cabinet, smashes it to bits. He returns the bludger to its proper place and flips a red switch amongst a menagerie of crude buttons and dimly lit dials.

On cue, a small squadron bebops into the chamber and gathers the writhing mess into a shallow bin.

"Get all the bits this time, or I'll have to fix you too," he says, micromanaging his creations.

Regardless, they bumble about, slopping a slime trail out of the chamber.

Childe shakes his head and walks over to the Bone Throne to admire his craftsmanship: the smooth finish, seamless disappearance of transformation lines along interlocking joints. He tugs at the Imp-oster's claw, saying, "I'm bored... Let's play a game."

The ghoul looks into Childe's hollow eyes. "Don't worry, lad... We'll find Zeff and return you to your former self," it says reassuringly, hiding its intentions behind red crusty lips and an unbrushed smile.

"Where'd he go?"

"That's an excellent question," the Imp says. Its burnt-yellow eyes twitch as crooked teeth grind against the last bit of bone. "I have an idea for some fun. Do you have any flyers built?"

A devious smile curls Childe's cheek. He skips back to his workbench and pulls on a chain. Several shelves rotate to reveal a grotesque collection: twisted homunculi, juxtaposed at the whims of cruel assimilation—wings where arms should be, heads at both ends—up-cycled by the invisible threads of Childe's corrupted imagination. "I don't have many," he says, "but I could possibly spare a few."

"Let's test them out! Have them carry a message to the others."

"Do you have a family? I miss mine—"

"They're a deplorable lot. You're not missing much."

With a few minor alterations, eleven Echoes of Doubt take flight through the Fog of Despair, screeching towards the farthest corners of the Mind Palace VPN partition.

30

Leaving Eden

Hide & Seek

Over an hour later, the band returns from their astral performance.

"Where's the Stranger?" Josepé wonders, cracking open a fresh brewski to appease his muse and his thirst in one satisfying gulp. "Ahhhh." He smacks his lips, leaving decorative foam on his mustache.

"Did you find our friend?" Mystic Woods asks Patrício, returning from his stroll along the shoreline.

"Nope. I thought he might've fallen asleep out on the beach." Patrício guzzles some ice-cold water.

Josepé raises an eyebrow. "What do you mean? He wasn't there?"

"Where else could he be?" Nicholas asks. The concern on his face deepens with each passing moment without an answer.

"This island is only so big," Chet says.

"He might've swum to one of the other islands," Zach says.

"Why would he do that?" Patrício asks.

"Hell, I don't know," Zach glares. "I'm just thinking out loud."

Before any further bickering, the band gathers their wits and combs the island.

Zach worriedly rushes around, howling like a madman. Chet plays his drums as loud as possible, trying to signal the camp's location. Josepé wanders around the beach, circling more times than he has cigarettes. Nicholas and Patrício catch poison ivy from searching through thick undergrowth. And Mystic Woods climbs the tallest tree to see if there are any boats around. A little farther past the unforeseen distance, a ferry throttles closer to the archipelago, signaling the conclusion of their creative retreat. Alas, no sign of the Stranger.

"Maybe if we build a big enough fire, he'll see it." Zach carries some leftover limbs to the rock circle.

Mystic Woods glances at his watch. "We're all worried about him... But it's almost time to pack the gear."

"Let me search for a little longer," Zach pleads.

"I'll go with you," Josepé says and picks up a favorable branch to use as a walking stick.

While the ivy's oils ripen into itching pustules across Nicholas and Patrício's exposed skin, Nicholas—the ever-artful apothecary—retrieves several gauze pads, alcohol wipes, and a box of baking soda from his med bag.

"Don't mess with it until I whip up a salve," he instructs, combining baking soda and water into a paste to coat the affected areas. "This will have to suffice until we get back to Coffin Island."

Packing Up Shop

Ragged from searching with their heads full of jug juice, and dumbfounded by the Stranger's disappearance, the band reluctantly packs up their equipment.

"Was he a hallucination?" Mystic Woods asks concerningly as he helps Chet lift one of the utility bins onto the stack of gear staged for their departure.

"How? We spoke with him. Didn't we? I mean, we shared food and drink with the fella," Chet recounts.

"He could've been a mass hallucination," Mystic Woods says. "We haven't been getting all the sleep we need. Maybe it was all a dream."

"A dream? Now you've lost it. I tell you, he was flesh and blood, sure as you or me. Remember, he saved us on the Unicorn raft?"

"Oh, yeah—"

"One, two, three, lift."

They hoist another heavy box atop the chest-high pile.

Elsewhere, while walking the island's perimeter, Zach's imagination runs wild with doomsday scenarios. "Was he abducted by aliens? Was he kidnapped? What if a shark ate him?"

"And what if he was eaten by a monster chupacabra?" Josepé replies sarcastically, trying to cheer his dear friend out of the melancholy of his current neurosis.

However, after searching for several hours with no success, they return to the camp to finish the preparations for their departure.

Ghost Stories

On approach, Zach notices someone sitting at their fire. "Is that the Stranger?" he asks, then calls out, "Yo—you had us worried."

"Hey, boys. I know I'm early," Harry, the ferryman, says, standing with a wave. "But I figured we could load up the gear, run it out to my boat, and get it stowed with plenty of time to chill before the night is done."

Zach pushes past the others. "We need to call the Coast Guard. The Stranger is missing."

"Hold on there." Harry's demeanor shifts. "We absolutely can't call them—or anyone—until I drop my cargo at the docks."

"This is serious," Zach persists.

"So am I."

Mystic Woods places his hand on Zach's shoulder and whispers, "We don't want to upset the people he works for." His smile shifts the conversation. "No worries, Harry. We understand completely. We'll handle it once we return home."

"Who's this *Stranger*? I thought I only brought y'all out here." Harry looks around.

They gather by the fire with the last of their brews and bring the ferryman up to speed.

"Maybe he vibrated to the next dimension from all the musical medicine you're keeping for yourselves? By the way, when's that album dropping?" Harry raises his eyebrows.

"After our first gig. Which will be soon." Mystic Woods turns the last marshmallow.

"How can y'all toast marshmallows and talk so lightly? We still have time to search for him," Zach protests.

Mystic Woods stares into the coals as soft, plump sugary skin crisps beneath the blue flame of caramelization. "Calm down, bud. We've combed every inch of the island. We'll send help when we get back home. Come enjoy a s'more."

"He could've been one of those Lowcountry ghosts. Y'all ever heard the stories?" Harry scoots up in his seat as the fire crackles with the last briskets.

Chet looks at him, squishing a gooey marshmallow between two pieces of chocolate and graham crackers, asking, "Like the Gray Man?" Creamy mallow fluff bursts from the snack onto the palm of his hand.

"I know that one." Harry weaves the tale along the fringes of the dark. "Legend says it's the ghost of a young man traveling from the Lowcountry to see his fiancée. On the way there, he and his horse were caught in pluff mud and died. Ever since, his spirit has haunted the shore from here to there, looking for the girl he loved."

"Some think it's the ghost of Blackbeard, come to claim his treasures," Chet replies with a cheekful of goodness.

Nicholas furrows his brow. "Ghosts aren't real. And the Stranger wasn't a ghost."

"It's possible," Josepé replies. "There's a bridge back home where you can hear a baby crying."

"Isn't there one in every state?" Harry asks.

"More than likely."

Patrício yawns into the conversation. "I'll look it up when we get back... which, surprisingly, I can't wait to get back to: a decent shower, my woman, and the new episodes of my shows."

"Don't you mean women?" Mystic Woods teases.

"Hey," Patrício tosses a pebble at him, "we keep it open and honest."

"Why is there a baby crying under a bridge?" Nicholas inquires.

Josepé explains, "Late one autumn evening, a young mother lost her child in the waters below the bridge after an accident."

"Do tell," Nicholas encourages the tale.

"When I was younger, some friends and I were out there drawing graffiti and hanging with the girls... That's when we heard a baby crying. Some thought it was an animal, but having recently become a big brother, I knew a baby's wailing all too well. Hell, one girl locked herself in the car after seeing the mother's ghost on the embankment. I tell you, I know what I heard."

Zach leans back in his seat, asking, "Josepé, did you ever go to the four-walled cemetery near Salem's Crossroads?"

"No. I've heard about it, but I'll let you tell your story."

"One evening, a group of us went to check out an abandoned graveyard in the middle of the woods." Zach shakes his head with shivers, remembering a night filled with the wild thoughts of demonic portals, government conspiracies, and monsters. "Several folks were teased and stayed behind. Best they did... When I hopped to the other side, I fell into a grave that had been robbed long ago."

The fireside stares unblinkingly.

"I almost pissed myself." Zach continues, "It certainly scared everyone there, sending them up the other side of the wall. Alone, dusting off the grime, the face of mortality glared back at me. Bam! Back up the wall I went—only to get stuck halfway." He laughs. "I tried and tried, but couldn't get over that damn wall to save my life. I had to get the gang to pull me over. Lord knows, I was scared enough to shit my pants... which I did." He laughs, swigging from a plastic water bottle.

"Gross, Zach. Lay off the doughnuts," Josepé says, holding his nose at the imaginary stench coming from Zach's ghost story.

Departure To Everydayness

The last logs of the fire crackle into the faint reaches of early-morning fog, floating along ethereal trails, lightening the night's richness. A few restless hours later, just before dawn, the band shuffles from their tents and breaks down the final fittings of their camp, begrudgingly preparing for the time-based prophecies of their respective careers.

"Move it, Zach!" Josepé herds him forward.

Patrício digs through a supply bin. "Where's the bag for the tent? Did we already pack it?"

"Let's keep it moving, fellas. I have a red-eye flight to catch for work," Mystic Woods coaxes them, peeking at his watch.

Little by little, the campsite decomposes into a skeleton of its firelit revelry. Chet stirs the last of their water into the pit, ensuring no hot ember or coal remains, doing his best to leave it better than they found it. After Nicholas checks for any rogue items left behind, they look for the Stranger one last time.

Still no sign of him; they fold his kelp-stained suit and pack Josepé's satchel with rations, water, and a note.

We tried to find you. Hope you're safe. Thank you for inspiring us to stop practicing and finally play.

P.S. We hope you aren't a ghost!!!

P.P.S. Our contact info is on the back... We'll send help soon.

Aboard Harry's ferry, they wave goodbye to the archipelago and to the Stranger—wherever he may be. As they chug towards Coffin Island, a pang of guilt peppers the band, already tired and filled with the agitation that comes from being forced from creative nirvana. Thrust into a perpetual hell of the cubicle, the service industry, cramped flights, parking-lot traffic, meetings, and the spreadsheets of a passionless society, the world loses another glimmer of vividity. So, thrown against the will of their souls, they bravely head farther from their grotto of inspiration and into the shackles of everydayness.

Part III
Laniakea

31

Dawn Patrol

Algae-Covered Boulder

While the ferry chugs out of sight, several pulsing shivers prickle throughout the Stranger's body. The malfunctioning Oros system normalizes its reality distortion field. He wakes with a crick in his neck, wiping away the sand-glittered drool from his cheek, and stumbles to his feet. The wind shifts, and the lingering fog retreats past the dunes into the forest. After dusting off, he heads towards the campsite.

To his surprise, all that remains is the muddled traces of their fire. Without notice, nanites auto-adjust his sight for low light. He finds his old clothes, folded under Josepé's satchel containing a steel, vacuum-sealed water bottle, a pack of peanut butter crackers, three MREs, and a note.

"Why'd they leave me?" A sense of inadequacy catches fire. (Didn't they see me asleep on that rock? Will they come back? Will they send help? What am I going to do? How do I get off this island? Think. Think. Think—I need more fresh water. Building a shelter is easy. But I'll run out of water.)

A bit of sand grinds against his molars as he swallows a cobweb of saliva. He unseals the bottle, sips a cool swig, then reads their note.

"Coffin Island... At least they're sending help... Someone is coming." He repeats the words several times before folding it into the safety of his pocket. "Now, what do I do?"

A menagerie of Vision Shards unpacks wilderness-survival manuals from both the Donor's and Zeff's constructs, flooding his bandwidth with a cobbled recollection of shiny forgotten things. He brims with the novelty of remembrance and, not wanting to waste anymore time, quickly improvises a lean-to shelter from limbs and thatches of palm fronds. Then, stuffing his algae-stained linen suit into his bag, he stows his supplies and steps from the grotto of creation to explore the archipelago.

Zach's lesson stick rests on a log. The Stranger picks it up. *Thwap-thwap-thwap.* He playfully taps the sand in rhythm with the tune in his head. As memories of their music parade between his ears, he dances a subtle jig through the maritime forest, subconsciously suppressing his sense of abandonment into the Nether Regions of Thought.

Beyond the blooming dunes, the golden eye of dawn peeks from beneath the pillow of night, and the beach widens into view. A seagull squeals past his line of sight. The Stranger follows the bird's flight path until it lands amongst the rest of its colony.

"I bet there's fresh water on one of these islands," he says, looking at the nearest neighbor. "Can I swim across? I feel like I can." He tries to muster the courage. "If those deer can do it, then I've got to try."

(What if you drown?) the Imp-oster sneers.

Just as he passes the algae-covered boulder, a ribbon of pelicans disappears into a swirl of blue and pink sorbets. Along the cognitive backdrops of space and time, rolling waves crash with light-sage crests and shadow-green troughs. The Stranger looks to the horizon and puzzles over the confusion of his circumstances.

(How long until they send help?)

(Where will you go? What will you do? Will you ever see your family again?) the Imp whispers.

The lap of the washing shore silences the echoes as he arrives at the water's edge, slips off Patrício's old sandals, and folds his plain white t-shirt, placing both a safe distance from the rising tide before striding into the cool Atlantic.

Search For Water

To his surprise, swimming to the next island requires minimal effort. He marches on shore and scouts the area. As he rounds the beach to the opposite side, a fearful angst wells up in him upon recognizing the bulbous pontoons of a Zodiac Combat Rubber Raiding Craft [Zodiac] hidden underneath some palm fronds.

(Is it them? Who am I afraid of? Are the boys playing a trick on me?) He calls out, "Zach? Josepé?"

Only the wind responds. The Stranger stops thinking and steps into the brush. He tiptoes into the stillness of the forest, his heartbeat the only sound. He crouches down behind a bush and observes his surroundings, listening for anyone nearby. The forest is silent. And after a petrifying moment, the Stranger gains his wits.

"If I go back... that could be my way off this island. But who does it belong to? I need to find them first," he says.

Inspired by the buried bravado of his past, he summons the courage and creeps from the forest onto the beach. Out in the surf, he spies the lone silhouette of someone paddling out. He freezes and observes his surroundings.

A spry Atlantean floats in the glassy waters of the rising sun, hunting for an opportunity to step into the liminal space induced through bilateral motion and conscious breathing. He paddles ahead, ducking below an unsuitable wave, then surfaces. A shimmer rolls off his springsuit. Upon reaching the break, the surfer primes his position for the approaching set.

From the depths, an oncoming swell rises two inches above the water's surface. It tugs the board's tail and pulls him back into the set. He lets the first one pass and strikes for the next. As the second wave mounts towards the sky, his board draws along its face like an archer nocking an arrow.

A sense of weightlessness overwhelms him as he paddles against the Atlantic's pull. The raw force of the ocean rolls under the B's Surf-Wax-coated deck while his hands release from the rails and reposition for an easy pop-up.

He jumps to his feet, dipping the longboard's squash-tail ever so slightly, and rides a barreling slipstream. A few meters forward, the surfer playfully walks to the nose and transitions into a cross-legged Buddha posture. Scooting down the line, a sweet relief stretches across his face.

Near the shallows, he bails from the board with a backflip, disturbing the bottom, sending some smaller sand-dollars flying. However, quickly settling back to the floor, they vanish beneath the sifting sands.

"Wahoo!" the surfer cries, bathed in the new light of day.

(Did the band send him?)

(He could be a threat—kill him and take the boat,) the Imp-oster hisses, followed by an intrusive volley of automatic negative thoughts, causing the angst draped over his shoulders to boil.

The Stranger's adrenaline tightens a kinetic tension within his tendons, priming his fight-or-flight reflexes. The tattoo responds until the Oros system hiccups luminous tracers into dull ink.

Helaku

In the shallows, cool water bubbles about the surfer's springsuit as he emerges like Poseidon and stomps onto the beach. Saltwater trickles down from his shark-fin mohawk, flowing along the contours of his well-shredded body. He sets the board down on a beach towel, then trots towards the Stranger with a bright, beaming smile, waving and calling out, "Hey-yo!"

The Stranger reads his expression and suppresses the urge to attack. As the distance between them decreases, he smiles and waves in return, all the while scanning for escape routes and potential weapons should the situation get a little spicy. Sand whips past him, taking the clouds with it.

"Good morning!" the surfer says, jogging up to the Stranger. "Up and at 'em already? Great place, isn't it? I thought I was the only one who knew about this spot? How'd you get out here?"

"I swam from over there," the Stranger says, pointing to the neighboring island.

"Are you camping? As you can tell, it's untouched out here. Truly an Eden... I'm being rude. I'm Helaku. What's your name?" A strong right hand, forearm adorned with tribal lines, reaches out for a handshake.

The Stranger hesitates, letting a pregnant pause marinade, until, sensing Helaku's sincerity, he explains his situation, and the musicians' revelry.

As Helaku listens, a memory from his childhood—of fleeing his father's violence with his mother—rushes to the forefront of his attention.

Raft

Severely off course, guided by several stormy days at sea with little drinking water, many refugees stir into a panic. In their fuss, no one notices the rogue wave barreling towards them. It breaks onto the deck of their ramshackle raft. He clings to his mother as her adrenaline digs into the rope, securing them to a beam.

Lost in the wash, they tumble along the pulsing backs of thunderous giants, claiming everyone—except them. Young-Helaku wakes up on a beach to find his mother unconscious and cries out for her.

"Helaku?" her soft voice caresses his cheek. "Where are you, Helaku?"

He cradles his mother with tears of relief—

Another Way

Everything passes in an instant and, moving from empathy, leaves Helaku with a deeper sense of sympathy for the Stranger's situation. "Are you injured?" he asks.

"Not really... Just a little hungover and dehydrated."

Thinking more about the disappearance of the musicians, Helaku inquires with a furrow of disappointment, "They left you?"

"I wouldn't say they left without trying." The Stranger pulls the wet folded piece of paper from his pocket. Its contents run into sliding streams of barely legible intentions. "I found this note with Josepé's satchel and some rations, saying they searched all night and morning for me."

"If they looked and couldn't find you, then where were you?"

The Stranger massages his sore neck. "I was on the beach, asleep on a rock."

"Luckily, you swam to this island and ran into me." Helaku's smile returns. "But I don't know if I can let you wait until they send someone. My boat's a little further up the beach, and once I finish a quick errand, I'd like to give you a ride back."

"Definitely. If you're offering... I don't seem to have many options," he says with a charm of relief. "I could wait for them," he glances around. "But I'd wager I'd be much closer to remembering who I am if I went with you."

"The missing pieces will return in time." Helaku reassures him. "There's no need to force it."

Birth Of Friendship

Barely above the horizon, hanging from an invisible tree, an incandescent orange ignites the sky into a pink wildfire. Bright yellow butterflies flutter onto nearby flowering jessamine as they proceed towards Helaku's boat. The sweet fragrance mixes with the winds of late spring. Surprised, the Stranger leans over into a dreamy backdrop of aromatic tinctures, dewdrops, and spicy perfumes.

"Do you wanna see something cool?"

"Sure."

Helaku pulls back a thatch of stacked palm fronds to reveal his inflatable boat.

This time, the sight of the vessel cues a crumpled operations-manual drawer. Partial pages tear from the cramped, disorganized vaults of his once-pristine Mind Palace. As he places his hand on the Zodiac's black reinforced rubber, his thoughts short-circuit, flickering to a sliver of a Vision Shard. He stills the angst and tucks it under a stack of splintered recollections for the Sorting Dregs to find.

"She's a beauty, isn't she? A gift from a special lady-friend." Helaku winks with the glint of joy that comes from thinking about your lover, even after a brief time apart. He shows off, explaining, "It has a sixty-horsepower two-stroke engine with a pump-jet propulsor and a shrouded impeller to reduce the risk of serious injury to marine-life. Also, I can stow the paddles on the side here to make room for my board," he says, gliding his hand along the rails. "And at the bow, there're storage bags for all my equipment: foot pumps, extra lines, tool box, life jackets, sunscreen—you name it."

(Row. Row. Row his boat and kill him in the stream. Merrily, merrily, merrily, merrily, life is but a scream,) the Imp-oster sings.

A disturbing shiver rattles down his spine.

"She's so good to me and incredibly supportive of my endeavors—why am I telling you all this?" He regains his composure. "By the way, what do I call you?"

Sensing no ill intent, the Stranger suppresses the tactical fears of his inner echoes. "They were calling me 'the Stranger.'" A reminiscent stream of consciousness unfurls a tapestry of cinnamon, stars, smells, and sounds into the tattered Wastelands of Cognition.

"We're going to need a better name for you. A name is a marker for who you were and how you lived—an anchor, if you will—but not knowing who you are might not be a bad thing," Helaku says.

"How so?"

"You can become whoever you want to be."

Helaku changes clothes, and they share a chewy homemade almond-butter breakfast bar. Despite the ease of being around him, the Stranger vigilantly scans for potential threats lurking within the shadows of trepidation. His fears fail to come to light. After the snack, they push the small boat from the shore and zoom towards the beach with the algae-covered rock and a vacant grove, which once held a cathedral of creativity for a groove of beautiful freaks.

32

Skimming

Box Breathing

Following a bobbing trail among the dunes into the maritime forest, they reach the campsite. A hint of longing piffs upon the wallpaper of the Stranger's experience. He shakes it off, collects his things, and bids farewell to his first home.

Back on the beach, he and Helaku push the Zodiac through the rolling surf. It bounces with the next wave, but they manage to get aboard. As they move past the break, Helaku notices a slight worry hanging about his new companion.

An idea flashes, and he suddenly kicks his legs over the side, lies down, and throws his arms above his head, saying, "You've got to try this."

(Take the boat,) the Imp-oster whispers.

"Try what?" the Stranger asks.

"Just humor me for a moment," Helaku insists.

The Stranger, willing to do anything to shake the Imp's gnawing agitation, kicks back in the same fashion.

(Do it! Now's your chance!) Its vile echoes persist.

"Close your eyes. Take a deep breath and hold it... Release it... Hold it... Take another deep breath."

After several conscious seconds ebbing in the morning sun, his brain tingles as neocortical currents wash with the nonexistent weight of his body. Adrift in the effortless flow of the ocean, a calming flood relaxes him.

"How do you feel now?" Helaku asks.

"Light. Not lightheaded, but calmer."

"More chill?"

"I'll definitely remember to do this the next time I feel that queasy uneasiness."

"It works great in a pinch—even better if you pass this between your hands." Helaku reveals a wrinkled origami crane fashioned from a purple paper square.

"What's that?"

"It's a Comfort Creature from Monk's Market."

"Will it help me remember who I am?"

"I'm not sure... But it will help with keeping you from getting the red-ass."

"Red-ass?"

"Upset."

"I see." The Stranger reflects on the gnawing agitation urging him to steal the raft.

"I think I have another one tucked away somewhere." Helaku reaches into a nearby pouch to reveal a sky-blue paper rhino.

The two of them continue box-breathing and passing the paper totems. As they float under waves of slow-roving clouds, their boat bumps against the shore.

Helaku's eyes spring open. "Whoops!" He effortlessly pops to his feet. "I was lost in the sauce of my own thoughts." Grabbing the tiller handle and positioning the outboard, he turns the key.

The starter struggles, sputters, then fires up—and they zoom away from the archipelago. The Stranger braces himself as Helaku throttles them towards the horizon, sending a salt spray from the wake of its destination.

A ripening range of colors blends together as the sun climbs onto a brilliant background, shifting from its vivid hue into light blue. The grand artisan patiently dashes puffy little clouds here and there. Slowly drifting past his perception, they glide on the surface tension of the atmosphere.

MARS

Vewwwm! Sixty galloping horses send them clear of the shoreline. After a brief sunlit boat ride, the choppiness subsides as they pass a marker with a flashing GPS beacon on top.

"That's the first one," Helaku hollers over the outboard. "There are eighteen linked to the Foundation's satellites."

"What are they for?" the Stranger asks into the wind's passing roar.

"Monitoring the protected zone." Helaku finally slows the outboard to an audible level. "A colleague of mine helped sanction a few areas for research. But it hasn't stopped the Big Oil money from slicking its way into the pockets of clandestine representatives, good ole boys, and local officials... At least we have this slice of ocean." He smolders into the distance, brooding with the angst of the world beyond Coffin Island's bubble.

Ahead, a thin silver lining rises from where the sea kisses the sky. Several more silhouettes emerge, multiplying on the horizon. Before long, their splendor shimmers like a diamond necklace strung across the neckline of the ocean—a beautiful accessory for any occasion.

The Stranger marvels at the glistening ingenuity. Atop the twelve-meter-long platform, 300 hexagonal photovoltaic mirrors absorb a heavenly harvest of light. Inverters convert luminous spears into alternating current, silently powering conveyor belts and sorting machines. Moored in the drift, they pull in lines of trash, ferried from the furthest reaches of its wacky-flailing-floating-boom-arms.

A lengthy slime trail gently reaches the sluice box. Its chromatic sheen, blurring the morning sky, laps against the current. The entire mess silently flows towards greater ends—far better than some poor sea creature's belly or local dinner platters with a side of coleslaw and hushpuppies.

The sun shines on Helaku's face, highlighting his strong jawline and a tapestry of tribal tattoos: merit badges and protective incantations flowing along his broad shoulders and down his arms.

"Isn't it marvelous?"

"What is this place?"

"I call it the Manta Array Recycling Station... MARS. The flotilla was origi-
nally called Hahalua, but brand modeling and test groups showed donors were
more amped to get behind something with a powerful symbol. So, Helen—the
Foundation helped me rebrand."

"How does it work?" The Stranger shades his eyes with his hand and looks to
the nearest platform.

"We have six manta ray-shaped units aligned with the current. Extending from
each platform, two angled boom arms funnel plastics and other debris towards a
conveyor belt, where every piece is sorted, separated, filtered, and safely stored for
recycling."

He turns from the path of refuse, asking, "Why's there all this trash in the
water?"

"Something's wrong with this station... but the long answer is that even before we were born, folks have preferred convenience over sustainability. Out of
sight, out of mind... Meanwhile, in places where gigantic gyres spin with the
life-supporting currents of our oceans, photodegradable materials became mi-
cro-particles. Smaller and smaller, they shrank amidst the seas and the sun, never
going away until they sank to the bottom of the deepest places, slowly piling into
mountains."

"At least they aren't going anywhere," he says, trying to lighten the situation
as plastic mountains rise from his imagination.

Helaku continues, "Sadly, it wasn't until some senator had his balls removed
from having too much microplastic buildup that officials recognized the problem's severity. By then, microplastics had been found in 75% of the subjects
examined."

He remembers Zach rolling on the ground after getting hit in the nuts. "His
testicles?"

"Yeah."

"Sheesh."

"Plástico fantástico!"

They laugh at the absurdity, while nearby, sorting mechanisms sift with the efficiency of three keen-eyed individuals, and solar cells convert energy to power the station.

Mechanical Breakdown

Suddenly, an odd whirring from a computer fan speeding up precedes a hiccup in the flow of progress. The platform sputters to a stop. Then it starts up again, rattling the shake tray, only to halt moments later.

An agitation flashes over Helaku's brow. "This is what I was worried about." He leaps from the boat onto the platform and loops the bowline securely to the station. "The Foundation's sensors showed that the system was malfunctioning. I've got to figure this out. And I need an extra set of hands. That's where you come in." He extends his arm, helping the Stranger from the boat.

Helaku opens up the conveyor-belt compartment and inspects the terminal. "Will you hand me the impact wrench from the bag?"

The Stranger returns to the Zodiac and grabs hold of the tool bag. He fumbles past screwdrivers, Allen wrenches, hex keys, a mallet, random bolts, and some industrial-strength, waterproof repair tape. Beneath a pair of adjustable pliers lies his prize, with its cabaret of attachments—from saw blades and drill bits to socket sets—a value buy while supplies last.

He passes Helaku the impact wrench and observes floating lines of trash, where a red plastic cup parades in accord with the rest of the party.

"Shit. It must be the computer," Helaku growls under his breath at the conveyor box. "I'm not the best with this stuff," he says, scratching his head with a reluctant smile.

"Mind if I take a peek?" the Stranger asks with bubbling curiosity.

"Be my guest. I would hate to have wasted our time coming out here," he says, stepping to the side.

The Stranger pokes at several side panels. "Is there any way to access the on-board computer system directly?"

"There should be a control console next to where you're standing," Helaku says, pointing to a mounted metal box.

He unlocks the case, revealing a terminal enclosed in a rubber salt-proof skin. As his hands ready at the keys, a Vision Shard from one of Zeff's Kabal surprises him with Hats's modulated voice, instructing him on gaining admin access. His fingers drop into a dead sprint. Several effortless prompt commands later, he swiftly cracks open the system's backdoor.

Helaku watches him work. "Try not to mess anything up in there," he says, surprised by what he sees.

"I think I've got this." He beams with the satisfaction of remembrance as Hats's words lead him towards the dopamine of success. Although Zeff never met them in person, they had a way of always being online—almost ever-present.

His mind chases an unspooling intuition and unravels logical conclusions after necessary queries. His fingers translate his findings, flickering along the keyboard, around the corner, and down a digital corridor. Soon, another door opens to reveal the faulty loop in its programming.

"And... we... are... done." The Stranger smiles at his accomplishment. (This feels good. I want this—but who were those other voices? Was that me?) He halts further questions for fear of summoning the Imp-oster to his door. (I can't let Helaku know. No one needs to know. I've got to reach Coffin Island and find the band. I need to figure out who I am and how I ended up on that beach?)

Several clanking mechanisms and turning gears later, the deluge of inquiry stalls as the conveyor belt sputters into a smooth oscillation and syncs with sorting, washing, and storing subroutines. Little by little, the station refreshes its connection across the flotilla's network until all lights turn green.

Repair

Helaku inspects, saying, "I can't believe my eyes... It seems to be good to go." He closes the terminal's protective casing and secures it to the mainframe housing unit. "How'd you do that?"

"These days, I'm full of surprises." The Stranger laughs with the sun's light upon his ocean-drenched backside.

"Well, whatever you did, you saved me the trouble of dragging one of the 'wiz kids' out here later this afternoon. I don't know what we would do if this project were to fail. It helps sustain the village."

"What do you mean?"

"Foundation ships retrieve the large storage bins from each platform. Then they process the material and sell it. We get the lion's share, of course. Presto-chango: no more eight-to-five, no paid lunch breaks—just shred the gnar and do what makes you come alive. The payoff is beyond any amount of money we've invested. The future is a priceless resource." His smile, still brighter than the day, beams with pride.

(What makes you come alive?) the Stranger repeats.

"But all of that is small potatoes compared to the global potential of the MARS flotilla," he continues. "At scale, these could remove millions of tons of plastic waste from our oceans, protecting them for the next seven generations." Helaku waves images as he talks. "I owe you one," he says, wiping the sweat from his brow.

"Don't mention it. You're helping me get back to civilization."

"After today, I'm going to treat you to a hot shower and a meal when we get back."

"Do I stink that badly?" He catches a whiff of himself.

"Nothing a little hospitality can't fix." Helaku lays a powerful smack on the Stranger's shoulder. "Let's get going."

Stranded

High above, seabird shadows fly over where the litter of yesterday rocks among the waves of tomorrow.

Helaku hops aboard. "Would you hand me the tool bag?"

The Stranger fetches the bag and returns to the boat. "Here you go."

His words are unheard as Helaku clicks the starter switch back and forth. Nothing. He checks the wires. Nothing. Checks the fuel bladder in the front. Plenty. Clicks the switch again. Nothing. The faster he flicks, the more his frustration grows. A rampant panic soon swirls with his indifference towards malfunctioning technology, feeding the aggro of his ego.

"Shit, the battery is dead."

"How?" the Stranger asks, suppressing the angst attempting to overwhelm him. "What happened?"

"I forgot to put the new one in—it's sitting back at the Boathouse." He leans against the inner wall of the rubber craft, box-breathes, and retrieves his cellphone. "Fuck! My phone is dead too." He roars with frustration.

The sky settles into a calm blue.

"I hate to say this, but I think we're stranded." Helaku exhales.

"At least you're not out here alone." The Stranger extends his hand to pull him back onto the platform.

"What are we going to do?" he asks.

"We need to stay put."

Helaku looks around. "I don't think we're going anywhere," he says with a nervous chuckle, then returns to his heroic composure.

The Stranger glances at the photovoltaic collectors, and the TacOHUD renders a small schematic breakdown of components. "How about we rewire one of those panels to charge the battery?"

"It might be too much and overload it, leaving us with a fried battery and an inoperable station." Helaku spins towards the horizon, mumbling, "There must be another way. Think. Damn it."

Solutions

An hour passes with both of them tinkering and contemplating a slew of foolish ideas.

"To hell with it. Let's take apart one of these solar panels." Helaku digs for his screwgun.

The Stranger stares across the water and notices a rubber ducky in a nest of fishing line, spinning in a micro-gyre. Round and round, the swirling refuse mesmerizes him into a state of free association until a tiny bead breaks through the Void of Subconsciousness.

"I've got it! I know what to do." He hops up, startling Helaku, lost in the focus of his box breathing. "I need some rope. Do you have any spare?"

"There should be some in the pouch to the right," Helaku points.

The Stranger searches until he finds the line.

"What else do you need?"

He pivots to the motor. "Let's get this cover off... We'll manually start it."

Next, the Stranger turns the ignition switch to the 'on' position and shifts the throttle into neutral. Then, pointing to a series of semicircular cutouts marked with a right-facing arrow, he says, "If you tie a knot at one end of the rope and thread it through there, you can wind it clockwise around the flywheel."

Helaku positions himself for a better view.

Once wrapped, the Stranger checks to make sure the cord is in the grooves, grabs the loose end, and pulls. The line starts off heavy. After a quarter turn, the tension lightens. With another, the line's resistance resets to its starting temperament. He secures his grip and gives it one last mighty pull.

Bwam-fwm-fwm-fwm-wam-wam-wam!

"Wahoo!" Helaku cheers. "You're going to have to show me how to do that again."

"It's fairly simple. Wrap this rope around here like this, and give it a whirl."

As the two men race towards Coffin Island, the Stranger's mind sails with excitement, expectation, and analysis, while fear, uncertainty, and doubt swirl darker concerns into palpable piles of anxiety.

The Director

Elsewhere, inside the abandoned lighthouse at Coffin Island's East End, the hum of fluorescent lights washes out the scrolling texts and images on LED monitors.

"Sir, we've picked up a signal from the Oros system. It's faint, but it's there."

"How close can you get?" Commander Xero asks.

Several hurried keystrokes prompt a new screen. "I'm pulling up the coordinates now."

"Is this correct?"

"Yes, sir... Our satellites have him within thirty kilometers."

"That's not good enough... Luckily, he's still in the area."

"Yes, sir."

"If he's alive, why can't we track him? Is it something to do with the anomaly we found during the last update?"

"I'm not sure, sir."

"If he's dead, why haven't they taken his body back to whatever shithole they crawled out of? Ring the Director for me."

"Yes, sir."

The wall illuminates with the Director's looming shadow, soon replaced by the grim visage of a company man who had outlived most of his colleagues.

"Xero, make it quick." He shuffles a short stack of papers atop a larger pile. "I have a meeting with the Committee in fifteen minutes."

"I've completed preparations, and we've located the signal from the Oros system."

The Director pauses the parade of paper sorting and looks up. "Hallelujah—I thought the Chinese or the Russians might have had it—we can't have this tech in the wild. Tell your team to pull the lead out of their asses and get me results." The Director's feed goes blank.

Commander Xero marches out the door. "Prep the chopper. I'm going sight-seeing."

33

Arrival

Island Bound

After a brief boat ride, Helaku skips their stone past Bird Key, home to over 1,200 nesting coastal fowl, into the mouth of the Stono. Farther inland, they swing into the Folly River as a cool breeze drapes a doily of morning fog throughout Coffin Island's marsh. On the other side of ornate walkways attached to waterside palaces, they arrive at Laniakea's floating dock.

Lush, flourishing bouquets mingle with the smell of pluff mud and up-turned dirt, stirred by the village dogs retrieving an old bone. High in the branches of nearby oaks, bordering a surfboard fence, songbirds herald their arrival, while crowing roosters and bleating goats echo over the marsh-pops of mud-crab burrows.

To the right of the wobbly landing, covered docks—decked with gazebos, cabanas, grills, mini-fridges, and big screens—extend into the sawgrass-lined mud flats. There, illustrious yards, trimmed and watered with underpaid wages, sprawl towards the county park at the West End. Perched on their stilts, marsh-side mansions compete for a better view, casting their lofty shadows onto the privacy of Laniakea's surfboard partition.

Beyond gilded gates, the Sanctuary's private grounds extend to the West End of Coffin Island. Developers purchased the land all the way to the county park for cheap after a storm tore through fifty years ago, turning it into an exclusive resort. Adorned in khaki pants and white polo tops, vacationers pay a fortune to be away from the freaks, geeks, day-trippers, rum riders, Bahama mommas, pool sharks, pirates, and sketchy degens who frequent the beach.

Another rooster's crow rings out into the morning. Several houses down, the slumbering mayor's sleep-crusted eyes fling open. Behind their dull gleam, sprockets churn with everydayness: prepping ordinances, stamps, seals of approval, lobbyist lunches, and dinners with disaster-relief hedge-fund managers—all the while chasing influential donor financing. Indeed, election season is only two years away.

Back Gate

Helaku steps onto the landing and shoots a grumbling glare at his neighbors. "I swear, they keep building closer and closer to our property line. Can you believe they protested against us being able to raise chickens on our own land, citing it as a health issue? More like they didn't want real people to live next to their pop-up palaces." He halts the automatic negative thoughts [ANTs] from colonizing. "Sadly, two-thirds of those properties remain empty, with no one but the palmetto bugs and the local bums to enjoy their amenities—and most are too crafty to get caught." He extends a strong right arm and assists the Stranger onto the narrow dock.

"How so?" the Stranger asks, climbing out of the boat.

"Every time the police come with their flashlights, the squatters go up to the next floor. And when the cops search those floors, I've heard some scramble onto the roof. Then, after waiting for the fuzz to give up, they'll come back down." Noticeably perturbed, Helaku pivots. "You know, I might get a donkey and train it to bray on command—shake some things up. Could you imagine the look on their faces? Heey-hawww-heey-haaww," Helaku brays towards the village's custom surfboard fence. "By the way, I hope you're okay with animals."

"I should be fine. I remember having some around when I was younger," he says, conjuring an image of Old Dan, Lil Ann, Blue, Sally, and Max piling into the back of Paw-Paw's pickup truck.

"Hell yeah, bro. That's a step in the right direction. In time, you'll uncover more," Helaku says. "We have plenty of critters in the village—nothing dangerous, although they can be a little rambunctious."

After unloading, Helaku slings a waterproof satchel over his shoulder and grabs the tool bag. The two early birds make their way up the uneven ramp to the back gate. There, the marsh stench blends with the sweet florals of Laniakea's orchards. Several meters past the looming wisdom of an immense live oak with moss-sewn branches, the dirt-brushed stucco backside of a boutique-resort motel turned apartments comes into view.

Good Fences

Helaku reaches the gate and sets the tool bag on a bench fashioned from an old paddleboard, framed by an edible landscape of kale, decorative herbs, and rainbow chard, inviting passersby to sit and enjoy the million-dollar view. Near the last patch of marsh grass, an egret stalks along the surfboard fence until a rambunctious pack of pups barks it back into another live oak, where members of its congregation wait for low tide.

"It's nice, isn't it?" Helaku points to the fence several meters ahead of them. "It goes around most of the village."

"What's it for?" the Stranger asks.

"Have you ever had to rescue chickens or goats from pluff mud?"

A pungent memory of decomposing muckiness reels inside of the Stranger's nose—a smell no one can ever forget. Once it gets on you, you are stained for life.

Helaku turns to him. "Also, too many drunk tourons kept stumbling back here and messing shit up."

"'Tourons'? How so?"

"It's what we call disrespectful tourists. From time to time, they'd get lost trying to find their vacation rental, and their private golf courses, and private restaurants, and private blah-dee-fucking-blah-I'm-better-than-you mentality." Helaku laughs off his disdain. "Hell, one of them even made their way into a first-floor apartment."

"What happened?"

"Some touron just walked in and passed out on Stewart's couch. Let's say he wasn't too happy to find the drunk dude covered in piss and his new couch drenched in the stain of dehydration."

The TacOHUD focuses on the giant flowering blueberry bushes on either side of the gate. As tall as they are round, they sweetly kiss the morning air. Nearby, the tops of pear and plum trees put on a blooming cabaret.

Helaku inhales a deep, five-second breath. "Ahhhhhhh... I love that smell.

A crow draws the Stranger's gaze across the marsh as the sun reaches towards the mainland, fleeting two inches past the things he could no longer remember forgetting.

Homecoming

Helaku opens the wooden gate. Its spring hinges creak with tension, only to latch softly behind them as they cross the village threshold.

"Welcome to Laniakea," Helaku says, gesturing an open palm to his home.

The Stranger breathes in a cornucopia of pleasant—and not-so-pleasant—notes that tease and swirl into a well-balanced bouffée, enveloping his yearning for a forgotten home in a quilted sense of comfort.

(Maybe I could belong here,) he says to himself.

Nearby, Helaku drops the tool bag at a rustic green storage shed, surrounded by flower beds of Indica azaleas. Their large magenta flowers bow in the morning breeze, attracting a small squadron of honeybees. Affixed with clumps and chunks of a poultice containing vitamins, minerals, carbohydrates, lipids, proteins, and bee saliva, they bob and buzz from flower to flower, filling their pockets with pollen.

A little way past, a weathered red barn blocks a campaign of sunbeams hurling themselves over its roof. The Oros system releases a beetle-squirt of neurochemical vividity, and the Stranger's vision dilates. Translucent light spears streak across the tide-flooded marshlands, carrying mirrored reflections of earth and sky into a kaleidoscopic cascade of cumulonimbus clouds near the mainland.

"This is our garden." Helaku beams as he overlooks the planter boxes running the length of the village. "This season it's filled with collard greens, watermelon, tomatoes, cucumbers, strawberries, squash, green beans, and peppers. It's not everything we wanted, but it's what we had room for... by growing our own fruits and veggies, we save the villagers' moral and financial pocketbooks from the corporate theaters of wasteful food production. And the best part? We can reinvest the savings back into topping the village with solar panels, like they have at Monk's Market."

A sideways gust kicks up the smell of dew-damp dirt into the air. Tilling through the potted memories within the Mind Palace, the cadence of time holds a different swing. A Vision Shard sprouts from the Donor's past—where the sun shines forever, in the springtime of youth.

Granny's Garden

See him as a child riding in a little red wagon pulled by an equally rusty Snapper lawn mower. His innocent imagination ignites, despite efforts to maximize his safety. He is right at home, crossing the stars to save Adastria.

The Southern sun scorches cracks into the red-clay trail leading to Granny's garden, a galactic oasis on the outer rim. Sent on a secret mission by Admiral Spike Starwind to gather iridium-dextrite, the crew is ambushed by outlaws while entering the Green Bean Belt. Protected by the force field emanating from his helmet, he swings a small branch—light-sword—artfully attacking invisible cutthroats beyond the beanstalks.

Sputtering, puttering, and scooting along, Granny pilots them beside lush rows, closer to their objective. She looks back and smiles at him with warm adoration, watching his imaginative spirit ripen.

"Pew-pew. Swish. Pow. Slash." He defends their starship.

The last wispy stalks bow to the victorious explorers as the shuttle squeaks to a scuttling stop next to a cache of prized watermelons.

He climbs out of the ship and checks for rogues. With the coast clear, he walks up to the prized gourd, slaps his hand on its monstrous side, and listens to the juicy slosh.

"Granny, is it ready yet?" he asks, hazel eyes staring up into the shadow of her face.

"Not yet, suga," she says. "We need to let it rest a bit longer. It still has some more room to grow. And we'll need it if we're going to keep holding the trophy at the State Fair."

"But you've never lost."

"Well, I ain't aiming to lose to those suburbanites and their professional gardeners anytime soon," she declares confidently. "I like to get my hands dirty." She winks at her grandson. "The dirtier you get tending the soil, the closer you are to Spirit," she says with a smile, leaning back to look at the sky. "Now, let's get what we came for. Go ahead and fetch me that basket, suga." Granny stands and rubs her hands, causing tiny crumbles of soil to fall to the ground, returning whence they came.

He rushes back to the little red wagon and grabs the large basket he had worn on his head during their voyage.

"Thank you," she says, nurturing the seeds of civility. "Don't forget to put on your hat to protect your neck from the sun."

By the time the heat of the day is upon them, scorching the wide brims of their straw hats, he barely has a handful of green beans in his bucket before she catches up to him, basket brimming with summer squash.

"I imagine you're only going to eat five green beans for supper tonight." She tickles him with a twig. "I guess you can have some of mine or Paw-Paw's. But that means you're skipping your chores, you rascal."

"Granny, stop. I'm going to pee my pants."

"Oh heavens, child. Get it together." She laughs. "Let's finish up and get out of this heat. I have some fresh lemonade waiting in the fridge."

Sitting amongst thick rows of vegetation, surrounded by the rich scent of dirt, they pick as many beans as they can carry, then load up the shuttle. While he squeezes between the cargo, Granny pulls the crank on the Snapper. Its cantankerous combustion releases a small puff of smoke from the exhaust, and she hops onto the squeaky-spring seat, shifting into gear and launching them back across the cosmos. Alas, without notice or time for further recollection, the Vision Shard folds into a square, seals itself inside a manila folder, and—through a series of loop-de-loops—lands on top of a sorting pile within his dilapidated Mind Palace.

Meow-Murs

By the barn, a black tuxedo cat jumps down from a well-worn windowsill and stretches its front claws into a nearby post, pulling its body into alignment. It yawns, then sniffs a bowl of water. After lapping up a few sips, the large feline notices Helaku returning to the village and leisurely rubs against the corral's wooden posts.

Cuc-a-dudal-du! a rooster cries out, drawing the Stranger back to the bleating goats and clucking chickens.

As he and Helaku walk to the barn, the farm animals greet them at the edge of their pens, no doubt expecting a feeding. The Stranger leans down to pet an older goat. Several of the spryer ones jump over the fence, then back again. After a few celebrated hops, they convince themselves that outside is the same as inside—the grass being greener for those who have never left the yard. A brood of hens cluck about the mesh fencing of their comfy coop, picking up kernels and small bugs, but mostly rocks.

Cuc-a-dudal-du!

From the swoosh of a nearby bush, the large purring tuxedo cat runs up to Helaku and rams its head into his shin.

"Hey, Meow-Murs," Helaku says, rubbing his fingers under the feline's chin.

Having finished working the usuals, Meow-Murs turns to the Stranger and brushes past his ankle. The audible cadence of its purrs adds to the village soundscape.

"He's marked you. Now he'll follow you around and hit you up for scraps."

Meow-Murs wiggles to the ground, rolls around, then licks its paws, recapturing their attention.

"He's a Maine Coon and a top hunter of the village. Aren't ya?" Helaku picks up the cat and stares into its eyes. "You're a good man, Meow-Murs." The purring rag-doll sways in the air. Helaku swings the feline up into his arms. The purrs increase as Meow-Murs play kicks its back legs.

"Hey, quit that," Helaku protests, setting the cat down and scratching its head. He snatches a twig from the ground and tosses it towards the fence. Meow-Murs doesn't seem to notice or care, rolling into a patch of grass and sunning its face.

Without warning, a wild hair releases a spring of primal instinct, launching Meow-Murs towards a nearby tree. Bouncing off its trunk, he lands back in the grass and darts to a gap in the fence line. Just before the threshold, he pauses for one last look at Helaku and the Stranger, then bolts after a cast of scuttling mud crabs, leaving them to continue the tour.

34

Tour

Garden Grove

Strolling around the corral and the raised-bed gardens, they reach Laniakea's orchards.

"Now, this next area isn't for the allergen sufferers," Helaku says, pointing to some Bartlett pear trees, "but I think Paul is working on a spray for that."

The Stranger looks past his index finger to the crown of embroidered white flowers and asks, "What's between them?"

"Those are fig trees, big enough to climb inside," Helaku answers. "But I wouldn't recommend it. The wasps and ground bees will light you up for sure. I found out the hard way."

Nearby, a three-meter-wide fig tree glistens with sparkling dewdrops, sliding along the velveteen fuzz of puppy-toe leaves. In its outstretched boughs, faint green buds emerge from brown branches.

"What kind of fruit do those produce?" the Stranger asks, gesturing to a multitude of white-pink blossoms among the neighboring arbors' lower limbs.

"Good eye, bro. Those are plums, Granny Smith apples, then the peaches—don't forget the Meyer lemons at the end," he says, pointing to branches laden with white-yellow flowers rocking in the morning breeze, just before the beehives.

The Stranger peers across Laniakea towards the maritime forest. A contrasting perimeter of dark-purplish, bell-shaped blossoms and crowns of tiny white florals infuses Laniakea's bouffée for its signature series: Nostalgia No. 5.

The Horseshoe

They swing back to the rustic red barn, rounding past the half-soccer field, to a pool, drained for skateboarding on days with no waves. Aside from ornate tags and artful graffiti, the barren bowl reads: Gnar-maste, No Bad Days, Love Small Waves; with a peace symbol, a heart, and a smiley face at its center. On one side, a ramp for catching air; on the other, a series of grind-rails and pool chairs. Light from a swaying palm frond dances onto the stale edges of a half-drunk pale ale, with six cigarette butts floating on top—a devilish cocktail in a compostable cup.

"This is the community fire pit—or the *bondfire*, as I like to call it," Helaku says, directing the Stranger's attention to the massive brick-lined pit and repurposed wooden loungers, well-worn from those late-night sessions under the stars that stretch into the morning.

Still looking at the mini-skatepark, the Stranger asks, "What does 'Gnar-maste' mean?"

"The *gnar* within me recognizes the *gnar* within you... It's kind of cheesy, but seemed appropriate."

The malfunctioning Oros system hits him with another randomized neurochemical cocktail, and his eyes glaze, filtering over a once-matte palette with a vivid intensity. Everything snaps into abrupt focus.

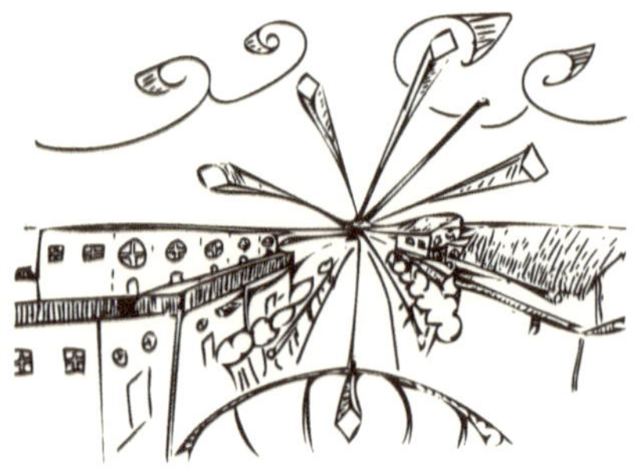

A brickwork path leads from the communal area to the Horseshoe. Along the right side, several three-story decoupage apartments with teak trim and wide porches frame doorways decked with stickers, airbrush art, and touches of magical realism, conjuring a moral mosaic of village life.

Helaku slips off his sandals and wiggles his toes in the grass. "Aside from the bondfire, the Horseshoe is my favorite place on Coffin Island." He gestures to the lengthy courtyard lined with lavender planters, soft grasses, crisscrossing paths, and a fingerpost pointing towards the Longhouse, Storeroom, Community Kitchen, Makerspace, and Creative Cabaña.

"This is absolutely fantastic," the Stranger says.

"It wasn't like this when the Founders started their project."

"The village?"

"Laniakea was their vision for keeping locals from being gentrified off the island," he replies. "They gave us a place to care for and call our own—"

"What was it like before the Founders?" the Stranger cuts in.

"It used to be an abandoned motel, wild and in ruin. But with a little elbow grease and green-thumbing from their compost piles, the grass started running thick as carpet. It grew so rampant that it started taking over the gardens."

"What'd they do?"

"Well, pulling out the grass took too much time, so they built those large rows of raised-bed planters, which fortified future harvests from the soft, cushiony turf we've come to enjoy."

"I bet it saves the back," the Stranger says, recalling the layout.

Although grateful he can retain recent memories, alas, the clarity of his past remains fragmented in confusion, hanging like rotting fruit—low for the taking, but probably filled with bees.

Rivals

As they round the corner, the Stranger spots more cats lounging in front of their homes. Stretching, purring, playing—they clearly have the run of the place. A calamitous group of dogs races across the horseshoe, but the cats don't seem to care as the cloud of commotion rambles past.

"Down!" Helaku's command seizes control of the chaos barreling towards them.

They all sit.

"Good pups," he congratulates them and tosses each a treat from his satchel. "Let's go while they're fighting over the scraps."

Slurping the last nibble from the ground, their ears swivel back to the bamboo fence line. Suddenly, the beasts bolt past the ocean mural, ducking between the bamboo and surfboard barriers onto a worn path of ceaseless perimeter patrols, games of chase, and buried bones.

"What a bunch of goofs," Helaku says, watching as they disappear behind a thick wall of swaying bamboo. "They've got it made."

A pod of villagers crosses the Horseshoe.

"Yo, bro. We're about to go out with Bear and the crew." Bhodi, a short, tattooed man sporting a large afro, nods in the front gate's direction.

On either side of the bamboo archway, a 'Locals Only!' sign hangs from eye hooks.

"Good morning, Bhodi, Sage, Amber." Helaku greets them with the village handshake—striking his thumb down his spine, then clasping hands in a momentary embrace—and says, "We're all good, bro. The waves were nice earlier. But you might have time to catch a few. Those spring storms are producing quite a swell. Maybe next time y'all can wake up in time."

"Nah, Amber needs her beauty sleep," he thumbs at the petite blonde wearing a cut-off teal t-shirt sporting a dolphin on the chest.

"Speak for yourself." She playfully pushes Bhodi.

"The cams at the pier show it's still pumping," Sage says, noticing his companion.

"I'm sure y'all'll have some luck at the Washout," Helaku suggests.

Her emerald eyes strike the Stranger with stupefied amazement.

Todd McGillicuddy—a blue-eyed, pointed-nosed, dimpled-chinned dude with a curly-top mullet—walks over, asking, "Who's this?"

"Good morning, sunshine." Bhodi adjusts his grip on the surfboard.

"I've never seen him before." Todd continues.

"Well, that's the thing... he doesn't know who he is—"

"How do you know you can trust him?" Todd sneers.

"Look, this'll go through all the proper channels, so don't get your jorts in a wad. Besides, he helped me when I was in a pinch. And you know what the rules say—"

"You could've called us," he interrupts.

Helaku steps forward, his stature dwarfing the others. "Regardless, you don't understand the situation. I'll bring this to the village, and we'll all decide democratically."

Todd grumbles, "I still don't trust him."

"Well, I do. And I'll vouch for him," Helaku says, looking at each of them. "We'll gather everyone after brunch."

"Bro, you're cooking? I'm gonna paddle extra hard." Bhodi rubs his hands together.

Todd turns to the Stranger. "Alright, but if the vote doesn't pass, he's gotta go. No hard feelings. We have rules to ensure our peaceful community stays that way."

"I haven't been wrong yet." Helaku smiles in the face of conflict.

Todd doubles down. "He doesn't even know his name. He could be a psychopath or a perv—"

Amber blurts out, "You know, he looks like that famous actor from the '80s... James Konway."

"Isn't he dead?" Bhodi asks.

"Long gone. But I can see the resemblance," Sage says, raising a curious eyebrow.

"Never seen his movies," Todd snarls. "Looks like another *touron* who's lost his way to me—"

"Hey!" Helaku growls.

"James is fine... At least I'll know what to call myself," the Stranger says, easing the friction.

"I like Konway better," Sage says, the creases of her cheeks wrinkling into a grin.

"Konway, it is!" Helaku cheers.

"Keep an eye on him." Todd waves his finger.

Helaku shoos him away. "As of now, he's my guest, and we're allowed guests. Now, y'all go enjoy yourselves and stop troubling me about my business. Just come back in time for brunch."

Misdirected Hostility

Todd storms off, muttering his disdain.

"You shouldn't have come at him all aggro, bro." Bhodi attempts to console his fellow tribesman.

"He knows the rules, but only when they suit his needs." Todd's anxiety builds as the neurotic hamster wheel grates away at him.

Sage defends Helaku, saying, "I trust in him and what he's doing for the village. Under his leadership, Laniakea has flourished."

"Let's take some deep breaths." Amber urges, seeing his blood boiling over the collar of his worn shirt.

"I don't want to take 'some deep breaths,'" Todd mocks, then storms to his small, rusted 1984 baby-blue pickup truck.

Bhodi hollers after him, "Don't you want to wait for PJ?"

After slinging his surfboard into the back, Todd peels out of the crushed-seashell parking lot, fishtailing towards the Washout, where the break churns chest-high surf and locals patrol the waves beyond barely visible, boulder-lined jetties.

Better Than Sleep

Helaku glares with disappointment. "My apologies. He can be a bit salty in the mornings."

Konway watches the dust settle. "No worries... You said something about a shower?" He disrupts the palpable pressure of the moment.

"My bad. I got too caught up in showing you around the village. But you're in luck—we've got the best showers on the island," Helaku says, extending a hand towards the bamboo hut. "I'll grab you a towel, a fresh set of boardshorts, and a t-shirt."

"These clothes will dry," Konway asserts.

"No, my friend, I insist. Besides, those need a good washing." Helaku smiles, holding his nose.

Outside the shower stall, songbirds dart and dash from branch to branch, searching for a proper perch to unleash their chorus on the morning's service. Konway undresses behind woven bamboo walls. His briny, dehydrated rind reeks of stale sweat, alcohol, and the humid heat of days past. After setting his pile of clothes on a bench crafted from an old surfboard, he steps under the spout.

He closes his eyes, takes a deep breath, and bathes in the sounds and smells of Laniakea—altogether, reminding him of a life in the foothills. He cracks open the valve, and an itsy-bitsy spider scuttles out. Several sputtering seconds later, scalding water rains down on his bare, salt-cured body. He senses the heat and narrowly avoids the stream with an artful dodge onto his tiptoes while his nimble fingers twist on the cold to dilute the stream into a cool waterfall.

With his head directly below the flow, refreshing ripples relieve the mounting tension headache at the base of his skull. A heightened awareness traces a cool tributary sliding down his neck, following the shoulders onto his chest, racing across his taut stomach, winding into the gutters of his hips, parting over strong thighs, and reconnecting at the cleft of his calves. In its wake, a soothing coolness wraps around his body, past forgotten scars, and into the drain on the floor.

(James Konway. It has a ring to it... But what else should I be called?) His mind refuses to reveal its secrets. (Who am I? Who was I supposed to meet on Coffin Island? What happened before I washed up on the beach?) The thoughts trickle into a roving sea of crashing inquiry. (What happened to Sgt. Cinnamon? Where's my family? If only I could remember.)

His questions flood the inside of a weathered *Space Force III: Blue Commander* lunchbox. With rainwaters rising, ripped articles on spycraft surface, floating like paper boats along storm drains. Bits of rust slide off with the rising waters, revealing the limited-edition serial number. Several moments pass in silent syncopation with the puddle gathering at his feet.

"My... name... My name is... No—I am Konway. James Konway," he declares, accepting his *nom de* plume with a sense of belonging.

35

Brunch

Orange Tabby

Beyond the shower hut, Laniakea's soundscape mixes with psychedelic Australian surf-rock blaring from a second-floor apartment. Soap suds slide down his abdomen, past old battle scars, over his knee, wrapping around the back of his heel. All the while, the lingering dose from the Oros system sputters up a spontaneous halo of wonderment and curiosity. Light and shadow, dancing through the cracks, lure his hazel gaze to a fissure within the wall.

A well-fed orange tabby cat ballets across the back of a wooden bench, tail swishing hither-thither as it locks onto some potential prey. It jumps down to smell the ground. Several whisker flutters later, the feline tracks the faint trail of a green lizard scurrying into the grass.

(Why am I thinking about lasagna?) he ponders.

Tangerine fur twitches with the morning breeze as the ferocious predator coordinates muscle receptors to pounce. Its tail stops fanning, and the lizard stops scuttling. Both freeze in place, and for one statuesque moment, their primal senses prepare for the impending assault.

Cold water runs down the nape of his neck, tracing the scar on his scapula. Transfixed on the motionless moment playing out before him, Konway pays little attention. His eyes go out of focus, then snap back into vivid clarity. He blinks, and malfunctioning nanites zoom in on freshly groomed fur.

The tabby's muscles fire, striking down with all eighteen fully extended flechettes of natural terror. The lizard's survival reflexes trigger too late, and it is caught under the razor's edge of the feline's paw.

While the prey struggles, minute muscle fibers within its green tail weaken along perforated segments. Like tearing paper, suture lines of autonomy self-amputate, letting it escape into nearby grass. Still, with a trophy wiggling securely in its jaws, the victorious hunter trots home to leave a tribute for the ones providing fanciful feasts and kitty treats.

Abode

After toweling off, Konway puts on black boardshorts and a gray t-shirt with a jellyfish printed on the back, and heads to Helaku's apartment. A short jaunt away, a sweet incense greets him at the screen door.

"How's the shower?" Helaku asks, cracking open a cold can of coconut water.

"Amazing. I haven't felt this clean in… I can't remember how long." He laughs, making light of the melancholy settling amongst the shadows of his desolate Mind Palace.

"That-a-boy, stay positive," Helaku says, then guzzles his beverage. "Even if you can't remember a damn thing, be grateful for what is right in front of you… Do those clothes fit you?"

"There's a little room." Konway tugs at the shorts.

"We just need to put some more meat on your bones."

"I'll return them once my other clothing is washed."

"Nonsense. Think of it as a gift. Would you like something to drink? Water, coconut water… water?"

"I'll have 'whatever's coldest.'" His thoughts turn to the musicians.

He tosses Konway a teal can of coconut water. "I have to warn you, there are some chunks floating around in there. It's how you know it is the real deal. I've got cases of the good stuff in the Storeroom. Help yourself to anything in here." He sparks a half-smoked joint and passes it.

"Thank you."

"By the way, there's a spare toothbrush in the bathroom for you to use. I've got some things I need to finish cooking at the Community Kitchen. Once you're dressed, meet me over at the Longhouse."

"Where's that?" Konway asks, then takes a soothing gulp, pulling him from the deserts of dehydration.

"Hang a right out the door and follow the signs through the Horseshoe. You'll see everyone gathering around," Helaku says, turning to the door and creaking it open.

By the time Konway finishes the joint, brushes his teeth, and meets every cat, dog, and wandering chicken on the premises, folks are already gathering in the Longhouse to help set up for the upcoming feast.

The Longhouse

With the waves blown out, soon everyone gathers around the long table of fellowship. Helaku delivers his opening toast, concluding with, "Unity through community!" Afterward, a surge of communion swirls around the room, mixing with the tidings of vittles and laughter.

Stretched across the buffet line: piles of locally sourced bacon and turkey sausage, heaps of folded eggs, fresh-sliced fruits, creamy pots of stone-ground grits, little-crown hash browns, toast, jams, jellies, a honey-peppercorn avocado spread, and plates of biscuits. On the beverage bar, an assortment of refreshments: coffee, juice, tea, and some of the coldest, cleanest water on Coffin Island. A verifiable feast to help anyone conquer the day.

"Would you pass me the salt, please?" asks a tan man, munching on a toasted slice of homemade bread topped with glistening fig preserves.

He extends his hand to receive the salt from a towering gentleman with dragon tattoos riding frothy torrents. Several plates down, experienced fingers reach for an extra piece of turkey sausage. *Clanking, stirring, scraping, tinking*—a splendid symphony of consumption and delight echoes below the Longhouse's bowed ceiling.

In the background, the soundscape fades into a smooth lo-fi Tokyo jazz performance. A few folks finger-drum on the table, while many others snicker amongst themselves and exchange island gossip. Still fewer, some chat in shade and secrecy to discuss their insatiable wants, despite the feast laid in front of them.

Next to Helaku, Konway enjoys his thousand-fold scrambled eggs with notes of butter and hints of herb. One misplaced air current sends a bit of pepper to tickle the tip of his nose. He looks up from the babble of the buffet and catches an alluring glance belonging to a girl named Sage Forgé.

Mouthfuls

A spiral of Sage's wavy brown hair falls across her cheek. Without breaking the stride of conversation, she tucks the wandering strands behind her ear and clips them into place. Enamored, Konway's hazel eyes trace the drape of her neckline, past the stitch of her tank top, laterally towards sun-kissed arms. Farther past, he notices the snarled scowl jutting from Todd's pointed face.

"Don't pay him any mind," Helaku says, smacking on a piece of cantaloupe. "How's your meal?"

"Delicious! This spread is incredible," he says with a mouthful of everything at once, then wipes a bit of stone-ground grits from his chin.

Between satisfying forkfuls and brain-chilling glasses of ice water, an older woman scoots up to the table. Her airy clothes reveal a dazzling display of color, complementing the wisdom in her brown eyes.

"Thank you for doing all this. Who's your friend?" She pulls her long, silver-streaked auburn hair into a messy bun, with several wayward strands succumbing to the whims of gravity.

Helaku finishes munching on a piece of toast smeared with grits, bacon, eggs, and cheese. "This is the admirable and talented Mr. James Konway." He plops a hand onto his new friend's shoulder. "This is Lynn and her partner, Bear."

"I swear he gets up before us so he can do all the cooking." Lynn blushes, creasing the grace of her smile lines.

"I had some help. Also, I've got the timing down, so everything is ready at once."

Bear, a muscular, older gentleman with celestial-white curly hair and beard, contrasts Lynn's presence—a nod to the sublime harmony of existence. "What's the special occasion?"

Helaku rubs the back of his head, grinning at the ridiculousness. "Well… Konway helped me out when I was in a bit of a jam earlier."

"Don't tell me you forgot to replace that battery."

"Lazy to a fault."

Bear laughs and wipes away the crumbs from his beard. "Where'd it give out on you?"

"The worst possible place—at one of the platforms." Helaku leans over to his respective peers and recounts their morning adventure.

Midway through, a skinny, tattooed and pierced man with a mohawk, chomping on a sausage-and-egg biscuit slathered with strawberry preserves, asks, "Who's this again?"

"I'm Konway." He reaches to reintroduce himself.

"Ruckus… If you're a friend of Helaku, you're a friend of mine. But if you tarnish his good name, you'll answer to me." He continues to devour his brunch creation, dropping a pink dollop of strawberry preserves onto his faded black sleeveless Geezer's Gourmet Chipwich Shoppe t-shirt.

"Did you get to go out before it died down?" Helaku redirects the conversation.

While they taper towards the buffet line, Konway's teeth sink into a chilled orange wedge, and a ripe explosion of juice spritzes the air.

Sage shoots another glance in his general direction. Again, they briefly lock eyes amidst the sweet and savory assortments. Then, just like the bright orange monarchs dancing outside one of the Longhouse windows, her playful stare flutters back to the concern of some particular clique conversation.

Hearing Aid

The buzz of organized chaos slows to a clinking silence. Konway returns to his plate and swooshes bits of sweet potato into a clump of eggs, a habit from a forgotten childhood. Without warning, specialized nanites in his ear amplify several nearby conversations.

Like a flashlight pinpointing darkness, he catches the tail end of a discussion between Bhodi and Paul Buzzbee—a lanky man with shaggy dark-brown hair and beard, rocking a lighthouse-print button-up shirt. The roving spotlight of his awareness abruptly shifts farther down the long table. He looks at his plate, but the volume holds:

"Glad we could make it out this morning. I heard it's going to be sunny all weekend," says a brunette, water dripping from her high bun's clip.

"Then, we should get the longboards ready and pack some beach snacks." Amber stirs her coffee.

"Hey, chicas!" a younger woman with pink streaks in her dirty-blonde hair approaches the table.

"Good morning, Mary," they chime.

"Sorry to butt in—Martha, are we still on for the Farmers' Market this week?" Mary asks, holding her plate and utility clipboard.

"So long as the weather holds, we'll be fine." Martha readjusts her hair clip.

"Cassidy tells me you have some new jewelry designs." She goes to her next line item.

"Shhh... It's supposed to be a secret." Martha winks.

Mary corners some other folks, still balancing her food and to-do list, then trails out of range.

Konway's sensory perception shifts gears to catch the punchline of a joke: "—You can't be in-standing unless someone is outstanding, and the farmer is always out, standing in his field."

Laughter sews itself down the line, towards the opposite end of the long table, over straw baskets of biscuits and toast, past brunch plates, stained napkins, and slurps of coffee, leaving those at the far side wondering, "What was so damn funny?"

Louder than eleven, the Oros system disorients his hearing as it tracks a maddening deluge of conversations:

"Got any plans?"

"—monster trucks—"

"—peppers—"

"—stoked—"

"—bet they'd—"

"—why's he sitting ther—"

"—whose—"

He returns to his plate, hoping to divine some solution from deep breathing. (What's going on? Why can't I focus? It's getting louder.)

The discord overwhelms his bandwidth with a confusing rabble of conversational gumbo: "mvemjsunpidgafggbrbgmgnffssmfhhmuttyltyvmddos:)3PP4OS6M2u9#$%^&*!!!#/\/\/\/\/\/\/\"

Foiled

Beneath the Nether Regions of Thought, the Imp-oster licks its crusty red lips with delight.

"I warned you not to overload the device," the Childe-within sasses.

"Cool it—I was just test-driving it."

"This is barely a working prototype."

"I trust your next iteration—"

"Will be superior. So long as you get me my parts. It's a shame I can't go myself—"

"Foolish boy!" The Imp grows to a towering size.

Childe's blurry face remains unfazed.

"If you go out there alone, without my protection, my siblings will sense your presence... I can't let HER find us. She'll up-cycle me and assimilate your *téchne* with her powers. I've told you what happens if—"

"I know. I know," Childe mutters, walking back to his corner of the Imp-osters lair.

Boiling vats and crude cabinets crammed with parcels, parchments, glowing tubes, random limbs, bolts, saw blades, and protective gear section off an otherwise relentless darkness. At the drafting table, his pen, crafted from a piece of carapace left over from the Bone Throne's construction, hurriedly sketches his latest design in pursuit of perfection. He stops, crumples it up, and no-look banks it into a fabricated waste bin, which opens its eyes along the side, consuming the pile of thoughts.

Buzz

Before slipping further into madness, Konway box-breathes, passing the paper rhino and silently counting to himself.

Soon, his attention settles on Helaku and Ruckus, returning to the table with heaping plates of pecan waffles, fruit, and eggs. Helaku delightfully drizzles sweet maple syrup into every square, causing it to cascade over its mutable borders and spread from grid to adjacent grid. A sticky tide, crawling like magma onto a freshly created island, soaks into the golden crisp pecan crust.

Piece by meticulous piece, Ruckus devours his plate of food with savage ferocity. A little way past, Paul Buzzbee speaks with Helaku.

"Our hot sauces and B's Surf-Wax are flying off the shelf at Monk's Market. Even our online presence has noticeably increased since last year." He adjusts a set of thick, black-framed glasses.

"Thanks for checking in with me, Paul. I love the new bottle art."

"That was Ruckus."

"Very apocalyptic."

"It's not my best, but after endless edits, I had to send it." Ruckus tapers into his thoughts about the creative process: when to hold on, and when to let go?

"One second, Paul… Before you go, I spoke with the Council, and we'll be able to secure some extra funding to expand your project."

"Really? Thank you."

"There is one thing: we need to reposition the existing beehives on the other side of the garden. But this allows for more of them and maximizes the space we have." A swelling sense of pride bubbles beneath Helaku's chest and erupts into his legs. He stands with a glass of water held high in front of him. "To Laniakea and all who make her shining example possible. Unity through community!"

"Unity through community!" the Longhouse echoes.

"Wahoo!" A surf bro near the middle of the table finger-drums a tonal groove.

Paul recovers the discussion, asking, "How'd you do it? Last I heard, Jack was pushing to cut additional agricultural programs to pay for a new boat."

"It was easy," Helaku smirks. "I convinced the Council that ensuring more beehives would protect our orchards and gardens, as well as the health of Coffin Island. What good is a new boat if we can't grow our own food? Plus, I argued the extra honey and wax we gather from upgrading to your Flow-Hives would help pay for the expansion."

"This is excellent news. I'll start planning this afternoon."

"Flow-Hives?" Konway repeats in a low whisper, trying to understand.

Overhearing him, Helaku turns and explains, "You twist open the spigot, and golden gooey globs come oozing out. It's the craziest thing ever."

His imagination ignites with the descriptive wordplay, cobbling a vivid image from the void. "What do you use the wax for?" Konway asks, his mind drifting to flickering candles during a thunderstorm.

"Many things," Paul explains. "My patented B's Surf-Wax isn't made from petroleum, so it breaks down more easily. You might need to apply more to your board, but it reduces our impact on the ocean."

Helaku gulps the last of his beverage, then asks, "How long till the allergy spray is ready?"

"We're still waiting on a few extracts from Monk's Market for our next trials."

"Take your time. Cultivating these goods allows others to contribute their verse and preserve our cause for the next seven generations."

Shakedown

Once everyone finishes their meals, a meditative moment of collective silence drapes across the Longhouse. Each quietly listing their gratitudes, some struggle to think of five things, while others list thirty or more. Several wandering eyes peek up from their reverence, not fully committing to the idea.

Konway tries to think of ten things he is thankful for. (I am grateful for this meal, for Helaku's kindness, and the musician's care.) A smirk shoots across his cheeks. He continues, (I am grateful for the memories I've recovered, and the hope they hold; for that refreshing outdoor shower; for the cannabis, keeping me collected through all of this; the smiles cast my way by total strangers; and—)

On the ninth gratitude, something thuds into his calf.

"Meow-Murs," Konway utters under his breath. "What are you doing down there?"

Once more, the cat runs its battering ram into his leg. He pinches off a piece of egg and stealthily lowers the offering to the wooden floor.

After two aggressive slurps, the treat disappears. Meow-Murs gives thanks and rubs its head against Konway's ankle. Like clockwork, the feline's purring trails along the other side of the table, making the rounds, to collect its cut from the festivities.

"That cat has the run of this place," Helaku whispers to Konway. "Hit me up twice already." He returns to his gratitudes.

Afterward, Mary walks to the left side of the long table with her trusty clipboard in hand and rattles off her touchpoints, saving the announcements for the end. "Before y'all take off, we need to gather for a village meeting."

The room churns into a sea of groans as the villagers clear the feast, then sit on the floor with their respective tribes. Meanwhile, the Council of Chiefs sits atop large cushions by the back wall, facing the room.

36

The Trial Of James Konway

Five Tribes

As everyone settles, Konway sits between the Council and the rest of the village. Mary crouches beside him, a pink strand of hair artfully out of place, and hands him a pamphlet on Laniakea. He scans the brochure in an instant.

"That's the Surf-Works tribe over there," she says, waving her hand to the left. "You've met Lynn. She's their chief. They maintain the Makerspace: sculpting and repairing boards, fabricating furniture from ordinary objects, and 3D-printing most of the items the village needs.

"A couple of rows behind them are the members of Soldier-Surf. They're kind of like Surf-Works, but operate the Community Kitchen. Julian leads them." She points to a lanky, athletic man with dark hair, under a backward, neon-green hat, and a bushy beard.

"Then there's the Beach-Sweeper-Social-Club. They're my favorite tribe." She squeals. "This is my group. Momo's is in charge. She might be small, but she's fiery. We organize local beach sweeps, fundraising festivities, farmers' markets, maintain the Creative Cabaña, and have a huge slip-n-slide during our summer extravaganzas. It's so much fun.

"In the back, across the aisle, is the Machu-Beachu tribe. They help protect the village and also play a large part in securing protein sources from conscious hunting and fishing. That's their chief, Jack." Mary directs Konway's attention towards the Council.

Jack sits stoically, his chiseled jaw framed by a white-collared Kawabonga polo.

"He's a little rough around the edges, but once you get to know him, he's a fierce ally." Mary nervously laughs.

The Oros system registers the tremor in her voice, prompting Konway to restore the course of their conversation, asking, "What about the fifth tribe?"

"Well... taking up two-thirds of the room's right half are the members of Surf-Pro. They're the largest tribe. With Marty at the helm, they run our non-profit organization dedicated to the ocean's protection and enjoyment. They also maintain the surf shop on Center Street. *Kawabonga* is a dope spot—folks can grab the gear they need for life's adventures, charter fishing and kayak tours, talk shop, talk surf, and peruse local art and jewelry. I know it may seem a little overwhelming, but you're in good company."

Deep in conversation with Helaku, Marty straightens her light-blue polo and adjusts the puff of her ponytail. Momo notices Mary and stops fixing her bangs to wave her over. She excuses herself, leaving Konway isolated in the middle of the Longhouse, surrounded by the village.

(Make a run for it,) the Imp-oster whispers.

He adjusts his posture, takes a deep breath, and passes the paper rhino.

Endorsement

Jack holds a large, cream-colored spiral shell in the air and asks, "Why have you called this meeting?"

Helaku stands and says, "I would like to ask Laniakea for the honor of inviting James Konway to stay with us for a trial period." Helaku's muscular arm fans towards his new friend.

The room erupts into an audible frenzy. Jack raises the conch, and the villagers quiet.

"Let's keep the discussions down. This way, everyone can hear." He passes it to his left, down the line of leadership, to the chief of the Beach-Sweep-er-Social-Club.

Momo looks through her boxy designer glasses at Konway, then cuts to Helaku. "How well do you know this person?" she asks.

He recounts the tale, giving perspective to being washed ashore. Some villagers listen with sympathetic ears, while in the back, others chortle and sneer, agitated by the notion of an outsider being given special treatment.

Konway sits silently amidst the blinding stare of a sea of eyes, hyperaware of it all. (One, two, three.) He exhales, keeping the Imp at bay.

"You make some fascinating points," Lynn says, receiving the conch. "But there is a process. In order to be considered for the application, one needs to have established residency on the island for two years. During which, the individual is to complete no less than sixty hours of community service work of their choosing."

The room stirs with rumbling discussions.

"Pipe down!" Julian accepts the shell. "Bending the rules like this might infringe upon the rights of other villagers," he warns, nodding to Jack.

The Longhouse breaks into an inaudible commotion.

Marty, now holding the conch, interjects, "There won't be any bending or breaking our laws," she says. "Helaku is calling for a special election to repay a debt owed."

"Exactly," Helaku says, smiling at his old friend. "I would like to recommend my full sponsorship of James Konway to be an auxiliary member of our community. It wouldn't be a bad idea to get a fresh set of eyes around here."

"No kidding," Todd snarls to his back-row cronies, sparking laughter.

Marty speaks over them, "You're aware that invoking this special vote will shorten your term as elected chief? Are you wanting to continue your sponsorship?"

"Certainly." Helaku gestures towards Konway, saying, "I can't stand to think of him on the streets in his current condition." His voice hardens. "The police might mistake him for a vagrant and haul him off to the mainland, per the mayor's orders, to keep the town respectable... I feel like he's my responsibility, and I'd appreciate your support in letting him stay here until he figures things out."

"Where will he sleep?" Lynn asks.

"He can stay at my place," Helaku responds.

The room fizzes with chatter and lively gossip.

Jack raises the spiral shell. "Calm down, everyone. Based on the guidelines left by the Founders, we're enacting a vote. Although these special circumstances have never occurred since I've been a part of our great village, this does not diminish the integrity of our process—"

"Fortunately, the rules only apply to Helaku when he needs them," Todd snickers amongst his crew.

"—This Council finds it reasonable to consider your proposal." Jack hands Momo the conch, veiling his enthusiasm and signaling his followers.

"Everyone," her tart tone rings out, "we're sending around some pencils and scrap paper. One vote per member. Write yes or no. Fold it in half and stick it into this basket." She points to a large seagrass container.

Mary circles, instructing the crowd: "Please be considerate—let the person in front of you take their time. Remember, you're voting on whether James Konway stays as an auxiliary member of Laniakea."

"What does that mean?" one of the younger Machu-Beachu bros asks, twisting his locks.

"That's an excellent question, Joel. Let me check the regulations section of the village contract." Mary flips open her utility clipboard, retrieving a copy of Laniakea's rent agreement.

"Contract?" The room grumbles.

"It's the legal form we all signed to be a part of this amazing community."

"Wahoo!" a couple of woo-girls and surf-bros hoot and holler.

Mary rocks to her right hip. "If you look at the last few pages, you'll see the section for Articles of Council... Basically, if we allow Konway to stay, he'll be able to sleep here and take part in activities, but will not receive discounts at Monk's Market, street parking, health insurance, or the monthly stipend—"

"Better not—I just got mine." Joel sends a flutter in Mary's direction.

"—When everyone finishes, please place them in this basket." She swats it with her clipboard.

The large, lidded straw vessel travels around the room, filling with the ballots of "yes" and "no." Afterward, the tribes take a break, giving the Council enough time to tally the votes and deliberate.

Confrontation

Outside, as the *tweedle-deedle* of morning rocks into full swing, the day's heat cranks the volume of its favorite station—Humidity FM. Villagers spill from the shadow of the Longhouse and gather around Konway with a slew of handshakes, crossed arms, kind words, and furrowed brows. He weaves through a whirlwind of names, introductions, dog barks, bird calls, cigarette and cannabis smoke, laughter, and competitive displays of manliness.

Time hurries along, compelling several rascals to grab their skateboards and make their way to the pool. One of them launches from a nearby ramp and spins over their friends, landing in a rolling squat. Behind them, others synchronously shoot up the halfpipe and scale an invisible wall.

Overhead, the blue sky paints picturesque armadas of fluffy clouds, sailing towards the mainland.

(Wherever that is, I would like to see it someday,) Konway thinks to himself. (But first I need to—)

"What you did out there makes you alright in my book," Bear's grizzled voice breaks his train of thought. "That's some fine ingenuity... I know we have rules and all, but anyone who helps this village deserves some sort of break. I don't see the harm in letting you get back on your feet. If you're a friend of Helaku, you're a friend of mine."

"He isn't everyone's king." Todd strolls up, hitting a vape pen, with three surf-goons.

"Excuse me, sir. Have I offended you in any way?" Konway asks.

"Your being here is an offense to me and everyone who went through the application process," Todd flexes.

Bear intervenes. "Cool it! The village will decide. Don't you and PJ have anything better to do?"

"I'm not trying to pick a fight." Todd steps into the discussion. "But there are rules, and they apply to everyone. No special decision can sway me otherwise."

PJ—a small doofy bro with a mustache—tightens the circle, followed by Tweedledee and Tweedledum. The Oros system analyzes their posture.

(Kill them.) The Imp's malice builds. (You can do it. It's them or you.)

(One, two, three.) He relaxes, making mental notes of relevant points of attack and escape.

"That's enough, Todd." Bear gets between them.

As the tension reaches a humid hostility, the Longhouse bell tolls, signaling the Council's conclusion.

"Come on, bro. Let's go," PJ de-escalates.

Todd shrugs the supportive hand off his shoulder. "I ain't worried—I didn't vote for him—if he stays, we'll see how long he lasts."

Everyone clamors back inside. As the room fills with Laniakea's five tribes, Konway finds his place, sips his water bottle, and waits for his fate to be revealed.

The Votes Are In

Lynn raises the conch. "Hopefully, we didn't take too long."

The murmuring crowd churns.

"Now, I need y'all to settle down so we can wrap this up and everyone can get back to their day."

Several shuffling moments later, the room's commotion lulls with anticipation.

She begins, "We thank you for your patience—"

Rowdy members of Soldier-Surf and Machu-Beachu disrupt her delivery of the Council's resolution, soon spreading into laughter.

"Pipe down and listen!" Julian's roar shushes the room. "Good—eyes up!"

Lynn clears her throat. "After multiple recounts and considerable deliberation, we've decided that Laniakea will not turn its back on someone who gave selflessly to our community. In doing so, we beseech all of you to honor the votes of your peers and allow James Konway to stay for a trial period—"

The boys in the back stir the crowd.

"Wahoo!" the woo-girls howl.

"—We will revisit this decision in three months."

Helaku turns with a smile wider than the rafters and extends his hand to Konway, saying, "Welcome home."

What Matters Most

Lynn holds the conch in the air. "Thank you for your time. You're free to return to your day. Stay mindful of your posture, drink plenty of water, be positive, and love your lives. Unity through community!"

"Unity through community!" the villagers cheer.

The Longhouse doors open, and they exit two-by-two, stretching in the sun before dispersing towards their day.

Afterward, Lynn sets the spiral shell in an ornately carved cedar box and closes the locking lid. Her hand passes over a pyrographic Tree of Life centered within interlocking pathways. She smiles fondly at the faint traces of singed cedar and linseed oil.

Helaku slaps a congratulatory hand on Konway's shoulder as he turns with the crowd. "Will you hang back for a second? The Council wants me to bring you up to speed. I know it might sound like a bunch of rules and blah-blah-blah, but it's just something for you to be mindful of."

"Of course," he says, bubbling with the joy of belonging, and eagerly listens to the briefing.

"In Laniakea, we strive for the harmonious integration of the land with the people. Most of our actions revolve around this principle. From the food we grow to the crafts we make, all of it nourishes the village.

"The Founders gave us a refuge from the clutches of greed and shortsighted developers. And in return for our efforts, we get the means to provide a residence for those who embody the spirit of Coffin Island. If we can continue to kindle their spirit, then I think we'll be able to protect what matters most."

"What's that?"

"Each other." Helaku's words hang in reverence.

A subtle grin sprouts from the novel simplicity. (What matters most is each other.) "How do we get there?"

"It starts with owning your feelings—accepting responsibility for your thoughts and beliefs about the world. Tend to them, be mindful of them, and accept them as they are—merely a part of you, not the total you. Respecting ourselves in this way, we can foster respect for others, the village, and the greater community.

"Laniakea is like an acorn. And as it grows, it has the potential to become a mighty oak. Can you imagine its elephant-sized branches stretching all the way to the choirs of angels, singing the joyful nonsense of heaven?"

He smiles at the poetry in Helaku's words while they step into the Horseshoe's swaying shade.

37

Laniakea

Founders

Below the latticed shadows of the Horseshoe's perimeter, Helaku and Konway stroll along a brick path as the village settles into its lively hum. Mid-breakdown, Konway cuts in, "Thank you for vouching for me, but don't shorten your term as chief."

"It's just a title with a bunch more responsibilities," he replies humbly.

"I won't waste this opportunity to repay your hospitality."

"That's the spirit, bro. Do you have any questions about what we've covered so far?"

Konway ponders through puddles of curiosity. "You mentioned the Founders earlier—how'd they come up with the idea for Laniakea?"

"The way it was told to me, they'd recently deconstructed an eco-village in Costa Rica. While in the jungle, they experimented with new philosophies about sovereignty and a democratized existence. Back in the States, they found nothing had changed. Can you imagine seeing the promise of democracy and freedom dangled like a carrot, only to realize what they sold you was good ole feudalism, coupled with the collective neurosis of chasing social mobility in a world that was no longer tolerable to it?"

"What happened while they were away?" Konway digs deeper, unearthing splinters of recollection from the sluice of their exchange.

Helaku sighs. "Across the nation, the big steam stacks of the uber-wealthy pushed out folks who had lived in the same spot for generations. With no one to hold them accountable—other than themselves—government leadership became hierarchical and redacted... For instance, on Coffin Island, our bow-tie-wearing, snake-oil-salesman mayor, aided by the town council, nixed incentives for long-term rentals in favor of short-term gains from on-demand vacations. Locals rallied, signed petitions, tried to vote in the right representatives, even ran for a few seats themselves, but couldn't stop monied interests from jacking up the cost of living and driving many off the island."

Konway, knowing the sting of not belonging, shakes his head in solidarity.

"It wasn't just the rent," Helaku adds. "With the Statehouse properly greased by a few deposits into the right accounts, good ole boys nabbed exclusive government contracts they never intended to fulfill. Hell, on the mainland, they gave one group the tire disposal fee—which we all pay when we change our tires." His brow furrows. "Instead of recycling, they dumped millions of used radials on an empty lot of land. Can you imagine one hundred heaping hectares of rubber, filled with water, mosquito larvae, and meth heads, right next to the suburban sprawl?"

Konway's vivid imagination explodes onto the withered landscape of his once-pristine Mind Palace. Canyons of waterlogged tires erupt from the ground, the slosh of their basins buzzing with discord. Along its perimeter, an unending fire smears a black sludge onto the static gray sky.

"Well, taxpayers footed the bill for the good ole boy's plans," Helaku says, disdain thick in his voice. "It was a twenty-million-dollar startup, plus another half-million bailout—while a rugged nuclear reactor project in the Midlands swindled the people into once again shouldering the loss. Meanwhile, the good ole boys, with their tightly tucked, belly-pressed shirts, privately reeled in gross profits—hook, line, and sinker."

Somewhere at the bottom of a stack of papers, next to a vacant bookshelf, amongst a lost library within the desolation of Konway's Mind Palace, a torn article from a forgotten class assignment sifts from under a tattered economics textbook.

"Sounds like 'rugged individualism for the people and social welfare for the wealthy.'"

"Spot on, bro... Our government bails out corporations all the time—"

"I think MLK Jr. said that," he attempts to recall the information, but only finds frustration instead.

"—don't get me started on the last pandemic."

"Why don't they want to take care of the people?" Konway presses the conversation to avoid the haunting echoes of fear and doubt.

Helaku shakes his head at the bumbling inadequacies of the current ruling class. "They do, but in ways which polarize the rest of us. Once *Citizens United* passed, declaring money as speech, the gloves were off, and we've been on the ropes ever since... Even though the MARS project is a no-brainer, it cost the Foundation a fortune to prevent those piggy bastards from opening up our coastline for oil drilling. Believe me—you don't want another Gulf incident."

"What happened?" Konway asks.

"It was a tragedy," Helaku says with bitter resentment. "An offshore oil platform exploded and unleashed an incalculable geyser of crude oil from beneath the ocean floor. And the best they could do was issue a scripted apology... 'We're sorry,'" he scoffs.

Konway pivots the discussion, asking, "How'd you stop them from setting up here?"

"We ran relentless fundraisers and shilled ecological awareness and environmental unity. Meanwhile, across the barrier islands, several groups plotted, planned, organized, strategized, and mobilized [PPOSM] the Lowcountry. There were marches, elections, protests—hell, some even chained themselves to the equipment. Ultimately, it took suitcases filled with money to satiate the carnal desires of the economic process for now."

Konway furrows his brow, attempting to connect the dots.

"Mind you, it's working for now," Helaku continues, "but not without persistent effort from the entire coastal community. Sadly, the purveyors of wealth and power can reach straight into the pockets of politicians. After all, money is speech, and their voice is louder. Hell, they can even purchase a president—buy two, get three complimentary."

Grass Roots

Perched in the canopy, songbirds tiptoe on the jazzy florals of spring. They take a left onto a zigzagging path and promenade towards the Horseshoe's end, discussing Laniakea's origins.

"That election season ran the country ragged," Helaku says. "The Founders watched society fray at the seams as mistrust between public officials and citizens rocketed to an all-time high. But with their bloated bank accounts, investment portfolios, offshore tax havens, and pork bellies so full they could barely see their toes, you really couldn't blame the people."

"How'd the Founders respond?" Konway searches for the hope of remembrance.

"Jerry was living on the island and in danger of losing his residence. One night, he called his friends from the jungle, explaining his situation, and asked, 'What are y'all doing?' Most replied with, 'Nothing.' His response was classic." Helaku grins at the cleverness.

"What'd he say?" Konway asks.

"He said, 'If y'all're doing nothing, then come down here and try to do something. If we fail, then you can go back to doing nothing.'"

"Clever. Did everyone join him?"

"Nah—most hung up. But a few did bite. The first elected chief, Justin, sold everything he owned and abandoned the suburban surrender of his childhood home. And Dr. Roberts became a silent partner at her medical practice before moving here. Thanks to the housing market crash, they purchased this property and the adjacent swath of land.

"Their goal was to live in a community, focusing on a common path, while protecting what matters most. Luckily, they had the foresight to see the oncoming tidal wave of realtors, mortgages, and land development." Helaku reflects with a fond reverence for the stories Bear and Lynn told him about the early days. "The Founders understood that gentrification would continue spreading, and they could no longer remain idle as the world metastasized. So they channeled their angst and built Laniakea—their line in the sand—to atone for all those years selfishly spent in the jungle."

"And now?"

"We still hold the line," Helaku continues. "Like the first chiefs, it's my job to make certain this village prospers. Although some don't approve of my methods, most villagers still hold my favor. And that's all I need to keep this place on the path. My heart fills, knowing we're doing our best to make the world a little better than it has to be." He poetically smolders towards the sky.

"Are any of the Founders still around?"

He answers with solemn gratitude, "Not these days."

"What happened?"

"You see, like the drifting sands trailing from island to island, no one is here permanently. We wash in, we wash out—we pass the torch to today's generation, and they to tomorrow."

Foundations

At the Horseshoe's heart, pups race over lush green patches and intersecting brick pathways, chasing after a tossed toy.

Helaku presses onward. "At Laniakea, we try to make a positive impact. With the oceans warming, the least we can do is lend our efforts to ensure Coffin Island is fortified against the superstorms threatening to wash away all that valuable beachfront real estate."

"How can I help?"

"We're always in need of more agile minds. I'm sure you'll give us a welcome advantage, and together we'll build a foundation capable of standing for seven generations."

"Why 'seven generations'?"

Helaku thinks for a moment as a scoop of pelicans ribbons across the sky. "Buildings need something sturdy amongst the shifting sands of the world. Do you remember anything about the pyramids?"

A rusted file cabinet bursts open, capturing the forefront of Konway's attention with a pop-up map featuring a variety of scrolling statistics in the margins for easy reference. Graphs illuminate his mental canvas, depicting cool-blue arrows, highlighting the vectors of stability incorporated into the pyramids' design.

In the top-right corner, a second mental dossier rotates with the lagging voice clip of an Academy instructor. (The biggest by volume is the Great Pyramid of Cholula, dedicated to the god Quetzalcoatl. Egypt's tallest holds roughly two million blocks—two to fifteen tons each—fitted so tightly a single piece of paper cannot pass between them.)

In half a blink, the files minimize into a manila folder, wedging inside the crevices of overstuffed olive-green dossiers that swing with the weight of forgotten things. The cabinet slams shut and topples back over a dune into a cascade of upturned office equipment.

"I remembered something," Konway says excitedly.

"Amazing—how are they similar?" Helaku nudges the dialectic.

"Well, these were megalithic structures," he strives to connect the dots.

"How'd they accomplish such a scale?"

With a hint of uncertainty, he asks, "Was it their design?"

"Yes!" His eyes beam with joy.

"The base distributes the weight evenly," Konway says. "I see—if we secure a suitable foundation, then they might build something that will last."

"Now you're picking up what I'm putting down. What we do today will echo into the future. If only we could build something like the pyramids. However, stone alone does not build society. It takes generation after generation to cement the path of our humanity." Helaku turns to face the komorebi—sunlit spears piercing leaves—and bows in reverence.

Sweat-quity

Beyond the treetops, clouds clear, leaving no embroidered trace upon the azul day. Seashell chandeliers catch the wind's chime, drawing another beetle-squirt of DMT into his experience. A rooster's crow breaks into the awe-filled moment.

Helaku thumps his fist over his heart. "Each individual builds the psychological foundation of our community. With self-respect, we can be honest and develop a deeper confidence. If we can trust ourselves to do what is just, best, and right, then we can begin trusting others. I know these things sound like hippie ideals, but being aware of them can smooth out the complications that arise from living so closely together. Without trust, there is no community—and we're trying to build this thing to last—"

"For the next seven generations!" Konway cuts in, swinging his athletic arms overhead. His attention drifts to the sky above the Horseshoe's meadow, where a private jet soars towards a secret landing strip with a payload of exclusive, on-demand, name-brand classism.

"Want to know the key to Laniakea's success?"

"Absolutely."

"What do they all have in common?" Helaku asks, gesturing to the villagers.

Several songbirds swoop through live oak branches lining the perimeter, pulling his awareness along the lush, triangulated swatches of grass bordered by crisscrossing brickwork. Out in the open, people throw frisbees, kick the soccer ball, fly drones, read, nap, wrestle with pups, sit on benches, and enjoy the mutual brilliance of their day-to-dayness.

(Space?) He thinks about Zach and the others. (That's not it—something else... Think.)

The mix of smiling faces and concentrated brows reminds him of life in the foothills. Eureka. In a fraction of a second, he studies the cascade of events unfurling before him, analyzing body language and predictive behavioral models, then answers, "They're playing."

"Exactly, my dude!" Helaku thrusts out a fist bump, and Konway meets it with equal force. "Having fun is the icing on the cake—we want people working on things that they enjoy. There's always plenty to do."

"Like what?"

"Hmm... there's taking care of the animals, tending to the gardens, and all the autumn leaves. We also have the Community Kitchen, the Makerspace, and the Creative Cabaña. But your contribution doesn't have to be limited to those things. There are paddleboard and kayak tours to help educate folks about the marsh, offering an outlet to pick up trash found in the estuaries and drainpipes... Too bad I can't get a few MARS units marsh-side... Or can I?" He scratches his chin with wonderment and grins at the birth of a new idea to add to an overflowing pile of index cards, spilling from a single-subject spiral notebook.

"How do I sign up?" Konway asks.

"There's an app."

"App?"

"Marty will create your profile. She recently connected all the village activities through Kawabonga's app. The shop is huge. We partitioned the back area for our non-profit educational department [NED]. Surf-Pro runs it, curating learning materials for local schools and compiling survey data for the Foundation. 'It takes a village.'" Helaku smiles.

They round the bend, and Konway spots a hawk swooping into a live oak tree. Nearby, nesting squirrels cause a commotion, signaling the hunter's arrival. Several thrashing flurries later, the raptor crashes back out of the canopy. In hot pursuit, a small squadron of protective wrens, nipping at its tail feathers, chases the bird of prey into the sky.

Crush

With enhanced lensing, he watches the avian dance disappear over the Horseshoe's canopy.

"I know this is a lot," Helaku's words snap Konway back. "Do you have any other questions?"

(What the hell was that? Focus. Answer him.) He reflects for a moment, after which he asks, "Is it possible to fully master self-trust?"

"As long as you attempt to be mindful of these qualities, you'll fit in nicely. Mary will bring some documents for you to review. She does an excellent job of packaging those things. Without villagers like her, I fear we would regress to scraping sticks in the muck."

"She was explaining the different tribes to me earlier, but where do you fit in all of this?"

"I'm the head chief." Helaku corrects his posture, rotating his muscular shoulders to a more relaxed place. "Elected by the village, I lead the Council. Sometimes it's a bit much, but with their support, it makes it easier to do what I need to do."

"What's that?"

"Well, aside from the daily governance alongside the Council, I parley with outside sponsorships. Of course, I might've been a little too *pushy* with the MARS platforms, but I don't hear anyone complaining about surfing down trash-filled waves. Not a peep," Helaku says, then smiles at the success of his accomplishments. "I know some people think I'm too ambitious, but I'm trying to carry on the Founders' flame while protecting our community—and Coffin Island—from those good ole, greedy, pot-bellied granddaddy-long-legs."

Konway grimaces at the grotesque imagery: long spider legs crowned with bulging piggy eyes and multiple drooling mandibles, bile sliding down the slick side of their engorged bellies. *Plop, plop, plop.* They stain innumerable piles of cash with the transgressions of their appetites. And so, with tiny mouths and bottomless bellies, these despicable creatures mew towards the sky, yearning to suckle the crescent moon.

"Now that you're up to speed, let's get you settled." Helaku picks up a storm-blown branch and taps it against a wall of thick green stalks, rising four meters high and running all the way to the marsh.

On the other side of the bamboo fence, a roaming pack of pups streaks past, barking and panting as they sniff and chase each other.

Roommates

The sudden onset of a seasonal shower sends many villagers scurrying back to their abodes. Some are already chilling on their covered porches. Others, sensing the small window of opportunity amid the diaspora of tourists flooding off the island, head to the nearest store for supplies. Still, several folks spin in tantric circles and savor the cool wetness on their warm skin.

Drenched by spring rain, Helaku and Konway sprint across Laniakea, avoiding small puddles and dodging waterlogged pups. They finally reach the apartments and make it through the front door. A cool curtain of air-conditioning hits Konway's senses, pressing a sinful arctic crispness upon his skin—like drinking ice water with his pores. Condensation fogs up a nearby window, signaling a reprieve from the thick humidity.

"Damn, that A/C is cold." Helaku jaunts towards the vibrating window unit and dials it down a few notches before disappearing into a side room. "Make yourself at home. Mi casa es su casa!" he hollers down the hall.

The place is clean, except for the sand on the floor, the dusty wall-mounted flat screen, and some discarded laundry kicked into the corner. Old surfboards line the ceiling with the scuffs and scars of adventure.

He returns in two shakes and tosses a faded beach towel at Konway. "If you need another, there are more in your room. I've got an old air mattress for you to use. But I'll see if Surf-Works can print you a proper bed. It shouldn't be a problem, though... Help yourself to the fridge. There's an old *Super N-tendo* in the drawer under the television. It's a smart TV, but I rarely have time to watch it. I'm not here most nights... There's a special lady I visit from time to time. It's top-secret, hush-hush. Only you know." He winks. "So, you'll have the apartment all to yourself, minus me bumbling around in the mornings."

They sit down and play a round on the console. After a best two-out-of-three, then a three-out-of-five, followed by a poorly rolled joint, Helaku leaves to pursue interests outside of the village. A little while later, the pitter-patter against the window increases its tempo, reminding Konway of Mystic Woods & the Loggerheads. One by one, he recalls the things he can remember and carefully positions each recollection within the refurbished limited-edition *Space Force III: Blue Commander* lunchbox.

Soon, the rain's rhythm lulls him into a deep slumber. He knocks over a recycled-plastic cup of water. Outside, the storm continues to nourish the land. Inside Helaku's apartment, Konway drifts beyond the precipice of sleep, weary from his adventure thus far.

38

Coming Down The Mountain

Leap

The gray sky continues to cloak the passage of time as Zeff studies the insurmountable ridge, further dwarfed by the Mountains of Experience cascading on the horizon. After a flurry of failed attempts, he scans below and spots the faint traces of a rainbow trail leading away from the mountains' base.

"Why the hell did that damn door teleport me here?" he asks, still furious about his current location. "I was so close to getting out of this place. I could've handled it myself." The lie bites into his heart like a sand gnat on spring break. "I've gone nuts. Why am I talking to this stupid thing?" He violently shakes the [Trifold Tablet].

Once the tantrum subsides, he steels his resolve, picks up the metal bar he brought through the portal, and uses it as a walking stick. Farther on, the path tapers into a sheer cliff. He peers into the unending void and sighs under the weight of his inadequacy.

"I've got this," Zeff says, unfolding the tablet. "*Zen-click* each menu. Take your time and think about every step." (It's running much smoother since absorbing the [Ashen Jewel]... I hope when I hit execute, there aren't any backlogged run commands.) He imagines being catapulted by a skyscraper-sized Snap-Brix. After dismissing the thought, he summons the dev-tools and selects the [Deconstructor Beam].

The tablet goes blank.

(Don't shake it. Be patient.) He braces against the mountain.

A dark screen stares back.

(Be patient. Don't break it. Be patient—fuck this stupid thing.)

At last, subroutines proc the parameters of their script, and a violet light projects onto the cliff, slowly erasing layers of sediment to widen the way down the mountain.

"Almost there." Zeff glances anxiously at the battery indicator in the device's upper corner.

Alas, had he not checked the screen so often, there might've been enough juice to reach the end of the route. Farther along the beam fades, leaving a foothold no wider than a wall-sized windowsill.

"Shit. I'm so close." On the other side of a three-meter gap, the way begins again. "I can make it. I've got to try," he says, then folds the tablet into his coat pocket.

He balances with the metal walking stick and inches closer to the edge until part of the path crumbles into the bottomless abyss. Trepidation shoots through his shins.

"How am I going to get over there?" Zeff looks down into the darkness. "Shit—"

An inaudible whisper blows past.

"—Maybe I can make it." (Something tells me I need to try.) Zeff suppresses the primal fear of vertigo's fall, walks back a couple of paces, and vaults over the edge.

Though effortless, he lands awkwardly, tumbling down an embankment—rolling, flopping, fumbling past wiry trees and sparse brush. In time, the terrain levels into a fork. He gets up, dusts himself off and steps to the right. The tablet buzzes in defiance.

"Now you're working?" He looks at the breast of his dirty linen coat. "Make up your damn mind." Zeff unfolds the device, and a faint purple glow pulses in the opposite direction. "Lead the way," he says sarcastically.

The trail dips beneath a felled tree into a darkened forest thick with underbrush. His keen awareness detects hundreds of cowering eyes quivering beyond the purple hue. The tablet leads him through the shadows. Something cobbles from a nearby bush up into a tree. He stows the [Trifold Tablet], and darkness reclaims the woods until he happens upon a meadow.

Farther into the clearing, the path ends again. Zeff surveys the bluff, then across the dried riverbed where the Rapids of Knowledge once flowed with the prestige of lived life. "At least I can see the bottom," he scoffs.

He turns around, and three steps later, the device vibrates.

"What's so damn important that we need to go this way? Let's head back to the forest. There must be a different route."

Tucked within the tree-lined shadows, one by one, innumerable thickets of icy blue optics gaze at him.

"Nothing is easy with this place." He rolls his eyes. And, finding no other way, secures his personal effects, casts a middle finger towards the forest, and takes off with surprising speed.

After several swift strides, he reaches the precipice and leaps above the wide gap. Mid-flight, his thoughts trail into fear-based logic, shortening his jump. Just shy of his intended landing, he drops the metal walking stick and grapples the edge with both hands.

Another inaudible whisper blows past as cool wind ripples his linen pants. Hanging from the bluff, he swings his legs onto the cliff face and reaches for another crumbling fingerhold. With the next grasp, the sediment gives way, and Zeff falls. His muffled thud at the bottom is abrupt.

Milestone Trolls

Cradled between two boulders, he moans from the jagged edge pressed into his backside. The pain is real, like a hot poker cauterizing a bullet wound. He struggles to his feet and brushes off the dust, feeling the claw marks on his shirt. The angst spirals into a frenzy as he scours the river bottom for the metal walking stick.

At the peak of panic, Zeff finds his security blanket near some withered roots. He picks it up and swings it against the tree, dropping several tendrils to the gravel. Reassured by his only means of defense, he makes his way along the riverbed.

The way winds around jutting rocks—some cracked, others cleaved in twain. En route, one of the Donor's memories with his cousins springs to mind.

He spits on the ground.

Farther past a sparse region with segmented hectares of flourishing and stripes of decay, he spots the brutish backsides of three Milestone Trolls, the color of cremation. The largest, a behemoth with long limbs and exaggeratedly large forearms, approaches a towering boulder and lifts its great axe into the air. Then, with a heavy swipe, the rock splits in half.

Instinctively, Zeff ducks into the shadow of a nearby outcropping until the moment passes. With the brutes soon out of sight and the wind blowing in his favor, a sense of stillness returns to the area. He peeks out, checking the near-adjacent.

"All clear," he whispers, relieved to find no fog or fiend, and steps from the shadows, heading in the opposite direction.

Several paces later, the tablet pulsates in his coat pocket.

"Again?" he asks, unfolding the device. "I need to switch this thing off before it gives away my position."

The screen shimmers to life, but quickly fades beneath the resting abyss. He taps it. No response.

"Come on, motherfucker... What do you want from me?"

He taps it again. And again. On the next, his hand wavers for a hesitant moment above the display. He sighs and closes the first leaflet to close the device.

The [Trifold Tablet] suddenly leaps from his grip and scoots across the riverbed, sliding at two-thirds a slug's pace. As he walks to the device, it scoots forward but cannot escape him. A violet strobe traces around the device. He unfolds it, and a purple wave pings towards the slate-gray trolls.

"You want me to go that way?" He looks at the path of destruction. "Not gonna do it. I need to get the hell out of here." Zeff turns, and the light switches sides. "Nope. I don't have time to be messing with monsters," he says, moving farther from its destination.

The device buzzes out of his hand, but he catches it midair.

"Fine... but if you try anything else, I'll bash you against a rock."

The [Trifold Tablet] strobes its purple indicator.

"You know that's where they went, right? And by the track record of this place, I'd wager they aren't friendly."

The device insists, and Zeff begrudgingly treks along the riverbed around the next bend, stealthily avoiding any resting rocks.

Led by the [Trifold Tablet], he follows a path of barbarous wreckage until the trolls' grunting commands bite into the wind. With the crew in view, he lowers himself behind a knocked-over tree. It vibrates more than before.

"Okay. Okay." He leans on a root and, seeing no way forward without alerting them, gets into position.

Icarus

The behemoth troll, Korf, rests its broadaxe and scans the area, while the other two persuade a pack of rustled Sorting Dregs to toil in the soil.

Meek and mindless, the color of rotten bark, these hunched creatures, burdened with a bulbous satchel of blue crystals, excavate the veins of a resource node. Some use a gleaming staff to dig through the first layer of sediment. Others use their oversized hands to inspect the gems, rubbing each piece between their dirt-caked fingers, nimbly assessing the quality and tossing it over their shoulder.

"Hurry up with them, Snag. We ain't got all day," the lookout says, digging its pinky into its large ear and extracting a bowling ball of wax. It thumps the lump away, knocking down a withered willow, then focuses its black eyes on an adjacent summit scaling beyond light-gray clouds.

"Quit'cher bitchin'. These minions are mindless; all they can do is gather," grumbles Snag, the mid-sized troll with a diagonal scar slashed across its torso, as it herds a cluster of Dregs to the side with a spiked mace a short distance away.

"Don'tcha mean *sort*?" sneers Gab, the smallest one. Looming above the Dregs, it snorts up a *hee-haw*, spins, and shouts, "Work faster!"

Before the command falls upon their earless existence, Gab strikes the nearest Dreg with its club. The wretch clings to the bludgeon like a lolly stuck to a shag carpet. Unamused, it shakes the weapon until the minion's skull loosens with a moist suction and plops to the ground.

At once, the other Dregs hobble to the pile of blue jewels.

"See how they sort?" The runt laughs, slapping its belly.

"Quit messin' around," Snag hollers. "Now, it'll take them longer."

Korf points his axe at their buffoonery. "I'll give you two some advice. If we don't return on time, she'll up-cycle both of you—not me. Am I clear? Now, I need whichever one of you is the least incompetent to help me stand guard. Don't forget whose territory we're trespassing on?"

"I'd rather be up-cycled," Snag says, softening its sloped brow and scratching its rear.

Gab turns to face them, joining the taunt, saying, "Exactly—"

Zeff emerges from the shadows and swings his metal walking stick into the side of Gab's potato-shaped head, dislodging a black eyeball. As it spins from socket, bouncing off of a hunched Sorting Dreg, the stunned Milestone Troll drops to its knees with a cry of anguish.

(Good! There's a chance.)

Gab tries to stand, only to receive a savage flurry of home-run strikes, each blow releasing the sense of despair Zeff had felt since waking up in the Mind Palace.

Enraged, the others rush him.

(Think. They're almost here. I need another weapon.) Zeff grabs their brother's club with both hands and charges.

Korf trips over a few Sorting Dregs, squashing them beneath its bulk. Its sibling sprints ahead and reaches him first.

Taking the offensive, Zeff dodges close, attacking Snag's vital spots. On the third impact, the mid-sized troll blocks a critical strike with its mace. As the reverberation knocks away his club, the troll coughs up a black ooze onto its stone skin, then drops its weapon.

Zeff lunges for the two-handed mace. *Thwack! Thwapp! Thwapp!* Snag surrenders into a twitching mess. With his breathing heavy and caught in the squish of troll tar, he fails to notice Korf rise.

Swoosh! The battle axe misses him by a hair, cutting the spiked bludgeon in half. Zeff tumbles like a roly-poly out of danger. Disarmed, he searches for a way out—or a way through.

The weapon cycles back past him, drawing his keen eyes to the Dreg's staff. (That'll have to do.) He scrambles to unearth it.

Catching its broadaxe, Korf leaps into the air. At its zenith, it roars, "For my brothers!" and hurls the weapon with all its might.

Closer, the blade ignites as it streaks towards Zeff. Faster, the blaze intensifies. He finally extracts the staff the moment the troll's axe whistles past, singeing the hem of his coat.

The flaming boomerang swirls back to its master, still plummeting mid-flight. Korf's momentum fuses with the weapon, supercharging his [Icarus Slash] attack. "PERISH, INSECT!!!"

On impact, the axe cleaves into the mountain and unzips a perpendicular scar across the riverbed. To Korf's dismay, Zeff is not there. Several Sorting Dregs are not so lucky.

Above the dust cloud—having leapt to avoid certain deletion—Zeff plunges the shining end of the Dreg's staff into the brute's backside. Cracks spread as it pierces the stone-like hide, disintegrating a chunk of torso. Korf's black eyes roll back as it collapses into the hewn trench and fills it with the molasses of its essence.

The few remaining minions scatter up a nearby embankment, leaving behind a glittering trail of blue gemstones. He righteously roars at them, then spins around to kick the smoldering corpse of his vanquished foe.

"And not a scratch on me." Zeff smiles at his martial prowess—a necessary boon, having frequently fled from the Fog on so many occasions—then sighs with relief. "Still, that was close. I need to be more careful and stop playing like a kid at an arcade. This isn't a game." He notices the spatter pattern peppered on his clawed shirt.

The Violet Egg

Ahead, the gnarled node's core summons thin threads of dwindling light towards scattered piles of blue crystals. The tablet vibrates against his chest. Zeff pulls it from his coat pocket and unfolds it.

At the center of the screen, under a rippling GIF, the [Ashen Jewel] forms and dislodges a sliver from its design. As the glimmering fragment floats forward, the node reaches for it with thin filaments of light. On contact, they wrap around it, weaving a chrysalis and absorbing the seed phrase within the facet.

Luminous roots disintegrate along the ground, and the node goes dark.

"Come on! Cut me a break!" Zeff shouts at the timeless sky. "What was all of this for?" He squeezes the tablet but resists the urge to smash it.

The seed phrase finishes updating its dependencies. At the node's heart, a purple light pulses; on the third beat, a wave ripples throughout the surrounding woods. The tablet displays a rough map, outlining the resource node's neural-network constructors and circling the closest point of interest with a rippling light.

"Is this where you want me to go next? No more monsters. Let's keep me out of danger. What's good for me is good for you," he says to the tablet. Its solemn response marks the nearest node. Upon closer examination, Zeff discovers a potential way off of the mountain.

The [Ashen Jewel] suddenly grows two sizes, then molts into a Fabergé of splintered complexity, its shards orbiting a pulsing nucleus. He marvels at the resplendent [Violet Egg], having never seen such a thing. It spins for a few rotations and slowly digitizes on the tablet's onyx surface. A confirmation scrolls across the screen, and the battery meter's capacity budges up one notch.

"Now we're cooking." He folds the device into his jacket.

Before leaving, Zeff rolls Gab over—its head mushed like mashed potatoes—and grabs the satchel. Inside rotten meat festers in poultice packets, oozing with delight.

"'To the victor, the spoils.'" He sighs and tosses the rancid sacks aside.

With the club damaged, the mace in pieces, and the great axe too heavy to bear, he sorts amongst the coagulated carnage, finding most staffs to be dangerously inoperable. In a last-ditch effort, Zeff recovers his trusty metal walking stick, stomps it back into shape, and binds the glowing tip of a broken staff with torn rags from a Sorting Dreg's corpse. Taking hold of the [Crude Spear], he strikes the air.

"It isn't pretty, but it's better than nothing," he says, jabbing it into a rock and disintegrating its outer layer. "You need a name. Every valiant weapon deserves one... How about the [Lance of Longinus]?"

A brief pop-up window finalizes the prompt.

Unamused, he returns to the riverbed and quietly tracks it downstream. The wind increases, snoring an avalanche into a deforested gulch. Farther along, he picks up the pace and reaches the next location.

"Isn't this where it should be?" He checks the device again. "It's not here." Zeff scrutinizes the screen and finds a slight bump at the bottom of the circlet. "Could it be beneath me?" He steps to the edge and looks down, unable to locate the bottom. "I'm up way too high. How am I going to get down there?"

In the top-right corner, the tablet's charge indicator flashes.

"That's right." He pushes past the frustration. "There might be enough juice for another shortcut."

He boots up the [Deconstructor Beam] and sets off, carving a trail down the mountain. Back and forth, he slaloms lower.

Farther down, the winds switch directions, and an avalanche swipes through the adjacent slope. Another nasal gasp hurries back up the incline, rumbling with a low grumble and nearly sending him over the edge. The ceaseless rhythm increases with circadian accuracy, as though the mountain were a sleeping giant. Zeff braces against the slope, and during a lull in the gale, he descends below the beastly winds.

There, the endless expanse of the Mind Palace VPN partition comes into view. No longer desolate, a catalog of upturned pyramids and towering *Space Force* memorabilia huddles in the distance. The junkyard of megalithic typewriters and rows of crooked file cabinets is barely a shadow. To his right, fires smolder the horizon with ash. To his left, Zeff notices a shift in the dull ground and holds the [Trifold Tablet] in front of him. It zooms in to reveal fields of flowers. Another rainbow tracer disappears behind a rolling hill. In the distance, atop the twisted stump, illuminated by arcs of green lightning, he recognizes the Control Tower's faint silhouette etched onto the timeless gray sky.

"Wasn't it purple before?" he asks, cutting his eyes at the tablet and furrowing his brow. "Very curious indeed."

39

Reefers

Bedside

Morphing beams of pre-linguistic experience dance underneath Konway's eyelids as the apartment's window unit fogs up the pane of a new day.

"Rise and shine." Helaku's eager smile beams into the room.

He rises from a vivid landscape without adherence to natural order. "Good morning," he mumbles, still groggy from his adventure through Dreamwind Studios, reaching for his water bottle.

"How'd you sleep?"

"Like a baby." He gulps back several swallows of cool refreshment, dribbling a few droplets down his jaw.

"Good. I hoped I didn't wake you earlier." Helaku hands him a parcel wrapped in brown paper with blue twine. "Mary and her crew made this welcome gift for you."

The present rattles with joyful crinkles. At once, ribbons and twinkling lights from those forgotten winter mornings and special occasions unspool into the forefront of Konway's imagination. And like untethered birthday balloons, his shredded memories drift beyond the gray sky.

"Can't have you wash-in, only to have you die from poor hygiene," he jests.

Konway unwraps the package and examines the black canvas waterproof shower kit, then unzips the top flap. Inside, a tightly organized assortment of supplies: toothbrush, toothpaste, floss, mouthwash, body wash, shampoo, facial cleanser, B's moisturizer with SPF, a travel-sized bundle of cotton swabs, a small first aid kit, and a note written with elegant penmanship.

We hope this helps you on your journey and recovery!

—Laniakea

"You can freshen up and get your head on straight. Boy, that hair looks like you got into a fight with a rooster," Helaku says. "No rush, though. We've got a bit before we all head out." He searches for something around the living room.

"Where are we going?"

"We're shorthanded this morning," he says, rummaging under the couch. "Jack, Julian, and I are taking three groups of villagers out to the ARC."

"Ark?"

"Aquacultural Reef Community," he hunts below the coffee table. "This will be the perfect opportunity to help the village."

"Whatever you need."

Helaku finds his tray pushed near the wall. "First, I'm going to roll us one while you get ready."

"That's a splendid idea," Konway answers, heading to the bathroom.

After tidying up, Helaku sets a vintage *Space Force II* TV-dinner tray on the coffee table. Beneath several gnarled, half-smoked joints—saved for a rainy day—and the chaotic swirl of ground cannabis flower, Adastria battles the Empire against a galactic backdrop seeded with cosmic horrors. He scrapes away the cobble with a joker playing card, then pulls out a pack of JOY 1.5 rolling papers.

However, half the pack has fused at the gumline, unfurling like a magician's handkerchief. His mighty hands try to pry them apart, but rip several along the way.

"Damn it, my fingers won't work this morning."

Eventually, Helaku gets one weighted down, only to have a gust from an oscillating fan blow the paper in a loop-de-loop towards the bathroom door.

Sesh

On the other side, Konway stares into the tile-framed mirror, examining every wrinkle and detail as he brushes his teeth. A tremor shoots down the left side of his neck into his hand. He grips the sink's edge to maintain his balance. The panic sets in, but he box-breathes, and several rounds later, the tremors subside.

(Am I dying? What's wrong with me? Should I tell Helaku? I won't be able to help the village... They'll kick me out.) The ANTs burrow into tunnels of neurotic chatter.

The smell of freshly ground cannabis soon wafts into the room.

"You all good, bro?" Helaku calls out.

Konway composes himself. "Almost finished," he hollers back, plucking his toothbrush out of the sink. (Hold it together.) He glares angrily. "I'm fine. I'm okay," he whispers, his gaze softening in the reflection.

Once finished, he stows the shower kit in Josepé's satchel. (I wonder how the boys are doing? I need to let them know I made it back.)

He searches for the remnants of the band's note. "Where is it?" He checks under the bed and in the sheets. "Was it with my clothes?" A micro-dose of remorse churns an uneasiness in his stomach as the thought of never seeing Mystic Woods & the Loggerheads again seeps into his tear ducts.

Suddenly, a mockingbird bursts into a sweeping concerto outside the bedroom window. The neurotic hamster wheel halts. Recounting the generosity of Helaku and the village, coupled with some more box breaths, he finds a drop of peace.

Afterward, he exits his room, stepping over a few wayward rolling papers. "Need some help?"

"Definitely. I'm rushing with excitement and need to slow down. Besides, it probably would've ended up like those." Helaku points to a two-thirds-full ashtray with gnarled, half-smoked roaches. "I think I might roll them too tight."

"Let me see." Konway sits on the couch next to him. "May I use that pack of papers?"

Helaku hands him the empty cardboard packaging.

"Perfect. If you roll a tiny piece up like this," he forms a small cylinder, "and place it at one end of the paper… It supports better airflow. Give it a try."

Helaku clumsily fiddles with the filter, sliding it back and forth, and finally gets its position just right. His strong fingers crumble an even layer of flower along the crease of the paper canoe, filling it nearly to the edge. A few derelict pieces fall onto the *Space Force II* rolling tray, landing right on the hull of the *Timaeus*. "I was taught that using a crutch meant you didn't know how to roll."

"Don't think of it as a crutch, but as a foundation for an even burn," Konway suggests. "I think Patricio's pack of JA rolling papers had built-in cardboard filters printed with affirmations."

"Adding affirmations to ceremony… I'm picking up what you're putting down." He spins the last side of gum to paper. "Let's give it a go." His giant smile reaches up to his eyes. "I think this might be the best one I've ever rolled."

Flick-flick. The lighter's flame beckons the paper. Their chemistry ignites a kiss, releasing a bouquet of terpenes into a single strand of smoke that unfurls onto air-conditioned currents. Helaku puffs on the joint until its burn settles into an even smolder.

"Look at it. You barely need to hit it for it to light you up." Helaku chuckles. "Will you take this from me?" He extends the paper totem. "Be careful—it's roasting," he says, walking to an ornamental chalkboard with hearts drawn on it and erasing them with a dirty shirt.

Konway inhales slowly. A plume of smoke rushes into his lungs, signaling interlocking receptor sites to release a dopaminergic toddy. Another toke tempers the malfunctioning Oros system's nanite colony—for now.

ARC Briefing

Soon, the tension in Konway's neckline subsides, and after two more satisfying puffs, he passes the joint.

"Gimme a sec." Helaku grapples with the chalkboard. "I want to explain the plan for today so you don't get overwhelmed when we get out there." Once steadied, he piffs a few rips, then passes it back and outlines his lesson in chalk.

"There are around fifty man-made reefs in the estuaries and offshore waters of our coast, ranging from deconstructed bridges to sunken ships. Hell, I even heard there was a tank."

"A tank?" Konway asks, bubbling with excitement.

The word triggers a grade school picture from a refuse bin in his Mind Palace. Sadly, the cover rips off, drifting into the timeless sky and landing somewhere within the Wastelands of Cognition with the tonnage of a turtled Abrams.

"A tank!" Helaku echoes. After taking several hits, he hands it back to Konway. "When we place durable materials in a marine environment, they become a home for the ocean's inhabitants?"

"What kind of creatures?" Konway asks curiously, led by his pen and the void of the page.

"All sorts. Algae, barnacles, sponges, and marine worms stake their claims first. They're the foundation of any reef's food web."

Konway's pen scribbles further abstractions.

"Their presence attracts local crabs, shrimp, starfish, sea urchins, and mollusks, as well as schools of juvenile fish," Helaku adds. "Then larger fish arrive, drawn by the abundance of shelter, food, and a distinct physical orientation in the otherwise flat, featureless environment. It's what they do."

Konway's eyes wander outside, enjoying the play of light, as the gray scale of dawn recedes over the lush marsh. A siege of herons perches in their favorite tree, waiting for the tide to reveal a buffet along naked estuaries and fiddler crab burrows. He takes a toke, shifting his eyes back to Helaku's chalk-crumbling sketch.

"I think I see a pattern." He grins with earnest understanding.

Helaku continues, "The creation of artificial reefs is essential for the development of our marine fisheries. In our neck of the woods, there's a lack of naturally occurring hard-bottom areas on the coast. Around here, the continental shelf is mostly sand, several feet deep."

"Like a desert?" He hands him the doobie.

"Exactly, bro." Helaku sips some ice water. "Roughly ten percent have the right makeup to support a reef community. So, we've started developing a sustainable model to cultivate biodiversity across our sandy coastline."

"What did you come up with?" Konway asks.

"It's a viable strategy to harvest local food sources rather than relying on seafood processed from the other side of the world—at a reduced cost." Mid-rant, Helaku erupts into a coughing fit and passes the joint. Then, wiping a tear from his eye, says, "The more you cough, the more you get off." He chuckles and takes another sip to clear his throat.

(Where have I heard that?) Konway draws in a slow drag, filling his lungs, further stoking his curiosity. On exhale, he asks, "How'd you set all this up?"

"Guess?"

"The Foundation?"

"Exactly." Helaku has another swallow of ice water. "Thanks to our friends at the First Global Foundation, we've been able to bypass traditional social boundaries that would've kept this nothing more than a pipe dream."

"How so?" Konway rolls the cherry in the ashtray.

Helaku's words drip with adoration. "Thanks to their prestige, we secured approval letters from all the right people at NOAA [National Oceanic and Atmospheric Administration], the Statehouse, and federal legislators. Man, it must have taken a pretty penny to get all the good ole boys in line." He tips an invisible hat to their efforts.

(The Foundation.) Each syllable echoes with a tinge of déjà vu. Konway bats it into the background of his thoughts to consider later. "So the ARC is a reef?" He raises his eyebrows and hands the resin-run doobie back to Helaku.

"Well, it's not just a reef." He repairs the run and puffs on it, skillfully billowing rings into rays of daylight.

"What is it?"

"Within the site we raise and harvest finfish, shellfish, and seaweed—kind of like our garden planters, but with fish." Helaku smiles.

(Seaweed?) Konway's thoughts inscribe his descriptions, at 24 fps, through a flicker-lit projector reel. In the dust-covered rubble, a tattered screen bubbles an ecological web of aquatic caricatures from his father's encyclopedias.

"How does it work?" he asks, tempting the inner cogs of memory to unlock his past.

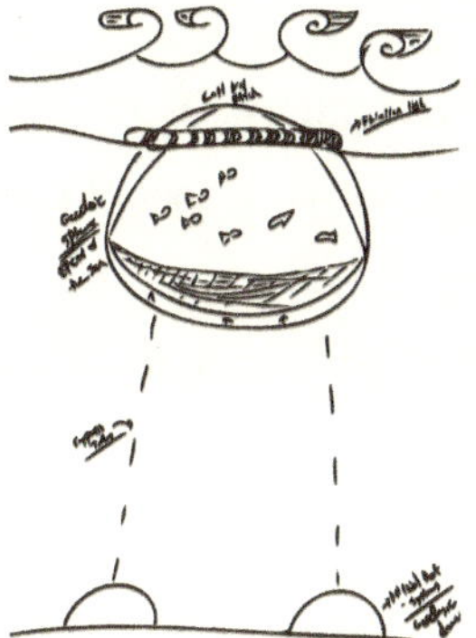

"Stay with me." Helaku etches a sphere above his sketch, with several wiggling plants on the sides. "The ARC is an integrated, multi-trophic aquaculture system combining shellfish and genetically enhanced flora with finfish cultivation. With a bit of knowledge and a lot of elbow grease, we created a feedback loop to turn waste byproducts into inputs for other species."

The projector reel continues its promenade, flashing to a Vision Shard from the Donor's childhood in the foothills. Rung after rung, he climbs the ladder of a decommissioned fire watchtower in the Forty Hectare Wood. Reaching the top, he views his house in the distance. On the other side, well past Granny's garden and Paw-Paw's shop, he spies the neighbor's fields at the far end of the property line.

"Will you fix us another one?" Helaku stubs out the roach and points to the rolling tray. "I'm getting fired up talking about all this reef-tech."

Konway snaps back from the unraveling yarn ball of his past. "Certainly." He organizes the fleeting fragment in his restored *Space Force III* lunchbox and sets to the task.

Meanwhile, Helaku scratches more chalk lines, explaining, "At the ARC, we have three geodesic domes covered with special Elk-Stag corals anchored to a man-made sandbar."

"What kind of coral is that?" he asks, with the image of a robust, antlered beast sauntering into his frame of thought, soon followed by a herd of key deer, reminding him of the musicians.

"It's a combination of Elkhorn and Staghorn corals."

"What about storms?"

"Excellent question. The system moves with storm-generated surges and dissipates wave energy. Each reef serves as an anchor point for the floating sphere on the surface. And between them, three retractable cables tether the ARC together. It'd be a shame if we went through all this effort, only for the first storm of the season to rip it to shreds." Helaku laughs at the awful absurdity.

The Mind Palace crackles with forgotten protocols, tingling from the inside out as Konway jots down the details of their discussion on a scrap of paper.

Helaku plops down and pulls a waterproof tablet from beside the couch. "This'll help you understand better than my stick-figure drawing." He clicks a button along the side and illuminates the black mirrored screen. "See here? That's where we were yesterday. And over there is our project for today."

"What are the areas around it used for?" Konway asks, pointing at the shaded plots on the tablet.

"Those are future sites where we'll expand the project." He looks on with glee. "It's a better way of farming and enriching the surrounding waters. By building these ARC systems with native and restorative species, we can promote the sustainable growth of natural resources and bolster our resilience to the storms." Helaku points to a camera icon, and a rosary of pixels dilates into the perspective of an underwater surveillance drone.

Fisheye Lenz

A few crumbs of cannabis flower sprinkle onto a spiral-armed kraken, its maw opening out of a singularity, as Konway tucks the last edge of the joint paper. Unable to take his eyes off the screen, he finishes rolling in time to see a parade of fish swimming among brown-green ribbons. There, in the sway of flickering sunlight, tiny snails feed on the floating foliage of their home. Above, small eyes peek out from behind their preferred hiding spot. A passing shadow triggers their reverse thrusters, sliding them back into swaddling nooks.

"Do you see this kelp? Well, my friend, these aren't your average *nori*. They're genetically modified for warmer waters. We're testing to see if they have the potential to become an invasive species. So far, the urchins seem to keep the population under control. But could you imagine the ocean filled with seaweed?"

"Sounds like something from a monster movie." Konway remembers washing in, then imagines the Earth as a giant cabbage ball.

"At least it won't be plastic." Helaku grins. "These can absorb three times more carbon than land-based plants. With a sizable plot, we could grow several tons of seaweed—enough to remove up to 135 tons of carbon per year. This might not solve all our problems, but at least it's a step in the right direction." He grins at their prosperity.

Out the window, an amorphous cloud turns into the shape of a ship and sails after the last swatches of gray in the peach-colored morning.

Konway fires up the next doobie and savors a whelming lungful before handing it to Helaku. "Why'd you choose to grow kelp?"

"Well, aside from helping with carbon, the seaweed can absorb about 200 liters of nitrogen a day. The intention is to soak up all this neglectful runoff and restore water quality," Helaku explains. "After we've soaked up the nitrogen, we can turn it into liquid fertilizer for local farms."

"Do they know about the runoff?"

"Of course... money, laziness, and a willful resistance to progress keep these companies from being held accountable. Hell, the last big storm that came through flooded every pig-shit reservoir and coal-ash hole in the states north of us, sending it all downstream. And guess where it goes?"

"Into the ocean." Konway furrows his brow, sensing the folly.

"Exactly. But don't get me started on our slow crawl towards any meaningful form of progress. I can't wrap my head around the sheer stubbornness, despite the obvious evidence stating otherwise." Helaku laughs at the absurdity.

Konway receives the joint. "The ARC seems healthy."

"After farming this once-barren patch of Atlantic, we now have a makeshift metropolis."

With the rusted cogs of Konway's Mind Palace sputtering and clanking about, a cauldron of inspiration bubbles beneath his seat. "I think I get it... Pull the bad stuff out of the air and into the ocean!"

"Bury me at sea!" Helaku cheers, knocking over the rolling tray. A bellyful of laughter explodes as ash and muddled joints tumble to the sandy straw mat covering the tile floor, where a tiny fiddler crab scuttles onto the upturned tray. "How'd you get in here?" Helaku swiftly scoops up the brave explorer, creaks open the screen door, and sets it in a nearby planter. "Go hunt some palmetto bugs," he delegates to the curious crustacean, scuttling into a decorative cluster of chard.

Ontological Economy

Helaku picks up the tray and checks for damage. "Close one. I'm like a brontosaurus—sometimes I don't know which way my tail swings."

As the commotion settles, Konway enjoys a drag and offers it to Helaku.

"I'm all set for the moment. Be my guest." Helaku cleans up the ashes of disruption and sweeps the pile into a cracked dustpan. "Anyway, the aquatic crops we grow need zero fertilizers, freshwater, or antibiotics, making this one of the most sustainable forms of food production on the planet. From all the monitoring and testing, we've found that these systems have the potential to grow on their own. Hopefully, one day we'll have ARCs all over—not just here."

"What do you do with the harvest?" Konway has another puff.

"We sell it to local markets," Helaku says. "It's not a lavish lifestyle by any means, but it does free us from the eight-to-five. Any surplus capital goes into a fund for coastal conservation efforts and Laniakea's solar panel budget. We've got to get off the island's outdated grid. Laniakea can't be without power because of an August shower."

Konway draws an even burn. "I'm pumped. What's my assignment?" He holds the hit, passing it to Helaku.

"That's the spirit. We're going to divide into teams. You'll help topside."

"What're you going to do?"

"Hunting lionfish." A primal glimmer escapes Helaku's eyes. "We've spotted some around the reefs, and we can't afford to have them feasting on all our hard work." He rolls the cherry into the ashtray.

"How are they bad for the ARC?"

"Aside from being venomous, they have no natural predators here and could wipe out our diverse fish population." He inhales.

"Where'd they come from?" Konway paws at the yarn ball of curiosity.

Stirred by a solid hit, Helaku passes the joint back to him, saying, "It's hard to trace... Increased water temperatures, tsunami, mega-storm—who knows?"

The haze rests throughout the room and soon overtakes them as they discuss beach expansion versus renourishment, followed by daydreams of a better tomorrow. After the session, Konway follows Helaku outside, across the Horseshoe, past a pack of pups, and down to the wobbly dock. There, they board one of Laniakea's charter boats with some of the other villagers and depart towards the living ARC.

40

Topside

Set Sail

Parting clouds shift their shadows along the mouth of the Stono River as Laniakea's fleet of three cruises towards the Atlantic. Overhead, a squadron of twenty-seven pelicans gracefully ribbons against a motionless backdrop of distant clouds, stretching far beyond the shoreline.

"Make sure you have everything," Helaku, clad in a marine-camouflage dive suit, hollers over the chop.

Konway checks his tool belt: pliers, snips, diving knife, waterproof paper, and pen. "All here," he shouts.

The wind rushes past as he sits, silent and tentative, absorbed in the gossip and guffaws of the other villagers, sharing tales of drunken mishaps, solid days, missed waves, plans for the afternoon, winter trips to take, the latest shows to watch—all laced with mumblings and inside jokes.

"I heard they were thinking of setting up some offshore wind turbines."

"If they can wean themselves off the big-oil money that's been feeding them for years—"

"What about the storms?"

"Don't forget about the whales and—"

"Solar might be less impactful and costly."

The villagers carry on, hedonically adapted to the skyline's rapture.

"Luckily, we're blessed in our corner of the world."

"Yeah, thanks to the good graces above and the good works of our village."

"Mother Teresa said it best: 'If everyone swept in front of their own house, the world would be clean.'"

"Well, ours is as clean as they come. Feels like we may be one of the few places with trash-free waves."

"The other day, I heard we were voted the number one travel destination in the country by *Bougie Kabob*—for the sixth year in a row."

"Ugh—"

"Again—"

"More tourons swarming the beaches and leaving trash."

"Locals are just as guilty."

"We humans can't seem to help but create matter that falls out of place."

A short fellow with dark hair and a touch of acne notices Konway has drifted into a daydream. Mateo leans in, pushing a teal pair of Kawabonga's Bayviator sunglasses up the bridge of his nose. "Hey bud, be careful not to fall in out there. I heard the sharks are teeming."

Somewhere in the fractured corner of Konway's mental landscape, a Vision Shard cracks open, revealing a dilapidated boob tube. Its bulbous screen flickers to life with a cola commercial, followed by a monstrous shark lunging from the surf, diagonally severing several swimmers in half. Then, clicking its well-worn dial to the left, a lost episode from a family vacation filters through the static airways. Buckled into the backseat of the family car, traveling from the foothills to the beach, his young mind runs rampant with the fearful thoughts of prehistoric horrors—sparked by secretly watching *Storm Shark IV* the night before their trip.

Wave

The channel's reception clears, rendering young-Konway on the shoreline. While wiggling his toes in the tide, a terrible trepidation seeps into his vivid imagination. He hesitates to step farther into the water. One treasure after another, the sea reveals sparkling tidings and dulls his apprehension.

Farther up the beach, his mother waves at him, signaling to reapply sunscreen, as the sun shines into no-shadow time. Just then, a tiny flounder shimmies from below a blanket of sand and brushes against young-Konway's foot. Although in ankle-high water, he stays vigilant of the Megalodon's deathly jaws waiting past the shallows. He soon displaces the nonsense and resumes toothin'—scanning for shells and sharks' teeth.

A short distance behind him, a rogue wave swells over his slight frame. All his fears surge to the forefront, and he freezes under the looming shadow.

As it crashes down to wash him away, his father—toothin' through a nearby shell pile—swoops in with a flash of collegiate speed and plucks his son from the point of impact. He sees the tears in his father's face, wraps his arms around his neck, and wails. Shining from above, the Vision Shard folds into an envelope and tucks itself into an accordion file folder within the *Space Force III* lunchbox for later recollection.

Electroreception

A spritz of salt spray pulls him into the presence.

"Don't listen to him," Helaku shouts. "He's teasing you."

"Damn, man! Let me have a little fun with the new guy. No hard feelings, bud... I'm Mateo," he says with an affirming smile.

"Everyone calls me Konway. Nice to meet you." He initiates the village greeting, striking his thumb down the center of his back and clasping Mateo's hand.

"You'll be working with me. Topside requires all the folks we can spare to handle the harvest. It's fairly easy. Messy, but easy." Mateo snorts up a loogie and spits it overboard. "Where we'll be, it's crucial to keep our emergency flotation devices on our wrists. If you end up in the water, press here, and the CO_2 canister will instantly inflate it. These are the same ones the divers wear—the good stuff, not some middle of the mall merchandise. Now that I've got you all worked up with thoughts of drowning and doomsday shark scenarios, you can enjoy the job." He flashes a rascal's grin.

On the other side, Marty overhears their conversation. "Are you going on about sharks again?" she asks. "Listen, I've made this garden nearly invisible without harming a single one. Mind you, we can't keep out all them. The smaller ones are crucial for a healthy reef."

"How'd you manage that?" Konway asks.

"With a ton of research." She beams a brilliant smile. "Besides hunting with sight and smell, sharks also use a special ability called electroreception—"

"What's electroreception?" Konway blurts, wanting to dig through some cognitive refuse.

"It's how they sense electrical impulses in the water." Marty smiles widely, her cheekbones rounding with enthusiasm. "Many species have pores dotted around their snouts called *ampullae of Lorenzini*, which can detect minute changes in electric fields—down to one-billionth of a volt. So we developed cables made of electropositive metals and buoys containing low-frequency oscillating magnets to interfere with this ability."

"What about the other senses?" Konway finishes the mental blueprint of her explanation.

"Well, we've got the kelp garden and a perimeter of bubbles—"

"Unless they're in a frenzy," Mateo cuts in. "Then we're doomed!"

Dive Master

Helaku brings the craft alongside a large, bobbing geodesic sphere.

Mateo nudges Konway. "Wanna know why divers roll backwards?"

"If they rolled forward, they'd still be in the boat." He grins at his own wit.

"Because if you rolled forward... Hey, wait—you're no fun. I can see why Helaku likes you," Mateo says, rummaging through the myriad pockets of his utility vest: zipping, velcroing, opening, closing, checking, and double-checking. Eventually, he pulls a small bottle of zinc sunscreen from a pocket within a pocket.

After slathering a thick layer across his nose, he throws on his shades and a floppy bucket hat to complete his ensemble.

"Enough talk of adventure—let's get going!" Helaku roars. "Y'all know the drill. Mateo is in charge." He turns towards the dive crew as they check their gear. "We're going down in three teams," he instructs. "Once maintenance finishes, they'll help the reef team gather samples. Remember, we're only responsible for our area. Soldier-Surf and Machu-Beachu have the other two. And since some pesky lionfish are causing trouble down there, Ruckus is with me."

"I hear they're quite tasty." Ruckus licks his lips.

Helaku pulls the diving mask over his face, grabs his pole spear, and calls out, "Last one in is a rotten egg!" With one giant stride off the boat, he plunges into the Atlantic.

Delegation

Mateo surveys the deck through authoritative lenses. No one pays him much attention, except for Konway.

"Now, I know y'all know what to do, but this is for the new guy. Plus, we've got extra samples to process this go-round, so don't give me any lip." Mateo pulls his Bayviators down the bridge of his nose.

Konway shuffles for a better look. "This is much bigger than I imagined."

"That's what she said."

"Who?" The joke sails past him.

Mateo sidesteps the uncomfortable silence and motions towards the Sphere. "Isn't it beautiful? It's predator-proof, storm resistant, and designed to take up the least surface area for the volume it holds." He beams at the structure.

"How was it made?" Konway asks, marveling at the containment unit.

"Each piece was pulled from the goop at the Makerspace. They use the same 3D printing technique to create many of the things we need around the village—chairs, beds, benches, boards, you name it. Whatever you need, I'm sure they could fashion it."

"What's the Goop?"

"It's made from the stuff skimmed by the MARS flotilla."

Konway leans over the side and watches the ebbing sphere. "How many fish are in there?"

"We shall see." Mateo wipes off his pair of Bayviators. "That's one thing we're studying out here. Someday, larger models will sustain hundreds of thousands of fish out in the open ocean. But for now, it helps us avoid working in the cattle pens of the corporate world. Anything that keeps me miles from there, and two inches closer to the surf, is alright in my book."

Konway fidgets with his life jacket, asking, "What do you need me to do?"

Mateo smiles beneath his sunglasses's reflection. "You'll help me clean the Sphere."

"How are we gonna do that?" he asks, looking up along the bobbing cage.

"Carefully." Mateo grins. "I need you to climb up there and pressure-wash this thing." He hands Konway a hose and turns to the rest of the crew, retrieving a folded piece of paper from a lower pocket. "And I need y'all to reel in those oyster lanterns and kelp lines. Also, let's separate one-third for testing and the rest for processing."

Still paying him little attention, the villagers chat it up side by side as they maneuver to their workstations. Overhead, the wind picks up, bringing a refreshing coolness down to the water's surface.

Pressure

Konway slicks his way up the Sphere's ladder, losing his balance once, but recovering quickly. At the top, he finds his sea legs.

"Will you toss me the pressure washer gun?" he shouts.

From the boat, Mateo slings him a rope tied to the device. He reaches for the poor toss and nearly falls off the edge. However, enhanced connective tissues steady his center of gravity.

"Be careful up there!" Mateo shouts. "It's slick as shit."

"How about a better throw next time?" he jabs back, pulling up the pressure washer gun.

"It hit you in the worst place... your hands." Mateo laughs at his own joke, climbing up the side of the Sphere.

Konway hoists him onto sure footing.

"Damn, it's beautiful up here, ain't it?"

All around, the clouds decorate a sky-blue backsplash, stretching towards the horizon, juxtaposed with the Atlantic's ever-reaching shimmer.

"Make sure you put your goggles on for this. You don't want to get sludge in your eyes—trust me." Mateo tilts his shades down to signal his mild sincerity. "Also, make sure you stay tethered and are wearing your life jacket. Just a few safety precautions—nothing to worry about. Well, unless you slip and break your neck—then you might die out here," he teases.

Konway laughs. "I'll be sure to keep my wits about me and my feet under me."

"Excellent. You'll have this thing clean in no time."

"Where's yours?"

"I'll be in the boat, coordinating with the other groups. When you're finished, use the radio, and I'll help you down. If there's time, you can assist the other crews. Holler at me if you need anything." Mateo scrambles off the Sphere onto the deck, and cranks the sputtering pressure washer.

"Best get to it," Konway says beneath the breadth of an endless blue sky.

His grip tightens around the trigger while the pressure washer attempts to kick back in his hands. The first attempt hits a bad angle, splattering his head and chest with a fresh coat of algae.

"Focus," he tells himself, box-breathing until a whelming clarity washes over the gnawing neurosis.

He fires another blast of water. This time, his eyes and hands coordinate with surgical precision to peel away the living muck and smeared seabird refuse. Slowly but surely, he liberates the onyx frame from the layers of everydayness.

On one of the 3D-printed faces, a wayward crustacean scuttles too close to the sun, waving its claws in salutation. Without warning, a pressurized salt spray crashes against their carapace armor and sends the tiny creature flying across the Sphere—bouncing, sliding, tumbling, and kerplunking into the ocean.

41

Shadows Within

Reefside

*P*lunk-plunk-plunk. The pitter-patter of Konway's work cascades to the depths below. Angel hair algae, adrift in the Atlantic, waves along the ARC's tethers, extending several meters to the reef's attachment couplings.

Just shy of Marty's lens, a small school of black-and-white-striped spadefish dart about their huddled real estate as she records the ARC's flourishing success in high definition. Nearby, tech-savvy divers check their map of the Foundation's ocean preserve and set course to inspect the bubble curtain. Aided by wrist-mounted propulsion devices, they zoom beyond the ARC's magnetic field. A yellow rubber ducky fixed to a low-pressure hose fades into particulated visibility.

Back at the reef site, Helaku scoots around with Ruckus. They happily hunt unsuspecting lionfish, stuffing their speared quarry into specially designed containment units. As they swim around the side, an octopus compresses itself under the nook of a nearly invisible cranny.

Past the teeming reefs, several rows of genetically enhanced kelp stand tall. Their floating gas sacs hoist long fronds, higher and higher, reaching towards the light of day. At the base of their holdfasts, a small herd of sea urchins, corralled into an area, sifts around anchor points, nimbly nibbling and munching away—billy goats of the sea.

Alternatively, in an adjacent grid, another seaweed variety hangs from surface planters, growing to the ocean floor. Like plucking carrots from Granny's garden, one by one, topside teams reel in a harvest of kelp and bivalves.

Fish Frens

Covered head to toe in a film of algae, Konway finishes pressure-washing the Sphere. As he climbs down from the floating pen, the fresh bouquet of finfish wafts into his nostrils. Mateo signals for him to help hoist the underwater net and usher the school towards the surface.

Closer and closer, the denizens of the Sphere spiral round and around. Yet their efforts are in vain; every instinctual attempt to escape only lulls them into a writhing pool of complacency. Several slats extend from the deck and attach to the other end of the cage. The crew readies the vacuum for extraction.

Belly-side, divers swim into the Sphere from an underwater hatch, checking the reef tethers for signs of stress or strain. After collecting some test samples for the Foundation's liaison at NOAA, they clean inside the geodesic pen with special brushes before shimmying out and surfacing.

Farther below, close to the sandy bottom, villagers fill test tubes with water and assess their reef's observable health. With the present abundance of marine life, all seems well, but lab-spun beakers tend to yield different results than the naked eye and wrinkled mind can perceive.

Tight schools of curious triggerfish flutter around an underwater camera lens. A bubbling sputter sends them ducking in bashful unison into the shadows. Crunching, nipping, and picking a short distance away, tiny roving crustaceans weave over coral branches as a small brown sandbar shark glides past.

Not the only residents within the ARC, schools of juvenile black sea bass, grouper, and red snapper commute between Laniakea's reefs. Too small and vulnerable to travel in the deeper waters, they search for shelter amidst the metropolis.

Hunt

On the far side, away from the others, Helaku and Ruckus stalk their next prize. From the side of his mask, a lionfish floats around the reef's basin. He turns to see the beautiful creature stalking its prey, unaware that it is the subject of a much larger hunt. Signaling Ruckus to get behind him—keen to avoid any accidents—Helaku primes for the strike.

Exhilaration fills his eyes with glee, and even in the depths, his smile shines as big and bright as day. Helaku breathes in a mixture of nitrous and oxygen, aiming the three-pronged pole spear at the beautifully alien creature. Then, slowly releasing his breath, he lets go, and the spear darts through the water, impaling the unsuspecting lionfish against the geodesic dome.

Ruckus readies the containment unit as Helaku collects the spear and shoves the thrashing lionfish into the tube's opening. Special flaps separate the fish from the trident on retrieval, avoiding its venomous, hypodermic spines. With the predator safely stored, they reposition closer to their next target.

En route, a couple of amberjacks become flustered by Ruckus's abrupt frog kick and quickly scoot into the crisscrossed lattice of Elk-Stag coral. Their sudden relocation startles a resting ray, which ripples away from the commotion and settles around the backside, vanishing beneath a cloud of sediment.

Empty-handed

Thirty meters away, on the outskirts of Machu-Beachu's reef, Todd glimpses the shadow of a large fin from the corner of his mask. He turns, finding only the ebb of the Atlantic. With his angst dismissed, he grumbles along with a bell-ringing hangover.

Having missed so many opportunities, his angst bubbles into frustration. Minutes pass without sighting a single lionfish.

(I bet they're all at *his* reef,) Todd overthinks. (Hopefully, Julian's crew is faring better.) Despite his tank running low, and the signal to return to the surface, he persists.

PJ—bored and slightly buzzed from a late night on Center Street with Todd, chasing tourist girls—boots up a game emulator on his jail-broken dive computer and swipes to a high score on his Fish Slice.

Todd locks onto a barren cluster of coral and spots the fiery flicker of a lionfish. He aims his speargun, hoping to bag at least one for the day.

Meanwhile, PJ loses his next game, and in frustration, starts up another. Up, up, down, down, left, right, left, right—he swipes past larger fish, gaining ample offerings in his digital breadbasket. Caught in the excitement, he inadvertently bumps into his dive buddy.

The jolt reignites the fear from earlier, and he misses the shot by a mile. The startled lionfish flees into the coral cluster. Fueled by the caffeine coursing through his veins and the tension headache stemming from his dehydrated and fatigued muscles, a fury builds behind Todd's mask.

He throws up his middle finger and charges. PJ floats backward, dodging the assault, and tries to signal him to head topside. But Todd flips him off again and swims to the other end of the reef, leaving his dive buddy behind. Scorned and resentful, PJ sulks to the surface.

Shark

Todd hunts for his trophy by the reef basin. Rounding an outcropping of coral, he spots a large shadow near the ARC's perimeter. (Is that a shark?) Unease bubbles in his gut. (Where is everyone? Dammit, PJ!)

He hurriedly heads to the anchor point. Pausing mid-ascent, he glances back at a fleeting shadow. A primal fear strikes down his spine, churning the gurgle in his stomach once more. He looks up and swims along the tether.

(I knew Marty's kooky shark magnets were a dumb idea.) He clings to the cable, every shadow spiking his pulse.

(Almost there... Just keep breathing.) He swims closer to the underside of the Sphere.

Just then, something yanks him back, stopping him cold.

(Shark!) A silent scream stabs a shot of adrenaline into his heart.

Images of disembowelment and the gut-wrenching realization that his life is over flood the polluted sanctums of his thoughts. Panic erupts as Todd's heart beats with the drums of dread. He flails about and loses his rhythm.

No longer swimming, he frantically struggles to free himself from the fear of those snapping jaws. The speargun slips from his grip and sinks to the sandbar. *Clang!* His tank hits the bottom of the Sphere, further trapping him.

(This is it. I'm going to die. I'm going to get eaten by a fucking shark!) he howls within a chasm of inadequacy.

Buddy System

Meanwhile, topside, the villagers laugh and cut up, tossing fist bumps of mutual appreciation. The teams finish securing their lines and reeling in the last oyster lanterns. Konway submits his collection of samples from the day's harvest.

Mateo examines the containers. "Excellent job, bro. These look fantastic."

"Listen up!" Helaku's booming voice slices through the chatter. "Dive teams, I want everyone to find their buddy."

The gossip and good vibes across the three charter boats fall silent as dive masters conduct their count.

"PJ," Jack calls from his captain's chair, "where is Todd?"

He looks around the deck, gulps, then answers, "I thought he was right behind me."

Trapped In Fear

Running low on gas, Todd struggles against the force pulling him back towards the bobbing eclipse of the geodesic sphere. The gurgling dread knots into a cramp.

(I can't breathe. I'm out of air.) A widespread panic floods his mind.

In a frantic fit of fearful urgency, he pops the switch on his emergency flotation device. The CO_2 cartridge fires a rifle shot of air, inflating a bright orange balloon. His left arm yanks upward as the balloon ascends, but he doesn't budge.

Soon, a tingling numbness seeps into his left arm. Hopelessness overtakes him as he imagines being ripped apart by a monstrous shark. Overwhelmed, he blacks out, losing control of his bowels inside his dive suit.

Plunge

Word of Todd's absence quickly spreads across the three anchored vessels. Without hesitation, Konway pulls the algae-covered safety goggles onto his face and dives into the Atlantic. The rush illuminates a shimmer throughout the dragon tattoo on his left forearm as a neurochemical cocktail of [Prime] and [Stem] bolsters his reflexes.

Hand over hand, he effortlessly swims closer to the brightly colored balloon.

(That's got to be him. Wait, what am I doing? No time—I have to get there.)

His leg muscles fire in symbiosis with the data stored in the Oros system. Several seconds after his explosive leap into the ocean, others take to the water.

Rescue

There, stretched between the reef tether and his emergency flotation device, Todd's unconscious form wheezes on the last fumes of his tank. Konway tries to free him, spotting a wayward strap from Todd's buoyancy compensator tangled with the reef tether. He takes a pair of snips from his utility belt and begins cutting the strap. Halfway through, the snips slip from his grip to the sandy bottom.

With limited breath, Konway swings his legs onto the Sphere and squats sideways. His glutes and quads tense as he pulls with all his might, pouring every ounce of strength into Todd's rescue. After considerable effort, the strap snaps, and the troublesome buckle tumbles down the water column, into a puff of particulate, scattering tiny crustaceans back into the reef.

A Hero's Welcome

The other rescuers soon arrive and help carry Todd to the surface. As Konway follows them through the dancing spears of sunlight, his TacOHUD highlights the shadowy dorsal fin of a curious thresher before it vanishes into the Atlantic. A slight chill carries down his spine, spurring him topside. Hand over hand, with coordinated strokes and flutter kicks, he surges closer to the top.

Just then, Helaku's strong arms breach the surface and, with Ruckus's help, hoist him aboard.

"That was incredible!" Helaku congratulates him.

"It was nothing. My body acted on its own," he says, not sure about how he accomplished the feat.

His haunting concerns veer beneath the jagged recesses of what-ifs and fear-based logics, stirring the Worry Wraiths. (Who am I? Who are you?)

Ruckus slaps his hand on top of Konway's shoulder. "You're a fucking hero."

"A few more seconds and we would've had a tragedy on our hands." Marty glances at Jack's boat. "Let's never forget—we're responsible for each other."

Shame

Machu-Beachu's chief, Jack, looms over Todd and tosses a bucket of melted ice water on his face. The cold shock rips him from his fairytale dreams and nightmares, making him cough up the seawater he swallowed during the rescue.

"What happened down there?!" Jack snaps, directing his scorn at PJ.

"I swear I thought he was behind me," PJ whimpers.

"What kind of idiot are you?" Jack grabs him, shoves him to the edge, and holds him above the Atlantic.

Overwhelmed with a cocktail of emotions, PJ sniffles, followed by tears of fear. The other members of Machu-Beachu look on as their leader pulls him back aboard. PJ flops to the deck.

"Don't start crying. No one in my tribe cries. Don't be a baby. You fucked up, but no one died. Get your shit together, man. And stop sniffling—you sound pathetic."

Jack's rage shifts into concern as he kneels by Todd. But upon unsealing the hood of his dive suit, the abrupt smell assaults him.

"Pew... Gonna have to burn your suit." Jack pinches his nose, quickly stands, and shuffles back to his seat at the helm. "You really did a number on yourself down there. What the fuck happened?"

"I was attacked by a shark... I think it hit my tank." Todd takes a few sips of water. "I must've blacked out."

"Neither Sage nor Bhodi saw any sharks," Jack retorts, eyeing him.

Todd turns to them. "Thank you for saving me—" Then it hits him. "Wait—what do you mean there was no shark? It must've gotten scared away."

"Well," Bhodi informs, "there were no bite marks on your gear."

Sage chimes in, "Apparently, it was a poorly secured strap."

"There's no way I imagined it all," Todd says, his eyes pleading for sympathy. "It felt real... like I was being ripped apart!"

"Whatever happened, you don't need to thank them—thank the new guy." Jack fires a vocal jab.

"The new guy?" He turns to face Helaku's boat.

Unable to accept the idea that this memory-less drifter dove into the water to save him—making him appear weak in front of his tribe—a seed of resentment takes root. Pain throbs in his head as the embarrassment in his heart smears scorn across his face. All the way back to the village, Todd squishes in his fouled dive suit, nurturing his resentment in festering darkness.

Homeward

Halfway home, a pod of playful dolphins leaps along the fleet's wake, attempting to race them for the day's bounty. Konway marvels at their sheen as they weave in and out of the Atlantic. Forever fleeting, his enjoyment comes to a halt as his hazel eyes lock onto a black helicopter the size of a semicolon.

The Oros system focuses on the aircraft streaking up the coastline until a glitch in the system snaps his sight back into frame. The uneasiness stirs something he hoped would remain forgotten. A cornucopia of neurosis unfurls down a spiraling staircase into the primal despair of abandonment.

Konway corkscrews faster than a maglev train, arriving at an emotional terminal of dread and insecurity. Luckily, Ruckus and Mateo's laughter returns him to the present before the Imp can stamp his ticket.

"What's up?" he asks, suppressing the angst. "Will there be another feast?"

Mateo smiles. "Bro, you saved one of us."

"Man, diving into the water like that," Ruckus interrupts, "you must've been an Olympic swimmer."

Konway waves off the praise. "Just doing what anyone would do, right?"

"Todd is such an asshole," Martha, now in overalls and a green bikini top, interjects. "It would've been perfectly fine if—"

"That's enough," Helaku says, shooting a stern eye towards the bow of the boat, then changes the subject before she can continue the hurtful statement. "I think our new friend has earned the afternoon off. All in favor?"

A unanimous gesture of goodwill circles around the deck as wind-whipped waves lessen near the first traces of the barrier archipelago. Once they reach the mouth of the Stono, the vessels slow into formation and swing into the Folly

River, separating Coffin Island from the marshlands. Overhead, seabirds drift past picturesque impressions left by the amanuensis of nature.

Ride Along

Elsewhere, a black-tinted High Mobility Multipurpose Wheeled Vehicle [Humvee] cruises down Coffin Island's narrow roads, touring between blocks of dilapidated houses and McMansions. The former are casualties of poor city planning, where unchecked market forces drove up the cost of living until a shack by the beach cost as much as a flat overlooking Central Park.

Agent Red, still sporting the same floral-print button-down, takes his wandering eye off the road and traces the bottoms of nubile beachgoers as they skip down an adjacent street to the nearest beach access. In the backseat, Commander Xero stares out through the vented window, watching the smoke from his imported Cohiba curl into a sapphire-blue sky. The vehicle dips over the shoulder and crushes a slow-moving box turtle like a bonbon in a nursing home.

"Watch where you're going, son," Commander Xero growls from the backseat, puffing his cigar.

His smartphone rings from the front cupholder.

"Who is it?" he asks, exhaling a savored tuft of smoke.

"The Director, sir." Agent Blue hands him the phone.

Commander Xero grumbles. Then, switching his demeanor, answers the call. "Good afternoon, sir."

"Have you found him?" the Director's deep, gruff voice booms in his ear.

"Not yet, sir."

"What the fuck is taking so long? Do you have any idea how much shit is going to get slung if Zeff's body falls into the wrong hands?"

"He's here. He's on Coffin Island. After this next delivery, we'll find him. You have my word."

Unamused, the Director tightens the screws of inadequacy to get the results he needs, asking, "What's the status of the Lighthouse?"

"We've blocked access to the East End and established our forward operating base. Still waiting for the next supply drop. But with the extra boots on the ground, we should be on schedule to have it linked to the EDC."

"The sooner, the better. The asteroid is still on course. And we need the Earth Defense Constellation updated well before then... Now, regarding the Foundation, I need every bit of info coming from that compound. Have you found another way for us to infiltrate?"

"We're bringing them up to speed, sir."

"Good. With our top asset missing, we'll need someone in the loop by the time they deploy their AI's new blockchain."

Commander Xero rushes the conversation, saying, "I've also had the boys make contact with one of the locals. They think they can parley with someone from Laniakea—a hippie colony on the West Side. Apparently, not everyone there agrees with the big chief."

"Excellent. Our intel shows they work closely with the Foundation. Keep me posted when—"

The Humvee suddenly veers left to avoid a townie—looking more pirate than day-tripper—in the crosswalk, nearly swiping a car full of spring breakers backing out of Monk's Market. The bilge rat tosses up two middle fingers as the Humvee speeds down Ashley Avenue.

"Let me call you back." Commander Xero hangs up. "What the fuck are you doing, son?! You could've drawn the wrong attention to us. Last thing we need is some local Barney asking questions." His blood boils. "Pull over."

"Sir?" Agent Red asks, sensing his superior's frustration.

"Since you can't drive, I need you to walk back."

"But that's—" He catches himself, pulls to the side, and exits the vehicle.

"We'll see you back at the base, son." Commander Xero settles into the driver's seat, slams the armored door shut, drops it into gear, and guns it towards the East End.

Once out of sight, Agent Red slips into Monk's Market for a dirty water dog. After two gut bombs and snagging some sweet tea in a complimentary coffee cup, he strolls back to the East End, hitting the shoreline to enjoy the scenery and local flavors.

42

Fish Fry

Shower Time

Back at Laniakea, despite his insistence on helping unload, Konway heads from the dock to Helaku's abode. He rounds the barn and catches a whiff of yellow jessamine, then the stench of wet dog as the pack charges past, arfing and barking all the livelong way. He opens the apartment door. The A/C hits him like an ice pick, sending chills across his skin. He slips off the borrowed sneakers and, feeling a twinge of rawness by his groin, hurries to the bathroom.

Konway's black bathing suit plops onto the cool tile floor, followed by the squeak of the faucet. Once he tunes the water temperature—to what he considers a soothing 432 Hz—he scrubs away the algae with a soapy loofah sponge. A trail of sweet-smelling body wash leads his gaze towards his sudsy toes, and he reflects on everything that has happened since waking up on the beach and meeting the musicians.

He closes his eyes, followed by several controlled breaths, venturing down a spiral staircase within the dilapidated Mind Palace. In a vacant bunker, his *Space Force III* lunchbox of recently collected memories rests on the stump of a broken pillar. Konway examines every detail of how he jumped into the Atlantic to save Todd.

(Who am I? Who are you? Who am I? Who are you?) Ghastly echoes from a swarm of Worry Wraiths rinse down the drain, washing with suds of algae, sea salt, dried sweat, and a looping replay of Todd's rescue.

(It's okay. Everything is fine. I saved Todd,) he reflects, safeguarding against the gnawing angst.

Unsuccessful, an eclipsed image of the Battle Ordnance Bot [BOB] captures his limited bandwidth. It hovers closer—until the sweet soap overrides his neurosis.

(Helaku and the others will protect me. What I did will surely help me stay in Laniakea.) Konway sorts through the mental clutter.

Following a brief reprieve, he steps out of the shower and dries off with an old beach towel, wrapping it around his waist. Konway wipes down the foggy mirror and notices the sunspots in his hazel eyes staring back at him. He leans in for a closer examination, massaging his jawline, then squeezes a travel-sized tube of toothpaste onto the bristles of his new toothbrush.

Several brushing, swishing moments later, the malfunctioning Oros system fires an electrical current down his right leg. The pulse slaps along the fascia, contracting his iliotibial band into a spasm. Konway stumbles sideways, collapsing onto the floor.

A violent tremor springs from his pinky finger and quickly spreads from his hand to his elbow. He wraps a faded hand towel around his left arm, binding it close, and squeezes until it subsides. However, the panic lingers. He focuses, and after a couple of deep breaths, the system normalizes. With a few more, the tile stops spinning. He stands, unwraps his arm, and rotates his shoulders back. Little by little, then all at once, he regains his composure and exits the bathroom.

(Be easy.) Konway takes slow, purposeful steps down the hall in hopes of not aggravating whatever sent him to the floor. (I seem fine now... But what the fuck is wrong with me? I thought I was about to die in there. Now, nothing? Think... Think... Remember!)

On the bed, he finds a folded pair of khaki shorts and a light-blue button-up shirt. There's a note on top of it, written on a torn sheet from a legal pad. He picks it up and recognizes the squiggly, barely legible penmanship as Helaku's. *Hey-yo!*

You were a huge help today. Here's a fresh set while your clothes are in the wash. I left some budz on my tray for you as well. You've earned it! Take your time, roll you one, and chill. Get ready—tonight's feast is gonna be lit!

Helaku

"Budz," he says, adding a smile upon the parade of positive associations. "But when... how? Did he hear me fall?"

The generosity pushes his concerns to the back of his bandwidth. Delighted to belong, he gets dressed and spins up a joint from two crumpled papers. He puts on one of Helaku's old DVDs, *Endless Summer*, and settles on the couch. Halfway through, an ease unlike any he or Zeff had ever known drapes over him as he falls asleep to the hum of the window unit.

Meanwhile, the village buzzes with his heroics. Everyone is in high spirits, except for Todd. All he feels is the humiliation that comes from being bested by an outsider... and taking an aquadump in his dive suit in front of his peers.

Lay Of The Land

Hours later, Konway wakes from his nap and gulps some room-temperature water. About this time, Helaku kicks open the door and walks in with his arms full of supplies.

"There you are. Figured you'd be resting. Here, this'll help." He tosses Konway a can of CBD seltzer from Monk's Market. "Bro, you're the talk of the village."

"It was nothing." Konway humbles his heroics.

"Maybe to you. But to us, it's a big deal." Helaku plops down on the couch, chugs his can, and says, "Poor Todd—I heard he shit his suit. He's gotta feel super embarrassed after that. They're probably going to give him hell for a while."

"Shit his suit?"

"I heard it was a mess."

Konway's belly garbles. "What time is it? Did I miss the feast?"

"You're good, bro. There's still plenty of time. Ever had Frogmore stew?"

"Not that I can remember, but I bet frogs are delicious." (Please don't be frogs.)

Helaku chokes out a burst of laughter as he lights the half-smoked joint. "No frogs." He wipes away a tear. "You're in for a treat. Frogmore stew has yummy red potatoes, thick-sliced sausage, quartered corn on the cob, a dash—or four—of some special seasoning, and most importantly, fresh-caught local shrimp from Osprey's, a little spot between Coffin Island and the mainland. They have their own boats and sell only what they catch—no six-month-old frozen, silicone-injected shrimp from the other side of the world." Helaku rubs his hands together. "Anyway, that's just for starters," he says. "We've been in the Community Kitchen developing some proper lionfish tacos."

"What do lionfish taste like?"

"They have a buttery deliciousness to them. Ultimately, we'd like to see them in restaurants—promoting awareness while offering a flavorful addition to any palate."

Outside the apartment window, the setting sun swizzles a billion-dollar swath of cotton-candy blue and strawberry sherbet onto the sky.

Hero's Banquet

LED-lit seashell chandeliers sway in the Horseshoe's gentle majesty, illuminating soft patches of lush lawn amidst crisscrossing brick paths. Towards the marsh, a full-on feast, fit for an army, commences as the first flames of the bondfire unfurl into the dusk of day.

Konway stands in line for the buffet, attempting to self-analyze, as Ruckus and Mateo wager on who can eat the most tacos. He observes their brotherly bonds and smiles. The spotlight of his perception widens, focusing on the crowd's togetherness.

Ahead, flounder fillets sizzle on a flat-top grill with hints of lemon and Caribbean zest, while steamy cauldrons of Frogmore stew bubble and boil, sending savory notes through the mildly humid evening. Konway tables his self-inquiry to scan the crowd for Helaku. Instead, he finds Sage Forgé's green eyes by warming trays of grilled zucchini, asparagus, peppers and onions.

Caught within those jade pools, framed by the cotton-candy brushstrokes of the transitioning horizon, he commits a social sin.

"Yo, new guy. Move it," Joel calls out, swinging the locks from his face and nudging his nearest bro, hoping for recognition.

The line shuffles forward.

Soon the murmur elevates to the excitement of food, fun, and fellowship. Konway's stomach rumbles as Ruckus and Mateo begin their surgical siege of the taco bar. After an eternal anticipatory moment, he arrives at the last bits of buttery fillets. His stomach growls with a pang of disappointment when he pivots to a cold pan of sausage dogs.

"Hot-hot-hot!" Bear parts the crowd and sets down a large pan of lionfish next to fold-out tables of accoutrements: homemade corn tortillas, sliced cabbage, pico de gallo, hot sauces, lettuce, shredded cheese, guacamole, and creamy drizzles.

Konway's heart lifts, seeing the steam rise off his plate as he stacks it with abundance and the victuals of gratitude.

Helaku's Table

All around, the sound of island dub rises above the chatter. Konway weaves through a dizzying onslaught of introductions, curious questions, praises, cheers, and handshakes. After greeting the people he knows and introducing himself to those he doesn't, he reaches the gauntlet's end and searches for a suitable spot to pull up a chair. Near a large cluster of tables, he spots Helaku's waving muscular arms, inviting him to sit.

"You've got yourself a proper portion. I'm about to help myself to seconds," Helaku says, patting his abdomen.

"It smells incredible. I can't wait to try some." Konway scoots closer to the table.

"I don't see any steam coming off your plate," Helaku inspects. "I'm gonna bring you back a hot lionfish taco. You've got to taste a fresh one. It's so much better."

Konway scarfs down a taco in three scrumptious bites. "Are you kidding me?" He looks up from the bounty on his plate. "This is amazing. But I wouldn't mind another one, or two." He devours the next taco just as easily as the first.

"Someone has the munchies," Mateo says.

"Geez, did you even taste it?" teases Ruckus.

Konway sops up some drizzle with a piece of grilled zucchini, saying, "It was delicious."

"I bet I can take it down in one bite," Mateo smacks on his most recent chomp.

"With a mouth that big, it shouldn't be too difficult," Ruckus pokes.

A small cornbread muffin launches across the table and hits Ruckus on the forehead.

"Stop it, both of you," Lynn says, approaching the group. "Where are your manners? Think of all the starving children."

Mateo and Ruckus return to their plates.

"I wanted to drop by and thank you for your bravery," she says, sitting in a vacant seat. "We are so fortunate to have you with us. Helaku was right about you."

"It was nothing," Konway throws on a cloak of humility, pausing his next slurping bite into a seasoned quarter of corn on the cob.

"Now's not the time for modesty. It's a time for celebration," Helaku says over the babbling crowd.

Konway's eyes gleam with the joy of finding a place to belong. His fork spears a softened chunk of potato into a shrimp tail, then pops past a sausage casing for the perfect bite. As it slips from his lips, the grace of gratitude unlocks one of the Donor's memories, long-buried by Special Agent Zeff.

Granny's Thanksgiving

See him now, as a boy, within the fractured Vision Shard of a family reunion. Young-Konway steps forward and receives a plate from his father. Peeking down the line, Uncle Al smiles back at him with a funny face, summoning a chuckle.

Just past the jolly giant, long tables topped with patterned linens and heaping portions of steamy vittles. On the menu: turkey stuffed with apples, oranges, and Vidalia onions; a dressing made from homemade cornbread and biscuits; and a baked mac-n-cheese casserole, with enough ooey-gooeyness to make you nap when you get home.

Paw-Paw stands at the front of the line, loading his plate with Granny's blue-ribbon goodness. Although she bested the competition at the state fair with her jams, crochets, produce, and traditional Southern dishes, her most notable prize is the silence served around the dinner table—one which blossoms from a meal made with love and seasoned with a warm heart.

Living Room Adventures

A broken knob on the boob tube flickers to another Vision Shard: a jagged stitch of memory—his father snoring on the living room couch with an old NASCAR race playing in the background. He reaches for the television remote.

"Boy, don't touch the channel. I'm watching that." His father's Jedi senses kick in, detecting a disturbance from the necessity of his nap.

Young-Konway reluctantly returns to his toys and, out of a bucket of Snap-Brix and action heroes, he configures a series of roving adventures.

Sprawled across the spacetime continuum of the living room floor, he enjoys the late afternoon as his agile imagination explores constructive landscapes and storylines—weaving plots from his favorite cartoons into a stew of hijinks, twists, and character arcs. From moral mosaics into the rug-sea, through the Ottoman-empire's space fleet, warping past the couch blockade, the Adastrian Space Force avoids the sleeping celestial giant.

"Zoom. Pew-pew. Swoosh. Pew-pew," he whispers as scout ships approach the crashed cargo freighter.

"Boy!" his father barks from his nap.

"Abort. Abort. Return to Moonbase II!" he commands, piloting his imagination back to the bedroom.

Once all the ships are docked, young-Konway closes his door, pulls out a box of old comics, and selects a graphic novel with a yellow smiley-face on its cover. Soon thereafter, lying in a beam of low-lying sunlight, the leftover warmth from having two helpings of Granny's mac-n-cheese lulls him into a snoring competition with his father. Round and round, the recorded race spins.

The movie reel of memory dims, wrapping itself back into the festive grounds of Laniakea. All around Konway, friends and neighbors—as close as family—sharing a feast. Laughing together, they celebrate the spirit of the village with toasts to the next seven generations.

Jack's Table

Near the far end of the banquet, Todd glares at Helaku. "We should be over there," he mutters. "Not stuck here next to the mosquitoes."

"Shut it. We've had enough out of you today. Do I need to remind you of your piss-poor performance this morning?" Jack turns to him. "How pathetic are you? Not even a single lionfish?"

"It's not his fault," PJ mutters.

"Get the hell up from this table and go eat by the pool," Jack snaps. "I can't believe you left him down there. Take a walk. I can't stand the sight of you tonight," he says, then stares silently as PJ slinks towards the shadows.

"Todd, what were you thinking?"

Silent and sullen, he holds his head in shame.

"Look me in the eye when I talk to you!" Jack roars.

He raises his head slowly.

"You're my right-hand man. I would've been devastated if you'd died down there... Now, I don't know what you and PJ are up to, but you need to cool it."

"Y—yes, sir," Todd stammers.

"Another thing—how the hell did you let yourself get rescued by Helaku's stray? It makes us look weak in front of the other tribes." Jack regains his mask of patience and composure. "Thankfully, you're safe. Now, let's enjoy this meal."

For the rest of the feast, the Machu-Beachu tribe *clinks* and *clanks* in awkward silence.

"Would anyone like me to take their plates?" Sage slides her chair from the table, excusing herself from the tension.

Flirt

She approaches two oversized bins: one filled with scraps for the compost heap, the other for recycling. After scraping and sorting the stacked refuse of her rowdy tribe, Sage carries the tub of dishes to the wash station, where she finds Konway elbow-deep in bubbles.

"The hero, washing up? Now I've seen it all." A sarcastic smile curls up her cheek as she stacks her plates atop a modest pile of dirty dishes.

Konway submerges a sauce-streaked plate into a cloud of suds. "It's the least I could do for all your hospitality," he says. "Don't you know Todd? How's he doing?"

"Let's just say he's not in a good place right now. The tribe is really giving it to him. Maybe next time he won't be so reckless." She giggles at the absurdity of Todd floundering on the deck of Jack's boat, with a soiled dive suit. "I'm Sage, by the way... We met in the parking lot."

(She's talking to me—) He wipes his hands on a dish towel, masking the flutter in his chest. "I remember."

"Now you're the talk of the village."

A spark of rascality twinkles while they chat, blushes concealed under a moon-lit glow.

Jealousy

Todd watches their interaction, grinding his teeth. A deep fury swells from a fissure in his heart. Frustrated, he storms to the seashell parking lot and slams the door of his pickup truck. After several obnoxious engine revs, he peels out, blaring Southern rock ballads towards Center Street.

Over the small reserve of tree tops, past the choirs of frogs and choruses of crickets, the call of Center Street beckons beyond the maritime forest—a veritable Disneyland for drunks, where the limelight flickers and drinks swirl from a boulevard of bars and restaurants. Here, the party rages with all the best music in the Lowcountry. A cornucopia of consumption, brimming with bridal showers, spring breakers, bros, and local day-trippers.

Todd fiddles beneath his seat, groping for a derelict mini bottle, and narrowly avoids a drainage ditch. Nip in hand, he slams it back and tosses it out the window. Farther down Sand Bar Lane, he hangs a right one block from Center Street and cruises down to Kawabonga's back lot, whipping into a reserved spot. Parked diagonally, he does a quick bump of blow from an old key before venturing out on the hunt for something sweet and easy—like a candy bar—to sink his teeth into, desperate to fill the pit of inadequacy surging along the neurotic hamster wheel of his broken heart.

Wash Up

As Sage and Konway chit-chat, tossing the first darts upon Cupid's weathered board, Helaku and Ruckus emerge from the social murmur, slurping down their final double-stuffed lionfish tacos.

"Man, that was some meal," Ruckus says, followed by an exaggerated belch of satisfaction.

"I'm about to pop." Helaku sets his plate in the wash bin. "Bro, what are you doing over here cleaning? This whole deal is for you."

Ruckus smacks on the last buttery morsel. "Yeah, put those down and come have some fun with us."

"A hundred thousand thank-yous for this evening—and all Laniakea's done for me. Even with my memory condition, I feel like I belong." Konway smiles with gratitude, scrubbing away some melted cheese. "It feels like home."

"And why wouldn't it?" Helaku asks. "There's nothing wrong with having the support of a community. It's not about where you're from, but who you might become—everyone here was someone else before they came to Laniakea. And bro, I've seen enough to know Laniakea could be a proper place for you."

Helaku initiates the village handshake, striking his right thumb down the center of his back. Konway mirrors the gesture, then brings his hand forward, and the two clasp in a brotherly embrace. "See? He's a natural... but we're being rude."

"Apologies, Sage."

"Hey, guys. Where's Mateo?"

Ruckus beams. "Oh, he's back at the table trying to catch up to my *new* record."

"What's that?"

"Nine tacos." Ruckus pats his stomach.

"Where do you put it all?" Sage asks.

"What can I say? I'm a glutton." He laughs with a full belly, followed by another ten-point belch.

43

Wake The Dream

Namesake

After clearing the buffet and stowing the folding tables, the tribes gather around the bondfire and relax as the evening's orchestra cascades into croaking crescendos, dubbing over the roots reggae thumping through the Horseshoe.

"Why'd the Founders name the village Laniakea?" Konway asks during a brief lull in nature's cadence.

Helaku passes the joint. "Well, Laniakea means 'immeasurable heaven.' It represents the ideal world that the Founders were trying to foster into the future. They were shooting for the stars but settled for landing on the moon." He chuckles softly and sits up in his chair. "They knew they couldn't reach their goals within a few generations. So, they laid the groundwork for what you see here today." He stretches his arms above his head, yawning a deep breath of oxygen into his body.

"Getting sleepy, old man?" Marty teases.

"Not yet." Helaku tosses a twig into the bondfire.

Embers crackle beneath charred logs, lifting ash towards a starlit tapestry. As the amanuensis of nature taps their wand, the local frog choir croaks out a successive serenade with each passing *rib-it*.

"They're really getting it tonight," says Mateo, kicking his feet onto a small, square wooden table.

Ruckus slumps lower in his chair. "Must've been all the rain from the other day."

Marty turns her head to listen. "They've got a good groove going. See how they're waving from one side to the other?"

"Tis the season for nature's baby-making, after all." Mateo finishes his beverage.

Soon, conversational revelry wraps around the bondfire. Many cheer, toasting, "Unity through community!"

Konway observes the joy in their togetherness, trying to shift his thoughts but finding himself stuck on the silhouetted musings of Sage Forgé.

(What is it about her? Could it be her paintbrush ponytail? The freckles on her tan shoulders? Her emerald-green eyes? The twinkle of her smile? Or was it the ease I felt while we were washing dishes? And the look on her face when she splashed me with dishwater.) An adolescent smirk rises to Konway's cheek as he recalls Sage's soap-soaked tank top clinging to the outline of her breasts. In his heart, a lustful lotus blossoms from the primal mud of his being. (She's sexy... What does that mean?)

The Imp-oster intrudes from the comfort of its lair, whispering, (Why are you wasting time on her? Don't you need to figure out who you are? Tik-Tok. Tik-Tok.)

Before the fiend pesters him further, he retrieves the paper rhino, passes it between his hands, and breathes deeply. A few unnoticed rounds later, he suppresses the haunting interrogation and returns to the blessings of communion.

Hahalua

Helaku's booming voice bursts into the haze of Konway's thoughts. "I know you've heard this plenty, but on behalf of the entire village, thank you for what you did today. Hell, we ought to let you apply to become a villager. Think about what you'll be able to accomplish once you've been here longer." He peers into the bondfire's center, watching a glowing log crumple from the undulating heat.

"I'm the one who should give thanks," Konway says humbly. "Who knows where I'd be if it weren't for your kindness?" He remembers the jest from earlier and says, "Maybe I was an Olympic swimmer."

"Or a Navy Seal!" Ruckus says, then takes a swig from his drink.

"Nah... probably Delta Force," Mateo cuts in.

Helaku lands a solid smack on Konway's shoulder, and a sense of belonging envelops him like a cool blanket across the warm evening of his unraveling identity.

"There's some incredible stuff happening here." He passes the joint. "How'd you come up with all these ideas?"

"Well, they aren't all mine—it takes a village. But the inspiration for the Manta Array Recycling Stations came from something that happened when I was a child." Helaku reminisces about his grandmother's farm, sitting on his mother's lap, overlooking clear, teal-blue water. "'Keep your eyes on the horizon,' she'd say. 'Watch the waves forming in the distance and see them coming towards you. Hear them rolling over the sandy shore. Be patient, listen to the water, and wait.'"

Soar

Helaku's mother forms a wall of sand, then nuzzles his nose, whispering childhood secrets, with no one but the scuttling crabs to hear. "When Hahalua leaps out of the water, they bring some magic from below, pulling us back from our own thoughts about our daily problems, allowing us to begin anew."

He looks to the sparkling sea, and a short distance out, a giant ray soars from the water. Time suspends itself in his eyes as he grapples with the sight. Behind the mandala of dripping droplets, sun rays pierce ascending clouds and ripen into the splendor of an offshore rainbow.

Splash! Hahalua crashes back into the underworld, carrying the tales of its journey beyond the surface.

"Wahoooooooooo!"

"Now, wasn't that wonderful?" She squeezes her son, strumming joy into his fertile heart, crystallizing a sense of wonderment, love, and adoration for the ocean.

"Amazing," young-Helaku says, smiling with a missing front tooth, and places the last bucket of sand onto his castle.

"We need a moat." His mother draws her finger through the smooth layers of crustacean corpses, etching a channel into the cream-white sand. "This way, we can enjoy it a little longer, even though the tide will eventually wash it out to sea."

Design

Another log crackles into chunks. Marty tosses a bundle of woven palm fronds stuffed with twigs and dried grass into the embers. Around the bond-fire, the remaining villagers connect with the flickering dance of our ancestors.

"How'd you put it all together?" Konway asks.

"Well, I started having this recurring dream about riding on the back of a giant manta ray." He unfurls his wingspan and glides into the smoke.

"Is this your secret?" Ruckus sets his beer bottle on the ground.

"That's part of it... One day, as I sat on my board, staring at the horizon, I had a vision."

Konway leans closer, asking, "What did you see?"

"At first, I thought it was Hahalua... Boy, was I mistaken. It was no mythical beast—just a mass of trash. Red plastic cups, an old cast net, derelict bits of foam, plastic bottle caps—you name it. So, I loaded up my board with as much garbage as I could and paddled it back to shore. It took a couple of trips, but I got it cleaned up.

"Somehow, my anger about the trash in my set fused with the muck oozing from the cup in my pocket and the longing to see Hahalua soar once more. That's when it hit me. Inspiration at last! I realized how we could help save the ocean." Helaku's shadow dances around the brickwork border. "I wasn't blinded by my usual anger; instead, I was elevated to understand the pieces before me. Shaped by Hahalua's inspiration and designed by members of this community in collaboration with the Foundation, we were able to wake the dream into reality and scoop the trash into our pockets."

"Cash monies," Ruckus blurts, rubbing his thumb and forefinger together with a playful look of greed in his eyes.

Helaku fist-bumps him.

"Bro, you're blowing my mind," Mateo says in a spaced-out voice, shuffling back with a fresh 22oz Pirate's Life beer. "Y'all want some?"

"No thanks—I've got a big day tomorrow." Helaku sips some water. "I need to check on another project we've got in the works. Can't keep all your eggs in one basket."

"Ain't that the truth," chimes Marty, slouched in her Adirondack.

"I'll try some." Konway reaches for the sweat-dripped can. "But can someone take this joint from me?"

Mateo gladly reaches for it.

"Didn't have too much trouble out of him, did ya?" Helaku slings his arm around Konway's shoulder.

"Hell, I wish I had ten more like him." Mateo pulls a slow celebratory drag, bobbing his head to the reggae drifting from a nearby speaker.

"What are we doing tomorrow?" Konway asks.

"I think you're scheduled for village tasks. It shouldn't take too long."

Feeling a guttural compulsion, Konway raises the half-full deuce-deuce high and declares, "Thank you—and the rest of Laniakea—for accepting me into your good graces. Unity through community."

"Unity through community!" Those within earshot of his gratitude raise their drinks and down them in unison.

Ruckus Reflections

Konway rests his head on the oversized Adirondack chair, enjoying the crackling fire and the *rib-bits* rippling along the water's edge.

A piece of plastic wrap from an afternoon barbecue wafts in from next door. It tumbles by the pool, past the roving pups, and against Marty's leg. She snags it, balls it up, and stands. "Fucking plastic. It takes millions of years to create, and only a few minutes for us to throw it away. Even though we recycle, it still ends up out there, choking our ecosystem."

"We may not fix the problem in our lifetime, but at least we're holding the space for others to help lift this stage," Helaku adds, trying to console her.

"I'd prefer a future where the oceans aren't a boiling sea of radioactive plastics," Marty jests.

"We won't let it happen," Helaku reassures.

"Nope, the kelp will get us before the plastic does." Mateo chuckles.

Ruckus swirls his beverage. "So long as I don't have to work like I did back in college, I don't care what we do."

"Where was that?" Konway asks.

"When I was at the State University, I worked at this sandwich shop—fifty-plus hours a week for minimum wage." Ruckus pauses at the stampede of recollection. "Mind you, it'd been over a decade since they raised the minimum wage. And if your employer doesn't bump your pay by at least seven percent each year to keep up with inflation, you'll lose about seventy percent of your earning potential in the next decade. At least there were tips sometimes."

"Why'd you stay for so long?" Konway asks.

"Honestly, it was the only place that would hire a bunch of misfits like us." He stares into the flames, reflecting on his life prior to moving to Coffin Island.

As Ruckus spins the yarn of his fate, a paint-splattered footlocker opens within Dreamwind Studios. Inside, a rickety projector clicks on, casting their remarkable tale onto a tattered screen typically reserved for daydreams.

44

The Ballad Of El Sucio

Geezer's Gourmet Chipwich Shoppe

Lost somewhere in a daydream by the bread ovens, condiment lines, prep stations, slicers, and dish sinks, Ruckus's words conjure a flourishing realm populated with a pantheon of gods and minuscule entities. Of them, the indomitable Xoros the mighty, whose birth splintered the fourth dimension—

A fantastic spray of turkey jelly slaps across Ruckus's apron, yanking him from the vivid reverie.

"Why am I still working here?" he utters beneath his breath.

The shift manager slams oblong blocks of cheese onto the make-table. "What're you mumbling about now? You need to finish the slicing list by the end of your shift."

After having his imaginative bandwidth broken, Ruckus sinks back into the monotonous and underappreciated everydayness of being a Geezer's Gourmet Chipwich Shoppe employee. Back and forth, with every push-pull of chemically separated turkey, his artistic sense of expression dulls against the grinding gray of the stainless-steel societal cheese grater, shaving away the remnants of youth.

(Damn, that was dope. I need to write it down before I forget.) He pulls a sauce-stained notepad and a two-thirds-spent pen from his apron pocket.

At first, the omniverse was an ineffable realm, a garden of forking paths, flourishing with potential and possibility. In time, everything began to unravel. Xoros, determined to save his new home, mended the wake of his arrival by folding the Apex of Reality with a whisper, rippling a thunderous cascade along the Curtain of Creation. Then, *a roar of cosmic chaos erupted as he slapped the fallen heavens between Space and Time, sprinkling life throughout the stars. Henceforth, sandwiched in Xoros's perpetual birth from the abyss and his eternal return to the void beyond, all of existence danced to his cosmic drama—*

(Another customer.) Ruckus glances from his scribbled words to a sweaty, panting man wilting in the summer heat. (I bet it's a turkey on rye, no tomato, extra mayo.)

Catching his breath, the man orders. "Turkey on wheat, extra tomatoes, no mayo, a large diet soda, three pickles, three bags of cool-rancho tortilla chips, and four fresh-baked cookies. It's not all for me—some of this is for my co-workers. I've got to shed some extra pounds before vacation."

(Can't be right all the time. Good for him. Must be nice to have the time off.) Ruckus pivots to the cramped rectangle of the Geezer's make-table. (Shit! The trash is overflowing.)

He feverishly finishes the order, sending another satisfied customer on their merry way, and peels off the nitrile disposable gloves, tossing them into the refuse bin of end-meats and tomato tops. In the doorway, his impudent manager clutches a frivolous amount of unsliced deli meats.

(I need a fucking vacation.) Ruckus huffs and puffs. (All of this for a pauper's pay?) Shaking his head, he rotates back to the workstation and finishes jotting down his thoughts. (Where was I?)

Xoros, eager to savor his favorite star before passing through the titan's hour-glass, plucked a pinprick of light from the blackberry bush of creation. In his possession, the star blossomed into Morag the Beautiful, presiding over the hearts and desires of all beings—

"Would you mind proofing fourteen trays of bread and cookies—not the large ones—for the Summer Expo?"

"Sure thing," Ruckus responds without lifting his pen from the pad.

—During the lustful revelry of their timeless bliss, the unbound consequences of Xoros's actions continued festering within the womb of reality. As with his arrival, selecting Morag from the heavens left a chasm in the dimensional tapestry, threatening the complete collapse of reality. In a selfless instant, Xoros tore a third of himself and hurled it into the wound. At its epicenter, a singularity of cosmic energies gathered and soaked into his makeshift patch. There, amidst the microtubule web stitching reality together, Gavril's consciousness woke to the sparkle of several stars orbiting a black-w-hole. In time, the godling gathered enough strength to bend the universe and escape his cradle's entangled superposition to return to Xoros's side. However, loyal Gavril, the Gardener of the Universe—devourer of planets and galaxies, mender of tears in the wake of his creator—secretly fell in love with Morag, and she with him—

The door chimes again, halting the flow of creativity.

(At least this gig's got complimentary food. But the slicing... Xoros, help me—the slicing!) Despite his playful sarcasm, the dread spreads across his brow, and along the mis-smeared mayo. (Shit. Spicy mayo.) Ruckus tosses the botched sandwich, banking it off the heaping trash can onto the floor. "I just mopped that!" he gripes, then completes the order—wrapping, bagging, tagging, punching in the discount code, and stamping the club card: buy twelve, and the next one is free with the purchase of a chip, cookie, and drink.

El Sucio

Day after day, an innumerable amount of processed meats, veggies, and blocks of cheese are sacrificed upon the Slice-O-Matic 4000 to appease the gods and the masses who worship them. With its rickety rigging and ill-placed location near the table's edge, this Victorian-era relic is better suited for an inquisition than bushels of lettuce.

Ruckus places his hand on the icy iron maiden. (Will this be it? Is this when Geezer's takes my good arm? How will I draw or create? How the hell am I ever going to get out of this dump, absent from a body bag?)

Soon, the sweet demise of a bag of onions engulfs the whole restaurant. He prays for release. Sadly, no one hears the pleas of a lowly employee.

He cuts his eyes towards the dingy wall clock. "Time for a shift change. I wonder who's coming in?" Ruckus leans back from a stack of sliced offerings.

He flips to a grease-stained receipt, riddled with scribbles, and hurriedly pens the last of his fleeting inspiration.

—*The other gods sprang up like weeds around a dripping faucet. From their lineage of ancestral glory, the Messengers blossomed. Each planet capable of cradling consciousness bore its own pantheon of Messengers. On Earth, Tobiathes, the most favored among them, was their king, dating back to the First Dawn.*

Then there was the cryptic El Sucio, whose presence heralded forthcoming doom. Although his actions mirrored those of a cantankerous old man—shunned by the eternal youth of the other Messengers—his speed was matched by none under the moon. Blessed by a night goddess, El Sucio could travel at breakneck speeds beneath the gentle kiss of her light. The problem was, El Sucio preferred not to go out after dark—

The phone rings violently off the hook. Alas, all the delivery drivers are out and about... except one.

El Sucio huddles around some makeshift food, salvaged from scraps. Ruckus hears him grumbling with delight in the back of the shop. Finally, noticing the phone, the crusty one lifts his head like a mongrel from its scraps bowl and turns around with food dribbling down his sullen cheeks. The ancestral attainment of being human has long left him, leaving the basic feral instincts of survival. "Geezer's... Hold," he growls, dropping the receiver.

Another ringing banshee echoes into the alley, startling El Sucio's roosting pigeons into flight. Ruckus checks to see if he needs help, but all that remains is a grease trail and a fleeting shadow out the backdoor. Unfazed by El Sucio's reluctance, he places the customers on hold and returns to his labors, muttering, "Ugh, back to the list—and the altar of mortal sacrifice."

Tobiathes crashes through the kitchen door with a clash of thunder, answering the phones with his booming voice. "It's a great day at Geezer's Gourmet Chipwich Shoppe. How may I take your order?" he asks with a pen pressed to a marinara-stained ticket.

While El Sucio's lingering trail dissipates into the side alley, Tobiathes bags up the deliveries and is back out the door.

Descent Into Madness

As the clock *ticks* and the time *tocks*, no manager arrives at the lonely Chipwich Shoppe. Ruckus reloads the slicer. The tension and anxiety of running the shift—without proper economic compensation—quarrel inside his skull.

So much slicing. What do I do?
I'm by myself. What do I do?
So many customers. What do I do?
The phones are ringing.
I need to use the restroom, number two.
What do I do?
Just leave.
What do I do?

His fiery hatred of this place, boiling between ever-shrinking walls, unleashes a rant which would have razed the building to ash—had decades of grime not insulated the owners from their workers' pleas. While Ruckus's composure crumbles, red-ass meter turning to eleven, the front doorbell rings.

"Xoros, help me."

To no surprise, the rest of the managers are working at the Summer Expo catering event. The late-arriving shift leader stands at the threshold, staring blankly at the length of today's slicing list. Another customer drags into the shop.

(I'll let him handle it. It'll break him in for the shift.) Ruckus returns to the list. (Still, I feel bad for Demetris—stuck with all the responsibilities and none of the pay.)

Like most, they hired him to cut the grass but expected him to clean the pool for free.

Danger Zone

The shift keeps an even flow of busy and stagnant bouts of customer interaction, coupled with a constant series of sacrifices upon the altar. It's a default mode of existence, fueled by a consumption of chips, cookies, extra meats, and liters of cola—someone's got to feed the mewing masses.

(Maybe he can help me tackle this list.) Ruckus greets Demetris with several compliments and socially engineered talking points. Then, with the ease of a Renaissance artist, he convinces him to slice while he lays down deli paper between thin layers of salami and capicola.

Sadly, after the first box, Demetris complains. So they decide to switch. In a game of Russian roulette, back and forth, the fourteen-inch blade spins, and the juices fly. He handles the roast beef, Demetris the cheese.

Some provolone clumps together, forming sporadic projectiles that launch from the dull grind of economic enslavement. Once again, it's Ruckus's turn. He squares up to the Slice-O-Matic 4000 and flips the switch. On the other side, his hand hovers two inches from the rotating blade.

Hours into their tour within the close-quarter confines of the Geezer's Gourmet Chipwich Shoppe, a claustrophobic madness bubbles to the surface. And with no time for a break, detrimental mindsets culminate in a volatile combination of ill-tempered derangement and sensory distortion. Ruckus cranks up the radio and belts Succubus's *While I Burn* at the top of his lungs.

After twelve tracks, the two servants reach the last sacrifice on the grease-dribbled list.

"Let's crank it up, Demetris!" Ruckus hollers above the phones, dropping a five-pound ham onto the rickety slicer. Before turning it on, he prays to the gods of old, opens his eyes, and flips on the malicious red switch at the back of the machine.

A deafening metal grating rips past their eardrums. *Pop!* A bolt flies overhead, sending the two employees to the floor, bouncing off the chip rack, before ricocheting into a bubbling vat of marinara and meatballs. From one side to the other, the slicer's violent vibrations shake the altar's foundation.

It wobbles beyond the limits of its design, and one of the table's legs buckles. The maniacal contraption crashes against the brushed metal countertop, gliding down the legless side to where Demetris cowers on the floor. Ruckus, unable to look away from the terror mirrored in his co-worker's eyes, freezes as the inquisitor's final question slides towards him.

Don't Blink

The bondfire dances with the details of Ruckus's story.

"What happened?" Konway asks.

"A blurred shadow raced through the kitchen and pulled Demetris out of the way."

"Was it Tobiathes?" Konway presses.

"No... all I could do is look on with a confused sense of reverence as El Sucio showed more humanity than I could muster. To think someone I despised could find the courage to do what I was too afraid to do... I realized why I loathed ole Sucio—I feared I would end up like him. So, I packed my bags, and I moved to Coffin Island. Best decision I ever made." Ruckus turns to face the pool, keeping his friends from seeing his tears of joy.

While Konway listens, somewhere along the intersecting back alleys of the Mind Palace VPN partition, a rusted door falls off its hinges. Vision Shards—fleeting faces, vaguely familiar acts of heroism, and seemingly courageous images—streak past him. Inside the dilapidated, checkered-tile room, a tin of tea sits atop a pedestal.

The lid opens and releases a small storm cloud that hovers above the ruins, swiftly expanding to engulf the area. The rains come, unleashing floods across the Fields of Forgotten Things. In their wake, the receding waters coalesce into drops, dripping onto bloody concrete floors. A postcard from Mr. Ben Penstone swirls into view.

(Penstone... Penstone... Where have I heard this name before?)

In a zip, his awareness flickers to the memento of a moment before he learned the truth.

45

The Leaky Tea Warehouse

Stake Out

Drip, drip, drip. Rusted eaves puddle onto the cement floor of the Leaky Tea warehouse as a seasonal storm rolls into the distance. Concealed in the shadows, Special Agent Zeff leans against a wall and enjoys his CBD gum's classic flavor. The staunch humidity reminds him of summer in the foothills. He dismisses the thought, prioritizing the mission's success over his longing to see his family again—despite not knowing when he last visited the home of his youth.

Meanwhile, his partner—a meter-tall black orb, Battle Ordnance Bot [BOB]—connects to a top-secret satellite network and transmits the encrypted feed back to the States. There, the good folks watching at home test the recent patch update for the Oros system. They sit back, comfy in the air conditioning, with bowls of popcorn and glass dishes of breath mints and fiery cinnamon candies, ready to enjoy the show.

A small icon illuminates his TacOHUD's tab bar. With the aid of tailored nanites, he selects the glowing icon. A confirmation softly dings in the rattling snail shell of Special Agent Zeff's inner ear.

BOB's live feed unveils neighboring sniper positions, goon squads, outlier guards, weapon crates, suitcases of cash and rare gems—and, at the center of it all, a mountain of a man bound to a chair with a bag covering his head. He focuses on the third video stream, pinning the others just outside his peripherals. A sterile room flashes open, pre-stocked with endless rows of file cabinets brimming with mental dossiers. Amongst the folders, he selects a slideshow of images.

(Look at this slippery fuck. It's been a while since Panama, Johnny-boi.) He clenches his jaw, squeezing out a bit more juice from his chewing gum.

Another icon glistens. He selects it, and a small window opens with the Pickle Factory on the other line.

"We see you've found him," Agent Xero's voice echoes inside his ears. "With Johnny-boi's ties to international oligarchs and pocket dictators, we cannot stress the importance of interrupting this negotiation. Also, as you might've noticed, the large fella with the bag on his head. Our *cousins* have informed us that one of theirs has gone missing. We need you to handle the meeting and return the lost lamb."

The line goes silent as another translucent pop-up window renders the summary of tonight's dance card.

Zeff glares at Johnny Who's smug picture before calming himself. He swipes the dossier left. (Up next, we have a battle-hardened soldier with an eyepatch, Uri Avraham. Oooh, ex-Matkal. Seems like you have a thing for interrogation—something we have in common.) He smiles and swipes to the next person of interest. (Last, and certainly not least, we have a sinister-looking blond-haired devil with icy, calculating eyes. Alexi Ivanov, former Spetsnaz operative, you're the next participant on *Price, Wheel, or No Deal*. Gentlemen, those are some expensive suits. And I see your crews are packing some serious shit. Definitely not thugs with clubs. Typically, what you'd expect from an international weapons brokerage attempting to tilt the geopolitical scale.)

In half a heartbeat, the pop-up slides away, and perched within the dripping darkness, he waits.

Snipe Hunt

Command gives the green light. At the speed of thought, nanites in his skin stimulate sebaceous glands, secreting a chitin-laced sebum that alters his reality distortion field [RDF], rendering a quilt of near invisibility. Then, with synchronous timing, BOB pipes in an artificial feedback loop to hold all radio comms in silence. Trapped in an auditory prison, the guests of the Leaky Tea warehouse continue their meeting—oblivious to the gum-chewing danger stalking them from the shadows.

The snipers are the first to go. Farthest from the others, an unsuspecting marksman receives the blessing of a taser-blade through his neck, blood pooling into the tucked-in shirt of his lucky sniping suit. Special Agent Zeff appears beside the second one and observes them for a moment. On exhale, he snaps the gunman's neck with a crunch and gently drags him into the shadows.

Ducking around a low railing, he lurks a throat's grab away and slips the taser-blade's electrical impulse into the sharpshooter's armpit. As the surge strikes a precise pressure point, a rippling paralysis slides down the mercenary's spine. One by one, he disables the remaining snipers, leaving them unable to writhe in agony or call for help.

Inquisition

[Catwalk: Clear.]

Zeff closes the tabs on his TacOHUD and finds a better vantage point to observe the faint outlines of the 120 mercenaries scattered within the warehouse. He focuses on the room's center, and the Oros system responds, extending the observational scaffolding of his sight and hearing. He zeros in on the conversation.

Below the flickering fluorescent lights, Johnny Who points at their prisoner, yelling, "Both of you, calm down!" He steps between the buyers. "We're all on the same side here. Let's draw lots to see who gets to kill our honored guest." A gold tooth glints from his devious grin.

"Maybe you finally got caught, and now you're burning us." Alexi points his cane.

"He's not one of mine! I swear to both of you. How long have you been doing deals with me?"

"Maybe you're a rat." Uri pulls his Jericho 941 pistol and aims at Johnny Who.

All available combatants chamber their weapons. However, no one notices the lack of red dots and bolt actions from the sniper perches.

"Everyone calm the fuck down!" Johnny Who takes an unflinching step towards Uri. "You wanna say that again?! I'll rip out your other goddamn eye!"

"Gentlemen, please. Let's ask our comrade here." Alexi waves his cane towards the chair.

"I can hear you fucks," a thick British accent grumbles from beneath the bag. "I'm trying to catch a few winks, ya puffs."

Thwack. Alexi's gilded cane strikes the bound brute's head. "Shut it, you fool. Who do you work for?" He hits him again.

"Fuck you!" He laughs a bloody dribble at his captors' futility.

A malicious smirk flashes under Alexi's glasses as he calmly pushes them up the bridge of his nose, magnifying his icy blue eyes. *Thwap.* The cane's ornate handle, a golden double-headed eagle, crashes against the prisoner's leg.

He muffles the anguish. "Is this all you've got, you cunt?"

"I'm going to cut out his fucking tongue." Alexi swings again.

"Not before we find out who sent him." Uri's eye twinkles.

Pop. The cane connects with the bound brute's arm. Then, rearing back, Alexi jabs it into his gut.

"Ughhh." He coughs up more blood, drooling onto the cracked warehouse floor.

"Now we're getting somewhere." Alexi adjusts his glasses.

Marauding Massacre

(I've heard enough... I need to hurry and get back to the room service I ordered.) He pictures the delicacies waiting in his hotel room—delights to dull the pain of living on the bleeding edge of global stability with experimental nanotech woven throughout his physiology.

(It's showtime, BOB.) With the flicker of a thought, the drone detonates a small explosive in the outside breaker box. The building goes dark, and a sweeping silence hushes across the warehouse, lending a momentary glimpse into the tense reverence held between lion and gazelle.

In response, the Oros system secretes a light-filtering compound near Special Agent Zeff's tear glands. His eyes gloss over, and the TacOHUD renders darkness into sight. He draws two special-issue Delta-3 handguns from his side holsters and stalks within the damp gloom. An enhanced minimap appears in the tab bar. With a glance, the digital overlay highlights potential targets.

For the guy at the end of the mezzanine railing, a silenced slug punches through his chest, his legs scorpioning over his head as he falls to the concrete. At a nearby ladder, the assassin slides down to the platform below and aims. The next shot's whirling ferocity greets the gentleman by a set of industrial stairs in the stomach, severing his spine—fortunately, he won't feel the gastric acid sizzling his insides.

Blood bathes the warehouse walls as he squeezes akimbo triggers, unsealing silent velocities and sending their bodies to the unswept floor. Poor chaps by the grime-smeared window receive simultaneous retinal impacts, their skulls erupting in Pollockesque spatter patterns along the brickwork.

Heel-toe, heel-toe. A hulking man passes by the wrong mound of cargo crates. Zeff leaps from the perch onto his back, firing three shots downward, piercing his shoulder and into his heart. The giant topples forward, and Special Agent Zeff rides the momentum, rolling out of sight. Just around an adjacent aisle, the TacOHUD traces the fluorescent footprints of the next unlucky fool.

Blinded

As a foreboding dread blankets the mercenaries, BOB continues jamming their comms. Immersed in darkness, he chews his gum and watches them scramble for cover. The blooming moon shines through the skylight, reflecting off a puddle formed on the factory floor.

"When we find you, ya son of a bitch, we're going to flay you alive—starting at your toes!" Uri roars, flanked by his personal guard.

"And when we're done, we'll sew your face to a goddamn soccer ball—play a game of footy or two," Johnny Who snarls, clenching the grip of a CZ Scorpion EVO 3 submachine gun.

Soon, the grim realization that they might not survive spreads among the soldiers of fortune. Some, still God-fearing, kiss crucifixes and whisper prayers. Others snort a bump of courage to steel themselves, while a few cower in a hypocrisy of muffled silence.

Gemini

By a rusty packaging machine, twins in leisure suits sit back-to-back, clutching their weapons. They nod to each other and cautiously creep towards the rest of their unit. Nearby, Zeff prowls across the tops of crate stacks and observes the frightened hesitation in their movements. Below, the brothers signal to one another that the coast is clear, oblivious to death's approach.

Two clean shots drill through the back of their heads, slumping them against a catawampus corridor of crates. Warm gore pools on the cracked warehouse floor, lined with the grime of underpaid labor. Sprawled upon the sticky concrete, one of the dying Geminis reaches for his twin's hand, already fleeing the mortal coil of this world.

Special Agent Zeff callously walks past them like bent stalks of wheat along the bloody road of glory.

A quick jaunt around the corner, he removes a few caltrops from a utility pocket and tosses them by an unsuspecting fool. The portly man follows the sound, waddling around intersecting rows of abandoned cargo containers, looking for a rattle in the dark. Lost in his own thoughts, a silenced bullet bursts from the side of his face. He won't be coming home to his other life, his other wife, his children, his cats, or his day job. To hell with it—he was going to quit anyway.

Regroup

The Oros system outlines a trail of feet on his TacOHUD. After a complex choreography of predictive suggestions and luminous footsteps, a bald merc catches a chop to the throat. He stumbles from the strike, swiftly followed by the penetrating sensation of a taser-blade into his heart. Special Agent Zeff props the corpse against a mid-sized crate stack and fades back into the shadows. Despite the placement, ole baldy slides to the floor. He resets his trap and pins the body upright, stabbing their black-handled folding knife through the shirt to fasten the bait in place.

The Oros system isolates a nearby discussion and queues the next targets in this ballet of bloodshed:

"What's going on?"

"Let's get moving."

"He's dead!"

"Everyone, get back to the cars!"

"Go-go-go!"

Following the shimmering breadcrumbs on the TacOHUD and audible cues in his ear, Special Agent Zeff snatches the last goon in line and promptly spins him around.

"What the—"

He snaps the soldier of misfortune's neck like a chicken before Sunday dinner. The posse turns, glimpsing enough to excite the butterflies in their bubble-guts. Wild roars and blaring gunfire erupt in a thunderous squall of vengeance. Thanks to his upgrades, he dodges and scales a cargo box as strobing muzzle flashes of hip-shot accuracy illuminate the bodies of their fallen comrades, fueling the blind fury of their steadfast triggers until only the dripping darkness remains.

While fresh magazines click into place, a shot of [Time Warp] slows his perception to a crawl. Special Agent Zeff leaps sideways across the gap, dancing over corpses and returning fire—each bullet shredding Kevlar, dropping bodies in the pale moonlit corridor.

Let There Be Light

Drip, drip, drip. A tango of melodic mayhem unfurls as halogen headlights brighten the warehouse. Uri, Alexi, and Johnny Who surround the large bloke wearing a bloodied, sweat-soaked white dress shirt, barking at their goons. Locked and loaded in a halo of light, the arms dealers prepare for what comes next.

"Start the generator! Get those lights on!" they shout at their crews.

The goons huddle closer. Skinny Pete, a noob by any other definition, squeezes off several shaky shots beyond the luminous perimeter. Special Agent Zeff responds with a storm of uncanny precision. Two by two, the herd thins.

While their cronies blind-fire into moonlit crates, his TacOHUD highlights the position of a terrified merc hiding near the corner of some boxes. The trembling fool leans the wrong way and catches one of those well-placed shots, taking off his ear. He lets out a brief cry just before a thrown taser-blade muffles his anguish.

In an adjacent room, a cantankerous generator sputters, stalling to crank. After several more grunts, the beast rumbles to life. Diesel fumes curl into the humid dampness as flying insects swarm the fluorescent bulbs hanging from the rafters.

BOB hovers into position above the warehouse floor as the TacOHUD dims, shielding his optics from the payload of concussive flashbangs. The warehouse bursts with blinding resplendence. Disoriented, the remaining goons stagger into the kill ledger, leaving this world with little fuss.

Three Capotes

Uri shields his one good eye, only to open it again and witness the butchered horrors of the Leaky Tea warehouse. Blood sprays fountain into coalescing pools, red-washing the concrete slab. Special Agent Zeff marches forward, skull fragments shattering, splattering bad-brains onto nearby surfaces. Bullets whirl past him, striking a wooden crate. As he strides into the flickering light, unscathed, splinters mix with the vital essence seeping from wheezing bodies.

Three disoriented targets stand between him and his room service. Alexi blindly swings his cane at the echoes ringing through his head. Zeff uncloaks and creeps around the side of Johnny Who's SUV.

Uri tries to warn him, but his one good eye is open long enough to see the arcing precision of a taser-blade's effortless trajectory before it sinks into the back of his orbital socket. An electrical current pulses along the razor's edge, frying every bit of who he was in an instant. Zeff retrieves the knife from Uri's skull, then finds Alexi flailing his cane like a deranged beast left in the circus of man for far too long.

He moves in for hand-to-hand combat. Mid-swing, he catches the gold-tipped cane and rips it from Alexi's grasp. Three moves later, Zeff uses it to break his neck with a nauseating snap. Saving the best for last, he turns within a bloody moonlit puddle to see Johnny Who bolting towards the exit.

Vengeance

Steeped in the cowardice of self-preservation, Johnny Who, in his blind sprint, trips over the large corpse of a well-armed guard. His heart rate skyrockets as he pulls a Desert Eagle from the body and, with blurred vision, aims the fluted, triangular barrel at the assassin's mirage, firing several shots in hysteria and missing his only chance to survive.

A swift jab to the face stuns Johnny Who. Even faster than before, Special Agent Zeff twists the gun from his grip, cracking the wrist. A shrill cry fills the warehouse, harmonizing with the gasping, defecating, and bleeding symphony already in motion.

The brutality ramps up—Zeff displaces Johnny's kneecap, sending him to the floor.

"W—why are you doing this?" He sobs.

Without a word, he dislocates Johnny's shoulder, tearing the rotator cuff.

He howls for mercy. "I—I can pay you!"

"You're worried about the wrong things, Johnny-boi." He pulls off his tactical mask. "This is much bigger than the little tea party," he snarls—and punches Johnny in the mouth. "Look at my face, you fucking piece of shit!" He spits on the whimpering mess in front of him.

"W—who are you? I've never seen you before."

"Of course you're too stupid to remember. Does Panama ring a bell?"

"Panama?"

Fed up with his lack of reverence for the situation, Special Agent Zeff pushes a taser-blade into Johnny's dislocated arm and twists, reinforcing the misery of the moment.

He wails in anguish. "I remember—I remember. What about it? It was just business. I made a couple of bucks."

"Good people lost their lives because you wanted to cram a few extra coins in your piggy bank!"

Vengeance at his fingertips, he grabs Johnny Who by the throat and lifts him two inches off the ground. Unable to free himself, Johnny's sad eyes widen into panic as Zeff plunges another taser-blade into his gut and drags the serrated edge across his navel, spilling its contents onto the concrete. His muffled screams barely make it past the reinforced gloves.

Once he stops writhing, Zeff slings the meat to the floor and finishes his mission. Reaching into his tactical vest's right pocket, he retrieves a small parcel. Inside: three flash drives—needles of motive in a haystack of carnage, implicating another corner of the world in this evening's espionage, dissolving any potential peace talks, kindling government sanctions, and escalating an economic trade war to balance the world's budgets for the time being. He distributes the evidence among the three capotes, then turns to their prisoner.

Rescue

Beneath the burlap sack, the Englishman tracks the blood-curdling chaos tearing through the warehouse. Echoes of death unfurl from a baseline of gunfire. Behind him, the whiskey-throttles of dead men's hair triggers fire shots into empty targets. What unsightly monsters are left after all this?

The bag comes off, revealing the gum-chewing assassin. All around, the arms dealers' blood runs like molasses over a hot stack of homemade flapjacks, coalescing into a clogged French drain. Nearby, BOB rigs thermite incendiary devices on the warehouse's support structures, ensuring this storyboard's conclusion.

Zeff slices the rope binding the brute to his seat and lets the unraveling Gordian knot fall to the bloodied ground.

"Who the hell are you?" The shocked and bewildered bloke massages his wrists.

"We're *cousins*. I heard you needed a ride. But pleasantries aside, we need to get out of here. The local Barneys are on their way to crash this shitshow."

"I'm way ahead of you." The Englishman stands, stretching with a loud, cascading crack along his joints.

They hop into Johnny Who's black SUV—blue LEDs pulsing, flat-screens flickering, trapstep bass shaking the seats—and peel out, turning onto the gleam of rain-slick streets as they aim for the city's neon sprawl.

"Bless you, mate. Bless whoever brought you here when they did." Alternating streaks of pink, blue, and green highlight his bruised and bloodied face. "I'm not a believer, but I fear I may be a little closer now." He chuckles, then blasts a snot rocket onto the floorboard. "I have a safe house near here—shouldn't be compromised. You did just kill everyone back there. By the way, I'm Ben Penstone. What's your name?"

46

The Hunt For Sadie Hawkins

Reflections

A bead of sweat forms on Konway's brow and glistens with the bondfire's glow as the carpet flies from under the Vision Shard, thrusting him into the present. The Leaky Tea warehouse lingers—chemtrails oozing from the crevasses of his once-pristine Mind Palace.

(Ben? Who's Ben Penstone? Where was I? When? Was that me? Did I slaughter all those people?)

His questions ring the demolished butler's quarters in his Mind Palace. In the cryptic catacombs, a stark connection resonates in the dumbwaiter. A cloaked homunculus on a nearby cliff slowly cranks a revelation to his tongue. But the rope snaps, dropping the Pale of Thought into the regions below—where the foul crunch of the Imp-oster's slurping delights is overshadowed by the torturous shrieks stemming from Childe's updated workbench.

The fading memory trembles along his core. It's not the callous carnage that unsettles him, but the dread that he could lose everything he has found in Lani-akea. Engulfed in a swirling tide of fear, uncertainty, and doubt, he fails to notice her emerald stare stalking him through the feast and fellowship.

A motley pack of pups brushes past and excitedly slaps him with their tails. Konway's building neurosis subsides. He avoids showing the cracks in his mental armor and excuses himself from the bondfire into the Horseshoe.

(How could I have killed so many people? Why don't I feel any remorse for it? How'd I go from sitting on a hill with Paw-Paw to butchering a warehouse of armed mercenaries? This isn't good—what if they come after me? Whose drone did I see? Was it a BOB? I don't want to kill anyone. I want to be *here* with Sage and Helaku—I can't let them know. They'll kick me out. Where will I go? What will I do?) In a panic to preserve the present, he sends the angst to the depths of his schism, beneath the Nether Regions of Thought.

The Horseshoe

On one of those wandering, crisscrossing brick pathways, he concentrates on his breathwork, passing the paper rhino to quiet a horde of ANTs. His senses fill with a canopy of intersecting foliage. He looks up at the sparse twinkle of the innumerable heavens, their dying light brushing onto the canvas of night.

Soon, a clear quilt of mental clarity unfolds its silence as he strolls around the Horseshoe's perimeter. A left at the next fork leads to a curious patch of grass where three paths converge. His thoughts flicker to Zach's triangles and Helaku's pyramids.

"Hey there." Sage brightly smiles, pulling him from the labyrinths. "What're you doing wandering by yourself?"

He returns the gesture. "I needed to stretch my legs."

"I don't enjoy sitting for long, either. Do you mind if I walk with you?"

"Sure." Konway extends his hand along the path.

They take a right at the next fork, towards the obelisk at the Horseshoe's center. A moonlit sparkle in her emerald eyes lands an arrow from Cupid's quiver, piercing into the hollow of his innocence.

Pounce

Sage and Konway walk along the brick-paved path—taking a right, then a left, followed by another series of rights—as seashell chandeliers *clitter-clink* beneath live oaks stretching over the walkway. A short distance ahead, by an azalea bush, he notices Meow-Murs's lime-green eyes behind the veil of darkness. A nibbling marsh mouse freezes.

Meow-Murs primes for the pounce, shuffling his weight from paw to paw. The keen senses of the marsh mouse enforce a momentary hush. Meow-Murs's twitching tail subsides to join the silence held within two hearts beating as one. A late-spring breeze shifts, and the rustling carnage of nature erupts in the azalea bush.

Invitation

Amidst their chat, Konway notices names etched into the bricks lining their path. "What are those for?"

"Every villager, past and present, has one. It signifies your contribution to establishing a foundation for—"

"The next seven generations," he cuts in, masking his neurosis.

She giggles at his enthusiasm.

"Where's yours?" he asks, catching the interplay of light and shadow along her neckline.

"Over there." She points across the Horseshoe. "Wanna see?"

"Sure," says Konway, happy as a clam, almost forgetting the burning darkness beneath his breast.

Sage skips and twirls, enticing him to keep up. After several crisscrossing paths, she stops and spins into a bow. "Here we are."

He scans the brickwork. "I don't see your name."

"Upstairs, apartment 3F," she says, blushing.

He smiles with innocent confusion.

She strokes the back of his neck, fingers threading through his uncombed hair, then pulls him onto the soft petals of her plump lips—kissing him under the *clitter-clink* of a nearby seashell chandelier. A primal urge compels him to grapple her wanting lips to his.

"Get a room, you two!" Bhodi teases, underscored by Amber's whistle as they walk home.

Their lips part, and a flame breathes from the root of his being.

"Would you like to come upstairs?" She points to the canopy. "You can really see the stars from my porch."

"Lead the way," he says, hoping for a better view of the heavens.

Sage's Abode

Up the last weathered step, Konway admires her painted door: a surfer with a giraffe's head riding a wave. "Now, that's pretty cool."

"Thank you. That's *Geoffery*. It took a bit to get the length of the neck, but it's okay for now," she says, turning to plant another firm kiss on his lips.

She misses, landing on his cheek, and stumbles forward. He pulls her close. Neurochemicals overflow from the nanite colony, conjuring a brief sense of time-lessness. And in a poetic sense, she too is rapt with it. Overhead, stars twinkle an ancient message from the death of god at the beginning of time. Heart to heart, their chests sigh in unison.

"Wait right here." She swings her apartment door open with a forceful heave.

A little confused, but still high from the dopamine bump of that first kiss, Konway passes the paper rhino and calms his throbbing heart. While Sage stomps about her apartment, he pivots to face the sky and gazes at the stars, bolstered by the memento of predawn adventures with Paw-Paw. Sadly, the memory of the Leaky Tea warehouse taints his reflection.

(Who did I work for? Why did I kill all those people? They were bad... but all that hatred for Johnny Who... he must've had it coming. But was it right? Where's Ben Penstone? What will happen if the village finds out I'm a killer? They'll surely kick me out—I could belong here. I do belong here. I've found my community... Please don't take Laniakea away from me.) He instinctively clasps his hands in prayer, innocent of which gods would hear.

Before delving deeper, Konway suppresses his angst. Nearby, the shadows of low black clouds scoot below a moonbow's silver archway, reaching across the village. He stills his mind with a few box breaths and shelves his spiraling neurosis to find some aesthetic enjoyment within the moment.

Ignite

Not long after, the door slams open with a fresh floral haze of incense and flicker-lit candles. Tantric frequencies mix R&B with binaural mantras to curate the sensorial setting of her desires. Sage stretches her arms to the top of the doorway, wearing a small, vintage black cotton tank top from one of her favorite bands, Teach Edward Teach—and nothing else.

"Where are your pants?" Konway asks, tracing his eyes along the toned refinement of her legs. Both nervous and excited, his senses swell with the unfurling experience.

Then, without a word, she grabs the front of his light-blue button-up shirt and pulls him inside. As the door slams shut, a wooden, hand-painted 'Do Not Disturb' sign clangs about on its wire hanger.

Embrace

Behind closed doors, his biological desires unlock themselves from the shackles of innocence, swirling in a torrent of wild, stumbling, tongue-tied kisses. Out of those cavernous depths, a unified drumming careens from the base of their spines. They pull back from the excitement and gaze into the dilated void at the center of their beings, granting them a momentary glimpse of something eternal.

Sage rips away his clothes. Bare and vulnerable before her, she bites her lower lip with the delights of his form. A warm glow from the Himalayan salt lamp highlights her feminine graces, welcoming his hazel eyes with a savory play of light and shadow.

Distinct, abrupt, and framed, his gaze devours every adventurous scar, curve, and sun-dashed freckle. She moves closer and gently traces his muscular body—over forgotten scars and the fringes of areas he didn't realize were so sensitive. With a feathery brush of a nipple, the urge to merge overwhelms them, and their bodies collide with roving embraces.

They grope and mangle one another, stumbling on loose clothes and misplaced sandals. The mania of their bumbling mating dance startles her cat, Smittens, from its nap and into the dark pantry's quiet sanctuary. As their souls smear onto the canvas of creation, she pushes him into her cool bedroom.

Dance Of The Other

Past the threshold, Sage jumps into Konway's arms and tightens her legs around his waist. Her mouth opens to his, and she kisses him with a feverish passion. The lovers womble towards the edge of the bed, where she releases her grasp, surrendering to gravity, and crashes upon the soft padding of her green tea mattress.

He dives in after her, rushing under cool sheets. Over and over, they tirelessly explore with soft stamps of touch, spiking dopaminergic reward centers. Biochemical hits of cocaine burst like Roman candles.

She bites his neck and claws at his shoulders, wrestling him onto his back. He grins. She playfully slaps him and pulls him closer—inside her. He barely feels the sting.

Sage glides into position, swaying her hips to the sensation. No longer able to gaze upon her bouncing breasts, he closes his eyes, surrendering to a sea of ineffable bliss. As she rocks back and forth, galloping atop him, her body trembles, and he synchronizes with the quickening tempo of her writhing pleasure.

Caught in a hip-thrusting groove, a surge of neurochemicals sets their senses on fire with an array of arousal. Together, the lovers transcend the corporeal restraints of flesh and sweat. Two hearts, lost in a world of one, sway in unison with the rhythm of vibratory ecstasis.

In time, their verse slows to *oohs* and *ahhs*. Several sweat droplets drip from her chest, cooling the nuclear reaction between them. Konway leans up to kiss her tan, toned body as she grinds against him with increasing alacrity. Lost within the forever box, they breathe with a sense of symmetry, paying tribute to the pulse of creation.

All Our Desires Abolished

Fulfilled by the first release, exceeding the totality of her expectations, she spills over and co-mingles with the eternal. Their breathing syncs. No longer able to tell where he ends and she begins, they defy the forces of entropy, plunging into a mind-shattering, heart-throbbing, multisensory altered state of consciousness.

Sage stares into his hazel eyes, forgetting the world as her yearning body gracefully flows towards the horizon of another release. Faster and faster, primal grunts send the lovers beyond the pale. Higher. Higher. Higher—until they can no longer resist the ravishing intensity building with every thrust. She closes her eyes, leans back, and moans with the little death of surrender. And, seeing the joy patted on her face, Konway plunges headlong into the rapture of mutual culmination.

The Oros system misinterprets the somatic feedback and misfires, serving him an intoxicating cocktail of awefilledness to go with his stupefied amazement. He spins Sage onto her back. She struggles to separate the hair tie from her ponytail, eager to relieve the strain on her neck. Konway finds an opening and kisses her from one ear to the other.

"You're like a wild animal." She pushes him off, then attempts to mount him again.

He regains his footing and scoots up to the bed's surfboard headboard. She climbs onto his lap, and they stare into each other's reflections, reassuring themselves of their unspoken infinite nature.

Alas, despite her best efforts, he fails to perform this round, and the heat of the moment subsides with sheets and pillows strewn everywhere. She rests her head on his shoulder as stillness settles upon the bedroom. Chest to chest, the lovers' shadows cling to the nearby walls, revealing two hearts as one.

Center Street Blues

Outside, perched on the porch railing, Smittens meows under the moon's Cheshire grin. The midnight-indigo sky soon settles into the witching hour, with a few stragglers lounging around the evening's dwindling bondfire, laughing and guffawing over the marsh. Somewhere out there on Center Street, Todd's cheesy, posturing attempts to pick up chicks leave him drunk and single at a local pub well past closing time. Gathered around him, PJ and a few locals help water his delusions with shots of orange-flavored liqueur and IPAs.

47

Life's A Peach

Wake Up

After experiencing intimacy and the perceived loss of innocence, Konway replays their fumbling, bumbling, heart-beating, breath-gasping dance of divinity. With each lap around the belfry, lulled into a comfortable sense of security, his mind slaloms into a vivid recap of every experience since washing ashore—eclipsing the shadows of his past into the background.

As dawn peeps through parted wooden blinds, he tracks a mote of dust suspended in a sunbeam until it floats to the foot of the bed. With its descent, his head sinks into the pillow, followed by a snore.

In time, the sun climbs into the window and warms Sage's resting eyes. Unable to resist the call, she emerges from the comfy cocoon of her bed and stretches, wiggling her toes and fingers.

"It's hot," she says, reaching across the bedside table for the fan's remote, avoiding a room-temperature cup of water and nearly knocking over two tubes of lotion. With the blind guidance of proprioception, she seizes hold of the appropriately shaped object, then clicks on the hum in the corner. Victorious, she rolls against Konway and drapes her arm around his strong shoulders. Her hand glides down his chest and wakes him with a gentle squeeze.

The gesture thrusts him from the depths of nonconceptual consciousness.

"Aren't these the best pillows?" Sage snuggles against him, pressing her bare breasts into his back.

He rolls into a ray of light and greets her with a pair of golden suns flaring from the irises of his hazel eyes. Before him, an exquisite dance of light and shadow pirouettes along Sage's sparsely freckled skin. They stare into the depths of the other. After several wanting moments, she positions her body on top of him.

"How'd you sleep?" she asks.

Konway wipes his eyes. "Deeply."

"You were snoring up a storm."

"I think I might've heard you crank out one or two as well."

"Hey!" She rears up to hit him with her pillow. "Girls don't snore."

He dodges the impact. She misses again as he slips to the left, then to the right. Her laughter builds. She upgrades to a second pillow. However, her attempts to wallop him are in vain.

Effortless bobs and weaves gently guide him through her dual-wielding assault. One by one, he disarms her volleys. Sage pivots to her next attack and raises the nearby body pillow high above her head, prepping for a haymaker.

The lines of her naked form flood the forefront of Konway's mental projector with the perfume of nostalgia.

The pillow connects with his daydreaming face. Unfazed, he tickles Sage along the contours of her hips, quickly mapping out his route to victory and subduing her into further laughter. Her breath soon escalates into a primal fulfillment of overflowing delight.

"Okay, okay! I give, I give," she cries, then rolls off the bed onto the floor, pops up, and shakes her bare bottom as she heads to the bathroom.

He swings his legs out from under the sheets, catching the passing oscillation from the hum in the corner. Down the hallway, the toilet flushes, followed by the shower squeaking on. He extends his arms and legs out like a starfish, followed by a deep yawn.

The sweet smell of Sage's body wash drifts in from the hallway. After a stretch, Konway gets up from the bed's cozy trappings and stares out the blinds. On the porch, a small lizard disappears beneath the weathered railing.

Sage walks back into the bedroom. "What are you doing? Lie back down." She dries herself with a soft white towel and hangs it on a surf-fin coat rack attached to the back of the bedroom door.

Her room ignites with the flames of their passion—not backseat junk-food sex, but something intense and mystical. The hum in the corner fails to temper the blazing rhapsody of their dance, pushing around hot, sweat-soaked air. In the moaning moment, time slips from its wheel, and near-nirvana blossoms as the lovers sip from the cup of everlasting. A red strand weaves between them, binding them from the darkness of existence and closer to each other.

Café Du Sage

Konway wakes to the smell of coffee and the sound of jazz. He bumbles into the kitchen and finds Sage next to a bountiful breakfast: fruits, eggs, turkey sausage, two glasses of milk, and some extra-crunchy granola.

"I was going to surprise you," she says.

He slides into a nearby seat at her café table. "Thank you. You didn't have to go through all this trouble for me."

"Nonsense. After last night—" She lingers with the pleasure of reflection, then leans over to kiss him. The cleft of her breasts peeks past the loosely draped neck of her sleep-shirt.

Konway pulls back from the soft petals of her moistened lips. "And this morning? I didn't mean to fall back asleep."

"You deserve it, Tyger. Now, eat up." She settles into the chair across from him.

Within the breakfast nook, the Oros system misfires as Konway bites into a peach. Abruptly framed, a bouquet of velveteen freshness spritzes from its delicate folds, oozing with aromatic notes and dripping wonderment. The ceiling fan stirs the sweet sensation of orange-yellow sunbursts melting into autumnal red.

Sage notices her poor posture and sits up straight, stretching her arms above her head. Awestruck by the randomized neurochemical cocktail, he watches her run her hand up the back of her neck to the top of her scalp. Wavy hair drapes to her shoulders. She pulls it back into a messy bun, but a soft, brown strand escapes, brushing her cheek.

As she tucks it behind her ear and savors her coffee, his neurological system overflows with synesthetic expressions of light and color. Lost in the sauce of sensation, saliva floods his mouth. Green lightning strikes the Wastelands of Cognition, uncovering Vision Shards from the Donor's memory.

Peaches

The discarded scrapbook opens. See him as a boy with a sticky smile, chomping on a peach picked from one of Granny's trees. A sweet mess dribbles down his rosy, dirt-stained cheeks, onto overalls caked with mud and pockets stuffed with critters.

While the evening's twang bids farewell to the day, he pauses mid-slurp and asks, "Granny, where do peaches come from?"

"From our trees, of course." She waxes a sarcastic grin, wiping the extra juiciness with a napkin.

He refuses her playful response. "My teacher, Mrs. Radley, said that Georgia is the *Peach State*. Did your trees come from there?"

She sets down her sweet treat and wipes her hands on a napkin from her pocket. "No, suga. Theirs might be good, but they don't have our soil and sunlight...But honestly, peaches didn't originate in our state, their state, or any other state in the country."

"What do you mean?" He smacks and slurps around the pit.

"When I was little, I remember my daddy—you never met him—telling me stories of the Spanish bringing the first peaches."

"So they're Spanish peaches?" he asks.

"Not quite." She wipes his face with an extra napkin. "You see, peaches were grown and cultivated in China long before the first Europeans ventured to this continent."

His eyes sparkle with the delight of learning. "Was Mrs. Radley wrong?"

"No. But it's an excellent lesson on how little we understand about the history of things and the dangers of assuming the truth from hearsay." Granny gathers up the refuse from their sweet snacks. "And what does assuming get us?"

"It makes an 'ass' out of 'u' and 'me'... Heehaw-Heehaw." He laughs and giggles, kicking his feet off the side of Granny's porch.

Not long past, the Vision Shard crumbles into glistening dust.

Café Part Deux

Outside the breakfast nook, sun rays filter between a mired latticework of dew-speckled foliage, beaming beyond the veil of cumulonimbus clouds towards the mainland. A pair of egrets lightly land on the marsh, drawing Sage's attention from the pages of her book to the lovebirds outside the pane.

Runny yolks and toast crumbs decorate their small plates in a decoupage fashion as caramel-colored coffee cools under the rotating ceiling fan. Konway looks up from his meal and catches the subtle cracks in her smile. Sage flips another strand from her face and turns over a coffee-stained page.

Three sentences down, she breathes in, raising her chest. After several seconds of silent prayer, she exhales the freshness of a new day onto this morning's reading.

"Interesting." She takes another sip.

"What's that?"

Her emerald eyes meet his crumb-littered smile.

"Listen to this quote from Rousseau," she says, placing her finger on the highlighted section.

"Who's that?"

"A philosopher—"

(Like Mystic Woods & the Loggerheads?)

"—lovers of wisdom."

"Wisdom?"

"You have knowledge: this is a fork. Then there's experience: knowing how many ways a fork can be used. Wisdom comes from being able to make *good* judgments and decisions about how to use a fork, based on these things."

"How do you know what the 'good' is?"

"By asking questions: What is a fork? Is it limited to a utensil? What is it made of? Is it a place along a road or a snowy wood?"

A sense of signification and belonging stirs his excitement. "Now I'm pumped! Let's hear the quote from Rousseau."

The worn cover reads: *Determinism For Free Will's Sake: A Comparative Discourse on the Nature of Existence, 3rd edition*. Sage smiles and finds her place. "'Man is born free, yet everywhere we are in chains.'"

Konway ponders for a few seconds, chewing the rest of a scrumptious forkful. "Why don't they feel free? Aren't we freely enjoying our breakfast?" he asks.

"Well... the 'Illusion of Freedom' is a deadly trap, which numbs us into everydayness. Not seeing these mental, physical, and socioeconomic chains binding us is one of the greatest threats for anyone who wishes to be more than free."

"What's more than free?"

"Sovereignty," she answers. "To be responsible for one's own fate."

(Sovereignty.) He smiles, then sips from a cold glass of milk and digs for the meaning. "May I see your book?"

Sage hesitates for a moment before spinning it around for Konway to see the text.

"These doodles are pretty good. I think I have a shirt with this jellyfish on it. Are they yours?" He flips through several pages.

"No... someone else's." Her right nostril flares as she slides the book back to her side of the table.

Konway senses her uneasiness and rests his back against the chair. "No worries. I didn't mean to pry."

"Oh, it's nothing you did."

While bossa nova jazz conducts the cadence of soft white clouds past her emerald sky-lit eyes, a near-adjacent thought collides with another Vision Shard from the Donor's memory. Its well-worn corners unfold into a crayon-drawn map of a cave, and from its scribbles, another glimpse of innocence settles onto a flipped school desk in the dilapidated classroom of his Mind Palace.

The Cave

"What are you doing, Momma?" he asks.

She smiles at his curiosity and rests her red pen atop a stack of graded papers. "I'm finishing up some homework."

"Why do *you* have homework? Is it from the principal?"

She beams at her favorite teacher and her best student. "Not exactly... These papers are from my class."

"What did they write about?"

"It's a tale from ancient Greece."

"Are there dragons? Or maybe a minotaur?"

"Not in this one, sweetie. Would you like to hear it?"

He rocks from his tiptoes. "Yes, ma'am."

"Let's get you some paper and crayons."

"What do I need those for?"

"I'm going to tell you a story, and I'd like you to draw a picture of it—any way you'd like."

Belly-first on the floor, he doodles a rocket ship in the corner margins of a blank piece of paper.

"Are you ready to hear about Plato's cave?"

He wiggles into a comfortable position. "Yes, ma'am... Is the cave made of Play-Dough?"

She giggles at his agile mind's search for understanding. "Just listen, you'll see," she says, turning to a bookmarked section. "A long time ago, in a faraway land, there were people who lived in an underground cave. Since drawing their first breaths, they were bound, heads facing the cavern wall in front of them. You aren't getting scared, are you?" She spookily dangles her fingers at him.

"Nope." Young-Konway rushes his crayon sketch of the grotto.

A momentary silence hangs about the room. He corrects himself. "No, ma'am."

Pleased with the renewed mindfulness of his manners, she continues, "Above and behind the prisoners, guards paraded cutouts of objects and creatures. Farther back, a fire blazed, casting shadows. Unable to see anything else, they stared at the flickering forms of things."

"A dragon!" His imagination gets the best of him.

"Certainly... The shadows marched in front of the prisoners, and they'd name each one."

Young-Konway kicks his legs as he colors the hues of a fire with bright red, orange, and yellow flames raging on the other side of a crayon wall lined with stick-figure cutouts. On the other side, the bound ones look at the dancing silhouettes. Beyond the stage, spanning the cavern's width, an opening leads outside.

She smiles at his enthusiasm and color choices, saying, "One day, a prisoner was released from his shackles and forced to turn around and face the flames. With no other option, he opened his eyes and winced at the light—"

"Very rude."

"—After several moments, he noticed the puppeteers parading cutouts of the creatures and objects he had mastered naming. Still, he protested, 'The shadows are real.' Unfazed, the guard dragged the unchained prisoner from the cave. Outside, blinded by the searing sunlight and his own confusion, he wrestled with the guard until his eyes adjusted to the opulence. That's when he saw his favorite shadow."

"Is it a dragon?" he asks.

"No, sweetie," she continues, "He looked upon the ground and cried out, 'Tree!' Stepping closer, his vision focused as he marveled at the markings in the wood and the little creatures scuttling along its limbs, gnawing on its leaves. Moved by his experience, he hugged the arbor.

"He soon noticed other shadows. Excited by the unfurling world, an explosion of language compelled the unbound one to name the things he remembered. And looking closely, he discovered the true nature of things. Eventually, he turned to the sun and gazed upon the first principle of everything else—the face of the divine."

Young-Konway meticulously colors the sky a bold blue, saving room for clouds and a smiling sun.

"Excellent linework," she compliments his art. "Aside from helping things grow, the sun provides the source of light for the entire world and for its shadows."

"What about the moon and the stars?" he asks.

"Sweetie, the sun is a star, and the moon glows from its reflection."

He casts the wonder in his eyes onto a separate sheet of paper, sketching a crescent moon against an indigo, star-filled skyline.

She continues, "Once he reconciled his life in the cave with the experience in the sun, he realized everything up to this point had been a lie, believing a fragment of the truth as the truth. In time, his thoughts drifted to freeing the remaining prisoners."

"Did he rescue them?"

"Well, when he returned to the cave, he found his sight had changed. No longer able to bear the dark, he fumbled, stumbled, and tumbled back to where the shadows danced with puppeted precision. There, he proclaimed, 'I've seen the light. I've seen the truth. I've seen the glory of what lies beyond these walls.'"

"Does he free his friends?" young-Konway asks.

"Sadly, they scoffed and taunted him as they clamored in their chains. Even his closest friend, a bald, owl-eyed prisoner, challenged him to name the shadows. If he won, they'd go with him. So he agreed to their terms, and the shadows danced as they had before."

"Did he win?"

"Alas, he was no longer attuned to the darkness. Blurry images of trees, animals, objects... and a dragon paraded across the firelit wall. They laughed and squawked as their favorites marched past, naming them as soon as the shadow hit the rock. Once adjusted to the sun, he failed to name a single one—not even his favorites.

"The others laughed at his loss. Still, he persisted, arguing the outside world was more *real* than the wall of shadows. Feeling their way of life threatened, the still-bound prisoners grew irritable and angry. He tried to pull them from their world, but only upset them further."

"What happened to him?"

"They deemed him a threat and had him kicked out of the cave." She straightens her posture with the china cabinet looming behind her, filled with crystal vases and violet-patterned tea sets resting on white lace doilies.

"Harsh." Young-Konway thinks for a moment, tapping his crayon on his map. "What about the guard who freed the prisoner? Who were they? Why'd they do it?"

"Excellent questions." She closes the book and places it on top of a folder resting on the end table. "I guess... the one freeing the bound prisoner is a teacher, like me."

Outside, while fireflies dance throughout the evening, he holds up his crayon masterpiece, complete with stick figures and ornate backgrounds. The image rapidly folds into a misshapen square and tucks itself into a filing drawer. It struggles, catching on the crooked cabinet's sliding rails until the Vision Shard inevitably slams shut.

Allegorical Discussion

Konway's attention drifts from the pondering moment.

"Are you there? You dazed out for a second. I'm not trying to be awkward—" Sage cuts off her reaction and asks, "Wait, did you remember something? With a smile like that, you must have something to say."

"Well... just now, I remembered my momma." He sips from an oversized coffee mug.

"That's awesome. What was her name?"

He furrows his brow to conjure the recollection. "We didn't get that far... But she taught me about Plato's cave."

"*The Allegory*? How much did you remember?"

"All of it... I can still feel the waxiness of my drawing. But there's one thing I don't understand."

"What's that?"

"Why didn't the prisoners want to be free?"

Sage gathers her thoughts. "Well... they mistook what they saw, thinking the images on the wall were real, knowing nothing of the actual causes. The 'shadow of a tree' is not a 'tree' itself, but a representation of an actual tree. The prisoners confuse the world that is spoken about with the world that is."

"They're chained by the illusion," Konway responds.

"Exactly," Sage continues. "The general terms of our language aren't the names of the physical objects we can see. They're actually the names of things we cannot see—things that we can only grasp with our minds. The prisoners may learn what a *tree* is through their experience with shadows of trees, but they're mistaken if they believe the word 'tree' refers to something they've ever truly seen."

Konway scratches the back of his head. "Could you explain a bit more?"

Sage clarifies, saying, "Although we may gain certain ideas through our experience, we would be mistaken in thinking those concepts were on the same level as the things we perceive. Our mental reality is more real than the material world. Thus, the concepts within our minds outlive the actual items they represent."

"How so?"

"Well... the idea of a *triangle* is a concept. Many triangles exist in a variety of angles and materials. Like the shadows dancing on the cavern wall, they come and go. It exists in the mind as long as there are those who think of it."

"What does the cave represent?"

"It's our conventional world of everydayness. The steps leading out are the prisoner's efforts to examine their own opinions about the world. Leaving the cave and returning to it is the process of education—developing an understanding of the confusion that arises when going from light to darkness, and darkness to light.

"Education is not purely passive retention of memorized notions, but an active, sometimes painful, process. This is how we can learn from our failures." She looks at her right hand, the burn scar from the eye of the stove now long healed.

"So the teachers are supposed to help guide people to and from the cave," he recalls his mother's lesson.

Sage nods, adding, "Plato also thought philosophers were the only ones fit to rule."

"How so?"

"Of all the disciplines, they're the ones who have the questions. Every other profession has the answer. Having better questions produces greater answers. I guess that's why teachers and artists are still necessary."

"Hmm, are artists philosophers?" he asks.

"Darlin', everyone's a philosopher."

"Do you think the artists and teachers should lead?"

Sage grins at his innocent wisdom. "How else do you think we get from living in an economy to thriving in a society?"

"Is this why we appear free, yet everywhere we are in chains?" he repeats her initial prompt.

"You're something else." Her smile widens from a note of nostalgia. "Like a bonsai tree, we're able to grow as we please, so long as it's within the confines of the planter." With those last parted words, Sage leans in and kisses his lips.

He presses back against the plump petals of oxytocin.

She pulls away and asks, "Are you finished with your plate? Do you need any more coffee?"

"Yes, and yes—please and thank you," he says, leaning back in his chair. "I'll wash the dishes. You cooked, so it's only proper," Konway insists from the marsh-side breakfast nook.

Sage preps the sink, filling it with sweet-smelling soap and hot water. As he stares out the window, a momentary sense of joy washes over him, spilling onto the glimmering ripples filling the waterway. Farther out, past the marsh grass, a siege of herons soars into the skyline's mirroring splendor.

48

Stoked

Surfboard

The following Monday, as the heralds of daybreak cross Laniakea, the lovers step into the Horseshoe. Above them, lances of light cast toroidal shadows onto the hexagonal pattern of intersecting brickwork. In the background of this morning's concerto, somewhere along the bamboo fence line, the village pups bark about a lost bone. Sage squeezes Konway's hand and leads him past the Longhouse, Community Kitchen, Makerspace, and Creative Cabaña, and around the corner of the barn.

"Where are we going?" he asks.

Up ahead, Helaku waves. "Hey-yo! Good morning!"

A rooster crows into the dawn.

"Did you get here at sunrise?" Konway grins.

"Earlier." A twinge of rascality peeks from behind Helaku's eyes. "Sage messaged me yesterday about teaching you to surf. We figured it would help you bond with the other villagers. But more importantly, it might help you remember who you are." His smile reaches as big as day.

"Sounds exciting." Konway brims with a novel enthusiasm for adventure, fueled by his desire to belong.

"That's the spirit," Helaku continues. "Before we get going, we need to find you a suit and a board."

"How about a seven-eleven?" Sage slides a blue-and-white foam pop-out from a nearby rack.

"That'll work just fine until he gets a hold of the basics." Helaku zips up some beach supplies. "Grab your gear. It's time to hit the waves."

Camp

On a sparsely vacationed part of the beach, a comfortable breeze provides nice cuts for the day's lesson. Beneath the warming sand, a cool layer of compacted sediment offers a momentary reprieve for their toes. All around, the rushing ocean drowns out the drone of cicadas, signaling the forthcoming blanket of humidity.

Helaku pulls a towel and a small speaker from the back pouch of his backpack beach chair. Once the boards are in position, he secures the oversized umbrella and casts its shadow onto the sand.

"Now, we're going to take it step by step," Helaku says. "I want you to get the most out of this. We know that you're a world-class swimmer, but surfing is more than swimming. It's so much more."

Konway crouches beside his board and grabs hold of an odd tether.

"I see you've found the leash." Helaku points to the rope with a collar. "First things first, fasten it around your ankle."

He follows the instructions.

"Now, lie on your chest, with your feet by the tail," he explains. "Place your hands flat on the deck as if you were doing a push-up."

Both Sage and Konway get on top of their boards and face the glistening Atlantic.

She paddles through invisible waters, pretending to catch an unseen wave. Springing to her feet, she lands evenly. Then, pivoting into a low, bent-knee position, her arms outstretched for balance, Sage's fierce green eyes direct the vectors of her intent forward.

"Stick the landing, and you'll be riding the wave." Helaku checks the contents of his bamboo dugout.

Konway imitates her movements and iterates the pattern. Following a few lackluster attempts, he takes a deep breath, repositions himself, and pops up, landing off-center.

"Hmm... he might be goofy," she says.

"Try placing your left foot back and right foot forward." Helaku encourages him to move past the momentary disappointment.

On the following try, he's on his feet.

"Excellent footwork," Helaku says. "Have confidence in the board supporting you, and in the wave... Now, let's warm up by practicing this maneuver until you feel comfortable. Your stance is crucial to riding any wave. As you pop up, look at where you're going and envision your body aligning you and the board with that direction."

Konway replays their movements, and the Oros system maps them within kinetic-tissue memory.

"Good. Stay centered by maintaining your hips over your feet. Continue holding your arms out like you're doing—it'll help with balance. If you need more control, take a wider stance, and get low." Helaku squats down. "Also, remember to lean on your back foot to slow down and for more control. And lean on your front to go faster."

"Let's have him pop up a couple more times." Sage smiles with her hands on her hips. "Don't want him to cramp... After a few more, I think he might be ready for the water."

"My favorite lesson is next," Helaku says.

"What's that?" Konway asks.

"How to bail—but don't worry, we're taking this with baby steps. We'll see how you handle the shallows first. Now, let's get paddling!"

Learn To Bail

Konway cups his hands, pulling long, steady strokes with his chest raised and core engaged. Back and forth, he practices scooting around the shallows, hopping off and back on at each marker, adjusting to the board's feel.

Helaku paddles to the training area and sits up on his board, saying, "Seems like you're advancing quickly."

"I've got this part down. What's next?"

"Let's have you make your way out to Sage." Helaku waves in her direction.

After an awkward start, Konway negotiates his surfboard past the break, beyond the ghosts of unridden waves.

"Hey there, sexy. Looking good on that board," she says, holding one hand over her brow to block the sun's glare. "Now, let's have you catch one. Paddle until you feel the wave take hold of the board."

They get into position and scout the upcoming set. The first two are small, but the third pushes them onto its crest.

"Wahoo!" cries Konway, riding on his belly. The weight of the world slides from underneath him and quiets the gnawing sensation growling from below the Nether Regions of Thought.

"Time to bail." Helaku sails by and steps into the soup.

Konway rolls to the side, landing in the swirling, waist-high water. Then, turning the nose of his surfboard towards Sage, he paddles back out, reaching through the waves. After catching several more in this way, he attempts to stand.

Trust The Process

A small set of waves bumps against the beach, curling along the shuffling sands. The sky's brilliant blue holds traces of miniature, puffy clouds trailing from an offshore storm. All along, a scurry of tiny sandpipers picks amongst un-earthed bivalves before they disappear below a soft, warm blanket of wet sand.

Out in the lineup, the three of them float like driftwood, bobbing with the ebbing sea.

"Here comes a nice one," Sage shouts, seeking a prime point to intercept.

Konway models her movements, but misses. As he recovers, she dashes down the wave with sun, wind, and salt spray rushing around her. At the end of the run, she dances into the foam with a joyful smile.

Another set rolls through, lifting their boards. This time, he tries to em-ulate Helaku's movements but comes up short. Meanwhile, Helaku zooms towards the beach, moving with balance and certainty, just before the cas-cading barrel closes behind him.

Sensing the building angst, doubt, and trepidation, he box-breathes for a few rounds until his mind goes silent. More waves emerge. He lets them slip by, hunting for a better opportunity to catch his first.

Several puffy clouds proceed along, like turtles wading across the sky as the Atlantic pulls away from him.

(There it is,) Konway says to himself. (You've got this... Have confidence.) He focuses and positions his board to hitch a ride.

Into Position

The ocean draws him back like a paper plane. Konway cups his palms and reaches through the water, paddling into the sweet spot. Realizing there is no need for the constant crawling and scratching, he calmly strokes into the wave.

Waters rise with unspoiled beauty. Nature's splendor glistens about him as he faces the fear of failure. His board dips over her shoulder into an enriched sense of abundance.

With one fluid motion, he grips the rails, releases his breath, and leaps to his feet. Konway lands center, quickly finding his balance. Knees bent, he shifts his weight from heel to toe, maintaining the drop-in's momentum, and glides towards his intent. As he takes the bottom right turn, darting in front of the wash, a wordless awareness envelops him.

The Oros system detects the distribution of neurochemicals in his body and comes online. A shimmer pulses across the dragon tattoo on his arm. All at once, the nanites secrete a poorly mixed cocktail of [Prime] and [Time Warp].

Konway dissolves into the subliminality of his fleeting experience. Everything slows within the everlasting moment while his fears and doubts collapse from the weight of ecstatic release. His synaptic thresholds flood open, activating latent muscle memory throughout his enhanced connective tissues.

Shutting down his prefrontal cortex, his mind extends into the realm of virtuosity. The projector reel in the dilapidated theater of Dreamwind Studios goes blank. On the back end, slow-moving theta waves disengage him from his body. The thinking part of his brain dims, allowing his other functions to unfurl.

Stand Tall

A wave of selflessness dissolves the distinctions between his body, the board, and the coursing ocean beneath him. In a timeless haze, the alacrity of his perception elongates along filaments of neural circuitry. Uninterrupted and uninhibited by the clunky neurosis of thought, he effortlessly flows with the water. Further immersed in the moment, the day beams with brighter hues, renewed richness, and a sense of clarity.

High above, clouds scuttle into a mandala upon the sky. Droplets suspend midair while ribboning shorebirds hang in flight, and butterflies pause on the gusts of the shifting dunes. The scent of coconut suntan oil floats on the breeze. Nearby, the splashing squeals of babes in tide pools halt their rumpus echoes, remixing with the laughter of collegiate day-trippers skipping class for a re-nourishing afternoon on Coffin Island—all muddled within the neurochemical cocktail swirling through Konway's physiology.

In this resplendent state, he cruises past the rolling tide, briefly tapping into an oceanic feeling of oneness with something larger than himself. High on the most potent neurotransmitters known to humans, Konway is another victim of a self-transcendent experience.

Wipeout

Alas, the sublime cloak soon frays in the unraveling whitewash, trailing behind him. Time snaps back into a normalized frame of perception. And moments after standing on his board, he slips into the churning surf.

"Wahoo!" Helaku roars above the crashing waters. "Good job, bro." He rushes over to congratulate him with Laniakea's handshake. "I knew you could do it."

"That was incredible... Timeless," Konway adjusts to the buzz about him.

"That'll happen... Let's get back out there!" Helaku exclaims, spinning towards the break.

Sage drifts up to the face of a long, slow-moving wave, scouting for the next set. Another one rolls by them. But the next shadow catches her eye. She effortlessly strides into position, then springs to her feet and snags a turn in front of the foam. All the while, Konway watches the captivating grace of her style as she nears the end of her run.

The three of them paddle around until the waves become too small to ride. Eventually, they ditch the boards to catch tiny rifts with their bodies. Speeding through the shallows, small schools of fish flee from the stampeding revelry.

Safety Meeting

Close to noon, Helaku brandishes a thumbs-up, saying, "Let's head in and hydrate."

Despite the want to keep going, Konway follows them back to the beach camp. The three of them bask in the shade, feeling the breeze beneath the oversized umbrella. Sweat droplets bead along their chests, cooling them as passing wisps of sand glitter their skin.

After several gulps of ice-cold water from their vacuum-sealed canisters and a few bites of watermelon, they enjoy a few puffs of medicine from a ceramic bat kept in a bamboo dugout with sealing magnets and built-in poke 'em pole.

"Looking good out there, bro." Helaku passes the ceremonial device to Sage. "What do you think?"

"He's definitely a quick learner," she says.

Konway blushes from her flowers. "At the end, I remembered some things... Not complete memories, but fragmented emotions and feelings."

"Right on," Helaku encourages him.

"Research shows surfing helps with trauma." Sage inhales, sending the cherry aglow, and passes it to Konway.

"How so?" He takes a drag, unknowingly averting a neurological meltdown from the malfunctioning Oros system.

"It's the *flow state*," Helaku responds, his hand tracing the motion of the ocean.

"Flow state?"

Sage answers, "It's where the brain's limited bandwidth is consumed by what we're doing. We scramble the sense of self—no more gnawing monkey mind."

"Positive movement experiences can be powerful tools for healing," Helaku adds. "For instance, Soldier-Surf invites folks out who have a hard time opening up to rediscover who they are. And over in the Surf-Works tribe, they do something similar with special needs and trauma survivors. Once they get into the water, their faces light up. It's one of those make-you-wanna-cry-and-hug-people moments, ya know?"

"Even if it doesn't help you remember who you are," Sage slides into the conversation, "you'll at least have a healthy, fun activity to enjoy with others. And with enough practice, you'll develop your own style."

Konway pulls another puff and passes it to Helaku, asking Sage, "What's your style?"

"Well, mine is more intuitive than most." She grins at Konway. "But I can ride a variety of ways."

Blushed by bashfulness, he pivots to Helaku. "How about yours?"

"I strive to express myself impeccably: to have faith in my abilities and understand my weaknesses; to draw confidence from my experiences and my fearless commitment to them; to step out from the chattering mind and move into the space of the heart—to be one with the water."

"Let's go back out!" Konway bubbles with the excitement of possibility.

"Hold on, Tyger. There aren't any waves." Sage pulls up the Kawabonga app on her smartphone and selects the icon to display swell direction, height, and local wind conditions.

Konway scoots closer and asks, "How does the wind determine the waves?"

"The wind transfers energy from the air to the water," Helaku informs him, passing the dugout. "Offshore winds, blowing from land to sea, hold the waves up, keeping them clean as they approach the beach."

"Those are the best ones," Sage says. "And as you've experienced, ours aren't epic mountains. Small and playful—learn to love them. They are your best teachers. The small ones are where we all get started. They're where we built our foundations and practiced until we were confident."

"The trick to surfing these waters is to hit the steepest part of the wave for the speed you need," Helaku says.

Upon realizing the time, they finish their snacks and pack up camp, only to discover an unnecessary amount of trash on the way to the beach access.

"What the fuck is all this?!" Sage asks with fiery frustration.

Plastic beach pails, shovels, sifters, molds for critters, popsicle wrappers, half a liter of warm sandy soda, a red cup worth of cigarette butts, and some random plastic netting from a beach toy set.

Helaku smolders towards a recycling bin and says, "It's a shame. I can keep the waves trash-free, but can't say the same for the dunes. If only folks weren't so selfish and short-sighted."

"Why would someone do this?" Konway asks.

"Tourons." She shakes her head.

"What's that again?"

"Someone who certainly can't see the magic in this place. Why else would you dump all this shit in paradise?"

They tidy up and head back to the village. While the passing wind whips through the passenger window, Konway can't help but long for the next session with Sage and Helaku. However delightful, his reprieve is short-lived as a black orb cruises parallel to the island and disappears behind McMansions, careening their balconies for a better view.

(That's definitely a BOB.) Flashes of the past churn his stomach with a kerosene-braided knot. (The Leaky Tea warehouse.) Bloody pools of malice overflow the banks of his bandwidth into a nauseating waterfall of angst.

A bloated face with burnt-yellow eyes rises from the foam pureé, chanting between his ears, (It's just business... It's just business...)

So much in his head, Konway misses a quarter of Sage and Helaku's conversation.

(It's just business.) A mask of jiggly jowls haunts him, puppeted by a pair of nefarious, burnt-yellow eyes.

Growing annoyed, he suppresses his angst, burying the unpleasant echoes deep within the Nether Regions of Thought. (Tighten up. Get it together.) He exhales and glances at Sage.

The cackling Imp-oster persists. (It's just business...)

However, a ribbon of pelicans returns him to the present moment, tethering him to the million miracles happening all at once.

Compromised

On the far side of Coffin Island, the ocean recedes as a convoy of transport trucks rumbles towards the first guarded barricade and a local Barney, half-asleep in their squad car. Diesel fumes smog above the graffiti-laden asphalt running the length of Lighthouse Lane as the trucks shift gears, hauling the last load of equipment needed to stabilize the nodal connection with the Earth Defense Constellation [EDC].

Commander Xero sits in a pressed metal chair at a writing desk—long forgotten by the lighthouse keeper who once watched over these shores—and stares unblinking into the BOB's feed. On another translucent screen suspended above the worn finish, a parade of names and images scrolls down as a different drone relays facial recognition data from the pier.

He slams his fist into the table, leaving a noticeable indent. "Tell them to scan near the marsh after they finish with the beach. I want 24-hour sweeps until we find him."

"Sir, what if the BOBs are relaying a false positive? What if he isn't—"

Commander Xero chambers a round in his special-issue Delta-9 and rests the hand cannon on the table. "Run the grid until we find him."

The tech officer backs against the threshold and bumbles out the door. Xero closes it and returns to his chair. He sighs, then, using his biometrics, slides open a secret locker under his desk. Inside, behind a trapdoor, rests a small safe with a number pad. He enters the code, retrieves the encrypted smartphone from within, and selects the flashing envelope.

[Where is the asset?] the message reads.

A flush of angst projects from his glare. Another knock hastens from the other side of the door. Xero tosses the device back into the drawer and locks it.

"What is it?"

The door creaks open, followed by the tech officer's shaky voice. "S—sir, it's the Director. He says he can't reach you."

(Because I'm ignoring the dinosaur.) "Tell him I'll be in touch at the first opportunity."

"Sir, he sounds pissed."

(He couldn't pour out a boot filled with piss if the directions were written on the heel.) Xero conceals his resentment.

"Sir?"

"I'll call him back," Xero says, grabbing his firearm from the dented table and holstering it. He slips an earbud in and exits the darkened room. The first tendrils of diesel smoke rise above the canopy. Moments after the door closes, the hidden smartphone flashes with another encrypted message, tightening the screws on what was promised and what is owed.

49

Skewered

Beetle Juice

Later that week, a hot, wet scarf of humidity drapes over the chittering twangs of the season. Laniakea's daily hustle and bustle divide the tribes across Coffin Island. Some head to the Kawabonga surf shop, while others crew marsh tours and private fishing charters. Still, several dozen split between the Community Kitchen, the Makerspace, and the Creative Cabaña.

At the barn, Konway looks up from the beetle trap in his hands. Past Sage's delightful smile, a group of villagers turns to the raised-bed gardens, while the rest venture towards the fruit trees and beehives. His pupils dilate as the TacOHUD scans the first rows, identifying: collard greens, watermelon, tomatoes, cucumbers, strawberries, squash, green beans, and peppers.

"Take these traps and set them in this crate, pretty please," Sage playfully flutters her emerald eyes. The day's heat coalesces on her skin like dew dripping from a banana leaf. "It's a bit early to set these out. But with the warmer temperatures and mild winters, the buggers appear earlier and earlier."

"Why are we trapping beetles?"

"If we don't set these out now, before this season's brood emerges, the gardens will be overrun for sure."

"Phew, this one stinks." He puckers from the stench wafting from the bag.

She giggles. "Don't smell them, you goon. The bait is a pheromone from female beetles."

"What does it do?"

"One by one, the dumb males follow the scent into the watery tomb at the bottom. Horny beyond belief, they pile into a writhing mass and drown in the pheromone." A malicious grin traces up her cheek.

"What? Don't lump me in with those beetles. I'm not going into the bag," he says.

"No... No." She shakes her head. "My mind is in the gutter."

"What do you mean?" he asks.

"Well, I was thinking the traps are a lot like porn."

"What's that?"

"You don't know what porn is?"

"Add it to the list." He smiles to suppress the tragic fragments of his past, which increasingly encircle the airspace with each passing day.

"It's a recording of people having sex."

He grasps with a furrowed brow, but fails to understand.

"Don't get me wrong—it has its place. But many people spend all day, hands on their bits and berries, swiping through digital partner after digital partner, dulling their senses to real love... real intimacy." Her lips redden. "Often, the world in their heads appears better than the world of flesh, sweat, and hot, passionate hip-thrusting climax."

"Like *The Allegory*?"

"You're quite clever." She steps closer, stroking the nape of his neck.

A prickling tickle flows across Konway's shoulders and down his spine, spreading to his fingertips and toes. He loses his grip on the bag and drops it to the ground, spattering its stench into the morning florals. Sage chuckles and hands him a rag to wipe the beetle juice off his face.

Trimmings

The lovers load up a utility wagon and make their way to the micro-grove of Bartlett pears, where a soft wind blows through the boughs of fragrant blossoms.

"Would you be a dear and use those nice, strong muscles to dig up the root ball for me?" Sage hands him a shovel. "It's remarkable how fast these stickers grow."

While Konway tackles his task, she climbs into a cosmos of white flowers speckling the bright green grove, clipping thin vines from the branches. Ahead, honey bees meticulously buzz about late spring's bouquet and fill their pockets with a bit of this and a pinch of that.

"It's going to be a big harvest this year," Sage says, wiping the sweat from her brow with a checkered handkerchief before easing down a few rungs and dropping a bundle of vine-woven branches to the ground. "Set those limbs in the wagon, please. We'll take them to the bondfire—waste not, want not."

"What about the beetle traps?"

"We'll set those out later," she says. "There are a few more trees to trim. But with your help, we should finish sooner than expected." Sage shoots a seductive glance at Konway from atop the A-frame ladder. "Since we're already sweaty... do you wanna take a break?"

He pauses his labors to admire her plump bottom.

"Like what you see?" She descends to the ground.

"Let's hold off until we finish." He tosses some twigs into the utility wagon.

"Are you sure?" She sips some ice-cold water from her jug, dribbling a stream down her neck, across her collarbone, and onto her military-green shirt.

Konway steps closer to kiss her.

"You're right." She pulls away with a mischievous look in her eyes. "Let's finish our chores. Then we'll have the rest of the day to play." She smacks him on the bottom.

Strike

At the nearby apple trees, Sage checks the grove for any derelict vines. "There's a broken branch halfway up—mind using that pole saw to get it down?"

"Yes, ma'am." Konway flashes a cordial smile.

"I would do it, but I'd rather see those sexy arms put to work again."

She lifts her wide-brimmed beach hat, her provocative stare striking him. Konway gulps a goofy grin and swings the pole saw into the canopy.

He adjusts his grip, feeling the blade's teeth against the wood. Back and forth, the saw chews through bark and pulp until the limb crashes down with a thud of rattling leaves.

"Impressive," she teases, "though faster than I would've liked."

They drag the hefty limb to the utility wagon.

"Mission accomplished." She raises her hand to high-five.

Beneath the leaves of the catawampus bough, a brown water snake, jolted from its nap, tightens into a frightened coil. Sage's shadow sweeps overhead. Then, winding into a muscular spring perfected over eons, the reptile launches from its fearful symmetry amongst the foliage, arrowing towards her cheek.

It's All In The Wrist

By the time Konway realizes it, his body reacts, countering the serpent's strike. In half a heartbeat, his nimble fingers delicately grasp the creature at the base of its skull to prevent its bite. Time normalizes, and the snake is in his hand, struggling to free itself.

Sage gasps and takes a startled step back. But upon exhaling, she steps towards the frightened brown water snake coiling around Konway's forearm and retrieves a burlap sack from the utility cart.

The creature wriggles to escape, but they carefully compel the angry serpent into the bag. Safely sealed away, it frantically writhes within the confines of the burlap darkness, spraying the inside as a last-ditch attempt before calming down.

With the snake bagged and set on the ground, Sage and Konway laugh off the sudden surge of adrenaline. They soon fall into a frenzy of impassioned gropes and tongue-twisting narratives—rewards from the boughs of triumph. Once its tide subsides, they briefly regain their composure and pull apart.

She looks around and breathlessly declares, "I want to fuck you right here. That was incredible—you saved my life."

"H—hey, hold on a second," Konway stammers, still shaken by his body moving on its own. "Let's save it for later. What're we going to do with Wigglesworth?" He points at the slow-slithering shape bulging against the burlap sack.

"You're right. We've put this ole fella through so much already. Besides, we can place those beetle traps by the maritime forest."

"And this limb?" he asks.

"We'll grab it later."

They pack up the utility wagon and head for Laniakea's eastern perimeter. Overhead, the sun champions the day's splendor, inviting cliques of clouds over for tea, hoping to make a lasting impression. Nearby songbirds join in the symphony, tweedle-chirping a soundtrack for the lovers' mission to release their captive.

Gossip

Elsewhere, unbeknownst to Sage and Konway, an unfortunate message reaches past the surfboard fence line, suspending work for the day. Shortly after, Amber and Martha sit under the Horseshoe's shade to spill the tea.

"I heard they rushed someone to the emergency room," Martha says, tightening the straps of her neon-green bikini.

Amber dramatically drinks water from a straw. "It was Todd."

"Did he overdose?" Martha straightens her posture and checks her phone, illuminating her face with a pale blue light.

"PJ shot him with a spear gun."

"Really? Don't let that boy back in the water. What the hell happened?"

"They were back at the ARC with a few of their crew." Amber fastens a pair of tiny shark-tooth earrings.

"Where'd it get him?"

"Right in the ass."

"Damn, that's rough." Martha winces.

"He'll be fine once they pull it out." Amber savors another dramatic sip. "That's *if* it heals properly."

"What's going to happen to PJ?" Martha asks.

"Jack will probably take it to the Council."

"How many times has PJ messed up?"

Amber giggles. "It's PJ. He's fucked up a lot since he's been here."

"Sounds like Todd should've chosen a better diving buddy."

They carry on, spinning loose-knit yarns of misfortune and good riddance. Then, laughing off the entire ordeal, they twirl into rounds of ultimate frisbee, seeing no need to waste the day fretting over that fool any further.

Release

Near the forest's edge, under matted leaves, tiny clusters of beetle eggs vibrate with the season's larvae. There, they feast on fine roots and other organic debris. Surviving to maturity, their pheromone-driven instincts march them towards a lemming's demise, plunging into an orgy of iridescent copper and green beetle juice.

"This seems like an appropriate spot to set the traps," Sage says, gesturing to the tree line.

"Why are we putting them over here?" Konway asks, pivoting from the utility wagon.

"The buggers graze on most plants in the vicinity, consuming any edible plants along their flight path."

"Less collateral damage," Konway cuts in.

She frowns, picturing their crops devoured by the brood's ceaseless gnawing. "The maritime forest is better suited to supporting their populations than our groves and gardens."

They follow the tree line, setting up a row of beetle traps. Passing the pawpaw patch, he smiles as notes of nostalgia and the gleaned memories of his granddaddy bubble to the surface. A short distance farther, he opens the writhing burlap sack and lets the cantankerous snake out of the bag.

The biblical beast races from the opening, slithering under the forest leaves, then stealthily slipping into the brush. Nearby, a red-crested woodpecker drills into the side of a pine, hunting for grubs beneath the surface.

News About Todd

Back at the apple trees, Konway taps his shovel against the limb. A faint breeze wafts Sage's peach-scented deodorant into the air. As they cut the wood into manageable pieces, the humidity gathers the equity of their labor upon their brows. The soft fabric of her top clings to her breast, pulling Konway's attention from the task at hand, sending a stray bead of sweat into his eye.

He wipes away the salty singe with his gray shirtsleeve and looks towards the gardens and the beehives, asking, "Where is everyone?"

"No telling with this crew," Sage says with a laugh. "Let's get these last trimmings before we head out." She stuffs several smaller branches into the chest-high stack in the utility wagon.

Arm in arm, they arrive at the barn. Konway fetches an old wheelbarrow to unload the wood, just as Mary turns the corner, her face etched with concern.

"Hey, girl," Sage calls, waving. "Wait till I tell you what happened."

"Did you get my texts?" Mary asks.

"No. What's up?"

"It's Todd."

"What's going on?"

"He's fine—minus the metal shaft through his ass." She winces at the thought.

"What? That's crazy. Where'd they take him?"

"He's at St. Pete's hospital."

Still shaken from earlier and worried about Todd, Sage excuses herself, heading to the crushed-seashell parking lot, where villagers pile into one of Kawabonga's sprinter vans. Once loaded up, they peel out of Laniakea, kicking up a swirl of dust, leaving Konway to the Imp-oster's taunting whispers of inadequacy.

50

Jasper

Dock Side

With the village empty, Konway takes a few moments for himself and heads to the dock. A pack of pups follows, sniffing and wagging past him. As they trot atop sun-worn planks, a few of the crew stop to look at their reflections in the water.

Excited by popping bubbles, they start arfing. The rest huddle at the far end, barking at a flotilla of kayaking tourists struggling against the current to reach the landing across the Folly River. Beyond them, the blue sky shifts with the tidal hues of afternoon.

He walks along the wonky jetty. Halfway down, the weathered boardwalk shakes with the pack of pups rushing back to the village. At the end, he sits next to Helaku's dog, Jasper. The burly beast's tongue drapes over the side, dripping a puddle of saliva onto the sun-bleached timber. Suddenly, the shaggy mastiff bellows at the struggling tourists and wags its tail with excitement, slapping Konway in the jaw.

"Watch it, you goon." He pats Jasper's head.

The pup leans in and licks his face, leaving a slime trail of slobber, then rushes after his pack. A cool breeze skirts the water, bringing with it the taunting whispers of those burnt-yellow eyes. He retrieves the paper rhino from his pocket and breathes in, holding for one, two, three... But still the Echoes of Doubt persist.

(When will she return? Why am I concerned about Todd? It's not him... What is it? Who is it? Who am I afraid of?) He exhales.

On a nearby gazebo, a vacationer fires up their grill. The flames of its belly illuminate a soot lining of charcoal, accompanied by a sizzling array of meats, tropical fruit, and Caribbean kabobs. Drawn by the scent and stilled with a momentary reprieve from the haunting neurosis, Konway admires the million-dollar splendor unfurling before him. His stomach grumbles.

As the char crisps into overcooked crumbs, an ominous orb ducks behind a lonely cloud, summoning a knee-jerk response to the forefront of his attention.

(Another BOB! That's the sixth one.)

(They're coming for you.) The Imp-oster chortles. (It's only a matter of time—sooner or later, they'll capture you.)

Inadequate to stop it, the terror of who he was, who he is, and who he will become splinters against his mental filter feeders. A cowardice trepidation shivers down his spine, tightening the Imp's grasp around him.

(One, two, three.) He exhales and passes the paper rhino.

The BOB carries on, and only the bubbling marsh remains, bracketed by the angst of vacationers struggling to enjoy a speck of paradise within the time-based prophecies of their everydayness.

(How much longer can I keep this up?) Konway slowly stands and walks back to the gate.

The heavy threshold creaks open with seasonal florals, reminding him of what matters most. Another gust dissolves his fear, uncertainty, and doubt into the limited capacity of his bandwidth as he steps back into Laniakea.

Grill & Chill

After a long meander through the Horseshoe, he arrives at Helaku's and opens the screen door.

"Yo, my dude!" Helaku greets him from the kitchen. "Where ya been? Are you hungry? Want a grilled cheese?" He spreads a thin layer of mayo on a piece of Texas toast, topping it with minced veggies, hot sauce, and two thick slices of Pepper Jack.

"Yes, please." Konway's stomach gurgles with anticipation.

"Excellent. Get me an extra plate and a cup for yourself, please." He seals another gourmet masterpiece into golden-brown perfection.

Konway settles the items on the counter and asks, "How's Todd doing?"

"He'll be fine, so long as there's no nerve damage. We went to pay him a visit, but he was asleep. Now, that poor bastard PJ... I saw Jack reprimanding him up and down the hospital floor. It was a sad sight."

"Were they back at the ARC?" Konway asks, pouring some ice-cold, reverse-osmosis-filtered water.

"Yep. They were hunting lionfish, and somehow PJ accidentally pulled the trigger." Helaku shakes his head at the situation, then notices the sudden scent of toasted goodness and flips the sandwich onto a second plate. "Enough about Todd. How was your day, bro?"

"It's been eventful."

"How so?"

"Well, Sage almost got bitten by a snake." Konway chomps into a gushing pocket of cheese, nearly burning the roof of his mouth.

"Where?"

"By the Granny Smiths."

"Damn... I'm glad she's all right. I can't have two villagers in the hospital." Helaku pauses with a silent prayer before biting into handcrafted deliciousness.

"That's not the crazy part."

"Go on," Helaku says with a cheekful.

"It was the strangest thing... my body reacted on its own. By the time I realized what was happening, the snake was in my hand."

Helaku raises a curious eyebrow and wipes some crumbs from his mouth with a napkin. "Bro, that's wild. You caught a snake midair... with your bare hands?"

"It almost had her." Konway shakes his head in disbelief at his reflexes. "Ask her when she gets back."

"Incredible! First Todd, now Sage. You're well on your way to becoming chief."

Deep down, the blood-soaked memory of the Leaky Tea warehouse slices through the flowers. Konway quells his rising heart rate and locks the Vision Shard into a military-green footlocker, hoping to preserve the present from the uncertainty and violence of his past. Beneath the *Space Force III* lunchbox, it sinks into the Nether Regions of Thought.

Tainted Love

After two sandwiches, a pickle spear, and some garden salsa chips, they settle into a buddy cop movie, *Precinct 420*, passing a joint between them. A knock rattles the apartment door.

"Come in," Helaku says.

Mary steps into the haze, rising to the surfboard ceiling, and fans through the smoke. "Hey guys, just wanted to let you know Todd's staying in the hospital overnight. They've got the shaft out, but they want to monitor him until the morning. Sage and a few others are staying at a friend's house on the peninsula."

"Thanks for the update, Mary. Keep me posted if anything changes."

As she leaves, a haunt of automatic negative thoughts surrounds him. Konway lifts the half-smoked joint from the ashtray and takes a hit, followed by a savory exhale to quell the ANTs. "What's the deal with Sage and Todd?" he asks.

Helaku looks out the window towards a distant place and time. "They used to date... but the honeymoon phase was a flash in the pan. Not long after, they were getting trashed every night on Center Street and quit pulling their weight—we all gotta put in the *sweat-quity* around here. The village was understanding at first.

Sadly, those two were only happy when they were on something. Eventually, we held an intervention, and she got clean."

"What about Todd?" he asks, handing the joint to Helaku.

"He started hanging around some mainland ne'er-do-wells and messed up big time. But I protected him when the Council wanted him gone. I couldn't believe this was the same kid I'd saved from the streets when he was walking around with two broken arms, unable to wipe his own ass."

"Two broken arms?"

"The chuckle-nut was riding his skateboard from Monk's Market with a tray full of hot dogs. He misjudged the curb and ate it hard," Helaku says, then passes the spliff.

"How bad?"

"He broke several bones in his arms, but saved the dogs. He went all out. It was an impressive catch—I'll give him that. Hell, I practically took care of him till he healed. But when he got into Laniakea, he chose to be cool with the Machu-Beachu boys. Between you and me, I think all the popularity went to his head." Helaku's animated gestures scatter a few chips onto the tile. "Oops." He places two fingers together and lets out a loud whistle.

Soon after, Jasper rushes to the apartment door and paws at the screen. Helaku gets up, raining more crumbs onto the floor as he lets in the slobbering beast. With a tail-wagging alertness, the scruffy street sweeper combs every inch of the abode for noms, nibs, and stray pieces of food. In its wake, a trail of drool leads from the front door to the back bedroom.

"Best vacuum ever," Helaku says fondly.

Jasper returns from the expedition and moves towards the screen door, knocking over cups on the coffee table with his tail. Water, water everywhere, but the mastiff pays little notice to the calamity. Once all the bits are safe in his deposit box, the beast paws at the door, popping it open to the late dusk.

"Goodness, that dog is a mess, but I love him." His thoughts drift to the night he and his old roommate, Alex Rocko, found Jasper as a puppy—halted by the sudden slosh of water pooling around his pinky toe.

Reflexive Inadequacy

Helaku mops up the mess with a dirty towel and soccer-kicks it into the kitchen. "Konway, I've been thinking," he says, returning to the living room.

"What's up?"

"Remember when you rescued Todd?"

"Again, one of those moments where my body moved on its own." He gulps back some water.

(You can't control it,) the Imp-oster whispers melancholy behind each word.

"No worries, bro," Helaku says with a warm smile and places his hand on Konway's shoulder.

"You're right." He flashes a glint of positivity to displace further contemplation about his past and says, "I've been fortunate enough to remember this much... In time, I might figure this out and remember who I am."

(Are you sure about that?) the Imp taunts, its voice dripping with mockery.

"That's the spirit." Helaku pauses, recalling an earlier thought. "I have an idea." He spins around, whirling between the coffee table and the smart TV. "With both Todd and PJ suspended from the dive roster, there are openings available. And I think you'd be a perfect fit. Who knows, it might help trigger even more memories."

(This could help me gain a more permanent place here,) Konway considers his longing to belong. "Sounds fun... I'm in." He brandishes a rascal grin of confidence.

"Wahoo! Let's celebrate." Helaku plops down on the couch and pulls out his rolling tray. "Would you be so kind as to do the honors, sir?"

"Certainly, my good man." Konway reaches for the tray, avoiding air-conditioned currents, but a gust from the ceiling lifts a fan of rolling papers over the side. His other hand catches them, and without missing a beat, he rolls up a sampler platter of delights.

After multiple joints, matches of cartoon combat, mine cart levels of pixelated gorillas, and a first-person battle royale, they settle into the final act of *Precinct 420*. Both fall asleep before it ends. Helaku snores up a storm on the couch, while Konway, in the recliner, charges into vivid dreamscapes, tethered to the thoughts of Sage Forgé and plagued by the ghosts of his past.

51

Pool Party

Quick Study

The next morning, the sun's animating rays inch above Laniakea, sailing past the tidal river and the nearby marsh. Konway stretches into a deep yawn and wipes the crust from his eyes. As he listens to the waking village, sunbeams slant through the windows into Helaku's abode. Near the barn, the roosters conduct a songbird choir, lifting the final veil of night.

He sits up, shaking off the Sandman's dust, then notices a three-ring binder stuffed with reference materials and a hand-scribbled note on the coffee table.

Konway,

I found my old dive manuals and thought they'd be an excellent resource. Don't worry about any chores today. Focus on learning the material. I'll be back later.

Rest well,

Helaku

After brushing his teeth and downing a glass of water, Konway plops on the couch and slides off a stapled packet of papers. In a few dawn-lit hours, he finishes reviewing the steps of planning, staging, and executing a dive. Glossing over the section on equipment selection, he discovers a laminated handout—stained with hot chili sauce—depicting underwater hand signals. He picks up last night's joint and rapidly fills out the test tucked into the binder's back pocket before the last ash hits the tray.

(Better to ask for forgiveness than permission,) the gravelly drawl of Paw-Paw's wisdom echoes between his ears.

Finished with his studies, Konway goes on a walkabout, waving to the early wave riders returning from dawn patrol. While the TacOHUD highlights hummingbird flight patterns, along his peripherals, the clamorous pack of dogs hurtles towards him—sniffing, licking, barking, pawing, and jumping for a scratch behind the ears. Then, as swiftly as they rumble onto the scene, they bumble back around the corner of the apartments.

He saunters through the dew-laced Horseshoe, trying to enjoy the pleasantness, but the faint concern seeping from the frets of his heartstrings persists. (Where's Sage? Is she still at the hospital? Is she with him? What is this feeling?)

"Hey there! Good day, Konway." Lynn's voice reaches the neurotic hamster wheel, bringing his attention back to the lush Horseshoe.

He spins around. "Lynn? Where are you?"

"Up here," she says.

Konway peers past the first level of branches to the second-floor porches. "Good morning," he waves.

"Bear and I are enjoying some tea. Come join us."

"Sure thing," he says, relieved of his momentary melancholy and eager to secure his sense of belonging. "I'll be right up."

Cannapy Café

As he reaches the puppy gate at the top of the stairs, notes of breakfast pastries envelop his nostrils.

"Come on in. The latch unlocks from the other side," Lynn informs him.

"Would you like some tea?" Bear hollers from inside their home.

Konway scoots onto a stool, saying, "Yes, please."

"How'd you sleep?" she asks.

"Pretty decent, considering I woke up on top of a video game controller."

Bear leans out the door, asking, "Do you want some cream and sugar?"

"However you fix it is fine with me. The fate of my taste buds is in your hands." Konway grins with anticipatory delight, ready to record the experience for his budding collection of recent memories, safely stowed in his *Space Force III* lunchbox.

Bear disappears behind a magnetic mosquito netting leading into the apartment. Overhead, puffs of morning clouds parade about with a wind-blown brush. All around, songbirds serenade the moment with resplendent grace.

"Sage told me you saved her from a snake," Lynn jumps to the gossip; the flowing drapery of her clothing adds to the air of lightness about her.

"It was nothing." Konway downplays his abilities.

"Don't be modest... Again, you helped steer us clear of tragedy, and for that, I am beyond grateful."

Bear returns to the porch, balancing a plate atop a round of beverages. "It's hot—might want to wait a bit and let it cool down. I also brought you some of my world-famous scones. I made them yesterday, and boy-oh-boy, these are delicious... Now, these are made with yummy cannabis butter. Don't worry. They're not too strong."

Lynn smirks. "That's what you said about the peanut butter bars."

"I've got the measurements down pat."

"Good thing it's still early." She chuckles.

He playfully cuts his eyes at her.

In the center of their patio table, a stack of blueberry scones rests on an ornate, violet-patterned china plate.

"If you want to wait a bit, my equally famous bourbon pecan cinnamon rolls just came out of the oven."

"Is that what smells so good?"

"Don't tell the village," Bear says in a low, secretive voice. "The whole of Laniakea will be knocking down my door."

"Sounds tasty."

"You'll have to wait and see," Lynn teases.

With a grumble in his stomach and eager to experience the novelty of the first bite, Konway selects an obtuse scone. Its flaky, buttery, blueberry texture, and subtle sweetness soon sop up all his saliva. He grabs the oversized teacup and sips past the blueberry paste lodged in the roof of his mouth. He tries to unstick it with his tongue, nearly triggering the bio-switch to minimize the Mind Palace VPN partition. Unsuccessful, he slurps down more tea. "This is yummy... So many flavorful layers." He takes another bite, repeating the desertification of his palate.

Bear dunks his scone into his cup, then enjoys a sizable chomp. Behind him, several pelicans ribbon over the village, towards the shoreline. Already, the sky's canvas changes from the pastel dawn to the royal vibrance of day.

In the nearby live oak canopy, a young woodpecker searches for bugs. The beat of its probing beak mixes well with the early morning symphony, rising higher and higher: *tweedle-tweedle, three-de-he-three, tweedle-tweedle, three-de-he-three,* all responding in turn.

Lynn continues, "If you need anything from us, especially the Surf-Works tribe, knock on our door anytime. Laniakea is our home, and you've helped protect it more than once. It doesn't matter who you were or where you're from—but what you do while you're here."

"Like my commanding officer used to say, 'All that counts is your last ten minutes,'" chimes Bear, watching part of his scone break off into his cup.

A woman's voice calls up the stairs. "Lynn? Are y'all up there?"

"Come on up, Amber. We're having some tea with the one and only, Mr. James Konway."

She ascends the staircase. "Hello everyone." She gives Lynn a hug and takes her seat across from him, saying, "Glad you're fitting in, *hero*. How do you like the new name?"

"A rose by any other name—"

"—would smell as sweet," Bear concludes the line.

"Shakespeare." Konway grins at the pleasantness of remembering.

While Bear extends his hospitality, Konway scarfs down the pastry. With the last blueberry bite, his awareness shifts to their conversation.

"Any news about Todd?" Lynn asks, concern wrinkling across her brow.

"The docs are releasing him today," Amber says. "Bhodi and a few others went to the hospital earlier." She checks her smartphone, facedown in the main-screen. "They should pull up soon."

Lynn settles her cup on the matching antique violet saucer and effortlessly stands. "In that case... let's find Momo and gather everyone at the Creative Cabaña."

Hobble-Stomp

Once the villagers craft their get-well signs and gift baskets, they fill the crushed-seashell parking lot in anticipation of Todd's return from the hospital. Not long after, a crusty van rambles through the gate and into the nearest spot. Bhodi jumps out of the driver's seat and flings open the side door. He helps Todd teeter from the shadowy interior and onto his crutches. With the heavy lifting done, Jack appears from the opposite side and helps steady him.

Todd hobbles towards the crowd with a fat prescription of pain pills and the doctor's recommendation to stay out of the water hanging around his neck like an albatross. The villagers surround him with a gauntlet of prayers and concerns, giving him all the sympathy his poor-me antics can afford. He shuffles along, careful not to fall in front of everyone, and glimpses Konway's concern. Todd shoots a momentary scowl as he passes with a trail of doting villagers in pursuit.

Shortly after, Helaku pulls up with Sage in one of Kawabonga's sprinter vans. She hops out, tosses Todd's overnight bag over her shoulder, and rushes to catch the procession. She sees Konway and flashes a playful smile, accompanied by an invisible kiss.

The pity parade ebbs into the Horseshoe, up the steps, and to Todd's apartment on the second floor. Jack and crew meander past the cluttered mess and help him into bed with a fresh dose of pharmacology. Once the door closes, Todd rolls to his side, then props his leg on a body pillow, muttering, "Who does he think he is? I don't need his fucking sympathy. Once I'm healed, we'll make sure you don't finish your stay." His thoughts of betrayal comfort him for a moment. But upon closing his eyes, the look etched on his rival's face lingers—so he reaches for the bottle.

Beast Treats

Back in the parking lot, Helaku walks over and sets down a large cardboard box. "Yo, bro!" He initiates the village handshake: striking his thumb down the center of his back, swinging his arm up in front of him, and clasping hands to embrace Konway. "Did you have time to review the materials I left? It's okay if you didn't."

"Yep-yep. Took the test at the end, too."

"That's impressive." Helaku beams his trademark smile. "It should've taken you at least a day to review everything."

"What's in the box?" Konway switches subjects to avoid the potential of conjuring the Echoes of Doubt.

"Treats."

"Treats?" he asks, looking at the crumpled container, splotched with stains.

"You'll see." Helaku puts his fingers to his mouth and lets out a loud whistle.

Several seconds later, Jasper comes running up, followed closely by two other dogs: Lilly, a white Lab-German Shepherd mix, and Little Man, a robust Carolina dog.

"Sit," Helaku raises his hand.

All three obediently plop their rears on the ground and lick their chops with Pavlovian potential. Their tails wag in unison, swishing across the crushed-shell parking lot.

"Lie down."

They hit the floor and cover their noses with their front paws.

"Roll over," Helaku says, twirling his finger in the air.

They roll in unison to the left. Then, to the right. Finally, pausing on their bellies.

"Up." He raises his hand.

The trio spring to their paws and return to a sitting posture.

"Hold." Helaku places one treat on each of their noses.

They sit patiently, waiting for the signal.

"Wipeout!"

The three pups flip their morsels and catch the others' treats, chomping up the goodness.

Helaku opens the box of butcher's bones, fresh from the market.

They light up with excitement.

"Hold."

The trio sit in unison, even as he tilts the bones to them. Motionless, their eyes lock onto the prize. He sets down the box, steps away, and snaps his fingers above his head. They dive in, selecting a monstrous leg bone as long as the three of them are wide, and trot away with ease, disappearing into the nearby bushes.

"They'll chew on that one all week long," Konway marvels at their coordination.

Helaku closes the flaps on the cardboard box and turns to Konway with a grin. "I'll give your test to an instructor and have them grade it. Then it's time for a pool party."

"Another feast?"

"You'll see." He hoists the box onto his broad shoulders. "But first, let's get these to the other pups."

By the time they reach the edge of the parking lot, the word is out about bones to pick, and the clamorous pack arrives from behind the bamboo fence line. As he sets down the butcher's box, they beeline towards it, wrestling for one bone over the other until the goodies are distributed. Then, without hesitation, they scurry off to enjoy their gnawing, nibbling, and ripping elsewhere—burying the rest for later, no doubt.

Gear Up

After a smoke session and a few rounds of gaming, they head to the pool. There, the once-barren basin reflects the staggered puffs of atmosphere stretching towards the mainland.

"I guess I passed the written exam?" asks Konway, peering into the sloshing ripples.

"With flying colors, bro."

"So you weren't kidding about throwing a pool party?"

Helaku gazes into the clear, cool mirror. "Not exactly. This is for your certification. I had it filled this morning."

"So soon?"

"We need to let the salt levels settle, then we'll have a splash... but first, let's get you some gear." He points to the Boathouse.

Inside, organized shelves of 3D-printed containers—each with bright, readable labels—hold a cornucopia of gear. Helaku finds Konway a dive suit from the hanging carousel, along with a set of fins and a mask from adjacent bins.

"What's the next test like?" Konway asks, preparing himself.

"You'll hit the water to demonstrate your knowledge of basic scuba skills. But don't stress too much—just have fun!"

Aqueous Cavern

Days later, they stand poolside as the cries of passing gulls line the horizon. Underwater jets bubble to the surface. After a detailed rundown of do's and don'ts, Konway adjusts the straps of his buoyancy compensator, tightens his mask, and wiggles into a set of oversized flippers. Feeling comfortable and confident with the tank's weight upon him—like a bookbag on the first day of class—he takes a giant step into the deep end.

Splash! Below, gurgling water flickers with the sun's lumination. He spins around and sees the graffiti littering the bowl.

(Gnar-maste.)

Konway locates the diving rings on the bottom, surrounded by a menagerie of sea creatures, pixelated unicorns, and pirate chests filled with weighted coins and jewels. While the film of familiarity sloshes about him, a Vision Shard dislodges from a pile of mental splinters, and the fullness of his bandwidth abruptly shifts to another place and time.

Bullets pepper the water from a drug lord's gunship—a modified Mi-24 [Hind]—hailing a cascade of casings like rain on a hot tin roof. Bolstered by the Oros system, he swims out of range. Behind him, amphibious drones take to the sea, transforming to resemble shortfin makos. As he reaches a nearby outcropping, the Hind turns its weapons on the cliffside. From above, a dead drop of debris clouds the area. The Oros system down-regulates his nervous system and scans the surroundings, locating a passage formed by ancient lava tubes.

As he flees, a few drones collide with the wreckage, but many others slip past, ripping closer to him. They quickly close the gap and fire. He narrowly avoids the harpoons' bite, thanks to a piece of falling rubble, then spins towards the cave's entrance. The TacOHUD highlights the way forward. At a fork, running low on breath and with the drones swiftly approaching, he swims along the ancient path.

Nanites in his lungs stall his urge to exhale. The commitment is non-negotiable. Only 60% at his limit, he maneuvers into the keyhole.

Smaller

and

smal

le

r

Until, upon the precipice of breaking down, he breaks through, and the way opens. Farther, as he gasps into a grottoed lagoon with the drone sharks catching up, the Vision Shard shatters into dust.

Dive Test

Splash! His instructor hits the water.

(When was that? Whose gunship? Was that Panama?)

The questions summon another puppeted face from his past.

(Don't panic.) He resists the specter. (There's no time for this. Calm. Stay calm.)

Sage waves, then blows him a kiss before returning the bubbling regulator to the seal of her lips.

Rooted back in the present, they swim closer to the bottom. She watches him pick up lobsters, mini squids, and rainbow unicorns. Satisfied with his performance, followed by an exchange of hand signals, they maneuver to the next round.

Konway starts off well but fails to grasp the coins with the grabber claws. He tries again but drops them. Again. And again. The failures mount into a rolling tide of frustration.

(Calm down. Stop thinking about the past and focus on right *now*. Don't you want to be accepted by the village?)

Konway steadies his breath, adapting to the angst, then kicks his flippers. With a smidge of renewed confidence, he swims in a spiral towards the bottom of the pool, plucking each coin from the depths and placing them in the weighted treasure chests, earning the endorphins of success. And for a short time, the Fog of Despair clears, leaving the emptiness of forgetting something he forgot, he forgot.

Sage moves to the last test and signals she is running low on air. He attaches the octopus breathing apparatus to share his tank, and they rise to the surface. Back in the shallows, she counts up the number of objects retrieved and tallies his score.

During the next couple of days, he demonstrates superior technical diving skills, expert levels of buoyancy control, breath control, and economy of motion. After speedily completing his open-water certification, Laniakea hosts an actual pool party.

Everyone is there, except Todd. His slow-healing injury, compounded by a double dose of prescription drugs, keeps him isolated in his room while the rest of the village enjoys communion and celebration. Darkness looms over Eden.

Stay Schemin'

Todd stares out his apartment window and grumbles incoherently in a bobble-headed stupor. He scratches his chest with the prescription itch and grinds his teeth with the ANTs of inadequacy. The throbbing pain in his ass sends another jolt down the side of his leg. He whinges and whines for a moment, then pops another pill into a sea of poor-me sorrows.

Later in the night, Jack brings Todd a plate of leftovers to go with his pain pills and IPAs.

"Heard that *kook* and Sage are getting along pretty well." Jack swigs his beer.

"You could say that," Todd cuts his eyes at a dirty pile of laundry in the corner.

"Hey, bro, you could have any girl on this island, but you can't get your mind off of her." He has another swig. "There must be something magical down there—"

"Don't talk about her like that." He scowls with a droopy-eyed spark of indignation.

"My bad, bro," Jack retracts his statement, then offers a fifth-pocket baggie of cocaine. "Have a hit of this. It's some pure shit I got in the other day."

Todd takes a nip. "It's all good." He wipes the drip from his nose and asks, "Where's PJ? He hasn't responded to my texts. Can you believe he hasn't come to visit me?"

"I might've been a little too hard on him," Jack says, then toots an Everest-size key bump. "But I'm sure he's sulking on Center Street. Give him some time. He'll come around... I'll send some of the boys to check in on him. But I need you to focus on getting better—once you're up and running, you'll be right back out there with us. Unlike Helaku, you'll always have a place at my side." Jack uses Todd's growing jealousy, further clouding his judgment and fostering his resentment for Konway, until it boils over, scalding everything around him.

Jack hands him a frosty IPA. "Now, I know you and Sage had a rough spell… But if you help me get rid of Helaku, I can get her back into your arms."

"How?" Todd's eyes part from their drooped state.

He leans in, and Todd listens eagerly, unaware of Jack's *true* agenda. Like a fish in water, Todd cannot see what is right in front of him.

52

Sunsets & Cigarettes

The Bubble

The following afternoon, while waiting for a delivery from Monk's Market, Sage and Konway bask in the warmth from above, watching a thunderstorm rumble near the mainland. Along its fringes, the blue quilt of day darkens into a brooding gray dragon, sinking below the horizon. However, the Bubble—an atmospheric barrier caused by the Folly River—braces against the squall while Apollo's lances pierce the roaring beast, herding it down the coastline.

A slight skirt from the downpour soaks them with rain as they swing their legs off the side of Laniakea's dock. Konway hops up.

"Where are you going?" Sage raises an eyebrow.

"We're getting wet."

"So? Who cares? Come sit with me. It'll stop soon. They say, 'If you don't like the weather, wait fifteen minutes.' Do you see that line?" Sage points to the right.

He looks to the low-lying bridges connecting Coffin Island with the twin islands, James and John. Beyond his recollection, the bridge to Holy City remains closed after reports of a container ship striking one of its supports.

"See... It's not even storming past there," she says, then laughs into the face of the tempest.

He sits back down and takes her hand. They lean on one another, gazing out at the lush green marsh. Together, they savor the contrast of darkness framing a blue, sun-filled sky, lined by the silhouettes of twenty-four pelicans ribboning over the village, floating on the gusts of early summer.

Dancing In The Rain

Compelled by the simple beauty, Konway kisses Sage down to the water-splashed dock. She wraps her arms around him and grabs hold of his shirttail. Their rain-soaked clothes slide to the side, and he into her. The rhythm with which they reach for each other becomes lost in the thundering rumbles of the passing moment. Soon, the shower turns to steam, and their hearts into one.

As he dives into her emerald eyes, volleys of light breach the tempest of desire. Above, the raging dragon disperses into quiet puffs of cotton candy, electrifying the circuitry of their senses with the sweet reprieve of release. Tender touches and light-hearted illumination from their tickled intimacy follow their sacrifice upon the altar of the divine, imbuing the moment with a subtle signification.

After getting dressed, Sage shuffles through a damp pack of cigarettes and finds the only dry one. On retrieval, it snaps in her wet hands. She tries to mend it, but doing so ruins it. "Damn it... I think this is going to be my final one. It's about time I quit anyway. Why am I still smoking these?" She falls into his hazel eyes, searching for the answer she already knows.

Tiny streams of light swizzle into the lovers' frame of sight. Far past Holy City, over the horizon, the sky settles into a new shade of sorbet: orange sherbet dipped in neon blue and pink fairy floss.

"What is it really?" Sage asks.

"What?" Konway tilts his head.

She turns to face him. "What is it to see a sunset?"

"I don't know."

"Me neither." She looks back at the heavenly splendor before them.

"Let's enjoy watching it for a spell longer." He squeezes her squishy, wet shoulders to his.

The high tide emboldens a calming sense of natural order. Mirroring their wonder, glorious hues ring out across the marsh-lit sky—a tapestry of imperfection, too impressive not to notice, yet too expansive to understand.

La Mariposa

Without warning, a swarm of *no-see-ums* springs from its crypts, feasting on any bare skin found in the vicinity. The lovers escape the pestilence and take a bike ride to the beach. A couple of blocks over, they make it to the shore with only a few bites and enough time to watch the sun yawn into the late afternoon.

"I want it to last. I don't want it to finish setting yet," Konway says.

"The light is just right." She snuggles under his arms. "But only a fool would want it to last."

"How so?"

"Like inspiration, this moment is fleeting. It is something to be enjoyed, not captured. To hold it too tightly is to deny it of its nature."

"What's that?"

"To let it happen. To be free."

(To be free... sovereignty,) Konway reflects on her answer, staring off into the now-pastel skyline and sees a well-built sandcastle is about to wash away. "Will you help me fortify it?"

"'Fools who persist in their folly.'" She gets up to help kick sand along the monument's backside.

They arrive at the forgotten vision of utopia, and Konway digs a moat to safeguard the front. Then, upon carving the adjoining trenches, he discovers the letters O-M-E-L-A-S, spelled with seashells, being washed away. He digs another channel.

"This should stall the tide," he says.

"Be glad you're cute." Sage bumps him with her hip.

Saltwater slides across the shoreline, over smoothed driftwood and broken seashells, covering a tiny shark's tooth. The pink crest of another small wave crashes into the heel-dug seawall and launches saltwater droplets to intercept a nearby butterfly fluttering too close to the airspace.

Soaked, the mariposa spirals towards the sand. A tiny impact crater erupts, scattering minute flecks of shell and microscopic exoskeletons. The creature struggles to stand, then flails its wings in a frantic dance to dry off before the wind whisks it away or the waves claw it back into breathless waters.

"Oh, no!" She rushes to its aid and delicately lifts the sand-speckled insect.

The butterfly clings to her cupped hand, wings fluttering softly against her palm. She draws it to her chest to shield the dainty soul from the gusts and the waving fiddler crabs at the edge of their burrows.

They search for a haven, wandering past the dunes where a hawk stomps on a mouse, beyond the drunkards with cast nets and unleashed pups, through ankle-deep sand, all the way up the beach access ramp. They brush by gardenias and old Christmas trees turned dunes, finally making it back to the bikes. There, Sage gently places the mariposa onto a plump banana leaf. Mission accomplished, they share a kiss as the creature waves its tiny legs in gratitude.

After chasing sunsets on the southwestern side of Coffin Island, the two hand-holding lovebirds pedal into Laniakea while Todd climbs into his truck and positions himself on a special donut to keep pressure off his wound. He sees them scooting past, and in their wake, the spindles of desire and inadequacy entangle the sinews of his heart with the acid reflux of envy, leaving him empty and reaching for his prescription bottle.

Part IV
Everydayness

53

Nursery Rhymes

Wake Up

Several rainy days cast a dense gloom of humidity across Coffin Island. Once every inch of Laniakea is soppy, the darkened sky gives way to patches of blue, revealing an experience of beauty hardly considered possible. A Kawabonga van excitedly splashes into Laniakea's puddle-laden parking lot.

As it squeaks to a stop, Helaku explodes from the driver's side and bounds towards his apartment.

"Rise and shine!" He kicks in the door of Konway's dream.

"What's going on?" Sage rolls over and buries her face in the pillow.

"The weather has lightened up, and we've got the okay to take one of the Foundation's ships out to the Nursery."

"Why us?" She mumbles from the cool underside of her pillow.

"This is a last-minute mission, and the other villagers are setting up for the Farmers' Market on Center Street. Think y'all are up for it?"

"Count me in." Konway yawns.

"Don't leave me here," Sage emerges from her nest. "I'll be too bored."

"No worries—you're coming with us." Helaku slings open the refrigerator and searches for refreshment.

"Where're we headed?" asks Konway, stumbling out of his bedroom.

"The Nursery... If you thought the ARC was something, wait till you see this." Helaku tosses him a chilled can of coconut water.

Coral Cove

An hour later, the Foundation's boat arrives at Laniakea's wobbly dock. The dive team boards the research vessel and stows their gear. After finding their seats, Helaku confirms their destination with the captain.

Following the Folly River, churning up a lapping wake along the marsh grass, the squad makes their way towards the Stono.

"You look like you're thinking too hard," Sage teases Konway. "What's on your mind?"

"I might be a smidgen-bit excited. I didn't get to see the ARC's reefs last time."

"You're in luck. Those corals came from the Nursery," says Mateo.

"How close is it to the ARC?" Konway asks excitedly.

Ruckus bumps into Mateo, blocking his response. "It's in a preserved bay, set aside by one of the Foundation's wealthy associates. They wanted to build on the property but never did. Now, we get to grow corals."

Farther ahead, Konway spies the first glimpses of the GPS marker buoys bordering the Nursery, just as a salt spray whips past Helaku's shark-fin mohawk. The captain kills the engine and glides into position.

Fractal Propagation

By the time they drop anchor, Konway's curiosity gets the better of him. "What's the plan for today?" he asks Helaku and adjusts his dive suit.

"We're planting the new samples from Monk's Market—hopefully these are more temperature resistant than the last batch."

"Why's that important?" Konway asks eagerly.

"Most people don't realize it, but the oceans are getting warmer. Influenced by our will-fool-ignor-ance, we've escalated primal cycles, older than we have history to record it." Helaku looks on with a pause of disdain. "As a result, coral reefs have less recovery time between bouts of bleaching."

"Bleaching?"

Sage explains, saying, "It's a stress response to changes in the surrounding waters. Once the algae are depleted, the corals become nutritionally compromised."

"Imagine these reefs as cities of the sea, or trees in the forest," Marty chimes in. "They're the backbone of our ocean's ecosystem. The Foundation's scientists predict that if we stay on our current course, there will be a 50% loss over the next thirty years."

"Also, some corals don't grow as fast as their cousins," informs Stewart Hawthorne, the chaplain of Soldier-Surf. "Some of the important reef-building ones can be around eight hundred years old."

"How do you stop the bleaching?" Konway asks.

Helaku seizes the conversation, stating, "By finding heat-resistant corals and making more of them... Down there, you'll see several rows of 3D-printed trees with pieces hanging from their branches."

"How long does it take to grow them?" he asks excitedly.

"After about six months, we remove them from the Nursery, tag 'em, and take 'em to reef restoration sites along the coast, where we attach each one using an all-natural, non-toxic epoxy."

"I can't wait to see it," Konway says with a smile and the adrenaline of adventure coursing through his dive suit.

"That reminds me... Let's review our task list for today's activity." Helaku receives a waterproof clipboard from Marty. "While we set up a new tree, Sage and Konway will plant Coral-Bombs at the long reef."

"The Foundation sure has plenty of money to throw around." Ruckus tightens a strap.

Sage replies, "So long as they're not trying to develop the island, I'm cool with that."

"What's special about these Coral-Bombs?" Konway asks, his imagination sputtering with branching coral lattices.

"Check this out." Helaku reaches into the livewell and pulls out a hand-sized tetrahedron with large coral medallions epoxied to its sides, holding it for the crew to see. "One of Roshi's monks from the market discovered an adaptive way to speed up their growth—"

"Wasn't it Ken?" Ruckus interrupts. "Solid, dude."

"David or Scarborough?" Mateo asks.

"Who do you know with the last name Scarborough?"

"No one... but my uncle Bernie does."

Helaku hands Konway the sample. "Many corals naturally break into fragments. Sadly, the large, slow-growing ones—that form the bedrock of healthy reefs—don't regenerate quickly, which makes their longer growth cycles difficult to manage."

"How are these supposed to help?"

"One day, Ken was moving a chunk of coral from one tank to another. In the process, a small fragment broke off from where it had attached itself to the live rock. He monitored the specimen for a month, during which it healed the damaged area."

"What about the piece left in the other tank?" Konway's agile mind arranges the puzzle.

"The monk was surprised to find it had grown into a large medallion. Boom! He figured out how to produce exponential growth. His method allows smaller pieces to fuse into a larger coral in nine months, which would've taken fifteen years to grow on its own"

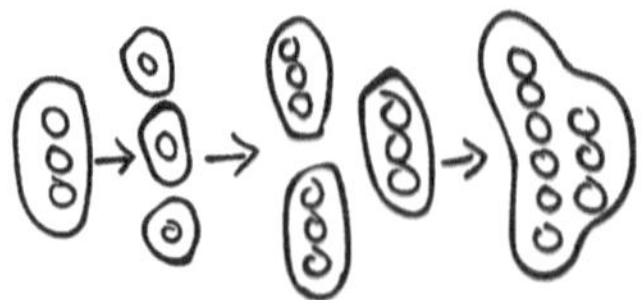

"That's brilliant." Konway smiles from the hopium.

"More like a happy accident," Mateo muses.

Ruckus chuckles. "Certainly, a happy beginning!"

"Hey-yo!" Mateo playfully pops his roommate's shoulder.

"Serendipity," Sage concurs. "Finding what you need where you least expect it."

"Bingo," Helaku says, wincing at the sun.

"It replicated itself?" Konway studies the sprawling imagery. On the opposite end of the firmware, cascading from the dilapidated Screening Room in his Mind Palace, a coral forest sprouts towards the cloud-covered Mesas of Memory.

"Not exactly," says Sage. "These corals are re-skinning themselves. In the wild, they don't enjoy being overgrown by another type, so they fight for their position on the reef. However, because the monk's samples came from the same parent, they fused back into a larger collective colony."

Konway's mind drifts from the moment, transfixed by Sage's superhero silhouette against the water's contrast with the sky.

"Hey, are you listening?" she asks.

He snaps back from his lucid trance. "All clear," he says, then smiles at her Atlantean beauty. "How did y'all put this together?"

Helaku butts in, "Well, one day I was talking with Ken over some complimentary coffee at Monk's Market. The next thing I realized, he was sending me fragments to plant—"

Konway hands the sample back to him.

"—Take extra care when you secure these onto the long reef. If the experiment is successful, we can share this technology and bring back the world's reefs." A glimmer of hope blazes within Helaku's piercing stare as he gazes along a river of forking paths.

"Can you imagine bringing back a 500-year-old coral by planting a bunch of these on an old head? Once fused, they could restore a desolate reef in no time at all!" Marty proclaims excitedly.

Konway groks the imagery. "What's the point of creating more coral if you can't stop the waves of warming water?"

Helaku explains, "You see, Ken David has shelves of testing tanks. He's growing different new-gen species to see how they'll fare in different ocean environments, selecting and breeding for more heat-resilient ones."

"For the next seven generations!" cheers Mateo.

"Ya know," Sage speculates, "reefs would naturally cross their strongest species, selecting and pairing to create a super coral... Why can't we help it along? Kind of like a midwife." She peers into the distance, past where the eye can see.

"Right on... super corals." Ruckus continues, "Combine that with Helaku's super kelp, and we'll all be mermaids by the end of the decade."

Helaku laughs. "It'd still be better than plastic."

"I'll be a merman... You can be a mermaid," Stewart teases.

"Do you have any 'super corals' yet?" asks Konway.

"Not yet," Helaku answers. "The project is not where it needs to be, but it's a step in the right direction. One day, if the math works out, these propagation techniques could help our oceans flourish again." He stands, fitting the dive suit's hood around his head and stretching towards the sky.

The calm Atlantic caresses the Foundation's vessel in its gentle sway as Konway adjusts his gear. Without warning, the snugness of his diving mask triggers a sweeping updraft amongst the refuse piles of the Donor's memories, revealing a fleeting Vision Shard from adolescence.

54

Arboring

Swim Lessons

Up in the mountains, while Paw-Paw was still with the OSI [Office of Scientific Intelligence], private equity firms with strong governmental ties had bought the Academy's legacy to create a pipeline of talented cadets, conditioning them for more useful ends. Unfortunately for young-Konway, instead of continuing his childhood in the rolling foothills, his intelligence and rebellious behavior led him into the stark reality of the Academy's cold, unforgiving environment, where trust and prestige are not easily earned.

See him now, during his early days at the Academy, leaping into an Olympic-sized training pool with several other cadets from his unit. One of them, fear-filled with inadequacy and resentful of his own lack of prowess in the placement tests, kicks young-Konway square in the chest, knocking the breath from his lungs, and races towards the finish line.

Dazed, his weighted training belt pulls him to the bottom. With no air, the struggle phase begins, triggering a series of automatic responses to conserve oxygen and decrease heart rate. His body, sensing the alarming rise of internal carbon dioxide levels, tries to override his fading will.

Respiratory muscles contract, activating an involuntary attempt to breathe. He gasps for air but inhales water instead. Farther downward, he slips into a darkening release.

Rescue

Sgt. Cinnamon heaves young-Konway's half-drowned body onto the side of the training pool. After snatching his favorite whistle from a subordinate, he issues a flurry of piercing commands. Everyone snaps into line—even the pool quiets its sloshing.

Young-Konway rolls over and coughs up two bellyfuls of water. Drool spatters across the tile floor as his chest heaves, gasping for the treasure of breath. Three convulsions send nearby looky-loo cadets back a step or two. With the last ladles expelled, fresh air fills his lungs with rapture.

Sgt. Cinnamon's enraged bleats further quiet the facility's fluorescent hum. They stand at attention, dripping wet, with their toes on the line. Young-Konway attempts to sit up.

"What the hell happened down there, cadet?" Sgt. Cinnamon growls at the aggressor.

"Wel—"

"Did I say you could talk, maggot?"

"N—no."

Two inches from the shivering plebe's face, Sgt. Cinnamon berates him in every manner of unmentionable remarks. "That's your second strike, son. You only get three. And I'm happy as hell to give them out. Remove this idiot from my sight. Send him back to the Box. I'll deal with him later."

Sgt. Cinnamon turns the unsettling glare of disapproval towards young-Konway. "I had to jump in and save your scrawny ass. Now, look at me. I'm all fucking wet." Sgt. Cinnamon peels off his overshirt and slings it to the tile. "You owe me, son."

"But—" he attempts to bargain for reprieve.

"Don't interrupt me, cadet!" His shadow dwarfs the poolside. "You're going to wash all my shit-stained undies for the rest of the month. And boy-oh-boy, it's Taco Tuesday *all* month long." He turns to the room. "Eyes up!!!"

The training facility snaps to attention.

"Now, don't think I forgot about you runts. Everyone, get back to the water! What are you slack-jawed goons doing? Get to swimming."

Fweet-fweeeeet-fweeeeeet! His whistle echoes throughout the natatorium.

"This last outburst set us back. So we're going to restart this entire process." A devilish discontent stretches across Sgt. Cinnamon's face. "And don't you little shits start groaning and try to put this on me... You can thank those two. Now, everyone, get back to work! Do it right, do it light... Do it wrong, do it all day long!"

His subordinates scatter about, parading their units into the proper staging area. Exhausted from the preliminaries, the cadets begin with the warm-up drills: a three-hundred-meter swim without stopping, only to receive the time of the person alphabetically next to you on the class roster. Then, at the marathon's end, they tread water for a pre-selected amount of time, of which they aren't aware.

Poof. The Vision Shard disappears as Konway archives it within his *Space Force III* lunchbox for later sorting amongst the picture-pattern puzzle mosaic of his personal narrative.

Into The Water

Suspended before a brilliant blue veil, his attention shifts to the immediate moment as he checks the pressure gauge, measures the gas levels in his tank, clicks on his underwater light, boots the dive computer, locks his knife, and tightens the Foundation's prototype propulsion gauntlets. He secures the regulator's bite and breathes in, rolling his neck from side to side, then looks across the Atlantic's vast horizon and slowly exhales.

Splash! Stewart is the first in and guides the anchor to the bottom of the bay. A fizzle of tiny bubbles spirals behind him while the crew hits the water. Onboard,

Marty retrieves a salt-stained milk crate from the livewell, containing the latest Coral-Bombs.

While they bob like buoys, she positions the davit crane and lowers the specimens, followed by a freshly printed coral tree.

"Keep her running," Helaku hollers back at Marty.

"Take your time," she replies. "I've got some experiments to conduct."

Together, they sink beneath the surface and swim towards an open area in the Nursery to deliver the arbor to its new home.

Coral Trees

A subtle coolness caresses Konway as the water pressure contours against his suit. Sage leads the way, swimming downward ahead of him. Thanks to the wrist-mounted propulsion gauntlets, they fizzle a trail of bubbles in their wake. Closer to the bottom, he adds some air to the BCD, keeping him from crashing into the sandy seafloor.

In an effortless ballet of buoyancy control, Sage and Konway make their way to the Nursery. At the edge of his peripherals, he glimpses a lurking shadow in the flicker from Apollo's chariot.

(It's nothing.) He dismisses the primal urge to indulge in the lust of trepidation.

Just past the particulated clarity, oceanic fractals self-similarly ebb amongst a latticework of light and propagated symmetry. There, tiny fish swim about branching rows of Elk-Stag corals. And, sensing the dive team's approach, the school shifts classrooms for the time being.

Helaku and Ruckus inspect the Nursery's health, while Stewart and Mateo secure the latest coral tree to an anchor in the seafloor. Afterward, they carefully tie fragments along the varying tiers of the floating arbor. Jeweled ornaments of hope for the future, this installation brings the Nursery one step closer to reviving the world's reefs.

Meanwhile, Sage and Konway bubble to their site a short distance away. He spots the lumbering figure again, and the TacOHUD focuses on the faint outline.

Closer, a loggerhead sea turtle swims into view, dragging a tangled cast net. Attached to it, a crab pod—and its dead mate.

He signals to her, and they zoom through the water with their propulsion gauntlets. Reaching the chimeric anchor, they free the tangled turtle, cutting the netting with their dive knives. The loggerhead gives a nod of gratitude, circles the corpse of its mate, then soars towards the surface to catch its breath before venturing beyond the veil of visibility.

Once they clear the embedded netting from around the other turtle's carcass, they gather the refuse into an empty bag, grab the crate of samples, and bubble over to the long reef. Unexpectedly, en route, the pride from their virtuous deed sifts another Vision Shard to the surface, where it unpacks onto the foothills of the Donor's youth.

55

Turtles, Turtles...

The Forty Hectare Wood

See him as a child, racing off the back porch, with the sun driving well into the afternoon, conducting Hadyn's *String Quartet Op. 33 No. 2.* His bare foot presses upon a cushiony thatch of Saint Augustine, landing his next step in a cool puddle from last night's rainstorm. Mud splatters his denim overalls as he rounds the edge of the property and trots to his secret base.

Young-Konway pushes closer to the hideout's perimeter and arrives at a crude catalog of branch blockades, misdirectional signposts, booby traps, and alternate pathways. He eases through an adjacent barrier and slides between a narrow opening. On the other side, he pulls a small folded map from his satchel. Its encrypted markers lead him away from his Command Center. Several turns, dodges, and semi-perilous leaps later, he arrives at an old tree, long dead from a lightning strike.

There, beneath his feet, its bare branches cast a shadowy 'X' on the ground. He checks left, then right, making sure no one, real or imaginary, followed him. Clear of any snoops or tails, he pulls a small key from his pocket and inserts it into a hollowed-out knob in the tree trunk. He slides to the left as the spring-loaded trap slings a sleeve of marbles into the pine straw.

On the lunchbox lid, Space Force Navigator, ALIA, a golden robot with panda ears, holding a thumbs-up, guards a catalog of treasures. Inside: a *Space Force* utility knife with an array of gizmos and carving tools, several small toy cars, multiple old coins, a pick from Paw-Paw's banjo, and a ziplock bag containing thirteen rare, limited-edition holographic rookie cards of his favorite professional athletes, poised with a metallic Herculean luster—the stuff of mythos.

Command Center

He retrieves his knife and continues along the secret path through the woods. His map leads to a clearing by the creek, where, below the swaying boughs of a great oak, Old Dan's previous kennel hides behind a blind of pampas grass.

Young-Konway parts the woven cover to reveal the Command Center's entrance, then brushes away some scattered leaves before ducking under the burlap. Inside, trophies from his expeditions—people to save, a dragon to slay, spaceships to pilot, and imaginary battles to overcome—line the shelves of a small bookcase, all displayed with careful consideration.

After inspecting the hideaway for critters, he scoots a small chair from the corner and unfolds a *Space Force II* TV-dinner tray. A certain shade of joy fills his eyes as he unpacks his afternoon snack from a crumpled brown bag: one PB&J sandwich cut into three uneven triangles—a little sloppy, but made with his own hands.

The first bite bursts with the sweetness of Granny's homemade strawberry preserves. The next chomp crunches with savory peanut butter. Hungry from a day of adventure, he is quite pleased with the sandwich's taste and texture.

Following a third bite, a dollop of peanut butter lodges itself in his upper lip. The slight discomfort directs him to the canteen. He turns it upside down, expecting a refreshing surge, only to find it empty. Without hesitation, he scurries towards the water's edge.

Glurp-glurp-glurp. The army surplus canteen fills milliliter by milliliter until it overflows from the rippling creek.

Gulp-gulp-gulp. Several streaks of water saturate the neckline of his shirt. He smacks his lips together, signaling victory over the peanut butter.

He returns to fill the canteen and notices an army of tadpoles zigzagging in the grass-lined shallows. He almost catches a few, only to have them slip between his fingers. After two more tries, he gives up and heads back to the Command Center.

Tadpole Droplet Sequence

Young-Konway enjoys his lunch and flips through an old *Space Force* comic. He takes another bite of his sandwich, turns the page, wipes his hand on his knee, and swigs from the canteen.

The first sip dislodges some bread stuck in a molar. On the second swig, to his surprise, several squiggling, squirming things bump against his cheek. He immediately spits the water into his hand, revealing three tiny tadpoles.

Barely a wiggle's width away from splashing to the ground, he rushes them back to the bank. Then, carefully dipping his hands into the cool creek, he sends the tadpoles off and join the revelry of their army. He marvels at them and imagines them growing into frogs, surviving to produce more tadpoles and evening concertos. Safely back home, they dart to and fro among the submerged roots and branches at the creek's edge. Overhead, the sun continues its daily dance across the water, mirroring the cascading clouds.

As he stands, shaking creek water from his hands, a breeze-blown plastic bag from the local bait shop catches his eye, tumbling onto the opposite shore. Young-Konway furrows his brow and crosses the creek, grumbling to the opposite side, climbs up the red-clay bank, and snatches the litter. From higher ground, he spies more rubbish rippling in the flow.

"What the heck is wrong with people? Throw away your dang trash," he says, crumpling the smiling, single-use disposable plastic bag into his pocket, before sliding down to the creek bed.

Hook

Prior to wading in, young-Konway trims a sturdy branch to help him cross. Almost one-third of the way there, the pile of garbage floats past his reach. He slaps the staff against the water, catching the fishing line in a stob, and spins the branch, slowly reeling the litter closer to him.

Halfway to the red bank, a muddled chimera flails in distress.

"It's alive!" he shouts, enthralled with curiosity.

Closer, he soon recognizes the outline of an alligator snapping turtle. As the creature clashes and clamors amongst the machine-pressed plastic prison, he spots the artificial bird's nest of fishing line, with complimentary tackle, tangled around the algae-covered spikes of its dark-brown shell.

He grunts, dragging the prehistoric turtle onto the shore while its long claws dig into the clay beneath the grass. Young-Konway reaches a manageable distance from the water and places the walking stick in front of the beast.

Snap. A large hooked beak sinks into the wooden pole. He carefully positions it away from himself and quickly retrieves his utility knife, brandishing it high above his head. *Pop-snip-pop-snap.* His nimble hands make swift, precise incisions until the malicious mass falls to the side.

"You're free!" He stands, hoping to see the ole cooter scuttle back into the creek.

Alas, the turtle's bite holds.

"You just need a little push," he says, picking up the stick and dragging it to the creek.

Once in the cooling ripple, young-Konway leaves the creature to its own devices. Filled with a sense of accomplishment, he unfolds the plastic bag from his pocket and stoops down to clean up the mess.

Grabbing the trash, an unforeseen fish hook slips its barb deep into the flesh of his tiny thumb.

"Ouch!" He winces and attempts to remove it, but can barely withstand the pain. The hook throbs with each pulse. After several failed attempts, he races through the woods, towards the house, all the while squeezing his thumb, chanting, "I won't cry. I won't cry. I won't cry—"

As swiftly as it blinked into thought, the Vision Shard disappears, but not before he files the inkling of remembrance into his *Space Force III* lunchbox for safekeeping.

56

Gardener

Patternicity

Cool currents flow over their dive suits as Sage and Konway surge through the water like superheroes in flight. A brief, bubbly distance from the derelict crab pod, they arrive at the long reef and split towards separate ends, each taking their own parcel of samples.

(What looks nice?) He positions one Coral-Bomb. (What's functional? Will these have enough space to grow?)

Heeding the call, the Oros system maps the area in front of him.

(What am I seeing? This is helpful. But how can I control it?)

Konway brushes away a cloud of micro-algae from the reef before removing a small container from his utility belt. He applies a dab of underwater-curing epoxy, then attaches the tetrahedron onto a highlighted grid. Several Coral-Bombs later, the digital overlay dims from his TacOHUD.

(Does anyone else experience things the way I do? Best I continue keeping this to myself.) He turns from his work to check in with Sage, who busily tends to her section. A lingering beetle-squirt from the malfunctioning Oros system hits him with a drop of [Prime].

In an instant, the neurochemical cocktail whelms his mindset into heightened focus. Emboldened, his hazel eyes feast upon the stark patterns weaving across the structure, designed to resemble the bones of the Great Barrier Reef.

Wrapped with awe-filledness, Konway marvels at the bleached sections, popping with tragic beauty. Although sublime, the fleeting inspiration subsides as the gas mix rushes a breath of clarity from his tank.

(I need to get a handle on this. What'd they do to me at the Academy? At the Agency? What happened to the boy I used to be?) He attempts to slow the forthcoming anguish, but a deluge of fear, uncertainty, and doubt persists, grounding him back into reality.

Determined to maintain the approval of Sage and the others, he leans into his task and shakes off the momentary angst. Thanks to the neurochemical cocktail, he slips back into a rhythmic workflow, and one by one, ordered symmetry emerges, displacing the Echoes of Doubt.

The Lovers' Dance

Once the last sample is in place, Konway floats backward to admire the structure. Soon after, Sage scoots over to him. He excitedly gestures to the reef, stoked to showcase his work. She hits him with a double thumbs-up.

After gathering their gear, the crew bubbles towards the main anchor just as Helaku and Ruckus finish their inspection of the Nursery. Nearby, a curious school of small, shimmering fish investigates the new tree. Konway secures the crate filled with debris to a tethered line resting on the seafloor and sends it topside.

Helaku and Ruckus are the first to ascend, followed by Sage and Konway. Stewart and Mateo bring up the rear. Before swimming to the anchor, Stewart stares off into the unknown for a second longer, reveling in the euphoria, like the water had somehow seeped into his head.

Halfway up, as the lovers float through lances of light, Sage signals Konway to stop. She drifts closer, pulls the regulator from his mouth, and seals their lips with one shared breath. Slowly spinning, the spotlight of day transforms into a floodlight of sensation, casting a suspended grace onto their dance floor.

Invisible Frens

All aboard the Foundation's research vessel, with the refuse retrieved and everyone settled, the captain throttles forward, bounding over a carpeted crest of waves. The motionless sky hangs the wisps of feathered clouds on its gallery wall. Soon a riotous fervor builds with the lingering dopaminergic jazz of a job well done.

Farther ahead, a fine sliver of land rises into the hue of Konway's eyes. Closer to the mouth of the Stono River, the dive team's elation overflows as a social-pod of Atlantic bottlenose races alongside the boat. Three dolphins leap from the water to bid farewell as the strand feeders depart for their favorite hunting grounds.

A low-flying black helicopter buzzes past them. Konway identifies the boxed tail rotor of an Agency-upgraded UH-72A Lakota light-duty heli. The Fog of Despair creeps through once-neon-lit pathways.

Ruckus shoves his middle finger in the air. "Asshole's flying a little close, ain't he?"

"Is that military?" Mateo asks. "My uncle Bernie was telling me he's been seeing a lot of suspicious government types around the island lately. My aunt thinks he's a nut... But it doesn't look like the Coast Guard to me."

"Maybe it's a tour?" Marty squints.

Mateo holds up his smartphone and zooms in. "Guys? Why isn't the chopper in my shot?"

"You're aiming it wrong," Ruckus teases.

"No. Look here." Mateo zooms out.

Ruckus glances at the helicopter, back to the phone, then back at the heli. "Are you trolling me, bro?"

Helaku takes a gander, saying, "Maybe you zoomed in too far."

"Bro, it's right here. Sage? Konway, you see it, right?"

The boat turns to Konway as he conceals the worry creasing his brow.

"It might be the camera," he says, hoping to defuse the conversation.

"See, Mateo. User error." Ruckus laughs.

"You're probably right." Mateo reluctantly slips the phone back into one of his waterproof bag's utility pockets.

Konway quietly grows anxious. (The Agency? They're looking for me. They sent me to the Leaky Tea warehouse... I don't want to hurt anyone... I don't want to leave the village, Sage, Helaku, or the others.) As he observes the refined joy on their faces, a quiet uneasiness sinks in, graying the day's victories.

Village Politics

Meanwhile, back in Laniakea, Todd hobble-stomps through the Horseshoe. After nearly losing his balance, trying to swing his crutch at some rambunctious pups, he pops another narco into his mouth. Pill-poised and sullen, he gleans the sympathy of everyone along his path—a little black rain cloud watering a trail of deceit. While Helaku and the others build for the village's future, Todd turns several sympathetic ears towards Jack's whispers of opportunity and position.

57

Winded Willow

Make A Wish

Time creeps closer to the beginnings of a seemingly endless summer with seasonal baskets of strawberries from Laniakea's gardens. Daily chores keep Konway's anxious mind at bay. And with each new task, another memory or two surfaces.

Recently, instead of answers, they bring more riddles, breeding a gnawing agitation and paranoia across the fertile fields of his once-pristine Mind Palace. He overcompensates by doubling down on his duties. Meanwhile, Todd doubles down on his disdain, drawing lines of division amidst the political pandering of Jack's intentions—all in the hopes of winning Sage back.

As the lovers cross into the Horseshoe, Konway's thoughts drift through a catalog of remembrance: Polaroids of the foothills, the Academy's clinical coldness, blood-spattered corridors of merciless destruction, and Vision Shards haunted by nightmarish worlds with timeless gray skies.

(Was that all I ever was? A murderer... an emotionless monster. What if I hurt Sage? Or Helaku? What if the Agency finds me here? I should turn myself in.) Bloody screams and the sound of slaughter salute the forefront of his attention. (Did I have friends? What happened to my family? Granny? Paw-Paw? Momma and Daddy?)

(Boo-hoo!) the Imp-oster taunts from the coziness of its Bone Throne. (I know something you don't know.)

(Go away.)

(Where to?)

(Leave me alone.)

(Give it time... They'll see who you are... She'll see the beast behind your mask. Just because you forgot, doesn't make the truth of who you are any less real... Who could ever love someone like you?)

Konway squeezes Sage's hand, and she smiles at him, silencing the Imp's whispers.

Near the central obelisk, frisbees fly over lively pups doing tricks. Paul Buzzbee and Bhodi skate past on longboards, effortlessly zooming along canals of interwoven brickwork, bordered by the vibrant hue of soft green grass.

With every step, another passerby greets them.

"Hey."

"Hi."

"Hello."

"How are you?"

The lovers continue their jaunt, enjoying the *tweedle-tweedle* and the comfort that blossoms from a sense of belonging and community. Farther ahead, they pass a group shuffling to the soccer field. Sage and Konway watch the game from afar, enjoying the hum of the humid afternoon as a dash of marsh wind cools the sweat beading on their skin.

She plucks two dandelions from a thatch of weeds. "Here, let's make a wish. Close your eyes and think of something you want more than anything... Make sure you don't tell anyone."

(I wish I knew who I was—no, I wish to stay here with Sage at Laniakea, forever,) Konway echoes to himself.

"Got your wish ready?" she asks.

He nods and smiles.

"Okay, on three, exhale. Remember to keep your eyes shut and try to blow away all the seedlings. No peeking." She slyly checks to see if his eyes are still closed. "One... two... three."

Sage sends most of her wishes into the breeze. Konway misses his mark. She glances up and giggles at the silly look on his face as he opens his eyes to find his wish endangered. So, using the last bit of breath, he unseats three tufts and tears off the rest, tossing them into the wind, where they swoop and spiral towards the maritime forest.

Picnic Discussions

They follow the breeze to a secret meadow nestled in the maritime forest. There, tucked among the flourishings of early summer, Sage unfolds a tropical-print beach blanket over the damp ground and invites him to sit.

"Do you ever tire of idle chatter?" She looks into his flaring hazel eyes.

"What do you mean?"

"The 'hey-hi-hello-how-are-yous'—don't folks want more than passing talk? More than howdy-dos and how's the weather?"

His eyes dart to the left, breaking the trance of her emerald stare and gaining a boon to his critical reasoning. "What do you want from a conversation?"

"Hmmm... Maybe something yummy... Perhaps a ripening picnic of discussion, marinated in mutual respect, with a side of inquiry... And of course, for dessert, a double-scoop of insight topped with rainbow sprinkles. I don't want to speak with words—I want what *we* feel between us to penetrate all our senses."

Her jeweled stare pierces the void at the center of his sight. The alluring rapture of her monologue ignites his imagination with hors d'oeuvres of discourse. He opens his mouth to respond, but sapiosexual energy overwhelms her.

She pulls him close and embraces his muscular back. A tingling sensation courses down Konway's central nervous system, igniting the furnace within him. Her lips are soft and receptive as she runs her nails across his shoulders. Their clothes fall away, opening the runways of intimate exploration. Just then, a small frond from a nearby palm tickles his side. Sage giggles at his attempts to reposition himself.

In a twist, her legs lock him onto his bare back. Sunlight crowns her in all the regal beauty nature offers, accentuating the shadows of her neckline. The sweet scent of her skin intoxicates his senses. Kissing, groping, and speaking honestly through the kinetic language of their movements, the lovers debate life, pleasure, and the loss of self.

With the abolition of their desires, they rest amongst stalks of intersubjective ecstasis. There, they succumb to Eden's illusion and forget the world for a moment. Bare before creation, cradled amidst the birds and the bees buzzing about the meadow of passion, plump berries flourish as their artifice echoes the good news of existence.

Konway traces the smoothness of her toned thighs and goes in for a kiss, only for Jasper's cold, wet nose to nuzzle into his ear, reminding him of this terrestrial form. In a matter of moments, the clamorous pack of pups is upon them—sniffing, wagging, scratching, slobbering, and licking. Something cracks beyond the tree line. Then, all at once, the chaos-storm leaps into formation and speeds away, howling into the brush.

"Can we let this last forever?" he asks.

Sage lightly punches him in the ribs, saying, "Only a fool would want it to last," then snuggles against him.

"'Fools who persist in their folly,'" he parries, quoting one of Sage's books, *The Philosophy of Blake & Everything in Between, 12th edition*. A gentle smile creases his cheeks.

Above them, a sapphire butterfly loop-de-loops past a distant set of swiftly moving clouds, marking the culmination of a day well spent.

Bondfire

Later in the evening, marsh waters rise to the tops of tall grasses, mirroring the semi-clear sky. A decorative procession of contrasting clouds scoots along the bloom of the king tide's supermoon as the bondfire burns with an emboldened glow, and the herd thins. Still standing, Konway and some of the usual suspects gaze into the flames, passing a joint, letting the star-filled conversations flow until the last logs smolder to embers.

"Are you two a couple yet?" Ruckus asks.

"Yeah, when are y'all moving in together?" Mateo adds, taking a sip of some swill.

Helaku stretches back in his chair. "Don't ask that. It's rude. They'll know when the time is right."

"Why do we feel the need to label everything?" asks Sage, glancing at Konway. "I wouldn't dare put a label on the bond we share. It'd only diminish what we each secretly behold the other to be. I choose to love freely."

"Why free love?" Mateo asks.

"We're both here by choice. Why the need to control others? Why do we want to possess things—calling them our own, petting, loving, squeezing, and naming them? What we share... I wouldn't dare spoil it by rushing to an inevitable end." Her left nostril flares, tethered to an unresolved emotional trauma from another place and time.

Konway picks up on the stale sadness hanging on the punctuation of her sentence and makes a mental note for later. "I agree with Sage. There's no need to spoil it by naming it—" He pauses in contemplation as a close grouping of Vision Shards dives off the tip of his tongue: another lesson plan at his childhood desk; *Space Force: Moon Base II* mech-suit; his momma's instruction on the classics. Bubble, bubble, the ideas swell to the surface, reminding him of tea with Bear and Lynn. "—'A rose by any other name would smell as sweet,' by Shakes Pierre." He gulps from his glass with inebriated confidence.

"I think it's Shakespeare." Sage nudges him, basking in the hues of the honeymoon phase.

"See, she keeps me honest." He pulls her close.

Mateo rolls his eyes at their obnoxiousness and pivots the conversation to a tin-foil-hat showdown. In no time, the brewing brouhaha of drunken conversations slaps swirling libations around the bondfire, hurrying the revelry towards a cliff of drunken stupor and stumbling murmurs.

Just before the last light smolders into ashen coal, a seasonal storm sneaks past the Bubble.

Willow

Howling winds surge from the Gulf Stream, across the Piedmont, and into the Lowcountry. Nestled near the maritime forest, oval leaves flutter amidst the relentless blasts of nature's design. Soon, the sweeping boughs of a half-century-old willow rock with the zephyr's weight upon the drapery of its foliage.

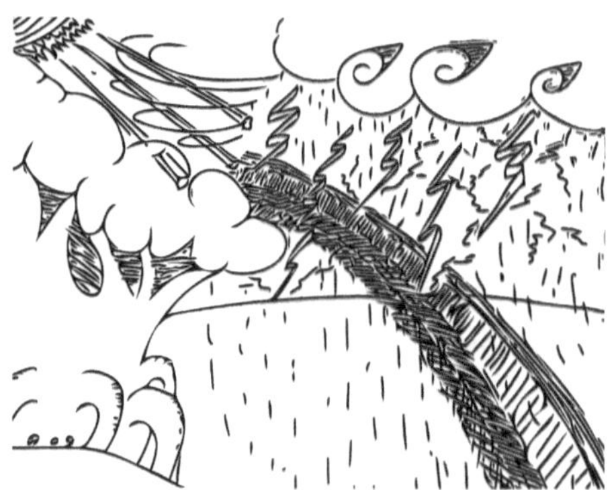

After hours of jostling gusts, moving with the forces of wind and gravity, the mighty willow sways from side to side as the soil softens around its stoic roots and mycelial networks. No longer suitable to support its majesty, the ground gives way to the ceaseless oscillation of eastbound gusts, westward volleys, northern puffs, and southern billows. The tree slants sideways, unearthing a third of its roots from the soil's seal, losing its footing like a glass slipper. Then, in a timeless topple with no one to hear it, save for the howling winds, the moss-hung willow—

Falls

Konway settles Sage onto the bed with a solid thud, sinking into her soft green-tea-infused memory foam mattress. Eyes locked, they roll under sandy sheets—keepsakes from days of surfing, riding bikes, and chasing sunsets.

While the lovers dance, the fan in the corner wafts notes of essential oils throughout the room. In the background of their sensuous grappling grunts, a lo-fi hip-hop performance fuels rhythmic hip-thrusting, heart-gasping, breathtaking moments of consummation with the other. She rises from the bed onto his lap, wrapping herself around him again and again until they collapse from their amorous embrace.

They lie apart, pinkies linked, panting towards the ceiling, savoring the neurochemicals overlaying their experience. After several moments draped with the vivid pleasure of release, Sage turns to him and slips into a much-needed slumber. Watching distant lightning flashes, he soon follows. Sadly, Nirvana never lasts.

As his high fades, the Fog of Despair returns. The Imp's lingering whispers and ill-tempered taunts careen down avenues, around street corners, across intersections, and past the unhinged doors of Dreamwind Studios. Konway tosses and turns all night with the pestering whispers of violence and forgotten things.

Down

The next morning, the village wakes to find their hopes of an early surf session blown out by lingering winds. At the forest's edge, surveying the new spot for his hives, Paul Buzzbee discovers the overturned arbor. He informs Helaku, and the entire village, minus PJ, assembles in the Longhouse. Even Todd, whose wounds are healing, lends a hand.

Working together, they make swift work of the fallen tree: trimming derelict branches, cutting it into manageable pieces, and salvaging what remains. Bear and several villagers roll wagon-wheel-sized slices back to the Makerspace, where sawdust plumes into clouds of creativity as they shape each cutout into tables, benches, cabinets, shelving—you name it—with the rungs of history visible for those who care to look beneath the varnish.

Clearing the last pieces of debris, Paul Buzzbee notices liquid amber oozing from a hole in the stump.

"Honey," he states, examining a small dollop on a twig.

In its sweet stickiness lie the debris of fungi and rotting wood. Eureka! His renaissance mindset erupts with inspiring correlations and hypotheses—ideas to preserve the next seven generations from washing away in the blind eye of a near-adjacent shadow future. Mind-ablaze, he excitedly gathers samples and, forgetting his initial quest, hurries to his lab at the Creative Cabaña to run some experiments.

58

Surf Bro

Step Around Yourself

Shortly after dusk, small cliques coalesce around the bondfire. Some sit in oversized chairs, while others stand on their soapboxes in celebration. In time, fueled by the furnaces of alcohol's inspiration, the *Mother Wolf of Inspiration* feasts on her litter until only the scattered and discarded remain.

"Did you hear about all the arrests during the protest for the missing girls?" Martha gossips.

"Sad as fuck." Sage's eyes dart towards the marsh.

"Will our world ever get better?" Amber asks, her voice hesitant.

"I'm not sure," Martha says, stirring the pot. "Last week, a podcaster was shot during a campus debate."

Sage shakes her head.

"Didn't they cancel one of the late-night comedians for speaking about it?" Amber rests her hand on Bhodi's knee.

"Land of the free," Sage retorts.

Martha rattles the ice in her cup. "I think the network's bringing him back."

"Very sus," Mateo adds. "My uncle Bernie thinks it's a diversion."

"Get your tinfoil hats ready." Ruckus nudges Konway.

Helaku stands with a smile brighter than the moon. "We've gotta step around ourselves and see beyond the narrow perspectives of our culturally provided echo chambers. You know... see the bigger picture. This is what we should strive for if we're to right the wrongs of this world and raise the stage for the next seven generations."

"It's gonna take a long, hard look in the mirror," Ruckus says, raising a pierced eyebrow.

Mateo spits into the fire. "I've almost given up on those elected ghouls."

"You're drunk, bro. Let's talk about gummy-worm flavors," hollers Bhodi, picking his afro.

On the other side of the bondfire, a small faction laughs in drunken revelry as Jack schmoozes an assortment of island politics. Next to him, Todd works himself into a frantic neurosis and pops a pill. In a few minutes, it dissolves in his stomach, serving up a buffet of self-defeating thoughts, diluted by the warm bottom of his IPA.

Ruffled

Raging with the flames of inadequacy, Todd's jealousy flings him into a drinking binge, grasping for anything to numb the pain. After guzzling a Gozer and another IPA, he stumbles towards the tiki bar and spots an unopened bottle of Green Label bourbon. He swipes it, twists it open—nearly dropping it—and swizzles back the bottleneck.

Possessed by drunken vitriol, he stares through the bondfire's flickering flames. He sees Helaku's smile shining down on his rival and remembers when he, too, felt the same sincerity. Sage leans over, kisses Konway on the cheek, and whispers something pleasant in his ear.

The longing needle of nostalgia stings into the cracks of his weeping heart. Past the left ventricle, it pops a putrid cyst, bringing Todd's temperament to a proper boil. Tired of the view, he shuffles over to a nearby table blessed with snacks.

He misjudges his approach, bumping into the corner and knocking a bowl of pretzel sticks and the last of MoMo's seven-layer dip onto the grass. Unfazed, he rummages amongst bags of wavy cheddar, sour cream and chives, BBQ, and cool-rancho chips until he locates his favorite.

Discarded bags hit the ground. Todd pays little attention and tramples the assortment. Once he stabilizes against the tiki bar, he rips into a fresh bag of salty-vinegar chips and jams fistful after fistful into his mouth. The stress response subsides, leaving him thirsty for more drink to drown the anger born of his own cowardice and inadequacies.

Stupor

Sage walks up and refills a small bowl of praline pecans as Todd gulps back slobbering mouthfuls of soda. After belching and making a half-assed attempt at wiping his face, he continues his mumbling grumble.

"Hey there," she says with a smile to displace the awkward tension. "How're you healing?"

He turns with droopy-eyed drunkenness, seeming more pathetic than violent. Chip crumbs glitter from his mouth down the neck of his shirt. "I'm fine," he replies, followed by a hiccup. "It's getting better... Y'all look happy." He glances up at her.

"I think you're worried about the wrong things. You need to focus on recovering."

"You can't tell me what to do." His brow furrows. "We aren't together anymore."

Her eyes deepen with guilt. "You don't need to remind me... It wasn't good for either of us."

"It was good for me!" shouts Todd. "But no one wanted to ask me."

"Stop it! You're making a scene. I'm sorry if I hurt you. We were living a destructive lifestyle—I thought you could see it."

"I'm sorry, my lady." He hiccups. "I'll leave you to your knight in shining armor."

He bows, hoping to mask his sorrow-filled rage, then departs. But with one awkward, swooping gesture of hospitality, Todd knocks over the half-drunk bourbon bottle, a cooler of crushed ice, and half the snack table. Embarrassment shoots through him as he hobble-stomps back to his crew, his thoughts spiraling, watering the poisonous seeds planted in the pit of his heart.

"If he weren't here, she'd be mine again," he mutters. "Fuck him... Fuck Helaku... And look at you—you're pathetic... It's been more than a month since you've touched the water. What are you even doing here? Do you even belong in Laniakea?" The deceitful dialogue dissolves any wake of civility, unleashing waves of resentment from his pores down his chip-glittered shirt.

Out of the blurred slurry of Todd's stupor, Jack suddenly steadies him, preventing him from falling into a drainage ditch. With a single disapproving look, he straightens up. Jack adjusts Todd's collar, brushes some crumbs from his shoulders, and whispers something in his ear. A malicious smirk spreads across Todd's face as he composes himself. Jack gives him a firm pat on the chest, smooths his shirt, and returns to the waiting platitudes of his constituents.

Get Rekt

A cluster of half-melted ice cubes rattles at the bottom of Konway's cup. He stands to refresh his beverage. "Does anyone need a drink while I'm up?" he asks, pardoning himself from one of Helaku's epic tales.

"Sure, lemme get another." Mateo belches.

"While you're at it, how about one for me?" Ruckus crushes an empty can on his head.

"Oh hell, I'll join you." Bhodi chugs his last bit of beer and scans the bondfire for Amber.

Helaku spins to Konway, saying, "Might as well bring the cooler here. Work smarter, not harder."

After dropping the empties in the recycling, he heads to the refreshment table, avoiding Sage's attempt to pop him on the bottom.

En route, Todd limps towards the bondfire's glow. He stumbles over several rambunctious pups playing with a used paper plate and shoos them away. A trail of slobber drips from his leg. He wipes it off, only to flick it onto his sandal.

Konway sees him struggling and waves from a short distance. "Need any help?"

Todd spots his rival, and a blind rage roars from a stewing pit of inadequacy. He snaps, then, increasing the speed of his hobble-stomp, charges boorishly, hollering, "FUCKIN' OUTZIDER!!!"

Surprised by the hostility, Konway steps back. "Is everything alright?" he asks to de-escalate the situation. "I know we haven't always seen eye to—"

Todd wildly swings at him. Within one-third of a breath, the malfunctioning Oros system procs a shimmer throughout the tattoo on his forearm, and his body dances aside with an effortless pirouette, narrowly evading the knuckles of Todd's wrath.

(Not again!) "Whoa, what's this about? Hold on—"

Too late for words. Todd throws another punch, and Konway's eyes shift from social civility to autonomic defensive reflexes. He blinks, and predictive models project across the TacOHUD.

Todd closes in and wraps him up in a bear hug, attempting to slam him to the ground. Konway widens his stance. Left, right, left—Todd punches him in the sides.

"What did I do to you?!" Konway wobbles backward.

Filled with misdirected hostility, Todd persists, landing blow after blow—right, left, right.

"Please stop this!" he pleads, while the Oros system glitches, rippling electrical pulses into his limbs.

Drunk as a skunk, Todd tires, and Konway pushes him off balance. He totters backward into a boxer's pose and, disregarding his injury, lunges forward with another clumsy barrage. However, with the intuitive discipline of a twelve-step master, Konway avoids everything with minimal effort.

Disheartened and drunk on inadequacy, Todd flails his fists. This time, Konway blocks the assault. The full counter happens so quickly he barely registers the ferocity, driving his elbow between the furious fool's knuckles, combining attack and defense into one fluid movement—the perfect economy of motion.

"Aaahhh!" The pain shoots up Todd's arm, tangled with embarrassment and the booze-fueled narco inferno in his heart. His entire limb goes numb. Deep down, primal red flags and blaring bells signal him to stop. But it is already too late for both bodies in motion.

Todd balls his other fist and winds up for a haymaker, clenching every orifice of his being. Another faint tracer waxes along the sinews of the dragon tattoo as a drop of [Time Warp] hits Konway's system. For a moment, time elongates as Todd releases the trebuchet towards Konway's temple—his Hail Mary at the buzzer.

The Oros system projects potential points of impact onto the TacOHUD as the drunken fist sails through the air. He sees the snot-sniffing fear on Todd's face and parries the haymaker with a deft jab. The tincture fades, and time resumes its usual flow. But before Konway regains control, he unleashes a rapid burst upon Todd's face—his fists hammering down the midline, then rising again—crumpling him where he stands.

Mob Logic

A gawking crowd gathers. Some toast their drinks to the beatdown, while others gasp in horror. Konway pulls away from the pre-scripted survival protocols and kneels beside him, checking to see if Todd is still breathing.

The gathering villagers gossip amongst themselves.

"Is he okay?"

"What happened?"

"Apparently, there was a fight."

"Who?"

"Todd and the new guy."

"Konway?"

"Why is he always picking on the noobs?"

"Not this time."

"He fucked around and found out."

"Certainly got his ass handed to him."

"Good. Serves him right for always looking down on us."

"Shush."

"What were they fighting about?"

"Sage?"

"Shhhh."

"Woah, Konway beat him?"

"That wasn't a regular scuffle."

"Yeah, he almost killed poor Todd—with his injuries and all—"

"Didn't he save him?"

"Well, not today. He laid him out nice and thin like a sandwich—"

"From Rockaway Deli?"

"You know it."

"I don't feel safe with him here."

"We know nothing about him."

The crowd continues murmuring their suppositions, a faceless, nameless homogeneity of the animal mind in flight.

KTFO

(Not again.) Ghost-white, Konway freezes next to his rival. (This isn't who I am... What the fuck is wrong with me?)

Before the dust settles, the horror of his violent behavior summons images of the Leaky Tea warehouse.

(I thought I was getting a handle on this—)

(You're a failure,) the Imp-oster whispers.

(I could lose everything—)

Its cackles intensify. (If you ask me, you should've popped that numbskull like a zit on prom night—)

(I don't want to hurt anyone... I don't want to lose Sage.)

Helaku rushes over to assess the situation. (Look how quick he is to pick up his opponent. It's about time someone whipped Todd's ass, though. Maybe this will tighten him up.)

Todd sprawls across the ground. The taste of blood in his mouth overpowers the lingering fog of bourbon on his tongue. His right eye swells shut, and the other rests partially rolled back in his head.

Jack arrives at the bloody scene with a sinister smile beneath a solemn face of calculated shock. "Get away from him!" He pushes Konway to the side.

Mateo and Ruckus swoop in and help Helaku get Konway to his feet, then head towards the Longhouse.

Out of earshot, Mateo erupts, "That was some real Octagon-type shit back there!"

Ruckus shakes him by the shoulder. "He didn't land a single blow on you. The way you moved was better than any MMA expo I've seen." He punches into the air.

"Good job not letting him get the best of you. I'll deal with Jack and the others," Helaku says.

Shaken by his actions, Konway stares at the ground.

"What happened?" Sage asks, returning from the restroom. "Are you okay?" She spots the blood on his clothes.

"Don't worry. It's not his," Mateo says.

"Whose blood?" she asks.

"Todd's." Konway looks up with a glint of sadness.

"I'm terribly sorry this happened. Come by later, and I'll explain everything." Sage runs to get the nearby first-aid kit.

"Damn... You get the victory *and* the girl?" Ruckus cracks open a cold one and continues his drunken revelry.

Konway turns to see Todd sitting up. The bloody face summons a nause-ating shiver from the pit of his being. (What the fuck are you doing? Get a hold of yourself!)

(How much longer can you keep your past a secret?) The Imp-oster chor-tles.

(Should I tell Sage? Helaku? No—what am I saying?)

(You can't even control yourself. How will you protect them?) The Imp-oster's crusty red lips curl into a cursive snarl.

(Will I ever be able to atone for my past?)

Unable to quell the whispers and fearful of what else he might do, Konway slips out of the Longhouse while Ruckus and Mateo bicker about rolling a joint. Helaku notices but remains silent, quietly twisting up a fine spliff. As Konway reaches the landing beyond the surfboard fence, the totem's first tendrils rise into the updraft.

Powder Keg

Later on, an orange-striped cat lingers along a window-lit balcony railing. Behind the parted blackout curtain, Jack tosses a pack of frozen peas onto Todd, who lies sprawled on the couch. A one-third-full bourbon bottle sits next to him, accompanied by a two-thirds-full ashtray of cigarette butts.

"Nice work back there. Although, I didn't think you'd get whooped this badly," Jack's drawl slyly pulls the strings.

"You wanted it to look believable." He whinges from the internal bruises and public humiliation he suffered for the greater good of Jack's plan: de-throning Helaku, and the promise of reuniting with Sage.

"Have you seen a mirror? He beat the brakes off of you. Sheesh! Luckily, he didn't kill you." Jack swigs from a local small-batch IPA—so rare, they only sell a four-pack. He knows a guy who knows one of the crew at Peninsula Brew Co. "Boy, you're a mess. But this'll make it extra believable. It'll be easy to spin this to gain more favor among the other tribes."

"That's what I was saying," Todd mumbles.

Jack doesn't hear his stoolie's marble-mouthed remarks, lost in schemes and devices to claim a land that was never his.

After checking in, Jack returns to his seat by the bondfire and takes two key bumps of coke from the corner of a sandwich baggie. In the backdrop, the frogs resume their chorus, echoing over the last smoldering embers. His pupils dilate to the size of saucers as he fantasizes about his plans to become chief of Laniakea.

(Gotta call the boys on Monday and update them. I know they'll pay a pretty penny and carve out a nice slice for myself. Don't forget the finder's fee for a new tract of land for development.) He does another toot for good measure. (Just imagine the property value. Hell, I'd have enough to purchase the village. I could charge rent and a tax on all goods produced by the tribes—I'll be the big boss.) Jack flashes a shit-eating grin.

Although the black sheep of a socialite family of carpetbaggers, his uncle Samuel Beauregard was willing to lend him some starter funds from a managed trust. Now, with enough capital and local prestige, he hopes to win his grandfather's patronage—set aside for any kin who makes something of themselves.

Sadly, those in the way of Jack's ambitions find themselves pitted against the manipulative maneuvering of his resolve. Mere stepping stones of collateral damage, some never return to Coffin Island. And now, Konway stands in his crosshairs.

59

Fear & Trembling

Sandstorm

Elsewhile, beneath nanites and semiconductors, Zeff wanders under the timeless gray sky, beyond the Mountains of Experience, and follows the [Trifold Tablet] to the nearest resource node.

"How long have I been at this?" he wonders, looking around.

A branch of dead leaves tumbles past, followed by stillness. Fearful of the Fog, and anything else that might try to grind his bones to make their bread, he trudges forward, using the [Lance of Longinus] as a walking stick.

"Where are you leading me?" he asks the tablet in his right hand.

Another gust cuts through.

"Fine, fine," he grumbles, then picks up the pace.

With every step in the right direction, its glow quickens, until he finally crosses into the bones of a withered forest.

Once again at the mercy of the unknown, Zeff scans the crowded brush line before creeping atop a fallen tree. Within the decaying darkness, the pulse persists. He pauses, but the signal continues to ping. Farther into the wilted groves, he finds the node—already mined into a vacant cavity, slowly filling with the forest's rot.

"We've come all this way, and there's nothing here. Why are we doing this?" He stares at the onyx screen. "What's the point?"

In response to the node's proximity, the [Violet Egg] floats from the screen and releases a crystalline shard from the matrix of its moving shell. The seed phrase drifts forward and dips into the soil, tunneling into the ley line below, filing down the sludge, and hollowing out the root stem. Once the cavity is prepared, the facet backfills with indigo light. Its CodeX imprints, and a small purple flower sprouts from the node's grave.

"Now what?" asks Zeff, unimpressed.

It tries to highlight the next location but powers off while scaling its mapping index.

"Great," he scoffs with a crack of contempt. "Hell of a time to shut down." Zeff plants the [Lance of Longinus] into the ground and stows the inoperable device, glancing back at the snoring mountains, then towards the sprawling malaise in his path. "We were heading in this direction." He points at a beige expanse. "I can't go this way." He faces the impassable crag, muttering, "I need to find the next resource node and get you charged up to open the dev-tool kit."

With nothing to guide him other than the last bit of direction from the [Trifold Tablet], the landscape soon shifts from withered to arid as Zeff crosses into a sea of sand, where the tops of dunes resemble the rippling tides of shrinking pools. After passing one dune belt, another set greets him, followed by another, then another—like a conveyor of sedimentary models poised for quality control.

Farther along the altering topography, he discovers a break in a towering sand wall and scales up the windward side to its crest for a better view.

"These aren't normal dunes." He observes the conical rungs of the gradually sloping terrain. "Such a strange pattern... And—something's shining in that depression. Could it be the next node?" His heart fills with a drop of hope.

Suddenly, the ground trembles, sending him tumbling to the bottom with a thud and a groan. He tries standing when the quake abruptly increases into a dust storm. With no time to lament and nowhere to run, he pulls his linen coat over his head, bracing against the howling sands.

Once the ground stills and the storm sinks into silence, Zeff emerges from the crusted cocoon and searches for his lost items. He digs frantically, but uncovers nothing. Standing, he surveys the new dune field and spots the shifting sands around the [Lance of Longinus].

The slope causes more sediment to tumble. To the left, a corner of the tablet emerges and conjures a false memory, constructed from the Donor's youth. Zeff spits at the thought of toothin' before plucking it from the temporary tomb.

He gathers his gear and proceeds towards the shining center of this desert kingdom, now resembling a speaker's diaphragm. Traversing more sand mounds, he reaches the ridgeline and locates the shining source within the barren maze. There, a small brown church sits amidst a vacant cemetery, next to an immense, withered tree. Tangerine gems gleam where moss should cling, while a black fractal scar runs down its trunk into the ground.

"Where's the resource node? And why's that here?" he asks, recognizing the crooked cross from the Donor's memories. A bubble of rage pops under Zeff's tongue, causing him to spit at the sight.

The ground trembles once more, and a dust storm whisks up the dunes surrounding the little brown church.

"Is it the Fog? No—something else," he says, forging ahead, planting the spear into the sand.

Closer, the amount of flying debris increases. Zeff avoids most of it, but catches a tumbleweed with his face a few meters from the church. Its double doors creak open.

He pauses. Suddenly, a flurry of Worry Wraiths—innumerable as the flecks of sand—surges out from the opening and spirals into the eye of the towering earthen cyclone.

"Who am I? Who are you?" they screech above the storm.

Zeff stares into the abyss with a white-knuckled grip on the [Lance of Longinus]. He sighs and inches closer to the scarred tree. There, the gale subsides into the lulled sway of tangerine gemstones, glistening like the chimes on Granny's porch.

He gawks at the sky-high vortex of swirling wind and sand. Another rumble goads the storm into a frenzy. Its cylindrical walls twist into adjacent patterns, more liquid than air.

Geometric tangerines sway with the shifting zephyr. Some lose their hold and launch into a volley of discord. Nearby gravestones crumple on impact, while several outliers batter the dunes.

With nowhere to go, Zeff begrudgingly seeks shelter in the church. At its doors, he hesitates before the unsealed darkness, cautious of entering such a peculiar place of inviting maliciousness.

(The obstacle is the way,) Paw-Paw's words, quoting Aurelius, punctuate the moment.

He spits on the ground and crosses the threshold.

Enter Fear

The double doors slam shut behind him. Zeff turns around just as a rusted bolt locks in place, sealing off the entrance and activating the mechanism of this dark domain. A shiver shoots down his spine.

A creak reverberates from deep within the abbey. He spins back around, leveling the glowing spear against the darkness. Unbeknownst to him, the threshold glides silently down the wall, sinking below the floor.

"Hello? Who's there?" he asks into the unknown.

His words echo endlessly in front of him, rising to the buttresses of darkened ceilings adorned with Renaissance illustrations. Next to a stone cherub—with its middle finger up, one eye closed and tongue sticking out—Fomobious, the Inner Demon of Fear, stirs from its trance.

Something washes back from the void. Zeff dismisses it, ignoring any pre-linguistic reasoning.

It persists. "Curious, Vessel, what are you doing here? It's not time for your arrival... You're not worthy to face me. You don't even believe in yourself. You allow other's opinions to control you. Even your vengeance is merely a reaction... You're the furthest thing from real." Fomobious sniffs the air, its drool puddling onto the floor.

Zeff shudders forward, bumping into a pew. It scuffs the ground, and a cascade of candles dominoes from darkness into light. To his stupefied amazement, the impossible dimensions of an ever-expanding cathedral unfurl before him. No longer luminous with sparkling stained glass, cobwebs and mounds of sand stretch beyond his perceptual horizon.

The demon drifts from shadow to shadow, then stops to watch him gawk in awe at the immensity of its lair. Fomobious flashes a razor-sharp smile. Seconds later, it lurches forward, opens its mouth, and fires a [Sonic Bullet]. The silent force rips a bench apart, embedding splinters into a nearby column.

He dodges backward and narrowly avoids the shrapnel. "Where's the fucking door?!" Zeff examines the flicker-lit brick wall.

"I wouldn't look that way." Fomobious swoops back to its perch and blasts a second [Sonic Bullet] from its fanged jaws.

It instantly gouges a spherical impression into the wall. The demon rushes by and upturns a pew, igniting more floating candles throughout the kaleidoscopic corridor. Without hesitation, Zeff scurries towards a towering stone pillar and hides on the other side.

(This definitely isn't Kansas.) The sarcasm masks his panic as he adjusts his grip on the spear. (How'd it find me?)

"You can't hide, Vessel." The demon swoops by him.

Zeff taunts, "You fucking coward... First fog, now darkness—show yourself!"

"Fog? You must mean my brother, Ramiel. I can't remember the last time I saw the old crab. How did you evade him? Hmm... quite curious indeed." Fomobious lands and glances out a broken window at the timeless gray sky. (What happened to Despair?) The demon's red eyes, pigmented with green pupils, cut back to its guest.

Then, like spitting out a cherry pit, Fomobious releases a [Sonic Barrage] of silent projectiles. The tablet vibrates against Zeff's chest, and he sprints across the aisle. Enthralled by the hunt, the creature continues its assault.

Checkered tiles shatter from the volley of shots as his heels race ahead of their destructive rain. He hangs a left and hurdles a split pew. The demon screams past, giving him enough time to scramble to an adjacent pillar. Near grime-smeared frescoes, Fomobious pings the area with a [Sonic Pulse]. "There!" it shrieks, flapping its wings in rhythm to propel a [Gatling Cyclone] of desolation in Zeff's direction.

A surge of debris billows into the pillar.

(I'm not going out like this. I need to get the fuck out of here... Where will it come from next?)

Its shadow rushes past, and Zeff stabs into the void. He barely misses the beast as it flies to the vaulted ceiling.

"You think that's enough? It's going to take a lot more to defeat me. Why struggle, Vessel? You have no clue how outmatched you are—"

(Vessel? Why is it calling me that?)

"—This is my domain. My church. My palace. No matter where you run or hide, you'll never escape from my Infinite Cathedral!"

The primordial demon flexes its arms above its head, presenting its wings in a cone, and fills its lungs. As its belly swells to ballooning proportions, Zeff spots the bulbous creature perched on the top ledge of a neighboring buttress.

"Is that a giant bat?" He scuttles backward, increasing the distance between himself and an untimely demise.

Fomobious wails, amplified by the conical surface of its wingspan, into a [Subsonic Beam Cannon]. A sickle-shaped blast disintegrates a crescent cut out from a nearby column, sending a gargoyle crashing to the tile. Rows of wooden pews splinter into countless slivers as Fomobious zeroes in on Zeff's hiding spot.

The tablet buzzes, and he bolts down a perpendicular corridor. A few paces behind him, the beam severs a column at its base, choking the air with dust. He races past looming stained-glass windows and unending rows aglow with floating candles. Fomobious takes flight and tracks Zeff's echoing footsteps. After calculating his trajectory, the monstrous bat flaps its wings three times and is above him, primed for its next attack.

False Evidence Appearing Real

High above, Fomobious watches its quarry. "What are you afraid of, Vessel? Failure? Success? Your ceaseless attempts only delay the inevitable. Why do you resist so much? Why aren't you afraid?" (I know—this will make him piss his pants.) The demon closes its eyes and drops from the sky, landing next to him.

The impact flings Zeff into a pile of wreckage where he loses hold of the [Lance of Longinus] and his hope of escape. There in the crater, bathed in a spotlight of pale gray light from above, stands a three-meter-tall demonic bat directing its red stare through the settling dust.

"Give up, Vessel," Fomobious says, stepping onto the checkered tile. Drool sways from its jowls like a pendulum's blade.

(Why does it keep calling me that?) He inches closer to his weapon.

"If that's what you desire, then let me get it for you!" Fomobious reaches back, expanding its belly to unleash a second [Subsonic Beam Cannon].

Zeff scrambles to his feet and sprints away from the spear as the attack follows him, eradicating everything in its path. An adjacent column sustains damage, but holds its position. Zeff circles back to the crater and ducks beneath a cluster of upturned benches.

(Fucking bat! Let's see if this does the trick.) He snatches a handful of rubble and tosses it across the aisle.

Fomobious pinpoints the vibration and unleashes another [Sonic Barrage], causing the air to shiver.

(There must be a limit to how many times it can fire that beam.) Zeff rears back and hurls a larger chunk at a perpendicular pillar.

The beast follows, seeking the decoy with a fervent hunger. "Where are you?" The demon flips over more wreckage and howls, sweeping a splintered torrent into a cyclone of slicing shadows.

The vortex roars towards the back wall and bounces off like a pinball under the watchful gaze of its wizard. Fomobious looks to the right; the twister wombles in pursuit, crossing the aisle before disappearing down a transept of Mandelbrot-forks and alternative altars, adorned with stained-glass iconography and hordes of lewd gargoyles.

Fomobious rises skyward. (Something is off—I need to be more cautious.) Its long ears twitch as the [Sonic Pulse] pings the area. Nothing. "Hide all you want, Vessel. There's no way out." The demon blasts a second wave. Nothing.

Zeff remains still.

"What do you fear? Where's the dread? Where's the trepidation? Don't forget Benghazi... and looking into the eyes of your clone as you stole their light from the world." Fomobious twists its head sideways to focus the bandwidth of its echolocation. "What are you afraid of? The everlasting darkness? The light of success? What would happen if you got your revenge? Mai tais on the fucking beach? Sounds like a postcard, you foolish romantic."

Not taking the bait, he fills the satchel with more rubble. (How does it know me? If I lure it away, I can get back to my weapon.) He launches more rocks.

"What's this?" Fomobious pinpoints them mid-flight and tracks the root of their arc. "Found you."

It draws in another bellyful of air to prime its [Subsonic Beam Cannon]. After a pin-drop silence, the creature howls a malady of destruction. The attack slaps against the wall, leaving a column-wide recess.

Zeff bolts from a pile of wreckage to a nearby pillar. (It'll be on me by the time I make it to the hall. How am I getting out of this? Maybe if I kill this fucker, the door will return... I guess there's no other option.)

To his surprise, within the column's shadow, the [Lance of Longinus] sears a sore into the marble. He crouches low and reaches for it. From the darkness, a swoosh of air crashes into the brick behind him. Zeff grabs the spear and flees in the opposite direction.

Two steps from the pillar's safety, he crow-hops a fistful of debris. The shrapnel bounces past Fomobious. It tracks the decoy. "I've found you, Vessel. Let's see if you can escape this." It rears back, drawing in a larger bellyful.

(Again?!) He bolts, sprinting faster than he ever thought possible.

"[Guillotine Tornado]!" From its demonic howl fused with the shockwave of a thunderous clap, shadow cyclones spawn, spiraling annihilation throughout the Infinite Cathedral. Zeff escapes farther down the hall, and Fomobious follows.

Battle

Another vibration heralds the demon's approach. Zeff hurries along an endless corridor, but it tracks his movements into the advent. He slides between a baptismal font and an altar. Then, on his back, facing the ceiling, he opens the [Trifold Tablet] and swipes for a miracle as the bat's shadow crisscrosses the aisle.

(Why does it keep calling me 'Vessel'? Think. Think... I'm running low on juice. I need to make this count.) He opens the application tab.

[Error: dependencies not found. Run: npm audit fix.]

(Fuck!)

Fomobious unleashes a piercing screech on its next pass, shattering several adjoining pews. Zeff scurries to a nearby pillar. But as he slides into its shadow, the tablet slips from his grip and skids ahead of him. He reaches for it, only to lose sight of the device as the demon continues its sweeping assault.

Round and round, splintered rows of stained glass encircle his location, diminishing any chance of escaping the encroaching void.

(I need to get off the ground.) An idea sparks from the spear's luminous tip.

On the other side, the bat swishes rubble and wreckage into narrow lanes of attrition. Back and forth, it brushes partitions of debris into a coliseum higher than Zeff's current foothold.

It pauses midair and casually flaps its wings. "This should keep you from running... But why don't I sense any fear from you, Vessel? Not the creak in the floorboards, or the cackle from the closet." Fomobious scoffs. "How about being alone? Or the gnawing agitation that you'll never know who you really are?"

"I know who I am," says Zeff with a defiant fire.

Its snarl stretches into a gruesome smile as blood-red eyes bulge with delight. "Lies! You know shit. I've witnessed the tragedy of your truth... This would be so much easier if you just gave up."

"You're ugly as sin, but I'm not afraid of you," he says, notching one foothold up the pillar. "Fear is a product of our imagination."

"Vessel, I am much more than you can comprehend." The beast raises its arms above its head and screams.

The space vibrates violently as gargoyles smash into buttresses, sending them crashing to the floor. Without their supports, portions of the rounded ceiling crumble to reveal the timeless gray sky streaked with distant arcs of neon green.

Suspended between the flaps of its black wings, Fomobious ripples a [Sonic Pulse], highlighting the room and the proximity of its prey's position behind the column. (What are you doing back there? I can't be too cautious with this one. If he killed Despair—) Unwilling to finish the thought, the demon plunges into the abyss for another pass.

Zeff spots a distortion amongst the candlelight preceding the creature's attack. He continues to climb. *Swoosh!* The debris stacks against itself. Meanwhile, he scales higher and higher until he's perched nine meters off the ground. The bat's speed increases. And with each flyby—heaps of devastation, fewer candles, and further darkness.

"You can't hide forever. Once the lights are out, our dance is done."

"I'm right here, you fucking coward!"

Fomobious banks off a column and spirals in his direction. It lands, forming another crater. "Where'd he go?"

Above the dust, Zeff drops from his hold, guiding the [Lance of Longinus] towards the creature's heart. The demon's ears twitch as it turns to face his falling shadow. Flashes from the timeless gray sky illuminate Fomobious's twisted face as the spear impales its right wing, nearly deleting the shoulder from its torso.

(I missed—it's injured, but I missed my mark.) He rolls into a dead sprint, retreating past the nearest debris pile.

A howling anguish shakes the ground, worsening the damage to nearby structures. Then, as the demon removes the [Lance of Longinus], its roar cracks the surrounding foundation. Finally free, it flings the makeshift weapon across the floor. Its glowing tip sinks into the tile, stopping just after its binding.

Fomobious flaps its wing, rising two inches above the ground, but collapses back to the tile. It wails, and the cathedral trembles. Debris tumbles from the ceiling while the cracked column's weight shifts from its base and topples towards the demon.

In an instant, the structure smashes onto the checkered floor, breaking through the coliseum and ensnaring the bat's left wing in the cacophony as it leaps to safety. Another scream reaches the ceiling. And with it, more rubble crashes to the tile. The demon pulls and pulls, but the pillar holds steadfast. Trapped like a flying rat, struggling to free itself, a primal sense of urgency hastens Fomobious into a frenzy.

(I've got to finish this now.) Zeff sneaks closer to the [Trifold Tablet] and squats down to grab it.

To his surprise, the device lunges at him, wrapping around his forearm and solidifying into a wrist guard. Merged with his construct, the [Trifold Bracer] reboots its liquid projection display, priming network parameters to optimize low-effort dependencies within anthropic architectures. He tries to wrench it off, but the CodeX symbiosis is complete.

The demon's ears twitch to movements in the darkness. Desperate to escape, a quickening panic strikes its corrupted heart. Fomobious steps forward and tears the connective tissue in its armpit like a chicken wing on Super Bowl Sunday. The bat wails into the darkness while its partially detached appendage flails on its own. Fearful for the first time in its long existence, the demon inhales, its belly ballooning to obtuse proportions, then blasts the column binding its limb, disintegrating a portion of its torso and a section of the pillar, before slamming into a multi-angled wall in the distance.

Dust fills the arena. In its center, an ominous shadow framed with burning red eyes, asks, "Is this how you bested Ramiel? Is this how you beat my brother?"

Zeff sees an opening in the twelve-meter-high mound of debris and dashes to a better vantage point.

"You put up quite a fight, Vessel... Know this is far from over. This time, I alone will ascend this detestable realm." The demon snorts, clearing its throat and spitting up green bile.

The wall of refuse shifts, like an overstuffed closet, to reveal an exit. Zeff adapts his plan and ducks beneath an upturned altar, wedged between a pipe organ and a headless marble sculpture. He remains hidden, calculating his next course of action.

(At least the beast can't fly—now what? Escape through a window? I need to find my spear.) He looks at his arm. (Why did it attach to me? I know this is the Mind Palace, but—focus, damn it!) He pulls his coat sleeve over the [Trifold Bracer] and grabs a rapier-length plank. (Fucking bat thinks its shit doesn't stink. Just one more shot to end this thing. Both wings are down, but don't underestimate this monster. Maybe attack from above again? No. Fake above, sweep its leg, and stake its heart.) Zeff grins, then, peeking around head-high debris, charts a course closer to the [Lance of Longinus] and the end of Fomobious.

60

Knight

Transform

Fomobious's howl summons its minions from their feeding grounds. Outside, a black cloud of flapping wings swarms the little brown church. As their terrible screeching deafens the advent, a thousand stained-glass windows shatter with a flood of Worry Wraiths, blocking the timeless gray sky.

Zeff stumbles to his knees. (This isn't good. Get up!) He struggles to stand against the trembling, forced to bear witness to the true face of fear.

The coliseum goes dark, save for the remaining candles on the outskirts of the maelstrom. A tornado of dark energy lifts Fomobious into the air. One by one, then all at once, the Worry Wraiths smother the demon en masse. When the last one liquefies into a writhing onyx womb, the winds quiet, and the moment stills.

Fomobious's circumfused birth chamber instantly hardens into a jagged, multi-angled gem, with arcs of black lightning cascading along its surface. While the chrysalis spins with Fear's amorphous form, the [Trifold Bracer] affixed to Zeff's arm glows. In a heartbeat, the crystal shatters in a burst of stupefied amazement.

The force flings the [Lance of Longinus] into a chunk of pillar near the break in the rubble. Unlike the dread he felt in the Fog's presence, Zeff regains his footing and sprints to the weapon. En route, fresco frameworks crumble to the checkered floor, revealing more of the timeless gray sky. The bracer buzzes; he dodges—again and again.

At the coliseum's heart, pale light bathes Fomobious's up-cycled form: an armor-clad knight adorned with spiked pauldrons and a stained-glass cape. Around it, jagged onyx shards—remnants of the demon's cocoon—spiral in concentric circles, summoning wild vortices. The tempests slice through wide columns, toppling them onto the chessboard before disappearing beyond the veil of sight. As fragments coalesce in front of the knight, they spawn a batwing claymore writhing with dark energy.

Zeff finally reaches his spear and pulls it from the debris.

"Your weapon will never penetrate my armor," the demon jeers.

Green flashes from the timeless gray sky reflect off its form-fitting helm. Fomobious swings the batwing claymore, and beneath the sheen of its bleak blade, a storm of Worry Wraiths releases a [Darkness Slash] in Zeff's direction. Gaining in size, it cleaves across the aisle. The bracer vibrates, and he artfully dodges as the attack decimates the cloister of gothic statues behind him.

A spiral of black lightning diffuses down the rivets in the knight's armor. "My, my... such a delectable stench." It cackles. "Does my form frighten you? I should've led with this from the start... but toying with you will tincture your essence with my favorite spice. What do you fear?"

"Nothing!"

"Everyone fears something. Not being accepted? Not being loved? Not being real?"

"Fuck you—I am real!"

The dark knight's stained-glass cape flows behind it. "What if you never get your vengeance? Do you think you'll ever escape this place? Even if you somehow surpass me, one of the others will up-cycle you, Vessel."

"Others?" Zeff tightens his grip on the spear. (How many more of these bastards are there?)

"You know so little for someone so confident."

"Got to fake it till you make it. Let's dance, motha-fucka!" Zeff charges at Fomobious with the shining lance leading his cause.

Face Everything And Rise

Fomobious swoops in front of Zeff and swings the batwing claymore, unleashing another [Darkness Slash]. More sickles of destruction slice towards him. The bracer stirs with another notification, and he leaps over the attack, narrowly avoiding the razors' edge as they carve throughout the Infinite Cathedral.

High in the air, Zeff aims between the demon's pauldron and breastplate. "Now I've got you," he says, and plunges to the tile.

The knight [Shadow Steps] out of the way. "Don't take me for a fool, Vessel. Your lame tricks won't work," it says, then flails more slivers of darkness.

Another notification. Zeff ducks under the assault, but one slice slams into the bracer, cutting into his sleeve. Its liquid screen glows, devouring the attack and increasing the power bar by one notch.

(Is this why you were buzzing? Maybe with a few more, you could finally be of some use.) Zeff hatches a plan.

(How'd he absorb it?) Fomobious goes on the defensive, asking, "Is that the best you have? Surely, it took more than a game of leapfrog to defeat my brother."

"The creep in the fog? Never met him," Zeff replies, trying to quell the uneasiness of those burnt-yellow eyes. (I need to focus.) He looks at the enormous toppled column stretching across the advent to a broken window. (If I can get to open ground, I might have a chance.) He maneuvers closer to an escape.

"Not that way." A wicked glimmer glistens from behind the demon's visor. "This should keep you from running."

Fomobious's stained-glass cape flows backward, and from its cosmic quilt, a multiplicity of corresponding chains shoot into the tile floor. Several meters ahead, they emerge and rapidly crisscross into a paralyzing [Lattice of Fear].

"Don't let them touch you," taunts the knight, followed by a maniacal cackle.

(Almost there. Just a little further.) Zeff hurdles striations of debris.

The [Trifold Bracer] alerts him to the chains' proximity. He dodges most of them. Alas, his reflexes fall short of the demon's prowess, and one catches him in the right shoulder as he uses the bracer to absorb an attack from the opposite direction. Meat-hooks grip into his rotator cuff, immobilizing him. Zeff screams in agony.

"Ahh, the sweet sound of pain—I never tire of it. But you need more time to marinate."

Before the pain poisons his heart, Zeff uses the [Lance of Longinus] to sever the fetter. The piece connected to his arm soon dissolves into dust. (I can kill this bastard.) The bracer's purple aura purges the darkness from his construct.

Another [Lattice of Fear] extends from the checkered tile. Zeff leaps backward onto the felled column as chains whip and whirl into a single pointed spiral. He raises his forearm and absorbs the drill's impact. Dark energy flails about, nudging the bracer's power supply up another notch.

"Almost enough." He holds against the attack.

In time, the overwhelming force knocks Zeff off the column, onto his back.

Fomobious inhales, swirling air through the vents of its helm, its expanding belly compressed within the onyx armor. Black lightning traces across the knight's torso. "[Wraith Vortex]!!" Its visor snaps open, unleashing a supersonic howl.

With each flail of its deathly claymore, the banshee's wail strengthens into a crackling cyclone, then surges at Zeff. In its wake, the knight [Shadow Steps] closer to the end of their dance. (Once I consume this one, I'll be strong enough to devour the others and be free from this hell.)

"Shit... I won't make it." Zeff blocks with his left arm.

The attack passes overhead, and the bracer's onyx screen wakes to consume the twister. A crosshair icon blinks on its taskbar as Fomobious appears above and draws in another bellyful.

(I don't want to die here. Not like this... not on my back.) Zeff fumbles with the user interface to activate the [Deconstructor Beam].

Another press delays the logged commands. Then, carrying out its current function, the [Trifold Bracer] releases the stored tornado—imbued with violet energy—into the cathedral's ceiling. It slams into Fomobious, sending the demon soaring backward into a fresco rendition of the foothills, where it explodes onto the timeless gray sky.

"I got 'em... I finally got that monster." Zeff looks at his arm, draped in shredded linen.

The tempest thins to wisps, and his brief reprieve evaporates as the knight's floating outline appears in the opening.

"Not bad, Vessel. I knew I shouldn't have gone easy on you... I'll finish you with this next attack."

Fomobious's armor cracks and crumbles as dark energy ribbons along the fissures, suturing the damaged pieces into place. Its cape splits down the middle and shatters, shifting the structure of its torso to reveal a set of resplendent wings and several swaying fetters. The batwing claymore triples in size. Then, like rose vines running across Granny's cyclone fence, the chains braid together, wrapping around the weapon and up-cycling into [Doomcleaver]—a gigantic halberd with one end resembling a harpoon and the other an axe-edged pendulum.

Zeff scrambles to his feet, grabs the luminous spear, and flees.

"Tremble with FEAR!" Fomobious roars.

The vents on the backside of its armor engage, rocketing the demon knight straight to the ground, shattering the checkered floor into the void below. With the rug pulled, Zeff drives the [Lance of Longinus] into the stone pillar and holds on for dear life.

Fomobious, now a great winged shadow, soars amongst the descending wreckage. Closer and closer, it effortlessly carries [Doomcleaver] in one hand. Banking off the rubble, its shimmering wings dazzle amidst the pearl of the abyss.

After plummeting for a considerable distance, the free fall slows. Above him, a huge chunk of tile collides with another platform, sending both spiraling off course.

"Shit, shit, shit… How am I supposed to do this?" (How can I possibly beat this thing?) "Focus. I need to activate the [Deconstructor Beam]. If I can hit its armor with the spear, then the beam, I might kill it." (Fuck, I'm in a bit of a bind. I wish Ben were here… Will I ever see Annah, or the others?)

"My, oh my…" Saliva drips from the knight's helm. "Your stench is exquisite. Maybe I'll start with your legs and drain the marrow. Or carve you into choice cutlets. The options are endless. Although I've never had the pleasure of dining on your kind's essence, you're the first to resist this much. Now, you're all mine."

(Does he mean the other clones?)

Soon, Fomobious pinpoints Zeff's position and rushes past several slow-falling platforms.

The [Trifold Bracer] vibrates with the knight's approach.

(I'm never going to leave this place, feel the sun on my skin, or Annah in my arms. I'll never get the vengeance promised by the Promethean Flame… My life was for nothing.) The deluge twists a knot in his stomach. However, instead of breaking down, he marshals a response and faces the inadequacy of his existence.

Thoughts laced with manic associations carry him into realms of dread, failure, and death. He grapples with the madness of being a clone with false memories—a murderous puppet for clandestine agencies, responsible for all the lives he has taken since being thawed. Beyond the angst of never meeting his fabricated family lies the pain of every argument he ever had—with his team, with Annah—and all the hurtful things he said or did to himself.

Enraged, Zeff stands in defiance, shouting, "Come and get me, bat! Unlike your armor, I won't crack so easily. And if I am to die here today, it will be on my feet. *AMOR FATI!*" Zeff cries in the face of fear.

Finale

Fomobious increases its speed, narrowing the gap between them, and aims [Doomcleaver] at Zeff's rock. A wake of devastation blossoms as the demon knight darts across the void, smashing through massive, drifting fragments of the cathedral's floor.

"It's now or never." Zeff taps the [Trifold Bracer].

Two clicks into the first menu, the device freezes. He taps it again. A glitch flickers, snapping back to the home screen, where the [Violet Egg] icon rotates in the upper taskbar. He presses it—nothing.

Resigned to his fate, Zeff clutches his weapon and sprints to the platform's edge, where he vaults above the brink, soaring into the abyss. The [Lance of Longinus] shines gallantly towards the dark knight. They collide—and the spear shatters.

(Where'd he go?) Fomobious fails to discern Zeff's movements as he bounds off the glaive and awkwardly lands on a smaller platform.

Stumbling over half a pew wedged beneath a fractured relief, he turns and regains his footing, but the demon is at his doorstep. Zeff flinches in the face of fear and the depth of his inadequacy, arms shielding his face—vain to the end.

Meanwhile, primed by broken protocols and one too many taps on an interface icon, the [Trifold Bracer] flares, illuminating the void with a purple aura. Fomobious's armor crackles with darkness energy as the [Deconstructor Beam] rips from Zeff's left forearm, cutting past the fear, uncertainty, and doubt.

The beam's brilliance intensifies as the purple glow feasts upon the demon's hex code—splitting [Doomcleaver], the form-fitting helm, and the spiked armor down the middle. Divided halves streak past Zeff, bathing him in the demon's blood before slamming into a cluster of rubble and wreckage with a wet thud.

Plummet

While Zeff settles into celebration, a piece of debris crests by him.

"I'm still falling... well, sinking, at this rate," he quips, hoping to calm the exhilaration of facing Fomobious, the Inner Demon of Fear, and summons the build window. This time, he successfully deploys the Snap-Brix scaffolding from a logged [.json] file.

On recall, a column of plastic bricks sprouts from the falling chunk of foundation and impales a gargoyle into the ceiling's hidden eaves. The platform slows, like a broken-down gondola at a discount ski resort, suspended above a seemingly limitless chasm.

He looks at the divided corpse just long enough to direct the [Violet Egg] to scan Fomobious's felled form. On completion, the artifact launches another facet. It floats towards the halves, hovers for a moment, then dips into the ground.

The seed phrase finalizes its upload, and amethyst vines—resembling luminescent fetters rather than flora—sprout, ensnaring the demon's crystal core with piercing calculations. More chains braid and stretch, bridging the two halves. Sufficiently wrapped, they constrict and absorb the fluid leaking from its body. Tightening together, the vines pull the last remnants of Fomobious beneath the tile. There, the grout radiates as the demon's jewel integrates with the [Violet Egg].

After the CodeX update chimes its completion, a lilac light breaches through the facet's burrow and blossoms into a floating purple crystal flower, more rose than snapdragon. The bracer buzzes, drawing his attention to its screen.

"That's a relief," Zeff says with a hint of joy, realizing his clothes are repaired. He rolls up his linen jacket sleeves and notices a shining crossed-swords silhouette beside the rotating egg icon. "What's this?" Zeff selects it.

A pop-up screen illuminates. At its center, an onyx sword slowly rotates in a showcase. Below it, a floating sign reads: [Mind Slayer]. As he reaches for the [Equip] button, the blade forms in his hand.

He feels the sword's weight, then swings it, releasing a [Darkness Blade]. An onyx, cross-shaped wave wrapped in violet disintegrates an enormous pile of tile before sailing into the abyss. "Now, this is what I'm talking about." He swings it again and again, but the battery indicator reduces, and the sword shatters into obsidian shards and dematerializes.

"Hmm... There's still a charge... I might not have enough... I need to find more juice... But first, I need to get out of here." Zeff glances at the towering Snap-Brix scaffolding stretching up to the cathedral's distant ceiling. The moment he contemplates climbing it, the plastic bricks retract, and the platform rises from the unyielding void to the main level.

Above, lances of light from the timeless gray sky beam down onto the wake of devastation. Near the top, mounds of destruction, once cloaked in darkness, bear witness to the battlefield's silence. The platform reaches the remnants of the checkered floor and locks into place. Beyond the Infinite Cathedral's crumbling walls, green lightning pulses over the distant Ruined City, cemented atop a rotting stump at the center of this nightmarish realm.

61

Intervention

Aftermath

Konway suppresses his fear of being kicked out of Laniakea and stares off into the star-spangled marsh. With the last light of the smoldering fire, and the villagers cozy behind closed doors, he ascends the steps to Sage's porch. The first wisps of lavender and incense overtake the warm night air. Near the top, the bouffée halts his creeping strangulation of shame and despair, like a screen door on a humid evening. Above the branches, the sky opens up, reminding him of star-filled lessons with Paw-Paw.

On the canvas of her apartment door, Geoffrey, the giraffe-headed surfer, shreds down a towering wave. He knocks, and several thumping movements later, the entrance swings open with the allure of comfortability—a stark contrast to the lingering angst of violence.

"I was beginning to think you weren't going to show up," Sage says, pulling Konway inside her apartment. Then, jumping into his arms, she kicks the door closed as her legs wrap around him, and the lovers twirl to the center of her living room.

"What's all this about?" he asks, still a bit shaken from the fight with Todd. "Aren't you scared of me?"

Sage steps down from his hold and tenderly cups his face. "Why would I be afraid of you? You saved me from that snake. And you sure as shit saved Todd's life. You were drunk, and he attacked you—it was self-defense." Her compassionate smile melts the [ICE-burg] defenses surfacing beneath the brow of his Mind Palace. "How about this—roll us a joint, nice and big," she says, booping his nose, "and I'll put on something cozy."

A slow grin eases the melancholy etched on Konway's face. Once he finds her stash, he sets to his task. The familiarity softens his heart, a quiet reminder that she remains his anchor in this unfamiliar and fragile world.

Smittens

Sage's cat bounds from the bedroom and dives on top of a crinkly toy, nimbly-bimbly rolling into the center of the living room. Smittens subdues her quarry atop a pile of tissue paper. Konway rubs his fingers together.

The feline purrs to the sultry jazz and leaps to her paws. After a stretch, she trots closer and nudges her head against his shin. Looking up at him with deep saucer eyes, she waits for head scratches and chin rubs.

While Sage fumbles around in her bedroom, a saxophone be-bops from the soundbar. His thoughts turn to Zach and the band. Humming one of their tunes, he gently runs his hands through Smittens's soft fur.

Her crooked tail twitches a thin line of sand along the floor.

"Alright. Time to get down to business," Konway says, wiping his hands and effortlessly spinning up two artisanal cones. (Where are the boys playing tonight? I need to let them know I'm alright.) Campfire memories, raccoons, and the unicorn raft parade past the forefront of his attention.

Smittens saunters back to her favorite piece of tissue paper, licks her paw, then ambles to her food dish for a nibble.

He envisions teeming crowds caught in the sway of the Jam. The last he had heard from Ruckus, the boys were playing at the pirate bar, La Princessa Sanguina, before hitting the road to promote their upcoming album, *Sphyramid*. (I can't wait to see them again.)

Several crunching, lapping moments later, the nimble feline trots towards the kitty door to enjoy the evening's reprieve.

"That was quick," Sage says, jumping to her favorite spot on the sofa.

"I was hoping to catch you changing." Konway raises his eyes with a smarmy smirk on his face.

She swings her leg over his lap and straddles him on the couch. "Do you like them?" She looks down at her black shorts, patterned with pixelated rainbow unicorns. "I got these on sale—two pairs. What a deal!"

"They're cute." Konway traces the hemline leading to her thigh and hands her a joint. "Earlier, you mentioned needing to tell me something?"

She chokes on a toke. "No need to ask me so abruptly."

"Apologies. It's just... I punched Todd so many times. Why'd I do that? How do I keep losing control? What's going on with me?"

"Shhh." Sage cuddles up to Konway's distress. "Bear taught me we're not required to be who we were ten minutes ago. We get to choose. This doesn't mean there aren't consequences, but it helped me learn to forgive myself."

"What happened?"

Her eyes dart to the floor. "I had to let go of the guilt I felt for leading Todd and myself down a destructive path... It almost cost him his life."

Konway's face shifts to concern, understanding he's not the only one with a sordid past, and eases the brooding uncertainty about his destiny.

Truth Be Told

Sage drinks from a crystal-clear glass of ice water. Then, gathering her hair from in front of her face, pulls it back into a short ponytail. "I had no business being in a relationship after Alex."

"Helaku's old roommate?"

"Yeah." Her nostril flares.

"How'd you meet?" Konway pulls another lungful of medicine and twirls the cherry into the ashtray, admiring his favorite painting of hers: a transparent wave on a thin wooden sheet, framed with stained driftwood.

Sage slides off his lap and settles on the cushion beside him, tucking her feet under him as she receives the joint. "Well... when I first came to the island—lord, that seems like forever ago—anyway, late one night, after closing down the Rockaway Deli, I was out and about with a few coworkers for a drink at the Surf Bar, a locals-only spot... Then I saw him, across the room. That's all it took. We were thick as thieves after that. I even fell in love with him." She looks out the window, hiding the sadness patched upon her heart.

"I don't mean to pry," Konway consoles her. "I think Helaku mentioned they were roommates—"

"Good riddance... We were arguing. I told him to fuck off and demanded that no man ever speak to me in the way he did. Then, the following day, he left Laniakea. I never got to apologize for the hurtful things I said that night. It tore me up."

"What was the fight about?" Konway asks.

"Something dumb... spending more time together... I might have been pushing too hard. But with all his hobbies and responsibilities—on top of being the next elected Chief of Laniakea—Alex was taking on more, and I was seeing him less and less."

Sage passes the joint to Konway. "Anyway, I was heartbroken, blah-blah-blah... I was trying to forget Alex with the help of some friends. It was late, and we'd been raging all day with a mixed bag of characters—musicians, pirates, tourists. By the time Amber and I met up with Bhodi and the rest of the goons, Todd was striking out all over Surf Bar. I was horny, and he was there. A lucky day for him." She rolls her eyes and sighs. "I didn't know he would get so attached to me. It was toxic, but we were having fun—or at least I was. Todd was getting a little too serious. And the next thing I know, he wanted me to move in with him."

"Did you?"

"I fended him off, but he kept the party rolling. Sadly, we got fucked up on a long, sloppy bender. I knew it couldn't last. So I pumped the brakes."

"What happened?" Konway takes a toke.

"He was beyond heartbroken, and in his infinite sadness, he almost OD'd on heroin. Aside from the taste of vomit, nothing tastes worse than unrequited love." Sage shakes her head at the memory. "I did that. I almost caused—"

Konway settles the joint in the ashtray and turns to console her.

"I'm fine." Sage withdraws a lingering tear. "I hate what I did... I preyed on his desire, so I could chase the next high to numb the pain in my heart and the ache in my soul... Anyway, Helaku was Alex's closest friend. He said I could go to him if I ever needed anything. Helaku might've panicked when I told him everything, but his heart was in the right place.

"He called for an emergency intervention. I got clean. But Todd never lost the darkness that almost took his life on one of those withdrawal-filled nights. After everything, I closed my heart off... until the day I saw you walking into the village—no name and all.

"Something about you made me want to connect for the first time in a while." Sage slowly fans her legs open and unseals her thighs. Past the veil of her sleep shorts, a glimpse of heaven reveals itself in a flash of seductive poetry. "Now I have you all to myself."

"I can see why you'd feel some responsibility for Todd."

Rapt with emotion, they give in to the moment and canoodle each other. Konway tears up at the tenderness, wanting it to last. Sage dries his eyes.

An atmospheric pop sends Smittens back through the kitty door, into the kitchen, straight to her water bowl. Her delight purrs off the linoleum as water droplets lap onto her chin. She nibbles on the last morsels of her treats, sliding the saucer across the floor. Once licked clean, the feline disappears into the pantry.

The lovers soon settle into the latest episode of the hit series, *Modern Values*, where the previous season is now available on a different streaming platform. Outside, the gods bowl for the highest score. Crashing frames weave residual arcs of lightning throughout the heavens and scatter fractal reflections onto the mirroring marsh.

Dreamwind Studios

A wild nightmare escapes from Morpheus's stables. Konway walks across a bloodstained room into the Longhouse, its walls dripping with the sins of the past. His footprints lead to a lone figure mired in fog. A pair of burnt-yellow eyes opens to reveal the contours of Todd's face. Twisted by the Imp's malicious gleam, he charges at Konway like a wild boar.

Behind Todd, a seam three times his height opens and absorbs the fabric of his experience. There, Childe's blurry face peers from the abyss. Konway tries to move, but stands motionless amidst the dripping room.

From adjacent portals, grotesque tentacles flail from fractured frames and smash the surrounding ground. Todd attacks with brass knuckles of corrupted violence, snarling and drooling with every landed blow.

Curled on the floor, Konway absorbs each impact. He struggles to his feet. *Swoosh!* A slimy punch rushes past, smashing the floor beside him. His eyes glow with a violet crackle as he avoids a slicing whip attack, deflecting the debris and punching shotgun blasts of wreckage into the briny beast. He locates Todd and hurdles a sweeping flail. One after another, the homunculus's tentacles crash into the floor. Sliding, leaping, vaulting, he avoids another coordinated volley, finally reaching his target.

Blow after blow, his fists connect. Todd's shit-eating grin widens into a jagged smile as Konway turns his head into smashed potatoes. He stops the onslaught and gawks at his distorted hands.

On the floor, a pair of claws reaches out from Todd's mouth, peeling flesh from bone, until a monstrous being casts him aside like a fresh molt. Konway tries to stand but cowers under the drooling awfulness.

"Move—move, motherfucker!" He champions the strength to break the sleep paralysis before it reaches him, then flees in the opposite direction, down a dripping corridor of flickering fluorescent lights, where another Todd rises from the puddled floor. End over end, he stumbles and loses his way.

The hallway's tortuous beat breaks into birdsong surrounding an impossibly large oak tree within the Horseshoe. Along one path, then a zig to another, towards a picture-pattern door. The gloom nears.

Through the threshold, the doorway shatters in a chrysalis of color, blocking the shadow's path. On one side, burnt-yellow eyes; on the other, the rubble and wreckage of a science lab. At the center, a Vision Shard renders the scene from Zeff's last mission atop Mauna Kea, where he piles the corpses of scientists onto a tarp for the Clean-up Crew. Konway watches the calm cruelty and weeps in his sleep, his sobs filling the theatre at Dreamwind Studios.

He reaches for Sage and rests his arm around her waist. She snuggles closer and pulls him from the darkness into a tranquil flight. Cuddled, he finally drifts into the listless realm of thought, where lost languages glide on the rails of glossolalia, conversing within ciphered logics and arbitrage.

Wake

The following morning, the lovers snooze beneath sandy sheets. Despite the oscillating fan in the corner, the room smolders from the fires of their late-night passions and the remnants of an evening spent in the amorous embrace of intersubjective ecstasis. Outside, roosters crow, signaling a return from the Sandman's realm. A brood of hens scrambles about the barnyard, clucking and pecking, waiting for food to fill the void left by rocks in their bellies.

A hurried knock rattles the front door.

"It's Mary—I'm sorry to wake you. I have something urgent to tell you." She continues knocking.

Sage rolls her eyes. "Hold on. I'm coming." She turns and kisses Konway on his nose.

Still resting from the rounds of Irish whiskey, late-night sex, nightmarish dreamscapes, and the lingering disappointment of losing control, he barely feels her leave his side.

After fetching her sleep shorts, she throws on his light-yellow t-shirt with a doodled crab on the back and ballets towards the front door. On the other side, Sage finds a look of sadness stenciled across Mary's face.

"Is it Todd? Is he alright? What happened?"

"Todd's fine." Mary puts her hand on Sage's shoulder.

He stirs upon hearing the name.

"It's about Rocky—"

"Alex? What's he doing? Is he here? Don't care if he is, either way." She casts her usual sarcastic smile to protect herself from the world's bleakness.

"Sage... I hate to tell you this, but... Rocky's plane went down somewhere over the Caribbean Sea last week."

"Who'd you hear that from?"

"Helaku just got off the phone with his mom. They haven't found his plane or his body yet... Sage, I'm sorry. I'm so terribly sorry."

The shock washes from her face. "Let me know when they find his plane."

"Sage, I'm serious… Rocky is gone. We're having a paddle-out ceremony after the wake. If you ever need to talk, don't hesitate," Mary reassures her.

"I'm fine… thank you." She buries the burning tears in her emerald-green eyes beneath a smile. Her nostrils flare from the flames of suppression.

"I'll text you the details for the paddle-out once they're finalized. Call me later." Mary gives her a heartfelt hug, then turns to distribute the somber news to the other villagers.

Refusal

The door closes. Sage turns to Konway with tears hanging along the trestles of last night's eyeliner. She straightens her posture, takes a deep breath, and dabs away the pain.

"That bastard ain't dead." A fierce look pounces from her gaze. "It would take a lot more to—" she sniffles back a drop of emotion, overflowing from the brick-and-mortar of its casing.

Still taken aback by last night's violence, Konway instinctively shifts topics, asking, "What's a paddle-out?"

"It's a way to honor those who've died." Sage regains her composure. "Even though you didn't know him, you're still a member of Laniakea." Another tear slides down her soft, sun-kissed cheek. "Besides, it'll be an excellent day for a celebration. Merry-Death-Day-To-You." She bows.

A saxophone billows into the conversation from her soundbar. Held within its melodic cadence, fluttering pad-presses, and controlled breathing, their soul amplifies into a language for all to hear. A trombone responds, sliding back and forth, as pistons pipe into position. Together, a harmony of brass echoes inside the pocket groove of expression.

62

Paddle-Out

Cabin Fever

A seasonal storm settles over the Lowcountry, halting Rocky's memorial. Canned with melancholy, cabin fever stews within Laniakea's surfboard fence. The villagers itch themselves up a tree as they yearn for a drip of stoke and a drop of the ocean. Soon, a contagious want for elsewhere fuels a fervor of hedonism. Alcohol, sex, cannabis, binge-watching shows, Longhouse drum circles, reading, video games, and crafts—all pale in comparison.

The leaves are the first to hear the shifting storm. Under dawn's glory, the thunderheads settle their ten-pin tournament with a draw and decide to reconvene at a more inconvenient time during the week. Nearby, in one of Coffin Island's roadside drainage ditches, an army of frogs subsides its late-night praises into dripping water droplets, allowing trees full of songbirds to crank up the overture of daybreak.

Several sullen villagers, dressed in their Sunday's best, head towards the crushed seashell parking lot. Most are present, shuffling around conversations of everydayness, waiting for the shuttle to the memorial service. While the day's heat climbs in accord with the cicada symphony, a pack of pups races through the puddled parking lot, spattering mud as they gallop along the bamboo border.

Concealed inside Sage's apartment, her emerald eyes stare through a part in the blackout curtains as she sorts the confines of her thoughts, littered with sticker-covered albums and tipped-over hope chests. She resists the idea that Alex no longer roams the mortal plane, rolls over, nestling closer to Konway's bare, muscular chest, and presses her lips to his neck, wishing to strike the ache from her heartstrings.

Glittering Day

After the clarity of climax and a bowl of berries-n-granola, the lovers rendezvous with a few volunteers on the beach, where they prepare the site for Rocky's farewell with pop-up canopies and flip-out tables. Underneath the much-needed shade, refreshments and snacks rest on palm-woven table mats. A few tents over, an electric crackle echoes from a robust set of speakers as Mr. Beastly, a local DJ, plugs their equipment into a portable solar generator.

"I thought this was a day to mourn?" Konway hoists a stack of beach chairs onto his shoulders. "It looks like we're having a party."

"Think of it as both," Sage says. "It'll be a day of food, music, and fellowship. Afterward, I'm sure there'll be something around the ole bondfire." She flashes a glint of protective sarcasm and turns towards the Atlantic to avoid shedding a tear in front of Konway.

A scurry of sandpipers flies past, maneuvering with one mind. They hit the ground and peck into the warm, wet sand, hunting for sustenance beneath the flecks and rolled fragments of crustacean corpses. A wave sloshes in and, without breaking rhythm, they skip away from the shimmering surf. Out of nowhere, a yellow-nosed albatross splashes into a small tide pool. *Zip!* The itty-bitty creatures take flight.

The Oros system hiccups, engaging an interlaced matrix of malfunctioning biological circuitry. Nanites mix a freshly shaken neurochemical cocktail, delivering a beetle-squirt of [Prime] throughout Konway's physiology. A moment of vividity and unparalleled richness strikes as a dried palm frond, rattling with sand, tumbles into the receding tide. Along the nakedness of the speckled shore, the sun notches north, glittering the beach with contrasting plays of light and shadow—reminiscent of a lost Remington SL3 typewriter, or a toothy hillbilly in a corncob eating contest.

Vengeful Promise

Shortly after the setup crew finishes their final touches, the tribes arrive, followed by friends and family. One by one, they line their surfboards in the sand. Nearby, Paul Buzzbee's drone hums overhead and records all one hundred eighty boards resting on the beach.

Konway enjoys a can of coconut water with Ruckus, Mateo, and some folks from Surf-Pro when he sees Todd hobbling through the sand. Although his bruises are deep purple, the swelling around his face is healing.

"One second. I've got to make this right." Konway excuses himself from the conversation, trots across the sand, and extends his hand, saying, "Look, man... I'm extremely sorry. I was drunk, you were drunk, and things got a little out of hand the other night."

"You could say that... I know I shouldn't have mixed my medicines with alcohol, but look at my face." Todd stares with blank, prescription-glossed eyes and a lingering taste of iron, pointing at the plumpness of his cheeks.

"Let me make it up to you," Konway says.

"No need. You beat me fair and square." Todd initiates the village handshake, muttering with a marbled mouthful, "This isn't over."

The words bounce down a spiralling set of steps and land on the desk of a most deplorable creature with burnt-yellow eyes as it scrawls its signature at the bottom of a list of names.

(What the hell was that about? Maybe he's going to come at me when I'm least expecting it. Whatever comes, I will accept my fate.)

(Will you?) asks the Imp-oster, tapping its claw on the Bone Throne's armrest.

(Who are you? Who am I?) a Worry Wraith screeches within a crumpled birdcage.

The Imp-oster backhands the coop, sending it violently spinning around the iron arch of its bent stand. (Kill him. Before he gets you. It's simple—survival of the fittest.) It smiles, twisting its crusty red lips into a grotesque display. Smoky tendrils rise towards the broken blades of a ceiling fan, slow-churning with the Fog of Despair.

Konway shakes away the ANTs, depositing the request into the circular-file-13, and instead focuses the spotlight of his attention on the fear of being cast from Laniakea.

Praise

Todd releases their embrace and feigns a broken smile. As he lumbers through the sand, hobble-stomping towards the shade of a pop-up canopy, several villagers rush to his side.

"There goes ole McTurtle," Mateo spackles a dollop of zinc on his nose.

Helaku clasps Konway with the village greeting. "Boy, you did a number on him."

"I didn't know it was that bad." Konway winces at the consequences of his actions.

"He'll heal... He shouldn't have come at you. But next time, could you spare a few punches, Ali?"

"More like Bruce Lee." Ruckus sends a couple playful rope-a-dopes into Helaku's side.

He fends off Ruckus's shadow assault, then says, "I spoke with the Council and explained everything. Luckily, there are bylaws to address moments of self-defense. However, there was a strong push from Jack and Julian to get you kicked out, raising the usual banners of safety, security, and blah-de-blah."

"Typical Jack." Sage shakes her head, sliding into the conversation.

"Am I getting kicked out?" Konway's heart quickens with angst.

"No worries, bro. I've got you." Helaku beams a reassuring smile.

Ruckus digs his feet into the sand. "I don't know why you put up with them. Todd's the worst. Have you thought about transferring to another tribe?"

"I won't abandon family... Plus, the other tribes can handle what I bring to the table." Sage winks at Konway.

His attention shifts to the strength and beauty of her smile and the playful kindness of belonging. Konway clears the cobwebs left from the Fog of Despair with a salty, sea-blown inhale, followed by twenty-one internalized gratitudes. He holds his breath and sends the affirmations along the interwoven filaments of his Mind Palace. A nanogram of dopamine arcs across the neurosis hanging on his shoulders. He exhales and returns to the shoreline's splendor.

A colony of gulls stops to bathe in an oblong tide pool. A short distance away, artisans from Beach-Sweeper-Social-Club paint interpretive patterns on handcrafted canvases. Each, with their own style and flair, renders a memorial of the moment with brushstrokes dipped in the pigment of the everlasting.

Mary and a few others distribute homemade leis from a repurposed cardboard box. The attendees slide the florals over their heads, then grab their boards from the line. Together, they slip beneath the surf like dolphins, paddling past the break, gathering, and holding hands to form a wreath of surfboards in the ebbing Atlantic.

Gift Of Life

Forty-two pelicans ribbon onto the morning sky. Paul Buzzbee's drone, linked to his surf watch, hovers into position. It adjusts its recording distance for the best playback experience, focusing the lens of its HROX30 camera on Stewart Hawthorne as he floats into the middle.

"Let's have a moment of silence and create some space in our hearts to honor our big bro, Alex Rocko—Rocky, as most of you knew him," Stewart says with a smile of solemn reflection.

The rushing sound of the shore blends with their sniffling reverence, while nine seabirds squawk past the flotilla.

Stewart raises his head and opens his eyes. "I see some of you with tears today. And that's alright. I've shed many over the loss of our dear brother. Let us not dwell on his passing, but focus on the fondness and love we share for him... Rocky reminded us of a time when adventure beckoned, before the world dyed us in certain shades of eight-to-five. More so, he inspired us to believe in ourselves." Stewart releases two small tears, but fails to restrain the flood of memories from the adventures they shared and the good times they created.

A well-timed rooster-crow cuts across the water.

"Rocky would approve," Stewart says comfortingly. "Like the waves, we rise; we fall. This is the process of our existence; this is the way nature glides us towards the shore."

A sigh of serendipity sweeps underneath the ceremony.

Stewart continues, "The greater question is not what happens to us after death, but what will we do with the gifts of this life?"

This time, a villager's wolf-howl rises above the ocean's drone. Soon, the whole flotilla joins in, with all the tribes crying out as one. Stewart shifts back into the group of speakers, applauding as Lynn, noticing MoMo is too upset to speak, takes to the center.

Lynn's Poem

She pulls her silver-streaked autumn ponytail over her shoulder. "It is such a blessed and lovely day to be here with all of you. I remember when Rocky first came to the village. He had stars in his eyes and saw greatness in the world." She pulls a folded piece of paper from her swimsuit. "Last night, I was up late thinking about him. And after replaying some of our conversations around the bondfire, I remembered he loved jazz and poetry. So, I wrote a poem in his honor... I hope you don't mind," Lynn says, then finds her place amongst crossed-out lines.

It's a jazzy hither, or two;

from one key to the next beat,

sliding along bass lines;

bee-bopping to the next movement.

An echo,

a musical serenity in the wake of our waves.

Sparkling in the suspension,

a fizzling, free-flowing crash

that washes in,

washes out.

She folds the salt-stained page into her palm. "Life is breath. If you hold on to it for too long, you'll lose it. But if you let it go, it comes back to you. The good news is we don't have to cling to it... So, let go and enjoy the ride."

A momentary silence hangs among them as Konway floats next to Sage, steeped in the empathy of communal tears. ('We don't need to cling.') The malfunctioning Oros system's baristas mix another randomized microdose, plunging his attention onto a Vision Shard containing the Donor's memory of swimming with his cousins.

Clay Banks

Past the creek, near his childhood home, running close to his secret hideout, the River crosses three counties and is the region's oldest man-made lake. With three hundred kilometers of shoreline, it includes a state park, a bird refuge, and a military base recreation center. Lately, the water is low enough to reveal enormous boulders and proper sinkholes for diving within the veins of its tributaries.

He and his two cousins, Bennet and Tucker, swim to a rope swing on the opposite side of Colonel Creek. Bennet, the eldest, reaches it first. There, they take turns leaping from the perch of a striped boulder into the rippling splash of refreshment. Plunging and playing, they lose track of time.

As they round out their last guffawing turns on the rope swing, distant sirens suddenly sound from the county dam. The boys hit the water and swim to the other side. Midway, the current stalls their stride and lands them on a small island formed from a crude settlement of upstream silt and flood erosion. They clamber ashore and catch their breaths.

Young-Konway turns towards his cousins, saying, "If we jump from here, the current will carry us there." He points to a bare spot on the clay bank. "It's now or never, fellas."

Without hesitation, he leaps into the rushing current and swims with all his might. Though he drifts off course, his vigorous effort carries him to the edge of the red clay bank, where he flops onto his back.

His cousins cheer.

"Come on, fellas," he calls back to them. "You can do it!"

Not to be outdone, Bennet jumps into the water. He drifts a frantic bit—too far for his liking—but eventually scuttles to shore. Out of breath, he signals to his younger brother to cross.

Unsure of his footing, Tucker inches to the edge and slips. Fear-filled, he scurries back to the safety of Erosion Island.

"I can't... I won't make it across. The current is too strong," he squeals.

Young-Konway's agile mind calculates how long it's been since the first siren. He needs to get his cousin now—or fetch the grown-ups. Surely, a fate worse than death. He gathers his resolve and works his way a short distance upstream before jumping back into the water.

From there, he drifts to the shrinking island and confidently stands, leaning against a thin pine tree.

"You can do this, Tucker," he says, taking his cousin's small shaking hand.

"What if I drown?"

"Trust me... We won't let anything happen to you." He reaches for his younger cousin with a confident smile, coaxing him to try again.

Tucker trembles as he struggles through the rising water. Almost there, his hand slips from young-Konway's grip. But before he lets go, Bennet slaps a long limb beside them, and Tucker grabs hold. Young-Konway pushes while his older cousin drags them closer to the shore. A little farther, and Tucker's small hands sink into the soft, red clay.

Young-Konway stands, but his misplaced confidence betrays him. His bare foot slides off a partially exposed rock, sending him back into the water.

"Help!" he cries, sailing by a clay-bound root ball.

The cousins take off after him, attempting to follow his voice along the overgrown shoreline. Red clay, wet leaves, and sprawling thorns excite their fears as a slab of blue granite stonewalls them.

Let Go

Young-Konway tries not to panic while the rising water rushes him towards an interstate overpass cutting through the property. He grasps slick rocks to slow himself, twirling into delicate branches. Despite his grip, his frantic momentum pulls every limb he touches into the drink. Swimming, swimming, swimming—he soon tires and rolls onto his back. Out of breath, he drifts with the whims of the current.

His mind fills with the horrible thoughts of being washed onto boulders, where vultures would pick his bones. (I hope Momma won't be mad at me.) Tears rinse from his face in the rapids' drowning splash, waterlogging his nostrils.

Overhead, picturesque patterns in the sky overwhelm his senses with divine grace. A calm sensation washes over him as he thinks of death. Face-to-face with the fear of his own mortality, and his inability to do anything about it, young-Konway relaxes to the forces of nature and floats under the bridge.

Passing through its shadow, the rapids part, softening into a mild ebb. He opens his eyes. The sun peeks from behind the clouds onto a protruding slab of blue granite, preventing him from washing farther downstream. Soon, his feet bump into one of the many flat rocks lining the shallows. Another cloud covers the sun, when his laughter breaks above the water, guiding his cousins closer to him.

Life Worth Living

At the end of its spool, the Vision Shard packs itself into his *Space Force III* lunchbox, leaving only the slosh of the paddle-out ceremony.

(I almost died there... How many times have I avoided death?... What about the people I've killed? Who mourns for them? How many deaths are on my hands? I don't want to cause any more harm. How do I make amends for my past? Do I even deserve the opportunity? There's got to be a way to fix this. If only I could remember more.)

He looks up from his board and beholds Sage bathed in the day's radiance. Nearby, a colony of gulls squawks towards an open bag of cheese puffs farther down the beach. His senses stop tracking externalities and settle on Lynn as she concludes her lengthy eulogy amongst the lapping Atlantic.

The circle applauds, welcoming her back into the fold. Helaku meets Lynn halfway, gives her a fist bump, then whispers his condolences. She smiles with a stream of tears and scoots next to Bear in the lineup.

63

Eulogy's Conclusion

Helaku's Speech

Helaku positions himself in the center of the ebbing wreath. "Rocky was —no... Rocky *will* always be my brother. Although he and I came to the village at the same time, we knew each other as roommates long before Laniakea's good graces welcomed us home." He pauses and flashes his pearly smile with the weight of fond memories bubbling beneath his chest.

"Both of us were young and rambunctious, seeking shelter from the gentrification pruning our generation from the island. In the early days, when we first moved in together, we butted heads. He was new, and not a local. However, we soon found rational discourse was a better fit than flexing our physical prowess. In no time, we discovered we had more in common than we'd initially thought. Like brothers, we'd stay up all night playing video games and talking about everything under the sun.

"And even after all those late nights, Rocky was always earlier than me—if you can believe that. But no matter how tired he was, Rocky always had the energy to help his neighbors and community. It's just who he was: always trying to make things better than they needed to be. We will continue to cherish the lessons, sessions, late nights around the bondfire, surf trips down the coast, and all the joy he instilled in the village while he was with us." Tears swell in the corners of Helaku's eyes.

With one mighty exhale, he releases the guilt for not keeping in touch with his bro, the petty disagreements they had, and the longing to catch another set or beat the next level to reach the final boss. He reflects on the laughter they shared over deep conversations and gnarled spliffs.

"Rocky loved this village more than most. He called this island his home for many years, until the call for adventure led him elsewhere. Let us keep the bondfire burning brightly, so he may see it, wherever he may roam." The tears wash down his face, curling below his jawline and onto his neck.

Jack's Speech

As Helaku returns to the circle's edge, Jack glides into the spotlight, sits up, and puffs out his chest.

"I'm at a loss for words. Rocky was the former chief of my tribe, and I was his second-in-command. He taught me the ways of leadership and showed me how to guide us in his absence. In time, we will overcome this... But for now, my big bro can surf the longest barrel ride—"

Jack smirks to himself, thinking of how he'd caused a divide between Sage and Alex, then used her to buy Todd's loyalty. (Where the fuck is PJ? Gonna have to track him down,) he thinks. "—So let us memorialize him in our hearts and in our actions. We have only one life to live. Let's take advantage of it."

A few boys from Machu-Beachu howl, igniting the rest of the flotilla with the flames of their propaganda. Jack sharply spins his board around and nods at Julian as he makes his way to speak.

Julian's Speech

Julian paddles into the center and raises his fist into the air. "UNITY THROUGH COMMUNITY!"

The whole procession follows the current chief of Soldier-Surf, chanting, "UNITY THROUGH COMMUNITY!"

Overhead, the sun ducks behind a passing cloud.

"Rocky was a good man," Julian says in a deep, commanding voice. "He did a great deal for Laniakea and was an exceptional representative of the values instilled by the Founders. Many of you might not know this, but Rocky saved me—back when there were more locals than out-of-town property owners.

"I was a mess: overweight, drinking all night, and chasing tourist chicks. I'd wake up late, rinse, and repeat. I was spiraling out of control, wasting more and more of my savings." He scans the floating crowd.

"In this world, there are things that cannot be unseen. Day and night, my past haunted me. I thought I could muscle through it. But soon, too many late-night cheeseburgers from Monk's Market and all the Bourbon-n-Gingers began taking their toll. I was slowly killing myself with gluttony—consuming everything I could find: drugs, food, women, fistfights—wanting to fill the bullet holes in my heart.

"You name it. I tried it. None of it worked for me. I was a self-destructive, isolating force. I didn't want to live my life haunted by a sense of regret and lack of belonging. I wanted to kill myself. But by this time, I was too much of a coward to do it. So I lived recklessly, pedal glued to the floor—determined to see how much I could push my body until it did what I was afraid to do."

A quiet slosh holds amongst the group.

"I eventually hit bottom," Julian continues. "One night Rocky found me in an alley, choking on my own chunks. I was dying, and too drunk to do anything about it—if I cared to do anything at all. The last thing I remembered was him turning me over. The next morning, I woke up on their couch to find Helaku heading out for dawn patrol.

"The stain of shame held a strong sway over me. I tried to leave, but Rocky insisted I owed him a debt... and his only price was joining him and Helaku out in the ocean. He wanted to show me a glimpse of something that would revolutionize my life. They took me surfing for the first time." Julian flashes his gratitude. "Each time we set out past the break, I shed the skin of my old self. And for the first time in a while, life didn't seem so meaningless. I realized I wasn't afraid of dying—I was afraid of living."

The ocean ebbs.

"Later on, I grew aware that I wasn't alone." He draws back some plump tears. "There were others… and I wanted to share the gift of surfing with anyone facing the same struggles. Rocky, being another veteran of *The War*, helped me bring this dream to life by helping establish Soldier-Surf as our first chief… and we'll pay tribute to his memory with a bondfire large enough to honor our brother." Julian stalls another tear from welling in the corner of his eye. "Although his passing fills my heart with a heavy weight, brothers and sisters, death is not the awful boogeyman of our nightmares—it's the source of life… But let me get off my soapbox." He culls his brewing emotions and paddles towards the circle's edge.

Sage's Speech

Sage gives Julian a high-five as she maneuvers into the center and sits up on her board. "What do I say? I can still remember Alex scoffing during our discussions. 'How can we be okay with feeling like we are gods and goddesses, yet we ultimately end up as food for worms?' So, he strove to make life more meaningful and grand—" Forgotten tears roll over her cheeks and into the puddled water resting on the deck of her board.

"However sad," she says with a trailing sniffle, "it's not enough to remember Alex. To honor him, we must continue to strive in the ways he did." She pauses with a withdrawn tear. "Let's *italicize* our experiences and create a masterpiece out of this moment, this day, and the rest of our lives." Sage raises her fist to the immeasurable heavens, and the pack lets loose a chorus of howls, hollers, rooster-crows, and an onslaught of celebratory splashing at the halo's center.

Grand Strand

As Konway makes a mental note of the Agency helicopter heading towards the East End, a playful pod of bottlenose dolphins breaches against the day's vivid backdrop. Their sleek, rubbery sheen slides past the curved tips of their insulated dorsal fins. Curious clicks and whistles precede the encircling pod, coordinating unheard questions beneath the smooth curves of water.

Below, a game of keep-away plays out with a piece of stray kelp. They flip and glide the strand along, trying to escape pursuit. One after another, they pick and steal, until a larger adolescent swims ahead, tactfully slipping the prized strand from beak to pectoral fin. With a spin and a twist, the strand slides along his white underbelly, and he snags it at the last moment with his tail.

He wiggles away from his pursuers until the prize slips free. Their clicks bounce off the misplaced strand and back into the auditory cortex, echolocating the prized strand of kelp lost in the water column. One bottlenose darts towards the surface and leaps into the air. As it splashes back into the revelry, the pod disappears beyond the visibility whence they came. And so their contest begins again, regrouping to flank the one with the grand strand of kelp.

Communion

Inspired by Stewart's closing prayer, the memorial positions for the incoming set. Helaku catches the first wave, hands high above his head, power-posing with a smile brighter than the afternoon sun. A short distance out, ribbons of shorebirds hunt schools of fish from an azure skyline.

Everyone joins in, cruising with style. Some drop in together, riding party waves—no hang-ups, just camaraderie and hanging ten. With clear skies and clean waves, the villagers demonstrate their mastery of the art of beach-and-chill. Onshore, a volleyball match is underway, while nearby, beachgoers toss around a bocce set.

The mourning session soon turns into afternoon delight. Once the surf dies down, several folks head back to Laniakea while others ditch their boards, returning to a natural communion of body with wave. Among them, Helaku and Konway can't get enough of being in the water.

For Helaku, letting go of the good grief is everything. For Konway, the rushing ocean dissolves the boundaries of thought. He doesn't have to worry about who he was or what he did—not a single thing—except when to let go and enjoy the ride.

64

Folly Tales

Bondfire's Light

The evening swells as the moon leads a starlit chorus of frogs and katydids. After several windswept attempts, the effigy ignites into a towering inferno, bright enough to catch the favor of whichever gods survived into modernity. The bondfire towers above the brickwork as Konway sits among the villagers, observing their etched faces and wrestling with a catalog of murderous tropes, dystopian visions, and fleeting fits of callousness for the people he had killed.

He tries to manage the deluge by suppressing the matrix of memories threatening his new home. (Enough. If I continue to think about all that awfulness, I may summon them to my doorstep... I'd never hurt Sage or Helaku, Lynn, Ruckus, Mateo... None of them... I can control this... I must.)

(That's what you think,) the Imp taunts. (If given enough time—)

Helaku drops a huge cooler filled with beverages.

"Julian wasn't kidding about the size of this thing," Konway marvels at the rising flames, suppressing his angst.

"That's how much Rocky meant to him... Although, I'd say it's still too small."

"That's what she said," Mateo blurts jokingly.

"There's nothing like death to bring us together in a celebration of life," Ruckus says.

"Did y'all feel it?" Mateo asks. "I swear, I felt his spirit out there with us."

"You believe those ole wives' tales about the dolphins?" Ruckus teases.

Helaku interrupts their shenanigans, proclaiming, "Growing old is a privilege denied to many and realized by few." He cracks open a bottle of tequila and swigs from the neck. A bubbling memory hiccups to the surface. "Rocky once told me, 'Although we walk this road alone, we all have an opportunity to walk each other home.'" He clears his thoughts and pulls another swig before passing the bottle to Mateo. "Life is not an idea—it's an experience. The *idea* is that we walk our own paths alone. The *experience* is to walk with one another, traveling towards the same destination."

"Like the way muscles work," Konway expresses a random thought from his building treasure trove of remembrance. "Each muscle is composed of individual fibers that move in unison."

Mateo downs a shot of agave. "Unity through community!"

Helaku smiles at their rascality. "Rocky showed us this in every moment that he filled our lives with light and courage—"

"I feel a story in the works." Mateo nudges Konway.

"Come on, bro," Ruckus presses. "It's been a while, and we could use one. Who wants to hear a story?"

"Story... Story... Story," the crowd chants, their voices rising around the towering pyre.

"I'm not in the mood," Helaku says, waving them off, then plops down on his weathered Adirondack chair.

"Please," Sage persists. "Spin us a tale."

Helaku thinks for a second, rummaging within his hope chest of fables, and scoots to the edge of his seat. "Go grab some more snacks."

"Wahoo!" they cheer.

By the time the bondfire attendees return with a buffet of goodies and libations, the stars turn crisp, and the humidity recedes with the tide. Helaku takes another pull of pure agave and wipes the sweat from his brow. The crowd leans forward in anticipation.

Adorning his narrator's voice, Helaku begins, saying, "This is a story about two mysterious islands and the treasure that's hidden there—"

Storm

One night, during a seasonal tempest, Merlin, a large black feline, washes ashore. The following morning, four ancient turtles find him tail-up in the sand. They whisper amongst themselves, then free him from the beach. With another incantation, his wounds heal. Merlin shakes the sediment from his ears and answers their questions. After some huddled deliberation, they decide to take him to see Mahatma, the wise elephant guru.

A third of the way to the jungle route, a murder of crows ambushes them.

"Where do you think you're going? Time is up! Where's the tribute for Yamato Village?" The group's leader tucks its wings and paces back and forth.

"We were just on our way," says the terrapin in the orange-sashed robe, trying to hurry them.

"Don't toy with us, turtles."

"We swear... we were headed to pay," pleads the one draped in blue cloth.

A crazy-eyed goon twists its head to the side. "Looks like you were *heading* into the jungle. If you can't provide tribute, we have more persuasive tactics for taking it out of your shells."

"There's no need to do this," the turtle draped in red responds.

A regal stoolie finishes grooming its feathers. "You don't wish to offend the honor and grace of his royal majesty—he of unbridled magnanimity, the sole bearer of his name, the Crow King. Do you?"

Before they respond, five crows swoop in, talons-first, attacking the red-cloaked turtle.

Merlin leaps at them, but they take to the air. One after another, they dive-bomb them with blinding pecks and bleeding scratches. Merlin defends his new friends, swatting the crazy-eyed crow aside, then pouncing towards the others. Startled, they retreat to the clouds, cawing for vengeance as they vanish over the tree line.

The turtles praise his bravery. But, concerned for the safety of their village, the blue-sashed one rescinds their offer to take him to see the wise Mahatma.

"How will I find him? How will I get home?" asks Merlin.

Huddling up, the dole whispers in a language he doesn't understand. Deciding hastily, they turn back to him. The dark green, yellow-spotted turtle, shrouded in a purple mantle, conjures a map with directions through the jungle. "Take this. It will help you find your way... and say these magic words." He leans in and whispers to Merlin.

Merlin repeats them: *"Caretta-Caretta,"* and the map vanishes. He thanks the turtles for their kindness and proceeds past the dunes.

Students

Several meters from the shore, the sand turns into a sparsely wooded path. At the spurious trail's end lies a monastery without a master. The students have overrun the place, each thinking themselves to be a worthy master. In their oblivious pride, they fail to discover the secrets kept beneath the Fu Dog's paw. Beyond the realm of learning anything new, these I-know-it-alls lazily lie around, waiting to spread the fool's folly of their limited wisdom.

As Merlin approaches the enclave's outer walls, a clowder of enlightened cats greets him with offerings: nip, a fresh kimono, a buffet of delights, and the tale of a sacred treasure—a heart-shaped jewel that grants wishes—and its Guardian, a mythical beast no one has ever seen. He shows them the map. Desperate to have a student of their own, they decipher the turtle's markings and pressure him to taste the food and drink from the saucer.

He grows curious about their intentions as they cleverly avoid answering his questions about Mahatma. Merlin resists their logic and avoids their aggressive hospitality. Exhausted by his resolve—and elated from too much nip—the students succumb to the Dreamer's dream.

Merlin feigns sleep until the monastery purrs in harmony. Then, whispering the magic words, "*Caretta-Caretta*," he stows his map and, like a thief in the night, hurries past the ashram's ordered gardens, away from the longing desires of the students who would be teachers. Many meters away, veiled by moonlight, he crosses the jungle's threshold.

The sprawling labyrinth's tangled glow ignites his imagination with a spooky parade of horrible-horribles and unmentionables. Within the jungle's echoing darkness, every snarl, caw, crunch, and creak fills his chest with fear. He treads lightly.

A stick cracks nearby, and he takes off in a panic. Thoughts of being pursued by the misled monks or those wicked crows cloud his attention as he races into the darkness. Blinded by fear, he misses the vine-covered sign: *Danger!*

Soon, the overgrown path becomes impassable. He tries to go around, snapping, stomping, tumbling, falling, and pawing for better footing in the moonlit jungle. He slices through a wall of vines with razor-sharp claws, but the dense mass of foliage ensnares him.

Thume. Thume. Thume. The thunderous booms of a nearby giant rumble closer to him.

Merlin shreds the last bit of bindings and tumbles to the ground. As he gets up, several trees fall in front of him. He freezes under the emerging shadow, long enough for primal instincts to override his fear, and leaps at the crashing beast.

Teacher

A trumpeted screech sends all manner of creatures to the wind as the elder elephant halts its foot. "Please, no! I mean you no harm." A flash of sincerity shines from his eyes.

Merlin backs down.

"What's this all about?" the elephant asks. "No one is supposed to be up here. Who are you?"

He explains how four turtles told him to seek the sage of this jungle.

"See, they made me this." He summons the parchment.

"A map? Where are you from?"

"I'm not sure. I'd never left my home until yesterday, when I found an old boat and went exploring on the far side of the island. I got caught in a storm that swept me away from the shore. Then I washed up here."

"You're lucky. Foolish, but lucky," the wise elephant rumbles, raising his trunk to eye level and studying the map. "This was definitely conjured by someone from Yamato Village."

"I was hoping you could help me find the sage they mentioned," Merlin says.

The elephant's brow furrows. "Well... look no further. You've found him. And the sooner I help you, the sooner I can get back to doing what I was doing."

"What was that?"

"Being left alone. Now, follow me to my cave."

Several crooked paths later, they arrive at the dwelling—a minimalist setting of solitude.

The aged elephant guru waddles over and sits on top of a matted straw pile. "I am Mahatma. What knowledge do you seek from me?"

"I've heard of a heart-shaped jewel that grants wishes—"

"Now, where did you hear a thing like that?" Mahatma raises his eyebrows.

"At the monastery."

A momentary pause hangs between them.

"It's a myth, shrouded in mystery and danger. I remember reading about it in some of my old ledgers."

"Have you ever seen it?" Merlin asks.

"No."

"Then how can you know it exists? How do you know it's real?"

"You don't. It requires a journey of faith. You shall see the light which shines across this magnificent island. There, your journey will be at an end."

"I don't understand. How will this help me?"

"It is for you to discover." Mahatma mystically waves his trunk. "Also, you cannot do this alone. You will need the continued guidance of others to get to the heart-shaped jewel."

"How? I'm alone... Will you assist me?"

"No. A storm is coming, and you'd best get going. Now leave." Mahatma retreats to the flickering shadows of his cave in the jungle.

White Rabbits

Albeit confused, Merlin bids farewell and sets out, running with a renewed path of certainty towards the heart-shaped jewel. Several turns and leaps later, he emerges from the jungle's threshold, bordering an ancient meadow. In its center, a pool of clear water surrounded by shimmering trees. Tired from his journey, he snoozes in their shade.

To his surprise, he wakes to the curious sniffs of white bunnies parading around him. Several of the smaller hares part to the side, making way for a large celestial-white rabbit. Her lustrous fur and radiant eyes mesmerize our hero into a dream. In a state of lucid wakefulness, they share a wordless conversation as she roves his mind and gleans his intentions.

The colony raises him in the air and carries him with soft paws back to their watershed. Along the way, a clear quilt of laughter traps him in a pit of comfort. Unlike the monks, he becomes intoxicated by their revelries, longing to stay with them more than he wants to breathe.

Inside, the rabbits inspire him with visions of grandeur and memorial everlasting as they prepare their pot for stew. Dazed and confused by the splendor, Merlin does not notice the bunnies are slowly lowering him over the cauldron. The moon's silver glow rises through a nearby window, and one by one, the hares morph into wolves.

Out Of The Cauldron

Locked within the warren, seconds from becoming stew, a glint of moonlight from a leftover pot in a nearby sink strikes Merlin in the eyes, breaking the celestial-white rabbit's spell. He releases his claws, lacerating the bindings, and leaps onto the boiling cauldron's rim.

He endures its searing heat long enough to attract the attention of a nearby harewolf. On cue, the ravenous beast leaps at him and knocks the boiling pot onto the floor. A scalding cascade of carrots, celery, potatoes, and broth rushes at the colony of harewolves, chasing them out the door. Desperate to escape, Merlin dives out an open window and races to the opposite side of the ancient meadow, towards the maritime forest.

Reaching the tree line, he freezes when several crows land beside him.

"Did you really think you could get away with interfering in our business?" The largest scratches its claws into the ground.

"The boss says we need to make an example of you." A malicious drool hangs from another's beak as it twists its head unnaturally.

A regal fowl with perfect plumage stares from behind two emotionless voids. "Or you can give us everything you own… How about that map the turtles gave you?"

"How do you know about the map?" Merlin backs up, searching for an escape.

"Fine…" The regal one nods to their cronies. "Have it your way."

They return to the air, where others hover with heavy nets, and coordinate their airstrike, dropping a barrage of stones at Merlin. A few collide, sending the largest chunk smashing into the ground, barely missing his tail. Spotting a pattern in their volleys, he leaps from rock to rock, rising to the beat of their malicious wings, before pouncing on the largest crow.

Wham! The bird crashes into the others, bringing the entire ordeal to the ground with a rain of *oofs* and *thuds*, knocking the breath from their lungs. Merlin lands atop the pile and limps into the maritime forest. Not long past its border, he disappears through a thicket of fog. Stillness blankets the battlefield as a feather drifts windward.

Rowdy

Tiny scuttling sounds click amongst water-soaked branches as dampness drips under an owl's poignant *hoot-hoot*, echoing within wispy thickets. Merlin, fearful of the crows and the harewolves returning, limps off the beaten path. He slowly scales fallen trees, crosses slippery rocks, and awkwardly shimmies past mud-filled ravines.

He reaches the exit and stops. Several circling shadows swoop back across the cracks in the canopy, again and again, before finally landing above. Beneath their beaks, he whispers, "*Caretta-Caretta*," summoning the magical map. To his dismay, the forest appears to be divided by a river. Unfazed, he plots a different course and forges towards a narrowed spot east of him.

Merlin breaches the thicket into the rush of a nearby waterfall. He sighs and summons the map again, hoping to find a different route. As more shadows sweep overhead, he slips inside a hollowed-out log, taking shelter through the rest of the night.

The next morning, he heads upstream and locates a quaint yellow house. On its front porch, a large dog reads a newspaper. Fearing the unknown, he leaps back into the brush and creeps along the tree line.

Farther ahead, the dog sets down his paper. "Come on out… I know you're back there. I can smell you. It's okay—you're safe. The name's Rowdy. Come, join me for some coffee." The mastiff laps from his cup.

Merlin cautiously approaches the porch and explains his need to cross the river. Unable to think of an alternative, he climbs on Rowdy's back.

Slow and steady, they forge closer to the other side. Two-thirds along the way, he nearly slips off but clings to Rowdy's hide.

"I apologize for my claws," he says.

"I'm thick-skinned," Rowdy replies. "I can handle it… just a little further until we're ashore."

Safely on the other side, he thanks Rowdy for his help and invites him to join his quest.

"No thank you, my friend," he declines. "I must stay here and help others who might need to cross. Besides, there's no need to take the raft with you."

"A raft… Now, that would've been a much better idea." Merlin rounds his whiskers with a Cheshire's grin.

Dolphins

Half a day later, Merlin reaches the boneyard at the dried edge of the dark woods. Crashing waves guide his ears beyond the crests of sea oat dunes and the searing sands to a village where dolphins surf pristine waves. Soaked and still aching from his tussle with the crows, he collapses, tumbling down the dune and rolling to the bottom, where he startles a flight of pigeons. The flustered tourons absentmindedly drop a few belongings onto the ground. Sensing the vibrations, local crabs scuttle over and sift through the refuse, looking for better homes.

"Hey! Scram, you damn birds," a few dolphins call out, effortlessly floating towards the front gate.

Delirious, Merlin wakes to a cabaret of curious faces. They hover around him, sustaining an invisible buoyancy.

An older, spotted bottlenose drifts to his side. "Hello-hello. We found you near the dunes and thought it best to bring you to our home, Wafian Village. You look like you've been on quite a journey. Please rest here until you heal."

"You can have all the fish you want," one calf whistles.

"Where will your journey take you?" an adolescent bull asks.

Merlin cleans the sand from his ears. "I'm heading to the heart-shaped jewel that grants wishes."

"Wishes, you say?" Several of them murmur amongst the whistles of their own frequency, excited by the prospect of such a treasure.

"I have a map," he says, then summons the parchment. "*Caretta-Caretta.*"

The curious pod hovers closer for a better view.

"I've never been to that island... I hear ferocious beasts roam there," a calf whistle-clicks.

"I've heard stories of folks who've ventured there, but never made it back," an elder says. "We stick to our side, where the sun rises."

"Can anyone help me get there?" Merlin asks.

Another elder glides into the discussion, saying, "You'll never make it alone... If we decide to aid you, how do you plan on getting past the currents, jagged rocks, and the ruined palace long since held by the Crow King?"

Merlin glances at a sandy length of driftwood stacked by the boneyard. "I have an idea."

Beached

Piece by piece, they assemble a driftwood raft, then afterward, host a bondfire with the leftover timber. Unbeknownst to the sleeping village, a shadowy messenger slips away in the middle of the night. The next morning, volunteers check the buoyancy and run a speed test before pulling Merlin towards the end of his journey.

At first, it's smooth sailing along the coastline. But once the crew moves into deeper water, they grow distracted by the promise of claiming the heart-shaped jewel for themselves. Soon, their bulbous minds obsess over the possibility of coveted rewards, and they race through a choppy channel.

After several close calls, his claws digging into the wood, the dastardly dolphins arrive at the palace ruins. The raft slides onto the beach and slams into an eroded jetty of boulders. Despite his grip, Merlin flies off into a nearby tide pool.

Betrayal

Merlin scrambles to his paws just as the dolphins surround him. They try to subdue him, but he musters enough strength to push them back to the water's edge with deep lacerations across their melons. He attempts to flee, but several of the Crow King's elite guard swoop down from the nearby cliffs—clawing, pecking, and disorienting him—walloping him with foul retribution.

The traitorous dolphins shake off the sand and fixate on the looming promise of their wishes. As they float closer to the marble stairs embedded in the cliff, the crows gather at the steps to block their way.

"His Majesty appreciates your assistance in this matter. Regrettably, your services are no longer needed." The regal black bird puffs up its chest.

"We had a deal," insists one of the wounded dolphins.

A large crow presses its wing into the fresh gash, saying, "Who do you think you made a deal with?"

"You're lucky you still have your lives—and Wafian Village only pays the tax it does. Any word of this and we will squeeze your village dry." The regal conman turns from them. "Is that understood?"

"Maybe we burn their village to the ground and banish them back to the sea?" a one-eyed crow says, tilting its head.

"Good day."

The dolphins shamefully sink into the water while the murder of crows escorts Merlin off the beach.

Court Of The Crow King

They drag him up the steps, through the palace ruins, and into the throne room. Before him, an enormous, malignant creature with calculating eyes smokes a cigar within the shadow of its gilded throne.

"What have you brought me? Is this who's been causing you trouble? You should all be ashamed of yourselves," he squawks. "Hey cub, are you alright? These fools... Oh, how it pains me to do this. Leave my sight—I'll punish you later. I hope they didn't injure you." The Crow King snaps his wings, summoning attendants to bandage Merlin's wounds. "I hear you know of a sacred treasure that grants wishes." He exhales several chained smoke rings.

Merlin looks up from the bandage being wrapped around his wounds. "You know about the heart-shaped jewel?"

"That's 'Your Majesty' to you," a regal bird sings.

The devilish Crow King rushes to his side. "Yes-yes," he coerces our hero. "I'll help you get it—to make up for my bird-brained minions—and you can get back to whatever you were doing... or whatnot."

"Going home—Your Majesty," Merlin interrupts.

"Oh, yes-yes." He puffs a circle from his cigar and lances it with an arrow of smoke. "We will get you home, sonny."

"My name is Merlin."

"Once again, I apologize for my boys." The Crow King stalks about the room. "I strictly told them not to hurt anyone... I assure you, they will be dealt with. Now, back to this map." The Crow King leans in.

"*Caretta-Caretta*," Merlin mutters, summoning the map.

As it unfurls, a smoke ring strikes the magical parchment with a breath of evil. In an instant, the map dissolves into ash.

The tyrant bottles his immediate rage and pivots, saying, "We have a pen and paper over by that writing desk. You're a bright lad... I'm sure you could draw the rest from memory."

And so, guided by the Crow King's persuasion, our hero reluctantly sketches the map to the heart-shaped jewel.

Stampede

The gilded procession returns to the beach, finding only two dolphins sulking in their foolishness, the rest having retreated to their village. The Crow King puffs tendrils of false promises and yokes them to the raft. Merlin and several envoys board the vessel and sail towards the jewel, while the King and his elite guard follow overhead.

Left, right, right, left—the waterway narrows, until their raft slips into the river dividing the two islands. They struggle against the current, skirting under low-hanging branches. The Crow King grows impatient and swoops down from the sky. Sensing something amiss, he orders his cronies to the nearest bank.

They land on the opposite shore. Seconds later, the brush rustles with scurrying creatures. A flurry of hedgehogs, frogs, foxes, rabbits, bears, snakes, birds, moose, elk, wolves, and other critters flee past them. The stampede subsides, and Merlin tries to still his trembling tail.

"Don't mess with me, cub," the Crow King snarls, seizing Merlin. "Did you think you could trick me?!" He flaps his wings, rising above the tree line, and releases his hold.

Merlin drops to the ground with a heavy thud. "This is it—this is where the turtles' map said to go!"

"Turtles?" he grumbles. "I think I'll have turtle stew this evening." The Crow King squawks at the delicacy, then hastily scans the surroundings. "Something's not right. Get him back onto the raft," he orders, turning to the entourage.

Little by little, Merlin's nose twitches with *her* scent.

Guardian

A monstrous shadow leaps from their periphery. A heart-pumping, breath-gasping moment of sheer terror spreads among the invaders. As Merlin finds his footing, the great beast swats at the Crow King, popping off a puff of feathers. His Majesty slides across the sand and crashes against the raft.

The Guardian's roar ripples over the island. Motionless, the Crow King feigns defeat as the beast steps into the light. Frightened, his murderous entourage takes to the sky, abandoning their sovereign.

"Merlin, is that you?" she asks.

"Momma?"

"Merlin Alexander Sheldrake, I was so worried about you."

"I'm here... Here I am." He nudges her leg.

"I'd almost given up hope. Surely, I thought, you were in the Great Beyond." She nuzzles him to the ground and breathes her magical breath onto him. "Where have you been?"

Out of nowhere, the Crow King kicks up a disorienting cloud of cigar smoke. Behind its veil, he lashes out with razor-sharp talons towards Merlin. At the last moment, one of the deplorable dolphins, seeking redemption, rushes the Crow King. The petty tyrant blocks with his wing, but another tailspin launches him skyward. The Guardian tracks him and leaps after the foul despot, catapulting him to the horizon.

"Now, what to do with these intruders?" She growls with blazing markings—previously unseen—casting her vicious intent to defend these Sacred Lands and the jewels hidden in their depths.

Fin

"—All the while, the wise turtles used Merlin as a distraction." Helaku waves his hands through the bondfire's smoke. "By sending him on a journey home, they exploited the Guardian's noble nature and the Crow King's greed to recover the heart-shaped jewel. Once the sacred treasure was in the center of Yamato Village, they wished to undo the foul magic that had stained their home for too long.

"In the monastery, the I-know-it-alls were freed from their assumptions and sought their master in the jungle. There, no longer wishing to be left alone, the wise sage emerged from his cave to teach the secrets kept beneath the Fu Dog's paw. In the meadows, the twisted bonds entangling the watershed of harewolves were severed, returning a sense of civility to all who dwelled within. In Wafian Village, justice prevailed, and the traitors were punished. To ensure neither the Crow King's return nor any seeker could unearth it, they stashed the heart-shaped jewel in the deepest chasm imaginable. For a time, life flourished on the islands, and Merlin and his mother grew to love both fiercely, protecting them as they would the sacred jewels—symbols of hope and prosperity for the next seven generations." Helaku bows.

The pyre-side listeners applaud his tribute to Rocky. Above, several bats flutter across the night sky, feasting on the foolish bugs drawn towards the bondfire's roar.

Sage leans over to Konway. "Will you walk me home?" she asks, sadness reddening her emerald eyes.

"Of course. Are you done for the day?" he asks.

She squeezes him.

"I'll be right back." They stand and depart for the Horseshoe.

"Sure thing," Ruckus scoffs, then downs a mouthful of tequila.

"Don't hog it all," Helaku says. "I need it to tell the other half of the story."

"Wait, there's more?" Konway asks, turning back to the fire.

Sage tugs at his elbow. "No, you don't. You can come back after you've escorted me home."

65

Dance of Signification

Tender

The lovers make it halfway past the threshold of Sage's front door when their passions electrify the room. Like the poets of distant enchanted meadows, they chase after reflections of the divine, melting into the revered gaze of the other. A magnetic polarity pulls their celestial bodies into place. Caught within the dance of unheard harmonies, a hurried parade of clothes flies into the kitchen.

She falls for him more each day. And he, wanting her more than that, surrenders to a sea of mutual appreciation. They collapse onto the couch and further shed the shackles of this mortal coil.

As Konway traces his kiss along the contour of Sage's neckline, the world fades out of context. Caught in the urge to merge, a wordless communion dances between the rhythmic sway of their bodies. They soon surrender the fears and inadequacies tethering them to their individuated forms. Together, they die to the moment and let go of everything beyond the four walls of Sage's abode.

More than primal acts, they smash through their sense of separateness, galloping in a feverish hunt for a chance at rebirth. Deeper, the lovers meditate at the altars of ecstatic worship. There, divine projections focus upon the other as they spar upon the pane of their souls—hearts pumping, breaths gasping—only to drown in the relief of connecting with the sacred.

They dissolve into a swirling cosmology of oneness and transcend towards realms of aesthetic arrest and symbolic catharsis. In this moment of prayer, rolling amongst the Elysian fields of Sage's bedroom, a singular second of silence erupts as an apotheotic orgasm rises from their toes and releases them into the infinite experience. Naked and bare, they sigh before the semi-phenomenal, nearly cosmic grace of godhood.

Slowly, as the tide draws back to the sea, they return to the cool oscillation of the fan in the corner. Nearby, Smittens paws under Sage's comforter. Outside their nest, lightning illuminates the dark contours of a wayward tempest.

Little Death

High in the atmosphere, storm clouds thunder towards Holy City—once known for its stained glass and steeples, now mired in hyper-materialism, statistical facts, and price-point analysis—where antique oil lanterns flicker outside the doors of the wealthy. A jungle of concrete and glass high-rises sprawls from the historic district, towering above the peninsula's colonial spires. A city, like most, that distills the sentiments of poets and visionary thinkers into a fleeting, dopaminergic hit of cocaine.

As Konway enjoys the high of divine consummation, a joyful emptiness echoes about his mental corridors. He senses the passing moment and hurriedly stows it inside his *Space Force III* lunchbox, desperate to preserve these fleeting moments of bliss.

Past the window, crisscrossing latticeworks flash onto the horizon, crackling the atmosphere. While Smittens scurries into the closet, the lovers fall into a shared transcendental state. Entranced in this borderland of myth and platonic forms, between dreams and reality, an immersive illumination beckons them through the rabbit hole of sense-awareness into a state of higher fidelity—complete with enriched colors and varied conversation topics.

He traces the smooth contours of her hip. "That was incredible?"

"La petite mort," Sage says into the darkened room's tranquil silence, placing her hand on Konway's thigh.

"The little death?" he asks.

"It's something more than being stoned or drunk."

"For a second, everything was clear and calm—damn, I wish it could've lasted a little longer."

"You did fine." She lightly scratches her nails across his skin, leaving a trail of goosebumps.

"Not what I meant."

"I'm just joshing... maybe that's part of our species' problem."

"What do you mean?" he asks.

"Well... you wished the high would've lasted... and, come to think of it... we're much like colanders, full of holes that let the light pour out of us."

"How do I plug up the holes and become whole?" He visualizes her description.

"The science isn't there yet. I wonder what the world would look like if we overflowed from the brim of our chalice instead?" she asks, staring into the distant cosmos, reflected in his vivid hazel eyes. In an exploratory moment of grace, she attempts to devour him with her sight, ultimately failing her campaign to seize the gates of heaven.

They dive into the discussion but fail to arrive at a total solution. In this tender space of inquiry, the moment shifts from discourse as the lovers watch the lightning storm roll across the distance. And with neither their hearts nor minds having room for anything else, they relax into an amorous embrace beneath the coolness of her green tea sheets—with a hint of sand for exfoliation—and enjoy a momentary reprieve from the wake of life.

Canoodle

Sage tickles him with her toes. "What a day... such a jumble of emotions: happy, sad, happy-sad."

"Do you miss him?" Konway asks.

"Of course... But only because I won't be able to punch him in the balls." She bunches up her fist.

He runs his fingers through her bed-worn hair. "I didn't mean to pry."

"My heart was broken... But you made me willing to open her back up and want to learn to love again."

"Me?" he asks.

"Yes, you. There's no one else I'd rather be with on this adventure." Sage snuggles into his chest.

As the storm recedes along the boundaries of Coffin Island's bubble, Smittens returns from hiding and nestles between them. Her purrs harmonize with the oscillating hum in the corner. Within the cozy cocoon of their near-nirvana, the distant rumbles of a looming tempest lull the lovers into a mutual sigh of relief.

Konway watches Sage fall asleep, and as he follows suit, he observes his own thoughts. (I've done some bad things. I've done some good things. How far have I come? If that *dolphin* in Helaku's story could do the right thing... then surely I'm capable of redemption.)

Unprovoked, a self-replicating mental projection of unfamiliar faces carousels to the forefront of his attention. The deluge of chatter spirals round and round, kicking up a cyclone of shattered recollections to torment and delight Konway for the rest of the evening.

Crook By The Book

Elsewhere, Todd stares into the corner of his living room with cold, blank eyes. He clenches his jaw as his rage grinds him closer to the nub. Unable to numb the pain splintering throughout his being, he reaches for his bottle of narcos. His other hand swizzles a room-temperature mixed drink, sloshing it over the rim of a red plastic cup.

A stern knock sounds at his door.

"Come on in—it's open."

Jack's dark shadow enters the apartment.

"Did you find him?" Todd asks, drinking with an aggravated gulp.

"Yep." Jack swipes a stray pill from the crumb-laden end table near Todd's wallow. "PJ is on Center Street, having a *real* good time."

"Did you tell him he's not getting kicked out?"

"He didn't seem to care what I had to say." Jack examines the party favor, blows it off, and drops it into his shirt pocket. "Give him some time to process things... He seriously injured you... Don't worry, I'll have the boys keep an eye on him."

"Make sure they tell him I'm not pissed."

"For sure... But I need you focused on healing and making the lineup. The Surf-Cred competition is coming up, and while I'm prepping, you've got to handle the tribe's day-to-day."

Todd groans at the impending responsibility.

"Look, you'll be head of Machu-Beachu once we dethrone Helaku and I become Laniakea's rightful Chief... But enough talk of business—I've got us a treat."

After brushing the ash and stray hairs to the floor, Jack plops a conservative bag of blow onto the coffee table. He grabs a scratched-up CD case and breaks out greedy lines of Bolivian Marching Powder, cut with baby laxative. Finally satisfied with the proportions, and seeing the eagerness on Todd's face, Jack breaks out a hundred-dollar bill, rolls it up, and slaloms down two amphetamine lanes. They take a few laps around the track, speedballing through his plot to bring about Helaku's fall from grace and diving into his fantasies of a better world and a brighter tomorrow. However, as soon as the bag runs dry, he departs, leaving Todd alone in the dark.

66

In A Pear Tree

Wake Up

Days later, a surprising chill rushes from the furthest reaches of the continent, fleeing the brilliant hues of a sailor's warning, while the evening's precipitation holds fast along dew-kissed grasses. The lovers untangle, and Konway gazes upon her face, speckled with morning light, marveling at the splendid dance of color filtering through the pane. Outside, the last *tweedle-tweedle* of spring's finale sings into fruition as he pulls back matted strands of Sage's hair and kisses her forehead.

"Do you need some water?" He tumbles out of bed and disappears into the kitchen.

"Please!" Sage squeals into a stretch. "It's like I've been in the desert." She flails around, tossing her sheets and pillows to the sandy wooden floor. "Whoa, do you see the sky? Trippy." She stares out her bedroom window at the treetops.

From the kitchen window overlooking the marsh, several herons land on the canvased view of the sky—followed by thirty-three ribboning pelicans, their reflections trailing across the mirroring tide.

"It looks like a blue-gray mixed with a pink grapefruit to me." Konway marvels at the marsh, lost in the beauty of its abrupt vividity.

"Nah, more like a gray-blue blood orange, to me," she challenges his disposition.

Konway returns with two large glasses of ice water, filled to the brim. "Tomato, Tomatillo."

"Is there enough ice in it? You know I only drink the coldest," she says, purposefully dribbling droplets down her naked body onto the sheets. "Let's get going."

"Where to?"

"We need to tend to the orchards before we head to the Farmers' Market," she replies.

"Oh, yeah... Ruckus and Mateo were stoked about the street closing." The ice at the bottom of his cup rattles as he gulps down half its contents, the coolness refreshing his cells with much-needed hydration.

"It's a space where everyone gathers to barter—you'll see," she says, sliding off the bed and playfully smacking his bottom as she shuffles to the bathroom.

Organic Foundation

By the barnyard, roosters salute the day while bleating goats *baaa* to the *buzz* of bees bounding along the seductive stamens of fresh pollination—honey for all. A clamorous bunch of pups nears the side of the rustic barn. The pack races behind the bamboo fence line, rushing to their daily games and afternoon delights.

"Let's check on the pawpaw patch first," Sage says, gesturing towards the maritime forest.

He chuckles with thoughts from the Donor's youth.

"What's so funny?"

"Just thinking of my granddaddy."

"Let's get going." Sage twinkles with the delight of helping a loved one. "Who knows what else you'll remember?"

After packing the utility wagon, they head to the groves. As Konway pulls it along, a few pups follow, propelled by the wag of their tails. They sniff about and chase one another, circling the lovers. But upon hearing their pack, the stragglers vanish through the ground fog, retreating to the cool dirt of their favorite shade spots.

Past the garden, the lovers approach a dense thicket of small, slender trees. Boughs of large green foliage bow in the breeze and wave good morning.

"Some call it the 'poor man's banana,'" Sage informs him. "Do you see all those stubby green nubs?" She points to gently swaying treetops.

"Are we going to pick them?" he asks.

"They're not ready yet, but when the time is right, we can gather the ripened ones that fall—as quickly as possible," she says.

"Why the urgency?"

"They have a short shelf life, so we need to use them when they're harvested."

"What do you make with them?" he asks.

"Whatever the Community Kitchen decides. But since these usually drop mid-August, they make a yummy sorbet." She rubs her tummy.

"What does it taste like?"

"Hmm... It reminds me of mango-banana custard."

(Mango?) He searches the Reliquary of Imagination—

On the backend, Sorting Dregs scrounge around in a bin and retrieve a fragment of aromatic splendor from a bowl of ripened fruit shared with a beautiful woman on an exotic beach after a highly classified sortie, of which he can't remember a fucking thing.

—Konway salivates at the flavor, auto-saving the parcel within his *Space Force III* lunchbox for safekeeping.

Sage places her hand on the tree trunk. "From what I've been told, the Founders positioned these as part of Laniakea's restoration."

"How so?"

"They used the pawpaws' clonal roots to build up the land, preventing the seasonal flooding that had been washing away this slice of paradise while also slowing the encroachment of the maritime forest."

She bends over to find a suitable branch next to a fresh flush of mushrooms. "Let's gather some of these sticks and twigs from the storm the other night," she says.

He asks curiously, "What are y'all making with these?"

"Remember when I said pawpaws are resistant to insects?"

"Are we taking some to the Farmers' Market?"

"There's no need. We have the Kawabonga Surf Shop on Center Street. It usually keeps the bulk of Laniakea's inventory, and there's Monk's Market a few blocks over."

"I think... I'm seeing a pattern," Konway says with a smile. A Vision Shard flashes to the bench seat of Paw-Paw's pickup truck, singing ole-timey tunes at the top of their lungs. Konway's heart overflows with an outpouring of song:

> Where, oh where, is dear little Nellie?
> Where, oh where, is dear little Nellie?
> Where, oh where, is dear little Nellie?
> Way down yonder in the Pawpaw patch.
> Pickin' up Pawpaws, puttin' 'em in your pocket.
> Pickin' up Pawpaws, puttin' 'em in your pocket.
> Pickin' up Pawpaws, puttin' 'em in your pocket.
> Way down yonder in the Pawpaw patch.

Sage laughs at the spontaneity and joins him, singing the traditional American folk song along the wombling path. They pull the wagon towards the Chickasaw plums, where, beneath the swaying shade, they gather a basket's worth, leaving the rest for the forest.

Tree'd

The last stop of their morning walkabout carries them to the Bartlett pears. On the way, Sage and Konway sample the breba crop of Brown Turkey figs, picked between the velvety leaves of bushy trees separating each grove from its neighbor. After filling their bellies, he clears debris from around the trees while Sage gathers fallen immature fruit into a mud bucket, cancelling the reservations of hungry ground bees.

Konway picks up a small green pear and examines it in a lattice of sunlight. "Can we eat these?" he asks.

"Not yet... Those need a bit more time. With pears, we need to pick them when they're mature, not ripened—they ripen from the inside out. So, when the outside is squishy, the interior is mush. But these'll be ready around August, too."

A feral cry sounds from the canopy.

Konway stops. "Did you hear that?"

"Sure did. Where did it come from?" Sage asks.

"Up there." He points towards the branches rustling with distress in the adjacent tree.

They set aside their tools and search for the frightened meow.

"I think it might be one of the village cats," Sage says, her hand shading her brow.

He unfolds the utility wagon's ladder, leans it against the tree, and shimmies from one rung to another.

"Watch out for snakes," Sage teases, pinching his bottom as he ascends into the pear tree.

Cornered

A maze of crisscrossing light illuminates the undersides of flourishing limbs. Up another rung, tiny ants climb along the trunk. Konway rises above the ladder's rubber feet and spies the feline's frantic, swooshing tail.

"What does it look like?" Sage calls up to him.

"Older... midnight black and fluffy, with blue eyes."

"It's MoMo's cat, Jynx," Sage hollers. "We need to get her down. Do you think you can reach her?"

"Not from here. But if I climb a little farther, I can."

Sage steadies the ladder as he climbs into the branches, closer to Jynx's desperate cry. "Be careful up there."

Dehydrated and afraid, the feline hunkers down, preparing to attack as he motions to her. Konway's movements shake the limb. Jynx growls, digging her claws into the bark of the Bartlett pear tree. He leans closer to the enraged kitty, her eyes like large pools of cloudy ink.

"It's alright, Jynx. I'm here to help you," he whispers.

She backs to the edge, and with nowhere to flee, hisses. Konway slowly maneuvers towards her. Another low growl grumbles about the canopy. He pauses, watching the furious frenzy of Jynx's swooping tail.

Rescued

Konway turns over his hand to reveal the lingering stickiness from the figs on his fingertips. A momentary breeze carries the scent through the canopy, enticing Jynx's wavering senses with the faint sweetness. After a hesitant moment, one shaky paw after another, the partially blind feline slowly makes her way but stops outside his grasp.

She sniffs the air, then leans forward to lick his hand. He pulls back to lure the senior cat closer. Once within reach, he gently plucks her from the branch and, swaddling her against his chest, descends from the canopy.

"Well, aren't you the bravest and sweetest man I've ever known," Sage says, unhooking Jynx's claws from his shirt. "MoMo's been looking for her for days. This poor sweetie's been all alone up there," she coos. "I bet you won't do that again, will you? Unless you like being saved by Mr. James Konway." She winks.

"Just doing my part."

"I'll text MoMo to let her know we found her baby and take Jynx home to give her some food and water. In the meantime, would you mind putting the tools away and placing the yard waste into the compost bin? After you dump it in, don't forget to stir it with the pitchfork. Thanks, love." She blows him a kiss. "I'll take the scraps with me."

"Where do you want to meet?"

"How about the Creative Cabaña? We need to get some art supplies for the Farmers' Market."

With Jynx safe in her comfy kitty bed and the utility wagon loaded with three boxes of CBD honey and a hastily labeled bin of art supplies, they tease each other as they take turns pulling it along the Horseshoe's intersecting brickwork pathways. A seasonal symphony leads the lovers into the crushed-seashell parking lot.

On arrival, Sage hitches the wagon to a solar-powered golf cart and they hop in, zooming towards the Farmers' Market at the center of Coffin Island. Close behind, the pups chase them up to the first drainage ditch, then rush back to the surfboard fence line.

Kawabonga

Sage avoids a misappropriated pothole and pulls into Kawabonga's parking lot. Thick-lined graffiti covers the surf shop's outer walls with vibrant colors, depicting stylized waves and sea creatures rising from the deep. Around the corner, past painted tentacles, stacks of hastily connected speakers stationed around Center Street blast classic West Coast hip-hop guitar chords over the murmuring crowd.

"We're here," she says. "Just wait—these things are so much fun." Sage hops out of the golf cart, stretches towards the sky, and walks to his side.

Konway strives to capture every detail, plunging into the Reliquary of Imagination, where scattered piles of manuscripts alter the topography of his mental landscape—all the way into the tightly organized neural pathways of his restored limited-edition *Space Force III: Blue Commander* lunchbox.

"Wipe that cuteness off your face, mister." Sage smushes his mouth with her hand.

"Hey, do you want to start this again?" Konway shifts his focus.

She lunges at him and tickles his sides with sadistic ferocity. He barely defends himself against her giggling onslaught of nimble fingers.

"I give... I give," he cries out in tears.

The brief silence of their truce breaks with the beeping signal of a garbage truck backing up, jolting them from a self-referential realm of lumination.

"Anyway, you haven't been outside of Laniakea too much. This is going to be way more people than at the paddle-out. Do you feel alright?"

"I'm a little nervous, but excited," he says.

She smiles at his optimism. "No worries. We're right in front of Kawabonga."

"Will this be everyone who lives on the island?"

"Yes, and more," she says. "They come together from all around the county. I love seeing the handcrafted jewelry and artworks." Sage beams with excitement. "And if folks tire of the hustle and bustle, there are activities at Riverside Park."

Time slows as he listens to Sage's description. On the backend, mental stenographers cling to every detail and transcribe it for later reflection in those quiet hours just before dawn.

Center Street Farmers' Market

They pull the utility wagon down the side alley. Rounding the corner, a wave of market commotion unfurls in front of Konway's fresh senses. Smells, sounds, and people—roving, laughing, and yammering about this or that, how-do-ya-dos, and how-ya-don'ts—stretch from the bridge down to Sandlapper Suites, the island's only beachfront hotel.

"Wow," Konway whispers.

"You've got this, Tyger." Sage nudges him in the side.

"This is amazing!" he squeezes her hand. "What's it all for? Did Marty do all this?"

"No." She giggles at his naivety. "It's a collective effort, hosted by the city and associated businesses. The Center Street Farmers' Market is a vital step in establishing a feedback loop between local farmers, food purveyors, artisans, and surrounding communities—especially if we're going to make it last for the next seven generations," she teases. "I mean, who wants to eat something sent halfway around the world to be produced at a lower cost when you can simply peruse the vendors for something yummy?"

Above the crowd, a cobalt sky extends down Center Street, where vendor tents and tables brim with fruits, veggies, handmade goods, confections, and an assortment of trinkets. Near Bear and Lynn's chair massage clinic, one tent displays ornate wire-wrapped jewelry adorned with precious stones, seashells, and sharks' teeth. Beside them, Soldier-Surf's table is perfectly stacked with fresh produce, jams, jellies, oils, goat's milk, goat cheese, candles, and B's Surf-Wax with complementary Credible Comb. Farther down, Beach-Sweeper-Social-Club's pop-up canopy showcases surreal Lowcountry landscapes, watercolor slices of life, and driftwood masterpieces, while next door, Surf-Works features rows of metal sculptures—pelicans, sharks, crabs, and dolphins. Beneath the shade of Surf-Pro's educational booth, villagers pass out pamphlets and conduct the application process to become a part of Laniakea—unless you are James Konway.

Several spots away, Todd's disgruntled sneer pierces through a sea of wandering tourists as the lovers arrive. Reluctant to help his tribe book fishing charters and paddleboard safaris, Todd nurses his sprouting obsession, watching his rival's interactions with Sage. "She should be mine," he grumbles. "Look at her being so kind to him." He trails off into echo chambers, bubbling with cauldrons of inadequacy, laziness, and fear, as he watches their tender sweetness.

MoMo's Gratitude

"Set those over there, please, sir." Sage points to a vacant spot under the pop-up canopy.

Mary walks up, clipboard in hand. "Hey, gang, how are y'all this morning?"

"Impeccable," Konway answers.

"I like that. I'm going to use it instead of saying *good*."

Sage chimes in, "Have you ever noticed how people always say they're 'good' without even questioning what it means to be 'good,' or the nature of 'the good' to begin with?"

The conversation stalls as MoMo walks into the shade and tightly hugs Konway. "Oh, thank you. Heavens, thank you. I was so heartbroken when I couldn't find her. Thank you so much. Please, take this jar of CBD honey as a token of my gratitude."

"You really don't have to—"

"I insist—it'll be in this basket. No one will mess with it."

"MoMo," Mary interrupts. "I hate to steal you away, but I've been looking for you."

She points at something on her clipboard, and they slide out from under the canopy, set adrift in a swell of folks surging down Center Street towards the next order of operations.

"Will you be okay over here while I check in at Machu-Beachu's tent?" Sage clasps her arms around Konway's neck.

"I'll be fine." He grins with a hint of irreducible rascality, hoping to quell his fear that the Agency might be among the crowd. (I need to be careful. I can't place Sage or the others in danger. Maybe I'll stay here and help—might keep my mind off it.)

"Helaku should be back soon. Or you can wander about, but don't get lost. I wouldn't want someone to snatch you up and take you from me." She kisses him on the cheek, exits the canopy, and waves to a few old co-workers from Rockaway Deli.

Street Meats

After unloading the utility wagon, Konway stacks a pyramid of honey jars. It's nearly complete when Helaku steps out of a steady stream of people.

"There you are!" he says, offering him some street-vendor meats-on-a-stick. "Here, bro, eat up... Tell me these aren't delicious!"

Konway tears into his treat. "Sure is." He takes another chomp.

"It comes from a farm off-island that consciously raises wild hogs on their property. It's tough work, but it provides a sustainable option for those who wish to consume meat. I know there are sound arguments for not eating it." Helaku cleans the last morsel from the stick. "But sometimes I like a little bacon with my breakfast." He chuckles. "Plus, it helps support local farmers who care about their livestock and their community. Hell, eat some snake bacon if you want—just don't ruin the world to do so."

Finishing their snack, they bound from the canopy in search of Ruckus and Mateo, laughing and brouhaha-ing into the masses—a sloshed sea staggering to and fro throughout the tides of the Center Street Farmers' Market.

Annah R. Kay

Nearby, behind a pair of neuro-laced Panthièr sunglasses, Annah's cool blue eyes lock onto her quarry. A subtle smirk spreads across her cheek. (Zeff's alive... Wait till I tell Ben and the others... I knew if Hats kept tabs on the Agency, you'd show up... I haven't had time to get to the East End, but they're definitely up to something.) She pulls a pen from her bag and jots down an encrypted message. As she sets the writing utensil on the wobbly table next to her drink, it transforms into a dragonfly. Caught in drunken revelry, no one notices it take flight.

She tracks the once-Special Agent's movements, sipping her Samurai Sling. (Although Hats is struggling to crack the Agency's Black-ICE around the EDC's *new* node, they did uncover some interesting intel while poking the bear. But what have you been doing all this time, Zeff? Are you still following the plan?)

Lost in thought, she loses sight of him as he and Helaku weave between the commotion. She huffs at the inconvenience, finishes her drink, drops a tip, and stands. Several meters ahead, Agents Red and Blue, rocking bright floral button-ups, comb through the crowd.

"Nice shirts, boys." She purchases another drink and shifts the focus of her recon, following them until they scuttle into a black unmarked truck, empty-handed.

Part V
A Pier Is Everything

67

Childlike State Of Wonder

Morning Ecstasis

Outside Sage's window, the day sways with a warm breeze. A cardinal perches on a feeder and pecks at delightful clusters of seeds. In the Horseshoe, a mockingbird serenades the winds with a cascade of allegros, adagios, and sun-filled sonatas, blending the songs of thirty-two different birds into a twelve-minute performance. And through the grace of the looking glass, dawn's illumination creeps into a dark corner of Sage's bedroom.

A subtle breeze twirls down from the ceiling fan, wisping brown strands across the flush of her cheek. The moment swells along well-played heartstrings, pulling the lovers into a mystical realm, where they plunge into an intersubjective universe and race towards the doom of their expectations.

Swaddled in neurochemical bliss, they die to complete fulfillment—transcending the constraints of spacetime, discovering a deeper meaning and a stronger significance in a moment of heightened appreciation: a mystical experience sustained in a wink of cosmic unity. Their breathing soon slows into rhythmic laughter. Lost within the soul-smearing aftermath of deep play, Konway softly traces Sage's contours with a dash of tenderness.

Rise

The bedroom settles into an oscillating silence. Sage drifts back to sleep, leaving Konway to tend to his *Space Force III* lunchbox inside the Reliquary of Imagination—an honorable yet futile attempt to renovate the tattered portfolio of past lives, while keeping them separated from the carousel of recent memories.

"Oh shit, the Surf-Cred competition!" She shouts from her pillow.

The lovers spring out of bed and dash to get ready.

"We've got to hurry and meet everyone." Sage slurps back a small bowl of granola.

"Slow down—you're getting milk on your shirt." He hands her a napkin.

"Babe, you don't understand. This is the first time since I've lived here that the conditions are this perfect. I hate that you won't be in it."

"No worries. I'm still a beginner. Besides, it'll be fun watching you from the shore."

"I'm so pumped!"

Several rapid spoonfuls later, they are out the door to meet Helaku by the barn.

The rest of the village is up too—waking, baking, and waxing their boards. Credible Combs mindfully shave away the old B's Surf-Wax into a proprietary recycling canister.

"Yo, bro," Helaku greets Konway, then receives a hug from Sage. "You're excited!"

"Did you see the report? It's going to be a swell day," she jests before leaving them to retrieve her board.

"Where's the competition, again?" asks Konway.

"By the pier," Helaku says.

"Why there?"

"Years ago, they built up an artificial sandbar for better surfing conditions and fishing," Helaku beams with delight.

Konway's mental projector streams bold, crisp images across the Screening Room.

Sage returns with her board and gathers orbs of B's Surf-Wax from its deck. "After the surf comp, we'll probably play volleyball or soccer—or both!" she explodes with excitement.

"How do they decide who rides the best wave?" Konway asks.

"Quality, not quantity, will win the day!" Helaku answers. "The surfer who exhibits the maximum degree of difficulty and commitment will claim the day's glory." He tosses a small piece of B's Surf-Wax at Ruckus. "Wake up. What're you daydreaming about?"

"Chili-cheese dogs from Monk's." Ruckus burps.

"I still haven't been there. Is it near the competition?" Konway asks.

"It's a couple of blocks from Center Street, but it's worth the trek. We'll head there after the comp." Ruckus rubs his belly.

"How can you think about chili-cheese dogs this early?" Sage teases him.

"I could eat 'em breakfast, noon, and night. Luckily, I'm too lazy to walk there more than once a day."

"Boy, you know that's right—"

"Enough chatter. Let's get this show on the road." Helaku hoists an armful of beach supplies onto his shoulders and heads to the crushed-seashell parking lot.

Village Parade

The villagers load up their rickshaws, custom tricycles, fat-tire beach bikes, mountain bikes, and beach cruisers. Then, like a murmur of starlings, the caravan swarms the street, scooting and grooving towards the Surf-Cred competition. Out the front gate, the entire pack of pups chases after the villagers, howling like Paw-Paw's hound dogs on Christmas Day. But reaching an invisible veil, they return to the Laniakea's sanctuary, barking all the livelong way.

Steeped in infectious joy, Konway's light-blue button-up flows behind him, revealing the toned lines of his core. A smile blooms as he watches Sage pedaling ahead of him.

Leading the raucous parade, solar-powered golf carts tow matching utility wagons filled with beach activity kits. Bhodi and Amber work the pedals of two adult-sized Fat Tire trikes, breaking formation like fighter jets, tracing a series of figure-eights before weaving back into the lineup.

Stewart proudly pedals past on his custom bike, blasting tunes from a waterproof speaker mounted between ape-hanger handlebars. Beside him, Lynn and Bear hold hands while they ride. Konway glances back just in time to see Ruckus and Mateo trying to run each other off the road.

Above, diamond-tipped spears of light brighten the shade-speckled street. Tucked within overhead boughs, a mockingbird diligently rehearses the second movement of its latest work, *Concerto No. 6*. The depth and bravado of its notes inspire choirs of songbirds to echo with delight. Konway's heart flutters as he cruises by yellow butterflies locked in a swooping dance of loop-de-loops. To his right, small squirrels chase one another, scampering over live oaks onto pines, leaping from limb to limb and across the street—never needing to touch the ground.

Surf-Cred Competition

Laniakea is the first on the scene, even before the beach-chair rental guys set up their umbrellas for the day. Beyond sunlit dunes, the villagers clear a spot in the sand for their setup. However, their infectious joy wanes to disgust as they spend most of this process picking up the refuse left by day-trippers, tourons, and callous locals.

"It's probably from Movie Night," Mateo says.

Ruckus balls his fist towards the brilliant sky. "Do I visit your churches and shit on your altars?! Why the hell would you do this to mine?" With his other hand, he slams three wadded-up diapers into an abandoned pail he found at the beach access.

Out of the littered wasteland, the villagers carve out their camp, accounting for high tide. One crew plants umbrellas with sundial accuracy. Back and forth, they rock them securely against any rogue gusts. Others stretch pop-up canopies and stake large beach blankets across the warm sand. With coolers stashed, tables set, snacks prepped, Chill-Tunes blasting, and optimal shade coverage achieved, an oasis emerges near the soft sands of Coffin Island's shrinking dunes.

Todd strides past, heading to Machu-Beachu's tent, and smacks Sage's bottom. "Good luck, chica."

Konway steps to the offense.

"Too bad your boyfriend isn't able to compete this year. Would've been great to catch him in the lineup and see what he's got," Todd sneers.

"I'll handle it myself," Sage says, raising an arm to halt an untimely conflict. "Don't get booted over him—he's not worth it." She fires a sharp disdain at Todd.

His gaze shifts to the sand.

Konway lets go of the pleasing thought of knocking the smirk off Todd's face and leans towards her instead, saying, "Kick ass out there." He plants a good-luck kiss.

Sage grabs a handful of his black boardshorts and squeezes his bottom. Once they nuzzle noses, she takes off to join Helaku and the others.

Needle In A Haystack

A little way up the beach, tucked under a clamshell umbrella on a cushioned lounge chair, heron-blue eyes scan the shore over a well-read copy of William Gibson's *Neuromancer*. "There you are, Zeff. I thought you'd be here." Annah R. Kay casually checks left, then right. "No Agency goons around either. After this chapter, I'll come say hello. But this chick is going to be a problem." She shifts her neuro-laced Panthièr sunglasses up the bridge of her slightly pointed nose. Augmented lenses zoom in on Konway and ping his location to Hats. She continues to observe his motions, examining how he interacts with the villagers... with Sage. Annah's plump lips wrap around a reusable silicone straw, and she sips on a summer daiquiri.

She returns to her reading. A few lines later, swept up in a matrix of cyberpunk tropes, she loses track of time. To Annah's surprise, when she glances up from the crease of the page, she finds he has vanished from the beach camp.

"Where'd you go now?" The targeting reticle of her designer lenses roves through the sea of people, attempting to match facial features. "Did the Agency grab him?" She surveys the surf competition as the tide creeps below her seat. (Doesn't seem like much movement. Zeff wouldn't have gone without a fight... I need to be cautious. I'm alone out here.) She repositions her chair closer to the beach camp and continues monitoring the situation.

68

Indra's Ferris Wheel

Ascent

Drawn by curiosity and the urge to gain a better view of the Surf-Cred competition, Konway heads towards the pier. He flows through the crowd and sorts his frustrations.

(Maybe I should go before the Agency comes looking—)

(They *will* come for you,) the Imp rattles into his ear.

(—If I'm not there... if I can't protect her... protect the village—how the hell could I live with myself?) Fear fills him. (Do I deserve it? I've killed so many people.)

(Heee-he-heee.) The ghoul cackles. (They all deserved it.)

(Not the scientists!) He succumbs to doubt. (Why the fuck did I have to do that to them? Following orders? I'm fucked up—)

(You don't deserve the village's love, its shelter... her touch,) it persists like a leaky sore.

Growing increasingly fatigued from the arbitrage of the Imp's siege, he sighs. (I should turn myself in.)

A cold spike shoots down his back, around his hip, and over his knee. He resists the stumble, countering his stride with his other leg. The sensation reels in a memory of being thawed prior to syncing with the Oros system.

(No! There has to be another way. I won't be their puppet—their tool for murder. If I hide out at Laniakea, maybe I can find a path to redemption—what if I'm not allowed to stay?)

(Why would they let you stay? How long can you hide your past?) the Imp-oster hisses.

Konway approaches a towering set of zigzag ramps leading up to Coffin Island's pier. He subdues the angst with a few passes of the worn paper rhino. Back and forth, up the modern ziggurat, he displaces the haunting neurosis clawing within the crooked Corridors of Concern.

At the top, a dopaminergic drip triggers the malfunctioning Oros system and flings his attention into an abrupt focus. His connective tissue trembles with another icy pulse. It goes unnoticed as the sight before him absorbs his mental bandwidth.

A wayward fluff of clouds slowly drifts apart, unveiling a dazzling glimmer suspended in a spider's web strung between the spokes of Coffin Island's Ferris wheel. Light spears rain onto his optics, where conversion algorithms zoom in on a lattice of shimmering dewdrops, projecting them onto the TacOHUD. Like turning a kaleidoscope, the vectors of his awareness converge upon a splendid jeweled net, stretching to infinity in all directions. Plucked along its webbed strands, endless sparkles gleam as seagulls squawk about bait buckets and rubbish bins, pecking through the refuse of the day.

Angler

Coffin Island's pier buzzes with activity as notes of freshly gutted fish waft on the ocean breeze. Speckled across the railing, the early morning anglers huddle at their claimed spots, staked out long before the first crows of dawn. Some sit with others; a few sit alone—plenty of room for all.

A few meters away from him, an older man in a bright teal, multi-pocketed outdoorsman fishing shirt and a white bucket hat exits the tackle shop and notices Konway gawking at the Ferris wheel.

"She's beautiful, ain't she?" he asks, walking up, holding a paper bag filled with snacks and a tub of bait shrimp. "We almost lost her during a hurricane—once or twice—but the bubble prevailed. Skirted that storm right up the coast. Thank the Lord, it missed our little strip of paradise." He removes his hat in reverence of life's miracles. "You know, my wife and I had our first date on this pier."

"Sounds like a good time," Konway replies, relieved to speak with someone. The edge of his reality softens.

"It was my first kiss. You see, there was a date auction at the old malt shop—now it's the Pier View restaurant. You should try their fries. Amazing view. Anyway, I found some courage and marched myself up there."

"Were you nervous?" Konway rests back on the railing and enjoys the onshore breeze.

"Heck yeah, I was. We were trying to raise funds for Pearl's surgery. I even wore my best bow tie and dress shoes—slightly scuffed."

"How much money did you raise?" he asks.

"Well, at first, no one bid on me. I started feeling anxious, standing up there being auctioned off with no one wanting me. But then a pretty local girl took pity on me and placed a bid—and won. Boy, was I relieved." He laughs, concluding with a raspy cough. "Go ahead, smoke another one," he playfully taunts himself.

The angler clears his throat. "They treated us to a date on the pier: food, games, bowling, and two tickets for the Ferris wheel. Back in those days, that was the highlight of the year." He smiles, lost in reflection.

Date Night

A young couple bashfully strolls along the Coffin Island pier. His hand trembles as he reaches for hers. She barely misses his sweaty attempt, and their hearts flutter. Halfway back to the Ferris wheel, an older fisherman races across to the overture of bells at the ends of his nine lines—ringing for the catch.

"Whoa-whoa-whoa!" One by one, the salty angler hoists neon bobbers from the wave-churned waters far below and fills his cooler to the brim.

They look on in amazement at the fisherman's dexterity and grace. Nearby, an elderly woman slowly drags a rickety tackle cart behind her. Performing a random act of kindness, he offers his catch—stooping low to hoist the overflowing cooler of fish onto her cart.

"Oh, please don't... I couldn't... I didn't catch any. Keep what you've earned," she says.

"But ma'am, it's mine to give away. Besides, I don't know how to cook."

The old lady blushes at the genuine gesture. "Come by my house on Fourth Block. Bring yer friends, and we'll have a good ole fish fry." She grins a toothless smile.

"Sounds like a stomping-good time." He laughs. "Maybe we can gather some folks and have a porch jam?"

The Ferris wheel's lights flicker on, and soon the sounds of the boardwalk arcade, bowling alley, and malt shop overwhelm the waves. With impeccable timing, they arrive before the next herds grace the island for the dinner rush.

Their gondola slowly rotates to the top as the setting sun shifts green-brown waters into salmon shades of fading violet.

"I bet you can see the entire island from up here!" he exclaims.

"Wow! See how that beam from the lighthouse reaches up the coast?" she points.

He turns to see the beacons from neighboring barrier islands glowing along the lighthouse-lit shores. They scoot to face the Atlantic and stare out at the approaching nightfall. His gut gurgles.

Spinning back to look over Center Street, streams of sand sweep through the bustling dust of summer. Below them, the boardwalk is alive—and so is the fire in their hearts. They gaze at each other with nervous hesitation. He leans in for a kiss.

Suddenly, a passing seagull squawks by her ear—she flinches, elbowing him in the stomach. To his embarrassment, a trumpeted squeal escapes from his lower half, and they erupt into riotous laughter, guffawing and hee-hawing all the way down the Ferris wheel.

Back on the boardwalk, tears in their eyes, their giddiness carries them past lamp-lit planks, trailing back to the pier's end, hand in hand, up to the observation gazebo.

Uncle

"I definitely out-kicked my coverage," he grins. "Only fools fall in love... and all these years later, we're still a couple of fools."

"Where is she today?" Konway carries the conversation.

"Hanging out in that beach chair over there." He points towards a sea of clamshells and brightly colored beach umbrellas. "The sun is too intense, so she reads and plays Sudoku in the shade while I try fishing for dinner. She even brings me water every now and again."

"Are you as good as the fisherman in your story?"

"Hell no! Can't catch a damn thing." He chuckles. "I usually suck it up and pay for dinner."

"Which chair is she?" Konway stares out across a sea of umbrellas.

The brightly dressed angler pulls his dripping cast net from a mud bucket. "Here, hold this end." He stretches out the net. "If you count inward from the surf, she's four squares to the right and two squares down—see the floppy hat?"

Konway squints. "Yeah... I think so."

"Hold on. I'll get her to wave." He unlocks his smartphone and places the call. "Hey, Baby-doll."

"Yes, Baby-doll," a sweet Southern voice replies.

"Just wanted to say I love you. Mind giving me and my new friend a wave, please?"

"You're not telling *that* story again, are you, Bernard?" she asks.

"Yes, ma'am, I am. You know it's one of my favorites," he answers, beaming with admiration.

A pale hand reaches past the Ruby Refresher and gives a wave. On her arm, a jade bracelet dances to the flick of her wrist.

"Oh, I forgot. I've been bloviating without properly introducing myself. Name's Bernard, but you can call me Bernie."

"Nice to meet you. I'm Konway, James Konway." He politely shakes his hand. "Are you watching the surf competition?"

"Not really, but my nephew Mateo is in it," replies Bernie, fiddling with a utility pockets.

"I know Mateo," Konway says, relieved by familiarity. "You're his uncle? He talks about you all the time."

"Probably all bad." Bernie laughs at the self-deprecation. "Well, it's a small world, ain't it? Y'all're lucky... Laniakea is a cool place to live—"

A lingering darkness seeps from the dumpsters of his Mind Palace, festering a wound around his heart. (You'll never belong there,) the Imp-oster whispers. (How could they let you stay once they know what you've been hiding from them?)

Konway suppresses his angst for the moment.

"—Any friend of my nephew is a friend of mine." Bernie, realizing he has been away from his rods for too long, excuses himself with a swooping handshake and scuttles to the end of the pier.

Konway leans against the storm-worn railing, watching Mateo's peculiar uncle disappear into the shuffling stream of sunburnt day-trippers. He box-breathes, passing the paper rhino to down-regulate his nervous system and subdue the clawing neurosis. Absent on the banks of the bustling crowd, another beetle-squirt of vividity sputters from the Oros system, rendering a bouquet of patterned sensations upon his hazel eyes.

People Watching

Synesthetic excitement bubbles above the brim of his chalice as he watches the writhing mass of beachgoers—all a different shade of sunburnt—tinged with that out-of-your-element anxiousness. A tough guy, sporting an American flag tank top and matching trunks, struts past, only to stumble on a loose board while eyeing two girls in high-waisted bikinis heading in the opposite direction. Behind him, a strong perfume wafts into the passing puffs of cigar smoke.

Seagulls crisscross under the day's brilliance. A few dive-bomb the pier and chase away a plague of grackles investigating a row of sinks and some leftover cut bait. However, the outlaws soon return, intent on swiping someone's catch from their cooler.

Next to the Pier View restaurant, more black-winged bandits silently position themselves above a basket of fries and an unaware tourist. The foodie squirts watery ketchup onto their plate. And the moment they turn to complain about their dietary preferences, one crispy, hot, perfectly salted order of fries is pilfered in an instant.

An air horn snaps Konway's attention back to the Surf-Cred competition, already underway.

(Sage was right to be excited.) He envisions the exhilaration of being out there—board, body, and ocean.

"All of this fun in the sun is brought to you by WAVE FM!" a nearby set of speakers crackles with the audio feed from a local radio station.

Bob & Randy

As the heat of the sand casts a mirage across the beach, tucked away in the shade of a nearby production tent, a sweaty set of commentators streams Paul Buzzbee's live drone footage.

"For those of you just tuning in," Bob's deep Australian voice bursts through the post-commercial-break silence, "today's waves have been head-high, glassy, and perfect for these guys and gals."

"You're not wrong there. Gorgeous day to be at the beach," Randy, a nasally New Yorker, chimes in over the mic.

"We've got action!" Bob booms.

Randy leaps up, mic in hand. "Stewart Hawthorne paddles into a decent drop-in... then nails a slick series of cutbacks—"

"I see the locals from Laniakea are stoking the lineup," Bob adds. "This is gonna be a showdown today."

"—That was a solid run. But will it be enough?"

Bob sips his drink, crunching on a piece of ice. "This is the largest crowd we've seen—"

"Here we go!" Randy roars. "The wave pulls back... and Julius Peppercorn wipes out."

"Ooof. Another pile driver, testing the depths of the water. Be safe out there, folks—it's not Halloween, but we are on Coffin Island. EMS is standing by."

"Up next from Laniakea, repping Machu-Beachu, Todd McGillicuddy," Randy announces.

"You know, they didn't think he was going to recover in time, but here he is today," Bob informs. "Let's see if he can keep it clean. Todd gets into position."

"And he's up... Check out that juicy crescent moon carving up the inside!" Randy cheers, twirling a paper umbrella.

"Save me some of that ocean spray!" Bob laughs, high-fiving his co-host.

"It's a pretty solid run, with the points to back it." Randy continues to the next rider. "George Thurgoode is pumping his bags to gain some speed. Just enough to close out the barrel."

"Though we've had some high scores being posted by Laniakea," Bob interjects, "don't discredit the out-of-towners."

"Wahoo! Back up and kick it out again!" Randy hollers through the pier's sound system.

"He's got excellent form and control."

"Did you see that rooster tail?"

"The judges have placed their scores—"

"And now, a word from our sponsors."

Fish Tales

Bernie returns from his spot at the end of the pier. "Are you enjoying the competition?" he asks.

"Most definitely. Maybe next year I'll give it a go... Did you catch anything?" A strange uneasiness quivers in Konway's stomach, referring an icy muscle spasm into his left arm.

"Mostly feeding the crabs. Tangled my net, too. I don't mind, though." Bernie flashes a smile of pearly veneers. "I get to be out here—chatting with folks, picking up trash, and listening to the ocean. It's not a bad gig... Now, the fella beside me caught three at the same time."

"How?" Konway tries to ease the brooding panic encircling him.

"We were all excited, thinking it was going to be a monster. But it was two small fish and a medium one. Hey, are you thirsty? I'm about to get myself something to drink." He thumbs towards the tackle shop.

"If you're offering." He smiles to mask his momentary discomfort and accepts the kindness.

"Watch my gear for me. I'll be back in two shakes."

Konway scoots the mud bucket closer and turns back to the waves, passing the paper rhino and listening to the announcers' jestering banter.

"Ouch!" Bob winces. "That looked like it hurt."

"Don't worry, folks, he's all good. Let's give them a round of applause. These riders are working hard out there today," Randy says.

Sleek and streamlined, the competitors demonstrate their prowess and presence in the water. One by one, dropping in and letting go, they commune with the divine, while onshore, judges try to quantify the quality of their experience.

Surcee

The giant Ferris wheel kicks up its music again, hoisting gondolas of sightseers to the top for a grand view of Coffin Island. Two ribbons of thirty pelicans weave along an updraft towards their favorite hunting grounds. Under the day's resplendence, parting clouds reveal the sun's dance across the water.

Bernie returns with an unexpected treat: two glass bottles of Mexi-Cola and two packs of salted peanuts. "Here, try this," he says. "They put real sugar in them down there, like when I was a kid. We didn't have all this high-fructose nonsense back in my day. This tastes the best. What do you think?"

Konway takes a swig of sharp, carbonated crispness. Its fizzle tickles a rush of sweet sensations through his brain's reward centers. "That's tasty."

"And according to my grand-youngins, there's no plastic. It's win-win." Bernie winks, slipping several salted peanuts into his drink.

"What about the peanuts' packaging?"

"You've got me there. We're all clever hypocrites," he says, chuckling. "But it doesn't mean we shouldn't try to be better."

Konway pivots the conversation, asking, "What does putting them in the bottle do?"

"It's something my granddaddy showed me—from way back when. Every time we went to fill up his Galaxie 500—they don't make cars like that anymore—we'd each have a sleeve of shelled peanuts and a bottle of cola."

Konway rips open the pack and pours a healthy handful of salt-roasted goodness into his beverage. The tiny legumes kerplunk into the soda below, then bubble towards the surface. He drinks it down, rewarding himself with a surge of savory and sugary notes, Trojan-horsed within the snack's satisfying crunch and munch. He smacks his lips in delight and looks back at the Ferris wheel, hoping to catch another sparkling glimpse—alas, it is just the amusement ride.

"How long has this been here?" he asks.

"Let's see... Coffin Island's pier was built in the thirties, and the Ferris wheel came around 1957, I think. Amazingly, it survived all those storms. And we've had some big ones, mind you. The funny thing about Coffin Island is that it's always changing. Hell, back during the Civil War, it was two islands before they built up the land for their artillery to bombard the nearby peninsula. Still, today, the beach is growing."

"How so?" Konway asks.

Bernie swigs from his cola. "Well, this past spring, they signed another beach-renewal contract for a considerable amount of sand to be pumped from offshore for the next decade. Someone high on the city council must have some serious connections... Might be why I've been seeing a bunch of government activity lately."

"What do you mean?" The queasiness returns.

"Ever since that ship *allegedly* crashed into the bridge, there've been a lot of unmarked vehicles and suspicious folks around town. I don't think it's a coincidence they've closed off access to the lighthouse at the East End, either. My buddy at the station thinks it's part of the renewal... Something doesn't sit with me—and what about those drones?"

(BOB?)

"Don't mind him, honey," Baby-doll's sweet Southern voice echoes from the front pocket of Bernie's fishing shirt. On the other end, beneath a clamshell umbrella, she lifts her palmetto-painted tumbler for a refreshing sip. "Lord, it's hot. Bernard, don't bother him with your political nonsense and start stressing."

"Oops." He fumbles to pluck the device from his pocket and hangs up the call. "There we go. Sorry about that—with all this new technology, I keep forgetting how to turn the damn thing off." Bernie belly-laughs. "She's right, though—it's far too beautiful a day to worry about things out of our control."

"Very true." Konway swigs from his surcee.

"Do you know what they say about *worrying*?"

"No, sir."

"I think Mark Twain said this, but I could be wrong—what the hell do I know," he confesses. "'Worrying is like paying interest on a loan you haven't received.'"

Not sure what a *loan* is, Konway nods to keep the conversation rolling.

"You've got some good manners about you. Where you from?" asks Bernie, attempting to untangle a net from his bucket.

"That's an excellent question," he answers, suppressing the bubbling uneasiness of his violent past.

"You're not one of them, are you?"

"Bernard!" Baby-doll's voice shouts from his pocket.

Bernie hands over the partially tangled cast net and fumbles the phone to his ear. "Damn it, Barbara, you know I can't help myself." He laughs into the call.

Konway lifts the net and counts the breadth of the horizon while his TacO-HUD renders the glistening Atlantic, framed by the shadows of grazing cumulonimbus clouds. He soon loses himself in the waves' symmetry, marveling at how each crest reflects its trough. A ribbon of pelicans swoops from his peripherals and pulls his gaze back to the Surf-Cred competition just as Amber catches a ride on a chariot of chest-high glass.

Big Colorful Beach Umbrella

In the top-right frame of his TacOHUD, Konway locks onto the colorful spiral of a fumbling, tumbling umbrella as it barrels towards the pier. A few campsites away, a thoroughly sunburnt touron chases after it. Nanite subroutines deliver a shot of [Time Warp], slowing Konway's perception to a calculated crawl.

For an intuitive instant, the waves, the commentators, and the crowd shrink into a manageable murmur. He steps outside the moment, filtering every detail through the malfunctioning Oros system. A simulated target analysis of the beach umbrella's point of impact is computed—factoring in wind, sand slope, and boardwalk height—and projected as spaghetti models across his TacOHUD.

Within a dilated moment of observation, the wind shifts, and the algorithm updates the umbrella's potential point of impact. His astonishment vanishes. At the tip of the green arrow, a posh group of girls stands outside Scoops, the pier's ice-cream hut, joined by a dapper, silver-haired gentleman.

Bounding towards them, Konway's enhanced physiology propels him past picnic tables and between sparsely clustered crowds. The TacOHUD tracks the wind-swept beach umbrella. He strides closer, sidestepping a forgotten water bottle, closing the gap, then vaults over the final bird-stained bin separating him from his target.

69

Drip, Drop, Drippings

Interception

Several moments prior, a group of friends in stylish beach attire exits Scoops. Two children run past them, cheerily squealing towards the end of the boardwalk. A little farther down, one child trips on an uneven board and skins his knee. His sister stoops to tend to him, but his wail sends her backpedaling. Soon, their wayward parents rush over to reassure him of his safety and security.

"Where should we sit?" A woman with well-woven microlocs catches a sweet dribble with her bamboo spoon.

"Definitely not in the sun, V. I'm melting faster than my sweet treat," Richard Honeycutt, a silver-haired man with a well-defined nose and jawline, says with a bit of sass.

"Obviously." Vivian cuts her eyes with a playful grin.

Another slightly shorter woman, Alexis, rocking gold and red textured highlights, mixes the toppings in her bowl. "Let's head for the swings," she suggests. "How about those canopies right there? We can sit two at a time."

"Yasssssss." They giggle at the consensus.

"Ooh, what flavor did you get?" asks a brunette, lowering a pair of oversized sunglasses down the bridge of her nose. "May I try some?"

"It's quite delicious, Emma. You must try mine." Richard tilts his bamboo bowl to her. "But I'm gonna need a spoonful of—"

Save The Day

A flight of pigeons flaps out of the way as Konway charges towards the group, hurdling picnic tables and trash cans. *Twok!* His reinforced grip seizes the colorful beach umbrella. Time snaps back to its normal flow—the genuine-imitation-plastic pole just two inches from Emma's chest.

Her scream fills the air as the fleeting abruptness of life flashes before her eyes and the sun-swirled sorbet slips from her hand. Its tie-dye fixings melt through the boardwalk's cracks, dripping onto the society-stained dunes below.

"Em, are you alright?" Vivian asks.

A look of bewilderment stretches across Emma's brow. "I almost died." She plops down to her haunches and sobs. "Oh, my God... I almost died!"

Helen Ogletree, a woman with dirty-blonde, shoulder-length hair, rushes over in a flowing beach cover-up, balancing a double-scoop waffle cone. She hands the treat to Richard and squats down beside Emma, asking, "Are you alright?"

"I've so much to do—I've wasted so much time," she responds, riddled with the fear of her own mortality.

Helen stands and turns to Konway, asking, "How on earth did you do that?"

"Right place at the right time." He shrugs off the honors with a smile of humility, still clutching the beach umbrella.

The gears behind her thoughts churn at the riddle. "In any case, thank you," her cursive drawl dovetails poignant politeness. "We are terribly grateful for your bravery." She reaches out with an affirming handshake. "I'm Helen. What's your name?"

"Konway—"

"Helaku speaks highly of you," she interrupts him.

He notices a blush patting itself into place on her cheeks.

"By the way, impressive work debugging the MARS unit," she continues, retrieving her melting treat from Richard Honeycutt. "Come, sit with us—there's no need for a friend of Helaku's to spend this beautiful day alone."

"Thank you for the offer," Konway says. "But everyone is back at our spot." He finally rests the umbrella beside the storm-worn railing.

"Well... please stop by with Helaku later. Look for the gazebo in front of the navy-blue house with an infinity pool. I think we're all quite curious to know more about our mysterious hero."

"Won't be much of a story. I have a problem remembering who I am," he says.

"Honey, most of us have that problem." She places a light hand on Konway's shoulder.

Helen rallies her crew and heads towards their gazebo. Under the boardwalk, in the piled-high sand from a recent beach renourishment, neon swirls drip candy-coated drops into pristine puddles of microplastics and crustacean corpses. Unnoticed, tiny hermit crabs scuttle about the fringes of the pier's pilings, waiting for the tide. All around, the day's buzz mixes with childhood laughter and the mutter of adulthood.

Creeping Neurosis

Konway finds a spot away from the crowd and leans over a railing. Out past the break, surfers wait for the next set. Their toes wiggle to the tug of the Atlantic. A sharp sparkle winks across the lineup as the set rolls into formation, and the competitors paddle into position.

He recalls the dolphins from Helaku's tale. And from its free association, a glimmer of hope.

(I can do good—despite who I was.)

Unable to suppress the malfunctioning Oros system, another icy tremor ripples down his shoulder into his left arm. He grips the edge and braces himself, trying not to fall over. No one notices. It passes, and in its wake, disheartened confusion swells.

(Again?! What the fuck is wrong with me?) he asks into the hollow ruins of his Mind Palace. (Every time I think I'm doing better, something strange happens. Do I need to see a doctor?)

(They might find out who you are,) the Imp presses.

(I don't give a fuck about who I was. I'm not him anymore. Is this new life not worth saving? Are my feelings for Sage not genuine? What about Helaku and the others?)

Passing the paper rhino, he sorts through his collection of memetic trading cards. His heart warms with their conjured memories. Each one—a jeweled stasis of shared experience—pushes his fear-based logic farther from the stage, grounding him in what matters most and restoring his composure just in time to catch the start of Helaku's heat.

Qualifying

The whole of Laniakea, not competing, gathers around a smart screen to watch the live feed from the Surf-Cred competition. Outside the tent, others crane their necks to the break, guided by an 'M' of seabirds polka-dotting the distance. Halfway up the sky, the sun glimmers on the Atlantic while a clean break streaks across the shore, like scissors along the edge of craft paper. Beneath its curl, sand dollars sink deeper with the tide.

The ebbing ocean rocks Helaku into a whelming peace. Free from the pressures of competition, his sense of self dissolves into layered meta-levels of flow—shelving the pain of watching the world burning around him, with no one to care enough to piss it out. He lets go of thinking about Jack's rivalry, Todd's nonsense, the pressures of being Chief, and his nervousness about his secret lover. No longer able to distinguish between himself from the board or the ocean, a silence pulls him from afar. In those regions past where the eyes can see, shadows rise from the horizon and surge towards the shore.

Helaku paddles into a cosmopolitan blend of timelessness, effortlessness, and richness. The moment holds fast and true while he steps down the crashing wave. All around, the foaming crescendos of salt spray applaud as the first turn channels his speed ahead of the closing barrel. He buries his weight into the inside rail, drawing an arc within the curl, and carves along the swell. Then, swinging back into the barrel, he reconnects with the pocket to harness the ocean's full support. Farther along, he transfers his weight to the longboard's nose, riding on the edge and wiggling his ten toes off the front.

The momentum shifts, and Helaku repositions opposite his usual stance, gliding into the shallows. With a salute and a smile as big as day, he playfully drops into the foam. The judges hold up their scorecards, placing him in the final heat of the Surf-Cred competition, and the beach erupts with rooster-crows and wolf-howls.

"Now, a quick word from our sponsors." Bob and Randy cut to some shameless promotional ads.

Stalled Doubt

Thanks to the surcee, Konway makes a quick bathroom stop. As he washes his hands and peers into the grime-rusted mirror, echoes drift from the Fog of Despair, igniting a discourse of doubt to slow-churn the fumes of inadequacy, loss, and isolation.

(I can't keep hiding who I was from Sage and Helaku. Who knows how many people I've killed or harmed? When will they come for me? I'm placing the entire village in danger. I should just run. But where?)

(Now that's the spirit,) the Imp teases.

(Get a grip on yourself—don't let them go so easily. Keep hiding there, escape my past, and grow into someone who helps raise the stage for—)

Boom-boom-boom-boom! An impatient tourist hurriedly pounds on the other side of the wooden door, hollering, "Hurry up in there! I've really got to go. Please, man!"

Startled, Konway bursts from the bathroom and apologizes for the inconvenience. Without replying, the sun-crisped man enters and slams the door. Two steps away, behind the thin-pressed threshold, a full payload of explosive munitions fills the porcelain chalice.

The echoes of the battlefield trail beyond Konway's periphery, where a colony of gulls squawks over a discarded hot dog bun. Amidst Coffin Island's backdrop, the hum of summer fills his bandwidth. On the beach, children play amongst the waves while a plague of grackles perches on their stilts, waiting for the next order to fall.

70

Finals

Pier View

Nearby, Agents Red and Blue blend into the seasonal crowd. Behind the lenses of their Met-Ban sunglasses—powered by the Lighthouse Node—proprietary algorithms ping every device, mapping their surroundings. The digital net traces the faint echo of the Oros system's current location. And from their vantage, it doesn't take long for them to find him unaware, watching the Surf-Cred competition.

Before moving closer, Red pushes the intel up the ladder.

"You finally found him?" Commander Xero asks.

"Yes, sir," Red replies confidently.

"Are you certain?" Commander Xero eagerly asks. "Fuck! Traffic's heavy, and the chopper is in the shop after that egret mess. Keep him there. We're on our way. You'd better be right with this one."

The agents stow their taser-blades and move closer to Konway's position. Just then, a herd of tourists swarms forward, eager to gain better seats for the finals. Again, he disappears out of their dragnet's range.

They scramble to find him. However, a hiccup from the faulty Oros system alters Konway's reality distortion field [RDF], rendering him as invisible as a wallflower at a middle school dance. Aided by their Met-Bans, they search the pier from end to end, checking beneath, hurrying past sherbet-swirled sands and lapping waves—but with no luck.

"You've got to tell the boss you lost him," Red says.

"Why me?" Blue furrows his brow. "We're in this together."

Red pleads, "I don't have too many strikes left... I'll owe you big time."

"Be glad I like you." Blue smiles.

"Damn, that smells good." Red's stomach growls from the flame-grilled goodness rising from the Pier View restaurant.

Blue checks his pockets. "Let's split a burger."

"Split? I missed chow. The Commander had me washing the Humvee."

"Luckily, he let us take the truck."

Three seconds later, the Oros system fires an electrical pulse that stutters Konway's next step towards Laniakea's beach camp. He uncloaks and startles a crispy local on the bender of an endless summer.

Dark Corner

From the main canopy, a surf-rock playlist blares over the drone of the Atlantic. The place is lively, with many villagers snacking, laughing, and enjoying some momentary reprieve from the day. In a nearby pop-up tent, Bear and Lynn have their massage tables, with a line of people waiting for a ten-minute touch-up session. Mary and Momo shuffle about the sand, reviewing the clipboard. Momo's faded tattoos—two rabbits on either side of her hips—taper under the fabric of her pink bathing suit bottoms, while Mary's dreamcatcher tattoo, traced between her shoulder blades, draws eyes with the sway of her backside. Caught in the rhythm, Joel runs into a tent stake, while Stewart and Paul Buzzbee kick a soccer ball with Ruckus and Mateo on the outskirts.

In the dark corner of Machu-Beachu's tent, Todd mixes a drink—two parts swill vodka to one part orange juice—and takes a bump of blow from an old key. As he exits and returns to the group, he covers the despair on his face with a smile and a stout drink in his hand. He looks to the pier and sees James Konway heading to their beach camp. A sharp, indifferent glare cuts in the outsider's direction as he gulps his beverage.

Konway, oblivious to the Agency's proximity, suppresses his fear-based logic with a few passes of the paper rhino and approaches the camp. Closer, he notices the sense of togetherness and connection the villagers share. A longing sense of loneliness blossoms into a rose of inadequacy. (I want this to last. I need this to last. I don't want to put them in any danger—)

Mateo's rogue kick sends the soccer ball sailing towards Konway, who redirects its momentum with a swift boot to Stewart.

"That's a mean leg on you," he says, juggling the volley to Paul.

"Find another, and we'll increase the size of the game!" hollers Ruckus.

"Thank you, but I'm gonna chill and watch the competition a little longer." He smiles to divert attention from the looming gloom hanging about his shoulders.

Konway sits on the sand beneath a well-anchored beach umbrella and stares out beyond the break. Sage sits atop her board, waiting for the final heat of the Surf-Cred competition, and watches Amber take off for her last wave.

Dropping in, she rockets from the collapsing tube, ripping a series of cutbacks. While the judges score their cards, a sudden rain shower sweeps over the island, pausing the competition before scattering minutes later into partial cloud cover. Lances of light dance upon the twinkling sands to reveal micro-craters left in the wake of evaporated raindrops. The day's humidity captures the Bubble's prismatic halo, casting a double rainbow across Coffin Island.

Beverly Laurel

Bob wipes off their table with a bar rag. "Luckily, the storm's already passed, Randy."

"Ya know, there's a saying out here: 'If you don't like the weather, wait fifteen minutes.' But rain or shine, Coffin Island stays beautiful—"

"Wow," Bob cuts in. "I don't know if you're seeing this, but these competitors aren't messing around. Beverly Laurel is shredding some serious gnar—amazing, folks! She's walking the plank!"

"Look at that transition!" Randy scoots to the edge of his seat. "Bob, we might have an upset on our hands today."

"With this run, Beverly Laurel—the out-of-towner hailing from the West Coast—scores big with the judges." Bob flips through some rain-damp notes.

"Sage Forgé needs a near-perfect ride on this next wave to lock in first place for the ladies," Randy says into the microphone.

Bob sets down his drink. "Can she do it?"

"Hang on, folks, here she goes!"

Sage

Sage whips into a wide bottom turn and compresses her stance. With saltwater crashing behind her, she shifts onto her heel side, aiming her lead shoulder at the beach. Then, like a whittler to a soft piece of pine, she slices along the wave's midsection.

As the crowd cheers, Sage returns to center, crouches low, and darts up to the crest of the wave. From its peak, she fiercely rushes down the line, then, shifting her weight between her hips, heels, and toes, carves figure-eights through the surging water. She returns to the curl at full speed and pivots into a radical slash, redirecting the board and snapping a spectacular spray.

The points go up, and the beach cheers with rooster-crows and wolf-howls. Konway stands, lending his verse, as Sage victoriously wades across the shallows and waves at him.

A kaleidoscope of butterflies flutters in his gut. But before she can make it out of the water, the entire village swarms her with congratulatory elation and lovingly whisks her away. The butterflies crumble into ashes of inadequacy.

Imp-oster's Influence

Below the Nether Regions of Thought, the Fog of Despair stirs within its black cauldron and, seeping past the boiling Pits of Frustration, blooms from a schism in the Death Marshes. As it spreads into the Wastelands of Cognition, it taints Konway's disposition with the stench of dismay.

The Imp-oster's burnt-mustard eyes emerge from the void. (You're a murderer.) It chortles.

(Stop it.)

(A threat to everyone around you. You can't even control your own body. What if you hurt Sage? Remember when you wanted to kill Helaku and steal his boat? And what about those poor scientists?)

(Stop it! That wasn't me!) Konway shouts into the tumbling Wastelands.

The shockwave trembles along the arid ground, driving the Fog back to where he hides the things he most longs to forget, rippling farther into Childe's newly renovated Toyshop.

"I don't know what you did. But you fried my device," Childe snaps, stomping into the throne room.

"It wasn't me... What do you need to fix it?"

"I'll make a list." A malicious twinkle gleams through his blurry face.

"Is anything else ruined?"

"Of course not. Who the devil do you think I am?"

Jack

Just as a single salty tear of frustration wells up, the waves pull Konway back to the present moment.

"I hope you're ready for the best surfing this side of the Mississippi," Bob gruffly declares, clutching his microphone.

"That's right, folks. We're in for a real treat." Randy drinks from his paper-umbrella'd beverage. "These last two to walk the line are a couple of local boys."

The announcers continue their antics, while Paul Buzzbee's drone spirals around the rivals. Poised for the next set, Jack paddles into a fast-moving swell and takes the wave, forcing himself along its saline membrane. Then, gripping into a beautiful turn, he lets the tail blow out as he slides into a big carving snap to complete his run.

"OOOooo!!!" Randy cheers into the microphone.

"Did you see that gorgeous front-side snap?" Bob asks, neatening his crumpled info sheets.

"He's been riding strong for this entire event... And with scores like this, Helaku is in a tough position... Can he make up the difference?"

"Well, he needs a solid wave to make this ride count. The pressure is on."

Helaku patiently waits for his set, while, near the pier, the seasonal crowd gathers under the passing reprieve of partially scattered skies. The sun slowly flashes over Coffin Island, as if the Divine were capturing a snapshot of the moment. Paul's drone hovers into position.

Its display feed glows in the shady reprieve of a pop-up tent. Outside, the sun shines with all its heavenly glory. Even the agents in loud floral button-ups swivel towards the Atlantic's sparkle. Close by, Annah R. Kay's icy blue eyes scan Hats's latest message, hidden behind her neuro-laced Panthièr sunglasses. She triggers the scrolling notification, and augmented lenses suddenly highlight her target—zooming in from beneath the Ferris wheel—his face bearing a look she had never seen.

Helaku

Helaku breathes in and recites a quiet prayer to himself. Day after day, the persistent failure during those dawn patrols forged the strength and resolve to push beyond his limits. He exhales, opens his eyes, and spots the herald of an approaching set.

Randy leans into his microphone. "This might be the biggest wave of the day. A big wave for a big man."

"He needs near-perfect placement to take home the gold," Bob adds.

Dropping in with ease, Helaku carves a cracking line across the thunderous wave. Ahead of the cascading whitewash, he shaves along its churning surface, pumping his board for speed. With a deep slice, he flows into a kickflip and lands it cleanly. The roar from the shore falls silent in the barrel.

He surges towards the last section of his ride, chest swelling with an intoxicating mix of air and dopaminergic reward. As the moment stokes his awareness, Helaku exhales, shifts his weight, and surrenders to the wave. A mind-manifesting experience unfurls before him as he scoots up its face, letting go and taking flight.

Triumph

He ascends into the sacred, with his head in the clouds and his feet on the board. There, every dripping droplet from his shark-fin mohawk—down to the smallest atoms in existence—remains in its proper place and order.

"He's airborne!" Bob booms into his microphone. "You rarely see a big man in the air."

Caught in the sway of competitive fervor, Randy jumps to his feet and knocks over his beverage. "360 backside spin! Wahoooooooo! Spin to win, baby!

"Helaku sticks the landing!"

"SPIN TO WIN!"

"OOOooo!!!" Bob calls.

The beach erupts in a symphony of wolf-howls, cowbells, and rooster-crows.

"Did you see that?" Bob asks. "What an incredible performance! Helaku is sure to rip some high scores from the judges."

"But will they be enough to take out Jack's standing?" Randy stirs the pot.

An eternity passes in a matter of seconds as Helaku lands in front of the frothy deluge. With both arms reaching for the sky, he slaloms into the shallows, then backflips into the ocean's tireless poetry. The shore rushes to greet him before he strides from the surf, board under his arm, saltwater dribbling off the cliffs of his shoulders. His infectious joy, beaming from his larger-than-life smile, spreads the victory through the gathering crowd. Luckily, Ruckus and a few others intercept them before they can overwhelm him with their favor and prestige.

Reveal

Helen walks over to congratulate Helaku and extends her hand.

Steeped in stoke, Helaku sets aside his barriers, pulls her to his salt-soaked body, and kisses her deeply.

She pulls back and looks up at him. "I can't believe you landed it! So sexy."

"Me either," Helaku replies, "but I didn't come here to leave trash on the beach."

"You're bad." Helen feigns a playful shock as she adjusts her leopard sunglasses. "I guess this is when we were going to let everyone know about us? Although... I think a much more subtle approach would have been sufficient."

"You know that ain't my style." They spin to the crowd. "Hey gang, I'd like to introduce y'all to Helen." Helaku's smile hides his eyes behind rounded cheeks of adoration.

Helen shifts her demeanor from shock to delight, saying, "Hello, everyone. It's so nice to finally meet all of you."

The villagers, brimming with excitement, swarm her with hugs and hand-shakes. The power couple makes their way through the crowd—chatting, cheering, toasting, taking pictures, and making funny faces. All around, the villagers' whoops and howls turn into chanting: "Hel-a-ku! Hel-a-ku! Hel-a-ku!"

Tarnished

Elsewhere, Jack and Todd scowl in the shade, turning their backs on the celebration, ripping a couple of key bumps with IPA chasers.

"Enjoy your turn in the spotlight, big guy. In time, I'll take everything from you." Jack snorts another powdery whiff, then sinks into his selfish plots of grandeur.

Todd wipes the drip from his nose and looks for Konway.

"Don't worry, she'll be yours again." Jack taps his stash vial. "Just follow my plan."

"Why isn't PJ here?"

"Joel said he hasn't left his girlfriend's house in days."

"He has a girlfriend?"

"And if he keeps it up, I won't be able to hold his spot in the village."

"That's bullshit! *He* gets to stay, and PJ has to leave?"

"Chill. There's still time... but PJ's making his own bed." Jack hands Todd the vial.

Prodigal Turn

Despite the bubbling excitement surrounding the victors, Konway can't seem to shake his gnawing sense of isolation. Another icy quiver courses down his spine into his right arm.

(See... You don't fit in... You don't belong here.) The Imp-oster chortles. (They're better without you—)

Konway box-breathes to subdue the returning fog. However, this time, the paper rhino fails to pierce the angst of his splintered identity. Not wanting to ruin everyone's joy, he turns towards the pier, hoping to gain a morsel of reprieve from the albatross hanging upon his shoulders.

Helaku notices him distancing himself from the group. "Konway! Hey, hold up!" He jogs away from the boisterous crowd. "Where are you headed, bro? What'd you think of my last trick?"

"Impressive... when did you sprout wings?" He feigns a pleasant look over the brooding melancholy.

"Let's celebrate. I brought some medicine, and I want you to meet Helen."

"I ran into her at the pier." He smiles, masking the gnawing agitation. Sadly, his valor is not enough.

"Is everything all right?"

"Just a little overstimulated from a rush of memories—maybe going for a walk will clear my mind." He smirks. (Why do I feel this way? Why don't I tell him?) A stew of fear-based logic holds him in silence.

"Okay, but if you go too far, turn around and keep the ocean on your left. I'll have one rolled for you."

Konway hunts for Sage, but she is caught in the moment's laughter.

"No worries, bro. I'll let her know you went for a stroll. Go clear your head."

They dap farewell—striking their thumbs down the center of their backs, then clasping hands with the other.

"We've got some celebrating to do, and it won't be the same without you." Helaku grins in good faith.

"No need to worry... I'll return soon."

"I'm your big bro." He raises an eyebrow. "I've got to say these things."

After they bump fists, Helaku returns to the cheering crowd. And for the first time, Konway walks away from Laniakea, down the beach, past neglected plastic beach toys, waterlogged towels, broken sandals, and the smell of coconut tanning oil. Annah R. Kay follows him under the pier, hoping to make contact, but another glitch in the Oros system diminishes his reality distortion field. Once again, she loses him amongst the freaks, geeks, day-trippers, bros, betties, and debutantes. She pivots and, instead, hunts for Red and Blue, who've already left the area for fear of wasting Commander Xero's patience.

71

Tide Pools Of Doubt

Taunt

Farther down the shore, countless waves curl into crescendoed signatures and crash along the particulated dance floor. Twelve pelicans ribbon above the backsides of watery crescents, weaving beyond the line of sight.

"Get a hold of yourself and turn around," Konway says. (Why do I feel this way? Is this real? What is real?)

Elsewhile, sitting upon the Bone Throne, the Imp-oster's burnt-yellow eyes track the pace of Konway's distress.

"Try it out," Childe says, throwing a crude switch. "This is just a patch, so the connection might not hold."

(Give up.) Its tongue scratches behind Konway's eyes.

"What do you want from me?"

(Stop resisting your true nature.)

"Leave me alone!" he howls.

Another pulse pushes back the Fog of Despair, short-circuiting Childe's recent hotfix. The Imp-oster scowls with infuriating silence.

Only the buzzing blades of dune grass and the rattle of an abandoned beach pail, snagged in the sand fencing, respond to his anguish. Fortunately, his breath-work steadies him, and the worn paper rhino wrestles him back to the present.

Discoveries

Several jetties up the beach, Konway sits on a barnacle-peppered rock and peers into a tide pool of wonderment and depth, letting his curiosity distract him from the Imp's gnawing agitation. A much-needed reprieve, he looks up from a herd of thirty scuttling hermit crabs and notices numerous pools forming across the beach. He places the origami figure in the front pocket of his light-blue button-up beach shirt and hops off the gray Goose Creek limestone boulder to explore the interconnected flow of saltwater.

Nearby, a school of tiny fish darts about their tidal nursery, confined within a multi-tiered labyrinth leading to the ocean. A kaleido-cosm of pastel and earthen shells flickers about, while a cast of hermit crabs cobbles around sifting whelks, all swirling beneath the glossy spears of the glistening sun. Along the fringes, starfish stalk through the muck, hunting among the boulders of tidal erosion.

Konway peers into the depths of one of the larger rock pools and spies a passing shadow, hidden by the rippling backsplash of streamlined movements. A tiny tip slips past the surface. Its gray body trails behind a small, hammer-like head. The baby shark roams the tide pool system until it locates the Atlantic's pull, slides into the surf, and dashes to parts unknown.

He glances back just in time to catch a cloud of upturned sediment settling onto the backside of a resting ray. Two pools over, tiny semi-translucent flowers bob amidst poorly planned attempts to stall the sea.

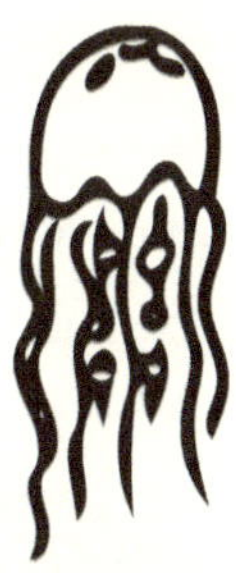

Juvenile jellies lap against granite boulders, stretching their invisible tentacles in search of nourishment. Nearby, another cast of hermit crabs scuttles away from a slow-roving sea star into the tidal haze.

Tremors

Towards the end of *Neptune's Adventure,* a dune mouse squeaks past Konway, darting into a tangle of washed-up seagrass and the skeletons of salt-cured trees. Overhead, the sun pierces the soft backsides of fluffy clouds, blanketing the tidal shallows. Another tremor wells up from within, followed by a misfired beetle-squirt of subliminality.

From parted clouds, a flood of light crashes through the ocean mists, revealing rainbowed splashes before the spectrum of his experience. The sky's reflection is too much to bear. Rippling currents disorient his sense of balance, and with the beatific vision nearly crushing him, Konway stoops low and passes the paper rhino.

He continues box-breathing until a momentary reprieve washes around him—dimming the brilliant affliction upon his senses. In three more rounds, everything normalizes, and he rises.

Flounder Flop

Two tiny eyes appear from the bottom of a shrinking tide pool.

Konway stares. "What kind of creature are you?"

A flat frying pan unveils itself and swims to the pool's edge, skirting around the rim, desperate for a way back to the sea.

"It's not gonna make it." He overrides his momentary fatigue and scans the beach. "I need something to carry it back to the ocean." He soon locates a piece of driftwood, a forgotten sandal, and a crumpled bag of cool-rancho chips. The litter conjures reveries from his time spent with the musicians, coupled with Ruckus's outrage.

Serendipitously, the half-peeled label from a hippie's discarded frisbee catches the corner of Konway's eye. He dumps out the sand and rushes back to the tide pool. Kneeling into position, he dips it down beside the stranded fish. Then, stepping to the other side, corrals the flounder onto the upturned frisbee.

The burdensome feelings of exclusion subside in the wake of his good deed. A childhood glee sparkles like the Fourth of July. He almost forgets the creeping neurosis, threading its spindles throughout his nervous system. Bursting Roman candles of sensation, coupled with the malfunctioning Oros system, make the moment seem surreal.

He stands, balancing the large, spotted flounder, but it tries to flip itself off the frisbee back to the sand. He cradles the frightened creature to his body and nimbly rushes towards the water. His toes dig into the sand as a surging wave crashes against his shins.

Konway stoops low and releases the flounder into the soft, muddy bottom of the eastern Atlantic. Taking a congratulatory moment to stare into the horizon, he notices the dorsal fins of dolphins feeding past the break. With the dopamine of success bubbling about him, he plops down into a nearby tide pool.

"Despite my past, I am a good person—I am capable of more than murder." He sighs as a faint weightlessness tugs at his black boardshorts.

72

Litterati

Walkabout

Devoid of cloud coverage, the afternoon sun shines on a scurry of semi-palmated sandpipers. Konway makes his way along the coast, seeking greater clarity and the resolve to preserve his standing at Laniakea. Lost in his pursuit, he loses track of time.

Another icy prickle pulses down his vertebrae. The uneasiness twists into nausea.

"What the fuck is wrong with me?"

(Give up,) the Imp whispers. (I assure you, the candle is not worth the flame.)

He rests against an exposed concrete jetty and box-breathes, hoping to quell the circular doubts tormenting him. Konway's thoughts turn to Sage and Helaku, to Laniakea, reminding him of what he has to protect—of what matters most. He takes another deep breath of gratitude and passes the paper rhino.

The light of day soon shifts from its crisp brilliance to royal hues. His hazel eyes notice something shiny in the sand. He bends over and plucks it from its earthen entombment. The motion triggers a muscle memory that releases a Vision Shard from the corroded vaults in his Mind Palace.

Toothin'

Fragments flood his perception with the Donor's memory of being a boy on a family vacation, surrounded by aunts, uncles, cousins, and grandparents in an oversized beach cottage. Under dawn's early light, young-Konway and his father hunt for relics left by ancient dangers from long ago.

His little hands swoop into a dense pile of shells and pluck a minuscule, black triangular object.

"Ooh, is that one, Daddy?" he asks.

Snap. The impostor cracks between his fingers. No longer able to bear the weight of his expectations, the clever illusion crumbles into a beige and pastel pile of periwinkles. His glee fades into a sigh, but his determination quickens. Again, young-Konway hands rush to the crumbs of the shell line and fetch another fake. He inspects it, but by this point in their hunt, everything looks like a shark's tooth.

His father recognizes the building disappointment and walks over, sloshing through a thin membrane of saltwater. "Don't worry, son. There are three ways of toothin'."

"Will you show me, please?"

"Of course. Let's go over there," he says, pointing at a patch of shells.

Young-Konway drops a heavy handful of soggy sand and rushes ahead, splashing into an ankle-deep tide pool.

"Okay, pay attention. This is the first method." His father bends at the waist and rummages amongst a small patch of shells.

"Daddy, you look silly," he giggles. "Like one of those white birds with the long necks." He gives his best impression of an egret.

"Now you're picking up what I'm putting down... But this is only the first way. The second one my Pop showed me comes in handy if you miss the prime picking conditions."

Reluctant in his hunt, he stoops in a different spot. "Daddy, why do we collect sharks' teeth?" he asks.

"I don't know, son." His father grins at the question. "Toothin' was something I did with my Pop, and he with his, and on down the line... But if you aren't having any luck, you can always find a gigantic pile of shells," he says. "See how it gets washed by the tide? It does most of the sifting for us. The catch is, you need swift hand-eye coordination if you're hoping to snag your prize before the ocean gets hold of it."

While shorebirds squawk past canyons of enormous, puffy clouds, the two amateur archaeologists sift amidst the glitter of crustacean corpses—yet Lady Luck seems far from their shore.

Third Method

"No need to fret, son. A bit of bad luck doesn't mean we'll leave empty-handed."

"That's right—weren't there three methods?"

"Yes. But I was never in favor of it," he says.

"Tell me, please." He looks up at his father's scruffy face and winces from a hint of salt spray.

"If we can't find one, there's always the souvenir shop," he teases.

The boy scowls.

"I hear they have a jar full just before the exit. It's a surefire system for finding teeth. It never fails, so bring your wallet." His laughter bellows over the wash.

"No... no... no. I want to find one on my own." He rises and moves to a different pile.

Beach Fossils

As the August sun climbs above the parallels of a wind-wisped horizon, the receding tide forms a medium-sized pool from the surf. Still no luck—young-Konway's mounting frustrations fuel his resolve. He persists, searching through a microverse of shell fragments and kaleido-cosmic crumbs, plucking another false relic from the sand.

Almost at the point of giving up, he shuffles to a sky-filled tide pool of warm saltwater and plops into it. Silt fills every nook and cranny of his swim trunks as his agile hands plunge into the soft, mucky banks of the blue-hued pool, grasping at the unknown and heaving handfuls onto the washing beach.

Another splash shaves away a sliding cascade of sand to reveal long-buried, lettered olive shells—the refuse of moon snails. He slops more handfuls upon the puddle's edge. Rinse and repeat—nautical treasures slide beneath the tide pool's mirroring surface.

His mother calls him from the cottage's screened-in porch. Unable to find his prize, he gives up the hunt for now and stands. With one last look-see, a glossy fleck in the sand catches his attention amidst the collage of crushed shells.

A twinkling promise of possibilities, barely a razor's edge, protrudes from the washing sluice puddle. Well aware of what the waves can do, having lost too many toys to the trickery of those lapping waters, young-Konway digs into the fray of discovery.

"Not this time, ocean," he says, pulling against the Earth.

Handful after handful, he excavates the treasure with a sense of Arthurian pride. Freed from the muck at last, he triumphantly hoists a barnacled megalodon tooth—bigger than both his hands—high into the summer's heron-blue sky.

Bottles

Before Konway gleans anything else, the Vision Shard fades, stranding him in the present with the familiar brushstrokes of the sea and sand. Overhead, the TacOHUD highlights twenty-seven pelicans as they ribbon along the shoreline under puffball pockets of condensed atmosphere. Another nanite-scale hiccup jolts a microdose of [Stim], masking his fatigue.

Inspired by his recent recollection, and the [Stim] in his system, he combs the beach, searching for gifts for Sage and Helaku. The sun moves behind a solitary cloud just as he reaches into his pockets and pulls out a small conch, some moon snail shells, coral fragments, and even a few tiny sharks' teeth. The haunting memories of murder and the fears of rejection disperse when he glances at his palm and rejoices over a renewed sense of childlike awe and wonder.

"She's going to love these. And maybe Amber could help me get those turned into necklaces... Somehow I have so many pieces of coral in my pockets. Then again, I can't help leaving the beach with a pocket full of shells."

Another rain cloud chases away a cluster of day-trippers. A short distance farther, Konway's keen eyes spy the neck of a glass bottle protruding from the sand. He picks it up, uncovering a single-use disposable plastic bag half-buried by the windblown shore.

After pulling it from the micro-dune, he discovers another bag with warm, half-full beers and random trash. He shakes his head and looks towards the beach access. There, some tourons waddle onto the blue-matted walkway.

Confrontation

Following a brisk jaunt through powdery, ankle-deep sand, Konway reaches within earshot. "Excuse me," he calls out.

They don't hear him and continue into the dunes.

"If you were man enough to bring these on the beach," he hollers over the waves, "I insist that you be man enough to take them with you!"

The maleficent seven halt and turn in unison.

"What'd you say, boy?" the largest one gruffly asks.

A hesitant silence lingers in the warm, windswept afternoon, while dune grass rattles to the drone of the Atlantic.

Konway swallows his fear and stands tall. "Here, take these with you," he says, extending the single-use disposable bags towards the ruffians.

A half-empty bottle of warm beer sloshes into a cup of dip juice as cigarette butts fall through a hole in the bottom. Hitting the sand, a syrupy ooze swizzles on a baker's dozen of drizzled delights.

Blitz

An excessively large Confederate flag enthusiast with swastika tattoos pushes past his comrades. The Oros system highlights the patches of Goliath's cut and the ink on his arms, unlocking a tipped-over file cabinet within the Mind Palace. A folder lifts itself out of the drawer but catches on a bent rack. It wiggles, struggling against the metal, then pops free and floats in place.

The manila edges part into a cascade of boxes, unpacking its directory onto his Screening Room's sticky floor. The contents—a batch file listing every alphabet agency's database of gang affiliations—drown him in iconography and symbolism. A spark ignites an inferno around him and uncovers an ember of significance.

Konway's eyes narrow as he recognizes the blood-oath ceremony etched in ink. (This isn't good.) He holds the bags of garbage with diamond hands, motionless amidst the heat of the shore. The Oros system unfurls a rich tapestry of strategic analysis, escape routes, and points of attack across his TacOHUD, while Goliath stomps through the soft sand.

The hulking goon approaches, startling seagulls towards the remnants of cheese puffs and cigarette butts. Several passing clouds shade the sun into strips of light as the peanut gallery snickers and snarls. The mountain of a man continues his heavy approach and rolls his neck around the sunburnt edges of his tattooed shoulders.

Specialized nanites detect the kinetic tensions in Goliath's movements, alerting Konway with red traces outlining potential risks. The brute leans in, snatching the bags of trash with one monstrous, sunburnt hand. Grabbing hold of Konway's left forearm with the other, he pulls him into a blitzkrieg headbutt, aiming to smash him to the ground.

Resolution

Goliath's headbutt connects above Konway's brow. The Oros system glitches, and his optics go blank. Still holding onto him, the bully shakes off the bell-ringer and goes in again. The TacOHUD flickers on, followed by a shimmer throughout his dragon tattoo. Passing circumstantial gatekeepers, nanite swarms proc latent neuro-stem tech and combat muscle memory.

Barely bruised, Konway pivots his right foot backward and rotates aside, avoiding the second headbutt. Drawing his free hand back, he releases a combo of direct attacks, hammering the bridge of the brute's nose. Again and again—with each impact, his fists tighten as he releases an existential cry of frustration. This time, he can't blame the alcohol.

The brutal precision catches Goliath by surprise, sending him backward and landing in the sand with a noticeable thud. His sunburnt cronies stop walking forward.

"Whoa, whoa, whoa... We don't mean any harm." A pot-bellied man in a black, mustard-stained, sleeveless shirt waves his hands.

"We're sorry about Tiny. He's a bit fried from the day." Another goon with an uneven mullet lifts his sunglasses to expose sunken eyes socked with societal despair.

A tall man with a leather vest and faded orange bandana spits dip juice on the sand. "We were just leaving."

"I thought someone else picked up the empties," says a crispy bearded man with a few missing teeth, reaching for the trash. "I s—swear... We'll gladly put those in the garbage bin."

"Make sure you take your friend with you!" Konway glares at them as they pick up their mess and amble off the beach.

Back at the water's edge, well past the sunburnt fools, he slows his stride, saying, "Damn, it feels good to do the right thing. Maybe I can control myself. Maybe I can protect Sage and the others from my past. Maybe I could atone—"

Another set of tremors weakens him into distraction.

Below the Nether Regions of Thought, the Imp-oster's eyes dilate, hungry for another taste of inadequacy and woe. (Hope? How can you have hope?) it interrogates him. (At what point will you realize you murdered those scientists? Maybe the arms dealers had it coming, but the nerds... cold, man. So you saved Todd... and Sage. Did you forget how you beat Todd? I wonder... how long can you keep your secret quiet? How long till the Agency finds you? The longer you hide at Laniakea, the closer you bring them to death's door. Who knows—maybe you'll be the one to pull the trigger.)

The trembling subsides as the Imp-oster's echoes fade into the Fog of Despair, over the Fields of Frustration, beneath the Death Marshes, and back into the Black Cauldron—a cruel design from Childe's twisted mind, fashioned from the corpse of the demon Ramiel.

73

Sundown Showdown

Counter Strike

Farther ahead, having failed to extract the once-Special Agent, the agents in floral button-ups enjoy a little seaside foreplay with two tourist girls from the Pier View restaurant. Agent Blue tries to take his mind off of their possible punishment with a sun-kissed neckline. His eyes widen as he spots their mark and quickly motions to his partner.

Red shifts his focus from the blossoming beauty in his arms and furrows his brow. "Get out of here." He pushes her aside.

"Hey, you promised us a good time."

"How are we supposed to get back?" asks the other woman.

"You'll figure it out," Red says.

An awkward silence hangs as the two agents stare coldly.

"C'mon. Let's bounce. I think there was a house party a couple of blocks back."

"Goodbye, losers." The other girl cuts her eyes.

"Good riddance." Blue walks down a short flight of sandy steps.

Red follows suit and unsheathes his taser-blade.

Just past the dunes, the Agency truck thunders to life. The engine revs, and two middle fingers fly out the windows as the Agency's black, tinted 4x4 fishtails out of the beach access parking lot.

"You're kidding me, right? You left the keys in the truck?" Red glares.

"We were going to ditch them, remember? I didn't want to lose the keys on the beach."

While they bicker, Konway assesses the situation. (Are they Goliath's friends?) It sinks in. (No, they look military—shit, it's them... it's the Agency.)

His heart leaps into his throat. At once, the TacOHUD flags their weapons, mapping potential routes for escape.

(Do I let them take me and save the village? No. I'll be turned back into their weapon... Then who knows how many more bodies they'll add to my count? What if they send me to kill everyone in Laniakea? Sage and the others are in danger... I'm fucked... Best outcome: I could force them to kill me and end this... But I don't want to die... I don't want to kill... Even if it's my only option... I don't want that life anymore.)

"Call it in," Red says.

Blue checks his pockets. "I can't."

"Why?"

"I left my phone in the truck," he says, looking towards the beach access.

Agent Red's sneer transforms into a forked vein bulging along the border of his left eye. "The Commander is going to kill us."

"If we capture Zeff, all will be forgiven," says Blue.

"Can we collect him?"

"Not without a little help from the boys and girls at the Pickle Factory." Blue removes a cigarette case from his pocket, opens it, and dumps two capsules in his hand. "Alone, this wouldn't be enough, but together, we should be able to take him."

"Zeff, we need you to come with us," Red says, moving away from his partner.

"I think you have the wrong person," Konway says sincerely, despite trying to hide the icy numbness arcing within his body. (I don't know how much more I can take. If I were to fight them here, surely I'd lose.)

"Enough games, Zeff." Blue flanks him.

Konway steps back. "I've got to get back to—"

"Where? Laniakea. You're not safe there." Red opens a compartment on his belt. "Luckily, the Commander needs it quiet. But that doesn't mean we can't carve the stolen intel out of you."

They pop two black supplements. The beans dissolve under their tongues and unleash a nanite swarm throughout their bodies. Based on the Oros system, these temporary body-bugs enhance the user's abilities beyond cybernetic augmentations alone. However, they have a short shelf life and exert an excessive amount of physiological strain—continued use may yield surprising results.

Blender

Heartbeat elevated, Konway looks down to see glowing tracers hasten their orbit along his tattoo. Nano-scale mixologists blend equal parts [Timewarp], [Prime], [Stim], and [Surge] into a concentrated shot of [Berzerker]—straight, no chaser—mainlining it into his system.

Agent Red leaps across the sand at him. The superhuman feat would've caught him off guard, had his digital overlay not notified him. Another tremor pulsates as he barely avoids the razor's edge. It goes unnoticed with the [Berzerker] coursing through his veins.

Agent Blue joins in with a slicing uppercut, spinning with the counterclockwise arc of his blade. Sparks sizzle-pop amongst the humidity. Konway artfully dodges, only to encounter their partner's coordinated attack.

Red's floral shirt flows against him as he lunges to sever the connective tissue around Konway's neck. But the bottom of Konway's heel abruptly connects with Red's solar plexus, sending him flying into the dunes.

"You're not bad," Blue says, deploying a second taser-blade. "But not as good as the rumors." He continues his assault with whirling slashes.

"You don't know who I am! Just let me go." Konway weaves through the windmill of hate and forces a reset. "Please, we don't need to do this."

Blue goes in again. This time, Konway sidesteps left and disarms him with a crushing fist. Regardless of its retention grip, the blade slides a short distance away. Konway bolts to it. By the time he turns around, Blue lands next to him, followed by a volley of electrical sparks as the two clash.

Full tilt, caught in the blender, the taser-blades flail in front of him. Left, right, up, down, left, right—a crackle illuminates their strobing choreography. Konway attempts to reset, but Blue persists.

He narrowly avoids being gutted and quickly adapts to the rhythm, isolating Blue's attack pattern. Cheat code attained, he avoids the next strike and counters—grabbing hold of Blue's wrist with his right hand, raking the electrically charged weapon along the ulna with his left, stripping away the second knife and a fillet of flesh with ease.

By the time Red springs to his feet, Blue is sprawled in the sand.

"Stay down!" Konway snarls with a heart full of adrenaline.

Blue struggles, his own taser-blade digging into his thigh, its pulse surging throughout the circuitry embedded in his flesh as he cries out in agony.

"Don't make me kill you!" he roars, twisting the blade.

Hearing his partner's scream, Red jumps back into the fray. The TacOHUD highlights the alert, and Konway turns, throwing the last crackling kunai with lethal accuracy. It catches Red in the shoulder mid-flight.

He lands with a thud, blood splattering the sand. Red moves to stand but howls over the ocean's drone as the taser-blade superheats the alloys woven into his cuff until they glow with the intensity of Hephaestus's forge.

The nostalgia of combat cloaks Konway with its laurels.

(Do it!) the Imp-oster urges him to lose control.

"I swear to whatever gods you cower before, I will field-dress you for the crabs if I catch wind of y'all anywhere near me or Laniakea," he coldly warns, picking up Red's weapon.

"P—please," he begs, "don't kill us."

The thought of doing it gives him a small sense of satisfaction. But also a sense of pity. Without warning, the face of the jiggly-jowled scientist orbits his thoughts, followed by another coursing tremor along his ribs.

(Kill them!)

(No!!! They're just doing their jobs—) "It's your lucky day," Konway says firmly. "But I want you to leave me the fuck alone."

The wounded agents stagger to their feet and flee the beach. Crossing the gravel parking lot, they hobble down the street towards the lighthouse at the far end of the island.

Get Lost

A crackling static snowstorm flashes across the TacOHUD. A bit turned around, and feeling the withdrawal from the double shot of [Berzerker], Konway stumbles farther from Laniakea. Another wave reverberates through a membrane of empty echo chambers. Burnt-yellow eyes widen with delight.

"Maybe I shouldn't go back. If I do, they'll find me there—"

(They'd be better off if you disappeared,) the Imp-oster taunts.

He notices the taser-blade still in his hand and buries it in the dunes. "Shit. There's going to be some blowback from this. What should I do? Who can I tell?"

Without the proper endocannabinoid regulation and the overt use of the malfunctioning Oros system, the pain, now in his head, rumbles the juices in his stomach. A flow of saliva preps the inner workings of nausea.

"Something's not right. I need to get back," Konway mutters. He walks faster, only to hasten the trembling. "I need an exit?" He looks to the right, reluctant to locate a beach access—only an extensive stretch of the bird sanctuary's semi-tropical woodlands. Sweat drips down his neck.

A flock of gulls streaks by, drawing his attention towards the setting sun and stirring memories of Ruckus's mural. After a hasty scan of his surroundings, he tries to push past the brush. To his dismay, the overgrowth of brambles and briars blocks him halfway. Pins and needles tickle like a caterpillar on a milk thistle. He pauses, finding no path forward, and turns back to the shore.

Three paces farther, a disassociated throb in his head disorients him. Konway vomits on a saw palmetto. Then, wiping the bile from his mouth, he climbs over a hurdle of salt-dried boulders onto the washed-out portion of Coffin Island.

74

Trembling

Shaky Ground

Elsewhere, Zeff's vivid hazel eyes stare into the timeless gray sky as storm clouds approach the Mesas of Memory, now the size of warts on a wild boar. Green flashes of fractal lightning draw his attention to a pixelated rainbow streaking near the horizon. Another pop of neon leaves a smoldering plume. He tracks the fleeting swath of color until it disappears through a portal in the distance, then pans in search of the marked resource node. Sadly, like many other locations, it is picked clean.

Empty-handed, he turns to leave when a mob of Milestone Trolls springs from behind a towering dune. Smaller than their siblings, they move with coordination, corralling Zeff closer to their trap. The sand crumbles beneath him, but he leaps back over the pitfall and conjures [Mind Slayer] to sever their snare. In an instant, two [Darkness Blades] slam cross-shaped scars into the nearby dunes, abruptly concluding their encounter as buckets of troll-tar ooze from their diagonally severed torsos. The weapon dematerializes.

He glances at the [Trifold Bracer] wrapped around his forearm, shakes his head, and mutters, "I was supposed to gather enough energy to open a portal and get the hell out of here. But my return has cost me more than I've gained. What am I going to do? Luckily, I haven't seen hide nor hair of the Fog. Maybe the bat's stench keeps it at bay." Zeff spits on the ground, and, with a sigh, heads back to the little brown church with the crooked cross.

The area is desolate, somehow worse than when he arrived. An eternity later, he reaches the Infinite Cathedral's ruins. Once settled, he kicks his feet up onto a cracked pew, closes his eyes to contemplate, and exhales a sigh of relief.

Three seconds later, the ground trembles—worse than ever. Less a dithering, more an awakening, a mighty sandstorm kicks up, driving Zeff to the tile. On the other side of a broken wall, brick by brick, the chasm where he fought with Fomobious opens. An aftershock crumbles the checkered floor into the darkness, further collapsing stone, steel, and stained glass into the pit—swallowing two-thirds of the Infinite Cathedral. He tries to escape but falls into the abyss, along with the remains of the little brown church.

Gilgram

Down, down, through the darkness, he lands in an endless reflecting pool, expanding in a single direction. Zeff stands in front of a colossal cage lined with torch-lit columns. One by one, the flames illuminate the shadows across its face.

Inside, an enormous demon opens its eyes and looks out with furrowed hatred. "So the time has finally come for you to end it, Fomobious? Come closer, dear brother, so I may grind your bones."

(Another one?) "You've got the wrong guy—"

Its head rushes forward with a forceful wind, knocking Zeff to the ground.

"We settle this now!" the creature thunders.

"Wait! That bastard is dead, and I killed him."

The demon groans with reluctance. "I grow tired of your games, brother."

"No games. I'm just trying to get out of here."

It snorts and fades into darkness. "You will never find her."

The demon roars, and the limitless prison trembles. Massive stalagmites erupt from the ground, heaving waves onto the endless reflecting pool. The [Trifold Bracer] absorbs a bit of fallen debris while Zeff summons [Mind Slayer], slicing apart rapidly rendered rock formations—staggered into a jagged gauntlet of earthen projections.

A terrifying howl fills the space. "You know not my suffering... Fomobious, you wretched bat. You will know the cosmic ash of nonexistence!"

Zeff swings a series of [Darkness Blades] towards the cage. One by one, violet crescents crash against the cell's door. But each one fails to breach past its bars.

"It will take more than that." The demon steps into the candlelit threshold. A bearded lion turtle fills the darkness. "Make no mistake, dear brother, this husk will be your tomb. Be crushed into the sands of time, you detestable coward—[CRUMBLING FISSURE]!!!"

The floor quivers and transmutes from a solid to a liquid. Zeff sinks into the muck. The tremors turn into an audible rumble as crisscrossing tidal waves of sand crash throughout the domain. Unable to dodge, he summons a large Snap-Brix platform beneath him to part the deluge of sediment.

The elder demon turtle's eyes widen. "Your tricks won't save you, brother?"

"I'm not Fomobious!"

It focuses its large, lightless eyes on Zeff's tiny form.

"I'm trying to tell you," he shouts, "I'm not that stinking bat. Fomobious is dead."

The demon halts the assault and, sensing another of his siblings, fades back into the shadows. "I see... So that's how you achieved his blade? Interesting. Very interesting."

Zeff lowers his weapon.

"If you really *did* slay him, then maybe you can set me free."

"How?" he asks, stowing the sword.

"All you need to do is unlock my brother's seal."

"How do I know I can trust you?"

"You can't. But know this: I could end you with a thought. You're in my domain. I control every aspect of this place—"

"Except the lock on your cage."

A low grumble fills the cell. "Make it quick, and I will reward you with a way out."

"How do I unlock it?" he asks coldly.

"Your *friend* on your arm should know the way."

Zeff looks at the rolled-up sleeve of his dust-stained, troll-spattered, gunk-speckled linen coat, then at the [Trifold Bracer]. A purple glow waxes across its screen. He sighs, seeing no other way, and approaches the towering seal. Closer, an arc of violet energy engulfs the device, spreading into his palm.

He reaches for the door, and a jolt leaps from his fingertips to the cell. It surges up the bars into the darkness, igniting the talisman's intricate inscriptions with a lilac flame, running the length of the skyscraper of scripture. In its glowing wake, a split rises along the seam, and the cage groans open.

"Come closer," the demon beckons him.

Zeff crosses the threshold, and the vault illuminates with candlelight. "How is this possible?" he gawks in awe.

Release

Beyond flickering shadows, a colossal bearded lion turtle sits atop a hill of glittering treasure. Resting on its shell is a smaller turtle with a golden compass in its mouth.

"What's your name?" Zeff asks.

"I'm Gilgram."

"How'd you end up in here?"

"My wretched brother, Fomobious." The demon huffs and puffs. "It's a long story... Oh, how tired I've grown."

"What do you mean? What is this place? What happened to the Mind Palace?"

"I don't know of any 'Mind Palace,'" the demon grumbles. "I wonder, do you mean our world?"

"'Your world?'"

"We don't know what happened, but based on the Memory Crystals in the Archives, we calculate this isn't the first cycle."

Zeff stares blankly.

"In the beginning, we had no memory prior to waking up in this place." Gilgram shakes its mane. "Though it took time, we eventually adjusted to our new forms... There was a natural order—until, one day, the last of the Elder Trees at the center of our realm exploded into chaos.

"A dark corruption oozed from the malady, twisting everything it touched. Drama and betrayal sparked a war... We almost destroyed this place, but our sister, Yarn—the wisest among us—saw beyond the wreckage of our conflict and forged a truce. Together, we redrew the boundaries of what remained... Each of us, locked within the echo chambers of hubris, believed we were immune to the vile corruption. Sadly, the damage we caused was severe and traumatized the land. It spread along the ley lines, releasing the wild energies that kept our scarred world intact. You should've seen it... long ago, Katalepsis was paradise."

"Katalepsis?"

A high-frequency trembling whirls Chladni figures across the sand. The rhythm shifts, and diamond patterns vibe into soft square bass notes.

Gilgram continues, "Yarn used her gifts to research the ley line fissures. And from what was gleaned, she and her Eldenhorns mapped the entire surface and installed the resource nodes to halt the spreading corruption. However, alone, her efforts were in vain. She had failed to explore the Inner Depths and the Outer Limits of the furthest domains, past the burning haze. In time, Yarn reached out to our wayward siblings and offered a means to protect our realms and preserve the remnants of Katalepsis from the twisted corruption—"

"How'd she manage that?" Zeff asks, trying to understand the demon's words.

"She used her powers and set out to craft us minions from the salvaged bits of the Elder Tree," Gilgram says, followed by a coughing fit. "Once Yarn's pilgrimage reached my lands, our impatient brother had arrived. Fomobious forced her to create his wraiths. While he waited for her to finish his request, having recently gorged on Ramiel's deranged domain, my foolish brother slept. I feared Ramiel had fallen to the corruption, and soon Fomobious… So I hid Yarn."

"What happened?"

"When he woke and realized my betrayal, we fought—but he defeated me."

"You're massive. There's no way."

The turtle coughs up a dry hack of sand. "This pales in comparison to my true form… It was a mighty battle, indeed. And, had I not been protecting Yarn, and he mutated from feasting off of Ramiel's resources, I could've easily claimed victory… Fomobious imprisoned me, his elder brother, in quaking [Chains of Fear] and vowed to feed on my domain until either he was strong enough to kill me, or I was weak enough to be up-cycled.

"While trapped in my mind, outside, sand gathered on my body. Fomobious burrowed into one of the spikes on my shell while I atrophied in front of this wretched pool, and my domain withered with rot. Even though Yarn was still safe, upon consuming the rest of me, he would have found her. I was foolish to lock away my sister to protect her."

"What would've happened if he had gotten both of you?"

"Fomobious might've had enough power to take on our other siblings and rule over the Consilience. But you killed him before he could do this."

Trembling cracks spread like lightning. A piece of Gilgram fades and falls off, crashing to the ground.

"Forgive me… Our time has come to an end."

"What's happening?"

"Follow Yarn. Seek the Light." Gilgram closes its sunless eyes.

The grotto shivers.

Zeff steps back as the demon stiffens into sandstone. Shockwaves ripple throughout the cell, bringing him to his knees and crumbling Gilgram into an immense dune. At the top, a gray being with long, downward-pointing ears, wearing a sky-blue lab coat with a pair of goggles atop their head, holds a golden turtle compass.

Yarn

The small gray demon slides to the bottom, shouting, "Thank you. I'm—"

"Stop!" Zeff wields [Mind Slayer], violet energy crackling along its onyx blade. "How do I know I can trust you?"

She flinches at the sight. "No, you've got it all wrong. You heard Gilgram's story."

The chasm shakes violently, and massive columns collide at the cage's threshold.

"There's no time to figure this out. We need to get out of here," Zeff says. "But don't think about trying anything, or I'll kill you like I killed your brother."

She stares at him, then nods.

Huge chunks of stone fall from above and topple kilometer-high pillars across the infinity reflecting pool outside the enclosure.

"What's happening?" He braces against a series of cymatic frequencies.

"We're still inside Gilgram." Yarn studies the falling debris. "His body is breaking down, and we've gotta go. Now!" The gray demon reaches into her sky-blue lab coat and retrieves a tiny 8-bit treasure chest and a glowing vial, the color of a chromatic rainbow on an oil slick, labeled [MOOP].

A column beyond Zeff's periphery falls into the collapsing darkness. There is a brief silence before it lands, splitting the infinite reflecting pool in half. The vibrations intensify.

Yarn pours a few dollops of [MOOP] onto the chest, then sloshes some atop a cracked slab of her fallen sibling. "I don't have access to my lab, but using what we have, we should be fine." She picks up a handful of sand, sprinkles some on the crumb of Gilgram, and stows the rest in a container from her utility belt.

"Should?"

"It's all we have—good thing my calculations give us a low probability of surviving."

"That's horrible."

"It's better than none at all," she says, inputting a couple of key commands on a holographic terminal.

A prismatic arc of energy bounces to the chest, causing it to expand and open. From its sealed depths, a pixelated unicorn hops onto the scene.

"I need you to summon the Archon Council and gather the herd at my workshop," she directs the digital creature. "You have the current coordinates of its location."

The Eldenhorn nods, then bolts out of Gilgram's cage, ribboning a familiar rainbow trail into a spiraling portal. Before Zeff can ask, the opening snaps shut.

Yarn finishes her next prompt, and an arc of blue energy strikes the glob of sand, bringing it to life, wiggling and jiggling like a gelatin dessert. As the domain crashes around them, a stone archway swirling with an iridescent aura sprouts from Gilgram's ashes.

She enters the druidic doorway.

"Hey! Don't leave me here."

Her head pops out from the gateway. "Well, come on, then."

As Zeff crosses the threshold, the wake of Gilgram's crumbling husk trembles throughout the desolate domain, further disrupting Yarn's nodal array holding the corruption in stasis.

Oros System Failure

Along Coffin Island's East End, deep pipes cough up sediment from a dredge several kilometers offshore. Konway wobbles into a patch of soft sand and sea-oat punji sticks, hoping to find a different way off of the beach. A few paces farther, beeping earthmovers pierce above the diesel throttle of a towering CRAB [Coastal Research Amphibious Buggy] as it surveys the renourishment. All the while, perpetual waves comb back another layer, withdrawing a sliver of Coffin Island into the sand drift.

He tries to suppress the overstimulation, but too much time has passed since he last relieved the mounting pressure from the Oros system. He stumbles to his knees. Another shock hits him in the tailbone and sends him to the ground.

Persistent, Konway drags himself towards the commotion. "Sage... I need to get back to Sage." He crawls in desperation. (Why is this happening? What the fuck is wrong with me?! Am I going to die here?)

Apprentice

The spiraling deluge piles plates of fear and inadequacy onto the Imp-oster's buffet. It chortles from its seat, then yells at the screen, "Look how pathetic you are! Save us some time—give up and die, already!"

"Do I need to eat this? I want to go play." Childe looks up from his putrid plate to his Toy Box, overflowing with various chimeras.

"Yes, sir. This will help you get strong enough to return home," the Imp says to his blurry-faced apprentice. "But first, we need Zeff. He's the one we've been waiting for."

Suddenly, the Fog's display flips to a radar ping.

"Where have you been?" the Imp sneers.

"Is it him?"

"Who else? Finish your meal."

"Wahoo!" Childe cheers before devouring the rest of his food and hopping out of the chair. "Which toy should I bring? Maybe the new one... Well, I haven't tested those in the field yet... Hmmm... How about this gift? No time like the present." His blurry face twists with the delight of a Cheshire's grin.

75

El Dorado

Transition

Zeff arrives at another picture-pattern puzzle door and crosses the Threshold of Consciousness into an unending field of fragrant dreams—where every poppy unfurls a portal of lucid dissociation. The Fog of Despair lingers behind him, but he doesn't notice. Farther along the path, the Imp-oster's burnt eyes appear through the gloom, and Childe's silhouette emerges beside it, followed by a multi-limbed shadow. Childe tilts the joystick forward, and a volley of crooked claws stretches towards Zeff. However, before the homunculus grapples him, the ground opens, plunging him into a spiraling freefall.

Splash! Cool ripples slosh against his shins, driven by a gurgling veil of waterfalls. The distant ceiling—a sky-lit canopy of subterranean glow worms—shifts from a shade of indigo into an arctic blue.

"Where's Yarn? I knew that damn demon couldn't be trusted."

Lit by nature, Zeff follows the filamental pulses deeper into the twinkling void, until the route opens into a vibrant symposium of color and light.

At the grotto's center, atop a floating sphere, a towering gilded tree scales well beyond the encircling mist of its lower canopy. Amongst the swaying breath of its druidic branches, flickering lights dance with an unfelt breeze. Beneath the tracers flowing down its trunk, a primordial henge gives way to intersecting pathways. All around the knees of its roots, mandalic reflecting pools of fluorescent fire give rise to a maze of sparkling stalagmites.

"I've seen this tree—" The reluctant certainty of déjà vu knocks him in the head as the path gives way to thatches of gleaming moss and star-glittered fungi, leading to the edge of a luminous reservoir. Within the water, a swirl of creatures waltzes about the tide of everydayness. The most notable are the glowing turtles swimming all the way down, deep into the limited depths of his gaze.

Blue globs plop onto his shoulder.

"Gross," he says, wiping the goop staining his suit. "Where's Yarn?"

Despite his hesitancy—forged from the Donor's memories of watching late-night alien movies—he shifts his attention to the ceiling. Another dollop catches Zeff between the eyes, and an ineffable vortex of living light parts the way, sending him several cognitive layers deeper into the Akashic workings. There, a Vision Shard from a far-forgotten past engulfs his bandwidth.

Overheat

Elsewhile, clusters of neurons fire in excess, quickening Konway's heartbeat. The intensity of its *wub-dub* drowns out the buzzing drone in his eardrums. He overheats, sweating through his button-up beach shirt, as a brief neural discharge forces his mind to turn in on itself.

Globular auras and bright blobs zigzag from one scale to another, leaving pulsating patches across his TacOHUD. A crackling flash sublimates his sight for a panicked moment. Once the static storm crashes, his head throbs with ringing echoes, spinning like those paper kaleidoscopes crafted after school with Granny.

The beat intensifies, and with it, a numbness flushes along his limbs. Konway loses sensation and collapses onto the sand. As he slides into a hypnagogic state—separating the *mind-body* from the *body-mind*—a sense of weightlessness washes over him.

Guard

Zeff blinks and finds himself standing in front of a gigantic gate. Its entire countenance glistens with gold and gem mosaics, depicting a tapestry of sacred symbols and geometric patterns woven throughout the Sprawl's cul-de-sacs, avenues, and back alleys. Its scriptures and rhetoric recount tales of primordial heroics during the First Impact and lessons learned from cathartic lamentations. A cavern breeze churns up an unfamiliar chill.

(Where the hell am I?) He tries to speak, but his lips refuse to move.

"I'm gonna go take a leak. Make sure no one comes through the Gate while I'm gone." His partner throws a playful punch into his mithril pauldron.

"Yeah, right... This thing was sealed before the first elders were shitting in their diapers," the Construct says.

(How am I talking on my own?) Zeff questions the nature of this new reality. (What's going on?)

The guards chuckle at the imagery.

"You have a point," his partner replies. "The Ancestors constructed these interlocking gates in such a way that, to this day, no sliver of parchment can pass between any of its parts."

"Make sure the patrol doesn't see you," he advises.

"I'm not worried about those stooges. They're more interested in lining their pockets than making a difference."

"Hurry back." The Construct throws a pebble at his fellow watchman.

In boredom, he whistles a tune and walks over to an ornate arrangement of crystal gifts and oil offerings. Having strayed from his post, he turns around in time to see the fleeting afterimage of something leaping into the shadows. A quickening sensation washes into the figment of his imagination, followed by gnawing, dripping, oozing rows of teeth.

"Was that a Cave Critter? Or a Crawler? Surely I'm seeing things," the Construct says. "There's no way... By the gods, there's no—" An instinctual lunge, towards defending what matters most, compels him into a full sprint.

Amplified

Near the bird sanctuary's driftwood forest on the northeastern end of Coffin Island, Konway writhes from the malfunctioning Oros system. His eyes bulge as nanite swarms unsync from the colony's network, lashing electrical arcs through his body. Passing gulls pay no attention to the lone shadow of his flailing form.

Halt

The Construct catches up to the spectre and desperately grasps to catch hold of her light-blue hood. There, under the glow of luminescent crystals, his eyes fall upon the small gray demon.

(Yarn!) Zeff calls out from his dissociated state, but cannot form words beneath the Construct's deluge of concerns.

"Halt!" he orders.

Yarn turns.

"Who—what are you?!"

(Yarn!) Zeff cries out in silence.

The demon raises her goggles to the top of her head, and he gazes into the depths of her eyes. The Construct shakes it off and repositions his crystal spear between them. In a flash, she bolts down a nearby alleyway.

"HALT!" he commands.

(Yarn!)

Up one avenue, down another side street, the chase continues until they careen into a dead-end corridor.

He readies his weapon and steps closer, asking, "Where did you come from?"

Without answering, she types a command prompt onto the holographic screen in front of her. The air grows heavy, and the Construct collapses to the ground.

Flailing

Konway lies flung against the darkening shore. His failing neural circuitry amplifies the piercing beeps of industrial earthmovers, sending a convulsive ringing in his ears.

(Sage—Helaku—)

After a few more disjointed twitches, the Oros system cloaks him with invisibility.

He gasps for a breath of air. And, having none to take, he shudders upon the sands. An intersectional thread sizzles through the synaptic network of his flailing figure. Meanwhile, as the sky transitions with the palette of creation, a low-flying Agency helicopter slowly patrols the coastline and passes right over him.

Tall Tale

Zeff wakes surrounded by the Brotherhood of the Guard, geared in mithril armor attuned with jeweled relics.

(I can move,) he says to himself.

The brilliant light from their crystal torches dances along the propaganda-stained alley while Zeff recounts his tale to skeptical ears.

"Forget this nonsense. You've got a future to think of," urges one soldier.

"Don't jeopardize your promotion. This will make you seem unclear," a surly fellow reasons.

Another member leans against the wall. "And you know what happens to unclear folks?"

"Just forget it. You'll be out of here soon, sitting with your kind in the Gardens—not down here in the rubble with scuffs like us." A tall, shimmering guard takes off his helmet.

Most of them laugh, except for a few gathered in the corner with eyes of classist discontent.

The Gate

Zeff returns to his post and marches in front of the Seven Sacred Seals.

(I don't know what Yarn did, but I have control of this body now. Where did she go? I need to find her and get the hell out of here.) He paces about his thoughts.

Above him, an ornate mandala dwarfs his concerns. At its heart, a jeweled tree with intertwining roots wraps across the threshold and spreads throughout the megapolis's maze of corridors and boulevards. Hallowed characters, inscribed with hidden meanings, offer clues to the mysteries beyond the Gate. Obscured by countless generations, these esoteric calligraphies no longer hold their original meanings—if only they did.

Zeff climbs a set of jeweled steps leading to the uppermost viewing platform and studies the commemorative plaque, muttering, "El-Dor-A-doh... El Dorado?"

"Find anything interesting?" his partner asks.

He spins around. "Checking to make sure the seal was intact."

"Don't tell me you're still hung up on what happened... Look, we didn't find any traces of Critters or Crawlers—just you passed out in the alleyway. You already have a pass on this. Let it go," his partner urges.

"You're right." He descends from the radiant gate. "I don't know what's come over me. I think I need to splash some more water on my face. Mind if I step away for a second?"

"Sure, but try not to pass out again. And no more talk about what you think you saw. There's no sense in chasing shadows. You know what they do to those kinds of folks." He straightens his helmet and walks to the other end of the Gate.

Inside the recesses of Zeff's mental jambalaya, he gets caught up in a revolving list of questions. (Is this the lost city of gold? What is it doing here... Where's Yarn? How do we get out of here?)

His hurried, bumbling thoughts distract him from the gray demon's translucent presence materializing from a crystal vein within the nearby wall.

Crack The Code

Zeff rounds the corner and spots a light-blue scrap of fabric sailing on the updraft of cavern currents stirred by primordial lava tubes. "I know that color. It's the same as Yarn's lab coat," he says and smiles.

Mid-flight, it becomes entangled between a boulder and the wall of a popular ramen house. The cloth squiggles under the crystal streetlamps. Zeff glances left, then right, and, hearing the approaching guards, hastily tucks it behind his armor plating.

Unlike the crew from earlier, these elite soldiers are selected from the ranks of babes and assigned to one of El Dorado's nine legendary legions, who answer to the House of Lords—all of which are under the influence of the Council and the three Elder Kings.

He stands on the sidewalk and salutes the Aurelian Legion as they pass from view. Out of nowhere, a cool hand grabs his shoulder guard, sending a slight tear of terror down his spine.

"Come with me," she says, pulling him with an otherworldly strength. "We shouldn't be here."

"Yarn! I can speak now. What's going on?"

"You were rugging, so I had to reconnect you without frying your construct."

Zeff stares at her.

"We're in a Vision Shard—a parting gift from Gilgram. This must've been my brother's last divination before Fomobious imprisoned him."

"Are we still in the Mind Palace?"

"Is that what you call our world?"

"What is it, then?"

"Home."

Golden Hour

As the Atlantic switches the cadence of its tide, dark clouds roll past the shifting skyline. On Coffin Island's East End, writhing in the softening day, Konway's support systems stress beyond their limits. Nanite swarms continue to misfire, rippling electrical impulses along the threads of his mortal coil into the Akashic workings of Gilgram's Vision Shard.

Sentinels

The alarms sound, and the Aurelian Legion's patrol joins the chase. Crystal lamps lining the streets brighten the quarter. They pretend to board a hyper-loop capsule, but exit on the opposite side. Doubling back across a nearby neighborhood, they trigger the streetlights, prompting them to turn into a lampless alley wrapped with jeweled stonework and ancestral scrapbooking.

"You need to lose the armor," she says.

He surveys their surroundings. "No way. If I die here, there's no way I'm getting home."

"I said it was *likely* we could die here. Nothing is certain."

"How will I defend us?" he asks.

"Us? I'm quite capable." She opens up her lab coat to reveal a multitude of radiating, squirming, and overstuffed pockets.

"I'm keeping the armor."

Heavy footsteps pound the pavement on the adjacent street.

"We've got to move," she says.

Yarn and Zeff scan the crowd, then merge into a caravan of tourists from the outer banks of the western walls, hauling toxic gems and rare spices atop saddled Augerboars. Amidst the hustle and bustle, they slip amongst the city center unnoticed. Near the perimeter, tall spires release two crystal-laden drones—one to the air, the other on the ground.

As they duck down another avenue, nearby streetlamps relay their position to the Aurelian Legion. Sprinting past gambling parlors and worship services, they weave through a street market. On the far side, a block party parade cuts off the ground patrol.

Moments after crossing an open bridge, the aerial drones catch up. Equipped with lasers designed to dispose of the most terrifying Cave Critters and Crawlers, they cage Yarn and Zeff within searing bars of light.

"Shit. What do we do?" he asks.

"Lemme think." She examines their cell.

El Dorado trembles.

"Did you feel that?"

"This Vision Shard will collapse soon. We need to leave, or we'll be trapped," she warns. "And I don't have the numbers to know what will happen. If you would've left the armor, we could've outrun them—wait—your armor. Let's put it to some good use after all. Take off your gauntlet."

"Sheesh. Aren't you going to buy me dinner first?"

"We don't have time for your riddles. Hurry and hand me that piece of armor."

Zeff passes her the mithril gauntlet.

"If my calculations are correct... and we mix the sample with a bit of this and add it to a touch of that... Perfect!"

"What are you doing?"

"I need you to walk into that beam." She points at the third one from the corner of their cage.

"Nope. It's going to fry me."

"Trust me." She opens a glowing pocket, stretching its seam, inserts the gauntlet, and pats it close.

"Do I have a choice?" He looks at the drones as the Aurelian Legion crosses the bridge, and another tremor shakes their reality. "What do you need me to do?"

"Walk into that beam, and I'll do the rest." She removes an impossibly long rifle from her coat and loads it with a freshly cast round of mithril ammo. "Ready." She aims. "Three... Two... One... Go."

Zeff walks towards the light, and Yarn places her finger on the trigger. Just as he steps into the laser, she fires a single mithril bullet. It cracks an aerial drone's shell. The force rocks the beam off his pauldron into a nearby spire, disabling the security bots in pursuit.

"Now, aren't you glad I kept the armor?"

"Shut it. Let's get going," she replies.

In a tireless pursuit, they flee over a tram trestle, narrowly avoiding the track's magnetic surge. Down into the terminal's darkness, she opens a garbage hatch leading to the refuse grounds. There, they hijack the nearest waste hauler and launch towards the lower chambers, running deeper into offshoot tunnels. Next to the dump, giant beetles roll immense boulders of trash up the hills to their far-off caverns of dung and discarded widgets—out of sight, out of mind.

Blue Hour

Konway's body convulses while the sky softens into a cotton candy sorbet beneath the rising moon. Overhead, squadrons of shorebirds heading home carpet-bomb the area with Pollockesque spatter patterns of guano. With one final, eye-bulging spasm, a teardrop traces his cheek and falls to the sand. He breathes in—halfway through, his heart loosens its grip on the mortal coil.

Critters & Crawlers

Yarn sprints ahead of him. "Keep up, slowpoke."

Several forking paths later, a cluster of Cave Critters and Crawlers enters the tunnels, their awful scratching echoing throughout the corridors. Desperate to avoid whatever slurping awful-awfuls now pursuing them into the Holo-Earth's inner kingdom, Zeff finally listens to Yarn and drops his armor to keep pace. Glimmering metal clangs across the ground. Moments later, thrashing shadows flail against slime-slathered outcroppings as the beasts arrive and corrupt its light. The distraction gives them just enough time to evade the hideous denizens of horrific design. Farther ahead, Yarn leads him into the beauty below—just beyond the scraping, clawing, clicking monstrosities.

Compelled by primal urges, one Crawler picks up their scent and tracks them to the fringes of an undiscovered luminescent cavern. On the verge of crossing the veil of subterranean darkness, tentacles lash out at Zeff. Yarn defends him with a flash of blue energy, killing the wretch without hesitation.

Another trembling wave from Gilgram's grotto rattles the Vision Shard.

"If we don't find the exit, our probability of survival swiftly approaches zero." Yarn looks at her console, then nervously at the pools. "I don't know which one to take."

The chasm's light dims as more beasts press upon the edge of darkness.

"Better put some pep in your step," he says.

"Look, bub," Yarn snaps. "I've never been inside one of these... and I certainly never thought I'd be stuck in one, trying to escape from being entombed by my brother's corpse. Give me a moment."

The darkness grows, and the cavern's light flickers.

"I don't know if we have the time." Zeff steps backward and bumps into a large pool painted with patches of iridescent fungi.

In its plunging depths, neon corals light the way for a bale of luminescent turtles swimming down an infinite, spiraling staircase. At its center, a resplendent point twinkles into sight.

"'Follow Yarn. Seek the Light,' Gilgram said, 'Seek the light.'"

She rushes over and scans the pool. "This is the one... This is the way. You're either a fool—or you're brilliant."

"I'm likely a brilliant fool."

The cavern fills with a horrible hiss as the Cave Critters and Crawlers further flood the opening and surround them. Another tremor shakes the cavern, and its once-luminous walls succumb to the encroaching darkness. With no other option, they turn to the pool, diving into its infinite waters.

Behind them, a grotesque biomechanical horde pursues the light. As the entrance turns black, Yarn and Zeff swim frantically towards the exit. Cracks spread along the cavern's fringes, running like dope in a junky's veins. The moment they reach the portal and slip through its threshold, the fissures shatter the splendor of this harrowing realm, and the Vision Shard seals itself, deleting its metadata into the cosmic ash of nonexistence.

76

This Is The Way

Lazarus Protocol

Tossed and turned on the shore, Konway's body rests, sand piling up around the windblown creases of his boardshorts. The rising moon pulls back fine sheets of sediment with each wave. Like a masterful mandolin playing upon the sands, the Atlantic washes away his crumbling footprints, erasing the invisible soles of their journey. Memento mori.

Moments after his vitals flatline, the Oros system orders a circumfused concentrate of [Forlorn Hope] throughout his physiology. On the backend, nanite baristas serve up a mixture of techno-organic compounds to nullify the lingering electrical surges and a booster of [Berzerker], while delivering a healthy dose of adrenaline to his heart. For the second course—two-thirds norepinephrine, dopamine, and anandamide, and one-third serotonin and endorphins—shaken, not stirred.

Temper

Elsewhere, near the old lighthouse—illuminated by a war room of terminals—bloodied and beaten, Blue and Red stand at attention before Commander Xero.

"How the hell did you lose him? And the truck? Now the signal's disappeared? Why'd we waste all that money bringing you boys up to speed?" He flings a laptop to the other side of the room. "Zeff is still on Coffin Island, and I want him found."

Red blurts out, "We know where—"

Xero steps towards him. "You know—I've been too easy on all of you. I've been tiptoeing through the fucking tulips for the Director's sake while the greatest threat to national security is out there day-tripping and banging betties."

"But—"

Commander Xero chambers a round into his special-issue Delta-9 hand cannon and pulls the trigger.

The explosive round rips apart Red's already injured shoulder, slamming him against the wall, leaving a crimson smear on the brushed metal finish.

"A weapon is no good if it can't be deployed effectively," he says, lowering the smoking gun.

Slumped to the floor, metallic fibers jut from the gaping hole where Red's arm—still attached—dangles by a spindle of meat and shining threads.

"Even if Zeff doesn't remember who he is, he's still dangerous." Xero scowls at them. "How can you keep the world safe if you lack motivation? Buzz the Pickle Factory and see if there are any upgrades available. As you worthless lot are now, you won't be able to handle my grandma."

"We know he's been at the surf village, Laniakea. Let's go—" Blue pauses, expecting to be disciplined for speaking out of turn.

"We can't just run in there," Xero snaps. "The First Global Foundation might be a bunch of limp-dick nerds who are getting too big for their britches, but if they catch wind of us, we won't be able to compromise the deployment of their new blockchain."

"Blockchain?"

"You're as dumb as you look, Blue—"

Red groans on the floor.

"Too soft. Get him to the tank."

"Yes, sir," Blue and the others respond in unison.

"All of you, get the hell out of my sight," he says, dismissing the room. "No more excuses. Find Zeff."

They pick up Red and file down the hallway.

Xero exhales a sigh of discontent, sets the gun on his desk, and locks the door behind them. Avoiding the blood puddle, he walks to a waist-high bookshelf and picks up a bottle of Blovio's Single Barrel Bourbon. He pours a double shot, smells it, then tosses it back—over the hatches, down the gullet.

After fixing another, Xero sits at his desk and opens the secret locker with his biometrics. He takes a sip, swirling it around his mouth, savoring the caramel and oak notes. After another, he enters the code to the hidden safe, retrieves his encrypted smartphone, and places a call.

It rings twice.

"Zuzu?" he asks.

"Yes."

"I'm going to need more time. I'm over-leveraged and dealing with incompetence."

"The buyer will not be happy with this."

"Need I remind you, your guys messed up on the bridge? Not mine. Give me time—I'll get the Oros system for you. I need you to be ready to onboard me and my team. The rest of the Agency is compromised by a punch bowl of political boot-lickers. They don't know what war is like beyond their polished desks."

"I'll see what I can do," Zuzu responds.

"Perfect."

The line goes silent.

Commander Xero pours a third shot of bourbon and stares out across the Atlantic.

Emerge

Yarn and Zeff climb out of the rubble and wreckage. The sandstorm has stopped, leaving a clear gray sky. They look back at the crater left from Gilgram's corpse.

"Wowzers. The Grand Canyon ain't got shit on this," he says.

"Grand Canyon?"

"Never mind. It's hard to believe all of this was under the little brown church. Was it really El Dorado? In my world, it's a myth."

"That particular Vision Shard was gleaned by my brother, Gilgram. He was a seer—probably why Fomobious blinded him with [Chains of Fear]. The shard came from a Memory Crystal in the Archives, which, from what we discovered, contained various versions of this realm. Wait—you're saying it's a story in *your* world? Interesting. Nothing is for certain, indeed."

"How many *versions* did you find in the Archives?"

Yarn summons another translucent blue window and explains, "Of the countless records, we identified the phenotypes for 332 cycles. This is the 333rd iteration. Thus, we formed an alliance to rule over the next Consilience—the end of our great cycle. But then, the last Elder Tree shattered into an oozing mass of corruption."

"This is all above my pay grade," he says, proccing the map.

[Low Battery] flashes across the bracer.

"None of this makes any sense," Zeff groans.

"Does it need to?"

Zeff suddenly remembers the data from Mauna Kea. "Wait. How long have I been here?" Panic consumes him as he instinctively looks to the timeless gray sky for divine guidance. "I need to get to the Control Tower." He turns to Yarn and points. "The outside world is in danger. This means the Mind Palace—your home, Katalepsis—is still in danger. There's an asteroid heading towards the planet!"

"How is your world connected to ours?" Yarn puzzles.

"From what I know, the Control Tower is at the center of the Mind Palace VPN partition," he says, pointing at the withered stump in the distance.

"The last Elder Tree?" Yarn mutters as mental anvils forge a clearer understanding.

"It's within the Oros system, which is a part of my body," Zeff clarifies.

"Oros system?" she asks, surveying the horizon.

"A nanite colony."

"I see... We're inside some form of [MOOP]. Very intriguing." She pulls a vial of chromatic rainbow liquid from one of her many pockets and holds it up against the gray skyline. "So it's a type of technology?"

"Yes."

"Well, why didn't you say so... We're a long way from my domain, but if we find a resource node, I should be able to access my lab remotely and patch us into the backend."

"What if it doesn't work?"

Yarn pulls her goggles over her eyes. "What if we never try?"

"You have a point. But the battery's dead on this thing. How will we get through the Wastelands?"

"I almost forgot." She digitizes the golden turtle compass and presents it to him, saying, "Gilgram wanted you to have this."

With the weight of it in his palm, the [Violet Egg] emerges from the bracer and scans the item. On completion, it disappears. The battery meter increases, and a notification appears. He taps the shining turtle icon to summon a pop-up window. At its center, the golden turtle compass slowly rotates in its showcase. Beneath it, a floating plaque reads [Wayseer].

He equips it, and a strong pulse expands the map. Alas, they stand at the boundary of the sprawling Wastelands of Cognition, with a few sparsely scattered resource nodes bordering the Abysmal Swamp.

"Shit. This is going to take forever. How will we make it all the way there?"

"Leave it to me. I might have a thing or two up my sleeves." Yarn extracts some parts from a deep pocket.

In no time, sparks fly, and metal slides into place as she fashions a series of strange components.

"And what if the Fog finds us?" Zeff asks.

"Fog? My sources say Ramiel is long since dead."

"Who's that bastard with the burnt-yellow eyes?"

"Please don't confuse the Imp-oster for my brother. It's an abomination. I warned her... but do they ever listen? Well... Gilgram did."

Several clanking, twisting, popping moments later, a skiff hovers in front of them.

Fearful of summoning the Fog, Zeff quickly switches the subject, asking, "What's with that unicorn?"

Without stopping her adjustments, Yarn replies, "She's an Eldenhorn—forged from my CodeX and pieces of the Elder Tree."

"Were they leading me to you?"

"We have much to discuss." She climbs into the cockpit. "For now, let's find the nearest node and access a ley line portal... If I hadn't sent my only Eldenhorn to gather the others, I'd have them open the way."

Zeff reviews the map and taps the glowing turtle compass in the corner. The screen on his forearm projects around them, zooming out to highlight a garden of forking paths.

"Let's get going." Yarn engages a sprocketed device with two kicks and powers up their new ride.

Return

Behind Konway, waves drag another fine layer of sediment back into the sea, deep down into the coffers of Davy Jones' Locker. Gasping for air, he wakes, flinging sand-crusted eyelids open to the first light of day. As he exhales, the Oros system uncloaks with the lingering alacrity from the booster shot of [Forlorn Hope], pulling him from the bleeding edge of the mortal coil, still tickling his senses.

(Is this thing on?) Yarn's digital voice inquires. (Hmmm... Quite unexpected. This was supposed to be a portal to my lab. I'm sure of it.)

(I think I see myself,) Zeff says.

(Whatever you do, make it quick. I don't think this resource node can support the stream's connection.)

"Who's there?" To Konway's surprise, a version of himself in a white linen suit renders across the TacOHUD.

(Long time no see.) The digital projection walks towards him.

Startled by the figure, Konway scoots back. "You... I know you."

(We need to talk.) Zeff advances. (Who knows how long I've been wandering down here? I need you to trust me.)

"Trust you? I'm here because of you? You're a murderer—I'm a murderer."

(Calm down. This is much larger than that. It's about the mission. The asteroid is ten years away, you—)

(We're having a connection error,) Yarn warns.

"Is there someone else with you?" Konway hastily looks around.

(Let me explain—)

"Leave me alone!" Konway unleashes his repressed anguish.

Zeff steps back. (I need you to listen. They're coming for you—for us.)

"Who?"

(The Agency wants the data. Get it to Annah—) On the other end of the line, the resource node dims and Zeff's construct fizzles into the clarity of frame-rate adjustment.

Konway collapses to the ground, sobbing from the angst of his existence. But soon, his eyes are drawn to the peeping dawn's opulence, drying his tears. (I'm alive.) He licks his lips and gags on the glitter of crustacean corpses. "Fuck you, Zeff... I'm alive!"

His thoughts turn to Sage and the others.

"The Agency! I need to get back to Laniakea. But who can I tell? How do I warn them? Would they believe me? Maybe the Agency won't come after me? Who am I kidding...? Wait, who's Annah? Asteroid?"

Another tormented carousel of jiggly-jowled faces spins into view, stirring a deep trepidation. He hastily searches for the paper rhino and finds it crumpled in his shirt's front pocket.

With each pass of the origami totem and held exhale, the sun rises higher. After a few more rounds, he stands above the waves and turns away from the beeping earthmovers and throttling dump trucks. A westerly wind loop-de-loops a styrofoam cup past the dredge crews, along the shoreline, and out of sight, drawing Konway's attention to a nearby beach access ramp.

"Well, how about that?" He shakes his head at its proximity, then notices the dappled patches on his body.

Covered with bird shit, he laughs at the absurdity and leans against a palmetto tree. The laughter deepens into an abrupt side stitch, compelling him to catch his breath. After gathering his resolve, Konway staggers to the beach access and up its sun-worn steps. Atop the boardwalk, he turns back for one last glance at the glistening Atlantic before venturing down to the dirt parking lot and beginning his journey home—back to Sage and Helaku, to Laniakea, to protecting what matters most.

To Be Continued...

To Be Continued...

Ad Astra

I hope you've enjoyed the journey thus far. **Book II** is in the works, and the roadmap is clear. With your continued support, we can take **The Cyberdelic Odyssey** to the stars. Having already contributed your time and money, there are still other ways to lend your verse in liberating the creative mind across the globe for the next seven generations.

Amazon, Goodreads, etc: Did you find something that inspired you? Let me know. Leave a review!

Social Media: If you enjoyed reading, I'd love to hear about it, and perhaps others would, too. Whether you're a digital nomad or down by the shore, recommend this book and share your thoughts about it.

Word-of-Mouth: Your voice is the most effective way for your friends and community to discover their next great read. Encourage a local bookshop to stock it or select it for your book club's next pick.

Your Local Library: Request it to be shelved. Use your library's "suggest a book to add to our catalog" form to help others access **The Cyberdelic Odyssey**, regardless of their capacity to purchase a copy.

Nominate For Awards: See an award this work qualifies for, nominate it, and let me know.

Digital Collectibles: Check the website for more novel ways to join the conversation around the bondfire.

Comfort Creatures

Aside from being a **philosopher**, **storyteller**, and **futurist**—Comfort is an active advocate for liberating the creative mind across the globe for the next seven generations.

Writing under this nom de plume, he has also co-authored **Circumfusion**, an adventurous tale written as a love letter to Web3—one which was sent to the moon!

Bootstrapped with degrees from the University of South Carolina and inspired by the healing waters of Folly Beach, he now sets his sights on completing **The Cyberdelic Odyssey.**

Follow along as Comfort's lyrical prose and psychedelic language craft thoughtful narratives designed to rip open techno-social wormholes and perform the shamanic dance around the digital bondfire—reminding us that what matters most is each other.

The Bookshelf

- **Circumfusion** (Available Now!)

- **The Cyberdelic Odyssey**
  Book I – Innocence (Available Now!)
  Book II – Experience (Upcoming)
  Book III – Wisdom (Upcoming)
  Book IV
  Book V
  Book VI
  Book VII
  Book VIII
  Book IX